CONTENTS

Louise Bagshawe

TALL POPPIES

*They call it the tall poppy syndrome.
If you are too successful, you must
be cut down to size.*

*Nina and Elizabeth are tall poppies.
One a poor Jewish girl from Brooklyn
who becomes a top-flight business
woman, the other an English public
schoolgirl who not only succeeds
at business but also establishes
herself as an Olympic skier.*

*As both women make their mark,
there are enemies hell-bent on
destroying their careers.*

chapter one

'NO! STOP IT, we can't do this!'

Nina squirmed away. She kept her eyes down. Her face was flushed from wanting, but it was too soon.

'Come on, sugar, gimme a break,' Jeff said. His voice was rough, and she could see the outline of his hard-on through his grey flannel pants. Nina tried to be cool about it, like Judy or Melissa or any of those popular girls, and not think how much it would hurt if he put it inside her.

'You drive me crazy,' Jeff breathed, running his hands inside the burgundy school blazer, finding her voluptuous breasts under the thin cotton of her shirt. Jeff grinned with triumph as her nipples stiffened against his palm. He'd been after her ever since he'd come off the basketball court, thought he'd like a swim, and found Nina doing twenty laps. Christ! Nina Roth, scholarship girl, major nerd, charity case—had a figure like Playmate of the Month! When she had climbed out of the pool Jeff couldn't believe it—water streaming from her hair, trailing down across a cheap black swimsuit, outlining big firm breasts, a tiny waist and long, curving legs. That was three weeks ago.

'Not here,' she said, looking up and down the corridor, trying to back away. 'Someone might see . . .'

'So what?' Jeff demanded sullenly. Nina was hard work for a chick that never had a guy look at her before. Sometimes he wondered if she was worth it. 'Don't you care about me?'

'You know I do—' The bell rang for third period and she jumped aside, shaky with relief, as kids came streaming out of their classrooms. 'I have to go, I got physics. I'll see you later . . .'

Inside the quiet, gleaming classroom Nina Roth took deep breaths, taking in the smell of chalk and polish, trying to concentrate on what Sister Bernadette was saying. Normally physics was one of her favourite classes. But not today.

The class sat hunkered down at their desks, bored and restless. Rows of smart burgundy blazers and crisp cotton shirts, tailored flannel pants or neat, swinging kilts were turned towards the teacher, eyes staring glassily at the blackboard where Sister was outlining equations in chalk. The College of St Michael the Archangel was one of the most prestigious schools in Park Slope. Brooklyn's richest parents had been sending their kids here for decades, paying through the nose for the nuns, the uniform, the Catholic education. Most of the trust-fund babies ignoring Sister Bernadette were atheist or Episcopalian, but so what? St Michael's was all about cachet, not the Church.

'So, the sum of the angles is . . .?'

Silence. The kids shifted in their seats.

'Nina?'

Nina jumped, dragging her mind away from the feel of Jeff's hands on her breasts. She flushed a dark red. 'Excuse me, Sister?'

The teacher pursed her thin lips. 'Nina, you're miles away. How do you expect to get anywhere in life if you don't pay attention in school?'

Mean giggles from the class. They all knew that she was the only one here who'd have to work her way up.

'Josie?'

'Ninety degrees, Sister,' Josie Whitney said smugly, shooting a look of triumph at Nina.

But Nina didn't care, not today. Because *she* was dating Jeff Glazer.

Nina Roth was an only child, which was just as well, since her parents couldn't have afforded a second. Mark and Ellen Roth shared a dingy walkup on South Slope and an air of bitter disappointment. They also shared a daughter, but for as long as she could remember, Nina had only got attention during their endless fights. A pawn to be squabbled over. Dad was in his fifties, fat, squalid. He said he had retired from the police force, but Nina heard on the street he'd been canned for siphoning off confiscated money and goods for himself.

Then there was Mom. Nina thought she remembered a time when her mom loved her, took her walking in Prospect Park, bought her Italian ice cream on Court Street, or best of all, took her out to magical Coney Island in the summer, to ride the funfair and eat cotton candy.

But that was before Ellen started to drink. These days Mom only hugged her in a drunken stupor, with her breath rank and tears of self-pity streaking her thin cheeks. Ellen didn't really love her daughter, Nina knew that. She took comfort solely in a bottle, cocooning herself in an alcoholic fog from the misery of her life, often blacking out for entire days. She kept just enough control to staff the family store, a scuzzy deli. Ellen worked behind the counter and counted the money. Nina's father took deliveries and stacked shelves. The important stuff, like accounts and reordering, Nina took care of. She'd asked to do it when she turned thirteen. Somebody had to put bread on the table.

Nina was sixteen years old. She knew her classmates despised her. She hadn't been popular at Beth Israel Elementary, either, where she'd won the St Michael's scholarship, but she didn't give a damn, because school was the way out. Her whole life had one obsession: to get out of the South Slope, away from all the dirt and despair. Away from home.

Even so, it hurt, the way the other kids shunned her, never inviting her to hang out, sniggering at her patched-up uniform and secondhand blazers. Nobody ever asked her to sit at their table at lunch   at least, not until three weeks back.

That miraculous day, Jeff Glazer had actually strolled up to her locker after French, and casually asked if she'd like to go out with him.

At first Nina just stood there blinking, convinced this had to be some particularly cruel joke. Glazer was seventeen, school quarterback, the only son of very wealthy parents, and a major hunk. Muscular, tall, with Viking-fair hair and ice-blue eyes, Jeff had dated and dropped half the best-looking girls already. Nina Roth would as likely fly to the moon as be asked out by Jeff Glazer.

But he was there, and he was asking. When he'd sat next to her at lunch, Nina wouldn't have traded the envious stares of Melissa Patton and her crowd for all the riches in the world.

She pinned her compass to the paper in front of her and mechanically traced out a couple of angles. It couldn't last like this, she knew that. Jeff wanted to make love to her, and if she didn't let him, he was going to dump her. Jeff told her that everybody did it, she was way too uptight, and if she loved him she would *make* love to him.

Nina breathed in deeply, trying to stop her heart thumping so hard against her chest. Jeff was going to expect an answer in Prospect Park tonight. And the answer was going to be yes.

The turrets of Caerhaven Castle towered black as coal against the twilight sky, darkened from the rain and wind. The bitter storm had raged all day, but tonight nobody noticed the weather. Light streamed from every window in the medieval walls, and from the line of Bentleys and Rolls-Royces crunching past the stone dragons on the front gates and up two miles of gravel drive.

The Countess of Caerhaven was giving a ball.

'Goddamn it, Monica. Where is that wretched child?'

Tony Savage, thirtieth Earl of Caerhaven, tugged at the waistcoat of his immaculate white-tie suit. He hated being defied. Not only was he holder of one of the oldest titles in Wales and 700 acres of rich farmland, Tony was chief executive of Dragon plc, the family company, a pharmaceutical giant, with divisions worldwide. It was publicly held; Tony Savage had 11 per cent.

At his side Monica shrugged, offering her hand to a new batch of arrivals. Tall and elegant, the second Lady Caerhaven swished around in a sea-green Balenciaga, pearls looped round her neck, sapphire clips pinching delicate ear lobes. She smiled dazzlingly at every unfamiliar face: Cabinet ministers, industrialists and investment bankers. She was charming to them all. So important for Tony's business.

The earl nodded softly to himself. Monica looked wonderful, behaved perfectly. Never gave him a second's concern. She knew her place was at his side. None of that feminist claptrap had ever sullied her brain; she just liked spending his money, hosting his parties and dazzling the *Tatler* set every season. She was the perfect wife.

Monica Savage had done her duty in every way. There was Charles, Lord Holwyn, and Lord Richard; the heir and the spare. And if she no longer welcomed him into her bed, that was fine too: Tony Savage had women whenever he wanted them. Monica pretended not to notice and got her little baubles from Tiffany or Garrards as a reward. If he'd only chosen Monica first, he'd have had no problems whatsoever.

Tony glanced at his sons. Charles, Lord Holwyn, thirteen, was handsome and callous, calculating like his mother and ruthless like Tony, already cocky and self-possessed. It was easy to be confident: Charles was heir to a title, a castle, London property and a vast fortune. He had dominated Richard since they were tiny boys, and Richard never complained. Richard was popular and easy-going; he made average grades in school; he'd be a gentleman of leisure and do very well. The kid was only eleven but Tony could tell. Richard was the image of his mother.

The earl checked his watch and felt rage stealing over him. Elizabeth was late for her own ball.

Elizabeth. Daughter of Louise, Countess of Caerhaven, his first wife and the only woman ever to make him look a fool. To this day he hated her. Louise worked when he asked her not to, refused to play hostess and cuckolded him with Jay DeFries. His former best friend. Careless whether they were seen in public, Louise made Tony a laughing stock and then divorced him before he'd had a chance to divorce her. He'd hated everything about her, even his infant daughter. Little Elizabeth was just like her mother: the same downy, dark blonde hair, green eyes and long, lean body, not a sign of her father on her. Tony was sure she wasn't even his, but admitting his wife might have borne another man's child would have been too shameful.

When Louise died, aged twenty-seven, of breast cancer, the infant Lady Elizabeth moved back to her papa. She grew up a rebellious minx, an almost uncanny replica of her mother.

Tony ruined Jay DeFries. He took over his business, muddied the books, got the Fraud Squad in. His former best friend had gone down for eight years, bankrupt. He hanged himself in jail.

As Dragon grew bigger, the whispers grew smaller. Soon nobody dared to mention Louise or Jay; Tony Savage, Wall Street's Robber Baron, heard nothing but flattery. But young Elizabeth, running wild, flirting with the local boys, dressing indecently, blossoming into exquisite, dangerous beauty, was in his face every bloody day. The cuckoo in his golden nest.

Monica beckoned Charles over. 'Darling, go upstairs and find your sister. Tell her to come down here *at once*. It's *her* sixteenth, and David Fairfax has been waiting for her all evening.'

Tony Savage looked across the grey stone of the Great Hall to where the plump figure of a young man stood cradling a glass of vintage champagne. His Grace, the Duke of Fairfax, one of the most eligible men in Britain. Suitor for the hand of his only daughter.

'Can't think what he sees in her,' Tony said.

In her bedroom in the West Wing, Lady Elizabeth Savage leaned against the chill stone of the turret window and stared out into the night. She ignored the sounds of the glittering party below her and listened for the endless sigh of the sea. The cold air tasted of salt.

Granny was dead. Only two days ago she had been sitting with her in the East Wing, chatting about business, politics, and the roaring twenties. Elizabeth was fascinated by business, the only thing about her dad she admired. There was an almighty row the day Tony discovered she'd been sending away for Dragon company reports.

'What is this nonsense, young lady?' he spluttered.

Elizabeth hurried to explain. 'I'm just taking an interest, Daddy. I thought I could study how Dragon does its marketing—you know I'm interested in how people sell things—'

'How people *sell* things? What are you, a *salesman?*'

'I want to work in advertising at Dragon,' Elizabeth said stubbornly.

'Over my dead body.' Tony actually laughed. 'The *company* is going to your brother! Behave like a lady for once in your life.'

White-faced, Elizabeth had turned and raced away up the stone staircase, looking for her grandmother.

Elspeth, the dowager countess, had occupied the East Wing for twenty years since her husband died. She loved Elizabeth, although she too was convinced the girl was Jay DeFries's bastard. Her heart sank as Elizabeth grew up into a younger, prettier version of Louise. She knew Tony would never give the child a chance.

When Elizabeth sobbed out what her father had said about Dragon, the old lady gave her a hug. 'Never mind, Lizzy. He'll come round.'

'He won't.' Elizabeth buried her face in the stiff cotton petticoats. 'He doesn't want me to do *anything*! He said it wasn't ladylike . . .'

Elizabeth's face was blotched red and puffy from crying. Her son was going to crush this one, unless somebody stopped him. Elspeth smiled, slipping her wrinkled hand over Elizabeth's smooth one. 'So, you want to work? If that's what you want, dear, you shall.'

Elizabeth shook her head. 'Daddy said the company is going to Charlie. He won't let me anywhere near it.'

'But it isn't up to him. *I* own fifteen per cent of the stock. It would get you a seat on the board. I'll call a lawyer and change my will. You can have it on your eighteenth birthday.' Granny's face creased into a smile.

Elizabeth stared at her grandmother. 'Truly? What will Daddy say?'

'He can like it or lump it,' the old lady said crisply. 'Oh, don't worry, child. I'll speak to him tomorrow.'

She knew Daddy had called on his mother the same day.

When he went up to her again the following morning, however, the earl found Granny stiff in her chair. Dead, from what the family doctor called a 'routine coronary'.

Elizabeth resented every smiling idiot at the ball downstairs. All she wanted was to be alone, to have a little time to mourn. The wonderful news about Dragon was dust and ashes without Granny, she thought, blinking back tears.

There was a heavy creak as the ancient oak door to her bedroom swung open.

'Everybody's waiting for you', Charles said, his low voice full of disapproval. 'It *is* supposed to be your party, Lizzie.'

'Nobody asked me if I wanted a party!'

'You're spoiling things again, as usual. Mamma can't believe how selfish you're being. What's that dress you're wearing? That's not the gown Mamma bought you!'

He was annoyed, Elizabeth glanced back at the plain green Laura Ashley dress with the huge bow on the bottom, lying rejected over a chair. She'd known there was no way out of this horrible ball, so she'd sneaked upstairs to Granny's rooms last night. She'd unpacked the gown she wanted from Elspeth's chest of drawers; it was a cloud of the palest gold silk trimmed with cream lace, a whalebone corset tapering down to a billowing skirt over stiff petticoats of ivory lace, a discreet pattern in gold thread and seed pearls dusted over the bodice. It fitted Elizabeth's long, lean body snugly, pushing her small breasts together and lifting them up, the skirts sweeping gracefully with every movement. She'd pulled her tawny hair up into a French pleat, added topaz drop earrings and slipped her feet into apricot satin slippers.

Dad could try and ignore her *now*.

'It was one of Granny's,' Elizabeth told him. 'Please go away, Charles.'

'All right, I'm going, but you'd better get down there. Otherwise, Father will come and drag you down, in front of everybody . . .'

He would, too. Taking a deep breath, Lady Elizabeth Savage composed herself, opened her bedroom door, and walked slowly down the winding stairs to her sixteenth birthday party.

'I told you before. I can't come back early tonight, I have economics,' Nina said.

'Yeah? And what are we supposed to do? The stock needs checkin'.'

Nina shrugged. They were arguing in the tiny, cramped kitchen, standing shoulder to shoulder while Nina washed the dishes.

'You're never around,' Ellen whined. 'You're always studyin' or out with your friends. Don't even have time for your mom.'

'Mom, I have to go to school, and I took that job at Duane Reed,' Nina told her shortly. She was too tired for this. Scholastic Aptitude Tests were two months away, she worked weekends and two nights a week at the local drugstore, and three evenings saw Jeff. The deli was just too much extra grind. They'd have to work it out by themselves.

Mr David had been right. Nina's maths teacher had called her in last semester and laid out the facts.

'Nina, I have to tell you, I'm concerned about your grades trailing off.' He'd looked at the solemn little face bunched with worry under its mop of raven hair. 'Your concentration seems to be wandering, you're constantly tired, and Sister Agnes tells me you fell asleep during chemistry practical last week.' He paused. 'Are things difficult at home?'

Nina stiffened. 'No, sir.'

Peter David gently motioned his star pupil to a chair, wondering how to handle this. Nina Roth had an instinctive grasp of economics, the like of which he had not encountered since leaving Harvard. She was destined for great things. But now she was letting it crumble to dust. Her grades had plunged. Her essays had lost their sparkle. The Ivy League scholarships he'd assumed were sure things would go up in smoke if he didn't do something.

'You work for your parents, don't you?' Mr David asked gently. He knew all about the lazy father and the lush mother. 'Have you taken on any extra duties besides that? School clubs, for instance? Drama, volleyball, something like that?'

Nina smiled. Drama or volleyball, indeed. Before Jeff Glazer she hadn't had a social life, but that had changed, and now she needed more money for clothes.

St Michael's, Jeff and her parents all taught Nina the same lesson: money *was* everything. It was a house on the North Slope and your own business, versus a walkup on the South Slope and a run-down deli. Jeff's folks versus her parents. Hope versus despair.

Nina Roth knew that the worst thing in life would be to turn out like Mom or Dad, sitting around, waiting for rescue, waiting for something to happen. You made things happen yourself. When Duane Reed advertised for a junior clerk, Nina marched off to the interview, lied about her age, and was hired on the spot. That first week, she'd taken her pay cheque and opened an account at Wells Fargo. She spent only what she had to, and each month the balance crept up.

Money was independence, power, freedom.

Nina's eyes narrowed. No way was she giving up her job. 'I work at a drugstore part-time,' Nina said. 'I need the money.'

'Well, we all need money,' her teacher replied, surprising her, 'but you'll be giving up a lot more money if you go on this way.'

'I don't understand,' Nina said, but she was listening. She respected Mr David.

'You have your SATs coming up, assessments, reports. You'll need all that for college. Now, we both know that you're good for an academic scholarship to NYU, maybe Vassar, but you can do better than that.'

'Better than Vassar?' Her eyes widened.

'Sure. Sure.' Peter David nodded impatiently. 'I'm talking Harvard or Yale, Nina, but not the way you're performing now.' Her teacher brushed aside her protests with an impatient wave. 'No, stop giving me excuses. You are a student with outstanding mathematical ability. Your economics are fluid and perceptive.' He leaned forward. 'It amazes me that someone like you would sacrifice long-term profit for pocket money.'

Nina sat there, taken aback.

'Something's got to give,' Peter David said.

She pushed back her chair, stood up straight, and offered him her hand. 'I hear you, sir,' Nina told him. 'I'll work something out.'

Starting that day, Nina cut back on her hours in the deli. She told Dad he'd have to check the books himself; she told Mom she'd need to spend more time behind the counter. But they didn't like it, and every day they let her know.

'You spend way too much time with that fancy jock you're seein',' her mother snapped.

'He's not a jock, he's just athletic,' Nina said, her buttermilk complexion lighting up. She'd be meeting up with him in the park again tonight.

'He's not interested in you. He's playin' with you,' her dad grumbled.

'Jeff's in love with me,' Nina said fiercely.

'Oh yeah?' Her father's face creased in scorn. 'He take you back to meet his folks yet? White trash, that's what we are. Don't kid yourself.'

'You're wrong!' Nina shouted. She grabbed her coat from the back of the door.

'Where d'you think you're going, Nina Roth? You got work to do *here*!' her mother yelled.

'I'm going to meet Jeff.' The door slammed on its hinges behind her.

A fresh fall wind whipped around Prospect Park, sending golden leaves dancing across the paths as Nina hurried towards the Long Meadow. She drew deep breaths, elated to be out of the claustrophobic apartment, tantalised by the thought of seeing Jeff.

'Hey!'

She spun round, the wind lifting her coal-black hair, and saw her boyfriend lounging under an elm tree. She felt her heart jump. He looked gorgeous, all those muscles huge and hard under his navy sweatsuit. He was wearing the latest black Nike trainers, and a steel Rolex. Nina pulled her threadbare duffle tight against the chill and told herself clothes didn't matter.

'Hey,' Jeff repeated, when she caught up to him. 'Where you been?'

'Sorry I'm late. I had some trouble back home,' Nina apologised.

'No problem,' Jeff said graciously. He turned and started walking west out of the park, heading for the cheap hotel on Eighth Street they always used. Nina used to think that was so cool of him, the way he'd casually pay for a whole night although they only took a couple of hours. Often he'd order up room service, too, and that made her feel spoiled and exotic, even if it was only cheeseburgers and beer. The sex was usually OK, but after Jeff collapsed across her with that strangled groan, looking drained, she felt . . . unsure. Left out. It was being kissed by him, stroked, told how beautiful she was—*that* was what Nina loved. In bed with Jeff she was accepted. Desired. That made up for everything else.

But today Nina could still hear her mother's carping voice. Suddenly the hotel seemed a little cheap, a little seedy.

'Hey, Jeff?' She put a hand on his arm. 'Could we maybe do something else tonight?'

He stopped short, frowning. 'What d'you want to do?'

'I'd like to go to your house and meet your mom and dad.'

'Oh yeah? What for?' Jeff demanded, irritated. He could imagine the reaction if he took her home! His mother would go ballistic! A Jewish checkout girl from South Slope!

'It's a dumb idea. We can't just drop in on them like that.'

'Why not?' Nina asked stubbornly. 'Are you ashamed of me? That's what my dad said.'

'He's nuts,' Glazer said warily. Nina's body had nearly given him a heart attack once he finally coaxed her into bed, and there was no way he was letting her go now. 'Look, we can't go tonight, because, uh, we're having some people over for dinner. Let me talk to Mom and you can maybe come for tea, or something. OK?'

'Sure.' Nina smiled up at him, bursting with happiness.

He does love me, she thought triumphantly. He does, he does!

Murmurs rose from the crowd as Elizabeth descended the stairs, floating on a glorious cloud of pale gold silk. Monica's first frown of disapproval at Elizabeth's rejecting the Laura Ashley melted into a warm smile. The young Duke of Fairfax, at the door to the Great Hall, was gasping like a dying trout. The countess heard wedding bells.

'Happy birthday, darling. I must say you look splendid,' Tony boomed, moving to grip her elbow firmly as Elizabeth started shaking hands. He felt taken aback. His tomboy daughter looked enchantingly feminine. He thrust her forward briskly through the glittering crowd.

'Evening, David. Glad you could make it,' the earl said genially.

Elizabeth blushed scarlet. How could he be so obvious! She wanted to pick up her cascading skirts and scamper away. Anything rather than listen to her father suck up to David Fairfax while he showed her off like a prize heifer.

'Good of you to ask me, Lord Caerhaven,' Fairfax replied. His gaze swept approvingly across Elizabeth's figure-hugging bodice and lingered on the freckled swell of her breasts. 'Hello, Elizabeth. Happy birthday. Smashing dress,' he added with more spirit.

Elizabeth looked at him wearily. David had had a crush on her for ages. He was ordinary looking, with sandy hair and a strong jaw, and had graduated from college with a spurious degree in estate management. He was OK, but pretty boring, and he was twenty-four. She secretly thought he was a bit of a perv, chasing after a girl eight years younger.

Granny's spirit bubbled up mischievously inside her.

'Hiya, Dave. How's it hanging?' Elizabeth asked, grinning.

Her father stiffened, but when Fairfax laughed he just glared at her and moved off.

'Smashing dress, smashing,' David repeated. 'D'you like a dance?'

She surrendered to the inevitable. 'Sure, Dave, that'd be cool.'

David hauled her bodily round the draughty hall.

'I say, Bessie—can I call you Bessie?'

'No,' replied Elizabeth coldly.

'You're wasted at school. Really, you know. You're very pretty. Ever thought about gettin' hitched?'

Elizabeth withdrew as far as the waltz allowed her, but was caught by David's plump arm squeezing her waist.

'Definitely not. I'm only sixteen, I haven't been to college yet.'

The duke looked nervous but tried again. 'What does a pretty girlie like you want to bother with college for? Bet your pa wouldn't mind.'

'I wouldn't dream of it,' said Elizabeth sharply.

Suddenly he caught her to him as they whirled in time with the Strauss, thrusting his face into her neck and kissing it. Revolted, Elizabeth braced herself and shoved him away.

'What the hell do you think you're doing? Get off me!'

She was a strong girl. Fairfax tripped and fell sprawling, and there was an agonising crack as his head hit the floor. David Fairfax lay crashed out on the polished marble, groaning in agony. Blood was seeping out of one cheek.

There was a stunned silence among the assembled guests.

Elizabeth sat under the mossy trunk of an apple tree and winced at the memory. Her father's face had set like granite and the ball had started breaking up as of that moment. David, helped to his feet by the onlookers, gave Elizabeth an embarrassed nod and hobbled towards the door.

It had taken barely half an hour for the piles of fur coats and cashmere shawls to disappear from the cloakroom and, once the last guest had hastened outside, the earl sent his daughter to her room, the quiet menace in his voice worse than any shouting fit. Neither last night nor this morning had Tony wanted to hear her explanation. As far as he was concerned she was simply a disgrace.

Even the servants had given her stern looks at breakfast. Monica had been reduced to taking a tray of coffee and dry toast in her bedroom, while Daddy and that little prig Richard had glowered their way through the kippers without so much as a 'Good morning'.

My God, if he wasn't already leaving everything to the boys, he'd disinherit me, Elizabeth thought, then hugged herself. Granny had put a stop to that. She needn't be afraid of Daddy any more.

'Lizzie!' called a reedy voice.

'Right here, Richard,' Elizabeth said. Her brother came clumping through the trees, looking annoyed.

'Where on earth have you been? You'd better get yourself inside, sharpish. Father wants to see you in the library, right away.'

She got up, ignoring the gloating tone to Richard's voice. What an unpleasant little brat he was, he loved to see her in trouble.

When they reached the dark-panelled hall Richard turned pointedly away towards his mother's morning room, leaving Elizabeth standing in front of the library door by herself. She drew herself up bravely and knocked on the old oak door.

'Come in,' the earl snapped.

The library was a large room, tapestries and antique swords mounted between rows of dusty, leather-bound books. Her father was sitting at his writing desk with his back to her.

'Elizabeth,' he said icily without turning round, 'your behaviour last night was unforgivable. You disgraced yourself in front of all our friends. Your stepmother was so ashamed she has made herself ill.'

'David Fairfax kissed me. What was I supposed to do? He was slobbering down the front of my dress—'

'Elizabeth!' Her father spun round on his seat, glaring at her. 'Not another word, do you hear me? Stop lying!'

'But I'm not lying!' Elizabeth protested, feeling the tears well up despite herself.

The earl raised a warning hand, his expression dark. 'Why in the name of God a decent young man like that should have been interested in you, Elizabeth, is quite beyond me, but you could not even accept a small romantic gesture—'

'There's nothing romantic about being pawed by that baboon!' Elizabeth cried angrily.

Father gazed at her impassively. Then he reached down to his desk and picked up a piece of paper.

'This is a letter of registration, enrolling you at the Ecole Henri Dufor.'

'The Ecole Henri Dufor?' Elizabeth repeated blankly.

'In Saas Fee.'

'You're sending me to *Switzerland*?'

Her father nodded coldly. 'I am sending you to your stepmother's finishing school to learn some manners.'

Elizabeth stared at him in disbelief. 'This is the seventies, Daddy. Nobody does that any more. What about my A levels?'

'You can take the baccalaureate, for all I care.' He laid the letter purposefully in front of him. 'You have gone too far, young lady. I tell you that I will not permit you to make a mockery of this family.'

She thrust her hands deep inside her jeans. 'I won't go.'

'You'll go. Or I will cut you off without a penny.'

'I'll borrow money from the bank.'

'Indeed. Against what would you borrow money?'

Her father's expression frightened her, but Elizabeth stubbornly shook her head. 'You know perfectly well. Granny told you about her will the day she died. She left me fifteen per cent of the company.'

'Your grandmother left me her entire estate,' Tony Savage said. 'She did *not* leave you any stock.'

Elizabeth stood there trembling with shock. The bequest had been her protection; she had counted on it.

'Phone her solicitors, if you like,' her father told her coolly, indicating the telephone on his desk. 'They will confirm it.'

Fighting to stay calm, Elizabeth shook her head. 'She can't have got round to changing it, then,' Elizabeth managed, 'but you know she intended to, Daddy. She told you when you went to see her. She wanted me to have her stake in Dragon. You have to respect her last wishes!'

'Mother told me no such thing.' The earl's tone was flat. 'I confess I am sorry that you choose such a subject for more lies.'

'I'm not lying,' Elizabeth gasped. 'You know how much I loved Granny!'

'Did you? It sounds to me as though you were trying to influence a frail old woman for your own benefit. And I notice you never mentioned this so-called bequest until now.' He snorted with contempt.

Panic and doubt washed over her in a wave as she looked at her father's cold, certain face. Did he really think she would lie about

Granny? Was it possible that Granny had planned on telling her father later? And never had the chance?

'You *will* go to Switzerland, one way or the other,' the earl snapped. 'If you behave sensibly, we will continue your allowance at the Ecole. If, on the other hand, you decide to cause your stepmother any more distress, you will receive not one centime. Which is it to be?'

At least she would get away from him. 'I'll go to Switzerland.'

'**W**ould you like some ham, Nina?' Mrs Glazer asked.

Nina shifted uncomfortably in her seat. Jeff had mentioned that she was Jewish at the start of tea, and an extra chill had settled over the already icy table.

'No, thank you,' she replied quietly, taking a sip of her tea. The cup was made of bone china and rimmed with gold leaf, the cutlery was silver plate, the table made from some dark wood that looked very expensive. She'd known Jeff was rich, but it was still a shock. They might both reside in Brooklyn, but he lived in another world.

'It's a beautiful neighbourhood,' Nina said, trying hard to make conversation. Jeff was no help; he'd spent the meal with his head lowered, pushing blueberry pancakes round his plate.

'Yes, isn't it,' Mrs Glazer answered coolly.

'Nina, tell me about your parents,' Ken Glazer said. 'Jeff tells me they have their own business.'

'Well, uh, not exactly.' Nina coloured. 'My mom runs a deli.'

Jeff's mother gave a tinkling laugh. 'How refreshing. And whereabouts is it? I must pop in some time.'

Nina wanted to die. 'I think it would be out of your way. We're on the south side of Park Slope.'

Mrs Glazer pursed her lips. 'Yes,' she said after a moment. 'I'm not down that way very often.'

I'll bet you're not, Nina thought miserably. She gave Jeff a pleading look but he reached for another pancake, refusing to meet her eyes.

It was another dreadful hour before he lumbered to his feet, muttering something about football practice, and they were able to escape. Nina thanked her hostess for the tea in as dignified a manner as she could, and took her time about putting on her coat, as though it were a silver fox instead of her threadbare duffle. As she descended the Glazers' scrubbed stone steps, Nina turned round and gave the town house a long, cool look. Some day, I'll be richer than you are, she thought. I'll own a bigger house, wear better clothes and have the kind of success you've never even dreamed of. I swear it.

Her small fist clenched under her cheap coat. *I swear it.*

'God, aren't families the worst?' Jeff said lazily. His confident swagger had reappeared. 'That was lame. Come on, baby, let's go and make love.'

Beside him, Nina dropped her eyes so Jeff wouldn't catch the contempt glinting in them. Ordinarily, she'd have laid into him for letting her down like that, but not tonight. They had more important things to talk about.

'What do you mean?' Jeff asked her half an hour later. They were sitting on the bed of the same room they always used, but for once the coverlet remained straight, the sheets unrumpled. 'You think you're pregnant? You can't be.' He passed a hand through his gleaming fair hair, his body hunched up in tension and disbelief. 'We've been careful.'

'I'm late,' Nina said dully. She hadn't expected him to jump for joy— at least not right away—but this blind panic was making her nervous.

'How late?' Jeff demanded.

'Two and a half weeks.'

He shot up from the bed and started pacing the room. 'But you don't know for sure. And anyway, who says it's mine?'

'What?' Nina gasped. 'You know there's only you!' How could he say that to her? 'Have you got somebody else?'

Jeff thrust his hands into his jeans and shrugged defensively. 'Sure. I've seen Melissa Patton a few times. Why shouldn't I?'

Despite herself, Nina felt two huge tears well up and trickle down her cheeks. She felt like such a fool. 'I thought you loved me. I thought we'd get married,' she said bleakly.

Jeff gave a harsh laugh. 'You thought I'd *marry* you?' His stare was cruelly indifferent. 'Don't pull that with me, sugar. I'm not getting married at seventeen. And when I do, it won't be to some white trash.'

Nina couldn't speak. She couldn't take it in. Was this the same Jeff who had held her close all those nights, whispering sweet things in her ears? Was this the boy she'd spent hours daydreaming about, the lover she'd killed herself to get time with? Just a few hours ago she'd thought he was her Prince Charming. Now Nina saw him for what he was: an immature boy, a coward, a bully, a cheat.

And she had his child growing inside her.

'I shouldn't have said that. We'll work something out.' Relieved that Nina wasn't arguing, Jeff looked away. All that white-faced melodrama, he couldn't stand it. It was kind of a shame, but there was no way he was up for this. Marry Nina Roth! She must have been out of her mind.

'I know this guy works out of Sixth Avenue,' Jeff said, calmer now. 'Dr Fenton. He's sorted out some of the girls from St Mike's before—he's a real doctor, qualified, but he's expensive, like five hundred dollars.'

Nina was gazing at him, her face expressionless.

'Hey, I'll spring for it,' Jeff said magnanimously. 'I know my responsibilities. I'll get the money to you in school next week.' He paused. 'No hard feelings, Nina, right?'

Nina stood up slowly and reached for her coat. She let herself out of the hotel bedroom without looking round and closed the door behind her. As she walked slowly home, grief gave way to anger, and by the time she reached Third Avenue she had started to form a plan.

Nina went to her locker and opened it. The space behind the grille was empty; twice Jeff Glazer had stuffed an envelope full of banknotes in there, and twice she had returned it. Perhaps he'd finally got the message. She pulled out her running shoes, unzipped her sports bag and packed them inside. The rest of the space was full of the clothes she had taken from her bedroom this morning. She removed a sealed envelope, addressed to Sister Ignatius, the principal. A similar note was tucked under her pillow at home, for her parents. Without rushing, Nina stacked her textbooks neatly inside her locker. Then she carried her tote bag into the girls' rest room and changed into her skirt, a neat blouse, and a pair of flat shoes. She emerged with her uniform folded in a neat pile, laid it on top of the textbooks and closed her locker door.

Nina ignored the strange looks her classmates gave her as they hurried off to geography. She turned left at the end of the corridor and walked straight through the double doors, down the marble steps and out of the gates.

The bag was heavy but Nina marched down the street like she hardly noticed it. Yesterday afternoon she had gone to see Jo Kepler, her supervisor at Duane Reed, and explained that Mom had been taken ill. She was going to have to quit her job right away. She was terribly sorry for the inconvenience, but could Ms Kepler give her a reference?

'Sure, of course. I hate to lose you, Nina, but of course I understand,' Ms Kepler said, shaking her head. 'I'll give you an excellent reference, and maybe we'll see you back here when your mother gets better.'

The letter was tucked safely inside the outer pocket of her bag, and now there was only one task left. Nina headed for the nearest branch of Wells Fargo.

'Good morning, miss. May I help you?' asked the smiling clerk.

'Yes,' Nina said. 'I'd like to close my account.'

Five minutes later Nina was back out on the sidewalk with a brown envelope in her hand. It contained $627; all she had in the world.

chapter two

ELIZABETH COULD HEAR the maid coming along the dormitory corridor, tapping on doors to wake up the young ladies.

'Six thirty, my lady,' the maid announced, opening Elizabeth's door a fraction.

'*Merci*, Claudette,' Elizabeth said, quickly swinging her bare feet out from under the eiderdown duvet. She loved her bed and collapsed into it at night without a second thought. Yet it wasn't difficult to get up in the mornings, she had so much to look forward to.

'There's been a new snowfall.'

Penny Foster, her room-mate and the only daughter of a property tycoon, was standing at the window looking up at the massive horseshoe of mountains that ringed Saas Fee.

'Terrific!' Elizabeth grinned. 'More skiing. I can do a run straight back to the village.'

'Is that all you ever think about?' Penny sniffed, pushing a lock of red-gold hair out of her eyes. Penny resented Elizabeth's energy. She had a wild reputation, in school as well as in the village, where her nickname was *coup de foudre*, the thunderbolt. Elizabeth skied with ferocious passion, ignoring all the school rules about forbidden areas. Saas Fee had practically year-round snow, and even after the tourists departed admiring locals noticed Elizabeth's graceful young body in its snug lilac suit twist sharply down a mogul field or bomb down a black run, crouching into the trajectory like a brightly coloured bullet.

Six months of Switzerland had changed Elizabeth dramatically. Her curves had become high and tight, her legs powerful. Her glossy hair had grown longer and thicker and the mountain sun had highlighted it with rich streaks of gold, the colour of warm honey. Away from Tony's constant disapproval, the sullen rebellion had disappeared. There was a fresh flush to her complexion and a dancing light in her green eyes. Elizabeth practically glowed with health.

'Come on, we've only got twenty minutes,' Penny said, and the two of them scrambled into their school uniform and rushed out into the corridor to join the other girls.

The dining room was laid out with long tables and hand-carved, high-backed dining chairs, its windows looking out towards the pastureland and the dark, scented pine forests beneath.

Elizabeth rushed towards the buffet and loaded her plate: newly baked bread, warm croissants, a bowl of steaming hot chocolate and some fresh apricots.

'Hey, Elizabeth, something to interest you,' Vanessa Chadwick announced. Vanessa was a shipping heiress, a willowy blonde who obeyed school rules and found the Savage girl rather shocking.

Elizabeth grunted. 'I doubt that.'

Mornings at the Ecole Henri Dufor were spent practising music, dancing or deportment and then attending 'lectures'. These were supposed to broaden the mind but normally sent Elizabeth to sleep.

Vanessa sighed at this lack of school spirit. 'His name is Herr Hans Wolf. He helped organise the Winter Olympics here last year.'

'Not Hans Wolf the skier?'

Vanessa flicked back her shiny blonde hair and consulted her lecture notes. 'He coached the Swiss ski team, if that's what you mean.'

'Yes, but he was a skier long before that.' Elizabeth tore off a piece of croissant and dipped it in her chocolate, eyes sparkling. 'Back in the twenties, when people used wooden skis they tied onto their boots. It was incredibly dangerous. Hans Wolf set five downhill records that way during his career. How long is he staying?'

'Just to give the lecture.'

After breakfast the girls trooped into the music room for piano practice. Elizabeth was dreadful as usual but smiled engagingly at Madame Lyon; she wanted some new ski boots and that meant Dad had to receive good reports. As soon as they were dismissed—all the girls bobbing a curtsy to the old lady—Elizabeth rushed down the corridor to the lecture hall to bag herself the best seat.

Herr Geller, the headmaster, peered in to check that his flock was settled. He noticed Elizabeth Savage sitting centre front and raised an eyebrow; most unlike Lady Elizabeth to take an active interest in anything. Still, he was pleased to see it. It had been a great coup for the Ecole to land the daughter of Lord Caerhaven—titles always looked good in the pupil register—and in many ways, her ladyship had proved ideal. The earl had written him a frank letter before Elizabeth was admitted, explaining that she was a wilful girl and likely to cause trouble; on no account was she to be given business education, maths lessons or allowed to have marketing journals delivered. He wanted a young lady and not a tomboy to return from the Alps, he wrote. When Geller had called Elizabeth to him to explain her father's prohibitions, all he got was a nod and a shrug of the shoulders.

Elizabeth had resigned herself to the inevitable. For the moment, it was better to play along, let the family think she'd given in. But one day, she promised herself, she would work at Dragon. *One day*. That company was her birthright and she wouldn't let it go.

She should be studying for her A levels, but instead she was stuck in this relic from the past, learning cordon bleu cookery, flower arranging and ballroom dancing. Enthusiasm was asking too much, but Elizabeth dutifully stuck roses in jars and waltzed to the 'Blue Danube'. At the end of her first term her report said, 'Modest and well-behaved', and gave her average marks for everything.

Tony doubled her allowance.

Besides, Elizabeth was enjoying herself. She thought she would loathe Switzerland, but within a week she was in love—the soaring, white capped mountains, green Alpine slopes covered with edelweiss and grazing cattle, the belled goats and clear mountain air. The village of Saas Fee was enchanting, with its narrow, winding cobbled streets and gabled shops. She adored Swiss food, thick black bread, cuttlefish soups, fondues and *Kirschtorte*, or cherry tart.

Then she had her first skiing lesson, and her life was transformed.

Alone on the black runs from Felskinn and Langflüh, slicing down the glittering, pearl-white tracks, her blood racing, she felt more alive than she had ever believed possible. Elizabeth had two years of finishing school and from now on she looked forward to every second.

She heard the other girls rise to their feet as Herr Geller and his guest entered the room. Hans Wolf marched rapidly up to the lectern amid the polite applause, with the air of a man who wants to get something over quickly. His long stride and erect back were in strange contrast to his wiry white hair and the deep wrinkles scoring his face. Elizabeth knew he was seventy-six, but he looked fifty.

Sighing, Hans Wolf regarded his bored, beautiful audience for a second. Then he reached into his jacket pocket, fished out some crumpled notes and started to read, rattling on about the Olympic ideal and the healing powers of sport. Occasionally he glanced up at the faces in front of him. Most of them were staring at him with glazed eyes, except for a pretty, healthy-looking girl with bright green eyes in the centre front, who was leaning forwards, spellbound, on the edge of her seat. Disconcerted, the old man gave her a brief smile, lost his place, found it again and ploughed on to the end.

After a few prepared questions from the prefects about sporting behaviour, Herr Geller was on his feet. 'I'm sure we're all most grateful to Herr Wolf for that fascinating talk.' Dutiful applause.

'Many thanks, Herr Wolf. I'm sure that was very instructive for our young ladies,' Geller was saying.

Wolf picked up his notes. slightly disappointed the attractive blonde had not spoken. 'My pleasure, Herr Geller.'

Wolf felt a small tug on his sleeve. 'May I ask you a question?' Elizabeth said nervously.

Wolf turned to see the girl from the front row. Close up, she was even prettier. He was interested despite himself. 'Go ahead.'

'I was wondering, Herr Wolf, what it was like to break the record on the Hahnenkamm?'

'What?' Wolf stuttered, taken aback.

'In 1925,' the young girl added helpfully.

'*Ja*, I remember when it was,' Hans Wolf replied. He took a closer look at the pretty eyes and saw the pale ring of goggle marks. 'It was terrifying. Wonderful. You are interested in skiing?'

Elizabeth nodded eagerly and Herr Geller, wanting to impress a member of the Olympic committee, added, 'Lady Elizabeth is a very good skier, I believe, Herr Wolf. Our own instructors taught her. The Ecole has an excellent record in—'

Wolf caught the scornful glint in Elizabeth's eye and was suddenly vastly amused. Maybe he could take the young *Fräulein* out for lunch at a mountain café. It would be fun to tell stories from his youth. The Hahnenkamm in 1925! A lifetime ago.

'So I hear, Herr Geller. I would very much like to see for myself.' He turned to Elizabeth. 'Young lady, will you show me what you have learned? We could take the gondola up to Plattjen.'

'I'd love to, sir.' Elizabeth glanced at Herr Geller.

'*Natürlich*, go ahead,' he said expansively.

Wolf eyed the young woman speculatively. 'Are you good?'

'Very good,' Elizabeth said boldly.

Wolf grinned. 'There are some nasty mogul fields up there. We'll see.'

Hans Wolf leaned over the rail on the restaurant balcony, wondering if he could believe his eyes. Down the steep, unforgiving slope opposite him, Elizabeth's strong young body was flying around the moguls. The stick was planted firmly and removed cleanly, she jumped high and twisted sharply from the waist. No mogul seemed too large, no jump too high. The teenager moved with instinctive grace and skill. The technique was unpolished, but she was superb.

Ten minutes ago he'd been looking forward to an encouraging chat and a pleasant lunch. The *Engländerin* aristocrat was obviously passionate about skiing, openly admiring of him and funny about her school. He had settled on the restaurant balcony and told her to have a go at the short, steep mogul run while he ordered lunch. The first time he watched her descent Wolf thought he must be imagining things. He waved at her to do it again, to check it was not a fluke.

She was so good, it set his adrenalin going just to watch her. He beckoned to a waiter. 'I need to make a telephone call.'

'Of course, sir.' The waiter led him into the bar. Wolf dropped some coins into the slot and dialled the number from memory.

'British Ski Federation,' replied a female voice.

'This is Hans Wolf from Switzerland,' he said. 'Is the director around?'

Six hundred and twenty-seven dollars didn't get you very far.

'Fifty a week,' the landlord said.

Nina shrugged and looked scornful. She was staring into a cramped little room with damp stains on the walls, a chipped basin and one closet. The communal bathroom was down the hall.

'Thirty-five.' Nina locked into his eyes with an icy stare. 'It's all I got. If it's not enough, I'll need to go somewhere else.'

The guy frowned. 'OK, but two weeks in advance.'

She fished in her pocket, peeled off the bills from her small roll. He left. She sat down on her small bunk and put her head in her hands. What were her parents doing now? Calling the police? Did they miss her? They had to miss what she could do. But even so, Red Hook was a no-go area; the cops wouldn't find her here.

She felt surprisingly calm. Jeff Glazer had been such a stupid mistake. She'd trusted him, and look where it got her. She wouldn't make the same mistake again.

Nina got up from the bed and went to the grimy window. Outside was the bustle and noise of dirty, dodgy Brooklyn. She had $557 and the clothes she stood up in.

Tomorrow she would get a job. It was time to get out of here.

Nina spent two anxious weeks trudging down Flatbush Avenue and around the Civic Centre. Brooklyn was sunk in the late seventies recession. Nobody was hiring. She was desperate when she had her first stroke of luck. A boy named Leon was standing in front of her in a checkout queue, bitching about the health food store that had just fired him.

Green Earth was a small hippy-looking place. Fading paint peeled from its storefront and round the dusty windows, displaying an assortment of candles, vitamins and joss sticks. Not promising, but her heart beat a bit faster. A bell jangled as she pushed the door open.

'Hi, can I help you?'

The storekeeper was grey-haired, maybe sixty. He was sitting behind the counter, hunched over a stack of loose receipts.

'I hope so,' Nina said politely. 'I heard you fired Leon. I'd like to apply for the job.'

The man shook his head. 'I'm not replacing him. Third kid I tried in a month. All they do is sit around talking back to the customers.'

'I'm not like that, really. I've got experience and a reference.'

'Sorry, honey, try somewhere else.' Nina was about to leave when he added, 'What I need is an accountant. Or a magician.'

'What are they, your records?' Nina asked.

'Uh-huh.' The old guy shook his head again. 'Never keep a store, kid. You'll go blind before your time.'

'I can organise those for you,' she said, ignoring his disbelieving expression. 'Really. My folks kept a deli. I used to—' she nearly said 'do the', but changed it to 'help with the reordering and stock-taking.'

'Yeah? You good at maths?' he asked, interest creeping into his tone.

'Top of the class. Look, why don't you let me sort out those receipts? If you think you can use me, give me a month's trial. If not, I'll stop bothering you.' She fought to keep the anxiety out of her voice.

He paused for a second, then nodded. 'I guess it couldn't hurt.'

'I'm Nina Roth,' Nina said, weak with relief.

'Frank Malone,' the old man said, shaking her hand.

Nina started at Green Earth at six bucks an hour. Compared to the chaos of her mother's deli, Green Earth's simple product line was a breeze to keep track of, and soon Nina could tell her boss what was selling and what wasn't. She painted the storefront a cotton-candy pink and put up bold cardboard signs for special offers and discounts. Word got round fast, and more customers started coming in. Nina learned the names of the regulars and gave them all polite, efficient service. Frank was impressed.

'How come you work so hard?' he asked one night, as she combed through a pharmaceutical catalogue. 'You should be out having fun.'

'I like to work,' Nina said truthfully.

She had a million ideas for improvements, and Frank Malone was eager to try them all. A widower of seven years, the store was all he had left, and Nina made it an exciting, friendly, bustling place to be. She worked like a demon. She knew she had to make herself indispensable to Frank Malone before the inevitable happened.

When she'd left home, Nina had just one thought in her head. She'd get a place, find a job to cover the rent, and spend her money on an abortion. It was terrible to lose her scholarships, but she had to get out of Park Slope, away from her selfish parents, a million miles away from Jeff Glazer. She felt so lonely and hurt she'd thought she would die.

It was difficult to pinpoint the moment she'd changed her mind. After she started at Green Earth, Nina meant to make a doctor's appointment, but somehow she kept putting it off. Two months into her job, the third month of pregnancy, Nina found herself stacking jars of baby food. She froze as she stared at the label, showing a chubby baby with a gap-toothed smile. And she knew she'd changed her mind.

Nina *wanted* her child. No matter who the father was. She wanted someone to love. She wanted to give all the joys, all the caring, that her own parents never bothered with. It's going to be tough, the nagging voice of reason warned. But Nina had made up her mind. *Tough I'm used to.*

It took four months before Frank noticed.

'How's my favourite girl?' he asked one morning, as Nina unlocked the front door.

'Good. You know, Frank, we should think about advertising. Posters around town, the local paper.'

'Too expensive.'

'It'll pay for itself in a month.' She took off her coat and hung it up.

'Well, I'm glad to see that.'

'What?' Nina asked, turning round.

He gestured at her stomach. 'You're putting on a little weight at last. It suits you, you should eat more.'

Nina braced herself. He'd have to know some time.

'It's not that, Frank. I'm pregnant.'

The old man's face darkened. 'Boyfriend's not around?'

'No.' Nina's eyes were expressionless. It was clear that she was in no mood for explanations.

'You need any help?'

'No, but thanks all the same.'

'So, you'll be leaving, I guess,' Frank said anxiously. Nina had only been around for a few months, but it felt like for ever. He didn't know how he'd get along without her.

'No, I hope you won't be mad . . . I've decided to keep the baby.'

'That's wonderful.' His face blossomed into a vast crinkly grin. 'You'll be a great mom. I guess I'll have to give you a raise.'

He trundled over and hugged her. Nina wanted to cry. Nobody had given her such simple friendship for as long as she could remember.

Frank added, 'I've been thinking about giving you a share in the profits, anyway. Five per cent on top of your wages. Since we're making some, these days.'

'Oh, Frank.' Nina said. Frank Malone was a lonely man who felt paternal towards her, and she *had* made a big difference in the store. 'I shouldn't,' she said weakly.

'Take it.' Frank brushed aside her objections. 'I got a cousin in Queens, a lawyer. Did my will. I'll get him to draw up the paperwork.'

Nina hugged herself. Five per cent of one tiny store, hardly an empire. But it was her first step on the ladder. The future wasn't rosy, but perhaps it wasn't so black either.

Three days later Frank Malone had a stroke. He was rushed to hospital, but there was nothing the doctors could do. He died an hour later.

'Nina Roth?'

Nina looked up from sweeping the floor as the door jangled. A tall, stocky man in a homburg and a black overcoat stepped into the store, ignoring the 'Closed' sign. She frowned wearily. 'That's right,' she said.

'I'm Connor Malone.'

'Oh.' Nina blushed, wiped her dusty hands on her apron and came forwards to shake his hand. Connor would be Frank's son from Albany, the one he was always moaning never came to see him. She wished she'd been wearing something more appropriate than her tatty blue jeans and red-checked shirt to meet her new boss. 'Hi there. I'm so sorry about Frank, Mr Malone. He was always very good to me.'

She decided not to mention the 5 per cent. Connor Malone wouldn't believe her, she could tell that right away.

'Yeah, he was a generous guy,' Connor said vaguely, glancing around the shop. 'He really pulled it together since the last time I was here.'

Nina couldn't exactly say that it was mostly her doing, so she just nodded and smiled. 'Green Earth is doing really well.'

'That's good, we'll get a better price for it.' He was so pleased he missed the look of panic on Nina's face.

'You're not going to sell, Mr Malone?'

Connor glanced at her. 'Sure, who'd run this place now?'

'Why not me?'

'I don't think so.' He smiled politely. 'OK, well, thanks for looking after the place till I got here, Miss Roth. I know you didn't have a contract, but I'll see you get a full month's severance. That's only fair.'

'Mr Malone, don't you think you should keep Green Earth open? It's making a nice profit now. I did all the bookkeeping and ordered the stock. I could go right on doing that, and you could hire a junior to help me out.'

Malone looked at the earnest little face and almost laughed.

'Nice try, Nina, but no dice. Sorry. I'll get you that cheque tomorrow.'

Nina didn't attend the funeral. Instead she stayed back and organised what passed for an Irish wake, a restrained affair with a few glasses of Scotch and some tired sandwiches, which was what Connor thought appropriate. She worked methodically in the store before the guests came back, tidying the last few boxes of pills and bottles behind the counter. Somehow it seemed a better farewell to Frank than a bunch of flowers anyway.

She leaned back against the empty shelves and took a deep breath. On her own again. It was scary, but she did have some options this time. The local storekeepers knew her and a couple of them had been over making probing noises. But Nina had the baby to think of now; she had to hold out for something better. A career with potential.

When the mourners returned and pounced on the whisky. Nina was still thinking about her future. By the time pompous Connor took her aside and magnanimously announced he was adding one extra week to her severance pay, Nina had pretty much made up her mind.

A year's bookkeeping had shown her the kind of money that the prescription-drug companies made, despite lazy salesmen and lousy service. New York was hooked on its vitamins and potions, and it would stay that way. There were vast improvements needed in the pharmaceutical business. She'd been a customer and she knew it. Thinking about that gave her a *frisson* of excitement.

The drug business would be hard work, but it would provide better for her kid. As far as Nina was concerned, that was all that mattered.

Nina was writing a job application when it happened, sitting in Green Earth in the gloom. Connor had boarded the place up, ready for sale, but Nina had kept a spare set of keys. She sneaked in most nights and hammered out résumés and letters to the big drug giants. Until she landed a new job, she couldn't afford a typewriter of her own.

She was trying ICI when the first pain came, a sharp twinge in the gut. Nina pressed a hand to her taut midriff. God, it hurt, it really hurt. Gasping, she doubled forwards, clutching herself. There was a pause, then another wrenching, flaming stab. Nina staggered out of the door and onto the sidewalk. There was a payphone there and she dialled 911.

When the ambulance got there five minutes later, they found Nina clinging to the phone, tears streaming down her face. Her slacks were drenched. She knew what was happening. She was going to lose her baby, like she'd lost everything else.

St Jude's Blue Cross Hospital was staffed with brisk, fatigued junior doctors. A black gynaecologist saw Nina.

'I'm sorry you lost the child, but you're OK. No reason why you couldn't have another.'

'Thank you, Doctor,' the girl said quietly. 'When do you think I'll be fit to leave?' ·

Dr Kenmore shook her head. 'You're fit now, physically, but you should stay and rest, that's fine. We do Medicare.'

'I have to go,' Nina said, and pushed back the covers.

'Don't you want any counselling?' Dr Kenmore asked. 'We have a rabbi here, he could talk to you.'

'No. Thank you.' Nina Roth looked up at the doctor, her face beautiful despite its pallor, heavy, silky hair ringing her face. 'No counselling's gonna change what happened. I'm alive, I have to get on with it.'

Nina felt so weak she took a cab home. She let herself into her room, collapsed on the bed and cried like she would never stop.

Two days later, she got her first positive reply.

Dolan MacDonald was the tenth drug firm she'd applied to. The position was for an assistant sales manager at $21,000 a year; a pittance by industry standards, but a fortune to Nina. In her first interview, she answered questions on her work experience and Dolan. Today she was meeting her prospective boss.

Nina left the subway at the Jay Street exit and headed for Dolan's offices, a functional block of grey stone. It looked dull, but she was excited. She wanted the job so much she ached.

Her second interview took place in a drab room somewhere on the second floor, with Ivan Kinzslade, head of the Vitamins division.

'You made good grades. Why you drop outta school?' he asked without preamble.

'I wanted to get on in the world, make something of myself.'

'So why you join a tiny joint like Green Earth?'

'It was tiny, but it made a good profit,' Nina said defensively.

Her interviewer's eyes narrowed. 'Not when you joined.'

Nina sat up a little straighter, realising Kinzslade had been asking around. 'I couldn't get a job anywhere else. It wasn't such a great idea, dropping out of school.' The Russian laughed.

Kinzslade called her at home that afternoon to tell her she was hired.

Nina insisted on her first pay cheque in advance; she needed it for the deposit on a new apartment, a small one-bedroom off Flatbush Avenue. She was surprised that demanding the money didn't hurt her image, in fact it impressed her bosses. Nina found that if she acted seriously people respected her. For the first time in her life she had a respectable place of her own, she was doing good at work, she could pay all her bills. It was hard, though. Nina's creamy complexion was dull with fatigue by the end of each day. She could cook herself a meal, just about, but she was pathetically grateful when Mrs Minsky, her neighbour, dropped round with the odd apple pie.

'Lord, child,' Mrs Minsky said, sniffing, 'they work ya too hard, you're white as ivory. Didn't your momma tell ya you're too cute for this? Ya need a man to take care of ya. If those guys at your work don't ask ya out, they should be takin' their own medicines.'

Nina could have laughed. Ask her out! Like they ever did anything else! Almost every man on her floor had tried his luck already. Slowly but surely Nina got the word out that she wasn't interested. Nina got a skewed reputation. She was a major babe, but uninterested in men. She was ambitious, always hammering at her computer keyboard, but bored by office politics. Soon enough, the boys ignored her.

All except Ivan Kinzslade, who had an instinct about Nina. The job he'd hired her for was simple, form filling and number crunching. At first she seemed happy just to do that, but after the first month, Ivan noticed her calls to the field offices were taking longer, she was asking for more data.

First thing one Monday morning she showed up in his office.

'Morning, Nina, you gotta problem?' the Russian asked.

'An idea,' Nina said, coming right to the point.

Ivan liked it. Roth was more up front than any other young girl he'd hired. She seemed much older than her years. 'Go on, then,' he said.

'We're wasting a lot of money in the way we sell our stuff. Look at this,' Nina said, spreading out research in front of her boss. 'We tailor journeys to our salesmen. If we paid more attention to retailers, we could focus our efforts.'

Kinzslade glanced up at the grave young woman standing over him. 'I guess you can try it,' was all he said.

Over the next year, Nina crammed as much work as possible into an

eight-hour day. She tried to alter Dolan's sales, organising training pro-
grammes and policy around the needs of the customers, not the company. Orders picked up, and Ivan gave her a pay rise.

In her second year, Nina talked her boss into thirty new computers.
The expense was a black hole in the quarterly budget, but quickly paid
for itself. Productivity went up two per cent; clerical expenses fell.

It was hard work, trying to change a system that had been in place for
decades, but her colleagues listened when Nina talked. Nina climbed
quietly, seriously, relentlessly, without stopping for friendship or looking
back for love. She didn't care. She thought that stuff was for weaklings.

The phone trilled on Nina's desk. It was Edwin Jensen, a prestigious
firm of head-hunters who specialised in pharmaceuticals. She was getting herself a reputation, they said. Dragon was looking for a business
development exec. Would Ms Roth be interested?

Nina took a deep breath. Dragon. The big time. Dragon had pharma-
cies, drugstores and health-food places across Europe and the States.
Their executives were highly paid, on hefty bonus schemes. The head
offices on Park Avenue were a fantasy of marble and gold, burgundy
leather and mahogany, exuding old-world elegance.

She had never even considered the British giant. Dragon acted like a
gentleman's club. The dress code was strict, recruitment conservative:
clean-cut young men, the cream of the Ivy League. It wasn't big on
ethnic minorities, City College grads, or women.

Why me? Nina thought.

'So, would you consider interviewing, Ms Roth?'

'Absolutely,' she said. It was certainly worth a shot. At worst she'd get
a little flavour of life inside a market leader.

A week later Nina arrived at the Dragon building on Park Avenue,
wearing her best suit and shoes. Dragon's HQ was a palace. The reception area was a study in burgundy leather, mahogany and marble,
bustling with men in expensive suits. The receptionist looked at Nina
like she was gunge sticking in the sink drainer.

'Yes, miss, can I help you?'

'I'm here for a job interview.' Nina's voice sounded very small in her
own ears and she cleared her throat. 'My name's Nina Roth.'

The woman tapped her hi-tech keyboard and unbent slightly.

'Yes. You take the elevator to the thirteenth floor. You'll be seen by Mr
Gary Bellman from Human Resources, and Lord Caerhaven.'

The back of Nina's throat dried up. 'Lord Caerhaven, *personally*?'

'That's right. He's visiting New York,' the receptionist said blandly.

Tony Savage. She'd clipped countless articles about him at Dolan. Savage had ripped the heart out of countless small firms and research teams, invested brilliantly, fired thousands of workers, and turned his moribund family business into a global giant. Known everywhere as the Robber Baron, he was respected but loathed. The drugs business feared him. And adored him. What the hell was he here for? Why was he attending this interview? Nina buzzed for the elevator and tried to calm herself. Thank God, she thought, I don't have too much time to think about it.

Upstairs a secretary ushered her into Gary Bellman's spacious office. The two men were sitting casually on chairs behind a long table; one smaller chair was set in front just for her. It felt like a long walk before she could sit down.

'You're Nina Roth?'

'Yes, Mr Bellman, how do you do.' Nina shook hands.

The sandy-haired guy raised an eyebrow. 'How do you know I'm Bellman?'

'Because I recognise Lord Caerhaven.'

Tony Savage grinned. He liked to sit in on odd meetings; lightning visits to keep his people on their toes. Today he was inspecting Human Resources. Bellman, his new guy, liked to pick people from different backgrounds to the norm: scholarship kids, entrepreneurs, cherry-picked youngsters from Glaxo or ICI. This girl, Roth, was clearly terrified, but putting on a good act. It impressed him; her lovely face and sexy figure impressed him a lot more. 'Tony Savage,' he said.

His strong, fleshy hand gripped hers like a vice, dark eyes sweeping across her body like they could X-ray her.

Nina blushed. Savage was physically overbearing, large and muscular. He had an air of ruthlessness that matched his reputation. She had to fight not to flinch under his stare.

'Thank you for seeing me,' she replied coolly.

'Lord Caerhaven has some questions for you, Ms Roth,' Bellman said.

Tony Savage looked at Nina for a long, luxurious moment, careful to keep his eyes expressionless.

He fired a question. Nina answered it sharply. He fired another.

Nothing seemed to faze her. As Nina talked, Savage's thoughts drifted. He wondered if his hands would fit round that tiny waist. What colour the nipples were on top of those creamy breasts. She looked uptight: great. Not the kind to sleep around.

A challenge.

Tony nodded coldly. Nina Roth had a great future with Dragon.

chapter three

ELIZABETH ARCHED HER BACK. Gérard's grip was firm, one hand expertly brushing across her breasts, the other stroking between her legs. He was so lost in lust for her incredible body he never noticed her eyes were closed. His own were fixed on the mirror opposite the bed, its ornate frame reflecting Elizabeth's firm body curving back against him, his cock pushing in and out of her . . . too hot to wait, Gerard felt himself speeding up, his breath coming shorter, starting to thrust. He gasped.

'Chérie, chérie, je t'aime . . .'

She said nothing but he felt her press against his hand. In time to his thrusts, he brushed his fingertips lightly back and forwards, the way she liked it. She moaned, and his touch got faster. He felt his orgasm gathering, struggled to control it as he pressed hard against her clitoris and heard her cry out. Groaning with pleasure, Gérard exploded inside her and collapsed. They slumped back together onto the silk sheets.

Elizabeth panted as her climax subsided, coming out of her fantasy. For a few seconds she was dizzy, disorientated. Then she felt Gérard slip out of her, snapping her back to reality. Once the pleasure had ebbed, she found she always wanted to be alone.

Elizabeth stretched out as though exhausted. 'Better get back to your own room. I need some sleep before tomorrow.'

'OK, sure. I understand. The races come first.'

He was too eager to please, pulling on his clothes right away. She knew he'd be at the bottom of the black run that plunged down from Diavolezza tomorrow, waiting to hug her for the cameras after the ladies' downhill. His enthusiasm annoyed her. It was boring.

Elizabeth stirred restlessly. 'See you tomorrow.'

'A demain.'

After Gérard left, Elizabeth wandered into her bathroom and ran a bath, pouring in a stream of scented oil. The fragrance of lavender and thyme filled the room and she willed herself to relax. The bathroom had a large window overlooking the lake, and as Elizabeth sank into the water she could see the turrets of the luxurious Palace Hotel in St Moritz, where Monica and her father would be checking in tonight.

Relations with her family had changed completely. When Elizabeth was offered a place on the British ski team, Tony agreed at once. Skiing was almost as good as showjumping. They could talk about Elizabeth at dinner parties again.

Soon it was clear they could do more than that. Elizabeth came second in her first slalom, actually won a downhill at Méribel. To the amazement of the Europeans, the British teenager came from nowhere to finish fourth overall in her first World Cup.

Elizabeth was an overnight sensation. Photos of Elizabeth smiling on the rostrum in her sapphire ski suit were splashed all over the papers; recession-bound Britain was in need of a bit of glamour. In the 'Winter of Discontent', sexy Lady Elizabeth Savage gave people something to smile about. To their amazement, Tony and Monica found Elizabeth was an asset, her black fleece washed white by the Alpine snow.

That Christmas, Elizabeth cautiously asked her father for a favour. She wanted to spend the summer working at Dragon.

Instead of the curt refusal she'd been dreading, the earl agreed. 'If it would amuse you, Elizabeth. I believe there are openings at head office.'

Elizabeth gaped with disbelief and stammered a thank you.

'I expect you'll enjoy it. As long as you realise the arrangement is temporary. You're bound to meet a decent chap on the winter circuit, and you'll be far too busy with wedding plans . . .'

Tony couldn't have been plainer. As long as she played ball and behaved herself, she could do what she wanted, but they were still planning on marrying her off. To underline the point, Monica gave her a diamond bracelet for Christmas, and on New Year's Day Tony quadrupled her allowance.

Elizabeth sold the bracelet. She opened a secret bank account in Geneva, and fed her allowance into it every month. The new star of the British team didn't need money. They booked suites at the best hotels and flew first class instead of club. For Elizabeth, nothing was too much. She ignored the British coach; and she stayed up all hours on the circuit, a butterfly playgirl in the skiing jet set.

It drove her teammates mad. When they were getting up at six to sweat in the hotel gyms, Elizabeth was lounging in bed with hot chocolate and a croissant. When they were slamming down the practice runs, being screamed at by the coach, Elizabeth would turn up late and do her own thing. When they were ordered to bed early before a race, Elizabeth would be downstairs in the cocktail bar, draping herself in the arms of the latest beau.

Janet Marlin, Karen Carter and Kate Cox, the other British girls, thought Elizabeth was a bitch who loved the limelight and rewrote the rules. Bad enough that Elizabeth was so gorgeous, without her showing up in sparkling diamond earrings and Perry Ellis cocktail gowns. And on top of that, she had a title. It was 'Yes, my lady', 'No, your ladyship', wherever they went. Even the press hounds called her 'Lady Elizabeth' when they were baying for a quote. But in the eye of the glittering storm, Elizabeth Savage felt lonely and empty.

She got a reputation as a playgirl. Soon she accepted one of the persistent suitors: Karl von Hocheit, a male model and son of a German car tycoon. Karl introduced her to sex. He was handsome, but he was blond and bland. She dumped him for the Hon Richard Godfrey, an Old Etonian, heir to a hotel empire; her parents were thrilled. Then Richard said she should win the title and settle down to child-rearing.

'Who cares?' he asked when she talked about Dragon. 'Lizzie, don't you realise you don't *need* to work? I'll take care of the cash.'

They broke up the same night.

Then there was Gérard, Comte de Mesnil. Gérard was a good lover and made no demands. She had stayed with him ever since.

In her second year of competition, Elizabeth took the individual silver for the slalom, gold for the downhill and overall bronze medal. The country went nuts, but she was bitterly disappointed.

That autumn, Elizabeth flew out to Davos to begin training again. She met up with Gérard and started to party. Once again, though, she began to feel a gaping emptiness inside her.

It was true that she loved to ski, but she didn't want to *be* a skier. Yet she wasn't equipped to do anything else.

All the flashbulbs, laughter and chiming champagne glasses in the world couldn't drown out the question pounding in her head.

My God. What am I going to do?

'Elizabeth, you have a visitor.'

Ronnie Davis, the British coach, studied his star athlete with an exasperated expression. Elizabeth had come third in the downhill at Val-d'Isère, trailing Louise Levier by a good six seconds. Shrugging, she had promised to do better at Méribel, but she'd still cut training yesterday. Her attitude drove him crazy.

'Is it Gérard again? Tell him I'm busy,' Elizabeth said.

They were standing in the lobby of the Antares, Méribel's smartest hotel. Janet was already strapping up for the slopes; Kate had gone to work out in the fitness room. Ronnie knew that Elizabeth would head for a café and a paper, despite the slalom tomorrow.

'No, it's not Gérard. Regretfully.'

'Hans!'

Elizabeth spun round to see a tall, white-haired figure standing behind her. She rushed to give him a hug. 'What are you doing here? I thought you retired last year.'

'It's true I don't coach, but they can't get rid of me that fast,' Wolf told her gravely. He nodded at Ronnie. 'An honour, Herr Davis. You have your country winning races again.'

'That's all down to Elizabeth,' Davis said flatly. He shook hands with Hans and headed for his room. Great, just great. Another hanger-on to tell Elizabeth how wonderful she was.

Hans took Elizabeth out to lunch. They rode the La Saulire gondola to the Pierres Plates, a chalet restaurant at the gondola station with breathtaking views down the valley. They sat on the sun-drenched terrace and watched the skiers swoop away down the black runs.

'It's a beautiful view, *nicht wahr?* The top of the world.'

'Stunning,' Elizabeth agreed.

Hans waved a wrinkled hand at the scene in front of them. '*Ja?* What do you see?'

'See? Skiers, I suppose.'

'Skiers. I am surprised you recognise them.'

Elizabeth glanced sharply up at the old man, and found the pale blue eyes were narrow with disapproval. 'If I was Herr Davis, I would send you home. I would not let you ski. You are a disgrace to your country.'

Hans Wolf was leaning towards her, his weather-beaten face angry and passionate. 'Everyone talks about you, how you do not train, you refuse all instruction. With these boys, always you are running around. You are not a skier, you are a tourist.'

Elizabeth pushed back her chair. 'I don't have to listen to this. Don't you read the papers, Hans?'

'*Ach*, the papers. Of course, you are a big star. *Coup de foudre*, the thunderbolt, yes?' He snorted with disgust. 'You don't notice the other skiers saying that. The pros. They know you are not trying. You have talent. So? Talent, you were born with. What matters is what you do with it.'

'Hey, I took fourth, then the bronze. I'll make gold this year.' Elizabeth tried to pretend she didn't know what Hans meant. 'Maybe I need a little polish—'

'Polish! You think taking gold is as easy as that? You are four, five seconds behind Heidi Laufen and Louise Levier, each race.'

'That's nothing,' Elizabeth muttered.

'It is an eternity. The Swiss girls train every day, while you go shopping. They rest every night, when you giggle with your young men. But they are not here to catch a husband; they are here to race. And win.'

'I'm not out here to get a husband, Hans.'

'Why do you resent the sport, then? I can't help if you won't tell me.'

Behind her sunglasses, Elizabeth's eyes filled with tears. Hans was deadly accurate: along the way, her love of the silent, plunging world of the skier had turned into a brooding resentment.

'Because I like to ski, but they're making me a *skier*. Just a skier. I want to be in business, Hans.'

Her mentor's face was a mask of astonishment. 'Is this all? You do that later, no? When you finish on the slopes.'

'No! I can't! My parents don't want me to work. I've got no degree, no experience, nothing. This is all I can do.' She gestured towards the crowds behind her, and then, to her embarrassment, burst out crying.

Hans Wolf handed her a handkerchief and coaxed out the whole story. 'So. You have no way to fend for yourself.'

Elizabeth shook her head.

'Well, maybe there are other firms you work for, not only Dragon. Perhaps the FIS, *hein*?' The Fédération Internationale de Ski was the sport's governing body. 'You are clever, Elizabeth. You are glamorous, well known. You could help promote the sport, but not if you continue this way.'

'OK, OK. I hear you.' Elizabeth felt a tiny ray of hope pierce the shadows. Sell skiing for the FIS? All it would take was one post, one job where she could shine. 'What do you suggest I do?'

'You stop wasting time this season and you start to train. You will need to sweat blood to get that five seconds back.'

'All right. I suppose I could try.'

'You will *succeed*. I will arrange for you to train with some of the men's teams. You must try to be the *best*. Not just as a woman—best overall. Then, you might take the gold. Anyway, this World Cup is a warm-up.'

'To next year's Cup?'

'No, idiot child. To the Olympics.'

When Hans arrived at five forty the next morning, Elizabeth Savage was already waiting. He had a flash of admiration. There was some spark about the girl he'd never forgotten; enough to make his blood boil when he saw her wasting her talents.

'How you feel? Muscles all warm and relaxed?' he asked as they jumped on the drag lift.

Elizabeth nodded, adjusting her goggles.

'After four hours with Brad they will be screaming for mercy,' Wolf told her smugly.

He could see her body in front of him tensing with anticipation.

For a second, Hans worried that Brad would get mad at him. Brad Hinds, the US men's coach, was training for the Super-G tomorrow. The demands he made of his boys would be a shock to Elizabeth's system, but if they took time out to look at their guest, she'd have them all crashing into the mountain.

'I can't believe you're making us do this, Brad. It's a waste of time.'

Jack Taylor leaned against his ski pole, six foot three, his two hundred pounds perfectly balanced, barely denting the snow.

Sam Florence, Rick Kowalski and Pete Myers had all been on the team longer than Jack, but they didn't resent him. Taylor was the great white hope for the Olympics next year. He'd taken the silver in his first World Cup, overall gold last year and was running a comfortable lead over his Austrian rival this year. Taylor's dedication took even champion athletes aback. He was up before dawn working out, ran five miles each evening, skied all year to train, following the snow across the globe.

The team admired him all the more because he didn't have to do it. Now twenty-four, Taylor had been tapped for the USA three years back, when he was skiing for Harvard at Aspen. That year he'd graduated magna cum laude in English and put off a business degree for the sport. He could only dedicate one more year to amateur competition—his one shot at the Olympics. But Taylor was never going to need the glory for a résumé. An only child, one day he would own 400 acres of prime Southern land, two Dallas hotels, a large stock portfolio, a colonial mansion and an exclusive stable of thoroughbred racehorses.

In addition to this, there was the slight matter of his looks. Not only was he smart, rich and athletic, Jack Taylor's tall, muscled body was crowned with a face that stopped girls in their tracks.

Taylor had jet-black hair, so smooth and glossy it looked like the flank of one of his mares. He cropped it close to the head in a severely masculine cut, which complemented the frank brown eyes with their dark, long lashes, the square jaw and the sensual, slightly cruel mouth that spoke of a hidden darkness, a pitiless male sexuality.

Girls fluttered around him like butterflies, but Jack was selective about the ones who made it to his bed, and he'd never fallen too hard. Six girlfriends at Harvard; six broken hearts by the time he left. Against the dream of Olympic gold, girls never stood a chance

'It's not a waste of time,' Brad replied. 'It's a favour to Hans Wolf.'

'Yeah? Why can't she train with the British guys? Or have Hans ask favours from the Canadians, not us?'

Brad Hinds shrugged. 'He wants her to train with the best. She's the women's bronze medallist. This year she wants gold.'

'Elizabeth Savage is no gold medallist. She's lazy, disruptive.' Jack's voice was ice. 'We don't need that attitude around.'

'So, not everyone's a fanatic,' Brad Hinds said doubtfully. He'd heard the same things. 'But it's only once, and we owe Hans. Come on, Taylor. He helped *you* out enough last year.'

Sighing, Jack Taylor nodded. Last year he'd pulled a ligament and might have been forced to drop out if Hans Wolf hadn't found him the best doctor in Switzerland.

'OK, OK. But don't expect me to slow down so she can study my technique.'

Rick laughed. 'You wouldn't slow down for the President.'

At that moment the drag lift pulled two figures into view, carrying them up the mountain to the top of the mogul run.

'Here already,' Hans said cheerily as he slid off the drag lift. 'Brad, it's good to see you. Hello, guys. Brad, can I present Lady Elizabeth Savage.'

Brad Hinds leaned forward and took Elizabeth's gloved hand. Christ, she was gorgeous. 'Uh, how do you do, my lady,' he said uncertainly.

'Please call me Elizabeth, Mr Hinds. It's such an honour to meet you. I really appreciate your making time for me today.' Her small hand shook his huge paw enthusiastically.

'Hey, no problem. I'm Brad, and these are Sam, Pete, Rick and Jack.'

'Elizabeth.' Sam Florence's grin was fit to split his face, as he stared in open admiration. Kowalski and Myers nodded hi.

Taylor gave her a cold stare, shifted impatiently on his skis. 'Brad, can we get going? We've hung around long enough.'

'Sure.' Hinds pulled out a stopwatch. 'You take the first run.' He turned to Elizabeth as Taylor settled into a crouch. 'Don't mind Jack. He's a little excessive about training.'

'Oh, I understand,' Elizabeth said warmly. 'Jack, you were superb at Garmisch—'

She never got to finish her sentence. Ignoring her completely, Taylor pushed off with a mighty lunge and tore down the mogul run.

'Jack Taylor is a real skier. He does not want to know you,' Hans whispered in her ear. 'You have to earn his respect.'

Elizabeth stood at the top of the run, her eyes narrowing.

That smug bastard. She was going to teach him a lesson.

Two hours later, Elizabeth was ready to drop. Hans had been right: training with men pushed her to the limit. After Pete Myers sliced his way down the mogul run barely a second behind Jack, Elizabeth took a go. Swooping, turning and jumping with ferocious concentration, she made the run three seconds ahead of her personal best.

She was miles behind the men. Taylor's stare was scornful.

Elizabeth listened to Brad's comments with unusual humility, but she was biting her lower lip with rage. On the second descent, she shaved off two extra seconds, but still trailed. The third time she pushed herself too hard and fell, bruising her hip painfully.

'Are you OK? Maybe you'd better take a breather,' the coach suggested anxiously. Ronnie Davis would skin him alive if the Brit's star girl was injured before her slalom.

'You made a great time for a woman, anyway,' Sam told her.

Jack Taylor caught her looking at him. 'The idea is to stay upright,' he remarked coldly. 'Don't bite off more than you can chew. Women's training is effective for women—if they bother turning up for it.'

'I'll go again,' Elizabeth told Brad furiously.

On the fourth attempt, she beat Pete Myers by half a second.

'Jesus!' Pete swore, disgusted with himself.

'Come on, Pete. You're way off today. Just concentrate,' Jack Taylor said loudly, belittling her achievement.

The girl flashed him a look of pure disdain, which Taylor pretended to ignore. He thought she was an arrogant bitch, and he wanted her to know it. Privately, he had concluded something else. Elizabeth was the best female skier he'd ever met. And she was the sexiest, best-looking babe he'd ever seen.

It was eight twenty when Nina stepped inside the Italian marble lobby of the Dragon building. It was her first day and she thought she would be early, but the lobby was full of Identikit young men striding purposefully towards banks of elevators. She made a mental note to arrive at eight tomorrow.

'I'm the new Business Development manager,' Nina explained to an elegant blonde receptionist. 'I'm due to report to Mr Jax at nine.'

The receptionist's gaze swept across the glossy black bob, the grey eyes and ivory skin. Then she stared almost rudely at the hourglass figure only half-hidden under the burgundy suit, and the long, curvy calves that tapered down to the neat pumps.

'Yes, ma'am,' the girl said thinly. 'Business Development is on the twelfth floor.'

'Thank you,' Nina said. Uncertainly, she picked up her briefcase, headed for the nearest elevator bank and pressed the button. At the twelfth floor the elevator stopped gently and the smoothly hissing doors opened onto a luxurious corridor. The floor was carpeted with a soft grey weave and on the walls were elegantly framed prints of Dragon products.

'Excuse me.' She stopped a young redhead carrying a freshly made mug of coffee. 'I'm new. Could you tell me where to go?'

'Sure,' the girl said neutrally, giving Nina a once-over. 'The typing pool's at the end of the next corridor. You should report to Mrs Finn.'

'No, I mean—I'm the new Business Development manager, Nina Roth,' she explained. 'Could you direct me to my office?'

The girl did a double take. '*You're* N. Roth?' Nina nodded.

'Yes, Nina Roth,' Nina confirmed.

There was a second's stunned silence, and then the girl said, 'If you'll follow me, Ms Roth,' with barely concealed hostility. She led Nina down the length of the corridor and to the right. A small group of offices nestled in a corner, with names stencilled on the doors. 'N. Roth' was in between 'S. Daly' and 'T. Robbins'. Nina was shocked to see that all three of them had the same status: Manager, Business Development. She had assumed she'd be the only one doing the job.

'This is your office,' the girl said, showing Nina into the cubbyhole of a room.

'Tracy Jones is the assistant assigned to you. You'll be sharing her with Mr Robbins and Mr Daly,' the girl continued. 'You can buzz her if there's anything you require. All the new managers have an appointment with Mr Jax at nine and his office is on the thirteenth floor.'

'Thank you,' Nina said faintly, opening her new leather briefcase and starting to lay out her documents. What tells me they don't have many women in management roles? she thought wryly.

Five minutes later, as she was busily setting up her computer passwords, there was a smart rap on her office door.

'Come in,' Nina called.

It swung open to reveal two expensively dressed men, both of them wearing big smiles and sombre pinstripe suits.

'Hi, I'm Simon Daly and this is Tom Robbins,' the taller, blond-haired one said, indicating his colleague. 'You must be Ms Roth.'

'Nina.' She stood up and shook their hands. 'Are you guys new here too?' she said.

'Yes, ma'am.' Simon, the blond, seemed more open and relaxed. He had a slight Chicago accent. 'First day of my working life.'

'Goes for me too,' Tom added. 'I majored in economics at Cornell and Simon did maths at Yale.'

Nina straightened up. 'I went straight into business from high school. I worked at Dolan most recently.'

'That's the reason, then. You don't have a degree and we don't have any experience. That's why we get forty-five thousand and all the others get fifty-two,' Simon grouched. He checked his Rolex. 'Ten to. Come on, let's get upstairs. We don't want to be late for our first pep talk.'

Nina nodded and followed them into the elevator, trying not to let her feelings show on her face. She'd thought thirty-five thousand was a fortune, but they'd hired these two guys with zero experience to do the same job as her. For ten thousand bucks more.

The thirteenth floor waiting area was already pretty crowded. Nina was relieved to see four other women, but as she introduced herself, the relief lessened. Two were in Human Resources, one was in Packaging, and one was assigned to PR. Nina sensed her isolation creep back. The girls had jobs that kept them well away from the bottom line.

The door swung open and they filed in. Small, gold-backed chairs had been lined up in rows in front of an elegant mahogany desk. All conversation ceased as Gerald Jax strode into the room. His grey hair was severely cropped and his dark eyes hard and uncompromising. The head of Dragon US, Jax radiated ruthless power.

'Dragon Chemical is the largest drug company in the United States. We aim for radical improvements in US market share. We pay the highest salaries and we expect the best. We're not easy to work for. We want results fast. Those who do not deliver will be fired. Those who do—will become rich. I expect to see tangible progress in the first month of your employment. Then we'll know who's intended for which fate.'

Dismissed, they rose from their chairs and began to leave. Nina stood up and headed for the elevator.

The speech might have been macho melodrama, she told herself once she was safely back in her office, but a part of her thrilled to the challenge. She had one month to come up with something hot. Dragon was richer than Dolan MacDonald, but it followed a lot of the same practices—shipping the same drugs at the same prices right across the States. There was huge wastage.

What if I could change that? Nina thought. What if I could get Dragon to invest in another mainframe, a computer that could track what drugs sold where? If we had a clearer picture of the market . . .

Nina titled the project 'Customised Response'. Her phones buzzed incessantly and the mailcart stopped by her door five times a day as data she had requested came flooding back. It was a mammoth task, and was made even harder than it had to be.

The reason was her assistant.

Tracy Jones had been assigned to the three new business development managers. A sexy-looking redhead with short skirts and long nails, she hated having to work for a woman. Tom's letters and Simon's charts always came before the work Nina needed typing. Nina didn't complain at first. She was new. But eventually she had to say something and told Tracy she wanted her reports assigned equal priority.

'They are,' Tracy insisted insolently, with a flick of her rosy curls. Nina flushed, hating the confrontation, but saw all the other girls in the pool slow down their typewriters so they could eavesdrop.

She knew she had to assert her authority.

'I'm sorry, Tracy, but I don't think so. I want these letters on my desk first thing tomorrow.'

'Yes, ma'am,' Tracy said icily.

The letters were delivered to her by mailcart at nine the next day. They had two spelling mistakes and a word Tipp-Exed out in each. Gritting her teeth, Nina retyped them herself.

Three weeks into the deadline, she got seriously behind schedule. Her proposal needed detailed statistics, and she'd have to check it before it went off to Jax. If she gave it to Tracy, Nina realised, it would be handed in late or be so messy she couldn't use it. She had no desire to be anyone's boss from hell, but, as the deadline got closer, she had no choice.

On Friday morning, Nina went down to the typing pool at eleven, to find Tracy sitting at an empty typewriter, painting her nails. As Nina approached, she brazenly continued.

'Hello, Tracy. I need this report typed up today. It's got quite a few statistics,' Nina told her, laying the sheaf of notes on her desk.

The girl barely glanced at her. 'Sorry, I'm too busy.'

Aware of the others watching her, Nina drew breath. '*Whenever* I need something done, you're always too busy. I think the problem is that you just don't want to work for me.'

At that moment, all the girls in the pool stopped typing.

Tracy shrugged, without looking up.

Nina tapped the paperwork sharply. She was red-faced, but her voice was firm. 'Tracy, I am leaving it on your desk and I'll be back for it at three. If it isn't done by then, I am going to fire you.'

'Oh, really,' Tracy said with a sneer.

'Try me,' said Nina.

There was complete silence as Nina walked back down the corridor.

Her heart was hammering in her chest, but she held up her head. She could feel the eyes of all the typists boring into her back.

Nina tried to get on with her research. It was impossible to concentrate. She didn't eat lunch and wondered what on earth she was going to do. At five to three Nina marched down to the typing pool to find Tracy languidly tapping at her keyboard. One look at the paper told her this was a letter of Tom's. Nina's own project was exactly where she'd left it.

The typing pool fell silent as Nina stood in front of her secretary.

Tracy shot Nina a defiant look.

'I gave express orders that my report was to be ready by three,' Nina stated flatly. 'Is there a reason why you haven't done it?'

'I told you. I'm too busy,' Tracy said rudely.

'And I told you. You're fired,' Nina said. 'Collect your papers from Gary Bellman in Human Resources.'

'You can't do that. You don't have the right,' Tracy challenged her.

'I've just done it. If your desk isn't cleared in ten minutes Security will throw you out,' Nina replied.

Then she turned on her heel and marched back to her office.

Breathing deeply to calm herself, Nina dialled an extension in Human Resources. 'Gary? This is Nina Roth in Business Development,' she said when he answered the phone. 'I've just fired Tracy Jones.'

'Nina, you can't dismiss anybody. You don't have the authority,' Gary Bellman said, sounding worried.

'Gary, I have fired her,' Nina told him firmly. 'And I have fired her in front of thirty-five other secretarial staff.'

There was a long pause.

'In that case, she's fired,' said the Human Resources director.

chapter four

HANS WOLF WAS RIGHT. The amount of work it took to claw back just a few seconds on each race was staggering. As the World Cup continued across the Alps, the British team watched Elizabeth's transformation open-mouthed. Ronnie Davis couldn't believe it was the same girl: she rose early in the morning to jog, practised with Karen, and turned up to training. She apologised to him for being so bloody-minded before.

'I was a jerk, Ron. I'm sorry. I'm paying for it now.'

'No problem,' said her coach, waving it aside. But they still had problems. If Elizabeth was ever going to get that gold medal, she needed to go an extra mile. Reluctantly, Ronnie concluded that it couldn't be with him; there wasn't much more he could teach her. He called the office back home and secured some extra funding. Then he called Hans Wolf.

Hans took over as Elizabeth's coach. It was the first time in her life she'd known what real work was. To her runs, he added heavy backpacks. In gym training he upped her weights. When she studied videos of Heidi and Louise, he made her write notes. The second an event was finished, Elizabeth barely had time to shower before she was being hustled onto a plane. If they got to the next stop ahead of time, Hans explained, there'd be an extra evening for practice runs.

'Don't I ever get a break?' Elizabeth gasped, as Hans rushed her away from the press after a downhill victory at Grindelwald.

'*Nein*. Plenty of time to sleep when you're dead,' Wolf told her briskly.

Travel, train, race. Travel, train, race. Elizabeth spent day after day lost in the brutal cycle of competition. But in spite of the punishing pace, she never considered cutting back.

Motivation was easy to come by. It was right there in the stocky form of Heidi Laufen, twice World Champion, and the aerodynamic crouch of Louise Levier, her heir apparent. The commentators called the two Swiss girls unbeatable.

Elizabeth sweated, strained, pushed her way forward. In one punishing month she wiped out Louise's lead. Now there was only Heidi to chase. The two girls struggled for supremacy across Europe.

Elizabeth found she suddenly wanted victory desperately. In the World Cup, her breeding and her bank account meant nothing. Talent was the only thing that counted. And she wanted to show she was worth something. She wanted to be the best.

Basically, Elizabeth admitted to herself, she wanted to be like Jack Taylor. She couldn't stand him, but she had to admire him. Taylor had blasted through the sport like an F-14 jet fighter, ruthless on a pair of skis. Over and over, the Stars and Stripes flew on the winner's podium. Hans forced her to watch tape after tape of Taylor's victories, pointing out the speed, the technique, the mastery.

He's the best, but doesn't he know it, Elizabeth thought, annoyed. Jack bloody Taylor, with his magna cum laude from Harvard and his blatant sexuality. Though she pretended not to care, his derision at Méribel had cut her to the quick. Elizabeth wanted his respect. She wanted his approval. The bastard could snub her all he liked, but she wanted him to rate her. As an equal.

When the women's and the men's events coincided, Jack Taylor turned up to the female event to cheer on Kim Ferrell and Holly Gideon, the US team. At those races, Elizabeth tried to squeeze a little more excellence from her performance. But though she took three wins and a second in front of him, he never offered her a word of encouragement.

The final slalom of the women's World Cup in Kitzbühel was a nail-biter. Elizabeth said a prayer at the starting gate and thrust forward. Plant, turn. Stick, slice. Nothing registered except the flagpoles and the snow. Concentrating furiously, her technique was perfect but she lost a little speed. She shot through the finishing line seconds behind her best time on this course. She led the field comfortably.

Elizabeth turned to the cameras to give her reaction. She kept it short. Nothing to do but wait for Heidi.

Finally, to roars of approval from the Swiss in the crowd, Heidi Laufen was called to the start. Time seemed to stop for Elizabeth as Heidi tore through the flagpoles. She wasn't as exact as Elizabeth, but she was quicker. With each gate Elizabeth felt her heart sink. Heidi came bombing through the finishing line over a second ahead.

Elizabeth could feel the eyes of her coach, her team and the press burning into her back as she walked over to shake the World Champion's hand. Now they were level. It would all depend on the downhill tomorrow—the legendary Hahnenkamm, the fastest, toughest, most dangerous run on earth.

Jack Taylor was standing with the US team. His eyes flickered over her body, but their expression was unfathomable. 'You could have done better,' he said.

Elizabeth stiffened. She pulled up to her full height.

'And I will. Tomorrow.'

On Wednesday morning, Elizabeth was up before her wake-up call. She'd tried to rest but hadn't slept much. Everything was riding on this afternoon. She selected a training suit in scarlet Lycra and dressed. Adrenalin pumped through her. Today she was challenging the world's best skier on the world's most dangerous course.

Rick Kowalski, the American number two, had agreed to let Elizabeth train with him, at Hans's request. Rick had arranged to meet her at the top of the Resterhöhe. Seven thousand feet above sea level, it was the highest ski area in Kitzbühel. Elizabeth was ready for some serious training. She looked around for Kowalski, but couldn't see him. She cupped her hands over her mouth and yelled.

'Rick?'

Suddenly, from behind her, a black-suited figure shot out of nowhere and sliced to a halt.

Elizabeth jumped out of her skin.

He raised dark goggles and regarded her steadily.

'Jesus Christ, Jack. You scared me,' Elizabeth said angrily. 'Where the hell did you come from? Where's Rick?'

'Good morning to you, too, ma'am,' Taylor replied. The Texan drawl was cold. 'Kowalski couldn't make it. He's in bed with flu. He asked me to come train with you. Rick never breaks a commitment.'

Taylor studied her for a moment, then lifted his stick and pointed off down the mountainside towards a dark pine forest.

'Brad found a route for me yesterday. It's got a sixty-five-degree sheer drop, a tough mogul run, some tree skiing, lots of powder on the straight.' He shrugged. 'Reasonably challenging.'

That meant white-knuckle terror, Elizabeth thought. A shiver of spine-chilling pleasure rushed through her.

'Stick with me. We'll be going close to a lot of mountain edges; concealed boulders, outcrops, stuff like that. Think you can handle it?'

'Hey. I do have a little snowcraft, Taylor.'

'You want to train with me? You *follow* me.' He was uncompromising. 'I'm not explaining to some English lord how I watched his daughter ski off the edge of a precipice.'

Elizabeth glared at him, but Taylor held her gaze calmly, refusing to back down. She swallowed her pride. 'I'll be right behind you. But this had better give me a workout.'

'Hey, Princess,' Jack said. 'After this, the Hahnenkamm's gonna look like a nursery slope.'

He pulled down his goggles and pushed off to the right, schussing swiftly down towards the forest. Elizabeth followed, gathering her body into an aerodynamic crouch. She caught up with him, crowding him, until there was just a few inches between them. Taylor swung sharply left. Elizabeth followed. He immediately took a hard right. She matched him, inch for inch. Fighting. Challenging. Competing.

Without so much as a glance at her, Jack leaned forwards into his crouch and disappeared. Gasping, Elizabeth found herself plunging down a sheer icy curve that had looked like an ordinary ridge a second ago. Instinctively she righted herself and hugged the gradient, while her stomach somersaulted.

Jack tilted away left, bringing his skis together. Why was he doing that? And then she saw it—two patches of dark shadow, bridging white ground barely two feet across. Shade like that could be covering a ravine, a crevasse. Elizabeth broke into a cold sweat as she swung her body violently, making sure she was behind him. Taylor schussed coyly across the strip of solid ground without even a hint of tension. Elizabeth followed, dry-mouthed with fear. Now she was across! She settled into a racing position, chasing the handsome silhouette in front of her.

'So, how are you doing, honey?' Jack asked as she drew level. 'All warmed up?'

Warmed up? 'You said you've skied this before.'

'Yes, ma'am.' The Texan drawl was relaxed.

'So when does it start getting hard?' Elizabeth asked casually. Two could play that game.

Taylor looked across at Elizabeth. This run would have beaten most guys he knew by now.

'Right about now,' he said, and shot over a mogul, executing a perfect helicopter spin. Elizabeth raced forward. Then she brought her knees together with a crash. Taylor had headed down the steepest, largest mogul field she'd ever seen.

Elizabeth followed grimly as he made for a boulder, shot over it, and soared into a twenty-foot jump due south, landing cleanly and hurtling forwards. Jack shot into the trees and Elizabeth, terrified, shot after him, hugging his trail as close as she could. Suddenly the bright glitter of the mountainside disappeared, and she was swallowed up by green, scented gloom. Instinct took over as she lunged, skied, and thrust round the trunks, making the fastest, sharpest turns she'd ever done in her life. No slalom ever invented could match up to this. Elizabeth tried to beat back the rising panic. A crash at this speed would snap her legs like matchsticks, wrench a shoulder from its socket! Not only would she lose the World Cup, she might never ski again!

Then, blessedly, there was light. The trees thinned. She swerved right, left, right again and schussed out onto the clear snow.

Jack Taylor had pulled up a hundred yards in front of her, nodding in admiration. 'Congratulations. That was some sharp skiing.'

Elizabeth sliced to a stop and ripped off her goggles. Scalding hot tears burst from her eyes, cooling instantly against her flushed cheeks.

'You bastard, you absolute bastard! Your stupid macho games could have fucking killed me!' she spat at him.

'Honey, I wouldn't have taken you any place you couldn't handle. I've seen how you ski.' He smiled at her. 'Elizabeth, I'm sorry, I—'

'Jack, do me a favour and get lost,' Elizabeth snarled, and thrust off violently, skiing away down the mountainside as fast as she could.

'Wait! Elizabeth, stop!'

Taylor's voice floated down towards her, but Elizabeth ignored it. She had no idea where she was, but the lights of Kitzbühel below gave her some sense of direction. She would schuss to the next ski area and ride a lift back to the hotel, calm herself down before the Hahnenkamm.

Jack had stopped shouting. Glancing round, she saw him settle into a crouch, as though desperate to reach her. As he saw her look at him, Taylor shook one pole frantically. She ignored him. Now he could try catching up with *her*.

She was hugging the mountainside, following the steepest gradient down. The world was returning to what she knew and loved—whiteness and silence—except for . . .

A faint rumbling sound like a growling stomach. Nervously, Elizabeth looked up. Out of the corner of one eye, she saw a rocky outcrop quiver. A pile of snow loosened and dropped heavily onto the slope.

Elizabeth slowed in an S-bend, suddenly petrified.

There was only one explanation for that sound.

Avalanche!

Elizabeth's body flooded with adrenalin. She pointed her skis straight ahead, crouching as low as she could. Skiing for her life, racing the snow. If only she knew where she was! Where this slope led!

Jack was heading hard right, motioning for her to follow. He knew the danger, and he came after me anyway, she thought miserably. And now she'd probably got him killed.

Her eyes were blurry with tears of terror. She had to be brave! If she lost control, she was history. Another huge rumble shook the mountainside. Elizabeth's head whipped round to see a vast, menacing wall of white sliding steadily down the rock face.

'Get to the forest!' Taylor shouted. 'This slope leads to a cliff edge!'

Elizabeth headed after him, rocketing towards another grove of trees. Behind her the avalanche had hit the slope and was cruising forwards. She didn't need to look round to see how fast it was gaining—a black shadow loomed over the ground in front of her, silent as death.

Jack was nearly at the trees now. She had another 200 yards to go. Desperately, Elizabeth pushed to the right, towards the trees at the edge of the cliff. Jack was standing three yards into the forest, his arms wrapped round a tree trunk. The breath stopped in Elizabeth's throat as she saw snow spattering across her skis. She'd failed by a few feet, she was going to die. Air shot out of her lungs as the snow hit her, freezing, heavy, and she waited to be swept into the void . . .

But something held her back. A hand, *Jack's* hand, his vast palm clamping her left wrist, strong fingers like a vice round it.

Elizabeth's body was flung forwards, her right pole ripped from her grasp, but she didn't fall. Jack Taylor was holding onto her wrist with a mighty grip. Her arm burned agonisingly as it took the whole weight of her body. For a few horrible seconds, the avalanche trundled over her back, pressing her down into the slope.

And then suddenly there was light, the weight bearing down on her slid away, and as she sucked air into her lungs the wave of snow teetered slightly and crashed slowly, unhurriedly, into the ravine.

Jack pulled her up, away from the cliff edge. Her shoulder socket screamed and she scrambled forwards. Taylor was holding onto a tree trunk with his left hand, his right hand clutching her. She could see every muscle in his arms rigid with the effort. He had been a human bridge, clutching her against the force of the snow.

Elizabeth flung herself into his arms.

'You didn't let go, you didn't let go!' She was crying, her whole body trembling against him. 'Jack, you saved my life!'

'We all make mistakes,' Jack Taylor said.

Then he tilted her face up to his and kissed her hard, the tip of his tongue tracing a fiery line across her frozen lips. Elizabeth felt burning warmth rush through her icy flesh as his body warmed hers. Jack was sucking snow crystals from her mouth as he kissed her and Elizabeth found herself flooded with a different kind of heat, a wet rush of lust that curled like smoke in the pit of her stomach.

Her muscles were melting with longing. She felt weak against such raw male strength. Pleasure fluttered across her groin. Despite herself, she moaned softly at the back of her throat, pressing herself against him.

Taylor's hand immediately slid up over the tight, cold red Lycra of her ski suit, his huge paw brushing her breasts softly. Elizabeth gasped as a burst of heat exploded between her thighs. Jack moved forwards to cover her, pressing her down against the tree roots. The rough bark prickled against her back, breaking the tension just long enough for Elizabeth to gather her thoughts. Firmly she pushed against his chest, shaking her head.

'Jack, no. We can't do this. You just saved my life. I—I'm not clear-headed. I don't even know you!' She was stammering out explanations. 'And we have to get back to Kitzbühel! I'm racing in three hours!'

Jack stared at her for a second, then sighed and stood up. He stood with his back to her and took a deep breath, trying to stamp out the fire blazing in his groin.

'Jack?' Elizabeth asked, scrambling to her feet.

'All right, Elizabeth. I'm not pushing you.'

'Thank you,' she said, hoping she didn't sound disappointed.

Taylor gestured to her boots. 'Fix your bindings and we'll get back.' Unhooking the ski pole from her left wrist he handed her his own pair.

'I don't need these—'

'Take them,' Jack said. She didn't argue.

When they reached the Thurn Pass skiing area, Ronnie Davis and the British team were standing by the gondola station, waiting for them.

Elizabeth glided to a halt and offered Taylor back his ski poles. He hadn't said a single word to her all the way down.

'Right on time,' Ronnie said. 'We're going to head back to the hotel. So, Jack, how was she?'

'She was the best female skier I've ever seen,' Jack said, without looking at her.

'Thanks for helping me practise,' Elizabeth said, blushing.

'My pleasure, ma'am,' Taylor replied softly. He nodded to the British team, turned, and schussed away down the mountainside.

The foot of the course was a zoo. Press, radio and TV crews from all over Europe were jostling for position, shouting out reports in ten different languages. Elizabeth waited with the others to hear her draw. Heidi Laufen was drawn number three to thunderous applause from the Swiss in the crowd. Elizabeth was drawn number fourteen.

She shrugged elegantly to the cameras, but she was very disappointed. Looking stunning in her signature rainbow suit, Elizabeth tried not to show her nerves. It was always bad before a race, but this time she had eels writhing in her stomach. Her parents were watching, Hans was watching, the world was watching . . .

'How's it going?'

Elizabeth jumped out of her skin. Jack Taylor was wearing dark jeans, cowboy boots and a black windcheater with the Stars and Stripes embossed on the pocket. Goggles had been replaced by black sunglasses. He looked just as impressive off skis as on.

The memory of his hands on her breasts sent a stab of wanting right through her. She blushed. 'I got number fourteen,' she said quickly.

'I heard, but it don't matter.'

'What do you mean, it doesn't matter? I—'

'Forests, ravines, avalanches,' Jack said, cutting her off. 'Remember? This is a walk in the park.' His easy air was infuriating.

An official marched up and tapped her on the elbow.

'You should get to the start gate now, my lady.'

'Elizabeth?' Jack said.

'What?'

He looked her right in the face. 'Just ski. Everything else is talk.'

Heidi Laufen made a textbook run. Dismayed, Elizabeth watched the spinning numbers freeze as she shot through the finishing line. A new record. Position: first.

Waiting was eternity. Elizabeth took deep breaths, tried to stay calm. Then finally her number was called. Instructions, technique, layouts raced through her mind as she settled into her starting crouch, waiting for the bell. Trying to remember everything . . .

The countdown finished. Three, two, one . . .

And then, as Elizabeth thrust off down the mountain, Jack Taylor's voice drowned out the theory. *Just ski.*

The run fell away under her, a steep drop before the first two gates. Flying by pure instinct, Elizabeth skied straight ahead. The run soared over a hill and she twisted to the right, ready for the Steilhänge—hard left, then down through the forest. Now the Stemmle stretch. Elizabeth swung hard towards the net, hugging the line, going at 90 miles per hour. She was soaring. Off at the Alte Schneise—nearly over, but here you could drop precious seconds if you lost position. Elizabeth held her crouch rock solid, every muscle screaming as she rode the bumps—a huge jump by the Hausberge! Elizabeth took it high. Landing swiftly, poles tucked under her arms, she fired past the finishing line, heart ricocheting under her chest, and sliced to a clean halt.

Panting, Elizabeth tore off her helmet and spun round, as the press did, as Louise did, as Heidi did, waiting for the announcement. She'd been fast, but how fast?

There was a second's silence as the time was announced.

Then pandemonium. Cameras flashing, reporters thrusting forwards, Hans fighting to get to her, and Elizabeth burst into tears.

She was twenty years old. She had just won the World Cup.

As she was swallowed up by TV cameras, Elizabeth caught sight of Jack Taylor, hanging back by the netting.

He nodded once, calmly. And then they both smiled.

Nina walked in to work feeling nervous. She knew she wasn't alone there: all the new Dragon managers had submitted their reports on Friday and today they got their results. Everyone was on a one-monther, so unless you got it renewed today, it was a case of clear your desk.

She was wearing a short dress with a cropped jacket, cream cotton with navy piping, and navy pumps. She'd taken extra care this morning with her make-up, her dark hair and eyes set off with subtle shades, charcoal round the eyes and matt plum lipstick. If she was going to get fired, it would help her out to look good.

It's not the project, Nina reminded herself, as she walked into her tiny office and set to work. 'Customised Response' was good. It was the fact that she'd exceeded her authority. Fired Tracy Jones last Friday, in public, forcing Gary Bellman to back her up. Gary Bellman, a division chief! Gary had been furious and she knew Jax would have heard what she'd done. She'd be seen as a troublemaker.

Sighing, she looked at her watch. Her meeting with Jax was at 10.00am sharp. Best get it over with. Nina picked up her bag and closed the office door behind her, heading for the elevator bank.

Jax's secretary looked at Nina gleefully. She must have heard about the Tracy thing too.

She recognised Jack Fletcher, new at Accounts, as he stormed out of the office, his face white. Clearly, he was off to clear his desk.

The secretary buzzed her boss. 'I have Nina Roth for you.' She listened a second, then, 'You can go in, Ms Roth.'

Nina squared her shoulders and marched into Jax's office.

The boss, sitting behind his mahogany desk, waved her to a seat. He had a file open in front of him; her project.

'This is good work,' he said.

Nina was so shocked she didn't say a word.

'Precise and focused,' Jax went on. 'You didn't try anything too flashy, but this could save us a good lot of overhead. It's similar to what you did at Dolan, but that's OK. We can use it.'

'Thank you, sir,' Nina said.

Jax looked the girl over appreciatively. A cool customer, this kid.

'You fired your secretary on Friday.'

'Yes, sir.' Nina's hopes sank again.

'You had no authority to dismiss another member of staff. Mr Bellman's office was furious.'

'But she defied me openly. It was the end of a long line of incidents.'

'I see.' Jax's voice was mercilessly cold. 'So you had previously discussed this problem with—which one of Ms Jones's supervisors?'

'I didn't.' Now, it sounded impulsive and childish. Nina blushed a rich red. 'I guess I thought I could handle it myself.'

'Well, your action was certainly decisive, Nina, but it was way out of line. Next time, contact somebody appropriate.'

Next time? It sank in: she wasn't getting fired. She felt light-headed with relief. 'Oh, yes, sir. I'll contact Mr Bellman's office right away—'

'It won't be Mr Bellman,' Jax said. 'It'll be Mr Keith Sweeney. In London.'

'London?' Nina gasped. 'I'm being posted to London?'

'That's right. The earl saw your report and requested you personally.' Jax leaned forward. 'That's not a problem, Nina, is it?'

'No.' Nina bit her lips to stop a stupid grin from spreading right across her face. 'Not at all.'

Elizabeth smiled and bowed for the millionth time that evening. They'd finally cleared out the photographers, and now the athletes were helping themselves to champagne, starting to loosen up, to celebrate.

It was the US team's victory ball. Schloss Lebenberg, the modernised castle that was their team's hotel, had been taken over. Everywhere from the casino to the pool was draped with vast Stars and Stripes. It was fun to come out and party. She'd almost forgotten how to do it. Elizabeth's dark blonde hair hung loosely down her back; her dress was a gorgeous, slim column of white silk and gold thread, spiralling into a loose fishtail. She danced the first waltz with Hans Wolf, to huge cheers, then whirled gracefully round with Ronnie Davis, Brad Hinds, Pete, Sam and Rick. Elizabeth told herself she was having a good time. She wasn't going to be put out just because a certain person hadn't come to find her. After the joint photocall, Jack Taylor had disappeared.

Who does he think he is anyway? Arrogant bastard!

She reached for another flute of champagne and then stiffened. Someone was resting their hand on the tight curve of her back. Angrily Elizabeth whipped round to be confronted by Jack, his tall frame bang up against her. His white shirt was unbuttoned at the top, displaying a tanned chest and just a smattering of hair. He looked relaxed.

'Congratulations,' Jack said softly.

'And to you.' She was stiff with him.

'You been looking for me?' Jack asked. He reached down and made to brush some hair away from her cheek but Elizabeth pulled back sharply. God! He thinks he's God's gift, the infuriating jerk! But Jack did look wonderful, the formal dark cloth picking out his eyes, the confidence, the aggression. Stuff had already passed between them that couldn't be taken back. She'd responded to him. He knew it. She knew it.

'And why would I be doing that?' Elizabeth snapped.

Jack laughed. 'Thought you might like to dance.'

'I've done nothing but dance.'

'With me,' Taylor insisted.

'Well, I've had to make do with the lesser gentlemen that were on offer,' Elizabeth answered icily.

They were standing close to the dance floor. 'Come on.' Taylor held out his hand, looking right in her face with insistent, come-to-bed eyes. She felt a new flood of lust, no doubt about it. The certainty that Jack would be great in bed mingled with the certainty that he'd done this to loads of women before, and that they'd all been eager to comply.

Her bodice was reinforced satin. Her hardening nipples would not betray her this time. *Right now he's acting like he's got some* right *to me*, Elizabeth thought crossly.

'I'm sorry. I'm feeling a little tired.'

Jack let his hand drop, annoyed. 'Please, girl. Stop playing games.'

'*Excuse* me?' Elizabeth said, coldly.

Jack bristled. This wasn't going the way he'd planned it at all. So he'd had a few drinks before coming to find her, so what?

'I booked a private suite here especially,' he said. 'There's no point, Elizabeth, I know how you feel.'

A private suite? He was planning on hauling me into bed? Elizabeth's brows knitted togher.

'Clearly, you've no idea how I feel, Mr Taylor.' She drew herself up. 'I wouldn't place too much emphasis on what happened earlier. It was a near-death experience, I wasn't thinking.'

'Yeah. I liked that,' Jack said.

They were interrupted by a waiter heading towards them with a salver. On it was a thin yellow envelope.

'Excuse me, my lady, but I have a telegram for you.'

'Thank you.'

Jack stood back, seething with irritation, as Elizabeth ripped it open. She read the message quickly, then looked up at him.

'I'm afraid I have to say goodbye. I've got to get back to the hotel. Daddy wants me to come home tomorrow morning: he's going to give me a job at Dragon,' Elizabeth said triumphantly.

Jack read the exhilaration in her tone. With an effort he made her a little bow. 'Then allow me to escort you home.'

'Thank you, I can manage.'

'I insist.' Jack took Elizabeth's elbow and steered her towards the cloakroom. Normally, when a girl got an attitude he lost interest, but right now he was dreaming up excuses to be in London. Maybe she'd blown him out tonight, but only tonight. He had her down as unfinished business.

chapter five

NINA LOOKED ROUND her new apartment and smiled. Two bedrooms, a tiled bathroom and neat, fitted kitchen, in a tree-lined Camden street. She had selected it from a list of company-approved flats, and 80 per cent of the rent would be coming out of her overseas living allowance. Then there were the relocation expenses and her rise for signing the new contract. Dragon had locked her up for five years, but they were paying handsomely for the privilege.

She'd had three days to settle in. Today was the first at work. Nina felt a rush of nerves. She was going to work in the heart of the company, directly for Tony Savage, the Robber Baron.

Nina picked up her briefcase and set off for the tube. She was over an hour early, and she couldn't wait. It was 1980. New decade, new city, new job. Maybe she was finally getting somewhere.

'Good morning, my lady.'

Elizabeth beamed at the receptionist as she handed over her security pass and a sheaf of company recruitment forms. Everything was great, even the wet, crowded streets, even the grey ugliness of the Dragon tower. She had been trying to gain admittance to this world for ever.

'New Products division is on the ninth floor.'

'Thanks.' Elizabeth nodded and joined a crowd of men in dark suits. They immediately parted and let her stand at the front. When the lift arrived, everybody waited until she had stepped in.

'Which floor, Lady Elizabeth?' a grey-haired executive asked politely.

Elizabeth brushed back her glossy hair and told him, returning everybody's beaming smiles. Of course they all knew who she was, she was famous. Everyone was going out of their way to be nice and welcoming. She felt super-confident. She was going to fit in here just fine.

Initial tests look promising, Frank.' Tony grinned, seeing the flash of greed lighting up Frank Staunton's eyes. They both knew the first firm to develop a safe slimming drug would own the biggest money-spinner since aspirin. 'Appetite suppressant, amphetamine base.'

'Could be big,' the head of New Products agreed.

Fifty-five, Staunton was thin and wiry, nicknamed the Terrier. He went after results like a dog after a rat, and he displayed utter loyalty to Savage, his master. Most of Frank's pay was stock options, so that Dragon's success was his success. Self-interest made him reliable.

'Your drones need to concentrate on this.'

Frank nodded. 'Including her young ladyship?'

Tony did not return the grin. He hadn't forgotten that Elizabeth was coming in today. Louise's bastard had forced her way into the heart of his kingdom. He grunted.

'And we have some others new in this morning.' The Terrier sensed his master's blackening mood and changed the subject. 'Joe Walsh, hot-shot analyst from Morgan Grenfell. Lionel White, a systems kid.'

'Nina Roth.' Tony leaned forward, animated. 'I forgot, she starts today.'

'She's working in the same area as Lady Elizabeth.'

Tony didn't listen. His pulse quickened as he flashed on the girl from Brooklyn, with her strong accent and dark, grave beauty. Intelligence and drive combined with great tits, a great ass and a handspan waist. His memories of the Roth girl sharpened into focus. She'd come up from the street, fast, still only twenty-one years old.

'Uh-huh.' He was casual. 'I'll take the first meeting with you. I'm going to be working with some of them myself.'

Nina was shown into Frank Staunton's office, where ten other people were waiting: nine men and a girl, probably a secretary. She was wearing a pretty little dress in a Liberty print, together with bracelets and earrings. Nina smiled at them all and began to introduce herself, but she kept one eye on the girl. There was something familiar about her, but she couldn't place her. She had a soft, rich look about her, a polish. Long, shiny hair worn loose, not even tied back for the office. Very beautiful and slim. Sleeping with somebody?

The men were all smiling at the girl. There was a nervous deference in their body language. Nina frowned. She *was* sleeping with somebody important. Women like that made it harder for all other women. This beautiful rich chick set her teeth on edge.

Elizabeth glanced up as Nina entered the room. A dark-haired, voluptuous woman, very young, wearing a tailored black suit, flat shoes and a steel watch. Immediately she knew this girl was wearing the right clothes. She felt embarrassed. Now the woman was shaking hands, briskly and impersonally. The others greeted her as one of them.

The girl came closer. Elizabeth heard an American accent. And then, she glanced right at Elizabeth and gave her a look of icy derision.

Elizabeth bridled. So she'd got the wardrobe wrong, so what? This girl looked her own age but *she'd* clearly been working for years. She hadn't had to blackmail her way into an office. Dad's company had hired her and given her a real chance.

There was only one empty chair, right at the front, by Elizabeth. Nina slid into it and sighed inwardly. There was no getting away with it. She offered her neighbour her hand. 'Nina Roth, just over from Manhattan.'

'I'm Elizabeth. I—well, this is my first job.'

The accent was plummy and patrician, accompanied by a little flick of the hair. The girlish gesture was out of place. What the fuck was she doing in New Products? It was a vital division!

'Elizabeth who?'

Elizabeth heard the hostility and bridled.

'Lady Elizabeth Savage,' she said coolly.

Nina looked at her sharply. Of course. The Brit skier. She'd seen her on CNN getting her medal. So, she wasn't a girlfriend, she was a *daughter*. Christ, she was just playing around on Daddy's patch. No messing around with experience or education for the boss's kid.

Nina knew she should be sucking up, like the men, but she couldn't do it. The thought of her own struggles boiled up in her like acid.

'And I'm *Ms* Nina Roth.' The sarcasm was unmistakable.

Elizabeth blushed a rich red. Bitch! Who did the Yank think she was? At that moment Frank Staunton walked in. Followed by her father.

Tony listened with one ear as Frank ran through the new protocols. Elizabeth was writing it all down, laboriously, occasionally looking up at him and catching his frown. She seemed uncomfortable, out of her depth. He bit back a smile; her defiant streak would mean trouble unless he found her some pretence of a role.

Nina Roth was sitting next to her. He liked what he saw. She wasn't writing, she was drinking it all in. Leaning forward, straining at the leash like a bloodhound, her thick, raven hair fell heavily round her high cheekbones, the pale skin dusted with excited pink. Under that sombre suit her body was magnificent, all curves. A go-getter. He knew she was aware of him, nervous in his presence. Her eyes kept sliding towards him, and if he caught her looking, she glanced back at Frank.

The earl was good at body language. Elizabeth sat stiffly next to Nina. For her part, Nina's eyes never even flickered towards Elizabeth's busy pad; the gesture was contemptuous, like, *I'll never need notes.*

Nina didn't know how he felt about Elizabeth. If she pissed off the chairman's daughter, she was taking a big risk. He wasn't used to females who did that. Tony smiled. He'd made it a rule not to mess on his own doorstep, but rules were made to be broken.

Elizabeth leaned over and pushed a button on her treadmill, pushing it up to maximum. The responsive growl from the machinery blasted her ears. Sweat dewed her body, her fringe was plastered to her forehead. Arms raised for maximum motion. Balls of the feet pushing off the rubber with every pulse. Elizabeth Savage lost herself in vicious, punishing speed.

In under an hour she'd be reporting to that utter bitch, Nina Roth. This was a pleasure in comparison.

The thought of Nina drove Elizabeth into a fury. They called her the Brooklyn Bomber in the office, the men, almost admiringly. She still hadn't worked out what Nina did but she sure was good at it. Barking orders and talking science gobbledegook Elizabeth couldn't work out. Never losing an opportunity to put Elizabeth down.

Dad had given her the job she begged for. Advertising on New Products. But whatever she suggested to Nina, the cow lost no time in vetoing. It was so unfair: Jake and Dino, the other advertising guys, loved her ideas but Nina stopped her work from getting anywhere.

Anger burned in her face as bright as exertion. Bitch! Nina was Daddy's bright-eyed little girl. She worked directly for him, she was his right-hand girl on the slimming drug thing. Elizabeth hated the way she smarmed up to Tony. Those two deserved each other.

She leaned forward to increase resistance. Elizabeth needed her fitness. While she was struggling at Dragon, Heidi Laufen was practising in the Alps.

Nina glanced at the scrolling text on her computer screen. The earl had assigned her to his own task force. That meant research, and lots of it. She had to find out who their most likely competitors were; how far their slimming projects had come; and what the distribution impact would be. Nina gathered facts all day.

Because she reported directly to Tony, the boys at Dragon fell over themselves to help her. She felt she was finally making inroads. The phone trilled.

'Nina?' She started as she recognised the cut-glass tones. Lord C. 'You're in early.'

'I've been at my desk for an hour,' Nina shot back without thinking, then bit her lip. Oh God. You didn't cheek Tony Savage.

'Glad to hear it. You should be up to speed on the Food and Drug Administration scan, then.'

'Yes, sir,' Nina said quickly. She glanced down at her dress, a dark red cropped affair with a long, slimming jacket. The earl expected all Dragon employees to look polished and pulled together.

'Then come upstairs to my office,' Lord Caerhaven said.

'Yes, sir. Right away.'

Nina replaced the receiver on the hook. One on one with the Robber Baron; the kind of chance she used to daydream about.

As she stood up she saw her hands were trembling.

Tony's office was fairly modest. Neat windows looked north over the Thames to Soho. The decor was light and modern; a secretary's annexe as yet deserted.

The earl was sitting behind his desk, waiting for her, wearing a dark suit, immaculately cut. His hair was close-cropped chestnut, only lightly speckled with silver. His eyes were hazel and he had a broad, strong chest. He looked powerful physically as well as financially, but there was something cold about the alert speculation in his eyes. He wasn't pretty, but his sexuality was magnetic.

She blushed. She couldn't believe it, she felt a ripple of desire. Something she hadn't felt since Jeff Glazer.

'Take a seat.'

Tony looked at the new kid. Short, but exquisite. He settled back languidly. 'Tell me about the FDA.'

Nina swallowed drily. She had news she was sure this man did not want to hear. 'They don't like drugs based on amphetamines, and even with those they sanction, you have class action suits. The appetite suppressant has an addictive effect and suppresses various autoimmune responses. I found over thirty landmark rulings over eight separate states.'

Tony watched Nina as she blasted through her findings. It was good work, well presented; no soft soap or small talk. He enjoyed the rhythmic swell of her breasts and the sharp little hand gestures she used. Despite the grown-up dressing and clever talk, she was very young.

'Hmm,' he said when she had finished. 'So the drug won't work?'

'Not in its present form.'

He leaned forward. 'I want a slimming drug they *will* ratify.'

'Yes, sir.' Nina didn't know what else she could say.

Tony looked at her; his gaze was hypnotic. 'And how are you settling in? Do you like London?'

'Very much, I—'

'How are you getting on with my daughter?'

Nina coloured. She felt fearful again. 'I, that is, she—'

Tony cut her off. 'You think she's a waste of space?'

Nina thought fast. Somehow, she knew that if she lied, this man would know. 'Well, Elizabeth's learning,' she replied.

Elizabeth. Tony noticed the deliberate lack of a title. This girl had balls, something he usually hated. In Nina it was erotic. Maybe it was the contrast, the rounded softness of her body and the hard coldness of her manner. 'I agree. I don't think work is any place for a young lady.'

Nina flinched. He didn't think she was a lady, then? On the other hand, he was looking at her like an equal. Giving her an amazing job for a new kid. Power and position she hadn't thought she'd get for years.

'No, no place for a lady—or a gentleman.'

Tony glanced up sharply. The girl was staring at him boldly, her pale cheeks flushed from her challenge. 'I could have you fired,' he said.

Nina lowered her eyes. 'Yes,' she said, 'my lord.'

He almost laughed. She was fencing with him. No female had tried that on with him since Louise. But Nina was no Louise; she was earthy, she was street, she was Jewish. Tony could handle her, easily.

'We still need to find a plan B for the drug. Do some thinking. We'll have dinner tonight at the Groucho, eight.'

Nina stood up. 'Right. Thanks for the invitation.'

'It wasn't an invitation,' Tony Savage said.

'This won't work.' Nina didn't hide her exasperation. 'It's too flashy.'

'It's a good idea.' Elizabeth burned with resentment. Her ads for their Soothex throat pastels were arresting, original. Dino loved them.

'It's not what I asked you to do, Elizabeth.'

'Lady Elizabeth,' Elizabeth snapped. She couldn't help it; something about Nina's dismissive attitude made her lash out.

The two girls glared at each other. 'I don't think so,' Nina said eventually. 'Social titles are not appropriate in the office. Not for a junior.'

Elizabeth flushed darkly.

Nina spoke up, so the rest of the room could hear her. 'If you have a problem with that, take it up with your father. Otherwise we'll keep it informal.'

There was a pause, then Elizabeth muttered, 'That's fine.'

Nina brushed a lock of black hair out of her eyes. Now she wanted to smooth things over. 'I love your bracelet, by the way. It's gorgeous.' She gestured to a thick silver cuff round Elizabeth's left wrist. 'Where did you buy it? I'd adore one.'

The other girl looked up at her. The green eyes were chips of ice.

'I don't buy jewellery, I inherit it.'

Nina stiffened. 'I'm sorry, I didn't realise you were so grand.'

'Don't worry, Nina. You couldn't possibly know about things like that. Considering your background.'

Nina paled as the insult went home. For a moment, the two young women just glared at each other. Then Elizabeth gathered up her rejected work and walked back to her own department.

Nina stepped out of the taxi and tipped the driver absent-mindedly. It had been a rush, racing home at a quarter to seven, tearing off her work clothes, fixing her face at the speed of light. A three-quarter black jacket covered her dress, a loose, flowing sheath of Thai silk in metallic blue. Nina's black hair fell thickly over a grey cashmere wrap. She was stunning, and she knew it.

Despite the long day and the rush at the end of it, Nina felt composed. Somehow, Lady Elizabeth's challenge had made up her mind. The confusion she'd felt in Tony's office had vanished long since. Nina knew what she was here to do.

Elizabeth and the well-heeled young men at Dragon looked on her as nothing. An upstart. Two years at Dolan, now Dragon, Nina thought, and no one to help me but me. She'd turned twenty-one a few days ago and hadn't even noticed until the evening. Birthdays just didn't seem important. Elizabeth Savage might be the same age as her, but she was lifetimes younger.

Nina pulled her cashmere wrap tighter against the bitter December air and ducked inside the nondescript entrance to the club.

The Groucho was full of media executives and stars; Nina recognised a couple of famous actors, a newscaster and a pop star. Tony was seated at a discreet table in a corner of the room, still wearing his work suit. He stood up when Nina appeared and waited as she shrugged off the wrap and coat, appearing in a slither of cobalt and silver.

She saw desire blaze into his eyes. She knew the gossip round Dragon was that she was his pet. Why shouldn't she take advantage?

'You look wonderful, Nina.'

'Thank you, Tony,' Nina said softly.

First class on a train back to London, Jack grinned to himself. He had just bought one of the finest colts he'd ever seen from a Gloucester farmer desperate for a cash injection. Piece of cake. What should he call the animal? A funky racehorse name. Maybe Easy Money. Taylor Stud, his fledgling operation in the UK had been as successful as everything else in his life. It was a buyer's market. Britain was tightening its money supply, and the medicine was hurting. The recession was biting deep. Luxury, high-end businesses—like racehorse stables—were feeling it. Closing down, selling up.

Jack bought himself a malt whisky and soda from the drinks trolley and smiled at the ogling waitress. He sipped the drink and watched rural England slide past him. To the victor the spoils. Jack had nearly everything he wanted. And finally, he had a chance at the one prize he hadn't been able to reach. Though she'd been refusing all his invitations, this one she couldn't duck. An order from Ronnie Davis, the British coach, to start her training again in preparation for the Olympics. The whole British women's team to meet in Kent at the weekend. And Ronnie, bless his cockney heart, had heard Jack was in town.

'Don't tell her I'm turning up.' Jack grinned as he remembered his own words. 'Let's keep it a surprise.'

Elizabeth tried to get her brain in gear. Skiing. The Olympics. It was important, she had to focus on it. A fortnight at base camp doing fitness routines and studying videos would be a good warm-up to the new training season, but it was hard to fight the sense of failure that swamped her.

Life at Dragon had proved to be one big disappointment. She was sure her ideas for ad campaigns were good ones, but Nina Roth was having none of them. And nobody was going to listen to her over Nina. Constant failure had worn Elizabeth down. She stopped presenting new ideas, and contented herself with reading company reports and typing market research.

Elizabeth never even thought about complaining to her father. Hand Tony that satisfaction? She'd rather die. He thought the sun shone out of Nina Roth's backside. He was happy to give her all the chances of real work, real satisfaction, he'd always denied his own daughter.

Elizabeth strode briskly through the crowds to Charing Cross, her Louis Vuitton overnight bag slung across her shoulder. She ducked into W. H. Smith's to pick up some reading for the journey. A Jilly Cooper and a *Standard*, that should do it. Her train was already at the platform and she secreted herself in first class, ready to try and relax with a KitKat and the paper.

She opened it at the sports pages.

There was a picture of Jack Taylor, his warm smile beaming brightly at her through the muddy newsprint. He had his hand on the neck of a young horse, a magnificent-looking colt. The caption called it 'Another score for Taylor Stud'. Jack had named the beast Easy Money. Elizabeth flung the paper into the luggage rack.

The Alpine Hotel was primed for their arrival. A giant Christmas tree in the lobby fought for attention over a huge display of banners welcoming 'Our Lovely Olympic Hopefuls'. Elizabeth signed in, furiously embarrassed, under a huge poster of herself.

'Mr Davis has left a message in your ladyship's suite,' the manager told her.' Let me get a porter for your bags.'

'There's just the one. I can manage,' Elizabeth muttered, lifting her bag. 'It's good for me, the exercise.' Elizabeth escaped to the lifts.

Her 'suite' was two rooms done up in tasteless pink and grey, with noisy air conditioning. A small note was propped on a table. 'Meet us in the gym at six thirty.' It was signed Ronnie Davis.

Elizabeth flopped down on the bed. She wouldn't even have time to clean up. The mirror opposite showed a cross, red-eyed young woman. In her futile efforts to make a dent at Dragon she'd let the gym work slide, and now she was unfit, out of condition and muscularly weak. She was tired and she looked dreadful.

'Welcome back,' she said aloud.

The gym was reserved for the team. Elizabeth could hear Ronnie's trademark growl as she arrived, in a sports bra and Lycra leggings over Adidas cross-trainers. No point trying to hide in baggy jog-pants, Ron would see right through that.

'Bloody hell, Karen, is that the best you can do? Pick it up, girl.'

Elizabeth stuck her head through the door. Karen, Janet and Kate were racing round a circular track, sweating bullets. The strident voice of her coach yelled scornfully as his athletes completed their endurance tests. Ron obviously didn't think any of them were up to it, and all three of them looked way, way fitter than she was.

'Hold it.' Ronnie waved Elizabeth over. 'Good evening, my lady, you've finally turned up.'

'Nice to see you too, boss,' Elizabeth said, waving at the girls.

Ronnie came forward and cast a critical eye over her body, checking her out like one of Jack's horses. Elizabeth blushed scarlet.

Ronnie frowned thunderously. He grabbed her wrist and took her pulse. 'You're jokin', aren't ya? Seventy-five beats per minute? I'm sorry, miss, you'll have to leave the gym. I'm expecting a World Champion athlete to show up at any second.'

Elizabeth paled. Seventy-five? Just three months ago she'd been a steady fifty-eight. Could she really have lost it that fast?

Ronnie threw a towel at her. 'Warm up. You got five minutes. Then we're gonna see just how bad the damage really is.'

Barely forty minutes later, Elizabeth was gasping for air. Her feet hurt, her calves were screaming. Christ, just a warm-up session normally, and here she was, totally worn out. Her sprint speed was still OK but her endurance was shot to pieces. Fifteen minutes of vicious squat thrusts had her in tears. Then Elizabeth had to endure the humiliation of a crunch and push-up routine in which Janet, Kate and Karen, three girls not usually in her league, outperformed her easily.

'Go and have your dinner,' Ronnie barked at them eventually. 'Not you, my lady. You ain't going anywhere. Drop and give me fifty.'

'Fifty!' Elizabeth gasped.

'Fifty, Elizabeth. Hans had you on sixty for routine—'

'But that was—'

'Back when you were a skier?'

Elizabeth responded to this with such fury that she didn't hear the gym door creak open again. She tried to ignore everything; the pain in her upper arms, the ache lancing over her back, Ronnie's cheerful hello to someone or other. *Come on!* She wasn't so bad that she had to take this shit. Surely. Fifteen, sixteen . . . She was sweating, gasping, grunting like a stuck pig. Twenty-two, twenty-three . . . but there was only so much that will-power could do. Elizabeth felt failure hovering over her like a vulture. With an agonised moan she swayed and collapsed.

'We've got a lot of work to do,' Ronnie said into the silence, 'if you're gonna go to the Olympics, let alone win 'em.'

Elizabeth nodded. She didn't have the breath to say anything.

'Oh, well.' Her coach's voice shifted back into a friendly, non-business mode. 'Time for supper. You can catch up with your mate here.'

A sudden sickening revelation hit Elizabeth as she stared at a second pair of boots. She raised her reddened, sweating face from the dust and looked up into a pair of twinkling brown eyes. The neat suit and Gieves & Hawkes shirt could not conceal the perfect strength and proportion of his iron, obviously superfit muscles.

'Hi there,' said Jack Taylor.

Elizabeth scrubbed angrily at her hair in the pouring shower. The fragrance of lavender and thyme drifting up from her Floris conditioner, and the burning heat attacking her soreness, could not wipe away the

sense of outrage. If she wasn't so mad she'd be crying. Seventy-five bpm,
looking like shit, flabby, weak—and Jack Taylor, watching her collapse
on the floor.

How could Ronnie do it to her? She was going to complain in the
strongest language. Get the bastard thrown out. What was a Yank doing
in the British training camp? What if word of her condition leaked out?
Heidi Laufen would have a very happy Christmas!

She switched off the water and started to dry her hair. Miserably she
wished she'd packed a few more cosmetics. There was nothing in her
bag but basic foundation, blusher and lipstick. Not much to counter the
first impression Jack must have got.

Elizabeth dressed in a simple jersey sheath from Sonia Rykiel. It was
OK. The pale pink shade matched her lipstick and that was about all
you could say. She didn't know which was more humiliating—looking
so ugly or looking so weak! Jack had been as polished and gorgeous as
ever, and he was clearly still at his peak performance. Most likely he was
laughing about it in the hotel bar, right now.

That thought stopped her hairbrush in mid-stroke. She pounced on
her telephone and stabbed out the number for Ronnie's room.

'Hi, it's Elizabeth.'

'Look, Liz, it's early days. No need to panic just yet—'

'No, no.' She cut him off. 'Jack Taylor, Ronnie! What the hell's he
doing here? I want him gone by tomorrow morning!'

'He's here because I invited him. He's going to be doing a little pre-
season training with us. It's just fitness.'

'Fitness, hell! He could report back to Kim or Holly.'

'Jack's hardly a spy. You didn't exactly complain about training with
him before.' Ronnie's voice was sharp.

'He goes! I'm not having it!' Elizabeth heard her own voice rise. She
felt like stamping her feet. 'I'm the World Champion, it's my team—'

'Hey! It's the British team, Liz Savage.'

'Bullshit! I'm the medallist here! I refuse to train with a foreigner. Get
him out of here, Ronnie, or I'll file a complaint to the Olympic Council.'

'All right, that's enough, Elizabeth. One more word about it and I'll
call in the OC myself. There's a minimum fitness standard for Olympic
athletes. If I have you tested tomorrow, you're scratched.'

Elizabeth took a deep breath, frozen to the spot.

'Jack stays. You come down to dinner in ten minutes, and we never
had this conversation.' Davis paused; his fury crackled down the line.
'Your attitude needs as much work as your body. You got two weeks to
get both in shape or believe me, my lady, you are out.'

chapter six

Nina pulled her Golf GTi sharply to the right and parked neatly. It gave her a little thrill to see her name stencilled in white against the wall: 'Reserved, Ms Nina Roth, New Products'. Last week she had passed her driving test first time.

The Golf had been the first tangible benefit. The day after that long, teasing dinner with Tony, Keith Sweeney from Human Resources had summoned her and had shown her a range of cars. She smiled softly as she left Sweeney's office. Dinner the night before had rewritten the rule-book around here. As she casually chatted about drugs, approvals, regulations, Nina made sure her body did all the real talking. Leaning into Tony, letting those hard eyes flicker over her bodice, her inviting smile and long legs. Nina knew it was throwing her principles to the winds to flirt like that, but Tony was the boss, and it was what he wanted.

For two weeks they had been circling each other; Tony with his diary crammed full of Christmas dinners hadn't had any evenings free since he took her to dinner. Nina, pressing her advantage, put together a file on freelance drug researchers that she hoped would blow Frank Staunton away. It was clear to her that the current slimming drug was effective, but not safe. If Dragon put a pill out there before it was ready, the company could be ruined.

Nina knew that in developing a slimming pill Tony was chasing his holy grail. But what if that was a mirage? Right here and now there was a lot more work to do. Inefficient customer response. Poorly advertised standard drugs that were losing market share. Nina made sure she had that stuff covered too. It wouldn't look good on her résumé if she spent all her time on a project that ended up a failure.

The building was half-empty. In the last week before the Christmas holiday, many staff had taken holiday time and gone home. Balloons sprouted from computer monitors and gaudy paper-chains looped across ceilings. There was a definite sense of unreality. In the States, Nina thought wryly, you'd get a couple of cards stood on a desk, that was it. The Brits did it differently; the Brits were like a bunch of school-children, watching the clock and waiting for the bell.

Nina threaded her way through Marketing. Lady Elizabeth's desk was unoccupied except for a huge pile of cards and presents. The staff sucking up. Sports fans' tributes, forwarded by the BBC. But Elizabeth wasn't here to pick them up, she was off at training camp in Kent.

Nina paused. 'This looks ridiculous.'

Dino Vincenza, senior marketing manager, looked up from his terminal. 'Lady Elizabeth is very popular,' he said silkily. 'Many people like her skiing. And her ideas.'

Nina heard the rebuke just as he meant her to. Popular, unlike you. And you're stamping on her. Technically Dino outranked her, but she was a high-flyer in a more important department, and a favourite of the Robber Baron.

'I'll call Maria in the postal office. Get this cleared. It may be Christmas, but that's no excuse for the place looking like a dump.'

'Of course,' Dino said sweetly.

Nina stormed off to her area with her cheeks flaming. She hated being mocked. Her own desk was fastidiously neat; since she was Jewish, nobody had sent her cards. Yesterday she had been pleased by this sign of respect. Now she found herself riddled with doubts. Was it respect. Or were they all snubbing her?

Angrily she switched on her computer and started to cross-reference.

'I'm efficient,' Nina told herself, pulling up a new spreadsheet. 'I'm working while the rest of the company sips sherry and stuffs mince pies.'

The phone buzzed on her desk, making her jump. She snatched it up. 'Roth, New Products.'

'Tony Savage, chairman's office.' The dry voice sent a shiver through Nina's stomach, an electric crackle like radio static. 'Do you have that report on the research teams?'

'I was just tidying it up.'

'I need it now. You'd better come upstairs and present.'

For a moment she sat frozen. Bastard! It wasn't even typed. He'd said tomorrow, hadn't he? But repeating that to Tony Savage wouldn't help her any. She collected together her notes. The virtuous smugness of a few moments before had evaporated.

The elevator arrived. Piped carols rang out annoyingly as Nina stood in the lift fidgeting. Tony met her as she stepped out.

'I have the basic gist, but it was due tomorrow,' Nina said. 'I had to do the sales projections first.'

Her boss frowned. 'I told you what your priority was to be. The slimming drug. Now go in there and present it.'

Reluctantly Nina walked into his office. A long table had been set up in the middle of the room and was surrounded by middle-aged men. She recognised Gerald Jax and Don Hadley, head of Finance US. Plus there was a banker from Crédit Suisse whose name she couldn't place, but his jowly face was familiar—a heavy hitter. Tony sat at the head of the table and introduced her briefly while Nina's heart flipped in her chest. These were men you seriously didn't want to screw up in front of.

'Thank you, Lord Caerhaven,' Nina said faintly. 'The first thing we have to face is that Steele Ripley, our current research team, is not up to the job. We must look for other R and D sources . . .'

Her throat was dry. Without orderly notes she was flustered, panicked. She forgot company names, track records. She fumbled questions from around the room. Sometimes she didn't even know the answers.

Nina couldn't look at Tony. She didn't look super-smooth now; these men were seeing just what she was, a young girl, floundering miserably.

'The B-28 damage isn't as bad as you're making out.' Heinrich Günther, Dragon Deutschland. The West German was bony and florid, anger making him more ruddy than usual. He'd discovered Dr Steele and Professor Ripley. 'Nobody has died.'

'Not yet, Herr Günther, but they would, long-term. Look, we might as well package up cocaine! You'd enjoy it, you'd get thin, at first you'd be fine. But in the end you'd be a useless junkie.'

There was a heavy silence. Jax lowered his eyes.

'Get out!' Günther shouted. 'You are wasting our time!'

Nina froze.

'Didn't you hear me? Get out!'

Shell-shocked, Nina grabbed her sheet of notes and bolted for the door. Once she was safely in the corridor, her eyes filled with tears. She ducked into a rest room to get herself together. Christ! What had she said? Was she really that bad? Was she going to get fired?

Tony watched Nina scarper like a startled doe. She'd been scrappy and scared, but she'd got the information across. He was pleased with the result. His lieutenants had something to think about. And Ms Roth had been scalded out of her complacency. He never liked a junior to think they were doing too well. Especially not a woman.

She was bruised now, he thought; that would soften her. That debacle with Heinrich was wonderful. Poor little Nina, how was she to know about his long-standing fondness for a snort of Charlie? He thought he was being deliberately insulted.

Tony reached into his breast pocket and pulled out a folded red spotted handkerchief. He threw it at Günther.

'Here, Heinrich. Terrible sniff you've got, old man. I should see a doctor about that cold. And now, gentlemen, let's consider the points Miss Roth made.'

Back at her desk, Nina typed furiously. She worked through lunch without taking a break. She couldn't afford to be caught napping twice. When the travel office sent someone upstairs with her air ticket for that night, Nina almost told them to check if she was still meant to be travelling. But if Tony wanted her out, she'd be out soon enough.

By the end of the day her stomach was growling and her fingers were cramped. She filed everything into a briefcase and set off for Heathrow, driving as fast as she could without breaking the law. She didn't want a ticket or a delay; no more black marks, please, God.

At the airport she checked in for Dublin with British Midland and was directed to the VIP lounge.

The earl was standing to one side in the middle of a knot of men, some of whom she recognised. For the second time that day she was taken aback. She'd thought she was the only one Tony was taking to Dublin, to attend a conference on distribution routes. But there were at least seven others!

Trying to hide her discomfiture, she walked over. 'Miss Roth. Good. I thought you were going to delay us,' Tony said coolly.

Nina smiled lamely. She didn't dare say a word. Tony wasn't smiling at her or glancing over; he seemed deep in a discussion with Harry Cohen from Planning. Clearly she'd got it very wrong. She was just one more junior exec; nothing special.

From Dublin airport they were ferried in limos to the Shelbourne Hotel. The Dragon contingent filed into a packed conference room to listen to speeches; they would be changing for dinner later.

Nina forced herself to listen. This was kids' stuff for her. Stuffed shirts from ICI, SmithKline Beecham and Glaxo droned on about healthcare providers. The room was warm from the packed audience, and Nina was fighting to stay awake.

And then it was his turn.

Tony Savage stood up at the podium and noted the immediate response. The packed room jerked to life. Whispers ceased.

He was the Robber Baron.

As he talked—with enough gravitas for a Lord Chancellor, rather than a takeover pirate—Tony felt the pleasure of it all flood through him like adrenalin. His quarterlies looked great. Recession? What recession?

Like Machiavelli, Tony thought, I'd rather be feared than loved.

As his speech raced to its conclusion, Tony let his gaze find his own people. The boys were watching with appropriate awe, but it wasn't them he was looking for. Nina. A flash of light blue in the drab browns and greys. She was watching him, and Tony was amused again. Because even though she quickly dropped her eyes, it wasn't fast enough to hide the blazing anger, the rage in them, burning in her dark pupils like fire.

After Tony's closing address, the meeting broke up to prepare for dinner. Nina rushed upstairs. The misery and rage would not be held back. He had lectured her and humiliated her. God knew how she was going to get through tonight.

She unpacked her overnight bag quickly, then repaired the damage to her exhausted face. Concealer under the eyes; a bronze slash of blusher painting the colour back into her cheeks, berry lipstick. It took less than five minutes. She pulled on a pair of dark-green mules by Ferragamo and grabbed her dress from the hanger. Full-length, bias-cut jade crepe, it was a creation by a hot new Manhattan designer, Donna Karan. When Nina slipped it on, adjusting the thick gilt clasp on the left shoulder, it clung to her curves then fell from the waist, making her look like a Greek goddess. And it moved like a sea wave.

Nina smiled softly. She looked beautiful. On nights like this one, you could put on your beauty like armour.

Downstairs the Dragon party had assembled already.

Harry Cohen coughed. 'Shall we go in? They've set our placings.'

Nina followed her colleagues. The plan had Nina on Table One. She checked it again just to make sure. Surely Table One was for the MDs and directors, wasn't it?

'Nina Roth,' she told the hovering waiter.

He glanced at a list. 'Yes, madam. Just over here.'

Nina followed the man right to the head of the table. She was two places down from the chairman of ICI. To her left was the Irish Finance Minister. The chair to her right was empty. She smiled and shook hands in complete confusion as she sat down. And then a shadow passed over the table and the waiter was seating her other neighbour.

Tony Savage had been born to black tie. He was lean, spare and muscular and looked great. Nina couldn't help but notice the table's reaction, how these grey, nerdy big shots smiled at her boss with their eyes full of envy and loathing. The alley cat was among the tame pigeons.

'I'm—I—good evening, Lord Caerhaven.' She didn't dare call him Tony. 'Aren't the delegates supposed to be seated separately?'

The arrogant tilt of his head looked down on her. 'They are, but I ordered that you be sat next to me.'

Nina swallowed.

'Is that a problem?' Tony asked. His eyes were dancing, observing her discomfiture. 'Would you rather be down there, with the others?'

'No, sir.' She was blushing. Although everybody at Dragon called Tony sir, in a work situation, there was something disturbing about it right now. Nina took refuge in a belt of champagne. 'I'm sorry about this morning, sir. I should have been ready.'

'Yes, you should have,' Tony said. 'I set the priorities. You follow them. Is that clear?'

'Yes, sir.' Nina swallowed the rest of her champagne. She was a mess of fear and desire. She blurted out, 'Am I fired?'

He grinned. His eyes flickered down the bodice of her dress, burning a wash of fire across her skin. Under the silk, her groin tightened.

'You're good. I can use you. You're just not as good as you thought you were. Don't act on your own initiative, act on my initiative. You're not at your five-and-dime store in Brooklyn now.'

The reference to her past jerked Nina's eyes back up to his. The earl was looking at her in that superior, maddening way Elizabeth had.

With an effort Nina nodded. Bastard, she thought. She turned to the Minister for Finance and made some desultory conversation, pushing her oysters round her plate. She couldn't eat. Tony Savage, on her other side, was lording it over the rest of the table.

Nina drank champagne for courage, enjoying the icy, bubbling sting in her mouth. She forced herself to take a little of the entrée. Grouse and roast parsnip. The earl was watching her. She felt his gaze on her shoulders, the curve of her waist.

The Minister turned to Tony. 'Lord Caerhaven, Miss Roth does you credit. She has a better grasp of EU regulations than my officials.'

Tony smiled. 'Nina's got a top-drawer brain, Minister. That was my first reason for hiring her.'

The alcohol made her brave. 'And what was the second?'

'The packaging,' Tony said lightly. Then he turned to his neighbour, and didn't speak to her again for the rest of the meal.

Once the plates were cleared the dinner broke up. The earl was shaking hands, but he broke off to pat her on the shoulder. 'Wait in the lobby. I'll be right out.'

Nina picked her way through the crowd, weaving and smiling. She was dizzy and carefree. Maybe she should have gone easier on the champagne, with an empty stomach, but what the hell.

Tony was out less than a minute later, striding through a crowd that seemed to part around him. He beckoned to her and they walked into the bar together. Nina found she was backed into a corner.

'I like your dress,' Savage said.

'I'm glad you like something.'

He laughed softly. 'Prickly. Let's see how good you really are.'

Nina caught her breath. The dark eyes and predator smile were fixed on her, and the desire in them was naked. So blatant she felt herself tighten in response. 'Are you asking me on a date?' she said.

'No, I'm asking you to bed. Don't tell me you're surprised.'

'I guess not,' Nina murmured. She kept her voice down, afraid people would hear them. 'And what if I say no? You sack me?'

He moved a step closer. Crowding her. Bending slightly, so his face was close to hers. 'You're a clever girl. And you want me. So let's not play games.' Savage held out his hand to her. 'Come with me.'

They rode up together in a stately, creaking elevator, joining some suits and a couple of dowagers. When the last of them left at the fourth floor, Tony turned to her, casually, and reached for her breasts through the silky crepe. Nina gasped. Her knees weakened. He didn't say anything but he smiled, letting her know he could feel her response. Tony moved one hand down to the flat of her stomach, resting it there, feeling the warmth of her burning through her gown.

The elevator juddered to a halt, and Tony waited politely for her to walk out first.

The penthouse suite was to the left. Tony reached for his key calmly, without hurrying, but Nina could see his desire was as strong as hers, he was just more used to it. How many women has he had? she thought. Every touch, every look of his was assured. Tony held the door open for her as he flicked on the light. Nina looked round a gorgeous room, crammed with flowers, baskets of fruit, and chocolates on a silver tray. The furniture was mahogany, Georgian antique, and a huge mirror dominated one wall.

Tony shut the door. 'Are you nervous?'

'No,' Nina said boldly.

He came over to her and steered her to the foot of the bed. Facing the mirror. Then he tipped her face up to his. 'Liar,' he said.

Then he bent down and kissed her. Nina breathed in cigar smoke, light, sexy masculine sweat, that expensive aftershave he used. His lips were brushing hers softly, not gentle so much as exploratory. Getting a feel for her mouth. Then he was rougher, using his tongue, biting her, his hands yanking her to him, moulding the roundness of her butt, stroking her breasts, her belly, pushing down between her legs.

When he broke off, Nina's breath was ragged. Tony reached for the clasp on her shoulder, unpinning it. 'Let's have a look at you, baby.'

Nina just stood there as her gown slithered to the floor. The dizzy, squirmy mixture of embarrassment and excitement was almost too much to bear. To want a man like this and to have him know it. A man you didn't even really like. Carefully she stepped out of her dress.

She stood naked apart from a tiny scrap of lace at the groin. She saw the light in Tony's eyes burst into flame. He groaned and pulled her to him. Nina felt his hands everywhere, tugging her panties down her thighs, his fingers sliding into her, feeling her arousal.

Tony couldn't get naked fast enough. His cock was throbbing in his pants, he was a teenager again, fighting to control himself. The girl was light-headed from the champagne, but even so, magnificently responsive, and naive at the same time. If not her first, he'd be one of the first. The thought was exquisitely exciting.

'God, you're beautiful.' He pulled her onto the bed. 'I could fall in love with you.'

'Bullshit,' Nina said sweetly.

Tony reached for her.

The phone buzzed. Elizabeth reached out to grab it. 'This is your wake-up call,' the recorded voice intoned. 'The time now is . . .'

Five forty-five. She dropped the receiver back on the hook and swung her feet down to the carpet. Elizabeth's morning routine was conditioned now. She showered, dried herself and pulled on her running gear. Four days in Tunbridge Wells had tightened her butt and strengthened her legs. Ronnie's threat hit home; whatever else happened, she had to be fit. The team had followed a set training routine, but that wasn't enough for Elizabeth. When Karen, Janet and Kate had finished, Elizabeth would change suits and head back out of the door. Five extra miles every night, then free weights. Seeing the other girls with better physiques than her fired Elizabeth's competitive edge.

And it was a good way to avoid Jack Taylor.

Elizabeth pulled on her sports bra, ignoring the little thrill of excitement and anger Jack always provoked. She hated him. His perfect body, his peak condition, his business success.

Elizabeth flung herself into a short warm-up routine, lifting her heels up to her butt to get the blood flowing round the hamstrings.

Last night, Ron had put them all through a second fitness test. Jack joined in. When Elizabeth hit the machines, Jack was watching her. She was clamped in place like a prisoner. And flexing, clamping her legs open and shut for the inner thighs, Jack had hung back and just blatantly stared between them.

Elizabeth pushed from the soles of her trainers, swinging her arms, blushing furiously. Remembering the betraying, ridiculous rush of sexual heat as she sweated and struggled, forcing her thighs apart, trying not to let that arrogant pig see what effects his little games had on her. It was killing her, that was a plain fact. If Ronnie didn't get him out of here, there was a terrible danger Elizabeth was going to crack. She'd lain awake for an hour last night, dizzy with longing.

She took a swig of water from an Evian bottle, stretched out her calves and hamstrings, and opened the door. The hotel was just stirring. Outside, the roads were still quiet in the morning darkness. Elizabeth's blood was flowing now and she was looking forward to her run. For forty minutes she was alone with her body, nobody hassling her. She was hungry to get back out there to the snow.

She jogged out of the lobby and stopped dead.

Jack Taylor was standing there, wearing pro Adidas trainers and a US Olympic tracksuit. 'What the hell do you want?' Elizabeth demanded.

Jack gave her a lazy smile. 'To go running, Sherlock.'

'I run by myself.'

'Well.' He shifted on his feet, a movement that reminded her of his skiing. 'I know you're scared of me, sugar, but—'

'Scared? Don't be ridiculous.'

'Sure scared. You've been avoiding me ever since I got here. Which I think is kind of unfriendly, for a guy that saved your life.'

Elizabeth gave him an icy stare. 'You're not built for speed, Taylor. Your muscles are all wrong.'

'Try me,' Jack said.

'OK.' Already she was turning the local roads round in her mind, rewriting the course. 'We'll start by the station, then up the High Street.' That was two miles of solid uphill work.

'Fine by me, Princess.'

She loped off to the right, heading for the pool of neon orange under a far streetlamp. Her feet were lifting off the asphalt, rising to the challenge. Behind her Elizabeth heard Jack's grunt of surprise and the heavy thud of him on the ground as he raced to catch her. Elizabeth effortlessly increased the pace.

'Come on, Taylor,' she said coldly. 'Let's see what you got.'

Thirty minutes later she was covered in sweat. Elizabeth was working at the top of her range but she could feel Jack really suffering.

'It's called muscle memory,' Jack gasped as he watched Elizabeth fly through the deserted streets of Tunbridge Wells, her long neck lifted, her haunches in front of him tight and fluid.

'What is?'

'Your fitness. Even if you lose it, you're not starting from scratch. You should be ready for snow work in a couple more days.'

'Well, thanks, Coach,' Elizabeth snapped. She was annoyed that Jack hadn't cried off yet, the stubborn bastard. 'Let's see if *you're* ready for this. Toad Rocks. Half a mile up this curve.'

Four minutes later she turned into a dirt track. The prehistoric rock formation thrust out of woodland, surrounded by sand. Overhead the sky was lightening, the pink and gold streaks of dawn creeping in from the east. She forced herself to bounce on her feet and breathe regularly.

Behind her Jack Taylor caught up, hit a rock, and collapsed, gasping. 'What's wrong?'

'God, it hurts. I think it's fractured,' Jack muttered, holding his ankle.

Guilt surged through her. If Jack's ankle was fractured, it was highly unlikely it would heal in time for the Olympics.

Elizabeth gasped in dismay and sunk to her knees by Jack. 'Oh, it's all my fault, I'm so sorry.' She reached out and touched his lower leg but Taylor flinched away from her. Elizabeth's eyes prickled with tears. 'Can I test it, Jack? I'll be very careful . . .'

He nodded, biting his lip, and spread his legs a little to make room for her. Gingerly Elizabeth draped herself across him, her breasts brushing his thighs, and reached forward with both hands. His ankle was lying in a pool of shadow from the rock.

'Gentle,' Jack murmured.

Elizabeth took his foot in her hands like it was made of eggshells and massaged it lightly, expertly, her long fingers working the muscle and bone, probing for any swelling.

'You seem OK to me—'

Suddenly Jack pounced, slipping one arm over the small of her back and tipping her into the sand. His legs kicked underneath her and his mouth fastened against hers in a deep, rough kiss.

'Bastard,' Elizabeth snarled. He tasted of sand and sweat.

'You play rough, sugar,' he said, looking right down into her eyes. 'I came to England to find you.'

'What, you can't live without me?' Elizabeth asked, sarcastically.

He grinned. 'Sure I can. It just wouldn't be nearly so much fun.'

Then he kissed her again, and again, covering her face and her neck and ears with downy, butterfly kisses, till Elizabeth gasped and pressed her body into his.

'Come on.' Jack hauled her easily to her feet. 'We'd better get back, or I'm gonna take you to bed right here.'

She trained that day in a fever of anticipation and happiness. Partly to prove something to Ronnie, partly to show off to Jack. None of the others could miss the way his eyes fastened on her all day.

Jack called for her after dinner.

'Let's go out for a drive.'

Elizabeth looked up at him in surprise, but Jack gestured to her tacky room. 'We can do better than this, don't you think?'

A hire car was parked in the forecourt, a sleek Mercedes. Elizabeth slid into the passenger seat while Jack jumped in beside her.

'Where are we going?' Elizabeth asked.

He smiled. 'You'll see.'

They drove out of town towards East Sussex, dipping up and down country hills. Jack drove smoothly, unfazed by the narrow woodland roads. At last he parked outside a cottage on the edge of Frant village. 'My country retreat. I stay here when I'm going to meets.'

Jack jumped out to open the door for her. His Texas gallantry made her nervous.

'Come in.' He flicked on the lights and ushered her into the cottage. It was beautiful, with timbered ceilings and wooden stairs curving upwards. Elizabeth followed him into a tiny sitting room. A careful pile of kindling, coal and logs was all ready in the grate. Jack took a box of matches and lit a firelighter. It crackled into flame at once.

'Cheat,' Elizabeth teased.

Jack turned his head and gave her a wicked smile. 'I'm not that rustic. Want a drink? Port, sour mash, champagne?'

Elizabeth shifted on her heels as he drew the curtains. She wanted to drink herself brave. 'Maybe a little champagne.'

They drank champagne by the fire, Elizabeth nestling her head in the crook of Jack's arm. He didn't make any move on her, and slowly the nerves started to fade. When he finally started to stroke her, Elizabeth wanted it, she was light with desire for him. They started to kiss, gently, then more urgently.

'Are you ready?' Jack whispered.

She nodded, smiling, and held out her hand to him.

'I got a better idea,' Jack suggested. Then he scooped her up in his arms like she was made of cotton wool, and carried her up the stairs.

chapter seven

SNOW LAY THICK on the ground in her tiny scrap of garden. Nina let herself out and set the burglar alarm. It was still a thrill to do that; the two-bedroom, three-storey house in Tufnell Park, ninety grand, her first property. Tony had recommended her to the Hong Kong and Shanghai Bank for a wonderfully low mortgage. Her Christmas present had been a diamond necklace and earrings from Asprey's, which Nina was planning to sell after a decent interval.

Nina climbed into her Golf and swung out into the traffic. January was a buzz; the capital seemed full of fresh vigour, as though desperate to make up for lost time. She knew her colleagues thought she was a crazy workaholic. They also despised her for her rapid promotion. Senior manager, that young? Nobody said anything to Caerhaven's new piece of ass, but the frostiness was there.

The irony was that she *deserved* the new slot, Nina thought, as she turned past King's Cross Station. She'd found an answer, to both of Tony's problems.

The last time she'd seen him was on Christmas Eve, in a suite at the St James's Club. He was taking a lunchtime InterCity to Cardiff to be ferried back to his castle, and he wanted to see her before he left. Nina was flattered by his hunger for her, but unsettled by the Christmas present. She took it and then him, straddling him on the bed, riding him almost violently. Tony was good in bed, and his power was a turn-on, but it wasn't like it had been the first time. It hadn't been that good again.

Dublin was the climax of a lot of things, she saw that now. Fear, and greed, and anger against a world from which she was permanently barred. Anger at Elizabeth, making her feel once again that she was just white trash. Well, she could go to hell. Nina had been furious when Tony had told her that the snobbish cow wanted him to fire her. 'My darling daughter isn't happy. She thinks you are stifling her creativity. She says you never consider her work—'

'That's because she never does any. I ask for market research on hospitals, she turns up with adverts for aspirin.'

'Do you look at her stuff?'

Nina seethed with resentment. 'Fuck no. I'm New Products. I want market research. Facts.'

'But you may have to humour her, I'm afraid. She's making good skiing times and she's in the next Olympics. She's talking about making a fuss in the press. Giving interviews.'

'And you don't want that to happen?'

'And that isn't going to happen,' Tony said, his voice light as silk round a blade. The darkness in his eyes made Nina shiver. 'Smooth things over, darling, would you? She is my daughter, after all.'

Nina spun her car into its new slot, closer to the building's entrance. She knew she was making a lot of enemies here, and Lady Elizabeth was at the head of the queue. To hell with them all. If she couldn't be liked, at least she could be good.

'Catch!' Jack spun the box across the room and Elizabeth's hand shot upwards to grab it. He thumped the table. 'Reflex like that, you should be in baseball.'

'Cricket, please.' Elizabeth smiled as she ripped off the wrapping and flicked open the small box to find a pendant, a platinum ski on a long chain. 'Jack, it's so cool . . .'

'It's not cool, it's romantic. Look.' He fished the matching ski out of his pocket. 'I'm keeping this half. Thought it was better than a split heart or a sixpence or something corny like that. It's a goodbye present.'

Elizabeth jumped on the eiderdown to kiss him. 'I love it.' She wanted to say, 'I love you,' but didn't dare. 'But what do you mean you're going away? It's nearly a month to snow training.'

Jack took the chain from her hands and looped it round her neck. He was quick with the clasp, it still amazed her, the guy was so big and yet so graceful. 'I got to go back to Texas. Check on my studs, check on the new orders.'

'Oh.' Elizabeth frowned. 'Can't that wait?'

'It's business. I have to go.'

'You don't have to, you want to. Whatever.' She was really pissed off. They'd waited so long, and now all she got was a few days snatched before and after Christmas. His business success was waved like a flag in her face, and Elizabeth felt miserably conscious that her own grand scheme had come to nothing.

'Hey, you'll want time at Dragon, right? You made your old man take you on, you might as well make it count for something.'

'You're right,' Elizabeth said. It was true. She had made Daddy take her on, and the power she'd had then she still had now.

Nina went up to see Tony as soon as she arrived. Mrs Perkins, his secretary, tried to brush her off. 'You didn't schedule an appointment? Then it won't be possible to see him now.'

'He said I should drop by any time,' Nina said, trying to smile. Casually, she fiddled with her cuff to flash her gold Cartier tank watch, another Tony bauble she could never have afforded on her salary.

Mrs Perkins went white. Bingo, thought Nina maliciously, and he probably sent you out to buy it for me, you uptight old bag.

'Mrs Perkins,' Nina said sweetly, 'I don't have much time. I'm afraid I must insist you buzz him for me.'

The secretary icily depressed her intercom.

'I'm sorry, my lord, but Ms Roth *insists* on my disturbing you.'

'Nina? Terrific. Send her in, Mrs P.'

'He'll see you now, Ms Roth,' Mrs Perkins said unnecessarily.

Tony was standing facing his windows, gazing out over the river that glittered in the weak January sun. He turned towards her, looking her over with sensual possessiveness. Nina found it arousing but disturbing, the way his eyes stripped her.

'You're wearing your watch.' He smiled. 'What about the earrings?'

'Too much jewellery's not appropriate for the office.'

'But I like to see you in them. Wear them tomorrow.' Tony gestured to the notes she was carrying. 'What's this?'

'I think I've found some answers. To the slimming-drug problem. And to Lady Elizabeth, too,' Nina said.

'Good girl,' Tony said warmly.

Elizabeth got into the office to find her friends genially welcoming her back. She smiled and asked them all about their Christmases, but she felt empty inside. Jack had flown back to America and she wouldn't see him for weeks. Then there would be a hard haul to reach Olympic skiing level, then the Games themselves. Elizabeth felt sick with nerves. Everyone was wishing her luck, treating her with a kind of awed respect that felt like a vice crunching her skull, the pressure was so huge. It was incredibly difficult to focus on anything else, but she knew she had to. Win or lose, by Easter the Olympics would be over and she wanted some kind of role to go back to.

The phone on her desk buzzed loudly. Elizabeth picked it up.

'Elizabeth, is that you, darling?' She tensed at the sound of Daddy's voice; the nice words flecked with sarcasm, the way he always spoke to her. 'Could you come up to my office? Nina Roth and I have a little suggestion for you.'

Elizabeth walked into her father's office.

Tony got up and walked across to kiss her on the cheek. Nina pasted a smile on her face as she watched them.

Tony waved both girls to sit down.

'Elizabeth, darling. Nina's had an idea.'

'Lady Elizabeth,' Nina nearly choked on the words. 'Do you recall that New Products were working on a new drug, B-28?'

'The slimming pill,' Elizabeth said.

'Yeah. That drug was a bust, but the research on it turned up some interesting side effects.'

'Part of the pill components were vitamins, and we believe vitamins may be the next big thing in retail,' Tony said. 'People want one pill for everything, and now we've got one.'

'We've found a way to combine iron and calcium,' Nina continued. 'Usually, calcium blocks the absorption of iron. So our new pill will be the most complete thing out there. And you are the perfect person to sell it. You could combine the campaign with your skiing career. You see, we're thinking of calling it Dragon Gold. As an Olympic hopeful, a World Champion already, you would be the perfect face for the brand.'

'You want me to be in adverts?' she asked her father.

'Only print ones, Elizabeth. I'd find television ads a little vulgar,' her father said. 'But you would also be in charge of the campaign. Designing it. Selling it. Overseeing the agency account, everything.'

Elizabeth was careful not to betray her elation.

'Is the pill gold?'

'Yellow, from the beta-carotene,' Nina explained. Elizabeth hated her patronising air. She thought she had a monopoly on anything needing a double-figure IQ.

'What do you think, darling?' the earl asked lightly. 'Right up your alley, isn't it?'

'Right up my alley,' Elizabeth agreed. 'If you mean it, about my having total control.' She leaned forward, looking at Tony challengingly.

'Of course,' Tony said.

'If I'm to control this line, I shouldn't have to report in to Nina.'

Nina sat perfectly still. She had no doubt Tony would cave in. All he wanted was the quiet life. And if that meant humiliating Nina then that's what he would do. She looked over at the girl so poised and polished in her upper-class clothes, and her eyes were flint.

'No. Nina will be supervising the actual launch, but your work will be overseen by Dino Vincenza. He's in charge of Marketing, after all.'

'Then that's fixed.' Elizabeth stood up, pushing herself up on the soles of her feet, perfectly balanced. It was a strong movement. She gave Nina a barely perceptible nod, then shook her father's hand.

'Well, that's all,' Tony said, dismissing the meeting.

Nina got up, unable to look at father or daughter. She followed Elizabeth into the corridor and waited by the elevator with her.

Elizabeth stepped into the lift. Nina followed her.

'You know, this works great for me,' Nina said. 'I really have so much work to do already, one less job will be a relief.'

Lady Elizabeth's green eyes fixed on hers. 'Nobody asked you if it would be great for you or not,' she said.

'That's right.' Nina couldn't help herself. 'I didn't go running to Papa to ask him to fix things for me. But then I'm not a part-timer. I really work for a living.'

'Yeah? Except when you go running to your boyfriend's bed. That's why he lets you do real work, sweetie. That's the only reason you made the grade. But don't get any illusions, Nina. Girls like you come and go, you're just a toy to him.'

'He doesn't give a damn about you. He's only doing this to shut your stupid little Sloane mouth up.'

Elizabeth smiled. 'You think I need you to tell me that? And you think I care? I've got a right to this company. I'll take my chance any way I bloody well can. And I can handle you. In fact I just did, didn't I?'

'Watch your back, kiddo,' Nina said.

Elizabeth laughed. 'Give it a rest with the melodrama, would you? You're in England now, you know, not a bit player on *Starsky and Hutch*.'

The lift slid smoothly to a halt and the doors hissed open. Elizabeth walked off towards Marketing in a soft swish of cashmere and tweed, her long, honey-blonde hair gleaming neatly down her back. Fury balled like a fist in Nina's stomach.

I might be in England, she thought, but I'm still playing by Brooklyn rules. And, girl, you just had your first and last warning.

'So. Tell me more about these *Wunderkinder* you've discovered,' Frank Staunton said.

Nina crossed her legs and leaned back in her chair. This time she could face Heinrich Günther, Don Hadley and the rest without a qualm.

'I've found a research team I think should replace Steele and Ripley.' Nina passed folders round the table. 'Dr Harry Namath and Dr Lilly Hall are currently operating in Zurich. They're freelancers and have supplied specialist work to pharmaceutical giants and biotech companies. They work on complex computer modelling systems. Dr Hall is the biochemist, Dr Namath the computer expert. Their ratio of success to failure is very good.'

'But slimming drugs, Miss Roth,' Heinrich Günther objected. 'Your folders refer to cardio, respiratory, anti-inflammatories . . .'

'If they already *had* a slimming drug, we wouldn't be having this meeting.' Nina saw the amused gleam in Tony's eye. 'The reason I propose we annex them is that they have recently done some very interesting veterinary work. A drug called Leptate has helped to slim pigs. It occurred to me to crosscheck animal medicine over the vacation.'

There, Nina thought. Now they'll stop despising me. That kind of lateral thinking is what's lacking over here. And with one brainwave I just got them closer than they've ever been before.

'We should move fast. Somebody else is bound to notice soon.'

'I agree.' Frank Staunton was looking at Tony, nodding.

'And I.' Seeing which way the wind was blowing, Herr Günther had decided to jump in there too.

'My daughter will be in Switzerland supervising a new product launch. As she's skiing in the Olympics, it will be perfect cover. Meanwhile Nina will be out there, ostensibly to cover sales and shipping, but actually talking to Doctors Hall and Namath.'

The meeting broke up. Nina noticed that the soft murmurs of congratulation were all headed Tony's way. She glanced angrily at the earl. Why did he want to steal her idea? He frowned slightly and Nina dropped her eyes. He didn't appreciate the protest. *I'm still the boss*, his dark eyes warned. *Don't fuck with me.*

As the plane dipped towards Kloten Airport, overlooking Lake Zurich, Nina's mind raced through the biographies of Dr Lilly Hall and Dr Harry Namath.

They were a strange pair. Dr Hall had been a full professor of biochemistry at the University of Western Australia. She didn't take time to publish her work and, when her college demanded more name recognition, she left for the private sector. Her work since then was ambitious, and often failed, but the scores she did make were serious. Her photograph in the file was ten years out of date; it showed a jowly woman in her forties, short, squat, with leathery skin from too much exposure to the sun. If there was a romance, nobody knew about it.

Dr Henry Namath. Pictured four years ago, nothing to write home about in the looks department—Buddy Holly glasses and facial hair—but a razor-sharp mind. Namath had been writing code and programming machines for ever. As a teenager he'd done two months in juvenile detention for crashing a state mainframe computer, causing all the traffic lights to stick on green all day. Later he picked up an easy doctorate at the London School of Economics. Now he was writing programs as a freelance. Clearly a maverick. Bumped into Lilly Hall at a hospital fund-raiser in London. They'd worked together ever since.

Both of them were arrogant, rebellious and probably as greedy as she was. Just the kind of hustlers I can do business with, Nina thought.

After customs she picked up her baggage and jumped in a cab. Tony had personally selected her apartment off the Storchengasse, which turned out to be a major shopping thoroughfare for the seriously rich. Hermès, Chanel, Cartier; it was thronging with women in silky furs. When the cab drew up outside a smart, flat-fronted building with a uniformed doorman, Nina stepped out with a sigh of pure satisfaction.

Wasn't this everything she'd always wanted?

'So.' Elizabeth dumped her skis down in the boot room for waxing and pushed her goggles up over her face. She clump-clumped her way into the hotel foyer and sat down to unstrap her boots. 'At least I haven't forgotten how to ski.'

'You could have fooled me,' Karen Carter sniped. 'Still four seconds off your best. And five off Louise's.'

Elizabeth shrugged. What the hell was your time? she wanted to snap, but bit it back. 'I'm improving every session.'

'Did you take a look at the *Sun* this morning?' Janet asked.

'Yeah, but it doesn't bother me.' The tabloids were all running nasty pieces about Elizabeth's lack of commitment, commenting on her Alpine rivals' current times. 'I'm heading out to Klosters with Hans tomorrow to start the real work,' she said lightly.

'Well, hold the back page,' Karen sniped.

Elizabeth smiled softly at her. What was the point? Did Jack get this crap from his teammates?

'Will you be packing all your advertising pictures with you?'

'Yes, I will.' Elizabeth had been spending every moment she wasn't skiing working on Dragon Gold. Nina Roth was due in Zurich soon and Elizabeth wanted to have something to show her.

'I don't think you should be doing anything but skiing, Elizabeth,' Karen lectured. 'It's not proper.'

Elizabeth squeezed her feet into trainers and eased into some deep stretches. 'England rugby players have full-time jobs. So have Jayne Torville and Christopher Dean. It's supposed to be an *amateur* event.'

'Amateur is right,' Karen muttered.

Elizabeth rounded on her. 'Yeah? Think you can do better? I don't *need* to train as hard as you, because I'm twice as good. I'm out here to do something for Britain. You don't have a prayer, not if you spend every day of the year on the snow. So get out of my face.'

Karen's mouth dropped open as Elizabeth stomped off.

'Snobby cow. She's had it far too easy for far too long,' Janet muttered. 'She's got it coming, that girl.'

Nina looked at her watch. Quarter to nine in the cold morning light, no sign of life. The grubby steel plaque read: Hall/Namath Consulting. She was in the right place at the right time, representing Dragon's global power and wealth. And nobody seemed to care.

This was the sleazy part of town, facing away from the lakeside. Nina shifted from foot to foot. The neighbourhood wasn't stirring yet. Otherwise, she'd have been scared to be stood here for fifteen minutes, wearing an expensive suit of dove-grey cashmere, a silver cuff bracelet and prim little studs. Nina wanted to look trustworthy. And rich.

She picked up her briefcase and depressed the buzzer again, a long hard push. It was freezing. She was going to have to leave and rearrange.

Angrily Nina took her finger off the buzzer and kicked the door.

It swung open, yanked back by a tall man with a broad chest, a square, clean-shaven jaw and handsome brown eyes. He was wearing a robe and not much else. He was very tanned. He looked furious.

Nina swallowed hard. 'Dr Namath?'

He straightened up. 'Yeah. Who the fuck wants to know?'

Nina flushed scarlet. She didn't dare look at him, he was almost naked. 'I'm Nina Roth from Dragon. I—don't we have an appointment?'

'You're who? Oh, sure, the drugs people.' He was still pissed off. 'What the hell do you want now?'

Nina was miserably confused. 'Sir, it's quarter to. I've been here since eight thirty. That's when you told me to turn up.'

Dr Namath paused, then shrugged and grinned. 'You're kidding. I meant at night. When we're done. Go have some breakfast, kiddo and come back at eleven.' He gestured to the thin paisley robe covering his bronzed chest 'I'd ask you in for coffee but I'm not exactly dressed for it.'

'Yes. Sure. Sorry I got the time wrong. In Dragon we tend to—'

'Eleven,' Namath said firmly, and shut the door in her face.

Nina went to the chrome and glass temple of the Container design centre and breakfasted on croissants and a bowl of wild strawberries. She buried her face in the *Financial Times*, still blushing with embarrassment and annoyance. He'd wrong-footed her, then called her kiddo!

Nina began combing through the financial reports. A small heading in the Marketing section caught her eye. A nice photo of Dragon Gold, the new vitamin pill, in new packaging. A raft of slogans jumped out of the text: Dragon Gold—Go for It; Gold not Cold; Golden Wonders. Despite her mood, Nina started smiling. Then she stopped.

The next picture was very familiar. Too familiar. Lady Elizabeth Savage, posing her lean, hard body in a new ski suit, black with gold detailing. Skis resting against her shoulders, holding up a bottle of pills and smiling that arrogant smile.

> British Olympic hope Elizabeth Savage launching Dragon Gold in Kitzbühel yesterday. Breaking her training to supervise the launch, Savage has commissioned a bold ad campaign that seems to have been an instant hit. UK retailers' advance orders are high, and with Savage also personally involved, Dragon Gold looks set to become an important retail line for the UK giant.

Nina felt a thin coat of ice settle on her heart. Elizabeth's launch plans had been faxed to her last week and ignored. She reread the piece and stopped dead at the order figures. Goddamn, they were terrific.

Nina called for the bill and pushed the papers away. How she longed to wipe the grin off that rich-girl face.

'Come in,' Namath said, opening the door for her. He was wearing a grubby white lab coat and tinted goggles, but she could still see a faint trace of mockery behind the eyes. 'Lilly's in the kitchen.'

Nina followed him inside. The kitchen was clean and functional with a reinforced glass window to the lab, where pigs and rabbits were crouched in wire cages and computers perched on tables strewn with messy notes. Dr Lilly Hall was wearing blue slacks and a red shirt and was sitting at the table sipping an Orangina. 'Dr Hall, I'm Nina Roth,' Nina said confidently, leaning over and shaking her hand. 'I'm with Dragon. We'd like to talk to you about a joint venture.'

'So take a seat. We're listening,' Harry Namath said.

Nina sat.

'You look pretty young to be a pharmaceutical exec,' Lilly Hall commented. She was clearly unimpressed by Nina's expensive suit. Nina also guessed she might be irritated by her looks. 'How old are you?'

'Twenty-eight,' Nina lied. Harry Namath snorted. Quickly she moved on. 'Doctor, we're aware of your recent biochemical work on pigs. We're very impressed and we'd like you to come and work for us, exclusively.'

She mentioned the fee. 'We have a heavy package on offer including your own lab and guaranteed non-interference in your research.'

'What do you want us to work on?' Harry asked.

'Same area. We can't be too specific before you're actually on board.'

'Well, I wanna know,' Dr Hall insisted. The Aussie accent was as thick as sourdough.

'Slimming pills, Lil.' Harry regarded Nina. 'That's what they all want.'

'Strewth!' Lilly laughed rudely. 'Is that right?'

Nina's fingers balled into a fist under the table. 'Yes, ma'am,' she said calmly. 'You've seen the benefits we're offering. Plus autonomy. You'll get full funding and remuneration but be free to do things your way.'

Lilly Hall looked up at her partner. Harry shrugged. 'I want to go back to London,' she said eventually. 'You cover relocation as well?'

'Yes, ma'am.'

'Then if we can work it out, legally, I'm game.'

'But we'll want more money. And a legal guarantee, we're in charge, you just own the results,' Harry Namath said.

'There's no more money,' Nina said authoritatively. 'You already have our absolute best offer.'

Dr Namath stood up slowly and looked her up and down. Then he opened the kitchen door. 'OK, well, thanks for dropping by,' he said.

'What?' Nina said.

'Come on, kid. We've both been round the block a few times more than you. You'll go, best guess, fifty per cent higher than your "absolute best", and believe me, you'll need to. Or I just get right onto Glaxo . . .'

'OK. OK.' Nina knew she was scarlet. 'It's negotiable.'

'That's better.' Harry Namath's face was straight but Nina heard the laugh in his voice. 'If we're gonna work together we've got to be able to trust what you tell us. Like, for example, how old are you?'

Nina couldn't believe it. She swallowed hard. 'I'm twenty-two.'

'Really,' Lilly Hall said, rather coldly.

'But I'm a senior New Products manager at Dragon, and,' she added with an acid stare at Namath, 'it was my research that discovered the breakthrough pharmacologies you've been working on.'

Dr Hall nodded. Nina got to her feet, leaving a couple of business cards on the table. She'd done it, she'd got them. That was what she should focus on, not the fact that the guy in the goggles and white coat who looked like Sean Connery with an American accent had just utterly humiliated her.

'I'll see you out,' said Harry Namath.

He walked her to the door. Nina offered him her hand.

Namath shook it. He had a dry, firm grip. 'Brooklyn, right?'

'Right,' Nina said flatly.

'I'm an American too, kiddo. You can't put it past me.'

'My name is Nina, Dr Namath.'

He fielded the rebuke easily. 'Only if mine's Harry. So, your lawyer will be in touch, we'll talk again.'

'Right.' She glanced up the street, looking for a cab.

'Hey, Nina,' Harry said, 'great suit.' He closed the door.

chapter eight

'YEAH, THE RESPONSE is fantastic.' Jake Ansom's voice crackled down the hotel telephone from the Dragon marketing department. 'Boots just put in another major order.'

'Brilliant.' Elizabeth grinned. 'What about the independents?'

Village chemists were important too. She wanted her pill to be flying off shelves everywhere, right now, while it was still hot. Once Dragon Gold was a household name, half the battle was won.

'You've got a real instinct for this stuff,' Jake said. 'Everybody's talking about it.'

Elizabeth laughed. 'Look. I want to launch in France. And put a major push into hospitals.' Elizabeth was brimming with confidence. The years of reading trade magazines were bearing fruit. And she had something to prove. By the time she was through, not even Daddy would ignore her any more.

Jake was still fretting. 'If you *insist*, but, Liz—you can't launch in France, just like that.'

'Why not? I've got total authority for Dragon Gold. But you're right, it's a waste to set up distribution in just one foreign country. We need to go across the Continent. It's OK. I spoke to Father this morning, he wants me to go ahead.' That was a lie, of course, but Jake wouldn't know it. Everybody at Dragon assumed Tony adored his only daughter.

'That's fine, then,' Jake said. 'I'll get our people in the local companies—'

'To call *me* direct. Father's very busy, he doesn't want to be bothered. That's why he gave me sole responsibility.'

When Ansom rang off she smiled. Maybe she was taking a risk, lying about Tony, spending millions, but someone else would soon discover how to link calcium and iron. Right now they had a unique product. And with the power and wealth of Dragon behind her, she could make a success of it Europe-wide before anybody had time to stop her.

Elizabeth launched herself into her warm-up routine, flexing, stretching. Outside a new blanket of snow had covered the mountains and she was late for meeting Hans and Jack. She was annoyed with the Texan for not calling her since she'd arrived, but she shoved that feeling aside. Today they'd be skiing again, skiing together. She twisted her glossy hair into a neat ponytail and picked up her goggles. No forests, no avalanches, God, this was going to be fun.

Elizabeth caught the cable car up to Gotschnagrat. Klosters dropped away beneath them, and Elizabeth's heart lifted along with her stomach; the sun was brilliant in crisp blue sky, new snow on the mountains glittering like powdered glass. Skiers were out in force, neon specks blazing over the runs. This was skiing, this was coming home.

Elizabeth stepped out at the Gotschna station, selected a flat patch of snow and buckled on her skis. Rossignol had custom-made these for her; they slid and turned like part of herself. Just a few brave souls were pushing off towards the start of the Gotschnawang, and she recognised Hans straight off; you couldn't mistake that ramrod stance, nor the incongruous shock of white hair.

She glided over with one effortless push.

'Elizabeth!' Hans smiled, clapping one mitt on her shoulder. 'You are well? Good!' He glanced her over critically. '*Ach*, not bad. It almost seems that you are fit. But fitness in the gymnasium does not equal speed on the slopes. All winter Heidi Laufen has been practising, and you are dabbling in business. What have you to show for it?'

Elizabeth grinned. 'Maybe something big, in a couple of months.'

The old man's face creased. 'In a couple of months, *you* will see something big. Heidi Laufen with an Olympic gold.'

'I don't think so, boss. I'll show you,' Elizabeth said cheerfully. She gestured down the plunging drops of the Gotschnawang run with a ski pole. She'd been looking forward to taking this on with Jack, his hard quads and glutes straining and pushing beside her . . .

'OK. We go.' Hans pushed off.

'Wait! Where's Jack?'

'Jack?' Wolf blinked; his mind was already locked into the run. 'You were late.'

'You mean he's *left*?' Elizabeth asked. 'I'm only fifteen minutes—'

'*Ja, ja.*' Hans was impatient. 'He is by now halfway down. He said, this is too important to waste time, he does not like waiting.'

'I see,' Elizabeth said coldly. She couldn't believe it. Son of a bitch, arrogant bastard! Fifteen bloody minutes! First he didn't ring her, now he wouldn't wait for her . . . She thrust off from the top. Instantly her reflexes took over as her body hugged the ice, her stomach floating fifty yards behind her as she flew behind her coach. Elizabeth flicked into ski mode like she'd turned on a light, keeping her eyes a hundred yards in front, hugging Hans's tracks so perfectly you could hardly tell there were two people on the snow. But Jack was still in the back of her mind, even while she concentrated on her technique. Maybe she'd been right the first time. Jack Taylor just lived for the chase. . .

Elizabeth swung right just a fraction too late in an ugly turn, the angle was huge. Hans glanced behind him and frowned as Elizabeth hung her head, abashed. Bloody Jack had put her off.

'Elizabeth, *lieber Gott!*' Hans grumbled, as she smoothly fell in beside him. 'Horrible, you ski like a farmer's wife, and slow as a cow.'

'Sorry,' Elizabeth mumbled.

'Sorry won't save you.' On a small flat patch Hans carved to a full stop, Elizabeth just fast enough to match him. 'Come, show me something, *Fräulein*, the World Champion I ski with! Where is your head? Not on the schuss.' The bright old eyes watched her clearly.

Elizabeth flung herself into the next barrelling drop before Herr Wolf could see the blush on her face. Was she really that obvious? It was embarrassing. And he was bloody well right, Taylor wasn't worth it.

She hurtled forward so fast it seemed her skis barely grazed the snow, flying over the ice crystals until the horizons were bleeding into each other. Hans dropped behind her, and all the world was whiteness and freefall, angles and sticks.

No posts announced the end of the piste. Elizabeth simply ground to a halt, a vertical wave of powder pluming up behind her like the tail of a giant white peacock. She ripped her goggles from her head and stood there panting, still recovering when Hans zoomed the last schuss a full nine seconds behind her.

'*Ja,*' Wolf gasped, breathing hard himself. His eyes twinkled. 'That is the girl I remember. You are now fast. But reckless. Speed *and* skill. That is what we need. But with much work we shall have it.' Hans waved at the café. 'A schnapps? We will celebrate, but it will be the last before the Games,' he said happily, as Elizabeth unlocked her boots.

Great, Elizabeth thought glumly, trudging up the wooden steps behind him. As Hans led her inside, the familiar waft of frankfurters, soup and cheese with black bread hit her.

'Hello, my lady,' Jack Taylor said. He was perched on a barstool, drinking mineral water, wearing the red, white and blue suit of the US team. He looked great, as usual: bronzed, huge, the dark hair cropped a little tighter than when she last saw him, the cruel mouth set in that maddeningly confident way. He looked like a champion. A world beater with the gold already reserved.

'Jack,' she said. 'Are you coming up to the Weissflujoch? We're just going to have a quick schnapps.'

Jack put some money on the bar and waved at Hans. 'No, I want to do some Strela blacks. You were late, Elizabeth.'

'It was only a quarter of an hour,' Elizabeth said angrily. 'You were rude, Jack, you should have waited for me.'

Jack shrugged. 'Sugar, I wouldn't ask *you* to wait. You want to drink schnapps, relax your schedules, ski tramlines? It's the Olympics. I never screwed up a schedule in my life, especially not for manners.'

'Nice to see you too.'

'Hey, I'm thrilled to see you. Look, if it was anyone else, I'd be on the gondola now, but I gave you guys an extra five minutes to get here.'

Elizabeth was furious. 'Don't do me any favours, Jack, all right?'

'I'm letting you train with me, Elizabeth,' Jack said softly. 'Wouldn't do it for any other female. This is—'

'The Olympics, yeah, so I gathered. But you needn't bother yourself,' Elizabeth snapped. 'I'm skiing a tramline run right now.'

Jack looked at her for a few seconds. Then he said, 'OK,' casually, waved at Hans and stood up. 'I'll call you tonight.'

Elizabeth turned away to pick up her schnapps. 'Like I said, don't do me any favours.' She picked up her glass and sipped it slowly, listening to Jack's heavy footfalls as he clumped out to the terrace.

'Problems?' Hans asked, but Elizabeth shook her head.

'Great, so we'll complete next week.' Nina was making notes as she talked to Frank Staunton in London. She rubbed her aching temples; it was the end of another long, busy day. She'd been setting up contracts and offices and new administrative structures.

A shadow fell over her desk. Nina looked up.

Dr Harry Namath, Dragon's latest contractual supplier, was looming over her. He wore a pair of jeans and a Yankees sweatshirt. Behind him Steffi Bierhof, Nina's new assistant, was looking outraged. Obviously Harry had barged past her. As usual.

Nina sighed. 'Hold on, Frank, Dr Namath's here, I have to go. Fax my apartment, right? I'll check the details tonight.'

She hung up. 'OK, Dr Namath, I'm all yours.'

'Great,' he said. 'Let's go find a restaurant.'

'We can talk here. I have too much work to do, and—'

'Nina.' Namath bent over her, his black hair and blue eyes seriously distracting. 'Let me tell you something. Biochemical principle. The human body needs food.' He pulled her coat from the rack.

'Really, I—' Nina couldn't stop a tiny smile as she accepted her coat.

'That's better.' Namath looked her over with a forty-watt grin. 'Come on, I got a table. Best place in town.'

Well, she *was* hungry, Nina rationalised as she followed him out.

The cab pulled off the Dörfli and Nina stepped out. Namath pushed her right and pointed. 'The Hard Rock Café.'

Nina laughed.

'I felt like Bud and a cheeseburger, I hope you don't mind '

They were shown to a cramped table in sight of the kitchen but Nina couldn't have cared less. A girl materialised right away and Harry asked for a cheeseburger, beer and fudge melt chocolate cake. Nina went for grilled chicken and Diet Coke, with a fruit salad.

'That's really going to do your cholesterol a lot of good.'

'So now you're worried about my cholesterol?' Dr Namath asked.

Nina blushed. Harry had been a hellish pain in the butt; he ran their lawyers ragged, wouldn't buckle on a goddamned thing. Lilly Hall had got the best terms any Dragon contractor had ever had. She had to admire Namath, he knew what he was doing.

'Well . . .'

'I can handle it. Or maybe you think I'm too fat.'

Nina was forced to glance at his body under the loose shirt. Nice, very nice. He was big but lean, well balanced.

'What did you want to discuss? Lilly's bonus? It's being credited to her tomorrow. The lab? That's ready to inspect Monday . . .'

'None of the above.' Namath dipped a handful of fries in barbecue sauce. 'I wanted to talk about us. You and me. Dates.'

'Dates?'

'Dates,' he said maddeningly, 'not the dried fruit kind or the calendar kind, you must have had some. Girls like you don't get away without.'

'Girls like me?' Nina repeated stupidly. It was dumb but with those sharp azure eyes looking right at her she felt like a teenager. Somehow she'd never expected this. Namath was mildly flirtatious with every female, and they'd fought so much, and she was the corporate enemy.

'Girls who are so radiantly lovely,' Harry said.

Nina blushed deeper. She had no idea how to react. Nobody had ever said anything like that to her in her life. She felt vulnerable and shy.

'I don't have boyfriends,' she said flatly.

'Good, I don't want you to have boyfriends, I want you to have me.' Harry said, taking a bite of his cheeseburger.

'No. It's nothing personal, but I tried it once and it didn't work.'

'Some guy treated you bad?'

'It's private,' Nina said coldly. 'Happened a long time ago.' Yeah, when I was a different person on another planet. Her strength, her hardness, had taken her from that girl to this one. Tony Savage she could handle. She wasn't scared of him. But right now she was very, very scared of Harry Namath.

'OK.' He accepted that, but wasn't put off. 'So that means what? You're going to punish every man you meet for the rest of your life?'

'I'm not going to punish anybody, I just don't want to deal with it.' Nina stabbed defiantly at her chicken. 'I'm trying to build a career.'

'Surprisingly enough, I had noticed that. But that's no way to live. Have you read Kipling? The *Just So* stories?'

'No,' Nina said, smiling faintly at the thought of her ever having time to read fiction.

'You should do.' Harry looked across at the young woman in front of him, groomed, self-possessed, lifetimes older than her age. There was something in that beautiful face he couldn't read, some veil those dark eyes were pulling down. He had ached for her since the second he first saw her, then his lust had mixed with something else; he'd never known a girl like her, breathlessly efficient, such a worker, so organised and pushy and quick. Nina was *it*. She was the one for him. And vice versa. Harry wanted to rip all that armour off and make her see it too.

'There's one about you. The animal who doesn't need anybody, just sways around all day, going, "I am the cat who walks by himself."'

'"I am the cat who walks by himself"?' Nina smiled.

'Even cats need company. Try being happy for a while, what could it hurt? If you don't like it you can always go back to being miserable.'

He winked at her and Nina felt a warm flush of desire lap around her belly and tighten between her legs.

'I can't go out with you.'

'You're in love with somebody else?'

'No!' That idea was so off-base she really did laugh. 'Definitely not. I just need my independence.'

'Independence, hell. You're terrified of me,' Harry said shrewdly.

Nina tilted her head. It was such an arrogant, lovely movement he wanted to reach over and kiss her. 'I'm terrified of nothing,' she said. 'But I don't want a man, Harry, it's not compulsory.'

'Then a friend. I could do with some company.'

'You've got Lilly.'

'Lilly? No, we're just professional partners.'

Nina weakened. What could that hurt? She'd never had a real friend since Frank Malone. 'But you'll just try and take advantage.'

'Nina.' Harry reached over and grabbed her hand. His fingers felt rough and calloused, covered in tiny scars and burns from acids or Bunsen burners. 'I swear to you, I won't do a single thing to you you don't ask for. In so many words.'

Tony rang Nina a week later. 'Getting on OK, darling?'

'Fine,' she said. She launched into a summary of the new division she was setting up, a restructuring of all their research projects.

'I know all that.' Tony was brisk. 'Stock's up two and an eighth. I'd like you to knock something out for the quarterly newsletter.'

'Sure.' Nina was pleased. Their newsletter for analysts was important; it led to big orders from the institutions. Now she'd really get noticed.

'Where were you last night?' he said. 'I got the machine. Same thing on Wednesday.'

Nina felt a soft chill dance across her spine. 'I was out.'

'Really?' Caerhaven's voice was measured. 'With whom?'

Never complain, never explain, Nina thought. 'With Harry Namath.'

'Of course, the charming Dr Namath. You went to the ballet, or the theatre? How delightful.'

Nina's heart thudded against her rib cage. 'Uh, we went to the movies, *An Officer and a Gentleman*.'

'Maybe we should get you home. He sounds like a bad influence.'

Nina changed the subject. 'I spoke to Lady Elizabeth's coach yesterday. She's moved up to Klosters, away from the team hotel, so she can train with Jack Taylor.'

That was a lie. She'd been too stretched to give the Sloany bitch a second thought, but Tony had asked her to report on the state of her relationship with Jack Taylor and he would explode if he thought she'd ignored his orders.

'That sounds promising, but you should go yourself. I'll call her and tell her you're coming.'

'OK.'

'You don't sound too enthusiastic, darling, but I think I can cheer you up,' he said warmly. 'I'll be in Zurich myself next Friday.'

On Wednesday night Harry found Nina crouched over her IBM, tapping away, sunk in her work. Frau Bierhof had gone home, the phones had stopped trilling and even the fax machine was silent. He threw her coat to her and pulled her down the stairs.

'OK, OK,' Nina said smiling. What the hell, it was nine o'clock. 'Where are we going?'

'To my apartment.'

She pulled back. 'Hey, Harry . . .'

'Where is the trust?' Harry asked rhetorically. 'I told you, you needn't expect anything from me until you ask for it. Maybe not even then.'

Nina gave him a suspicious look but climbed into the cab. So far Harry had been as good as his word: fun to be with, great company, but nothing more. A peck on the cheek was all she got when he dropped her home.

She was wildly curious to see Harry's place. A neat penthouse on the Niederdorf, a one bedroom with *Sports Illustrated* on the couch, a mess in the sitting room, and piles of computer paper everywhere. Not much luxury apart from a huge TV. But he'd set it up for her: two chairs in front of the screen, home-popped corn, chilled Millers, nachos, a large bowl of M&Ms . . .

Nina burst out laughing as Harry reached for the remote and pressed play. The screen flickered into life. It was the Superbowl, last year's final she'd complained to him she'd missed.

'Have a beer,' Harry said. 'I got chilli dogs waiting to be heated up.'

'Oh, this is great,' Nina said, smiling, 'this is so great—'

Harry walked up to her and kissed her full on the mouth.

Nina melted. Instantly. It was thermonuclear meltdown, weak at the knees, her lips parting, her back arching into his arms, his tongue—

'No!' She pushed him away, breathing hard, fought for control. For time. 'You said you'd wait till I—'

'I lied,' Namath said.

Nina forced herself to sit down and crack open a beer. 'Don't spoil it, Harry. Let's just watch the game, all right?'

Oh God, help me, Nina thought. He was so gorgeous. And so smart, and so sweet. Regret stabbed at her like a dagger. Harry liked her, because he didn't know her. He just had no idea what he'd be getting himself into.

She wanted him so badly. She wanted to cry.

Nina checked in to the Fluela at noon. She hated Davos. This was town as theme park: skiing, skiing and more skiing. Elizabeth's world.

She got her room key and went right upstairs. Last night with Harry had unsettled her, she felt nervous and edgy. She wasn't *like* this, her confidence gone and her armour dented. Tony was turning up tomorrow, and she didn't even know how she felt about that. Soon it would be time to transfer back to London . . . I'll see less of Harry, Nina thought to herself. I'll get back on track, it'll be great.

She thought about Tony as she dialled Elizabeth's hotel in the valley below. He seemed to miss her. That had to be a plus.

So why was she wishing so hard that he wouldn't show up?

'Hotel Möller, *guten Tag*.'

'Can I speak to Lady Elizabeth Savage? This is Nina Roth.'

It was a few seconds before Elizabeth picked up. 'Nina! Daddy told me I might have the pleasure.'

Nina felt a surge of anger. She said politely, 'I wonder if I could have a few moments of your time. Tony would like a progress report.'

'But of course. Would three o'clock suit?'

'Not really. If we meet then I can't get on a train until—'

'That's the only time I've got today.'

Nina bit her lip hard. 'Then three o'clock it is. I'll come to you.'

'Wonderful. I'll look forward to it.'

She got to Elizabeth's hotel at ten to three. Klosters oppressed her with its huge Olympic rings everywhere, the Games paraphernalia limbering up. A picture of Elizabeth herself, green eyes limpid, gazed out from an import cover of a British sports magazine.

Jealousy flashed through Nina. Elizabeth had all this, but it wasn't enough, she wanted her playtime in Daddy's back yard as well. Nina was forced to think about the loathsome prospect of Elizabeth actually winning an Olympic gold. Then she really would be famous, she'd be a heroine to the Brits. What would Elizabeth do with leverage like that?

It made her sick just thinking about it. The receptionist showed her to an anteroom and Nina settled down to wait. And wait. Her anger grew as the minutes ticked by. This selfishness was going to get her home at nearly midnight.

The door opened and Elizabeth strode in. She was dressed in some kind of sexy, clingy rainbow ski suit. Goggle lines marked her tanned face. She was glowing from exercise, tawny hair pulled back in a girlish ponytail. Elizabeth smiled defiantly and dumped a pile of fax papers on the table.

'Sorry I'm late. Got caught up in a crash on the Strela. Really vile, one of the Spanish girls twisted her ankle. She's out, most likely.'

'Oh.' *Do I care? Be polite, Nina, be polite.*

Elizabeth smiled. 'How's Zurich?'

'Busy. It's like setting up a new business.'

'Just like me, then. Why don't you have a look at my stuff, tell me what you think?' Elizabeth asked.

Nina took the pile of faxes she was proffered, pretended to look through them. 'It's doing very well back home. Sales are holding.'

'Yes.' Elizabeth nodded proudly. 'Did you realise that it's almost three weeks since our last TV slot ran, and they're *still* selling?'

'I'll admit, you seem to have a flair for advertising, Lady Elizabeth.'

'I do indeed. A talent you could have used.'

'I needed you to work on other things. Market research matters.'

'Yes, I realise that now,' Elizabeth said coolly. 'Now I know more than most executives about what our market *wants*. And when we tailor our work to that—bingo.'

Nina pressed her manicured fingers deep into the table mat. *Oy, I can't take much more of this madam telling me about the market!*

'Well, that's about it. How's the skiing coming along?'

'Pretty well, so far, but we'll have to see,' Elizabeth said vaguely.

'Are you training with your boyfriend?'

Elizabeth seemed to freeze for a second. 'I don't have a boyfriend.'

What? 'Isn't Jack Taylor your boyfriend?'

'No, Jack's just a friend,' Elizabeth told her. 'We do ski together. Sometimes. But if I get any free time I spend it on work, not socialising.'

She flashed Nina a brilliant smile from perfect white teeth and stood up, extending one hand. 'I must dash, meeting the coach at the Drostobel run and the queues are horrible! Say hello to Father for me.'

Nina picked up Elizabeth's notes with a sinking heart. *Just a friend.* Had they busted up? There were a lot of papers here; she was taking it seriously. Maybe in that bimbo's head she was involved in Dragon for real. Tony wasn't going to like it. And neither did she.

Elizabeth arrived at Drostobel feeling tense. It made her edgy when Nina asked about Jack. There was something behind that—Nina Roth wasn't interested in her love life . . . or lack of it—but she'd have to worry about it later.

Hans had been pleased with her progress so far. She'd shaved almost a second off her World Cup time for the Davos meet. Trouble was you couldn't count on that—the rumours were that Heidi and Louise had also come up with new routines. And there was more that upset her.

The Strela crash she'd nearly skied into: every skier's nightmare. Elizabeth's mouth dried up thinking about that. They were all just one fall away from oblivion.

Focus, focus, she warned herself. At the top of the lift she slid onto the snow and tightened her helmet strap. Somebody rapped on the Union Jack emblazoned over her visor. Elizabeth looked up crossly. 'Hey, cut it out! Oh, Jack, hi, I was looking for Hans.'

'He couldn't be here,' Jack said lightly. 'He asked me to help out.'

'Hans asked you to train me?' Elizabeth repeated.

'I guess,' Jack said, shrugging. 'I'm polishing Super-G this afternoon. I don't mind showing you what you're doing wrong.'

Hans, you bastard! Elizabeth thought. This would be good for her and Hans knew it—he didn't give a damn about anything except her skiing. It was murder to have to take it from Jack Taylor but she had no choice here at all. Jack's Super-G was outstanding.

'Thank you. That'd be great,' Elizabeth muttered. She'd been avoiding him since the day she arrived. It occurred to her that this would be the first time she'd seen him ski since the World Cup.

'OK,' Jack said evenly. He cursed Hans Wolf silently under his breath. He owed Wolf too many favours to turn him down, but the old guy didn't know what he was asking. Why should I care if some limey chick doesn't take my calls? Jack thought angrily. It bothered him that she was blanking him again. He couldn't forget that kiss on that freezing winter's morning in Kent, and then the cottage, and everything he'd imagined, but better . . .

Elizabeth was looking at him from under her helmet. Impatiently. That tilt of her head bugged the shit out of him.

Come on, Jack, that was it, she's a great piece of ass, but there are lots of those. Now you gotta train with her so let's get on with it.

Well, he *would* train her. He'd show her exactly what standard was required of an Olympic champion. What sweat bought you.

I'll show you, sugar, Jack thought.

'No.' Jack's voice was impatient, almost disdainful. Elizabeth smarted under it as under a whip. Bastard! She'd been dropping and twisting for hours, trying to follow Jack's bawled instructions, till her waist was sore and her butt ached and the whole world was a blur of flying snow and flapping flagpoles. '*Left* a little, then right, lean into the curve!'

Elizabeth screeched to a halt, skis digging into the ice. She was panting, red-faced under the helmet. Fucking bloody Jack, if only he had been a little less good at the Super-G and she'd got something to throw back at him. But his sodding technique was perfect. 'I'm doing the best I can,' she shouted.

Jack shook his head. 'You're gonna have to do better than that.'

Elizabeth ripped off her helmet and a great cloud of tawny hair tumbled down round her shoulders. Her green eyes were sparkling; Jack fought back the surge of desire lapping round his groin.

'Christ! I *know* that! Can't you be a little encouraging?'

'I could, but I won't.' Jack shrugged; his handsome face was glowing gently from exercise, like he'd completed a few pleasant strolls. 'I'm not British, sugar. I'm not here to fly the flag and get your autograph.'

'What the hell's that supposed to mean?' shouted Elizabeth.

'It's supposed to mean that you need a lot more work.' Jack lightly lifted his ski pole and touched her on the chest. 'You need to quit being late, quit skipping practice, quit playing shop.'

'I'm doing something real—'

'Oh, like hell.' Jack was too annoyed to take this bullshit any more. 'You've got some ego thing going with your dad, you're letting it waste the best chance Britain's got for a gold.'

Elizabeth said nothing.

'You got the talent, sister, you should stop fucking around, or you're not going to win, and that's the bottom line,' Jack said harshly.

'You know, you sound just like my father,' Elizabeth said.

Jack was angry. 'Fuck you, babe.'

'I don't think so, Jack. Once was enough.' She strapped her helmet back on and lifted the visor. 'Thanks for the workout.'

She lowered her poles and pushed off southwards, disappearing in a flash of iridescence down the Strela black that led down to Davos.

chapter nine

THE DOORBELL BUZZED. Nina jumped, startled. She'd only got to the tinted moisturiser stage of her make-up. Her watch said 8.00am. It couldn't be him, it had to be a mistake. She ignored it and rubbed pale concealer under her eyes; God, she was so tired. Up at five to wash her hair, but she'd got in at midnight and been forced to stay up till two, trying to think of some way round the Lady Elizabeth problem.

The buzzer again. Shit. Nina stumbled to her entryphone.

'Tony! Sorry, you're so early—come right up.'

She rushed back to the bathroom. Tony, oh God. Her heart started hammering, she felt a nervous sweat break out across her back. She spritzed herself with Joy, his favourite, and sprinted to open the door.

Harry Namath stood there, holding a video.

'Oh.' Nina gasped with surprise, then recovered herself. 'Er . . . Harry! Come in, sorry, I was expecting someone else.'

'So I gathered.' Harry stepped into the apartment, looking her over. '*Tony?* I thought it was always "the earl" or "Lord Caerhaven", some feudal bullshit like that.'

Nina wanted to die. 'Well, I usually refer to him that way to other people. He's the boss, I have to be respectful.'

'But privately you're friends?'

'I wouldn't say *friends*,' Nina said evasively. 'Not strictly friends . . .'

'That's good.' Harry's handsome, open face curled a little with dislike 'He's sharp, but I hear bad things about that guy.'

'Successful people always have enemies.'

'OK, OK, if you like him.' Harry handed over a cassette. 'Brought you the game. It's a goodbye present. Lilly's found a place in London. Says she's seeing some interesting results on the latest batch of mice.'

'But why does she need you with her?' Nina pushed her hair back from her eyes. 'You run the computers . . .'

'She's real insistent. I don't like to let her down,' Harry said. He moved a little closer. 'Don't tell me you're gonna *miss* me . . .'

Nina dropped her head so he wouldn't see the look on her face. A big wave of loneliness and loss rolled right over her. It dawned on her like a flash of lightning, how miserable it was going to be without him.

Namath walked up to her and cupped her chin in his hands, gently tipping her face up to his. Desire and frustration clamoured inside him. He wanted Nina so much.

'Like I'll miss a migraine,' Nina smiled weakly. She knew she should prise his hands off her face, but she didn't move.

'I guess I'll see you in a month.' Harry was still looking right into her eyes. 'Do I get a goodbye kiss?'

'Do you want one?' Nina whispered.

Harry looked at her for a second. Then he bent his head, very slowly, touched his lips on hers, just brushing them, an echo of a kiss.

'Is that it?' Nina whispered. Harry was hovering there, his mouth close to hers, she could feel the heat of him. Lust crashed over her like a wave, and she pressed her lips against his. Harry pulled her to him, kissing her over and over, not giving her time to think.

'God, you're so lovely,' he murmured.

Nina felt her knees give. She was arching against him, totally, helplessly responsive. His fingers flickered at her waist and then his hand was on her, pulling her shirt out, his palm moving upwards to the wire and lace of her bra, brushing over her nipples.

God . . .Nina gasped. She felt a sharper tug of lust shoot right down her body.

'Baby.' He was cupping her breasts now, groaning softly with pleasure, his thumbs stroking, just the right pressure. Nina forgot about telling him to stop. She couldn't say a word. A spasm of pleasure exploded across her groin, she felt herself moisten, he was almost too slow, she wanted this, *needed* it now.

Harry's other hand slipped down from her waist, past the tweed and gilt buttons and up her skirt. Tony's due at ten, what if he's early? flashed though Nina's mind but then right out again. She felt herself part her legs slightly and then his hand was on her, covering her, two fingers tracing the slickness, unbearably softly, Harry's breathing rough and unsteady, and then he pressed his whole hand on her and she shook, a light, sweet orgasm rippling through her. Nina's cry was muffled by his kiss, her legs gave, she was dizzy from the pleasure of it but still hungry, still tight with desire. They collapsed backwards onto something, the sofa, Harry pulling her up almost harshly, climbing on top of her, lying against her, kissing her, his fingers darting over gilt and silk.

'Your flight . . .'

'Screw my flight. I'll get the next one.'

'We can't,' Nina managed.

'How wrong you are,' Harry said, unstrapping his belt, dragging the shirt over his head. His chest was paler than his face, smattered with wiry curls. His powerful thighs pinned her legs down, she felt denim brush her as he threw off his jeans. Nina's stomach clenched with longing. Harry grabbed the hem of her skirt and shoved it unceremoniously up round her waist. His fingers trembled a little as he unsnapped her bra, revealing her incredible breasts, the nipples dark and tight like black cherries in cream.

He had to get inside her or he was gonna come. Nina couldn't think or move, the pleasure, the wanting was so huge now and she felt the sweet pressure filling her like a tidal wave rearing up, building, and then Harry's arms pulling her closer and he was taking her stronger and harder and the wave exploded, and she came, sobbing out his name.

Harry's orgasm burst from him like Nina had ripped it out of his heart. He collapsed against her, relaxed and perfectly happy.

'You've got to leave,' Nina panted.

Harry reached over and kissed the side of her neck. She was warm, soaked with sweat.

'Really,' Nina insisted. She kissed the top of his head, but reticently. She's holding something back, Harry thought uneasily. 'I have a meeting.'

'We'll do this again. When you get to London.'

'Sure.' Nina dashed round, picking up her stuff, as Harry pulled his clothes back on. 'Look, you can still make your flight . . . call me when you find a place.'

She pecked him on the cheek as he left. Taken aback, Harry found he was standing in her hallway, his sneakers unlaced.

'Gee, thanks for stopping by,' he muttered.

Nina waited until she heard Harry's footsteps on the stairs. Then she sat down weakly on the floor and started to cry.

Tony stepped into Nina's apartment with a smile. 'My dear, you look wonderful,' he said warmly.

'Thank you. I hope you had a good flight?'

'Quite acceptable, darling, thank you.'

'Great . . .' Nina pushed a stray lock of hair out of her dark eyes. 'Shall we get right to it?'

'Fine with me,' Tony said, making to slip off his cashmere overcoat.

'No.' Nina put her hand up to stop him. Tony looked down and saw that she was bright red. 'I didn't mean that . . .'

He looked at her sharply. 'What's the problem?'

'No problem, we just have a lot to discuss first, about work, and your daughter, and I think we should do it right away.'

'Right you are.' Savage shrugged himself back into his coat. 'We'll go and have some lunch; business before pleasure, I suppose.'

Tony took her to the Merci Hotel. While he confidently ordered for both of them Nina opened her file. Her mouth was dry and she felt her heart palpitating. She'd always known what manner of man the Robber Baron was. But when he was sitting in front of you it was different. She knew he had always watched her in the same way, that powerful rajah stripping her with his eyes. In London she'd enjoyed it, but that was before she'd met Harry. The jewels, the callous sensuality, started to rankle. What looked like generosity was something very different. He forced her to wear those jewels because they marked her out as his property. His plaything.

She could put a label on that uncomfortable feeling now. It was the way Tony made her feel like a high-class hooker. Oh, God, she thought. She was going to have to tell him it was over. She felt petrified.

Waiters set a starter before them, braised veal and truffles in a white wine sauce. It was delicious but Nina could hardly taste it. Nervously she handed her boss the copy for the quarterly report.

Tony leaned back and read it slowly.

'Very good.' The patrician tones were smoothly pleased. 'Very nice, exactly what the institutional boys are looking for.' He touched his champagne flute to hers. 'To Dragon. May she spread her wings and fly.'

She took a sip, then said, 'We'd better talk about Elizabeth.'

The tiniest cloud settled on Caerhaven's forehead as her name was mentioned. 'So when is the Taylor boy going to pop the question?'

Nina breathed in. 'I'm afraid I don't think they're together any more.' She watched Tony's expression darken.

'I don't believe it,' he said angrily.

Nina shivered. 'There's something else. It's about Dragon Gold.'

'What? Oh yes, her little pill. Managed to make a go of it, a few orders from Boots.' Tony took a belt of champagne, then refilled his glass. His flirtatiousness had vanished. 'Maybe I can give her a few UK products to play with until we *can* get her married off. At least she'll be content.' He almost spat out the word. 'And unnoticeable.'

'I'm afraid not. Not if I read the figures she's been giving me correctly. She's tried to bury what she's doing, but reading between the lines . . . Lady Elizabeth's trying to launch Gold in Europe. She appears to have got herself a budget from central funding.'

There was a crashing silence. Tony Savage stared at Nina.

'I see.' The earl's voice was ice. 'And with what authority is she doing this? How could she unlock our monies like that?'

'I believe she's doing it with your authority. She refers to you a lot in the correspondence I've seen. She's just giving orders, and they're assuming she has the right to do it.'

'You're serious.'

'Yes, sir. Dragon is a family company—nobody would dare challenge a Savage. It is fairly . . . unorthodox. And bold.' Nina had to admit it, she loathed Elizabeth, but you had to give it to her, it was gutsy as hell. And with someone less sussed than me, she might even have got away with it. She tried to smile at Tony. 'Like father, like daughter, I guess.'

The earl's head jerked up. His eyes stared right through Nina, the fury in them blazing like coal, so fierce she shrank back in her chair.

'I don't have a daughter,' Tony Savage said.

Tony stepped out of the limo at the airport concourse and motioned for Nina to get out.

'Sorry I can't stay, darling. I must go back and sort this out.'

So I gathered, Nina thought. Tony had called for the bill right away and bundled her into his waiting car. On the drive to the airport he'd made her go through the figures over and over.

Now his expression softened. He lifted one hand and tucked the wind-blown hair back behind Nina's ears, looking her over pleasurably. 'Really, darling, so sorry we've been interrupted. But you'll be home very soon, we can take up where we left off.'

Tony bent to kiss her, but Nina turned her head, so it landed on her cheek instead of her lips.

He pulled up sharply. 'What's the matter with you?'

'Tony,' Nina said, and her voice sounded a lot calmer than she actually felt, 'I'm sorry, but that side of our relationship has to finish.'

Caerhaven looked down blankly at her. 'Don't be ludicrous.'

'It doesn't feel right any more. I'm sorry, Tony. I'll return all your jewellery,' Nina said.

Tony almost laughed. 'Nina, Nina. You don't understand. *I* enjoy *you*. We stop when I get tired of it.'

'What?' Nina whispered.

'You heard me.' Tony checked his watch. 'Don't send me back the jewellery. Wear it the next time we go out.'

'I'm not going to see you socially any more,' Nina said.

Tony's hand cupped her face and tightened. He smiled deep into her dark, luminous eyes. 'I gave you everything and I can take everything. You'll be reasonable, darling, or it will be the worse for you.'

Elizabeth's feelings were mixed as she stepped out of the courtesy bus, its new gold paint emblazoned with the Olympic rings hoping to compensate for the ramshackle suspension. Apparently not even the thought of a glorious women's gold could persuade the BSF to part with hard cash, so the team arrived at Flims in a nicely painted old banger, courtesy of the Swiss Confederation.

'Did you see the French bus?' Janet Marlin asked as she grabbed her bags and dumped them onto the snow. 'It has bunk beds and everything. Just like rock stars use.'

'How would you know what rock stars use? Been in the back of the bus with Duran Duran?' Kate teased her friend.

'Forget about the French bus, did you see the American one?' Karen added, with a sly glance at Elizabeth. 'It's a bloody palace. Ford are sponsoring them and they've got a lounge area, a video . . .'

'What, don't they have their own mountain?' Elizabeth replied with heavy sarcasm.

'You should know, love, didn't Jack show you around?'

Elizabeth stiffened. She'd walked right into that.

'Why should he? I hardly see him any more.'

'Yeah, I heard something about that,' Karen said. 'Or maybe he just didn't want you to bump into Holly Ferrell.'

'Holly?'

'Yes, Holly. Didn't you know? He's been skiing with her day in, day out since they went to Grindelwald. Doing the Lauberhorn and the White Hare . . .' The main contenders for the medals spread themselves out among the courses by mutual consent.

Elizabeth couldn't help it, she paled. Jack training with someone else! Holly Ferrell, a blonde society babe who had never greatly troubled the timekeepers nor the sports writers. Holly would be Ms Perfect, a nice wholesome Miss America with white teeth and no personality . . .

The other girls were watching her.

'Why should I care? I've seen Jack ski, I don't think I can learn anything more from him.'

'Sure. It's all about skiing,' Karen said.

Ronnie Davis arrived from the back of the coach and the girls fell silent. He glanced from one flushed face to another.

'Catfights again? Just cut it out! Christ almighty, this is supposed to be a team.' Ronnie's bark was sharp enough to scare them all into silence. 'One more word from anybody and I'll report it to the Sports Council and FIS. Nobody talks in bars, and nobody,' he added with a sweeping look, 'speaks to the press. There are all the home comforts you'll need in these chalets, including a weights room.'

'Are there newspapers? I'd like to see how we're getting on in the Falklands,' Karen said smoothly. Elizabeth looked at her; there was something in Karen's tone that made her edgy.

'I can tell you that, love. We're winning. There'll be *no* papers, no radio, no distractions. From now on we're just here to ski.'

At six Elizabeth appeared in the dining room for supper, a tasteless fish and pasta thing cooked up by the team nutritionist.

'Protein, carbs, bit of fat, the boffins know what they're doing,' Ronnie Davis said cheerily. 'Here are your schedules, girls. Elizabeth, here's yours. Hans has called and he'll be meeting you tomorrow.'

Elizabeth dutifully wolfed her food while the other girls chattered.

Ronnie went to check the weights room, while Elizabeth was trying to rehearse the courses in her mind.

She took her plate to the kitchen and washed it up. None of the others said a word, but she didn't give a monkey's. They could try and send her to Coventry like a pack of bitchy schoolgirls; she was going to work out and then head straight for bed.

On her way through to the chalet gym Elizabeth paused in the TV room. There was a bunch of papers strewn prominently over the sofas. She grinned as she saw they were English, great! Ronnie's censorship hadn't worked that well.

Elizabeth flopped down and leafed through them, flipping to the back pages. Her green eyes flicked determinedly over the story topped by an unsmiling Jack Taylor, his cruel mouth set hard as a gladiator. Then there she was: big picture, her ski poles in one hand, goggles round her neck, hair pulled back from a chiselled face. Elizabeth recognised the shot, her triumph after a personal best Super-G in practice, back at Davos. At that moment she recalled the mix of triumph and annoyance, because it sunk in how much Jack's training had helped her. She looked gorgeous. She couldn't suppress a thrill of pride.

She soon stopped grinning.

'SNOW HELP TO BRITAIN,' sniped the *Sun*. 'TEAM SPIRIT SAVAGED,' screeched the *Mirror*. 'SELFISH, SECRETIVE, SAVAGE,' screamed the *Star*.

The articles were pure acid. Elizabeth was a playgirl who insisted on luxury hotels and refused to train with the team. Not a word about the fact that her training was agreed by Ronnie, that the hotels were to keep her away from the press . . .

'What the hell's this?'

Ronnie Davis reached down and tore the papers out of her hands. 'Don't pay attention to that crap, love.' He stuck his head into the kitchen. 'Ladies, get in here *now*.'

'What's the problem, Ronnie?' Kate asked innocently.

Ronnie shook the crumpled sheets of newsprint. 'This. I told you we weren't having the English papers. Somebody must have ordered them up here. I didn't want Elizabeth to see the crap they've been printing.'

All three denied it, Karen shaking her head like butter wouldn't melt.

Elizabeth made a real effort and shoved the lump back down her throat. Somebody had not only wanted her to see that, they'd been feeding the media those lies in the first place.

'It's OK.' She looked at the girls with measured calm. 'I won't let fish-and-chip wrapping put me off my stroke.' She paused and looked directly at Karen. 'I can promise you, it'll take a lot more than that.'

Nina's heart lifted as she stepped out of Swissair Flight 223. The sky over Heathrow was overcast and the plane was full of passengers wishing they were still on the slopes. But not Nina. A Dragon driver, mercifully untalkative, had been sent to drive her straight to the office. You had to give it to Tony. When you were with Dragon, life was smooth.

'Good morning, Ms Roth,' the receptionist said. Nina clocked the quick flash of hostility from one beautiful girl meeting another. She was pleased, that meant she looked good. Men she recognised smiled and waved. A good sign. They thought it was worth kissing up to her. The quarterly report must have made quite an impact.

The elevator hissed smoothly to a stop and Nina stepped out, smiling and glad-handing her way to her office. Her secretary, Anita Kerr greeted her with a mug of coffee and a mountain of notes. 'Frank Staunton wants to see you in twenty minutes. I'll buzz you, OK?'

'Fine.' Nina sat down and leafed through the memos. Only one page got her attention: a curt memo from George Gage, in Production, copied to New Products.

'Owing to quality control concerns, company product no. 87569 is being temporarily discontinued.'

Nina lowered her coffee and tapped her computer keyboard. Interesting—normally products didn't get out there unless they were super-safe. The cost of recall was huge.

Her IBM flashed up the name: 87569, product, Dragon Gold, executive in charge, Lady Elizabeth Savage.

She gave a low whistle. Goddamn, Tony really knew how to bear a grudge. Elizabeth's strategy had been groundbreakingly successful. Nina knew it could have opened the door to the vitamin market. He had wanted a way in for years, but he'd rather throw it away than take it from Elizabeth.

For a second she felt sorry for Elizabeth. Tony was a hell of an enemy.

'Come in, come in.' The Terrier gave Nina a thin little smile. 'The traveller returns. Good work, by the way.'

'Thank you, sir,' Nina said, as Staunton ushered her in. To her surprise she saw Harry and Lilly sitting in the room.

'A great achievement, the liaison with two of our prized assets.'

Liaison? I *found* them! Nina smiled as neutrally as she could at Harry and his partner. Lilly looked at Nina coldly, said, 'G'day, kid.' Harry sprang to his feet. He walked over to her.

'You look gorgeous,' he murmured. Nina flushed and shook hands. Harry traced a small line on her palm, one fingertip stroking the soft flesh between her thumb and forefinger. It was too sensuous. Nina yanked her hand away. 'Hello, Harry, I hope you're settling in OK.'

'No complaints,' Namath replied, his eyes dancing.

'Dr Hall was just going through her latest results with me,' Frank Staunton said.

'Then I won't bother you,' Nina said with relief.

'I'll drop by your office when we're done,' Namath said.

'That would be fine.' She smiled briskly.

Frank Staunton turned back to the dumpy woman on his couch. How delicious, her attempts to hide it were pathetic. Nina had something going on with Namath. He was sure that would interest Tony. Things were going to get a little hot around here.

In her office Nina pressed a cooling hand to her brow. Oh God, Harry, you shouldn't have let anything show . . .

Anita poked her head round the door. 'I've got the priority mail for you, and your copy of the quarterly report.'

'Great! Let me see it,' Nina said. She found her piece right away: 'A New Approach to Drug Research'. Nina felt victory flood through her. This would lead to another promotion. She settled down to read.

Two minutes later, her heart stopped.

For a few seconds she felt dizzy, so stunned and betrayed she didn't know what to do. Then Nina lifted her phone and tapped out Mrs Perkins's extension.

'Mrs Perkins. This is Nina Roth. I'd like to speak to Lord Caerhaven.'

'I'm afraid that won't be possible,' Mrs Perkins told her smugly. 'Lord Caerhaven isn't in the country. I can take a message—'

Which he'll never get. 'I see. Where is he?'

'He's out in Switzerland, Miss Roth. Cheering on Lady Elizabeth.'

'We'll stay for Elizabeth's races, then we'll go straight back,' Tony said. His face was expressionless as he stared up at the mountains.

He and Monica were staying at the Park Hotel, their suite the best Flims had to offer. TV crews swarmed over the resort like ants besieging the skiers' chalets and the Olympic Village. The competitors' chalets were fenced off; some common little man named Davis had curtly told him that Elizabeth had left the team chalet to move in with her coach.

'Oh, really, darling?' Monica murmured, admiring herself in the wall mirror. The Nicole Farhi in orchid lambswool clung to her concave stomach and slender shoulders. She knew she'd photograph wonderfully tonight. And tomorrow night. And every day that the cameras asked for comments from the proud parents. 'I think we should stay, don't you?'

'If you like,' Tony agreed absently.

The phone rang. Monica picked it up. 'Monica Caerhaven . . . oh, darling, it's you, how thrilling. Yes, he's here.' She languidly handed the phone across to her husband. 'It's Elizabeth, dear, for you.'

'Thank you.' Tony cupped one hand over the receiver. 'Darling, why don't you find Charlie and Richard and go out shopping for a while?'

It was a clear dismissal, and Monica didn't hesitate. Smiling blandly, she nodded and left the suite.

'Hello, Elizabeth,' Tony said. 'I've got some rather bad news for you.'

Elizabeth had slept fitfully, tossing and turning in the hard orthopaedic bed. The conversation with Tony had filled her with a white-hot rage that just refused to simmer down. He'd torn apart her work, her baby. No consultation, nothing. To stop her having any success, Tony was prepared to wipe out all their market gains and take thousands in losses. She felt the bitterness as strongly now as she had last night.

The desire for revenge was incredibly strong. It was blazing up in her. She started to march on the spot, swinging her arms and heels through the warm-up she could do in her sleep. She hadn't needed more incentive, but there it was—the gold would give her the means to get back at Tony. And Nina Roth. How had she figured it out from the notes I gave her? Elizabeth wondered, but stopped herself as she lifted one leg onto the windowsill, bowing into the stretch. Come on, girl, not now. You've got exactly one day to the start of the Games.

There was a sharp rapping at the door. Hans poked his head round.

'Hey, I didn't mean to wake you.'

The old man waved that aside. 'Only in the morning you ski, you must rest all afternoon.'

'OK, boss.' She planned to ski the Sogn Gion that morning, a dry-run for the Olympic downhill tomorrow afternoon.

'Do not be distracted, *Liebchen*,' Wolf lectured her sternly.

'Don't worry.' Elizabeth turned her head to him. Her green eyes sparkled with determination. 'Nothing is going to distract me now.'

Nina sat in her office and considered her future.

Her options were very limited now. She had to believe that Tony had some explanation. Without the newsletter giving her credit, it looked like this was just another success for Dragon's team. She wasn't even mentioned by name.

After a lot of pushing, Mrs Perkins had admitted that Tony was due back in England tomorrow. 'Could you try and reach him in Flims, Mrs Perkins? I need an urgent meeting.'

'About what?'

'I'm afraid that's really between me and Lord Caerhaven,' Nina said smoothly. Mrs P would probably assume Nina wanted to arrange a rendezvous, and it would be more than her job was worth to stand in the way of any pleasure of Tony's.

'Certainly, Miss Roth,' said Mrs Perkins thinly, then hung up.

When Nina came back from lunch there was a message on her answering machine. Tony telling her to meet him at the Halkin Hotel at 9.00pm. He sounded pleased, like she had finally seen sense. And he had nothing on the agenda but sex.

Elizabeth stood at the start of the Lauberhorn, waiting to be called. First in Super-G and the two Flims downhills, second in the slalom to Levier. Best of all, Louise had crashed in the Cassons race and Marie Le Blanc, the French girl, came second in Super-G, so right now, her competitors were spread out. The British tabloids were reserving judgment, but they'd stopped slagging her off.

Hans was icy cool. He let her give one-line statements to ITV and *Olympic Grandstand*, that was it. After Flims all he said was that she needed to work on the slalom. Good old Hans; Elizabeth knew he'd be down at the bottom right now eating his heart out.

This was the Blue Riband race. Women had never been permitted to ski the treacherous Lauberhorn before in any World Cup. There was no women's record for the Lauberhorn, so Janet Marlin of Great Britain had set the first; three minutes fifteen, the first and last record she'd hold in her life.

Louise Levier made three-eight. Heidi Laufen three-seven. Marie three-ten. All blazing performances. Elizabeth was next.

'Number eight, representing Great Britain, Lady Elizabeth Savage!'

Elizabeth stepped up into the starter's hut. The noise of cowbells and rattles was deafening. The countdown began, she felt strangely calm. Nerves that seethed minutes before you skied evaporated once you were actually up there. Out of the corner of her eye she saw the crowd packed behind the safety nets, Union Jacks waving brightly against the snow. She pushed off.

The schuss, leaning as low as possible, feeling the speed pick her up like a bullet and fire her down the track. She saw the jump, soared clear and landed smoothly. Now hug the trees, careful, careful, lower with the body—Elizabeth's tight quads steering her. Through the tunnel, bombing over the snow. Long, long right, she shifted left milliseconds before the turn. For a moment she thought she wasn't coming back up, her gravity was too low, but then she tilted, righted herself, she was upright again, too fast to see flags or register cheering.

Elizabeth thrust through the gates, couldn't slow down fast enough and tumbled over under her own tidal wave of powder. She felt like an idiot, scrambled to her feet.

For a moment they all just waited for the time to flash up. Hans walked over, put his bony hands on her strong shoulders.

Three-six point five-five. A roar went up from the crowd, Ronnie Davis jumped three feet in the air. Nought point four-five of a second faster than Heidi Laufen. The camera crews rushed forward and Hans gave her a little nod. Her lead was extended yet again. Less time than a heartbeat, but it said, Britain one, Switzerland two and three.

Camera lights shone brightly into Elizabeth's rosy face; microphones like fluffy marrows hung suspended over her head and handheld ones were thrust under her nose.

'How does it feel to win the first women's Lauberhorn?'

'I wouldn't know, I haven't won. Christy and other great skiers have to go yet. It was a thrilling course to race, and I'm just going to concentrate on the next slalom.'

'That's it, ladies an' gents,' Ronnie said, beckoning to officials to get the rat pack off his girl. 'Liz, that was brilliant, you were flying down the fucking thing, I thought you were going to take off!'

Hans Wolf gave him a reproving look. 'You lost control at the end.'

'Yeah, but only after I was through the gate.'

'If it happens on the run *glaub' mir*, you can die.'

Elizabeth lowered her head, annoyed. She was burning with triumph, she thought Hans might have been a bit more upbeat.

'Elizabeth, your dad's flying home today,' Ronnie said. 'He wanted you to give him a call before he leaves.'

Elizabeth smiled. 'I don't want to talk to him. If he asks again, tell him I can't be bothered, simple as that.' Tony could go screw himself. Once she had the gold in her pocket, she could make his life a misery.

'Still we have more work to do,' Hans said, like he could read her thoughts.

Elizabeth nodded and smiled. 'I know. It's not over yet.'

The words sounded blissfully unconvincing. Bring them on, Elizabeth thought, Heidi, Louise, Tony . . . she was going to blow everyone away. This was her moment. She was invincible.

Nina arrived at the Halkin Hotel at nine precisely. She checked herself out in the elevator mirror as she rode up to Tony's suite. Her raven hair was twisted up in a formal French pleat; her suit was Comme des Garçons, chocolate brown piped with cream. Low mahogany heels from Pied-à-Terre, no jewellery. Her make-up was shades of brandy, berries and gold. She looked beautiful, but serious too.

The elevator slid to a halt and discharged her. Nina started to feel scared. God, she wished she'd been able to get hold of Harry. They'd had just one Chinese meal together, the first night she got back, then he'd jetted off to France with Lilly. She could have done with a friend right now.

Nina pressed the doorbell outside the earl's suite.

Tony opened it and ushered her in, smiling softly. Inside the expensive Japanese minimalism of his suite someone had laid a table laden with plates of sushi, vintage Krug chilling in a silver ice bucket and vases of purple orchids. Nina's glance swept to the bed. There was a large, royal-blue box laid out on it, stamped with the gold crest of some jeweller or other.

She wanted to laugh. That was his answer to everything.

'I don't buy it any more, Tony.' She pointed to the box. 'Whatever it is, I hope you got a receipt.'

'Whatever are you talking about? Come on, darling, I hope you're not going to be difficult. You know how stupid that would be.'

'Are you threatening me?'

'Threatening you? You're really not that important.'

'I'm the reason Dragon went up five points in two weeks,' Nina said fiercely. 'That work was mine. But you didn't credit me.'

Tony reached for the champagne, popped the cork and poured out two glasses. 'It wasn't *your* work, it was Dragon's work. Done with our funds, achieved with our name.' There was an edge to his voice.

'You have to give me credit for that work. Nobody else in this company managed it. You owe me promotion and—'

'I don't owe you a bloody thing,' Tony said. He didn't shout, but there was a quiet menace in his voice that made Nina shrink inside. 'Come on, Nina, this is silly,' Tony said silkily. 'You want a promotion, more money—that can be arranged, I'll dream something up. Providing you stop all this nonsense about credit.'

Nina stared at him. 'You think I'd sell myself to you? My God, is that the kind of woman you think I am?'

'It's the kind of woman I *know* you are.' Now his eyes were black pinpricks of cold rage. 'You proved that in Dublin.'

'I wouldn't touch you again if you were the last man alive!' Nina snarled.

'Of course. You prefer something a little more basic. Like Harry Namath?' He laughed to see her pale in front of him. 'I wouldn't set much store by that one, darling, he's not interested any more.'

She felt sick. 'You told him,' she said dully.

'Of course I told him. In some detail,' Tony said lightly.

Nina said nothing. Her eyes flooded with tears.

Tony reached up and traced his finger around her jaw. 'But angel, you still have me. I can make life very sweet for you.'

Roughly Nina pushed him away.

'I don't think you understand. I'm not asking you for this, I'm telling you. Otherwise,' Caerhaven said blandly, 'it's over for you. You'll be fired. You won't find work at any other drug company, once I put the word out. People will assume that you're just another tramp, one who worked for me and whom I've now tired of.'

'I do understand,' Nina said, quieter now.

'Good.' Tony picked up a flute of champagne and held it out to her. 'So we can forget this unpleasantness, and you can look forward to a very pleasant life and a bright little future.'

Nina hesitated for a second, then took the glass.

'You were wrong about Dublin. I didn't sell myself; I used you for what you could do for me.'

'See? We're so alike, Nina, we're two sides of the same coin.'

Nina smiled back. 'Wrong again, my lord,' she said. Then she flung her chilled champagne right in his eyes, and walked out of the suite.

chapter ten

THE ALARM WENT at six as usual. Her head ached but she was dry eyed. She'd done all her crying last night.

Nina put on a little make-up. She didn't feel like it, but it was about dignity. She felt hollow with grief and loss, but she wasn't going to put it on a billboard. She fixed herself coffee and listened to the *Today* programme on Radio Four. At 9.00am she rang Dragon.

'Can I speak to Anita Kerr in Nina Roth's office, please?'

'One moment.' A brief pause, then, 'There is no such office registered here, madam. Anita Kerr has been transferred to another department. But she's on vacation for a week.'

God, that bastard works fast. 'Then Human Resources. I need to discuss collection of my personal effects.' She had personal notes and research papers, project studies on all the rival companies. Invaluable for when she was looking for a new job.

The girl put her on hold for a full five minutes.

'I'm sorry, but he's not available.'

'Then his deputy?'

'I'm sorry, nobody is available. Would you like to leave a message?'

Nina left her number and hung up.

At nine forty the doorbell buzzed. Nina opened it to find a spotty kid in a grubby T-shirt clutching a cardboard box.

'Nina Roff? Delivery for yer,' he said, thrusting the box into her arms. 'Sign 'ere. If that's your car out front, someone'll be round to collect it in a minute. And the furniture.'

'The furniture?' Nina said blankly.

'Yeah, it's all in the papers,' he said indifferently. 'See ya.'

She slammed the door behind him and sat down on the couch. The small box contained her pens and pencils, three postcards from Zurich and a thick envelope franked Berman, Graves & Bowler, Tony's legal firm. She ripped it open. A pink P45 form from the UK government, a 'you're history' form, fluttered to the ground.

Dear Miss Roth,
You are hereby advised that your employment has been terminated for cause, as verbally advised. You are prohibited from entering the premises of Dragon Chemical. Your work and contact notes are proprietary intelligence and will be retained. Your car remains the property of Dragon and you are required to return it immediately. Other personal items purchased for you by the company are also to be returned. The Home Office has been notified of the change in your residency status . . .

There was another sharp rap on the door. Nina jumped to her feet and opened it, to be confronted with five burly men in red and black Dragon Security outfits. A white van was parked outside.

'We've come for the stuff. You got the car keys?'

Nina handed over the keys to the Golf and stood aside to let them in. Silently the men filed past her and started to carry off her furniture.

Friday morning dawned crystal clear over Verbier. At the top of Veysonnaz the athletes stood around, shifting on the snow and not talking to each other. Most were following the monitors rigged inside and outside the hut. At the starting gate Elizabeth was ready to go. Her heart was racing as though she were halfway down already. Two minutes to triumph or defeat.

The news wasn't good. Her championship lead just narrowed. Heidi had led until Louise skied the race of her career. And the only thing between the Swiss girl and the podium was Lady Elizabeth Savage.

There was no time to think. The klaxon sounded and Elizabeth shoved herself forward, violently, launching due south like a rocket. How do you top a perfect run? You go *faster, faster*! Her muscles burned as she forced herself down for the vertical plunge, hugging the netting line for greater velocity. Wind howled past her helmet.

As she headed into the final furlong, Elizabeth took the last turn at a dangerous tilt, her chest inches from the ground, right by the netting as she—

Suddenly she was out of control! A small, sick lurch she tried to steady but was going too low and too fast to stop, and Elizabeth slammed into the side netting, screaming in pain as the tips of her skis thrust through the woven nylon, halting instantly as her body travelled forwards at more than a hundred and twenty miles per hour. Her legs were spread-eagled, flung against the solid grip of her boots, the world was a white and blue tumble of sky and snow, then cracking bone, her own distant screaming, and a warm red stream of blood on the icy ground before pain washed everything away in a terrible darkness.

All she wanted to do was crawl away and die, Nina thought. The sweep of events had hurtled past and left her behind, and she felt drained. Dragon was rewriting her history as ruthlessly as the KGB; she was a nothing, a non-person. Every day she saw the upward march of the stock. Little articles about Dr Hall's research appeared in the biotech sections of the papers. And big, commanding photos of Anthony Savage, Earl of Caerhaven, bravely coping with the tragedy in Switzerland as he ramraided yet another three companies.

That was the thing that saved her.

No matter how lifeless she felt, she had too much pride to look at those charming pictures and just take it. Nina clipped the photos and pinned them everywhere—above her kettle, on her mirrors, by her bed.

It worked like a voodoo charm. Soon grief was only her second emotion. The first was rage.

The first thing to do was sell the house. Then there were the jewels. Tony had refused to take them back and she needed the money. You had to have funds to go to war. And if the authorities didn't know where she lived, they couldn't serve her with any nasty letters. She rented a cheap flat in Highgate for cash, using a false name. It didn't have a kitchen, just a fenced-off little enclosure that was part of the sitting room, paint was peeling off the door frames, but Nina had lived in worse dives than that.

She bought a secondhand computer and fax machine from *Exchange & Mart*. Once they were set up in her cramped little bedroom Nina's spirits lifted just a touch.

Now she was ready to go to work.

She couldn't find a job. Glaxo, Wellcome and ICI turned her down flat. Tony Savage had been clever, very clever, she thought bitterly as she left SmithKline Beecham. He let her have a few interviews. Even a couple of job offers. She could never prove any blacklisting, but she knew just what was going on.

The jobs she was offered were suitable for an entry-level executive without a degree. They would mean years of working her way back up; the same frustrating struggle for promotion and recognition.

Nina couldn't live with that. She would have to find another way.

Elizabeth blinked dizzily, her mind struggling to the surface through pain and fatigue. She was desperately thirsty and there was a wrenching ache in her left ankle. Her body felt wrong. Unbalanced.

'She's coming round.' A clipped English voice, a grey-haired doctor leaning over her bed. 'Lady Elizabeth. Do you know where you are?'

Elizabeth whispered, 'Pain. Water.'

The surgeon lifted a beaker of water to her mouth and motioned to a nurse. 'Give her ladyship some pethidine.' He gave her a brisk, impersonal smile. 'I'm Dr Jopling, one of your father's regular consultants. He had me flown out here to attend to you after your accident. You're in the Clinique Reine Catherine, outside Geneva.'

The nurse silently injected something cold into her side.

Elizabeth stared at him. Images flooded back into her mind.

'I fell.'

'I'm afraid so. You had a serious accident and underwent several operations, but you're all right now.'

'No.' Elizabeth shook her head. The pethidine was working, washing away the pain, but something was very wrong.

'Doctor.' Elizabeth's voice was a weakened croak. 'I want to know what happened. Please tell me now.'

'Very well.' Jopling came closer to the bed and looked like he might be going to take her hand, but then thought better of such familiarity. 'You suffered serious internal and external injuries, including haemorrhaging, broken bones and fractures.' A beat. 'The worst damage was done to your left foot, which was broken by your fall and then sliced to the bone by your right ski. This injury was further compounded by your ski boot. It crushed the severed portion of the foot.'

He paused. There was no way to soften the blow. 'Every effort was made to reattach, but the nerve endings were beyond repair. I'm sorry to have to tell you that we amputated your foot at the ankle.'

Blood drained from Elizabeth's face as she glanced down to the end of the bed. Two feet seemed to point upwards under the blankets, but she only had sensation in the right one.

'A prosthesis,' the surgeon explained. 'It's plastic; attached to your leg with a metal frame, jointed on the ball of the foot to simulate as normal a walk as possible. The best on the market; your father insisted.'

He pretended not to notice as tears filled Elizabeth's eyes and trickled silently down her cheeks.

When she felt she had control of herself she buzzed for the doctor.

'I'd like to see Herr Hans Wolf,' Elizabeth said.

The name seemed to shock Jopling. His face creased just a fraction. 'Herr Wolf was refused permission to see you.'

'Refused permission?' She pushed herself up on her elbows and glared at Jopling with fiery eyes. 'Who refused him permission? You?'

'Not at all, my lady,' Jopling said hastily. 'It was Lord Caerhaven. He has control over all the arrangements here.'

I'll bet he does, Elizabeth thought. 'OK, Dr Jopling, please call Hans and ask him to come and see me.'

Jopling nodded. 'I believe Herr Wolf is staying in the city. He has called to check on your condition every day.'

Elizabeth started to cry, she couldn't help it. She brushed back the tears. 'Has anyone else called?'

The doctor spread his hands. 'Hundreds. The British team coaches, your teammates, many other competitors, and the media . . .'

'Did . . . did Mr Jack Taylor ask to see me?'

'He rang to ask after your condition, and he sent flowers, but he didn't request an appointment, no. I will call Herr Wolf.'

'Thank you. Doctor, who won the medals?'

Jopling looked at her with a certain amount of pity. 'Louise Levier took the gold, Christy Lansch the silver and Heidi Laufen the bronze.'

'And Jack Taylor took the men's gold?'

'Of course,' Jopling said absently as he checked the charts at the foot of her bed. 'There was never any doubt about that.'

The door opened at 3.00pm. Elizabeth sat up, hoping to see Hans, but it was her father. He walked over to Elizabeth with a vast bunch of blossoms in his arms, and laid them on her bedside table.

Elizabeth flopped back on her pillows, disappointed.

'Darling, you look terrible. Are you feeling OK?'

'I've lost my foot, I'm never going to ski again,' Elizabeth said flatly, 'and I've lost an Olympic crown I had sewn up.'

'We don't know if you had it sewn up.' The earl perched himself on the edge of her bed. 'Never mind about that now. I've come to discuss your future. I gather Mr Taylor is out of the picture.'

'Who do you *gather* that from? Your girlfriend?'

'I don't have one of those, Elizabeth, but if you're referring to Nina Roth, she's been dismissed. For insubordination.'

'You're breaking my heart,' Elizabeth said bitterly. 'You get good information, though. Jack was never *in* the picture. So I'll have to come and work at Dragon.'

'Yes.' Tony leaned forward and spoke softly. 'I've thought about that. I have some terrific openings for you.'

He reached into his jacket and handed Elizabeth a sheet of paper. Her eyes flickered quickly across it, then rose disbelievingly back up to his. 'Corporate Hospitality, Events Organisation—you have to be joking. I know you were angry I did Dragon Gold without your permission, but—'

'Angry? Yes, I was angry. What you fail to understand is that Dragon is *my* company. Nobody does anything without my approval.'

'I won't do those two-bit dressmaker jobs.'

'Then I'll give you a small allowance, as long as you behave yourself and keep out of the spotlight.' Tony's smile was full of malice. 'Do you know, I thought of you just yesterday. I was talking to Dean Bradman in the Sydney office, and he told me the most marvellous Australian proverb: you've got to cut down the tall poppies. You were a tall poppy, Elizabeth, you and Nina both.'

Elizabeth looked right into his eyes. She couldn't believe it. She was lying here with her foot shorn away, and this was what he was saying.

'I—'

Tony held up one hand. 'Don't spoil things, Elizabeth. You don't have the power to embarrass me now. You're not quite the national heroine you were. It seems the press are blaming you for reckless skiing . . . nothing official, of course, but that's what they're printing.'

'You *owe* me,' Elizabeth said fiercely. 'I'm your *daughter*. Don't you owe it to my mother?'

The earl sat up as though he'd been stung. He looked at her again, more carefully, a musing expression on his face.

'You look so like her,' he said absently, then, 'Those are my offers, Elizabeth. Take them or leave them. I don't give a damn either way.' He tapped the paper again. 'In fact, Elizabeth, I'm doing all this *because* I owe your mother.'

Elizabeth had nothing to say. She watched him as he left the room. He hates me, she thought. My God, he actually hates me.

Hans came to see her. Despite his stiff manner, he was brokenhearted and it showed. A light had gone out in those clear blue eyes. Elizabeth had sworn she wouldn't cry but it was no use; Hans Wolf's grief, contrasting with Tony's casual cruelty, opened the floodgates.

Hans's bony hand gripped hers fiercely. 'Never have I seen you ski that way. You had the gold in your pocket.' He snapped his fingers. 'Mademoiselle Levier was a dairymaid next to you.'

'You didn't say that at the time.'

'*Liebchen*, you know your old Hans. I was only being cautious . . .'

'Wish I had been,' Elizabeth said.

'Cautious skiers? There is a place for them,' Hans said stiffly. 'Teaching the snowplough to *Kinder* on the nursery slopes. There has never been a woman skier like you.'

Elizabeth looked away before the tears started again. The dreadful thing was, she thought that too. Deep inside, she thought she was the greatest, could have been the female Franz Klammer. But everybody would forget her now, not right away, but soon.

'Easy, when you have the best coach ever.' She tried to be British, brisk and impersonal. 'Anyway, I came to it late. I've only been skiing for a few years. There are other things that I can do.'

'What will you do? Work for your father?'

'I don't think that's going to work out. He and I have fallen out. He won't let me do the kind of work I want.'

'I see,' Hans said. He looked at her with a fierce protectiveness. 'There are many options for you. I can speak to the Swiss Sports Council. Or the FIS, they will be thrilled to have you market the sport.'

'I don't think so. Thanks, Hans, really, but no.' She shook her head and Hans saw a new gauntness in her face. 'Spend my life publicising

124

slopes I'll never ski again, writing puff pieces about Jack Taylor's next World Cup?'

'You have not heard, then? Herr Taylor has retired from the sport. After this gold. In one year we lose both our brightest hopes.' Hans bent over and smoothed her coverlet. 'But what about him? He loves you. He is a rich, powerful young man, he can look after you.'

'Oh, Hans,' Elizabeth said, stroking his hand. 'It's all over between Jack and me, it has been for ages. And anyway, I've had enough of being looked after. I'm going to take care of myself.'

Wolf looked down at his protégé. Under the misery there was something he had not seen in her before. A quiet fury, a cold chip of ice at the heart of her pupils. A certain foreboding mingled with his pity.

There were a lot of empty hours in the hospital bed, waiting for reflex tests and anodyne clinic food. Enough time to watch a lot of CNN or read months' worth of *Paris Match*. Or to brood.

Monica, Charles and Richard all paid dutiful visits. They weren't malicious like Tony, they just didn't care. Which made them and her about even. Ronnie and the others asked for appointments but Elizabeth told Jopling to make medical excuses. She wasn't interested in other people. She was interested in Tony.

Elizabeth started to eat. She did intensive physiotherapy four times a day, against the doctor's advice. It was hateful, having to stand between two poles, resting her weight on a foot that wasn't there. After years of instinctive balancing, every step felt like she was lurching drunkenly. And her foot. It was solid, plastic. She hated it. Elizabeth felt ugly, like her beauty had fled along with her hopes. Her body was changing too: from lean strength to slim, softer and weaker; she felt like a coat hanger. But through all the pain and frustration, and the nightmares, Elizabeth never wavered. She ordered a new wardrobe and stuck it on Tony's account; clothes in smaller sizes and specially made boots and shoes; her hair styled and dyed a radiant blonde.

She wanted answers. And she wasn't going to find them in the clinic. She insisted on being discharged after chopping the rehab period in two by her exhausting schedule. Then she had Mrs Perkins book her on a flight under a false name to avoid the paparazzi at Heathrow.

She made it through the airport in shades and a Burberry raincoat, so nobody recognised her except a respectful customs officer. He said he was sorry, and welcome to England. Elizabeth smiled bleakly. She got more goodwill from a total stranger than her own family.

It was raining lightly as the limo that Tony had sent to meet her purred up the M4, water spattering over the glass so the traffic slipped by in a soundless blur. Elizabeth switched on the radio so she wouldn't have to chat to the driver, and let the formless suspicions in her mind swirl into some kind of definite shape. By the time they pulled into the narrow country road that led to Caerhaven, Elizabeth had an idea.

'Darling!' Monica kissed her. 'You look wonderful, so glad you're better after such a shock. And the hair, well, it's *very* dramatic . . .'

You hate it, you think it looks too good, you cow, Elizabeth thought. She smiled back. 'It's nice to be home.'

'Jenkins will unpack your bags, and there's a wonderful salmon mousse crying out to be polished off.'

'I don't feel that hungry, really,' Elizabeth said. 'I think I'll just have a bath, change, make a few phone calls.'

'Of course,' Monica said with perfect disinterest. 'Do what you want.'

In her room Elizabeth stripped and grabbed a warm sweater, her cowboy boots and some Levi 501s. They were hanging off her, but she fixed that with a thick belt. Then she picked up the phone. Joe Sharp, an old boyfriend from the village, had a brother who worked on the *Bangor Courier*. She hoped he hadn't moved.

'Hello?'

She felt a silly relief. 'Joe, it's Liz Savage.'

There was a stunned pause, then he laughed. 'Christ! I haven't heard from you in years. *Shwd mae pethau?*'

'It's going OK, *iechyd da*, but could we stick to English? My Welsh is sort of rusty.'

'OK, OK, if you must. Not that your sort were ever really Welsh anyway.' The teasing changed to concern as he gingerly approached the subject. 'Liz, I'm really sorry, I heard—'

'Thanks, but I'll be fine. Things happen for a reason.' That sounded unconvincing even to her. 'The stuff in the papers was all bollocks, but never mind about that now, I need a favour from Aled, as soon as possible. I want to check some old press cuttings. Family history.'

'Anything for you, *cariad*,' Joe said. 'I was going to town to meet a few mates. I could give you a lift if you like.'

'Now?' Elizabeth said, a bit startled. She checked her watch; it was still only three o'clock. 'Sure, why not? Thanks, Joe, I really appreciate it.'

'I'll pick you up outside the front porch in ten minutes.'

Elizabeth slipped out to find a black Mini Metro and a grown-up Joe Sharp. He was bigger and thicker, and the caterpillar fluff on his chin had turned into thick stubble. He was ugly as hell but very coarse and masculine. She could see why she'd been attracted to him as a teenager.

Joe whistled as she climbed into the front seat. 'You've dyed your hair, you look great.'

'How do you know that?'

'Come on, girl, you're all over the papers. I won fifty quid when you took the World Cup,' Joe said amiably, shifting fluidly into gear and speeding off down the gravel drive.

Bangor was relentlessly gloomy as ever, though by some oversight it wasn't raining. 'The *Courier's* just down there,' Joe said. 'Aled knows you're coming in. I'm having a few jars with the lads, so come to the Royal Oak when you're ready.'

Elizabeth thanked him and climbed carefully out. A few people stared at her, then looked away again. The hair's confusing them, Elizabeth thought, and anyway, I won't be famous for long. She made it into the functional slab of grey concrete that was the local rag's office. Aled Sharp came and met her at the front desk. She quickly explained she wanted to check some old press cuttings.

'My station's over here,' he said, leading her to a beat-up IBM. He was blond and thinner than Joe, and he also seemed nervous. 'Just tap in the reference you want, and then press this, er, Lady Elizabeth—'

'Elizabeth. Please. You're a lifesaver, Aled.'

He smiled shyly. 'It's not strictly allowed, but seeing as it's you . . .'

'I just need half an hour,' Elizabeth said, then she had an idea. 'Look, tell your boss you did me a trade. Time on the clippings service, in exchange for an exclusive. I haven't talked to any national press. He can license it to the *Sun*.'

'Would you do that?' Aled's face pinkened with excitement. 'Oh, brilliant, terrific. I'll go and tell the editor.'

Elizabeth watched him go. Poor kid, it was probably the closest to a scoop he'd ever come. Quickly she entered into the database.

She tapped in EARL OF CAERHAVEN, and LOUISE, COUNTESS OF CAERHAVEN, 1956-60

CROSS-REFERENCE: LADY ELIZABETH SAVAGE

She thought a moment, then added one more name.

JAY DEFRIES

It took a while for the computer to scroll and select. Elizabeth read it over. Double-checked to be sure. Then with a calm she didn't feel, she sent it all to the printer.

'He wants me to come over and interview you tomorrow,' Aled Sharp told her eagerly when he came back. 'Find anything interesting?'

'Yes, I did.' Elizabeth said. 'I found the answer to everything.'

Nina sat alone in her office. Her premises were located on Wardour Street. Rent was high in Soho, but that was how it had to be. She had a tiny space in a good location. The office was two rooms, and it had come with peeling walls and filthy windows. Nina had rolled up her sleeves and painted the walls a soothing apple green, then scrubbed the windows until everything gleamed. The front door was stencilled: 'ROTH CONSULTING'.

Roth Consulting. It sounded so grand. Management consulting was the hot new business sector, and who knew more about European markets than her? Just a few contracts would let her hire staff . . .

Nina realised certain doors were shut to her. The big companies wouldn't need her help, and word had gone round from Tony. It was the little fish she'd set her sights on: outfits with one product; firms that Tony would never consider. Minnows.

Great theory. But lousy reality. The little firms she approached were too strapped for cash even to think about consultants. Meanwhile, the rent on the office, its equipment and her flat were eating up Nina's savings at a rate of knots. She needed a contract. And fast.

Jack tugged on the reins and turned round, his Arab stallion half rearing in annoyance.

'You ain't been listening to a single word, son,' John Taylor said wearily. He pricked his mount forwards, breathing hard. Jack had ridden him right off the course today, flying across the fields like he was riding for his life. Whatever Europe had done, it hadn't softened him.

Back to the States with a gold medal. The TV people and the papers making such a fuss. Jack should have been prouder than a peacock.

He wasn't. The one time he looked happy was when they looped that burnished disc round his neck. Saving that, he was moody and restless; no interest in anything, even the ladies. The Dallas babes were queuing up for it everywhere he went. But Jack was acting like a goddamned monk.

Today their ride round the ranch had ended ten minutes ago, that was how long it took John to catch up with their son.

'Sorry, Pa.'

Taylor Senior patted the horse's sweating flank. 'Boy, I don't need no shrink to tell me something ain't right. You'd better spit it out. I don't need no zombie round here.'

Jack looked down. 'It's Elizabeth.'

'Elizabeth? Her again? I am mighty sorry for a girl who has something like that happen, don't get me wrong, but last time you spoke you were sayin' how you were through with her, what a stubborn, ornery bitch she was. There's lots of pretty girls right here, and y'all know you got work to do.' He waved a suntanned hand around the rolling acres. 'The stud farm, the hotels and the land, it ain't going to nobody but you. You gotta start taking an interest.'

'Pa.' Jack looked down at him distractedly. 'I have to go and find her, tell her how sorry I am. In person. It's a skiing thing.'

'Back to Europe?' He snorted. 'Like hell, it's a skiing thing. Look, son, go if you have to. You want to waste thousands of bucks jettin' over to dry some chick's tears, be my guest. But then you get your butt back here.' He jabbed a finger at the stables behind him. '*This* is your future, Jack. Texas. Not London. You'd better have that real clear in your mind.'

The car came crunching down the gravel drive to park in front of the house. Elizabeth sat at her turret window and watched it come, Tony's sleek Silver Phantom Rolls-Royce gleaming whitely in the warm spring sun. Now he was actually here, Elizabeth's calm deserted her. She felt the adrenalin surging through her as she watched Monica glide out and offer her husband that reserved, passionless kiss. But she knew she was ready; it couldn't be postponed.

Elizabeth picked up her folded set of clippings and looked at her reflection. She'd chosen an outfit Tony would hate: black jeans, ankle boots and a tight green T-shirt by Donna Karan. It was aggressive and sexy. That had always bothered him; now she knew why.

She limped downstairs and walked stiffly across to where Tony stood, ignoring the ecstatic welcome of the dogs.

'Elizabeth, darling,' he said, his brow creasing at her new look. 'It's a bit too dramatic, wouldn't you say?'

'Not really. Look, why don't you step into the library, and we can have a little talk.'

He looked her up and down with that cold assessment that had been so hurtful before, but now just slid off her.

'As you wish.' Tony walked across the uneven flagstones to the library door, pushed the studded wooden door and held it open.

Tony sat at his desk and glanced at her. He looked utterly self-possessed. Elizabeth shut the door firmly behind her and sat down herself. At least she would have the element of surprise.

'You've always hated me, Tony. And now I know why.'

His Christian name. His eyebrows arched.

'Don't look so surprised.' Elizabeth smoothed out her list of cuttings and passed them over, seeing Tony's shock at the old articles. 'I never knew Mother, but I wish I had. She had you over six ways till Sunday.'

'Nobody had me over.'

'I look so like her, don't I? Nothing of you at all, Lord Caerhaven. Or of Jay DeFries, for that matter. But my, how awkward it would have been.' Her voice was thick with sarcasm. 'Whispers at the Athenaeum. Jokes in *Private Eye*. Tabloid fun at your expense. Of course, it simply wouldn't do, I see that. You had to take in the little cuckoo.'

'Well.' He did a creditable job of hiding the rage. 'You've become a PI, how inventive. You always were a little tramp, just like Louise—'

'A tramp? Because she wouldn't play dumb in the gilded cage? I can see just why she'd prefer Jay, even without money, or a title.'

'You cheap little bastard,' Tony said, with real viciousness.

'Well, that's the difference between us. I *know* you're a bastard. You don't know if I am.'

'You're no child of mine, Elizabeth. I have sons.'

'Lucky you, since we all know just what you think of females. Having been trampled by one of them.'

'She was a ball-breaking whore,' Tony snarled.

'I've always thought,' Elizabeth said slowly, 'that a man who could have his balls broken by a woman wasn't much of a man in the first place.'

'A pity Mr Taylor doesn't agree with you,' Tony said.

It was a direct hit. Elizabeth flushed. The earl pushed back into his chair and steepled his fingers.

'What do you want, Elizabeth?'

Elizabeth smiled. 'You'll like this one, Tony. I want out. I want enough money to look after myself. In exchange, I will always be Lady Elizabeth. A million pounds, that should do it. You wouldn't even notice it.'

He shook his head. 'No guarantee.'

'You have my word.'

'Worthless. I might agree to a trust fund. A million, paid at intervals over the next five years, conditional on your silence. You sign a contract; if you ever breathe a word, the money is repayable with interest.'

'Fine with me, old man, but I want something now. My cases are all packed; I don't want to spend another night under this roof.'

Tony stood up and drummed his fingers on top of the grand piano.

'Fifty K and Walgrave Road.' That was a beautiful mews house Dragon used for corporate hospitality. Elizabeth had stayed there once; it was a little jewel of a house tucked away in a tree-lined street in Earl's Court. 'There's a housekeeper who will let you in, the lawyers will bring papers round tomorrow. That's the first year. It's worth two hundred grand easy.'

'Fine,' Elizabeth said. 'Go out and tell your chauffeur he has a passenger for town.'

Tony nodded. 'So, darling, I suppose this is goodbye.'

'I suppose it is, Father,' Elizabeth replied.

'You'll keep that promise or lose everything.' He smiled thinly. 'You'll find out, Elizabeth—once you're outside, you stay there. I have a lot of enemies, and they all know the score. They hate me, but they don't mess with me. There's not a soul in London who's prepared to risk that.'

Elizabeth left the room without replying. At that moment, she wanted revenge more than anything in the world. And Tony's last bit of pomposity had put a name glowing into her mind.

The woman she'd disliked but respected. A blinkered workaholic with a razor-sharp brain. Someone who had been close to Tony. Someone who might know a way to bring him down. Nina Roth.

chapter eleven

HARRY NAMATH slowly pulled off his lab coat and looked over at Lilly. 'What?'

'I said she'd left the company.' Lilly tried to sound casual, but it didn't come off.

Harry frowned. It was dark outside, three in the morning. They'd just come off a gruelling session of proto-lipid tests. But the tiredness melted away when she dropped this little bombshell. He stared at Lilly.

'Don't overreact. She got us the deal, she's gone, so what? These corporate bods will get another suit to replace her.'

'She's a friend of mine, Lil. Why didn't you tell me?'

'I didn't think she was such a mate of yours.' This was so obviously a lie that Harry didn't bother replying. 'OK, fine, but you hadn't been speaking.'

'We were in France working.' Harry's voice was cold.

'I reckoned it was all over.'

'What would you know about that?' Harry's voice was cold.

Lilly sat up and glared at him. 'The earl talked to me too, all right? He told me the score. Little tramp. She was bad for you. I told the earl that too. He said he was going to can her, and I said good on him.'

'Lilly, you have no right to interfere in my private life.'

'Oh, don't I?' the dumpy woman said bitterly. 'When I'm the one who's been your partner for years! I'm the biochemist, Harry, they don't want computers. I could just have taken this whole thing for myself. But I carried you along with me and what happens, you run off with some floozy brunette, some career prostitute who slept her way—'

'That's enough!' Harry shouted, then calmed himself. 'Lilly, we hardly even socialise.'

'We're together enough,' she muttered.

Harry shook his head again. Lilly. Somehow she had managed to delude herself that their working together was a relationship. She'd never said a word. Maybe she didn't want to spoil the dream. He had shattered her illusion and now she was screaming about betrayal.

It was worse because it struck a chord. Lord Caerhaven had reached into his heart and squeezed a burning fist round it. The words in the laconic English tone were almost more than he could bear; ugly pictures of Nina, screwing Tony, on her back for a promotion. Harry was already halfway in love with Nina. Making love to her had been incredible. That memory had been tainted, corrupted with acid.

He had tried to shove Nina from his mind. But he couldn't forget her. He thought about it every day. How could she? Was she really that cheap?

Harry decided to get an answer. He wanted to confront Nina. To say all the things that were burning up in his chest. And now it looked like he wouldn't have the chance.

'Sorry, Lil,' he said, 'I quit.'

'Don't be a jerk.'

'Whatever you think we have, we don't. I'm sorry. And I don't like being played for a schmuck. Or manipulated.'

'If you go,' Lilly said meanly, 'you're breaking contract with me. Your work on our research becomes my copyright, and you'll lose all your royalties. Do you get that? You'll lose everything.'

'I'll lose this project.' Harry shrugged and reached for his overcoat.

'You're bluffing! What the hell will you do?'

He turned to the door and gave her a quick, dazzling smile. 'What I always do, Professor. Land on my feet.'

Elizabeth took the keys from the housekeeper on Tuesday night and signed the papers on Wednesday morning. Tony's lawyers came by at 9.00am on the dot. That was no surprise. He was as eager to be shot of her as she was to go.

She had got Walgrave Road lock, stock and barrel, so she spent a morning checking it out. There was everything she could wish for, from a power shower to a study that came complete with IBM computer, printer and fax machine.

She arranged to have all the bills transferred to her name and called Coutts & Co, where a smug functionary confirmed the deposit of £50,000. Then she went to the Lloyds round the corner and picked up an account transfer form. Stuffy pomp and circumstance were behind her now.

'We'll handle that for you, miss,' said the teller. 'Name?'

'Lady Elizabeth Savage,' Elizabeth said, and smiled briefly as he gave her a quick, embarrassed stare.

'Yes, my lady, right away.'

She wondered idly if that was really her name. In the end it didn't matter: Savage or not, she was out on her own.

Nina flicked through the pages of *American Scientist* and tried to pay attention, but it was no good. Yesterday she'd had her first break. Peter Meyer, president of a small bottling plant, had returned her call. She'd had dealings with him at Dragon. Meyer had been impressed then and invited her into head office. His firm was in trouble: one of their biggest clients, Tropex, was about to cancel a long-standing order, switching bottling function to another firm. Maybe, he said without optimism, she could come up with something.

Nina hadn't needed asking twice. She had extensive notes on both Meyer and the client company when she'd showed up this morning, wearing her most businesslike charcoal suit to go over the options. She had gone back to the office on a cloud of hope. It had lasted all of two hours. That was when Peter's secretary called her to say the board was minded to turn down the proposal.

'We'll give you a final answer by the end of the day, but I can't see them changing their minds.'

'I see.' Nina struggled to control her disappointment. 'Thanks for letting me know.'

Now she sat here facing the facts. The Meyer call was the first bite she'd got in weeks, and now the fish had almost wriggled off the hook. She'd offered him a no-win, no-fee deal and he still wasn't interested. If Peter Meyer didn't think she was worth the effort, even at zero cost, Nina stood no chance. She was going to have to give up. Pack in the office and take some menial job, entry-level like the ones she'd been offered before. Or maybe she should go back to America . . .

There was a knock on the door. Nina stopped dead. Somebody had got the wrong address.

'Hold on,' Nina called. She walked over to the door and opened it.

Elizabeth Savage was standing there. She had lost the golden tan and about a stone and looked more tired than when Nina had last seen her. She was still beautiful, skinny and tall, however. The startling blondness of her hair framed the sharp cheekbones like a glossy halo. She was wearing tailored slacks, a close-fitting military jacket and a pair of heeled boots. Nina couldn't help but notice the boots, glancing down involuntarily.

'Come in,' she said neutrally. Should she offer her sympathies? No way, that would sound as false as it would feel.

Elizabeth walked into Nina's office and looked round.

'It's not the Stock Exchange,' Nina said defensively.

'It must rent cheap.'

'Did you come here to gloat, my lady? If so, you can just leave now. Or is it a message from Tony?' Nina's brown eyes glittered with distaste. 'Because the answer is no, no and no. Whatever it is.'

'Neither one. Can I sit down?' Elizabeth asked, gesturing to a chair.

Nina's eyebrows arched. She looked hard at the other girl. 'I'm busy, but you can have ten minutes.'

'Sure, you look busy,' Elizabeth wanted to say, but bit it back.

'Nina.' She sat down and brushed the hair out of her eyes. 'I don't like you, you don't like me. Fine, that's a given. But maybe we could help each other out. On a purely business basis. A pact of convenience.'

'Go on,' Nina said.

'I have fallen out with my father. It's been brewing for a while but now it's final. I've left Dragon—I was kicked out, or as good as. I've moved out of the family home. He expects me to live off the pocket money I've got in exchange for that, but I have other ideas. I want to make money myself and I want revenge.'

Nina laughed. 'You expect me to buy that? Why would he do that to you? You're family!'

'He hates me,' Elizabeth said intently. 'Come on, Nina, you knew him, you slept with him. He disliked me intensely. You must have been aware of it.'

'Yes, I was.'

'Then you should believe me. He destroyed my life. I had no real education. I wanted to go to university—you have no idea how much—and I wanted to work, but he wouldn't let me do either. That way he could control my destiny, can you understand that? No degree, no experience,

I was qualified for nothing. Except winning races. Dragon Gold was *mine*. I made something of it, but Tony incurred millions in losses when he took it off the market—just to spite me.'

'It was pretty gutsy, faking Tony's authority like that. He was so mad when he found out he dropped everything to fly home.'

'I'll bet,' Elizabeth said softly. 'You can imagine what that was like. He did the same thing to you, and you were his girlfriend.'

'Correction. I slept with him. When I no longer wanted that to continue . . .' Nina shrugged.

'Then help me.'

'Look, Elizabeth, I don't know what you think I can do. If I could have hurt him, I wouldn't have waited for your permission.'

'OK.' Elizabeth's green eyes narrowed. 'I'm not the president of your fan club, but I have money and I can sell this firm. You *know* I can, because you've seen me work. We could make something together.'

Nina sighed 'It sounds good, on paper, but I can't take your money. There is no business. I got the first break I've ever had yesterday' She explained about Peter Meyer. 'That phone's going to ring any second to turn me down, and it'll be the first and last bit of business I ever do.'

Elizabeth leaned forward urgently. 'Let me call them,' she said. 'I've got an idea. If you're going to fold anyway, what could it hurt?'

'Come in,' Peter Meyer said expansively, ushering them both into his office. He smiled briskly at Nina and shook hands with Elizabeth. 'Nina, you never said Lady Elizabeth was on board with you.'

Nina nodded quietly. He had agreed to another meeting right away, because he was terrified of Tony Savage.

That little deception got Elizabeth through the door, but she'd need something more to get them any further.

'This won't take long, Mr Meyer,' Elizabeth said. Her voice was rather cold. 'I called as soon as Nina told me you were in negotiations. It's just a good-faith visit, really.'

'Good faith?' Meyer repeated.

'Yes. Lolland Jars have also replied to our pitch.'

Nina stiffened. Meyer sat upright and frowned. Lolland Jars were his biggest rival. He feared they were going to have their shot at the Tropex contract.

'They want to get their firm in shape for the future.' Elizabeth's smile was apologetic. 'So, if you could just sign the formal "no" from your board we'll be legally clear to start dealings with Rob Lolland.'

'Wait a second!' Meyer said anxiously. He hated Rob. What had he missed here that Rob had seen? 'You can't work for Lolland if you're in negotiations with me!'

'I'm sorry.' Elizabeth leaned back, an expression of confusion on her patrician face. 'I thought you were turning us down.'

'No, we were just trying to rejig the budget,' Meyer said hastily.

'I'm afraid we do need a fast decision. Mr Lolland needs an answer, one way or the other.'

Meyer glanced at Nina's briefcase. 'Do you still have that contract you brought round before?'

'Of course.' Nina unclipped her case and handed it across to him.

Elizabeth added, 'If you do want to hire us, we need expenses payments in advance. Two thousand for the first month.'

Meyer nodded and scrawled his signature at the bottom of the page. 'I'll transfer the funds across at once. I'm afraid you'll have to disappoint Mr Lolland. Meyer Bottling got there first.'

Nina and Elizabeth exchanged a quick glance. Nina took the signed contract, and they shook hands.

'Good to have you with us. I'm sure with such a capable deputy you'll make very rapid progress,' Meyer told Nina with relief.

'Thank you.' Nina smiled back. 'But Elizabeth is my partner.'

In the cab back to Soho, Nina looked at Elizabeth with amazement. 'Lolland replied to our pitch? They turned me down flat!'

'So?' Elizabeth grinned. 'That's a reply!'

Nina streamlined Meyer's operations and cut costs, while Elizabeth provided them with a marketing prospectus for fresh clients. Meyer retained the account they were about to lose, and entered into discussions with three more companies. Nina sent Peter Meyer pitching segments of the market he'd never even considered. He paid Roth Consulting, with a bonus. And he spread the word.

A month later, they had more work than they could handle.

Elizabeth and Nina found it hard going. They hired a secretary, a mature woman returning to work. Helen Potts kept them civil to each other: they couldn't snipe in front of her, although they were respectful of each other's talents. Elizabeth's effortless confidence and polished manners worked beautifully with clients, but they still got under Nina's skin, and Elizabeth hated the draconian way Nina ran the place, in at 8am out at 8pm. Plus, there was mountains of work, with little reward. All the money they saw went as fast as it came: hiring new equipment, moving offices to Hammersmith, paying lawyers and accountants as they set themselves up. Nor were their own fees large. They were

undercutting the big boys, and all their clients were baby firms.
It was a makeshift alliance, but bills got paid. Jobs got done.
They were in business.

'**M**rs Potts, could you hold the fort for half an hour?'
It was a cold June morning, rain pouring down on Hammersmith
Broadway. Nina could see it splashing on the red roofs of the buses that
crawled past their windows.
'Certainly, Miss Roth.'
Elizabeth glanced up from the transparencies she was viewing.
'Something up?'
'Let's go into your office a second,' Nina said. Elizabeth followed her
into the room and settled into a chair.
Nina seemed edgy and tense. 'I think we're in the wrong business.'
'Oh! Well, that's reassuring,' Elizabeth said irritably. 'Nina, we have
six jobs in hand and three more waiting.'
'Yes, but what are we getting out of them? We're not making enough
money. We're keeping ourselves afloat that's all, and since we can only
handle so much consulting work, that's not going to change. We've been
so busy we haven't looked at the big picture.'
'You're right, but I think we're working as hard as we can.'
'It's not about working harder. It's about working smarter. We need to
advise bigger firms, then we can command *real* fees. Sterling Health
don't need us to teach them how to suck eggs, but there's a lot of
wastage in their systems. What they need is computer help. I can pinpoint market improvements—did it for Dragon *and* Dolan.'
'Yeah, but you can't write a major computer program.'
'I know somebody. I think he'd go for it, but I'd have to offer him a
partnership. Do you agree?'
'Providing our decisions have to be made unanimously,' Elizabeth
said coolly. 'I'm not going to be outvoted by you and a friend.'
'Understood. Though I'm sorry to say he and I aren't exactly friends,'
Nina admitted.
Elizabeth gave her a small smile. 'Hasn't hurt *us* so far.'

Nina used Elizabeth to track Harry down. She knew the numbers for
Lilly's lab like the back of her hand.
'I'm sorry, Lady Elizabeth, I can't help you.' Dr Hall's Australian
accent was thick and rather sour. 'Harry Namath walked out of this firm
a few months ago. Don't tell me Dragon has more business with him.'
'Absolutely not.' Elizabeth played a hunch. 'Actually, he owes me

money. I loaned him twenty grand when he moved to England.'

'Well, that's different. Twenty grand?' Lilly laughed meanly. 'I have an address here somewhere and a phone number . . .'

Nina caught the tube to Charing Cross and picked up a cab at the station rank. She wanted to turn up looking successful. She had told herself she had to be strong and businesslike. It would do no good pleading with him to give her a second chance. Tony had told him the truth and he had been disgusted; that's why he hadn't called when she was fired.

I was right the first time, Nina thought. I should never have let another man into my heart.

For this meeting she had dressed with incredible care: a dark green Jil Sander pantsuit, crisp and attractive, with Stephane Kélian pumps and camel leather gloves. Simple gold studs in the ears, soft make-up. Nina wasn't going to hide from him. She refused to apologise for being attractive. Dr Namath could take her or leave her.

The taxi pulled up outside his house. It was a quiet street near the Oval, a pretty mews house with a cherry tree in the front garden. She could see a light burning in the upstairs window. He was there.

She paid the driver and walked nervously up the steps.

Nina rang the bell three times, pressing really hard. She heard him racing down the stairs. The door wrenched open.

'All right, all right, what's the—'

Harry jumped out of his skin. He was so surprised he didn't say a word. It suddenly occurred to her he might just slam the door in her face.

'I do have a telephone,' he said slowly.

'I thought you might just hang up on me. I've got a proposal for you, Harry,' Nina said.

'Well.' Namath scratched his head and gave her a strange look. He was wearing shorts and a T-shirt, which was plastered to his lean torso. His chin was peppered with two days' stubble. His face was glowing; he'd clearly been working out. She felt the sudden pulse of lust all through her body.

'You're making quite a habit of it.' He lifted his T-shirt. 'I'm as unprepared as the first time. Come in and wait while I have a shower.'

Nina went dry-mouthed. She said, 'Fine, thanks.'

Namath stood back to let her in. 'Kitchen's right through there. Coffee's freshly made,' Namath said as he bounded back up the stairs.

Nina went into the kitchen. She took her time with the coffee, noisily opening cupboards and choosing a mug. Trying not to think of him, standing there, with the water sluicing him down, pushing the soap across his armpits, and his back . . .

'So.' Harry's voice jerked her out of it. He was wrapped in a navy bathrobe and rubbing his hair with a towel. 'What's the story?'

'You broke the partnership with Lilly. Why did you do that?'

Harry poured himself a mug of coffee and took a sip. 'That's really none of your business. I guess you must have got this address out of Lilly. Don't ask her any more questions about me, Nina.'

She flushed. 'You're right. I apologise. I just needed to see you. I want to suggest something to you.'

'Oh?' Harry watched her neutrally. 'Business or pleasure?'

If I said pleasure, would he kick me out? Nina wondered miserably. Then she squared her shoulders and looked him right in the face.

'Strictly business. And believe me, Harry, this is perfect for you.'

'There is a train strike. Please make alternative transport arrangements. Contact your local tourist information office.'

Jack grinned at the announcements crackling out of the underground tannoy at Heathrow. Welcome back to Britain. He bought a paper, jumped in a cab and gave the guy directions to the Regency Hotel.

He wondered how Elizabeth was doing. When he'd called Dragon they had no information. Lady Elizabeth had left, under no circumstances could they release her address. Perplexed, Jack rang the castle. Monica Caerhaven had been vague; she muttered something about Earl's Court and put the phone down. Something was definitely up.

The British Ski Federation gave him her address with no trouble. Ronnie Davis, reduced to coaching third-raters like Karen and Kate, almost fell over himself in his eagerness to help. 'She's running some computer firm. Consultants . . . I got a number here.'

In his room Jack unpacked, dropped to the floor and did fifty stomach crunches to shake off the lazy feeling he'd got from the flight. Then he dialled the number that Ronnie had given him. The company was out in Hammersmith, west London. It was called Tall Poppies.

'Just a second, Mr Taylor,' Mrs Potts said brightly. She waved at Elizabeth, crossing to her office with an armful of ad layouts. 'Personal call for you on line two. It's a Mr Jack Taylor.'

Elizabeth froze. Then she said, 'Yeah, right, put it through.'

She put the layouts down and shut her door behind her. The red light on line two was blinking silently at her. She felt herself break out in a sweat, a light dew of fear. She picked up the phone.

'Jack! This is a surprise.'

'God, girl, are you ever hard to track down.'

'You could have tracked me down in the clinic,' Elizabeth said angrily, then kicked herself. Great, where did that come from?

There was a pause. Then he said, 'I've got to see you.'

'I'm really busy, Jack,' Elizabeth said negatively. Talking to him was one thing; she didn't know if she could handle a visit.

'Elizabeth Savage, I flew in from Dallas just to see you. I fought like a bobcat with Pa to let me go. Now I'm here I am *going* to see you, if it means campin' outside your door on the sidewalk. Now do I come over there and punch out your security guards or are you going to be a lady about this?'

'Be a lady about it?' Elizabeth chuckled despite herself. 'Jack, you don't know how to take no for an answer, do you?'

'No, ma'am, guilty as charged.'

'Come to my house. Twenty-four Walgrave Road in Earl's Court. I'll be there in forty minutes, but I warn you, I can only give you a little time.'

Jack smiled to himself as he hung up. 'We'll see about that, sugar.'

He found the place without any trouble. It was a cute little house, tucked away in a tiny corner hidden in the heart of the city. It struck him that he'd never been to a place of Elizabeth's before. That suddenly seemed so wrong and wasteful. Jack shook his head, smiling confidently. No more. Now he was going to rewrite the book.

He bounded up the small stone steps and hit the bell.

'Hey,' Elizabeth said. 'Did it insult your mother, or something?'

'And good morning to you too, sweetheart,' Jack replied.

She looked different. Real different. The athletic frame was gone, slimmed off her. No problem, she was beautiful either way. The competitive fire had also disappeared, but Elizabeth still looked tough and focused. She was wearing a tailored pantsuit in dusty pink, and her hair was coloured a dazzling blonde, layered all round her face in a feathery cut. She blew all the simpering Dallas debs right out of the water.

'Come in,' Elizabeth said.

Jack stepped inside the house. It was sparsely but elegantly furnished, a few old oil paintings on the walls, rows of leather-bound books, the normal rich-limey clutter. 'Very nice. Your pa give you some spares?'

'I bought everything you see,' Elizabeth said flatly. 'Tony and I have split for good. The house was part of the settlement.'

Jack walked over to a far wall and examined a small pastoral. 'Looks Pre-Raphaelite. What is it, Burne-Jones?'

'Very good, I've started collecting.'

'Without the earl's help? Come on, Elizabeth, where would you get that kind of money?'

Jack settled himself in a leather armchair and took another look round the room, paying greater attention. Sure the decor was sparse, but everything here was top quality stuff.

'I can't believe you, Jack.' Elizabeth sat opposite him and allowed herself to sound annoyed. That was simple, so much easier than actually confronting what she was feeling right now, a sort of dizzy joy combined with sick apprehension. 'You come over here, you drag me out of work, and all you can ask is how I pay for my paintings?'

'So you think I should ask you about your leg?'

'Shouldn't you?' Elizabeth demanded. He was totally wrong-footing her. She'd expected belated tears and hand wringing, and here he was, joking and squabbling with her like nothing had happened.

'Honey, there's nothing to say. You know how sorry I am. Of all the people in the world I do know what it would mean not to ski again.'

Elizabeth looked away before she started to cry. That was perfectly true. Only Jack, and maybe Hans, could have any idea. She swallowed hard to push down the dry lump in her throat.

He jumped up and grabbed her hands. 'You know I tried to visit. Your father told me to get lost. I flew home and tried to forget all about you.'

'And you couldn't?'

'I'm here, ain't I?'

'But I've lost my foot,' Elizabeth muttered. 'I've got a plastic foot.'

'So what? It was never your foot I was interested in.'

Jack's hands had left hers and were cupping her face now, one finger delicately tracing the line of her jaw and her cheekbones. His touch on her skin was like an electric charge. Her stomach was melting into a liquid, shifting pool, she wanted him so badly.

'Jack . . . it won't work, it never does.'

'It won't work? Baby, you know we ain't ever tried it.'

'What about Sussex?'

'Not bad for a warm-up,' Jack said, reaching up to the ivory silk at her neck and undoing one of the buttons. Elizabeth knew this was her cue to push him off but she didn't.

'But that's not a relationship, Jack . . .'

'Yeah?' He breathed it, bending down to kiss her, just brushing her lips. 'That's just fine with me, sugar. I don't want a *relationship*. I want you. In case you're too blind and mulish to notice. This makes twice I've flown round the world for you, and I'm not doing it again.'

'Jack—'

'Jack, Jack.' He kissed her again, briefly and impatiently. 'Is that all you want to say? Objections? Reasons we both should be somewhere else, right now? If you don't want me, Elizabeth, you just say so. Look me right in the eyes and say go.'

He tipped her face up to his. His eyes locked on hers were probing, intense. Elizabeth didn't say a word.

Jack pulled her closer still. Close enough to feel him hard up against her groin. 'That's what I thought,' he said.

'I can't believe it,' Jack said.

'Believe it,' Elizabeth answered. She showed him round the crowded offices packed with people, sixteen programmers hunched over their workstations. Tall Poppies had taken over two floors of the Hammersmith offices. Downstairs was Elizabeth's own marketing division. 'Yesterday was the first day off I've had in four months. We're growing so fast I'm getting altitude sickness.'

Jack stared at her. Elizabeth did look frazzled, but she was happy too. 'We're stretched to the limit, but we're making a lot of money.'

'And it wasn't working before?'

'Oh, it was working, but in a small way. We fixed that when Harry came on board. He's a genius programmer. He creates the software, Nina applies it to the market, I spread the word.' She tugged at Jack's hand. 'Come over here, see the boardroom.'

Elizabeth showed him into a small, well-equipped conference room, with a mahogany table and four chairs. Then she shut the door behind her and kissed him triumphantly on the lips.

'I'm deadly serious, Jack. This time it's working. And we're in charge. If it keeps up this way, I'm going to be a multimillionaire before I'm thirty years old.'

'Is Elizabeth still busy?' Harry asked, slightly annoyed.

'Is this about your new project?'

'Yeah. I need to know if we can sell it.'

The boardroom door was still closed and Nina smiled. 'Elizabeth's got a lot of history with Jack Taylor. I think you should just let her alone.'

'It's going to mean working late tonight.'

'So what else is new? Success is tough,' Nina replied.

It was true. Harry had given them everything Tall Poppies needed. Nina's cold efficiency was offset by Elizabeth's English-rose persuasiveness, and with the addition of the American scientist they had something fresh to offer. Computerisation. Tall Poppies became IT consultants to the UK drugs business. They were in demand right away. Nina made her first really big score, an efficiency programme for a division of Procter & Gamble. After that it was open season.

Nina was straining to go like a Doberman on a leash. She'd waited for this all her life. When Harry complained he was being pushed too hard, they hired more programmers, unorthodox talents the hi-tech giants wouldn't touch. Soon Elizabeth needed marketing help too.

Harry and Nina fought all the time. Blazing arguments the staff could hear through Harry's office wall. Elizabeth acted as a bridge between them, and there was too much work and new business to have it get in the way. Nina knew it was mostly her fault, but she couldn't stop.

It was torture, having him physically close all the time. But Nina couldn't do without Harry. He was the engine for her revenge on Tony Savage, and for her and Elizabeth both, that was the absolute priority.

Elizabeth had told her what Tony said: 'You've got to cut down the tall poppies.' Every job they landed, every new bill that got paid, was a slap in that bastard's face. Tony refused to comment on all the good-natured questions about his daughter's success. When Nina imagined all the journalists bugging him, it gave her exquisite pleasure.

'Yeah, success is tough,' Harry said. 'Just like you.'

'Me?' Nina tried to smile. 'I'm just a marshmallow. Look, is it really urgent?'

'Damn straight, it's urgent.' Harry ran his hands distractedly through his hair. 'And I've got a Unilever meeting in forty minutes.'

'Then how about I go over it with you tonight?'

'OK. Your place or mine? Or does that sound too much like a date?'

'Your place is fine. And no, it doesn't sound like a date,' Nina said with a touch of bitterness. 'Don't worry, I know better than that.'

'Let's go back to the hotel,' Jack said, kissing her forehead and eyebrows. 'You're turning me on, sugar, I swear.'

Elizabeth's creamy skin blushed a deep rose. 'Cut it *out*! This isn't some kind of sex trip, Jack. This is my business.'

'I know that.' Jack stood upright, letting her wriggle out of his arms. 'And I'm totally impressed. But come on, baby. You know things are changed now. When we're in Texas you and me can—'

'Wait a second.' Elizabeth held up one hand. 'What did you say?'

Jack shook his head. 'You're right, I'm all messed up. Going too fast. But I've had years of practice at that.' He dropped to one knee and took her hand in his. 'Elizabeth, you know I love you. And you love me, unless you're one hell of an actress. Will you marry me?'

'Maybe,' Elizabeth said.

Jack scrambled to his feet, frowning like thunder. '*Maybe?* You know, I had this scene all figured out.' He fished in his pocket and drew out a blue velvet box. Inside was a huge solitaire diamond, emerald-cut on a ring of white gold. 'And I have to tell you, girl, *maybe* wasn't a part of it. Are we still playing games? Aren't we done with that?'

'Oh, yes.' Elizabeth blinked back tears. 'We're done with that. Which is why I say maybe. I do love you, Jack, and I want to marry you.'

'Then I don't see the problem.'

She waved at the busy offices behind them. 'That's the problem, Jack. Tall Poppies. It's my thing and I'm not selling up. Not now. We're on the threshold of something extraordinary . . . I've been waiting for this all my life, to be somebody in my own right. I can't give it up and go back to . . . to Southfork and play at being Sue Ellen.'

Jack sat down heavily. 'Sweetheart, I don't have a choice here. I'm an only child. I got hundreds of acres of prime Texas land, two hotels and a stable full of the best studs west of Arabia. I can't sell it.'

'You can do whatever you want.'

Jack scowled at her. 'Honey, get real! You're saying you want me to *live* over here, like a goddamn househusband?'

Elizabeth blinked the tears back again. 'Look, thank you for the offer, truly—'

'No!' Jack shouted. He caught her hand and pressed it onto his heart. 'You can't say no to me! We were meant to be together!'

Elizabeth looked at him. She loved him so much. But she knew that if she gave up Tall Poppies to be with him, she would wind up resenting him so bitterly that love would turn to hate.

'God,' she said, and one big tear trickled out onto her cheek before she could get a grip on herself. 'I thought so too.'

Nina left Elizabeth alone for the rest of the day. It was strange, seeing Jack Taylor in the flesh; so tanned and Texan, he was a Marlboro Man in the flesh. She couldn't imagine him ever dating a cool customer like Lady Elizabeth. He was real courteous when Elizabeth introduced them, but he seemed distracted.

'Nice to meet you,' she said. 'Elizabeth, can you come round to Harry's house this evening? We need to check out his new product.'

'Sure. Sure.' Elizabeth turned to go. 'I'm not going to be in this afternoon. Is that OK? I'm going to drive Jack to the airport.'

'Whatever you need,' Nina said.

It was still light when she got to Harry's, the gold and pink streaks of the summer evening silhouetted behind the pretty Georgian houses in his street. The tree outside his front door was in full green leaf. She stepped up and rang the doorbell wearily. How nice it would be, just once, to have an evening off. She hoped whatever Harry Namath had dragged her out for was worth it.

'Hey, come in.' Harry led her into the kitchen where he liked to work at night. He had a terminal set up in the far corner. He looked so relaxed and confident. Nina was frazzled from clients, and her neck hurt.

'You look tired.'

'You got it.' Nina rubbed the back of her neck. 'Can we get to it? I'd like to go over what you're proposing.'

'Something I've been working on,' Harry said. 'Proprietary software. I'm calling it Home Office.'

'Home Office?' Nina repeated. 'But we do consultancy—'

'And we still will, but this is going to take us to a whole new level. You won't just sell to big drugs firms, you'll sell to every small business-man in the country,' Harry said.

'OK.' Nina knew better than to laugh at Harry when he got that look on his face. 'Layman's terms, tell me what you've written.'

Over the next couple of hours he explained it to her. Home Office was a software program you could sell in the high street. It would cen-tralise word processing, spreadsheet and inventory functions in one program.

'What are we doing?' Namath asked enthusiastically. 'We're reorganis-ing all these giant firms to make them more efficient. Well, that's some-thing *everyone* needs. The florist. The guy with the corner store. Didn't you tell me once you'd run a deli?'

Nina glanced up to see if Harry was being sarcastic; but he was just asking a question.

'Sure, south side of Park Slope, Brooklyn.'

Harry winced. 'You ever have inventory problems there?'

'Every week,' Nina agreed.

'Well, if you'd had Home Office, it would have done your inventory in ten minutes max.'

Nina looked at her watch. Quarter to eleven. 'Elizabeth's not coming, but I know what she's going to say.'

'She's going to turn it down?'

'She's going to love it.' Nina shook her head. 'It's brilliant, Harry, it *is* going to lift us to the next level. A factory, sales force, the works. That means we'll need money, capital. And that means bank loans. If we try to raise the money by going public we'll get taken over, and we're not ready for that yet.'

'But if we go for a bank loan and it goes wrong, we've lost this company. My credibility. Everything.'

'That's right. So will it go wrong?'

'Not the code, sister,' Harry said with a grin.

'Then we'll do it,' Nina said.

Namath let out a whoop of joy. Then he came over and started to massage the back of her aching neck. He was strong, his fingers were pleasurable, she wanted to melt into it, let him take all her pains away.

Roughly Nina pushed him off. 'Cut it out, Harry,' she snapped.

'Right.' He lifted his hands and spun away from her. 'Business, I forgot. That's all life ever is with you. Don't you want anything else?'

Nina got up to leave. 'It's a great idea, Harry.'

'Don't dodge the goddamn question.'

She turned at the door. 'You know what? You're right, they're all right. There's nothing but business in my life. I really don't see the point, because every time I've tried something else, I've always got burned.'

'By who?' Harry sounded furious. 'Tony Savage, the great heartbreaker? Are you going to pine after him for the rest of your life? Because he burned you?'

'Get this straight,' Nina snarled. 'If there's any burning between me and Tony, *he's* the one that's getting fried.'

She slammed the door behind her.

chapter twelve

WHEN NINA WOKE UP, it was a bright, cold morning, the early light crisp with the promise of great heat later on. This morning felt significant somehow. And then she remembered. They were going to gamble.

A million things could go wrong. Maybe shopkeepers would as soon fly to the moon as buy a computer program. If Tall Poppies blew several millions of pounds of financing, they were history. This was the biggest stake she'd ever risked. For the first time in her life, she had something precious of her own to lose.

What the hell. Nina jumped out of bed and into the shower. Make a decision, then go with it. Win or lose. She grabbed a towel from the rail, went into the hall and phoned Elizabeth.

'Hey, kiddo, I'm coming round. I've got some great news.'

She reached Elizabeth's thirty minutes later.

'You look terrible,' Nina replied. It was true. Her partner wore a defiantly pretty amethyst DKNY dress, and her blonde hair was gleaming, but she'd obviously been crying all night.

'I feel terrible,' Elizabeth admitted, then burst into tears.

Nina put aside her finance projections and gave Elizabeth a hug.

'Jack and I are through.' Elizabeth explained what she could, in between sobs.

'But that's terrible. Did he fly back to Texas?'

'Just to Dublin.' Elizabeth was distraught, almost choking on her tears. 'He said he's got stud business there and in England . . . God, if he comes back to London I don't think I'll be able to bear it.'

'London's a big city, babe, and he likely won't be here for long.'

'I don't know if that makes it better or worse,' Elizabeth said, wiping her hand across her eyes.

'Look, we'll buy you out if that's what you want,' Nina said bravely, wondering where they would get the money. 'You should be happy.'

'But that's the problem. I can't be happy in a gold cage,' Elizabeth picked up Nina's notes. 'Come on, tell me what's going on.'

'Are you sure? It's . . . a pretty big deal. Do you want to look at it now?'

Elizabeth nodded. 'My head's still intact. It's my heart that's broken.'

Outside Tony Savage's windows, all was calm. The sun glittered on the sluggish Thames, lambswool clouds bobbed across a periwinkle-blue sky. Inside the office, things were not so calm.

'They're doing *what*?' Tony barked.

Frank Staunton recoiled from Tony's anger, the Terrier shrinking from its master's boot. 'Bank financing,' Staunton repeated. 'Maybe they suspect that going public would see them taken over.'

The earl got to his feet and started to pace round his office. He'd kept tabs on Nina Roth's little adventure through a discreet but expensive private investigator; looking for the moment it got off the ground, so he could crush it. When he heard Elizabeth had hooked up with her he could scarcely believe it; didn't the silly little bitches hate each other? Evidently not so much as they hated him. Tall Poppies! Elizabeth's arrogant slap in the face. And now they'd gone out and picked up that unshaven, unbusinesslike slob, Harry Namath.

Yesterday at lunch Bob Cohen had teased him unmercifully. 'And you let them go, Tony! Talent like that?' The financier clearly enjoyed the joke as he speared his salad.

'They're riding a craze,' Tony replied tightly.

'You think?' Bob shook his head. 'If this new venture is as hot as the money is saying, all bets are off. Your daughter's company could be as big as yours in a year, Tony. You must be bursting with pride.'

Tony pleaded sickness and called for the bill. All round the Square Mile they were whispering and laughing about him. He hadn't felt such powerful rage since Louise ran off with that prick DeFries.

He dragged his attention back to the present. 'It *would* see them taken over, Frank. By me.'

I expect they know that, Staunton thought but didn't say. 'Of course, if the product fails—'

'We must make sure it does.'

'I don't see how we can do that, sir. Dr Namath is a genius programmer, the Roth girl seems to know what she's doing and the banks are queuing up to lend them money.'

'There's a simple way to stop them,' Tony said. 'There's always a simple way. Get out, could you, Frank, I need to think.'

Staunton glided out of the room and shut the door behind him. Tony stared angrily at the latest share prices on his computer screen. Dragon shares were blinking down another eighth.

And two young women were laughing in his face.

All he had to do was see that their product failed miserably. He recalled the smug face of Bob Cohen. 'Home Office. A Filofax for the PC. Tall Poppies will be the first ones out there. Nobody can catch Namath, and he's immune to poaching.'

The earl caught his breath. It was so damn obvious, he was amazed he hadn't thought of it before. 'Bob, you're a bloody genius,' he said.

They divided up the tasks between them. Elizabeth toured the finance sources, raising the money. Nina went round the country, interviewing software manufacturers for the subcontracting, and talking to sales reps. By the time Elizabeth had moved on to packaging and promotion, everything was in place. They were all waiting on Harry.

'Look, when I said it was ready I meant the basic code,' Namath said. 'We're still two weeks away from customer tryouts, a month away from production.'

'Who's in charge?'

'I'm doing the user interface—graphics, sound, all the stuff that'll make it attractive to the buyers. Tim Paris is finishing up the platforms. John Cobb is checking the code, and Lee Reddy's troubleshooting.'

'We should be ready earlier,' Nina fretted.

'OK, Nina. You want to write the program yourself, be my guest. Otherwise, it's one month. You just got to wait,' Harry said.

'Take a holiday,' Elizabeth said. 'Oh, don't look at me that way, Nina, just a week. Recharge your batteries. Like an investment in your energy.'

Harry grinned. 'She's right, Nina. She's going ahead with the marketing and I'm writing. What I need is for you to get out of my hair.'

Reluctantly, Nina agreed to a holiday.

It was a mistake. She tried turning up to work on the Wednesday, but Elizabeth pushed her back out of the doors again.

'But I'm going stir crazy,' Nina pleaded. 'I want to do something to help the company.'

'You really want to do something? Then go and see Harry,' Elizabeth told her 'Seriously. I mean it. Tall Poppies is going to take off like a rocket, but the rocket will explode unless you guys sort yourselves out. If you and me can wind up friends, so can you and Harry. Whatever the problem is, you need to talk it through.'

'OK.' Nina nodded. 'OK, I'll go round right now. Maybe we can work something out.' She pressed Elizabeth's hand. 'How are you? With Jack? Is he still around?'

Elizabeth's beautiful face took on a tight look. Her smile no longer reached her eyes. 'Yes, but he's going home next week, so I'll be able to forget all about him.'

Nina smiled back and turned to hail a taxi. She knew neither of them believed that, but there was no point in saying so.

'**H**ey, what a pleasant surprise,' Harry said wearily as he opened the door. He was wearing jeans and a faded blue shirt and he looked great, despite the red eyes from being shackled to a computer screen for days on end. 'What have I done now?'

'Nothing. Absolutely nothing,' Nina said, squeezing past him. 'It's OK, Harry, I've come to apologise.'

He looked at her suspiciously. 'Either this is a plot of Elizabeth's or I'm having caffeine hallucinations.'

'Right first time.' Nina went into the kitchen. Elizabeth was right, this was a conversation she had to have. She was scared.

'No way.' Harry followed her into the kitchen. 'You have some agenda, Roth, you're permanently on my case.'

'I came over to talk about that. To . . . apologise,' Nina repeated. Her mouth was drying up, this was a bad idea. God, he shouldn't be able to do this to her. Not still. 'We're partners, we shouldn't be at each other's throats like hyenas. I think you're doing a great job.'

'You think I'm doing a great job.' Harry looked at her searchingly. 'Jesus. Do you have any idea how clinical that sounds?'

Nina shrugged. 'What do you want me to say?'

'I want you to tell me the truth. You came over to clear the air, right?' Harry said mercilessly. 'So clear it.'

This was it. She couldn't stave off the confrontation a moment longer. It was so hard, though, with Harry standing there, looking so handsome, his gorgeous eyes with the thick black lashes staring at her so challengingly. He would never understand why she'd done what she'd done . . .

'OK.' Nina took a deep breath. 'I thought it was easier to be aggressive than let you look down on me. I know what Tony Savage said to you, and—it was all true.'

Harry nodded. 'I know that.'

'Then you must despise me,' Nina said, and to her horror she heard her voice break and felt her eyes film over.

'No. It's true. I wanted an explanation, but you made it very clear I had no right to one. You broke up with him, and I couldn't compete with some ghost. I hoped I might win you over, once we were colleagues again, but that hasn't exactly worked out.' He shrugged.

'You couldn't compete? I *hate* Tony Savage.'

'So you must have loved him once, right?'

'Wrong! Are you insane?' Nina said. 'I hate him because he told you, he took you away from me!'

There was a moment's dumbstruck silence. Harry just stared at her. Then he reached forward and grabbed her two hands in his.

'But you were having a relationship . . .'

Nina tugged her hands away. 'No. I slept with him. I was new and hungry, and everyone assumed I was sleeping with him anyway, so I thought, what the hell? He can be of some use to me.'

'So why did you break up with him?'

'Because it made me feel . . . bad. I realised I was talented, I had promotion due me anyway.'

'And he didn't like it when you walked.'

'First he threatened me. Then he told you. Then he offered me rewards. And then he fired me.'

Harry Namath looked like a man processing a lot of information, Nina thought bitterly. 'But you did find him attractive?' he asked.

'Yes, at first I did, but I never loved him.'

'And I made you feel there could be something more to it.'

'Yeah, well. That was obviously another mistake. Look, Harry. That's the way it was. I'm not apologising for it. You can judge me when you've walked in my shoes, and not before—'

'Jesus!' Namath said. He moved closer to her, lifted one hand and clamped it over her mouth. 'You know your trouble, honey, you never listen. I don't judge you. You don't love him?'

He lifted his hand. Nina muttered, 'No.'

'Then that's all I give a damn about,' Harry said, and he pushed her back against the cooker and kissed her.

Nina moved her stuff into Harry's, and every moment he wasn't working on Home Office, they went upstairs and made love. She got that same thawing feeling she'd had in Switzerland, only this time there was no fear, no ghosts lurking in the darkness of her past. Harry filled in something missing from her life she didn't know was gone. In his arms she felt safe and relaxed.

On the Saturday Elizabeth came round for a council of war and found them curled on the couch in their dressing gowns.

'Hey, don't mind me.' She held up a hand to block Nina's protests. 'It was always going to be when, not if. When's the wedding?'

'Whenever we have time,' Harry said, grinning.

Elizabeth looked horrified. 'You're going to wait that long?'

'So what's the news?' Nina asked.

'Thunderbirds are go, kids. The loans went through this morning. Our asses are in hock to the banks to the tune of four million quid.'

'I'm on schedule,' Harry said, 'if John Cobb and Tim Paris are ready.'

'Well, if not, they haven't said anything to me.' Elizabeth got up to leave. 'I hate to spoil the mood, guys, but maybe Nina should come into the office again. We need to be totally ready, and we can't afford to have Harry distracted.'

Elizabeth tried to analyse her feelings as she turned into Earl's Court Road. She hadn't felt so upset in a long time. She was happy for Nina and Harry, wasn't she? They were two of her dearest friends now, and the atmosphere at work would be smooth as silk. But she didn't feel happy, she felt wretchedly miserable. It was too saintly to try to rejoice for other people when your own heart felt shattered.

She parked the car and stepped out onto the sunny pavement. And stopped dead.

Jack Taylor was sitting on her steps.

Elizabeth's eyes lit up like floodlights. 'Jack!' She rushed over and hugged him. 'What are you doing here? I'm so glad to see you!'

He's changed his mind! He wants us to get married!

'You won't be, when you know why I've come,' Jack said.

Elizabeth pulled back and looked at him. 'What's wrong?'

'You're in big trouble, sugar,' Jack replied gravely. 'I'm real sorry.'

Elizabeth unlocked her door and took him inside. Jack told her everything he'd heard, and Elizabeth sat down, shakily.

'Are you OK?' He looked anxious. 'Let me get you a drink?'

'No. Thank you,' Elizabeth said, distractedly. 'I need to call Nina, and my lawyers. Look—thanks for letting me know.'

'Hey.' Jack pushed the phone towards her. 'You call who you want, but I'm not leaving. Right now, you need a friend.'

'They're going to do *what*?' Nina gasped.

'Put out a program of their own. "Executive Package." TV advertising starts tomorrow, a huge spend, commercials during the news and *Coronation Street*. Billboards in the City and the West End.'

'But that would cost millions!' Elizabeth said. 'It would swallow up initial profits—'

'He's got millions, and it don't look like he cares about profits,' Jack said. 'He just wants to be first. They've seen the response to your proposals, you see? They know people are waiting for this.'

'You mean to tell me we've just prepared the ground for Dragon?' Nina spat.

'Looks that way. I'm truly sorry.'

Elizabeth pushed her hands through her hair. 'If he takes the first wave of customers—'

'It could become industry standard,' Nina said dully. 'Nobody will buy a competing product from a baby firm.'

'But I don't *get* it,' Elizabeth said. 'Harry was way in advance of the pack on this. How could anybody have overtaken Harry's team?'

The two women looked at each other.

'Oh my God,' Nina said. 'I can't believe it. That slimy prick. He's poached one of our team. It's the only answer.'

'We need to call Harry. He's in the office, working on some last-minute stuff.' Nina punched in the number and Harry picked up right away. They talked quietly for a few minutes.

Jack looked at Elizabeth. 'If you want to hire lawyers, you can use my money, but I guess you wouldn't take it.'

'You guess right,' Elizabeth replied, 'but thanks, Jack. You've been a good friend.'

He nodded. 'I wanted to be a lot more than that.'

'Maybe you still will.' Elizabeth was on the brink of tears now. 'If my company isn't—if I turn into the most famous bankrupt in Britain . . .'

Jack lifted her hand to his mouth and kissed it softly. 'I hope you can believe I don't want you that way.'

Nina hung up and turned round, shattering the moment. Her eyes were bright. 'Harry doesn't think we should do anything. Just carry on as before. No statements to the press. No panic.'

'Pretend it's not happening?'

'John Cobb's gone,' Nina said. 'Left a message on Harry's answering machine. Tony hired him for over a million a year.'

'What?' Elizabeth's mouth dropped open. 'A million quid? We were paying him twenty-three grand! That's a hell of a pay rise! What does he have that's worth a million?'

'Experience.' Nina looked grim. 'He was in charge of checking Harry's code. He had total access to Home Office.'

'And Harry thinks we should carry on regardless?'

'If that's Harry's advice, we have to trust him.'

'You're right there,' Elizabeth said furiously. 'There's nothing else we can do.'

It was agony to watch. The mighty Dragon sales machine swung into action with devastating effect. TV screens were bombarded with ads. The computer press ran profiles of both systems and concluded there was nothing to pick between them. Except Dragon's was out first.

The press Elizabeth had courted were now hounding her wherever she went. The hacks who'd loved them last week were now full of scorn. Their bankers were on the phone every day, demanding clarification. When Tall Poppies' own campaigns, modest and well targeted, started to run, people poured scorn upon them. Scenting blood, the tabloids even got in on the act. The idea of a deadly rivalry between Tony Savage and his estranged daughter was just too delicious to resist.

Sales of Dragon's package, as predicted, went through the roof. Initial stocks soon sold out. More copies were rush-produced. Linguists produced interfaces in French, Spanish and German. For two weeks, Executive Package was the computer craze of the moment.

Tall Poppies launched Home Office on schedule, but they were way behind. Lukewarm reviews said there was nothing wrong with the product, but so what? With its no-nonsense packaging, no sales discounts and lack of publicity, Home Office was a moth to Tony Savage's glittering butterfly. Their loans were due in two months. It looked like the game was up.

Exactly twenty-one days after the launch, Dragon took a call. A sweetshop in Birmingham complained of a bug. Instead of printing out its normal spreadsheets, Executive Package was typing a nursery rhyme. Over and over. Nothing they could do would stop it.

Tony called the customer personally. He thought it was a masterly piece of PR.

'Must be a faulty copy. What's the message exactly?'

The man sounded embarrassed. 'It goes, "I'm the king of the castle, and you're the dirty rascal," uh, my lord.'

'What?' Tony coloured. 'Never mind. Just a glitch. We'll replace it right away.'

That same day, the Customer Services department received ten more calls. The next day, twenty. By the end of the week, they were flooded.

'Jesus Christ!' Tony said, raging at John Cobb. 'Fix this! Don't you understand, we have half a warehouse full of returned copies?'

Cobb looked helplessly at Frank Staunton. 'I can't fix it. It's programmed into the code. It, uh, appears to be a time-activated thing.'

'It prints the message three weeks after EP is turned on, sir,' Frank Staunton said smoothly.

Tony looked at his underling with loathing. The little jerk was enjoying this!

'If it's in the *code*, write new code! Change it!'

Cobb ran his hands through greasy hair. He looked like a man who hadn't slept. 'But I can't do that, my lord. It was Harry Namath's code.'

'Get out,' Tony snarled.

Cobb scuttled out. Tony sat down heavily in his carved chair and stared at Staunton. 'I can't believe it.' The clipped tones were tight with humiliation and fury. 'It's a trap. The little bitches have trapped me.'

'We'll have to recall the entire line,' Staunton said blandly. 'I'm afraid the television stations are starting to pick up on it.' He tossed Tony a copy of that night's *Evening Standard*. Twin shots on the front page showed Tony and a computer screen, blurting out the EP message. The headline was: DIRTY RASCAL TO LOSE HIS CASTLE.

'To do what?' Tony snorted. 'What are they talking about, Staunton?'

'I think it's a comment from Marcus Fitzallen, sir,' the Terrier said with undisguised pleasure, 'speaking as Chairman of the Board of Dragon. He says they want a word.'

'But he survived,' Nina said.

Elizabeth shrugged. The 'rascal' fiasco had cost Tony Savage a profits warning and a public reprimand. 'Of course he survived. Men like that always do. My father spent a lifetime covering his back.'

They were in the office, sipping champagne and leafing through the papers at a celebratory Tall Poppies brunch. When Tall Poppies went public, the issue was an immediate success. After the bank loans had been repaid, all three of them were millionaires, a few times over.

'What made you suspect John Cobb?' Jack asked Harry.

He grinned. 'I didn't. I just didn't trust anybody. I booby-trap every program I write against hackers.'

'Come on, sweetheart.' Nina beckoned Harry. 'Let's go home.'

'OK.' He briefly touched her cheek. 'I'll wait for you in the car.'

'Goodbye, Jack,' Nina said, waving to him.

'Nina.' He winked.

Elizabeth said, 'I'll walk down with you,' then ran over and threaded her arm through Nina's. 'We did it,' she said.

'We did the first part of it,' Nina replied, smiling softly. 'We've got a long way to go to get where I want to be.'

'Tony'll be back, you know? We made him look like a fool.'

'Yeah, ain't life grand,' Nina said, her eyes sparkling. 'We can handle him, no problem.'

'It's true: he couldn't stamp us out when we had nothing . . .' Elizabeth grinned. 'Living well is the best revenge, but misery and humiliation's pretty good too.'

They hugged, and Nina slipped out to where Harry was waiting.

Elizabeth walked slowly back up the stairs. Jack was perching on the edge of her office couch, wearing jeans, cowboy boots and a thick blue jumper. He looked so gorgeous. Bittersweet pleasure, because now, Elizabeth thought, he's got nothing to stick around for.

She walked over to him and sat down. Don't ruin the happy mood by getting all emotional, Elizabeth warned herself.

'So, I guess you'll be leaving soon,' she said.

'Hmm. Maybe.' Taylor nodded. 'But first, I got a business proposition for you.'

Business. Right. Elizabeth tried to look enthusiastic. 'Sure, go ahead.'

'Well now,' Jack said slowly. 'I spoke to Pa last night. Thought if y'all could make so much money with lateral thinking, we should give it a try. I was talking to him about property over here. The Viceroy Hotel.'

'The place on the river?'

'Yes, ma'am. We reckon it would look real good in the portfolio, but it'll need upgrading. We thought maybe Tall Poppies could do it.'

Elizabeth sat stunned. 'But that would take you—'

'At least six months. By which time, you'll probably need to open an office in the States.'

'Jack!'

He caught her left hand and pressed it to his mouth. 'Baby, I'll say it again. Will you marry me? We can be together, we'll work something out. Hell, you take all these dollar-and-cent gambles every day. Why don't you risk a little on something important?'

Elizabeth leaned up and kissed him. He tasted of sun and champagne and Texas, Jack, her Jack, absolutely the only man she had ever loved.

'Is that a yes?'

'Oh, yeah,' Elizabeth said, 'that's a yes, sugar.'

LOUISE BAGSHAWE

Louise Bagshawe is only twenty-six years old but has already carved a name for herself in the publishing world. From an early age she has been an achiever, particularly in the field of writing. At just fourteen she was the youngest-ever contributor to *The Tablet,* a Roman Catholic weekly magazine, and in 1989 she was chosen as Cadbury's Young Poet of the Year. A year later she was reading Old Norse and Anglo-Saxon at Oxford University, where she became president of the Rock Society, which established her as a figure in the music world.

Indeed, her first job was as a press officer for the classical music department of EMI records. Being a strong personality, however, she was soon having differences with the management. 'For instance, my bosses thought I was a bad influence on violinist Nigel Kennedy, encouraging him to play rock rather than to interpret Beethoven's violin concertos.' After nine months the company fired her, but she remains grateful to them. She explains, 'If I'd been less miserable at work I would never have started to write.' As it happened, she took the opportunity during this gap in her career to write a synopsis for a novel, which she then sent to a publisher. She was just settling in to what promised to be a jet-setting lifestyle with new employers, Sony Music Entertainment, when the publisher made her an offer she couldn't refuse. Within months *Career Girls* hit the bookshops and, at the age of twenty-two, Louise Bagshawe was on her way to becoming a household name.

Tall Poppies is her third novel. Anybody who has read the book and seen a photograph of the author will know that one of the heroines, Elizabeth—with her natural beauty and long blonde hair—bears a marked resemblance to Louise Bagshawe herself. 'It is not just our looks,' Louise confesses. 'In fact I went to school with many girls like Elizabeth and grew up with them. One of my cousins even lives in a castle and I have to say that I used parts of it to describe Elizabeth's family home.'

Louise Bagshawe also admits that ambition is another trait that she shares with Elizabeth, and her other heroine, Nina. 'Ambition is a constant in all my work,' she says. 'I would not be where I am today without it. In *Tall Poppies* I chose to write a lot about skiing because it is a sport that favours the ambitious. It conveys the power, speed, exhilaration and sheer thrill of competition better than anything else—and it is also so romantic.'

Unsurprisingly, Louise Bagshawe likes to ski, but she claims that, unlike Elizabeth, she prefers the easier slopes. However, she certainly does not spare herself when it comes to work. She is currently living in Los Angeles where, over the next three months, she plans not only to write her new book but also to finish two film scripts.

So where does she see herself in ten years' time? 'Screen writing, producing movies, writing books—and hopefully married with a few children.' Like her glamorous and ambitious heroines, she has to fit romance into her busy schedule and, like them, she is also a hopeless romantic. 'I want everything in a man—intelligence, good looks,' she says. 'But, for the moment, I have to live my romance through my books.'

JOANNA TROLLOPE

Other People's Children

This is a story of relationships—the tangled relationships that result when marriages disintegrate. It tells of three deeply affected women—Nadine, an abandoned mother; Josie, a stepmother with new responsibilities and Elizabeth, a would-be stepmother—and of the men and children that link their lives. Through exploring their feelings and experiences, the myths and truths that surround such difficult and heart-rending situations are clearly revealed.

Chapter
ONE

BEHIND HIM, SOMEONE SAID, 'They shouldn't be called weddings.'

Rufus felt his ears glow. He leaned forward and stared at the tips of the new shoes his mother had persuaded him to wear instead of trainers. The person who had spoken behind him had been a woman. She sounded vaguely familiar.

'Not second time round,' she said. Her voice was calm, as if she had no personal axe to grind, but was simply stating a fact. 'There should be another word for second time round.'

Rufus raised his head very slowly and transferred his stare from his shoes to the wall twenty feet ahead of him. The wall was covered with white satiny paper and on it hung a picture of the Queen in a white dress and a tiara. Just below the Queen was the neat brown head of the lady in the grey suit and gold stud earrings who was, Rufus's mother said, the registrar. Being a registrar meant you could marry people to each other. This registrar—who had smiled at Rufus and said, 'Hello, dear'—was going to marry Rufus's mother in a minute. To Matthew. Rufus did not let his stare slide sideways from the registrar to include his mother and Matthew. Matthew had a grey suit on, and a yellow flower in his buttonhole, and he was half a head taller than Rufus's mother. He was, also and above all things, not Rufus's father.

He was, however—and this fact lent added alarm to an already disconcerting day—several other people's father. He had been married before, to someone else whose name Rufus couldn't remember, and he had three children. *Three.* All older than Rufus. And *all*—Rufus

161

swallowed hard—people he didn't know. Actually standing beside him was Matthew's younger daughter, Clare. She was repeatedly doing up and undoing the bottom button of her black cardigan. Below the cardigan she wore a crumpled orange skirt almost to the floor, and black boots. She was ten. Rufus was eight. Rufus's mother had said that he and Clare would get on, but to Rufus, Clare was as foreign as if she came from another planet. So was her brother, Rory, standing on her far side, in a black leather jacket and black jeans. Rufus's mother had made him wear a tie, but Rory was wearing a T-shirt. He was twelve, and his hair had been shaved up the sides and back of his head, leaving him vulnerable and gawky—soft-looking, like a baby bird. He had played football with Rufus earlier that day with a Coca-Cola can, kicking it round the patio of the house that Rufus was now going to share with his mother and Matthew. And, some weekends and during school holidays, with Clare and Rory and Becky who was fifteen and who had—well, she didn't go straight down in front under her sweater. Becky wore a denim bomber jacket and every so often she gave the left breast pocket a little tap. Rufus knew why. She kept a pack of Marlboro Lights in there and she wasn't supposed to.

Rufus's grandmother, on his left side, stooped towards him a little. She was going to say, 'All right, darling?' He waited.

'All right, darling?'

He nodded. She tried to take his hand. Rufus liked his grandmother but he did not wish to hold her hand, especially not in public, with Clare and Rory and Becky in their enviable solidarity of being three, on his right-hand side. He put his hand in his trouser pocket. There was an acorn in there and the rubber stopper from a water pistol. He held the acorn. It was warm, from being in his pocket, as if it had a life of its own. He had picked it up on a school walk to the playing fields, in Bath, where he used to live, where his father lived now and would be, at this minute, at this very minute, instead of being here in this white room with the glass lights and Rufus's mother. Where Matthew was, instead.

Matthew took Josie's hand under the restaurant tablecloth.

'Mine.'

She smiled, entranced, but not daring to look at him because of all the other people sitting round that table looking at her.

'Oh, Matt—'

'Mine,' he said again, squeezing her hand. 'Can't believe it.'

'Now, now,' Matthew's father shouted jovially from the far side of the table. 'Now, now, you two.'

'It's perfectly legal,' Matthew said, 'as of an hour ago.' He sounded quite at ease. He raised Josie's hand from under the cloth and kissed her wedding finger. 'Legally Mrs Mitchell.'

'Good luck to you!' his father shouted. He seized a nearby champagne bottle and sploshed wine approximately into all the glasses he could reach. 'Drink up! Drink to them!'

'Good luck, dears,' Josie's mother said. She lifted her glass. 'Long life together, health and happiness.' She nudged Clare, who was next to her. 'Raise your glass, dear.'

'I don't like it,' Clare said. 'I don't like champagne.'

'You can pick up your glass,' Josie's mother said, 'can't you? You don't have to drink out of it.' She looked across at Rufus. He was sandwiched between Rory and Matthew's younger sister, Karen, who was a nurse. Rufus looked, his grandmother thought, as he used to look just before he sang a solo in his school nativity play and was certain something would go wrong. She indicated to him to raise his glass.

'Toast to Mummy and Matthew, darling. Come on.'

She glanced towards her daughter. Josie looked so happy, so pretty, in a cream silk suit with her red hair done up somehow behind her head, that it seemed downright unkind to have misgivings. But how could she not? As a divorced woman herself of thirty years standing, with Josie her only child, how could she not have terrible apprehensions about Josie's leaving Tom Carver and all the settled, acceptable comfortableness of that life in Bath for a secondary-school deputy headmaster with three uncouth children and an eccentric-sounding ex-wife apparently spitting tacks with rage from the hovel in Herefordshire she'd taken herself off to? It wasn't that Matthew wasn't a nice man, because he was nice, and quite attractive, but he—well, his position, to be fair, seemed so perilous beside Tom's. And he knew it. He'd said, when they'd had their first awkward prospective mother-in-law, son-in-law meeting in a local pub, 'I suppose, Elaine, I should apologise.'

She'd looked at him, startled.

'What for? For taking Josie? Josie's never done anything that Josie didn't want to do. You needn't apologise for that.'

'I don't. But I'm not the catch Tom Carver was.'

Elaine had thought of the house in Bath, of the long windows on the first floor, of the immaculate basement from which Tom ran his architectural practice, of the little walled garden behind with its statues and stone urns. Josie had told her that Matthew Mitchell earned £33,000 a year. She had also now seen the house they would live in, always two of them, mostly three and sometimes six. It had three bedrooms.

'No good pretending,' she'd said to Matthew. 'But no. You're not.'

She looked round the restaurant now. It was Italian, with rough white walls and rush-seated chairs and a menu that featured fifteen kinds of speciality pizza. That's why it had been chosen. For the children.

'Are you strong enough for this?' Elaine had said to Josie. 'Are you sure? Can you really take these children on?'

'Mum,' Josie said, 'I've been there and done it. I've been a step-mother.'

'But that was different. These children are younger and—well, not very amenable—'

'We'll do it together,' Josie said. She'd been brushing her hair, that astonishing coppery river that gave her a glamour disproportionate to the rest of her. 'I love him. He loves me. We'll cope with the kids together.'

Now, beside Elaine, Clare, Matthew's youngest child, said, 'What's this?'

'What, dear?'

'This,' Clare said. She jabbed her fork at her pizza.

'It's an olive,' Elaine said.

Clare dropped her fork.

'Yuck. I'm not eating it. Looks like a beetle.'

'Leave the olive, then,' Elaine said. 'And eat the rest.'

'I can't,' Clare said, 'I can't. Not if the olive's been there.'

Across the table, Rory was tearing at his pizza with his fingers, Rufus was just eating, steadily, looking at his plate. On Elaine's own plate lay a little mound of pasta shaped like bows in a sauce of salmon and dill. She didn't feel like eating it. She turned to Matthew's daughter, Becky, on her other side. She had a nose stud shaped like a tiny crescent moon and alternate fingernails on both hands were painted black. The pizza in front of her was completely untouched.

'Aren't you eating?' Elaine said. She had meant to say 'dear', but the word had not somehow emerged.

'No,' Becky said.

'Aren't you hungry?'

Becky turned briefly to look at her. Her eyes were a startling, pure, pale delphinium blue.

'I'm dieting,' she said.

Karen, Matthew's sister, tried to avoid her father's eye. He was overdo-ing it, drinking too much, shouting false jolly things across the table to try to cover up the fact that Matthew's mother had refused to come to the wedding. She'd not only refused to come but had made a continued and noisy fuss about refusing, culminating in shutting herself in her bedroom on the wedding morning.

'I'm not getting her out,' Derek said. 'I'm not even trying. There's disapproval coming from under that door like black smoke and she can just choke on it.'

Karen had a headache. She'd just finished eight days of night duty on the geriatric ward and was so tired she didn't really care who married whom. She thought wearily of all the seventeen years that Matthew had been married to Nadine, and the steady stream of abuse of Nadine that her mother had kept up, of Nadine's appearance and lack of housekeeping skills and wrong-headed (in her view) political commitment and endless student zeal to embrace new skills, new languages, new causes.

'When will she stop playing about and earn some *money*?'

But when Matthew had fallen in love with Josie, Karen's mother's tune had changed overnight. Nadine became 'Matthew's wife', 'the mother of my grandchildren', 'my daughter-in-law', as if she'd suddenly sprouted a halo. Nadine, to her credit, took no more notice of the change of opinion than she had of the original one, but Matthew was up in arms. He'd had blazing, bellowing, roaring rows with his mother, telling her that her real trouble was that she was jealous, plain, bald, ugly old jealous, because he had had the guts to leave a bad marriage for the prospect of happiness, and that she'd never had the nerve to do the same, but preferred to grind on as she was, taking her disappointment out on everyone around her in revenge. Karen sighed and picked up her champagne glass. It was true. What else, she sometimes wondered, but the spectacle of her parents' palpable unsuitability to spend a weekend together, let alone a lifetime, had ensured that she was still unmarried at thirty-six? She took a swallow of champagne. Beside her, Josie's little boy, Rufus, had put down his knife and fork and was sitting back in his chair, far back, as if he felt he didn't belong.

'You OK?' Karen said.

He was a sweet-looking kid. He said, 'I got tomato on my tie.'

'Shouldn't worry. Look at my dad. I should think he's got half his lunch down his. D'you want some ice cream?'

Rufus shook his head. He looked, Karen thought, so lost. He probably felt it. Karen had seen plenty of kids in his position in the hospital, trailing down wards to see parents who weren't their parents, who never would be or could be, except in the mere name society gave them, for its own convenience. A lot of those kids looked stunned, as Rufus did, as if they knew at some deep level of their heavy hearts how powerless in all this they were. Karen touched Rufus's arm.

'You'll like Matthew. When you know him better. He likes kids.'

Rufus bowed his head a little but didn't speak. Karen looked past him to her nephew, Rory. He had eaten all his pizza and was drinking Coca-Cola out of a can.

'You should put that in a glass, Rory. This is a wedding.'

He paused in his drinking to say, 'They gave it me like this.'

'That's no reason,' Karen said. Rory was a bright kid, all Matthew's children were, but he had, as did his sisters, Nadine's defiance. Nadine thrived on defiance: defiance of the orthodox, the traditional, the accepted way of thinking and behaving. It was this that had attracted Matthew to her in the first place, Karen was sure, because it appeared so fresh and vital and questioning, after the rigidly respectable limitations of their own upbringing. Nadine had seemed like someone flinging open a window to let great gales of wild, salty air into the confined stuffiness of Matthew's life. But then in time her rebelliousness drove him mad, so mad that, just before he met Josie, he'd gone to live in a bed-and-breakfast place, and they'd all had to cover up for him in case the parents at his school found out and thought he was going round the bend. He nearly had. It started when Nadine had gone off to join a women's camp at the gates of a military base in Suffolk almost eight years ago, and even though she came home again, she couldn't stop. She fell in love with being anti things—anti-motherhood, anti-marriage, anti any kind of order. She was, Karen knew, impossible to live with, but she had something, all the same. All that crackling energy, and the jokes, and the mad meals cooked in the middle of the night and the sudden displays of affection that won you over, time after time.

Karen stretched across and put a hand on Rory's arm.

'You should look after Rufus.'

'Why?'

'Because he's your stepbrother now and there's three of you lot.'

Rory said, staring across the table, 'Nothing's changed.'

'What?'

'Mum said. About this wedding. It doesn't change anything. She said.'

Karen took a breath.

'Excuse me, but it has. A lot's changed. You've got a stepmother and a stepbrother now and you'll have to get on with it.'

There was a sound between them. A tear, quite unbidden, was sliding down Rufus's cheek and he had flung up a horrified arm to stop it.

Rory took a last swallow of Coke and shoved his chair back. He said, without looking at Rufus, 'Want to play Kick the Can?'

'OK?' Matthew whispered.

Josie nodded. Despite her elation at the day, at being truly Matthew's, she hadn't been able to keep her gaze from straying permanently to Rufus. He looked to her incredibly small, much smaller than eight, as small as the first day she had taken him to primary school and he had said, looking at the playground, 'No.'

'Rufus,' she'd said, 'this is school. This is what you've been longing for. You'll love it.'

He had taken his hand out of hers and put it behind his back.

'No,' he'd said again.

He couldn't say no now, in the same certain, careless-of-opinion, five-year-old way, but he could look it. Everything about him looked it—the way he sat hunched over his plate, the way he wouldn't look at anyone, the way he only spoke in whispered monosyllables. Josie had seen Karen trying to talk to him and had then sensed some kind of little incident which resulted in Rory slouching away from the table followed by Rufus, with his head down.

Matthew leaned closer. She could feel his breath warm on her ear.

'Can't wait till later.'

'Matt—'

'Yes?'

'The boys have gone.'

'They'll be scuffling about in the car park. They'll be fine.'

'I don't think any of the children are fine.'

'No,' he said. He took her hand again. 'No, they aren't. But they will be. This is just the beginning.'

'Perhaps we shouldn't be going away—'

'Honey,' Matthew said, 'we are going away for three whole nights. That's all. And that's for us. Like today is.' He glanced round the table. 'Look. Your mother, my father, our children, your best mate, my sister, my best mate, all here for us, because of what we're going to make of the future, what we're going to repair of the past.' He shook the hand he held. 'I love you.'

'Same,' she said. '*Same*. I tell you, though, my best mate thinks we haven't done it quietly enough. She thinks we should have just sloped off at dead of night with a couple of witnesses.'

'Let her,' Matthew said. 'Let her. We're not marrying her. We're not marrying anybody but us.'

'I don't like being disapproved of,' Josie said. 'Not even by someone I know as well as I know Beth.'

'How lovely,' Matthew said. 'How just lovely that you *mind*.' He gazed at her, his eyes on her mouth in a way that always made her feel faint. 'Nadine would have relished every moment.'

On the other side of the table, Beth Saddler, Josie's oldest friend, asked Matthew's father if it would be all right if she smoked.

'Don't see why not,' he said. 'Ashtrays everywhere, aren't there?'

Beth took out a packet of cigarettes and a lighter from her handbag. 'I was at Josie's first wedding. It was the full white works, in church. Even though she was pregnant. Was Matthew's?'

'Nope,' Matthew's father said. 'It was registry office and a curry lunch.' He made a face. 'I can taste it still.'

'I can't quite take this talk of *weddings,* somehow. A second marriage isn't a *wedding*, it's just a second marriage. It ought to be so quiet you can hardly hear it. Is that how your wife feels?'

Matthew's father drained his glass.

'I haven't had the foggiest, for forty-five years, what my wife feels.'

Beth said, almost as if he hadn't spoken, 'I mean, it's this step thing. A step-parent must be a very unsatisfactory parent for a child to have. All today we've assumed that it's going to be all right, this wedding, this marriage, these children, that it's *natural*.'

'Seems to me,' he said, 'that there's good parents and there's bad parents and there's good step-parents and there's bad step-parents and the whole thing nowadays is such a bloody muddle that if you get a good one of anything you're pretty lucky.'

She's smoking,' Becky said, 'so I'm going to.'

Ted Holmes, who had met Matthew on a climbing holiday in France twenty years before and had remained a friend ever since, eyed her. She was tall for her age, with a pronounced bosom already and her mother's astonishing blue eyes.

'Who are you aiming to upset, then?'

Becky shrugged.

'No one.'

'Or everyone.'

'Who'd notice?'

'Your father. Your grandfather.'

Becky said, 'Mum doesn't care.'

'She isn't here,' Ted said, 'to care or not to care.'

Ted had always found Nadine a complete nightmare. Matthew had met Nadine soon after that first climbing holiday and Ted had been horrified.

'Boy,' he said to Matthew. 'Boy, don't do it. She's chaos. She's crazy.'

Matthew had gone ahead and married Nadine and then Ted had met a girl at his local squash club, and had embarked on a courtship so long and uneventful that he sometimes thought it would still be going on if she hadn't said she'd leave him if he didn't marry her. He liked being married, once he was. Penny was an even better wife than she'd been a girlfriend, and after five years she gave birth to twin boys who were now at home, with measles, and Penny was at home, too, nursing them, instead of being here with Ted supporting old Matthew.

'I think,' Ted said to Becky, 'that you want to leave that cigarette until you're on the train. You're going back to Hereford tonight, aren't you?'

Becky nodded.

'Mum meeting you?'

'If her old banger makes it. It's a wreck. It's all Dad'll give her.'

'Now, now.'

'It's got a hole in the floor in the back. You can see the road.'

'Your mother,' Ted said, eyeing Becky's piebald fingernails, 'she's got a job?'

'No.'

'If she had a job, she could buy a better car.'

'Why should she?'

'We've all got to try,' Ted said. 'We've all got to do our bit.'

'Not when it's all unfair.'

'Unfair?'

Becky said, not looking at Josie, 'She's got a new house, hasn't she? And their car is pretty nearly new.'

'And who's that unfair to?'

'Mum.'

'Becky,' Ted said, suddenly not caring, 'your mother wouldn't know something fair if she met it in her porridge.'

She glared at him.

'Pig,' she said.

He shrugged. 'OK,' he said. 'If it makes you feel better.'

She took a breath.

'Nothing does!' she shrieked. 'Nothing does! And nothing ever will!'

And then she burst into tears and banged her head down into her cold and untouched pizza.

'Ted said sorry,' Matthew said.

Josie, lying back with her eyes closed against the headrest of the passenger seat of the car, said why did he feel he had to.

'For upsetting Becky.'

'What did he say?'

'He wouldn't tell me, but it was something to do with Nadine. Some home truth, no doubt. He couldn't stand Nadine.'

Josie felt a small glow of affection for Ted Holmes. It warmed her, creeping across the chill that had settled on her, despite all her earlier happy excitement, at the moment of saying goodbye to Rufus. He was going to stay with Elaine, her mother, for three nights. He held up his face for a kiss, and his face was quite empty of expression as if he were being kissed by someone he hardly knew because he'd been told to allow it.

'Bye, darling.'

'Bye,' he said.

'Have a lovely time,' Elaine said. 'Don't worry. Don't think about him.'

Josie looked at her gratefully. None of this was what Elaine would have chosen, but she was really trying to accept it.

'Mum was good,' she said to Matthew now.

He reached out for her nearest hand.

'She was,' he said. 'And Dad was fine and Karen was fine and my mother was a disaster.'

Josie rolled her head so that she could see his profile and the jawline she so much admired.

'And the children?'

'Josie,' Matthew said. He took his hand away from hers and put it on the steering wheel. 'Josie, we've got three nights together and two days and, during those three nights and two days, we are not even going to mention the children.' He paused, and then he said in a voice that was far less positive, 'We've got the rest of our lives for that.'

Chapter TWO

ELIZABETH BROWN STOOD at the first-floor windows of the house she had just bought and looked down at the garden. Down was the operative word. The garden fell away so steeply to the little street below that some previous owner had terraced it, in giant steps, and put in a gradual zigzag path so that you could at least get to the front door without mountaineering. The whole thing, her father had said when he came to see it, was like living halfway up a staircase.

'I know,' she said. She loved her father and relied on his opinion. 'Am I mad?'

'Not if you want it.'

She did. It was unsettling to want it because it was not what she had intended to buy. She had meant to buy a cottage in the hills around Bath, a cottage that would be a complete contrast to the featureless London mansion-block flat in which she spent her working week. When Elizabeth's mother died, and her father decided to sell his antiquarian book business in Bath and move to a flat there big enough to accommodate the books and whisky bottles and cans of soup which were all he required for sustenance, he gave Elizabeth some money. Enough to change the shape of her hard-working, comfortable but uneventful professional life.

'You ought to garden,' her father said. 'Seems to suit women. Something to do with nurturing and producing. Look for a garden.'

She'd looked at dozens of cottages and gardens for a whole summer, travelling down on Friday nights to Bath, staying with her father in considerable discomfort among the book piles, viewing all Saturday and sometimes on Sunday mornings, and then returning to London on Sunday afternoon to order herself for the week ahead.

'There isn't an idyll,' her father said. 'You have to make those.' He'd looked at her. 'You're getting set in your ways, Eliza. You've got to take a leap. Take a punt.'

'You never have—'

'No. But that doesn't mean I think I'm right. Buy a tower. Buy a windmill. Just *buy* something.'

So she did. On a warm Sunday morning in September, she cancelled the viewing of a cottage in Freshford, and went for a walk instead, up the steep streets and lanes above her father's flat. The hilly terraces were full of gentle Sunday-morning life: families, and couples with the radio on, audible through open windows, and desultory gardening and dogs and a pram or two, and washing. Here and there were 'For Sale' notices thrust haphazardly into front hedges, but Elizabeth didn't look at them except to think, with the wistfulness that was now so much part of her daily thinking, how nice it must be to need to buy a house in a town near schools, to put a family in. How nice to *have* to do something, instead of wondering, with a slight sense of lostness that her friends loudly, enviously, called freedom, what to choose to do.

She stopped by a low iron gate. Beside it, a 'For Sale' notice leaned tiredly against a young lime tree. The garden, tousled and tangled, but with the air of having once been planned by someone with some care, rose up sharply to the façade of a small, two-storey, flat-fronted stone house in a terrace of ten. It had a black iron Regency porch and a brick chimney, and in an adjoining garden a small girl dressed only in pink knickers and a witch's hat was singing to something in a shoebox. Elizabeth opened the gate and went up the path.

Now, three months later, it was hers. There were no leaves on the lime tree, and the garden had subsided into tawny nothingness, but the lime tree was hers and so were these strange semicultivated terraces which were, Tom Carver said, full of possibility. Tom Carver was an architect. Her father knew him because architecture had been one of the speciality subjects of her father's bookshop, and had suggested to Elizabeth that she get him in to help her.

'Nice man. Good architect.'

'Well, I'm good at *this* sort of thing,' Tom had said, standing in the tiny sitting room. 'I'm good at making space.'

She nodded gratefully. It disconcerted her that she, who spent all her working life either subtly directing people towards decisions, or briskly making them herself, should feel so helpless in this house, as if it represented all kinds of possibilities that she doubted she was up to.

'I'm not sure I want a house at all, you know,' she said to Tom Carver.

'But you want this one.'

'I seem to—'

He was perhaps in his mid- or early fifties, a burly man with a thick head of slightly greying hair and a surprising ease and lightness of movement. He wore his clothes, she noticed, with equal ease, as if they were exactly what he had intended to wear. Elizabeth seldom felt like that. Work was fine, work was no problem because all it demanded was an authoritative but sober neatness. It was play that was the problem. She never, all her life, could quite get the hang of clothes for play.

'I think we should knock this right through,' Tom Carver said. 'And give you one really good space for living in. Then you'll have north and south light as well as room to swing an armful of cats.' He ran his knuckles over the party wall to the room behind. 'What do you do?'

'I'm a civil servant.'

'Treasury?'

She blushed, shaking her head.

'Heritage. Mostly—libraries.'

'Why are you blushing? Libraries are admirable.'

'That's the trouble.'

He smiled.

'Shall we make this house very bohemian?'

She was laughing. She said, 'I'd be appalled.'

'I'm not serious,' he said, 'but it doesn't do any harm to undo a few buttons. If we put the kitchen on the north side of this room, you'll have the south side for sitting.'

'I mustn't sit,' Elizabeth said. 'I mustn't. I must garden.'

I must learn how, she thought now, looking down at it. In the efficient flat off Draycott Avenue, there wasn't so much as a window box. I suppose I'm the age for gardening. Isn't rising forty when people start, when they realise it's the only chance they'll have to make living things grow and happen?

A car stopped below at the little gate and Tom Carver got out. He had a long roll of paper under his arm, the drawings he had promised to bring of her new living space, her new bathroom, her new ingenious guest bedroom made out of the old bathroom, her new patio at the back to be gouged out of the hillside and decorated with a table and chairs at which, Tom Carver promised her, she would eat breakfast in the brief morning sun. She banged on the window and he looked up and waved. She went down into the narrow hall and let him in.

'Bloody cold,' he said.

'Is it?'

'Much colder up here than where I live. How are you?'

'Fine,' she said.

He went past her into the sitting room and unrolled the drawings on the floor.

'This house isn't in the least regular. We always think of the Georgians as so symmetrical, but most houses in Bath are just approximate.'

Elizabeth knelt on the floor. The drawings were very appealing, all those orderly lines and shaded areas in faded indigo, lettered with a quiet architectural flourish.

'Did you always want to be an architect?'

'No. I wanted to be a doctor. My father was, and so was my grandfather, and I refused to consider it, out of pique, after my elder brother won a medical scholarship to Cambridge.'

Elizabeth ran her finger over the shaded rectangle that would be her south window seat.

'Do you regret it?'

'Yes.'

'Do you think that regretting it makes you a better architect?'

He squatted on the floor beside her.

'What a very nice question, Miss Brown.'

'Elizabeth.'

'Thank you. The truthful answer is that it's made me quite a successful architect.'

'And I,' said Elizabeth, 'am quite a successful civil servant.'

'Is that a reprimand?'

Elizabeth stood up.

'Just a little warning. Why haven't you put the sink under the north window?'

'Because I've put a door to the garden there.'

'But I don't want two outside doors in this room.'

Tom stood, too.

'Then we shall think again.'

'I'll need space for gumboots, won't I, and coats, and somewhere to be out of the rain when I take them off.'

Tom stooped and laid his finger on the plans.

'There.'

'Oh,' she said. 'Sorry.'

'And there's an outside door for all that there. This door was for the summer. To carry trays through. That sort of thing. A summer Saturday. Friends coming for a drink.' He stopped. He straightened up and looked at her. He said, in a different voice, 'You can't really imagine living here, can you?'

'No,' she said. She put her hands in her coat pockets. 'At least—I thought I could, when I first saw it. But perhaps that was partly seeing all the life that was going on around it.'

Tom gave the drawings on the floor a small, deft kick so that they obediently rolled themselves up again.

'Tell you what. I'm going to take you down to my house, which at least is warm, and give you some coffee, and we'll talk—'

'I'm not having second thoughts—'

'I'd like to be certain of that before I tell you how much I've already cost you.'

Elizabeth said, with some force, 'I want this house.'

Tom bent and picked the roll of drawings up. He glanced at her. 'I believe the first two words of that sentence,' he said.

Elizabeth sat at Tom Carver's kitchen table. It was a long table, of old, cider-coloured wood, and it had a lot of disparate things on it—a pile of newspapers, a bowl of apples with several keys and opened letters in it as well as fruit, a clump of candlesticks, a stoppered wine bottle, a coffee mug, a torch. The kitchen was a light room, running right through the depth of the house, with French windows at one end through which Elizabeth could see the painted iron railings that presumably belonged to a staircase going down to the garden. It was the kind of kitchen you saw in showrooms or magazines, where every inch had been thought out, where every cupboard handle and spotlight had been considered, solemnly, before it was chosen.

Tom Carver put a mug of coffee down in front of her.

'Your expression isn't very admiring.'

'I'm not used,' Elizabeth said, 'to being in houses where so much care has been taken.'

'That's my profession, however.'

'Yes, of course. I didn't mean to be rude.'

'I didn't think you were.' He sat down opposite her and pushed a bowl of sugar towards her. 'Why do you want to live in Bath?'

'My father lives here. I know it. It's easy from London.'

'Why didn't you buy a house in London, with a garden, and just come to see your father the odd weekend?'

Elizabeth put a spoonful of sugar into her mug and stirred it slowly.

'I don't know. I didn't think of it. My mind got taken up with this cottage-and-garden idea.'

'The Anglo-Saxon rural idyll.'

'Perhaps.'

'It's a very romantic idyll,' Tom said, 'very persuasive. Do you have an idyll?'

Elizabeth took a swallow of coffee.

'No.'

'Sensible girl,' Tom said.

'I'm not sure I am,' Elizabeth said, 'but after my mother died, I was very conscious of wanting to change something, do something new, add something. I didn't want to change jobs because I'm only a year or two away from something quite senior, but I felt—well, I felt that I might be turning into one of those women who taught us at school, and who we used to pity, in our superior and probably quite inaccurate fourteen-year-old way, for having nothing in their lives but us.'

Tom cupped both his hands round his mug.

'Have you ever been married?'

There was a tiny beat.

'No,' Elizabeth said.

'Have you ever wanted to be?'

Elizabeth looked down into her coffee. Half of her wanted to tell him primly that he didn't know her anything like well enough to ask such a thing and the other half wished to confide, in a rush of relief at being able to, that she only ever seemed to want to marry men who were already firmly married and that it troubled her that she only felt able to release herself into loving if there was no real danger she might have to commit to it. And yet—and this was an increasing pain—the loneliness caused by this inhibition was getting daily harder to bear. It was beginning to colour everything. When she had stood in the little house in Lansbury Crescent that morning, she had been able to visualise her solitude there, but not the scene that Tom had suggested, of a summer evening, with the garden door open and a tray of drinks on a table on the patio, and a group of friends. She had friends, of course she did, friends she went to the cinema and theatre with, friends who asked her round for Sunday lunch and failed to fool her, for a moment, despite their loud comical wails of complaint, about the deep proud satisfaction they felt in having children.

'I thought,' she said to Tom Carver, 'that we were going to talk about my house.'

'We are. I'm luring you into telling me if you really want to spend maybe fifteen thousand pounds on something your heart might not quite be in.'

'Why should it matter to you?' Elizabeth said rudely. 'You'll get your fee in any case, whether I like the house or I don't.'

Tom Carver got up and went across to the kitchen counter where he had left the coffeepot. He said equably, 'You're quite right. With most clients, I don't really care. But . . .'

'But what?'

'You're a nice woman,' he said simply. He held the coffeepot above her mug. 'More coffee?'

She shook her head. He filled his own mug. He said, 'Can I show you something?'

'Of course.'

He put the coffeepot down and went to the other end of the kitchen which was arranged as a kind of sitting room, with a sofa and armchairs and a television set. He came back carrying a framed photograph and set it down in front of Elizabeth.

'There.'

It was a photograph of a little boy, a boy of perhaps—Elizabeth was never certain of children's ages—about seven. He was extremely attractive, with thick hair and clear eyes and a scattering of freckles. He wore a checked shirt and jeans and he was staring at the camera.

'My boy,' Tom said. 'He's called Rufus. He's eight.'

'He looks angelic,' Elizabeth said.

'I rather think he is,' Tom said. 'At least, in his absence I do.'

Elizabeth moved the photograph a few inches away from her

'Is he away at school, then?'

'No. He lives with his mother.'

'Oh dear,' Elizabeth said.

'His mother left me,' Tom said. 'Almost a year ago. She left me for the deputy head teacher of a secondary school at a place called Sedgebury, in the Midlands.'

Elizabeth looked at the photograph again.

'I'm so sorry.'

'She's a teacher, too,' Tom said. 'They met at a conference on pastoral care in state education. He has three children. They were married last week.'

'I'm so sorry,' Elizabeth said again.

'Perhaps I should have expected it. Plenty of people told me so. She's fifteen years younger than I am.'

Privately, Elizabeth thought that this vanished wife might be about the same age as she was, herself.

She said, cautiously, 'Mightn't it be a matter of temperament, not age? My parents were twelve years apart, and they were happy.'

He smiled at her.

'In our case, it was both.'

The telephone rang.

'Excuse me,' he said.

He went across the kitchen to the telephone.

'Hello? Hello, darling. No. No, I've got someone here. No, a client. Yes, of course you can. Sunday morning. All well with you? Good week? I wish they'd get you a carphone with all that travelling. OK, darling, fine. Lovely. See you tomorrow.'

He put the telephone down.

'My daughter.'

Elizabeth looked up.

'Your daughter?'

He came back to the table, smiling.

'My daughter, Dale. This is turning into rather a confessional. I have a daughter of twenty-five and another son of twenty-eight.'

'How?' Elizabeth demanded.

'By the conventional method. My first wife died twenty years ago, from some virus contracted on holiday in the Greek Islands. She was dead in ten days.'

Elizabeth stood up.

'Saying what bad luck seems rather inadequate.'

He looked at her.

'But that's all it was. I thought, at one point, I would simply die of grief but even at the lowest ebb I knew there was no one to blame.'

'Did you bring the children up on your own?'

'Yes, until nine years ago, when Rufus was on the way and I married Josie.'

'But your first children were nearly grown-up then—'

'Nearly. It wasn't easy. Dale and Lucas—Dale particularly—were used to having me to themselves.'

Elizabeth turned to look for her coat.

'I've never had any competition for my father. Maybe I'm lucky—'

Tom said, 'Look, I really am very sorry. I never meant to burden you with all this. I never intended to do anything except discover what you really want to do about this house.'

She lifted her coat off a nearby chairback. He rose and took the coat from her and held it out for her to put on.

'I don't know now. You've made me think. Or at least, this morning has.'

He left his hands on her shoulders for a second after the coat was on.

'Have you enjoyed it?'

'Yes,' she said.

He came round to look at her.

'I would so like to give you lunch.'

'Now?'

'Right now,' he said.

'**W**ell,' Elizabeth's father said. 'All settled?'

'No,' Elizabeth said. 'At least, not about the house.' She looked round her father's sitting room and sighed.

'Why don't you tell me about the day instead?'

'I feel a bit shy about it—'

'Why?'

'Because I've learned a lot about Tom Carver.'

'Why,' Duncan said, taking his reading glasses off, 'should that make you feel shy?'

Elizabeth leaned in the doorway to the tiny hall.

'Because I'm not used to people telling me things about themselves unless they want to show off to me. And he didn't. He seemed to want me to know.'

'Ah,' Duncan said.

'Don't sound so knowing.'

'It wasn't so much knowing, as light dawning.'

'There isn't any to dawn. We had lunch in a wine bar and he talked much more than me.'

'That doesn't surprise me. You never were much of a talker.'

'Daddy,' Elizabeth said. 'I'm beginning to wonder if I should have bought that house. Tom asked me if I could imagine living there, and I'm not sure I can.'

'Dearest,' Duncan said, 'when you were five and we were going camping in Brittany, you said you didn't think you'd come because you couldn't think what it would be like.'

'What did I think when I got there?'

'You seemed to like it. I taught you how to ask for bread and you went trotting off to the baker's, looking extremely serious, and came back with the right loaf every morning.'

'But this is different.'

'Is it?'

'It's bigger.'

'Only proportionately. You're bigger, too.'

'I don't want,' Elizabeth said, 'to buy another chunk of solitude. I don't want to delude myself that I'm making a change when I'm only doing more of the same in a different place.'

Duncan stood up. Crumbs from the water biscuits he ate with his mugs of soup showered like dandruff from the creases of his cardigan. He looked like an elderly heron, his head thrust forward on a long thin neck, on a long thin body.

'You're an old bag lady, really,' Elizabeth said fondly.

He smiled at her. He said, 'And you're a nice woman.'

'Tom Carver said that.'

'Well,' Duncan said, 'at least he's old enough to know.'

When he got home, Tom Carver opened a tin of rabbit in jelly for the cat. He didn't much like cats, but this cat had been Josie's and she had left it behind when she departed, so that it became for Tom a kind of ally, a partner in abandonment. It was, in any case, an amiable cat, a huge, square, neutered tom called Basil who lay like a hassock in patches of sunlight, moving ponderously round the house all day as the sun moved.

When he had fed Basil, Tom went down to the basement. The room was austere and serene, a kind of artistic engine room, except that it was silent. It was pale and calm and furnished with immense drawing boards and long low cupboards, like map cases, into which Tom slid his plans and drawings. The lighting was immaculate. The only ugly thing in the room was the giant photocopier and it lived behind a Japanese screen of cherrywood and translucent paper.

He moved to the nearest drawing board and switched on the carefully angled lights above it. On it lay plans for a barn conversion. It was a big strong nineteenth-century barn, and Tom was having trouble persuading the owners not to fill the huge east and west gables, through which the wains had once driven, with glass. He slipped onto the stool in front of the board and looked at his drawings. They were good, but not wonderful. He thought of Elizabeth kneeling on the floor of the sitting room at Lansbury Crescent, looking at other drawings. He thought of her sitting across the table from him in the wine bar, listening to him. He thought how nice it would be if they were going to eat together again that evening, after a concert perhaps, or the cinema. He thought that perhaps he would ring her at her father's flat and suggest lunch tomorrow, on Sunday, before she caught her train back to London. Then he remembered that he couldn't. Dale was coming tomorrow. Dale had had a bad time recently, being ditched by that boy and everything. He would not, he thought, tell Dale about Elizabeth.

Chapter
THREE

BECKY WONDERED if, at fifteen, the cold could kill you. She knew if you were old it did, because you couldn't move about much and you got scared about turning the heating on because you couldn't pay the subsequent bills. Becky could hardly imagine feeling like that. In her view you did, in so far as you could get away with it quite easily, what you wanted or needed to do, and left the problem of paying for it to someone else. At least, mostly she felt like that. But not, oddly enough, lying rigid with cold as she now was, with all her clothes on in a bed in her mother's house that was so cold itself, it felt damp. If there'd been a heater in the room, which there wasn't, even Becky would have hesitated to turn it on, because of that awful scene downstairs two hours ago after supper, when Rory had said he was still hungry and Nadine, in a screaming rage, had emptied what was in her purse over Rory's head and shoulders, shrieking all the time that he could eat that if he bloody well wanted to because it was all there was until his fucking father got round to remembering his responsibilities.

Rory had sat there, ashen, with pennies and twenty-pence pieces sliding down his leather jacket and off his jeaned legs to the floor. He hadn't tried to pick the money up. None of them had. They'd simply stayed where they were, frozen, not looking at each other, not looking at Nadine.

'Two hundred quid a week!' Nadine yelled. 'Two hundred quid! How'm I supposed to live on that? How'm I supposed to look after you?'

The children said nothing. Very slowly, Clare drew her booted feet up under the folds of her orange skirt and held her knees hard against her. Dad had told her—and Becky and Rory—that there was enough money to pay the rent on Mum's cottage, and that he would buy their clothes and stuff for school. But Mum said that wasn't true, nothing Dad said was true, *nothing*. She said Dad was a liar. She also said Dad was a number of other things, not all of which Clare had understood. But shivering in this cold, cluttered kitchen with Nadine yelling and Rory looking as if he might throw up at any minute all over the money on the floor, Clare understood very well that, whether her father was a liar or not, his absence meant suffering. Real suffering, for all of them.

Once Nadine had started yelling, she didn't seem able to stop. She'd yelled about Josie and about Matthew, and about how they—her children—should never have been so disloyal as to go to their wedding, and about the state of her car and the state of the cottage and how her life was over. It had seemed to go on for hours, and then, as suddenly as it began, it stopped, and Nadine was hugging them and kissing them and telling them they were all the world to her, and digging in the cupboard to produce, triumphantly, a box of sachets of drinking-chocolate powder which only needed boiling water and not milk, which had run out anyway.

When they'd drunk the chocolate, Nadine said they should go to bed. Becky had protested, pointing out that it was only nine thirty, and Nadine had asked—with that alarming edge to her voice again—what Becky proposed to do at nine thirty at night in a dump in the middle of nowhere. Becky had clumped upstairs, wordlessly, behind Clare. She thought of asking Clare to get into bed with her for warmth, but she could tell, from the way Clare's shoulders were hunched under her cardigan, that Clare would say no, to punish her, because, after an episode like that downstairs, you just had to punish someone for everything being so awful.

They'd gone into their bedrooms, equally silently, Clare and Becky into the one they shared, and Rory into the crooked space under the cottage's eaves which he had chosen in preference to sleeping in the third bedroom, which Nadine had made into a kind of studio, full of paintbrushes in jars, and a small weaving frame, and bursting plastic bags of hanks of wool and cotton, and half-made sculptures of wire netting and papier-mâché. Rory had made himself a sort of tent under the eaves there, and in it a nest of old duvets and sleeping-bags. You could only get in by crawling. Becky watched him crawl in and knew that he would, as she would, sleep in all his clothes, even his boots.

She didn't think she'd ever been so cold, ever felt so paralysed by it, helpless. Across the room, Clare was a darker shape against a dark all. She was still now. Before, she'd been crying but when Becky said, 'Clare?' she'd said, 'Shut up!' Her orange skirt and black cardigan were lying in a jumble on the floor because she had undressed and put on an old track suit instead. It was a track suit Dad had given her long ago with characters from the Disney film of *The Jungle Book* stamped on the front in soft, flexible plastic.

The house was very quiet. Becky hadn't heard Nadine come upstairs yet. There'd been some bangings about half an hour ago or so, but since then, there'd been silence. It wasn't a serene silence but then, Becky supposed, a scene like the one they'd witnessed left the air a bit shaken up, like thunder. She rolled over onto her other side, shoving her hands down between her thighs and feeling the hard seams of her denim jacket press uncomfortably into her side and arms. Perhaps she should get up and find some gloves, some of those mitten things Nadine wore knitted from brilliantly coloured wools by people in Peru. Nadine had had a thing, last year, about Peru, about the corruption of the government and the extent of poverty and child prostitution in the capital, Lima. It was one of the last things Becky remembered Nadine and Matthew having one of their really big fights about, when he'd discovered she'd given £100 to a charity appealing for funds to help the slum dwellers of Lima. Nadine had flown at him, all nails and teeth, and he had gone from shouting to silence, utter silence, and had walked out of the house. Clare had tried to follow him. All those rows, all those horrible, howling quarrels with Matthew telling Nadine she was mad and Nadine telling Matthew he was worthless, always ended with Matthew walking out and Clare trying to go with him.

Until now. Becky pulled her cold hands up again and began to blow on them. Until now, when Matthew had finally married Josie and they had all known that there would be no more rows, for the simple reason that Matthew and Nadine would never live together again. Becky couldn't bear that. It gave her a pain so acute that she tried not to think of it at all, but to tell herself instead that nothing was final, nothing. There was nothing you couldn't change, if you wanted change enough. *Nothing.*

She sat up. It was hopeless. She was colder than she'd been when she came upstairs. She pushed the duvet back and put her feet on the floor. They were so cold, even inside her boots, that the soles felt lumpy. She stood up. She'd go downstairs and see if she could find something, somewhere, to make a fire with. Nadine hadn't let them light the fire in the sitting room because she said the chimney smoked, but Becky didn't care about smoke.

She opened the door. The landing and narrow staircase were in darkness, but, peering down, there was a line of light still under the kitchen door. She went down the stairs, stiffly, and paused at the bottom. The thing with Nadine was that you never quite knew what to expect. Becky put her hand on the kitchen door handle and turned it cautiously.

'Mum?'

Nadine was sitting at the kitchen table, wrapped in an old rug. She hadn't cleared away their supper things, nor their chocolate mugs. She was sitting with her head in her hands and her long dark hair falling unevenly over them and over her shoulders, and she was crying. She was crying in a way that made Becky think she had been crying for a very long time.

'Mum?'

Slowly, Nadine looked up. Her face was wretched, drowned.

'I thought you'd be asleep.'

'I couldn't. I'm so cold—'

Nadine said, 'It's awful, isn't it? I've never been so cold either.'

Becky came further into the room.

'D'you want some tea?'

Nadine said, 'There isn't any milk.' She found a tissue in her sleeve and blew her nose.

'You could have it black.'

'Thank you,' Nadine said. She was shivering.

Becky went past her and ran water into the kettle.

'I'm sorry,' Nadine said.

Becky said nothing. She leaned into the sink and stared hard at the water running into the kettle.

'It's just that it's so awful and I get so angry because I'm so powerless. This horrible cottage—'

Becky turned off the tap.

'You chose it,' she said.

'I did *not!*' Nadine shrieked. 'It was the only one we could afford!'

Becky closed her eyes for a moment, and swallowed. Then she opened them again, fitted the plug into the kettle and switched it on, staying by it while it spluttered into life, her back to Nadine. She shouldn't have said that, she shouldn't have answered back. It would just start everything off again. No matter that she was right, no matter that she and Nadine and Rory and Clare had driven round Herefordshire for what seemed like weeks, looking at cottages for rent, with Nadine saying, 'No, no, no,' to every one, even the decent ones with proper bathrooms and bus-stops nearby, and then at last, when they'd pulled up in front of this utterly doomed place which looked like the witch's house in a fairy tale—there were even mushrooms growing on the roof—miles from anywhere, she'd said, 'Yes.' They'd all groaned, wailing with incomprehension and horror. *'Yes,'* Nadine had said again.

'Did you hear me?' Nadine said. Her voice was calmer.

'Yes,' Becky said.

'It's true. This is the cheapest and the cheapest is what we had to have. You know why.'

Becky said nothing. She thought of the car, which Nadine had also spent a lifetime finding, with its rust patches and holey floor, parked outside in a mouldering lean-to of planks and corrugated iron. It was frightening to think that something so fragile was her only link back to the outside world, a world in which, at this precise moment, even school seemed attractive.

'I know it's awful for you here,' Nadine said. 'I feel really badly about it. It's awful for me, too.'

Becky put a tea bag in a mug, poured boiling water onto it, squeezed the bag against the side of the mug with a spoon and fished it out. She turned and put the mug down in front of Nadine.

'Could you get a job?'

'How?' Nadine said. 'How? With no one to get you all to school and back but me?'

Becky tried not to remember all the cottages they'd seen on bus routes.

'Could you get a part-time job, in Ross or somewhere, while we're at school?'

'Shop girl?' Nadine enquired sweetly.

'Maybe. I dunno. I wouldn't mind a Saturday job in a shop.'

'You're too young. Anyway, how would you get there?'

Becky shrugged.

'Bike, maybe.'

'And where will you get a bike?'

Becky opened her mouth to say, 'I'll ask Dad,' and closed it again, too late.

'From your father, no doubt,' Nadine said. 'Your honeymooning father with his nice new house to come home to.'

'It's not very new,' Becky said.

'But rather,' Nadine said dangerously, 'newer than this.'

Becky was suddenly very tired. She put her hands on the table among the dirty plates and let her head hang, feeling her hair swinging down, heavy and dark, like Nadine's.

'I wish—'

'What do you wish?'

'I wish—you didn't hate him like this.'

Nadine took a swallow of tea, and made a face at it.

'What would you do, in my place?'

Becky said nothing. She observed that her black nail varnish had chipped, and resolved that she would just let it chip until it all came off bit by bit. Then she'd paint them green.

'If the person you loved and had been married to for seventeen years—*seventeen*—suddenly told you he was marrying someone else, and that you would have to go and live somewhere else on almost no money, how would you feel?'

Inside Becky's head, a little sentence formed itself and hung there. It read: It wasn't like that. She said, 'But *we've* got to see him. We've got to go on seeing him.'

Nadine looked at her. Her light blue eyes were wide with fervour. 'Exactly. *Exactly*. And can't you just use one ounce of imagination and see how agonising that is for me to bear?'

In the morning, Nadine drove them all to school, Clare to the nearest junior school and Rory and Becky to the comprehensive. They had been at their new schools for two terms, ever since it became plain that Matthew really did intend to marry Josie and Nadine had decided that it was intolerable for her, and the children, to stay in Sedgebury. Matthew had wanted her to stay, so that the children at least had the continuity of school and friends and grandparents, but she had refused. She had been in such violent pain that she believed, passionately, that the only way she could possibly assuage it was by getting out, getting away from everything that was familiar, and was now denied to her. The children had complained bitterly, but she had told them it had to be. Nobody wanted this new life, but they had to live it.

'You must reconcile yourselves to it,' she'd said. 'You must learn.'

They didn't, she thought, much like their new schools, but they bore them. They were inevitably more rural than the schools in Sedgebury, and though no rougher, the roughness took a different form. Nadine thought the children had got quieter. When she was talking to them, or angry, she blamed this new quietness on Matthew and Josie, but when she was alone in the cottage in the middle of the day, she sometimes, and despite all the frightening turbulence of her feelings, admitted that it was not as simple as that. When she dropped them at school, she always said, 'Three thirty!' to them, as if encouraging them to think she was only seven hours away. Becky had suggested that she didn't drive them all the way to school, but dropped them at a collecting point halfway where they could join the school bus. But she'd said no.

'You need me,' she said to Becky. 'For the moment, anyway. You need me to be there.'

And I, she thought to herself, reversing the car badly in the gateway to Becky and Rory's school, need them to be there. I'd just drown without them.

When she got home, she resolved, she would clean the cottage and do some washing and put at least clean pillowcases on the beds. She would also, with the screwed-up fiver she had found in her jacket pocket, buy something for supper. Macaroni and cheese maybe, or potatoes and eggs. When she was a student, she'd lived on potatoes and eggs. Her skin had got terrible. She remembered it clearly, because she'd always had good skin, the kind of skin you didn't have to bother with because it seemed to take care of itself. It developed spots and rough, dry patches and went dead-looking, in protest. So she'd switched, with the kind of exaggerated enthusiasm that she'd always been at the mercy of, to a macrobiotic diet and ate bean curd and brown rice. Her skin took a pretty poor view of that, too. Nadine put her hand up and touched her face. Her skin had never recovered really. Matthew had told her, when she complained to him about it, that she'd gone too far, pushed it beyond its limits. He was always accusing her of that, always telling her that she pushed everything too far, people, causes, opinions, him. Matthew . . . At the thought of his name, Nadine gave a little scream out loud and beat impotently on the steering wheel.

She drove the car slowly up the lane to the cottage—they'd first seen it when the hedges were bright with blackberries and rosehips, but now they were only dark and wet with winter—and parked it in the lean-to. There were so many holes in the corrugated-iron roof of the lean-to that the car might as well have lived outside for all the protection it was afforded. But it suited something in Nadine to park it there, religiously and pointlessly, every time she returned to the cottage, forcing everyone to struggle across the neglected garden carrying school bags and shopping.

The kitchen in the cottage offended her by looking exactly as they had all left it over an hour before. She'd offered the children a breakfast of cereal softened with long-life orange juice out of a carton, because there was no bread or butter or milk, and they'd all refused. Clare had drunk another mug of powdered hot chocolate and Becky had found, somewhere, a can of diet Coca-Cola over which she and Rory squabbled like scrapping dogs, but they would none of them eat anything.

'At least I tried,' Nadine said to the kitchen. 'At least I *offered*.'

She went across the room and filled the kettle. It would be more economical to wash up and wash the kitchen floor with water boiled from the kettle than to use water heated by the electric immersion heater. It *ate* money. There was a meter in the dank hall, and it ticked away loudly all day, whether the lights or the cooker or the immersion heater were on or not, menacingly reminding Nadine that it was devouring money. She looked out of the window above the sink and felt a new wave of despair rise chokingly up in her throat at the prospect of being stuck here, alone with her thoughts, until the blessed necessity of going to get the children would release her briefly from her cage. She had never minded solitude before, indeed had sought it, insisted on it, told Matthew she would, quite literally, go mad for the lack of it, but now she feared it. Tears of fright and misery (self-pity, Matthew would have called it) rose to her eyes.

'Oh God,' Nadine said. 'Oh God, oh help, help, oh help.'

The kettle began to boil, its ill-fitting lid jerking under the pressure of the steam inside. Nadine wearily leaned over and switched it off. She went across to the table and stacked the bowls and plates and mugs scattered about into haphazard piles, and carried them over to the sink. Then she picked up the washing-up-liquid bottle. It was called 'Ecoclear' and had cost almost twice as much as the less environmentally friendly brand on the supermarket shelf next to it. It also, as Rory had pointed out, didn't work, dissolving into pale scum on the water's surface. Nadine squeezed the plastic bottle. It gave a wheezy sigh. It was almost empty.

Nadine went over to the dresser and unhooked the last clean mug. She spooned coffee powder into it and filled it up with water from the kettle. Then she found a hardened cellophane packet of muscovado sugar and chipped off a piece with the handle of the teaspoon, stirring it round and round in the coffee until it finally melted. She took a sip. It tasted strange, sweet but faintly mouldy.

Holding the mug, Nadine went back to the kettle and with her left hand poured the contents awkwardly over the dishes piled in the sink. Then, cradling the mug in both hands, she went out of the kitchen, down the hall past the ticking meter, and up the stairs to the landing. All the doors were open on the landing, revealing piles of clothes on the floors, and rumpled beds and the plastic carrier bags of nameless things that the children carried about with them. In the bathroom there were lumps of damp towel by the bath and the rickety shower curtain had come down, drooping in stiff, stained plastic folds.

Nadine went round the landing and closed all the doors. What she couldn't see, she might not think about. Then she stooped down, and holding her mug of coffee carefully so as not to spill it, crawled into Rory's tunnel under the eaves and buried herself there.

'We've been waiting nearly an hour,' Becky said. She climbed into the front seat beside Nadine. In the driving mirror, Nadine saw Rory slide in next to Clare, his face shuttered as it always was when he didn't want anyone to ask him things.

'I'm sorry,' Nadine said. 'I didn't sleep much last night, and I went to sleep this morning, by mistake. For too long.'

She glanced in the driving mirror again. Clare was yawning. Her hair needed washing, and fronds of it stuck out here and there, giving her a neglected look.

'I'm sorry,' Nadine said again. 'Really. I was just so tired.' She put the car into reverse. 'Had a good day?'

The children said nothing. Nadine gave them, as she turned the car, a quick glance. They weren't sulking, she could see that. They just didn't know how to reply to her in a way that was both truthful and wouldn't upset her. The car was moving forward again. Nadine gave Becky's nearest thigh a squeeze. 'Hungry?'

'You bet,' Becky said.

'We'll stop at the village shop,' Nadine said. 'I found a fiver. We'll buy potatoes and eggs and have a bit of a fry-up. Egg and chips. What about that? Egg and chips.'

There was a pause. Then Clare said, 'We had egg and chips for lunch.'

Chapter **FOUR**

DALE CARVER PARKED HER CAR with great competence in a space underneath the first-floor windows of her brother's flat. She fixed the steering-wheel lock, got out, pulled the back window screen over the car stock she carried all the time as a publisher's travelling rep, and locked the car. She glanced up. The curtains were pulled across the windows of Lucas's sitting room and there were lights on inside. At least he was home. He'd said he'd try to be home by seven, but that so many people at the local radio station where he worked had flu, he might have to stay late and cover for someone. Or maybe the lights meant that Amy was there. Amy was Lucas's fiancée. She was the head make-up girl for the nearest television station and they had met in the course of their work.

Holding a bottle of wine and the proof copy of a new American novel for Lucas—Dale found she couldn't help giving him these slightly intellectual presents in front of Amy—Dale climbed the front steps of the house and rang the middle bell. There was a crackle, and then Lucas's voice said, 'Dale?'

'Hi.'

'Come right up.'

'Ten seconds,' Dale said.

It was a game between them, to see how fast she could race along the hall—it depended on what she was carrying—and up the stairs, lined with old prints of Bath and Bristol (there was a penalty if she knocked one off), to Lucas's front door where he'd be standing, counting.

'Eleven,' he said.

'It never was!'

'Nearly twelve.'

'Liar,' Dale said.

He kissed her. He was wearing a black shirt and black trousers and an open, faintly ethnic-looking waistcoat. Dale indicated it.

'Cool.'

He winked.

'Present from a fan.'

'Hey. Does Amy know?'

'Yes, I do,' Amy said. She appeared behind Lucas, her blonde hair in the curly froth around her face which Dale sometimes privately wondered how Lucas could bear to touch. It had a faintly woolly look to it, like a poodle.

'I've brought these,' Dale said to Lucas, holding out the book and the bottle. He took them, peering at the book's title.

'Wow. Great.'

'It's brilliant,' Dale said. 'You think you never want to read another word about Vietnam, but this is different.'

'Thanks,' Lucas said, still looking at the book. 'Thanks.'

Amy took the wine bottle out of his hand.

'I'll chill this.'

She was wearing leggings and ankle boots and a big T-shirt. She went into the kitchen and called, 'Want a coffee?'

'I'd rather have a drink,' Dale said. She moved into the centre of the sitting room, between the twin sofas covered in rough pale linen. 'A drink drink. I've been down to Plymouth today. The traffic was vile.'

Lucas picked a vodka bottle off the tray inserted into a bookcase and held it up, enquiringly.

'Lovely,' Dale said. 'The very thing.'

'Why,' Lucas said, pouring vodka, 'don't you get a job that doesn't mean all this travelling? If you want to stay in publishing, why don't you go on to the editorial side or something?'

'It would mean going to London,' Dale said. 'I don't want to go to London.'

Amy came out of the kitchen holding a mug.

'It's funny,' Amy said, 'the way you two want to stick around your dad.'

Lucas handed Dale a tumbler of vodka and tonic and ice.

'We don't,' he said, 'not deliberately. It's just happened, because of the areas we got jobs in.'

'I couldn't wait to get away from Hartlepool,' Amy said. She sat down on the nearest sofa, looking at Dale, taking in her trouser-suit and her small jewellery and her smooth hair, tied back behind her head with a black velvet knot. 'Or my father. Nothing on earth would make me live within miles of my father.'

'We're not going to,' Lucas said. He looked at his sister. 'You're too skinny.'

Dale made a face. She sat down on the sofa opposite Amy and took a big gulp of her drink.

'Things haven't been brilliant lately. First Neil walking out—' She paused, took another gulp of her drink and then said, 'And now Dad.'

Lucas sat down next to Amy, leaning back with his arm across the sofa behind her.

'What about Dad?'

'He's got a woman,' Dale said.

Amy looked amazed.

'He hasn't,' Lucas said. 'I've seen him often lately and he's never said a word.'

'He hasn't said a word to me, either,' Dale said. 'But I know.'

'Come on,' Lucas said. He was half laughing. 'Come on. Josie hasn't been gone a year—'

'Men do that,' Amy said. 'They can't stand being alone, so when their wives die or push off, they just grab the first next one.'

'Dale,' Lucas said, ignoring her, 'you're making this up. There isn't any evidence. Anyway, Dad would tell us. Dad would say.'

Dale pushed an ice cube in her drink under the surface.

'He wouldn't say, if he didn't want us to know.'

'But why wouldn't he want us to know?'

'Because he'd know,' Dale said, 'that we wouldn't like it.'

'Speak for yourself. I wouldn't mind.'

'I don't believe you.'

Amy leaned forward and put her mug on the black coffee table.

'She's right, you know. You don't want other women moving in and taking what's yours. You've had Josie already.'

'She didn't take much,' Lucas said.

Dale said, looking at her drink, 'Rufus did.'

'Hey!' Lucas said. 'Cool it! Poor old Rufus. He's your half-brother, remember!'

'He wouldn't be,' Dale said, 'if it wasn't for Josie.'

'Look,' Lucas said. He leaned forward, his elbows on his knees. 'Look. Josie's gone. Josie's over. Dad doesn't have to pay another penny to Josie. He gave her some money to help buy a house, but he isn't supporting her because she's married this Matthew guy. He just has to support and educate Rufus as he did us and then Rufus'll find a job and be independent.'

'OK,' Dale said. 'OK, OK. Forget Rufus. It's this new woman I'm bothered about.'

'What new woman?'

'She's called Elizabeth Brown. She's a client of Dad's. Her father used to run that antiquarian bookshop off Queen's Square. The drawings of her house are all over Dad's office.'

'So what are you so fussed about? Dad has a client who happens to be a woman—'

'I heard him on the phone,' Dale said, 'asking her to have lunch with him. Or dinner or something.'

'Can't he have a meal with someone sometimes?' Lucas said.

'Of course. There was just something about his voice. You know. You can't hide it, in your voice, if you're talking to someone special.'

'You're jumping to conclusions.'

'I'm not. He looks happy.'

'He's that sort of bloke. He usually looks happy—'

'No,' Dale said. 'No. Not just things-are-OK happy, but things-are-exciting-and-wonderful happy.'

'So?'

Dale banged her glass down on the coffee table.

'Stop pretending you don't bloody *mind*!'

Lucas got up from the sofa. He went over to the drinks tray and poured a bottle of slimline tonic water into a glass, and then a splash of vodka and then a neat wedge of lemon and two ice cubes.

From behind him Dale said accusingly, 'Next thing you'll be saying is you didn't mind Josie!'

Lucas didn't turn. He looked at his bookshelves, at his collection of contemporary male novelists, of modern poets, of travel books. He hadn't minded Josie, in the end. In fact, once he had got over his eighteen-year-old shock that his father could give his love to anyone in the world but himself and Dale, he had begun, quite early on in his relationship with Josie, to feel that the house was better for having her in it. It felt more balanced, it had more vitality. And he had, from the first, liked Rufus. It was disconcerting to imagine Rufus's conception, because Lucas, deeply preoccupied with his own turbulent teenage sexual drive at the time, was thrown to think of his father being driven—even temporarily—by the same urges. But once Rufus was there, he seemed to make no special claims and, to their credit, neither Tom nor Josie made any special claims for him. He was the baby, like Basil was the cat, and in his father's attitude to Rufus—almost diffident at first—Lucas sensed an element that had never occurred to him before. He began to see, or thought he could see, that his father felt guilty; guilty for impregnating Josie in the first place, guilty about the carelessness that that implied over the one thing you should never, ever be careless about—human life. Maybe he'd married Josie out of guilt and that guilt had compounded another guilt about introducing as radical an element as a stepmother into the stable Carver household. All these thoughts had knocked about together for some years in Lucas's head. Once or twice, he'd tried to talk to Dale about it, to suggest to her the complex humanity that might exist in a father you thought you knew inside out. But there was something in Dale that couldn't hear him. She was deafened by what she felt for her father, by her need for him.

Lucas turned slowly from the bookcase. Amy had swung her legs up onto the sofa and was lying along it, her eyes half-closed. Dale was sitting back, her arms tightly crossed, as if she was containing something dangerous or painful. They might have been in separate rooms for all the consciousness they showed of one another. Lucas wished, and not for the first time, that his fiancée and his sister would realise that there was plenty of him to go round.

'Dale,' Lucas said.

She didn't look at him.

'Dale. Dad's not going to marry again.'

Amy opened her eyes.

'Think about it,' Lucas said. 'Just think. He lost Mum tragically and he was on his own for over ten years. He didn't try to marry anyone all that time, did he? We were there and we know he didn't. I think he had his reasons for marrying Josie, and they weren't, on the whole, just because he was mad about her. He was fond of her, and she was pregnant. You *know* that, Dale. You saw it. And then she left him, and he was shattered. He couldn't believe that anyone he'd done so much for could treat him like that. He was in pieces, wasn't he? We were really worried about him during the divorce. Remember? Now—' Lucas paused and took a breath. Dale was very still.

'Now,' Lucas said with emphasis, moving across the room to stand over his sister. 'Now, is a man like Dad, a man with a personality like Dad's, with two—in different ways—such bitter experiences of the end of marriage, ever going to risk it again?'

Dale unfolded her arms and reached for her drink.

'But he's lonely. Now we're living away from home and—Josie's gone, he's lonely.'

'Sure. But the solution isn't marriage, for God's sake. The solution, for Dad, is enough work, which he has, and the companionship of a few Elizabeth Browns. All the advantages and no strings.'

Amy said, from the sofa, 'Would you like that, Lucas?'

He took no notice.

'Dale. Dale. Dad is not going to re-marry. Do you hear me? Dad is not *going to re-marry.*'

Dale looked at her drink for a long moment and then she looked up at her brother.

'Promise?' she said.

After Dale had gone—she was plainly hoping to be offered supper, but Lucas seemed to forget to suggest it and Amy, though she remembered, certainly wasn't going to—Amy boiled some pasta and tipped into it a tub of pesto sauce from the supermarket and laid the island counter of their tiny kitchen with two mats and two forks and a candle.

She didn't drink alcohol herself—didn't like the taste—but she put out a wineglass for Lucas.

Then the telephone rang. It was the producer of the late-night phone-in chat-and-music show at the radio station to say that the presenter's three-year-old had been rushed to hospital with suspected meningitis, and could Lucas stand in?

'Don't,' Amy said.

'Got to,' Lucas said. He looked at her. 'Sorry. Think of the extra money.'

'I'd rather have you here—'

'Can't do it. Think of that poor kid, and how her parents feel.'

Amy thought how nice it would be if she believed Lucas ever considered how she was feeling. When they first met, his thoughtfulness was one of the first things she'd found attractive, but after he'd asked her to marry him and she had moved in with him, he didn't seem to feel that considering her feelings mattered so much.

'OK,' Amy said. 'You go.'

He leaned forward and kissed her.

'We'll go out tomorrow, promise. Or Friday.'

She nodded. He picked up his leather jacket and a bunch of keys.

'Sleep well,' Lucas said.

Amy went back into the kitchen and scraped the pasta off their two plates and into the bin. Then she put two slices of toast into the toaster and plugged the kettle in. On the draining board sat the mug she had been drinking from earlier, and Lucas and Dale's vodka tumblers.

Lucas had told Amy that Dale had been absolutely devastated by their mother's death. She'd only been five, and a very dependent, mummy-clinging five at that. When Tom told his children that their mother was dead, in the hospital, and would never be able to come home any more, Dale had rushed upstairs and burrowed into her mother's side of the double bed and refused to come out. Then she'd had hysterics. Lucas told Amy he would never forget it: the darkened bedroom with only one lamp on and his distraught father bending over the screaming, twisting child on the bed and he, Lucas, standing in the shadows full of a weight so heavy he thought he might just break into pieces.

Then Dale transferred her fierce affections to her father. She screamed when he wouldn't let her sleep with him. She would creep down in the night and try to defy him by getting into his bed when he was asleep and wouldn't notice her. Amy had wondered, aloud, why Tom didn't get some help with her.

'He did. There was someone called Doris who was there after school, if he wasn't.'

'I mean shrink help,' Amy said.

Lucas flinched a little.

'He knew what was wrong,' Lucas said. 'It was Mum dying that was wrong. He felt—'

'What?'

'Well, I guess he felt it was up to him to put it right.'

But he hasn't, Amy thought. Fathers can't. Fathers don't know how to deal with daughters because they're men and men never grow up really whereas most women are born grown-up. Except Dale. You could look at Dale now, all got up with her suits and briefcase, without a hair out of place, and still see that kid on the bed, kicking and screaming and scaring the hell out of her father and brother.

Amy took the two pieces of toast out of the toaster and flipped them quickly onto the breadboard. She liked Tom Carver; she thought he was a nice bloke and he spoke to her as if he could really see her. But when Amy saw something in Dale affecting Lucas, affecting him in a way that distracted him from everything but his work, that got to Amy where it hurt the most.

Dale lay in the bath. The water was scented with lavender oil—they'd recommended it to her, at the alternative health centre in Bath, for stress— and there was no light except a candle. She had her eyes closed and was trying, with a steady, rippling movement of her hands that washed the warm water across her breasts and stomach, to emulate that soothing, repetitive movement in her mind.

After she had left Lucas's flat, Dale had driven home to her flat on the edge of Bristol, with her mind still burdened. She had bought the flat with Neil, because he said his career chances were better in Bristol, with the theatre and big broadcasting presence, and she had agreed, partly because she liked agreeing with him and partly because she was delighted to find that, because of him, she could contemplate leaving Bath. Even for somewhere only a dozen miles away. But when Neil left, he seemed to take the charm of the flat in Bristol with him. He took very few things, but he managed to take a great deal of atmosphere. A flat which had seemed to offer stimulus, satisfaction, retreat and self-sufficiency dwindled overnight into just somewhere to live.

Dale thought about Lucas. She appreciated how patient Lucas was with her and how much he had genuinely, all her life, sought to reassure her. Even choosing Amy was a kind of reassurance in itself, because Amy could never be considered as a threat or a challenge to Dale, or to the relationship between Dale and Lucas. Even when she was jealous— 'And I,' she had told Neil once, laughing at her own ability to admit such a thing, '*invented* jealousy'—she acknowledged it wasn't because of anything Amy did or even because of Amy's presence. It was because she, Dale, was in a jealous mood.

Her jealousy, she sometimes thought, grew out of fear, the fear she had had all her life, that everyone she loved and needed would, in the end, leave her.

There had even been a small lurch of panic when Josie left. She had wanted her to go, had connived at it, but, when she saw the devastation Josie's departure wreaked upon her father, she didn't feel so much triumph as fear that Tom would leave her and Lucas and go off after Josie. Neil had grown very exasperated with her about that. Looking back, it was probably the beginning of the end of their relationship. He said it was impossible to live with someone who was so deliberately, intentionally irrational.

'It feels real to me!' Dale cried.

The bath water was getting cold. Dale stopped swishing her hands about and fumbled in the dimness for the soap. Her friend Ruth had said to her once, in those black weeks after Neil had gone, that she'd got to realise that love wasn't owning people, having them right by you in case you needed them; it was, instead, setting them free, letting them go.

'And another thing. There isn't a finite amount of love to go round so there's a danger someone else might nick your share. Some people can love only one person, some can love hundreds, but it doesn't mean it's the same amount of love in each case. I might fall in love again, mightn't I? So will you. But when I do, I won't love my kids any less, any more than you'll stop loving your brother and father.'

Dale stood up in the bath and reached for a towel. She wrapped it round herself, like a sarong, under her arms, and stepped out of the water. Then she padded across to the sitting room to where the telephone lay. She picked up the receiver and dialled Tom's number. It rang out and then the message on his answering machine clicked in.

'You have reached Tom Carver Associates. I am afraid there is no one—'

Dale put the receiver down and stood looking at it. Tom was out. She clenched her teeth slightly. With whom?

Chapter FIVE

'WON'T YOU COME IN?' Matthew said gently to Rufus.

Rufus sat on the low garden wall with his back to the house and kicked his trainered heels against it in a steady rhythm. Elaine had just brought him back. She had parked her car outside the house, and Rufus had got out of it slowly and submitted to Josie's hug, and then mutely declined to go indoors. He had, instead, moved out of her embrace to sit on the wall and kick his heels.

'I should leave him,' Elaine said. She raised her voice just a little so that Rufus could hear her. 'He can come in if he gets cold.'

Josie had looked anxiously down the street. It was an unremarkable residential street, lined with pairs of semidetached houses, all built in the late seventies, all just like their own. Some of the gardens were neat and empty, some were densely, busily planted, but most just indicated the random preoccupied nature of family life. Josie didn't know anyone in the street yet, didn't know what kind of street it was, whether it was safe for an eight-year-old to sit out in.

'Come in,' she said coaxingly to Rufus. 'Come in. We've brought you a present.'

He didn't look at her.

'No, thank you,' Rufus said.

Josie and Elaine went into the house. Rufus didn't turn, but he sensed, rather than saw, that they were by the sitting-room window watching him. He thought of getting up and walking off, but he couldn't quite summon up the rebelliousness for that. Nor did he want to frighten Josie. He just wanted her to know, in a way she could make no mistake about, that 17 Barratt Road might be the place she had taken him to live, but it was not his home. It was, instead, a very hard place for him to be and he wanted to make this extremely plain. To Josie, to his grandmother, to—Matthew.

It seemed a long time until someone came out to him, so long that he was really quite cold and was beginning to notice that it was getting dark. Some of the houses down the street already had their Christmas trees up and Rufus could see the lights. They were mostly coloured lights which Rufus knew were in some way inferior to plain white ones. He supposed they'd have a tree at No. 17. He didn't much want one but you sort of had to, at Christmas. Despite the sparkling trees in the street, Rufus couldn't believe that Christmas was coming. It didn't feel Christmassy at all, away from Bath and with the prospect of Matthew's children coming. Rufus kicked harder. Matthew's children were a problem to him that Josie didn't even seem to begin to understand. He heard footsteps on the concrete strips of the drive—not Josie's footsteps—and then he observed, out of the corner of his eye, that Matthew was sitting on the low wall about eight feet away. Matthew didn't speak. He sat facing the opposite way to Rufus and he had his hands in his pockets. Rufus hunched his shoulders.

'Won't you come in?' Matthew said after a while.

Rufus said nothing. He didn't want to go in, but he was beginning not to want to stay outside, either.

'I won't come in with you,' Matthew said. 'I've got something to do in the garage. If you go in it'll only be Mum and Granny.'

Rufus ducked his head. He muttered something.

'What?'

'It's not that—'

'No,' Matthew said, 'I don't expect it is. But it's all I can think of, at the moment, to help you.'

He looked at the house. The lights were on in the sitting room and Josie and Elaine were seated on the sofa and in an armchair, with mugs of tea. The armchair came from the house Matthew had shared with Nadine and Josie had found the sofa on a skip.

Half their furniture had been obtained that way, the half that wasn't Matthew's or didn't belong to Josie from her years in Bath. On the other side of Sedgebury, stacked in a local garage belonging to a friend of Matthew's who wasn't using it, was Nadine's share of their joint furniture. She had refused to take it to Herefordshire with the same vehemence that she had refused to use her share of the proceeds from the sale of the previous family home to buy a flat in Sedgebury. Matthew knew she had bought a car, but he didn't know what else she had done with the money. There hadn't been much of it, heaven knows, after they'd paid off the mortgage, but there was enough for Nadine to make a mess of, or even just to lose. She lost money like other people lost socks in the wash. It used to drive him insane.

He glanced at Rufus. It was quite dark now, but he could still see his face faintly, staring down at his relentlessly kicking feet. Rufus had come into Matthew's life with his own money, Tom Carver's money, which would feed him and clothe him and send him on school trips. It was, of course, right that it should be so, right that Tom Carver should support his own son, but there was something about Tom Carver's money being in Matthew's household that was difficult to bear. Matthew was worried about money—without Josie's help, he'd never have been able to put down the deposit on this house—but that didn't stop him preferring the independence of anxiety to the need to acknowledge that another man's money was helping him to scrape by. Josie had said that almost all the money she had put into the house was her own, money she had saved from her teaching job in Bath, but, looking at some of her clothes and her possessions, Matthew sometimes wondered if she was being tactful. Too tactful, perhaps, almost patronising, as if she thought that the truth about her money was something he couldn't be expected to handle. And he felt that, felt it keenly.

Cars were beginning to come down Barratt Road, their headlights swooping up and down as they negotiated the ridges in the road that the council had put there to slow them up. Some of them caught Rufus and Matthew in a brief yellow glare and showed Matthew that Rufus was shivering.

'You have to come in.' He stood up and came to put a hand on Rufus's shoulder. 'Come on.'

Rufus sprang away from him onto the pavement, then he ducked sideways through the drive gate and tore up the concrete strips to the house. Matthew heard the door open then slam. Then he saw, in the lit sitting room ahead of him, Josie rising to greet Rufus who was coming into the room very slowly, the picture of deep reluctance. My Josie, Matthew thought, stirred at the sight of her. Mine. He saw her try to put her arms round Rufus and Rufus gracefully elude her to sit on the sofa by his grandmother. Matthew turned away and began to walk towards the garage. Mine—and also someone else's, long before me.

Clare stood in the bedroom doorway.

'Is this where I'm sleeping?'

'Yes,' Josie said. She was smiling. It had taken her several days to get the girls' room ready, including extracting, from the locked garage, duvet covers and pillowcases that belonged to Matthew's children. She had laundered these, and made up the beds with them, and bought bedside lamps and a pinboard and put down a white wool Greek rug that used to lie on the floor of Rufus's nursery in Bath, when he was a baby. The results were very pleasing. Matthew, who had painted the walls and put up dark blue curtains patterned with stars which Josie had found in a charity shop, said the girls would be thrilled. They'd never, he said, had a room half so pretty. He had taken Josie in his arms and kissed her.

'Our first Christmas together. And you're putting so much into it.'

'I like doing it,' she said. It was true. She did like it, did relish the feeling that she was doing something to stabilise the lives of Matthew's children who, it was plain, had always lived in a very uncertain and irregular way. Josie had only had one encounter with Nadine, which had been brief and disconcerting but had left her with the hope that Nadine would not be a hard act to follow.

'They're afraid of her,' Josie said to Matthew.

He had looked doubtful.

'Yes, they are,' she'd said and then she'd said it again, insisting, 'They're afraid of her moods.'

'I think,' Matthew said unhappily, 'that they love her.'

Even if they did, Josie told herself, brushing out the fringe on the Greek rug, it wouldn't prevent them from seeing how good it was, how reassuring, to have meals at regular intervals and a clean, cheerful house and no rows. There would certainly be no rows. Rows, Matthew said, had punctuated his life with Nadine with relentless regularity, sending china and children flying. Josie had been shocked, listening to him. She and Tom had argued, certainly, mostly about Dale—but neither of them had ever thrown anything. It wouldn't have occurred to them and, if she had her way, it would soon not occur to Matthew's children either, as a means of communication. She would be very patient with them, she told herself, *very*, and not ask or expect anything in return for months. She felt, being in charge of the house and the family, that she would have endless patience with the members of it in return for that power, a power she had never really had in the house in Bath because she had walked into it already complete with the Carver family and all their habits and traditions, including—and this had been abidingly hard— the ghost of Tom's dead wife, Pauline. Pauline, canonised by dying so young and so unjustly, pervaded the house with a subtle strength that Josie would have respected if she hadn't felt so threatened by it. Nadine, by comparison with Pauline, was a most manageable opponent; she was clearly a rotten mother, a lousy housekeeper, and she was alive.

Clare dropped three or four bulging carrier bags on the floor by the nearest bed. Various grubby garments flopped out.

'Do you like it?' Josie said.

Clare said nothing.

'Those are your duvet covers and pillowcases—'

Clare gave the beds a cursory, indifferent glance.

'Are they?'

'Yes. Aren't you pleased to see them again?'

Clare began to fiddle with her bottom cardigan button. 'I don't remember them.'

'I hope,' Josie said, persisting, 'that I've put them on the right beds. I've put yours there, and Becky's on the bed by the window.'

'Becky won't sleep by the window,' Clare said. 'She only uses the window to chuck her fag ends out of.'

Josie smiled.

'Sorry, but I don't want her smoking in here.'

Clare sighed. She trailed across the room, stumbling over the Greek rug and rucking it up, and looked at the pinboard.

'What's that for?'

'Posters. Your posters and postcards and maybe paintings you do at school.'

'In my year,' Clare said, 'we do pottery.'

'Well, surely you've got some posters, haven't you?'

Josie stooped to flick the rug straight.

'Becky likes Oasis,' Clare said. 'They won't fit up there.'

'Clare,' Josie said, 'I'll leave you to kind of look about. Open cupboards and things. You know where the bathroom is.'

Clare shot her a quick glance.

'I'm not using the bathroom,' Becky had said that morning, on Hereford station. 'I'm not sitting where she's sat.'

'What you gonna do then?' Rory said.

Becky blew out a cloud of smoke.

'Crap in the garden.'

Rory and Clare had taken no notice of this. Becky had long ago lost the power to shock them. But Nadine, waiting with them until the train came, had cackled with laughter. Something in Clare had wished that Nadine didn't always make something much harder which was hard enough anyway.

Clare turned her head and stared out of the window. If she put toilet paper on the seat, maybe it would be OK to sit where Josie sat. As long as Becky didn't see her doing it.

'We haven't decorated the tree,' Josie said, 'have we, Rufus? We left it for you and Rory to do, didn't we?'

Her voice sounded false to her, bright and silly like a parody of a nursery-school teacher.

She said to Rory, 'Did you do a tree for your mother in Herefordshire?'

'No,' he said. He wore, as all the children did, the same clothes he had worn for the wedding. He stood beside the boxes of Christmas-tree ornaments and bags of silver tinsel, gnawing at a cuticle on one thumb. He had a spot, Josie noticed, on one side of his nose and a generally stale air, as if neither he nor his clothes had been washed for weeks.

'Come on,' Josie said to Rufus.

Rufus bent and picked up the box of Christmas-tree lights.

'These are new ones—'

'I know.'

He looked at her. He gave her a long, steady glance of reproach for having Christmas-tree lights which were different from the tremendously long string of little white lights, bought by Tom, which adorned the tree each year in Bath.

'I couldn't get plain,' Josie said. She should have said, truthfully, that the coloured ones, bought from a Sikh trader in Sedgebury market, had been the cheapest she could find.

'These are common,' Rufus said disdainfully. 'They should be white.'

Josie put her hands up to her hair and adjusted the band that held it back from her face.

'They're all we've got.'

'Where's the telly?' Rory said.

Josie pointed.

'There.'

Rory made as if to move towards it.

'When you've done the tree,' Josie said. 'Come on, it's lovely doing the tree.' It was too, once, with Tom in charge and tiny Rufus laboriously hanging things on the lowest branches and even Dale, in the end, joining in. It was one of the few moments increasingly, in the year, when Josie could feel that she had been right to marry Tom, that they had a good life together, that it didn't matter that she couldn't love him as she had always hoped she would love a husband, with that excited, triumphant love that she had tried to *make* happen, defiantly, marching up the aisle, nearly five months pregnant, in an ivory corded silk dress cut high under the bust, like a medieval dress, to disguise her growing bump. Now, of course, that kind of love was easy. She only had to think of Matthew, let alone see him, to feel a leap inside her, like a flame or a jet of water. She had wondered, at the beginning, if this exhilaration was just sex, but it was still here, almost eighteen months after that first meeting at the conference in Cheltenham, and not only here, but stronger. She loved Matthew, she *loved* him. And it was Matthew's child, standing in her sitting room, who was being so obdurate about a task which had always managed to lift Josie's heart.

'OK,' she said to the boys. 'OK. I'll challenge you. I'll challenge you to take these inferior lights and all the other tacky things that you so plainly despise and *make* something of this tree. I'm going to get lunch. What about spaghetti bolognese?'

Neither boy indicated that he had even heard her.

'I'll be twenty minutes,' Josie said. 'And then I'll come back in here and expect to be amazed, OK?'

She looked at them. Rufus, sighing, took the lid off the box of lights and Rory, still chewing his thumb, bent to flick out of the nearest bag with his free hand a skein of silver tinsel. Josie went out of the sitting room and closed the door. Rufus looked at Rory. Rory didn't look back. Instead, he dropped the tinsel and ambled over to the television.

'Where's the remote control?' he said.

Becky had been smoking. When she finally dawdled into the kitchen for lunch, she brought a strong waft of cigarette smoke with her. She was wearing her denim jacket and a long black skirt with a rip in it, and her hands were almost obscured in thick mittens knitted of black and fuchsia-pink and emerald-green wool. She was also carrying something screwed up in an old white plastic bag, and when she sat down she dumped the thing in the bag on the straw tablemat in front of her.

Josie, standing by the stove with a ladle for helping out the pasta, decided to wait and say nothing. This wasn't easy. Nothing that morning had been easy and tears and temper were knotting themselves up inside her chest and throat in a way she couldn't remember them doing since the early days as Tom's wife, when sixteen-year-old Dale talked incessantly and directly, to her father, about her dead mother. This morning's troubles had been different in kind, but no less upsetting in intensity. There had been no attempt by Matthew's children to unpack nor to evince the slightest interest in the house or the possibilities of the life they might live there. Becky had even left her bags outside the back door, refusing to look at her bedroom at all, and had then vanished. When Josie went upstairs to see if Clare was all right, she found the bedroom just as they had both left it and the bathroom floor mysteriously strewn with pieces of unused but crumpled lavatory paper. There was no sign that either soap or a towel had been touched. In Rufus's room, which Rory was to share, Rory's rucksack sat directly in the doorway, as if poised for flight straight back out again.

It was at that moment that Josie thought she heard the television. She went downstairs and opened the sitting-room door. On the floor, lolling on cushions dragged off the sofa and chairs, lay Rory and Clare. Rory was holding the television remote control and was flicking rapidly through the channels. Clare was sucking her thumb. Rufus, looking miserable, was looping tinsel and glass balls onto the tree, all on one side and as far away from the others as possible. He shot Josie a glance as she came in. Rory and Clare didn't look up.

Josie had taken a deep breath.

'Please turn that off.'

Rory took no notice. Josie stepped forward and took the remote control out of Rory's hand.

'Jesus—'

'What did you say?'

'Jesus,' Rory said tiredly. He rolled over on the cushions.

Josie turned the television off and put the remote control in the back pocket of her jeans. She said to Clare, 'Won't you help Rufus?'

Clare looked at the tree.

'He's done it.'

'No, he hasn't. He's only done one side.'

Clare got, very slowly, to her feet. She picked up a red glass ball and hung it on the only part of the tree that was already densely decorated.

'There.'

'That's no good,' Josie said. She tried to keep her voice light. 'Is it? Three-quarters of the tree is absolutely bare still.'

From the floor Rory said, his voice muffled by the cushion his face was pressed into, 'Who's gonna look at it anyhow?'

'We are,' Josie said. 'You four children, and your father, and me. It's a Christmas tree for—for the family.'

The moment the word was out of her mouth she wished she hadn't said it. Each child became suddenly and perfectly still and the room filled with a palpable air of cold offendedness. She bit her lip. Should she say sorry? Should she say oops, sorry, my mistake, shouldn't have said that word so soon? She looked at them. Then something rose in her, something that elbowed out of the way her first feelings of apology, of needing to acknowledge her first failure at being angelically, superhumanly patient.

'It's a word,' Josie said to the still children. 'Family is a word. So is stepfamily. Stepfamily is a word in the dictionary too whether you like it or not. And it's not just a word, it's a fact, and it's a fact that we all are now, whether you like that or not, either.' She paused, then she said to Rory, 'Get up.'

He didn't move.

'Get up,' Josie said. 'Get up and put those cushions back.'

With infinite slowness, he dragged himself to his feet and began to dump the cushions back on the sofa and chairs.

'Properly,' Josie said. Out of the corner of her eye, she could see Rufus silently imploring her not to antagonise Rory. 'Go on.'

Rory sighed.

'You heard me.'

Clare moved from her position by the tree and began to sort the cushions out. She kept her head bent so that Josie couldn't see her face. Rory watched her, his hands in his pockets.

'If your father was here,' Josie said, 'is this how you'd go on?'

Clare put the last sofa-seat cushion back, the wrong way round so that the zip showed.

'Where is Dad?'

Her voice sounded as if she were on the verge of tears.

'At school,' Josie said.

'I want him,' Clare said. Her eyes were brimming.

Me, too, Josie thought. Oh God and how. Me, too.

She tried to touch Clare and Clare twisted away and hid herself behind her brother.

'He'll be back soon. He'll be back after lunch.' She fought down the urge to scream and said instead, 'Shall we have lunch?'

'I don't want any,' Becky said now.

'Won't you take your mittens off?' Josie said.

Becky put her hands on the table.

'I'm cold.'

'But you can't eat in mittens—'

'I'm not eating,' Becky said, glancing over at Josie and the steaming pans on the cooker, 'that.'

Rufus looked blanched with tension.

Josie said, 'Everyone likes pasta. Everyone likes spag bol.'

Becky gave her a brief, pale blue glance.

'I don't.'

Josie took a breath.

'Did you have breakfast?'

'No,' Becky said.

'Have you had anything to eat all day?'

Becky said nothing.

'Look,' Josie said, 'if you left Hereford at eight something and it's now half past one and you haven't had anything to eat, you must be starving.'

She ladled pasta and sauce onto a plate and put it down in front of Rufus.

Becky began to fumble with the knot she had tied to secure the plastic bag. She said to Clare, 'Where's a plate?'

'I don't know—'

Clare looked across at Rufus.

'Where's a plate?'

Rufus turned towards his mother. Josie held out a plate to him from the pile in front of her.

She said to Becky, 'Do you just want salad?'

'No,' Becky said.

Rufus passed the plate to Clare and Clare, without looking at him, gave it to her sister. Becky put it on her tablemat and put the plastic bag on top. Then she went back to fumbling with the knot. Josie helped out two more plates of pasta and put them in front of Clare and Rory. Neither acknowledged that she had done so. They were watching Becky. So was Rufus. They were all concentrating on what would be revealed when Becky got the knot undone.

Josie gave herself a small portion of pasta and went round the table to the place she had deliberately laid for herself between Becky and Rory. She sat down.

Very slowly, Becky unravelled the last of the knot, peeled back the sides of the carrier bag and tipped onto her plate, with enormous care, a lump of greyish rice studded with smaller lumps of orangey red and soft-looking black.

Josie stared at it.

'What's that?'

'Risotto,' Becky said. Her voice was proud. 'Mum made it.'

She glanced at Rory and Clare, daring them to object, daring them to say that, when Nadine had cooked the risotto the previous night, they had all flatly refused to eat it and there'd been a row about that, and then another row a bit later when Nadine had found Clare and Rory under the eaves with a plastic bag of sliced white bread, cramming it wordlessly into their mouths in great hungry unchewed bites.

'I thought you weren't hungry,' Josie said, looking at the mess on Becky's plate.

'I said I didn't like spaghetti.'

'I see. So while we eat this hot, newly cooked food, you are going to eat cold risotto?'

'Yes,' Becky said. She looked across the table at Rufus. 'I've got more,' she said to him. Her voice was conversational, almost pleasant. 'I've got enough to last me till I go home again. I don't need to eat anything here.'

Chapter
SIX

'DAD,' DALE SAID, 'we've got to have a tree.'

Tom Carver took his reading glasses off.

'I'd rather not.'

'Why?'

'You may not like me saying this, but I don't want a tree because of Rufus.'

'But Rufus isn't here.'

'Precisely. But last year, he was. Rufus and I went out and chose a tree and brought it back and decorated it together.'

Dale stopped fiddling about with the liquidiser and came to sit at the table opposite Tom.

'Dad.'

'Yes.'

'May I point out that you've still got us? Lucas and me? Your first-born children?'

'I know. And nothing and nobody will ever replace you. But Rufus is my child also, and since he was born, I have never had a Christmas without him and I'm not looking forward to it.'

'Thanks a million,' Dale said.

Tom reached across the table for her hand. She removed it just far enough away for him not to be able to touch her.

'He's eight,' Tom said. 'Little boys—and girls for that matter—give Christmas another dimension. You know they do. And another thing. It's just too soon for me to feel that Christmas is as Christmas was when Rufus was here.'

'Well,' Dale said. She could feel her voice hardening and was not, somehow, able to stop it. 'Well, it may be too soon to play at Christmases again, but it doesn't seem to be too soon to play at having a girlfriend.'

'Elizabeth Brown, I suppose you mean.'

'Yes.'

'Friend. Not girlfriend.'

Dale said nothing. She got up and ladled a scoop of chopped leeks and vegetable stock into the liquidiser.

'How do you know about her?'

'I looked at the plans in your studio. I heard you on the telephone. And you haven't been here on three nights when I've rung. You're always here, always.'

'Dale, I have had two meals with Elizabeth Brown,' Tom said. 'And she has come down from London on three weekday evenings, once for a concert, once for the cinema, and once for a private view of a painter friend of her father's.'

Dale flicked the switch on the liquidiser briefly, and the thick greenish liquid swelled against the sides.

'But you've never done that before.'

'No. Because I was married. I went to concerts and the cinema with Josie and you didn't like that much either.'

'Josie was OK,' Dale said.

'You can say that now, because she's gone. But I need a life, Dale. I'm a human being, as well as being your father.'

She looked directly at him, smiling.

'But you're my father first.'

He smiled back.

'Of course. Always will be.'

She came round the table and leaned against him. He put his arm round her. She bent down and put her cheek against his. It was smooth and cool and faintly resilient, as Pauline's had always been.

'Dad.'

'Yes?'

'We can have a Christmas tree, can't we?'

'I'm so sorry,' Tom had said to Elizabeth, 'that I can't see you over Christmas.'

'That's fine,' she said. She meant it. She had known him after all for only a month or two, and only the last few weeks of those months had signified anything even faintly more than mere friendship. He'd simply seemed very pleased to see her each time they met, and had not said goodbye without arranging for another meeting. If he had suddenly said that he wanted to see her at Christmas, Elizabeth would have been surprised, even a little disconcerted. He had children, didn't he? And he knew she had her father. Christmas was such an accepted family time.

'What,' he said, 'do you and your father do at Christmas?'

'Oh, we go to Midnight Mass in the abbey, and we go for a walk and I cook something for him that isn't tinned soup and we have rather too much to drink with it and after it and go to bed quite early.'

208

'Very decorous.'

'Very. And you?'

Tom had paused. Then he said, 'I'm afraid we rather relive the Christmas we've always had. Crackers, tree, everything. Dale—Dale wants us to have stockings again. It was all perfectly seemly when Rufus was around, but without him I feel as if we're insisting that nothing has changed when it has.'

'But Dale is still your child—'

'Of twenty-five.'

Looking back on that conversation, Elizabeth had a small but certain feeling that Tom was in some way asking for her sympathy. He had suggested, with infinite lightness, that Dale was somehow too much for him, too strong, too decided in what she wanted and also in the implications of those desires. Elizabeth had seen photographs of Dale in Tom's house, and photographs of her older brother Lucas. They were not pretty, or handsome, but very good-looking with strong features and even teeth and shining hair. Tom had told Elizabeth about Dale, and how violently her mother's death had affected her. Elizabeth had listened politely. When her own mother had died, she had felt no depth of grief. When her father died, she knew it would be different and she would experience all the intensity of losing an extraordinary ally while having, for the first time in her life, no one to stand between her and the stars. She wondered at the raw need behind the outward poise that drove Dale to try to exert some kind of control through insisting on a stocking, still, on Christmas morning. She wondered, too, if behind Tom's 'Very decorous' comment on hers and Duncan's Christmas lay just a hint of envy. There was no glamour to the Browns' Christmas, that was quite certain, but there was an adult freedom to it. The thought that a man like Tom Carver could look at anything she, Elizabeth, possessed or did with envy or admiration gave her, to her surprise, a sudden thrill of tiny but significant power.

On Christmas Eve, Tom Carver said he would like to go to Midnight Mass in the abbey.

'Why?' Dale said.

'I feel that I'd like to.'

'But you never go to church. You don't believe in all that stuff. I bet the last time you went to church was when you married Josie and you only did that to please her.'

Tom picked up Basil from where he lay on the kitchen table and carried him over to the garden window at the end of the kitchen. He hadn't been in the garden for weeks and it had a wet, dark, flattened look, a winter sulkiness about it. Even the sweet stone statue of a girl holding a dove, which he so loved, looked as if she'd had enough. He and Josie had found her in an architectural reclamation yard just before their marriage and had pounced on her with relief, as if she was a symbol for them both, a symbol of hope and harmony. It was something of the same hope that had carried Tom into church on his second wedding day, an anticipation that by marrying Josie in such a place—whatever it did or didn't mean to him—would somehow open up the possibility of making his relationship with Josie as profound as his relationship with Pauline had been. He bent and rubbed his chin slowly across Basil's obliging broad head. He hadn't thought Pauline was perfect but he had preferred being married to her to being married to Josie. Except for Rufus. Whatever the lost perfections of Pauline, it was Josie who had given him Rufus. And it was something to do with Rufus that made the idea of an hour in Bath Abbey at midnight suddenly strongly alluring. He turned round.

'Dale.'

'Yes?'

'You've got your Christmas tree and Christmas stocking?'

'Yes.'

'So I am going to Midnight Mass. You needn't come with me. I shall be quite happy to go alone. But I'm going.'

Dale came down the kitchen towards him. She was holding a mixing bowl of brandy butter. She held out a wooden spoon.

'Taste that.'

Tom took a small lick. Basil craned interestedly upwards, purring like a traction engine.

'Excellent.'

'More sugar?'

'No. Definitely not. I think you should stop playing the perfect housewife and go see a friend or something.'

Dale looked at him, her head slightly on one side.

'I'll probably come to the abbey.'

'Good.'

'I just do wonder why you've suddenly got the urge to go.'

Tom shrugged. He bent down and let Basil roll heavily out of his arms onto the floor. He waited, with resignation and a degree of dread, for Dale to continue, 'I suppose it's because you hope you'll see *her* at the abbey,' but she didn't. He heard the click of her boot heels go sharply back up the length of the kitchen, and then he straightened up.

'I'm going down to the basement.'

'Lunch?' Dale said. 'Soup? A filled croissant?'

He shook his head.

'No, thank you. Sweet of you, but no.'

She smiled at him.

'No trouble,' she said. She began to scrape the brandy butter briskly out of the mixing bowl into a green glass dish. 'It's just when I'm here, I like to look after you. That's all.'

Elizabeth couldn't see Tom in the abbey. It was packed, of course, hundreds of people, and he had never indicated that he would be there, but something in his faint unspoken envy of her own projected Christmas had made her feel there was the slightest possibility she might see him. She had a new haircut—much shorter—and a new overcoat, with a fake-fur collar and cuffs, and she had achieved both these startling changes on an impulse, just a few days before Christmas, amazing herself. Her father had admired both.

'Very becoming,' he'd said of her hair. 'Very. You look much younger and far less responsible. And a red coat. Red! I thought you were colourblind to every colour on earth but navy blue.'

He stood beside her now, peering at his hymnbook through reading glasses she had mended that afternoon with fuse wire.

Elizabeth felt very fond of him. She felt, if she thought about it, oddly fond of everyone round her, too, and of this abbey with its profusion of eighteenth-century monuments, and of her new haircut, and the glossy black cuffs of her new coat, and of Christmas and of England, and life. She felt she wanted to sing lustily and in a heartfelt way, pleased to be part of such a congregation, such an occasion, with Christmas about to break upon them all, intimate and immense all at once. She turned to Duncan and smiled at him. He winked.

From some distance away, Tom Carver, with Dale beside him, realised that it was indeed Elizabeth Brown over there, in a red coat with much shorter hair. He glanced at Dale. She had her hymnbook held up, almost ostentatiously, in front of her face and was singing with apparently solemn concentration. Tom pushed his reading glasses down his nose so that he could see comfortably at long-distance over the top of them and, singing still, fixed his gaze upon Elizabeth.

'Hello,' Elizabeth said.

Rufus regarded her. He had Basil in his arms and the possession of this huge fur pillow seemed excuse enough not to say anything.

Elizabeth smiled.

'I'm a friend of your father's. He's helping me with my new house.'

Rufus rubbed his face against Basil. This friend of his father's looked nice, normal and nice, unalarming. She had on the kind of skirt that the teachers in his old school in Bath used to wear, with pleats, very tidy-looking.

'Did you just get here?' Elizabeth said. She sat down on the arm of one of the chairs by the television so that she was more or less the same height as Rufus.

He nodded.

'Daddy met me.'

He closed his eyes for a moment. It had been such a relief to see his father and his father's car in that lay-by, where they had all agreed to meet, that he had wanted, to his shame, to cry. But he didn't because he felt guilty about Josie. They hadn't said much to each other, his mother and father, but concentrated on getting his bag and his gumboots and stuff from one car to another, and when Rufus was in his father's car, he had bent his head for ages over the fastening of the seat-belt buckle in case his mother saw his face and saw what he was feeling, to be back in his father's car at last.

Elizabeth put out a hand and touched one of Basil's nonchalantly dangling paws.

'Did you have a good Christmas?'

Basil was getting heavy. Rufus had to let him slither out of his grasp onto the sofa.

'I don't know—'

'I know what you mean,' Elizabeth said. 'When you look forward to something so much, you can't really believe it, when it happens. And then you can't decide if it's as good as you'd hoped it would be.'

Rufus began to kick gently at the leg of the sofa.

He said uncertainly, 'It was weird when they went away.'

She said gently, 'Who went away?'

'The others,' Rufus said. He stopped kicking and put his hands on the back of the sofa and began to spring up and down, his coppery-brown hair jumping with him. 'Their mother rang. So they went.'

'Oh,' Elizabeth said. 'You mean your stepfather's children.'

Rufus nodded. The telephone call had come quite late on Christmas Eve, after he was in bed and waiting rather tensely for Rory to be sent to join him. He'd heard his mother shout, 'Becky, it's for you,' in the voice she used when she was in a temper and trying to hide it, and then there'd been mutterings for a while, and then he'd heard the phone banged down and there was pandemonium. Becky had screamed and Josie had screamed and Clare had cried and Matthew had shouted and Rory had turned the television up so loud that the people next door began to bang on the party wall and yell at them all to shut up. After a bit, Rory came tearing into their room and started to ram all his stuff into his rucksack. Rufus reared up in bed.

'Where're you going?'

'Back to Mum's—'

'But it's Christmas—'

'Does it matter?' Rory said. He kept his face averted from Rufus. 'Does it bloody matter *what* it is?'

Rufus watched him. Then he heard the car being reversed down the drive to the gate and all the children thundered down the stairs and slammed the house doors and the car went roaring off. Then there was silence. The silence was worse than the noise had been. After a bit, Rufus got out of bed and went out onto the landing. His mother was sitting on the stairs, with her head in her hands.

'Are you crying?' Rufus said.

She looked up at him. Her eyes were dry.

'No.'

'Why've they gone?'

'Nadine told them to.'

'Oh.'

Josie held out an arm.

'I'd rather like a hug—'

Rufus had gone down the stairs and sat next to her.

'Are you pleased they've gone?'

He said slowly, 'I don't know—'

'I know,' she said. 'Nor do I. I want to kill Nadine. Why did Matthew give in?'

Rufus didn't know. He didn't know now. Matthew had been very quiet all Christmas Day, and he had dark rings under his eyes. Josie said Matthew was disappointed. The odd thing was that there was something disappointed in how Rufus felt, too, and that was troubling in itself.

'It's hard for you,' Elizabeth said now. 'It must be.'

Rufus stopped jumping. He was slightly out of breath. He hung over the sofa back. 'It's hard for you,' she'd said. She'd said it quite ordinarily, not in a soppy, sorry-for-you voice, but as if it were true, a fact, something that no one should pretend was otherwise. A feeling arose in Rufus that some kind of thankyou was called for.

He said, not looking at her, 'Would you like to see my bedroom?'

Chapter
SEVEN

NADINE LOOKED at the piece of cold pork in the larder. She wasn't sure how long you could go on eating meat after it had first been cooked, and she'd cooked this almost a week before, on Christmas Day. She couldn't remember cooking pork before—it had been one of the many things on the hit list of foods she would never touch—but it had been a present on Christmas morning, from the farmer half a mile away, along with a sack of potatoes and a bag of Brussels sprouts. If he hadn't come, she didn't know what they would have eaten. Food had hardly been uppermost in her mind when she'd telephoned Matthew's house and begged Becky not to leave her alone, all alone, for Christmas.

She'd agreed to meet Matthew halfway and retrieve the children. She hadn't wanted to, she'd wanted Matthew to come all the way to the cottage so he could see how she lived, what she was reduced to. But he had refused. He'd said if he had to go more than halfway, he wouldn't bring them at all, and in the background Nadine could hear Becky pleading with him and Clare crying. She imagined Josie and her son smirking with satisfaction in the background, with the central heating on and a bulging refrigerator. Then Matthew put the phone down on her and, when she tried to ring again, the answering machine was on and she was so afraid she might miss meeting the children that she had leapt straight into the car and driven off into the night.

The children looked exhausted. She had determined she would neither look at Matthew nor speak to him, but she saw enough to reassure herself that he looked exhausted too. And he looked scrawny, and much older. He'd hardly said goodbye, even to the children, but just let them get silently from one car to the other, only helping Clare with her bags. Clare looked as if she had been crying for weeks.

And then, a mile from home, Nadine's car had stopped. Just stopped, dead, in the middle of the road and would give nothing but a faint groan when Nadine turned the key. It was very dark and they had no torches. Nadine said, as cheerfully as she could, that they'd have to walk.

'No,' Becky said.

'But—'

'I'm not carrying all my stuff, and I'm not leaving it in the car either. It doesn't lock.'

Nadine said, with an edge of sarcasm, 'So what are you going to do instead, may I ask?'

'Go to the farm. The one the cows belong to.'

'But we don't know them—'

'Not yet,' Becky said.

She had made Rory go with her, and they had gone off in the dark and returned, in a surprisingly short time, in a Land Rover with a farmer called Tim Huntley. He was youngish and grinning, with heavy shoulders and hands. He winked at Nadine and told her she'd run out of petrol. He had filled the tank from a can in the back of his Land Rover.

'You all right in that cottage?' he said to Nadine.

'No. How could anyone be?'

He grinned.

'We never thought they'd let it again.'

'It was all we could afford,' Nadine said. She saw the children shrink back as she spoke. In the light of the Land Rover headlights, Tim Huntley looked at them all, consideringly.

'Hop out,' he said. 'I'll start her up.'

He got into the driver's seat and pumped the accelerator. Then he turned the key. The engine coughed and turned. He got out of the car and held the door open for Nadine.

'I'll be down in the morning,' he said, 'to see if she'll still fire.'

'Thank you—'

'No problem. Up at five for the cows anyhow.'

He'd come at nine on Christmas Day, dumping the meat and vegetables on the kitchen table. He patted the pork.

'One of ours. Should crackle well.'

Nadine had been in her dressing gown, with her hair down her back, making tea and apprehensively counting bread slices, to see if there were enough. She smiled at him.

'You are really, really kind.'

'It's nothing.'

'I mean it. Thank you.'

He had blushed very slightly and slapped the pork again.

'Thirty-five minutes to the pound. Hot oven. Don't salt the crackle.'

She had suddenly felt extremely happy, standing there in her kitchen with such a reassuring bulk of food on the table. She gave him a deliberate quick glance.

'I wouldn't dream of it—'

Later, she heard her car being started up in the lean-to, and later still she found a pile of logs outside the door. She'd said to the children, 'See? See? You were *meant* to be home for Christmas.'

They'd eaten the pork on Christmas Day and Boxing Day and on the day after, and then the children wouldn't eat it any more. Nadine put the rest of the meat in the damp larder, and baked potatoes instead for every meal. In between baked potatoes, the children did things she asked them to—washed up or brought wood in or emptied the kitchen bin—but listlessly, and at every opportunity escaped upstairs to do things with Christmas presents they tried to pretend they hadn't got. Nadine could hear the whine and tattoo-like beat of battery-operated games and Becky, under her mitten, was wearing a silver ring shaped like a fish curled round on itself. It came from the Indian craft shop in Sedgebury, Nadine was sure. It was probably the one Becky had wanted for her birthday but which Matthew, in one of his suburban frenzies about money, had said she couldn't have. But plainly she could have it now, couldn't she? Now that Becky had to be bribed to love him, to stay with him and the Randy Redhead in their dinky little house.

'Mum,' Becky said, from behind her.

'Do you think we could curry that?' Nadine said, pointing at the pork.

'No,' Becky said. 'Can we go into Ross?'

Nadine looked at her.

'No. Why?'

Becky twisted her hidden ring under her mitten.

'Just—wanted to—wanted to go somewhere.'

'What will you do if we go to Ross?'

Becky shrugged.

'Go round the shops—'

'With what?'

Becky muttered something. She ducked her head so that her hair fell forward. Josie had given her a black nylon wallet for Christmas with a ten-pound note in it.

'Did she give you money?' Nadine asked.

'A bit—'

'Don't you know,' Nadine demanded, 'when you're being bought, when someone is trying to *bribe* you?'

Becky thought of all those meals she had refused to eat, the beds she had declined to make, the washing-up she had just left, defying her father to push her towards the sink, to dare to touch her. Nadine's unfairness, in the face of this steady opposition to her father's new marriage, made her eyes water.

'How can you be so disloyal,' Nadine shouted suddenly, 'as to take anything from her?'

Becky moved away from the larder door and slumped in a chair by the kitchen table.

She said, into her hair, 'It's all the money I've got.'

'Hah!' Nadine said. She marched past Becky with a handful of potatoes and dropped them into the sink. 'Welcome to the club.'

Becky leaned her elbows on the table and put the heels of her hands into her eye sockets. If she pressed, coloured flashes and stars and rings exploded against the blackness, and briefly, blessedly, cleared her mind of thoughts. Such as the thoughts that had pursued her all morning, which she sought to escape by suggesting an expedition to Ross, thoughts of her father, and how she wanted him to be there. Without her father, Becky had lost a sense of the future, a sense that round the next corner might be something other than just more of the same. She raised her head and looked at Nadine's narrow back, bent over the sink.

'Mum—'

'What?'

'When you and Dad sold our house—' She paused. 'Where did the money go?'

'Into the bank,' Nadine said shortly.

'Couldn't—couldn't we use just some of it?'

Nadine turned round. She was holding a potato and an old nailbrush. 'No.'

'Why not?'

'Because,' Nadine said, 'it's all the money *I've* got. All I'll *ever* have.'

Becky didn't look at her. She said in a rush, before her courage fled, 'Why don't you get a job?'

There was an ominous silence. Becky heard the potato and nailbrush fall into the sink.

'Sorry?' Nadine said. Her voice was cold.

Becky mumbled, 'You heard me—'

'Yes, I did,' Nadine said. She came away from the sink and leaned on the opposite side of the table, staring at Becky. 'I heard you. I heard you the other night, too, when you said the same thing. Do you remember what I said to you?'

'Yes—'

'Well. The same reason is true now. I can't work because of you children and where we are forced to live.' She leaned forward. '*Why* are you asking me?'

Becky said, to the table top, 'Other mothers work—'

'Hah!' Nadine shouted again. 'So *that's* what you're getting at! *She's* got a job, has she? She's got everything that should be mine and a bloody job, too?'

'No, she hasn't. Not yet. But she's going to—'

'Becky—'

Becky closed her eyes.

'Becky, how *dare* you speak to me about her? How *dare* you even begin to make comparisons when you think what I've done for you and she's destroyed? How *dare* you?'

'I wasn't comparing. I was just telling you. You asked if she'd got a job and I was just telling you—'

'Shut up!' Nadine yelled.

Becky pushed her chair back from the table, tilting it to get away from Nadine's furious face.

She said, persisting, 'You ought to get away from here. You ought to see other people than us. You ought—' She stopped.

'What ought I?'

Becky cried wildly, 'You ought to use your energies for something else than just hating Dad!'

'Right,' Nadine said. 'Right. That does it.'

She marched round the table and gave Becky's tilting chair a swift kick. It lurched and toppled, sending Becky onto her knees on the kitchen floor. She put her hands down to steady herself and waited, on all fours, for the next thing to happen.

'You have no idea about pain,' Nadine said. Her voice was odd, as if she was restraining a scream. 'No idea about suffering, about being rejected, about the end of love. You have all your life before you and what have I got? Nothing. Seventeen years' investment in a relationship and what do I have at the end? Nothing. *Nothing.*'

Very slowly, Becky sat up on her heels. She looked up at Nadine. She had no idea why she wasn't retreating into the silence that had always been, in the end, her only defence. But she wasn't. She was sick with fright, but she was going to say it. She was *going* to.

'You *could* have something,' she said. Her voice shook. 'You could have something, even now, if you wanted to. You could have had something, all along. But you wouldn't.'

There was a small, stunned silence, and then Nadine leaned down and slapped her hard, across her cheek. Becky gave a little cry. Nadine had never struck her before. She'd screamed and shouted and slammed her own hands or herself against walls and furniture, but she'd never hit Becky before. Or the others. Hugs, yes, violent cuddles and kisses, but not blows. Never blows. Becky put a hand to her cheek. It was stinging.

'Oh my God,' Nadine said. She yanked the chair upright and collapsed onto it, putting her face in her hands. 'Sorry. Oh, sorry—'

Very slowly, Becky stood up. She leaned on the table. She felt slightly sick. 'That's OK—'

'No,' Nadine said. She stretched out one hand to Becky. 'No, it isn't. Come here. Let me hold you—'

Becky shook her head. Nadine raised hers from her remaining hand and looked full at Becky.

'I'm sorry. I'm really sorry. I should never have hit you. It's just that I get so wound up, so angry—'

'I know.'

'Can't you understand?' Nadine said. 'Can't you see what it's like to have made such a mess of everything and then to find that you're stuck?'

'Whatever it's like,' Becky said, 'you shouldn't take it out on us.'

The kitchen door opened. Clare, wearing her Disney track suit and an old Aran jersey of Matthew's, came in holding the headphones of her new personal tape player.

'Rory's gone.'

Nadine swivelled on her chair.

'What d'you mean?'

'He's not upstairs and he's not downstairs.'

'He'll be outside—'

'It's raining,' Clare said.

'Perhaps he's in the car, seeing if it'll start—'

'I've looked,' Clare said. She had been impelled to go and find him because of the sudden silence from his burrow under the eaves. He was in one of his refusing-to-speak moods, but Clare had seen him, a couple of hours ago, tunnelling into his bedding with his new Swiss-army knife and a small log from the pile Tim Huntley had brought. For some time, Clare could hear chippings and whittlings, and then she put her headphones on and could hear nothing but the soundtrack from *The Sound of Music* which she only played when alone for fear of being mocked for listening to anything so creepy, so sentimental, so pathetic. But she loved it, she loved its sentimentality and its portrayal of a family as a safe haven, a happy unit, loving, unthreatened in their togetherness. When she had heard to the end, she took off the headphones and noticed that the woodcarving noises had stopped. She put her head out onto the landing and saw that Rory's leather jacket had gone from where he'd dumped it on the floor. She went across to his burrow.

'Rory?' she said.

There was no answer. She crawled in. On his pillow lay the log. He hadn't been carving it, he'd just hacked at it. It was full of gashes and slashes, as if he'd just tried to kill it with his knife. She reversed out onto the landing and did a tour of the upstairs and then the downstairs. Then she went out into the drizzle and looked in the lean-to and the awful shed where a stained old lavatory crouched in the corner like a toad. Then she went into the cottage and sought her mother in the kitchen.

Nadine looked as if she was about to cry.

'I can't face it—'

'It's OK, Mum,' Becky said. 'Don't panic. He can't be far.'

'I must go and look for him—'

'He's twelve,' Becky said. 'He's nearly a teenager. Anyway, what could happen to him round here?'

Nadine glanced at her. Then she looked at Clare. Then she took a deep breath and pushed her hair off her face.

'I hope you know,' she said, and her voice shook a little. 'I hope you both know how much I love you? All of you?'

'Hey,' Tim Huntley said. He'd come round the corner of the Dutch barn with the tractor and a movement had caught his eye. Someone on top of his great maize stack, someone not very big. And then the someone had moved again, and revealed itself to be the kid from what Tim and his mother called No-Hope Cottage. He was crouched up there looking down at Tim as if he expected to be shouted at.

'Hey,' Tim said. 'What are you doing up there?'

'Nothing,' Rory said. He was wearing jeans and a leather jacket that had seen better days and a T-shirt, and he looked blue with cold. Tim opened the tractor-cab door and swung himself down. He looked up at Rory, twenty feet above him.

'How long have you been up there?'

'Dunno—'

'You better come down.'

Rory hesitated. He'd climbed up on impulse, making toe- and finger-holds in the maize wall as he went. But getting down was another matter. Tim went close to the maize.

'I'll catch you.'

Rory shrank back.

'I'm not going to lam you,' Tim said. 'I just want you down.' He moved to stand directly below Rory. 'Lie on your stomach and move yourself over the edge feet first. There'll be a drop and then I'll catch you.'

Rory's head disappeared from view, and then his trainered feet appeared over the edge above. He manoeuvred himself until he was holding on only with his arms.

'Slowly,' Tim said. 'Let go!'

Rory fell. Tim caught him clumsily round the waist as he dropped and they both tumbled to the floor.

'Bloody hell—'

'Sorry,' Rory said. He scrambled sideways away from Tim's bulk and got to his feet. 'Sorry.'

Tim got up slowly, brushing down his boiler suit.

'So you should be. Why are you here in any case?'

Rory said nothing. He didn't know, except that he'd been driven from the cottage by a sudden desperation to be out of it, and the farm had seemed a simple destination.

'You know what trespass is?'

Rory shook his head.

'It's being on someone else's land or property unlawfully. It's interfering with what belongs to someone else. Suppose you knocked some of that maize down?'

'I didn't.'

'You could have.' Tim looked at him. He was shivering. 'I'll take you home.'

'No,' Rory said.

'Why not?'

Rory said nothing, just kicked at the dust on the floor of the barn.

'You in trouble?'

'No,' Rory said.

'Then—'

'I'll go,' Rory said. 'You don't need to take me. Thanks.'

Tim let a pause fall, and then he said, 'Where's your dad?'

'He's not here—'

'Working?'

'No,' Rory said. His head was bent as he watched the scuffing patterns his feet made. 'He lives in Sedgebury.'

'So your mum's on her own there, with you lot?'

Rory nodded.

'You better ring her,' Tim said. 'Tell her where you are.'

'No—'

'Why not?'

Rory couldn't explain. He couldn't tell this man he hardly knew that if he rang Nadine there'd be a dramatic scene. He said, instead, hurriedly, 'I got bored. I'll—I'll go home now—'

'Mind you do,' Tim said. He remembered Nadine distraught in the dark lane on Christmas Eve and then in her kitchen the next morning, cool as a cucumber in her dressing gown, as if she'd known him all her life. She must be over forty, to have these kids, must be. But she didn't look it.

Tim put a hand in his pocket and found a packet of chewing gum. He held it out to Rory.

'Hop it.'

'Thanks—'

'I'm going to ring your place, dinnertime. And if you're not home, you'll cop it.'

'Why did you go?' Nadine said.

Rory shrugged.

There were baked beans on the plate in front of him, and he was pushing them about with the blade of his knife, making a mess, not eating. It occurred to him to say that he was bored here, fed up, stuck in the cottage with his sisters and a television so old that, even when mended, it couldn't get a proper signal, but he knew it wasn't worth risking it. He'd only have to start talking like that and everything would blow up again and he was too tired for that. He was tired all the time, it seemed to him, tired of having nothing to do, nowhere to go, tired of tension, tired of having to watch what he said, tired of baked potatoes. He used to feel tired this way in the past, when Matthew and Nadine quarrelled, or Nadine went off somewhere and left Matthew to cope. Rory swallowed. He mustn't think of Matthew because it would make him start wanting him to be there as he used to be, just Dad, and not as he was now, only partly Dad because of what had happened, because of Josie and Rufus. Rory didn't hate Josie and Rufus the way Nadine wanted him to, but he hated what their arrival had done to his life. It had been a rough old life before, in a lot of ways, but at least Dad had been in it, at the centre, a necessary presence making tea, yawning in the kitchen in the early mornings, wearing an old plaid dressing gown. Tears pricked behind Rory's eyelids. He put the knife down and rubbed the back of his hand across his nose.

'Aren't you hungry?'

'Sort of—'

Nadine looked round the table. Clare had eaten half her beans, but Becky's and her own were virtually untouched. We're a sorry lot, she thought, a sad little crew of human rubbish, the bits and pieces chucked out when other people's lives change. Poor children, poor scruffy, weary

children with their disrupted lives and their dependency and their genuine desire not to cause me pain. I shouldn't have slapped Becky, I
shouldn't have. And I shouldn't shout at them for things they can't help.
They're good children, they are, they're good, loving children, and
they're all I've got, all the future I've got anyhow. She smiled at them.

'Eat up.'

Becky slowly shook her head.

'No thanks.'

'Look,' Nadine said. She leaned forward, her forearms either side of
her plate, and spread her hands flat on the table. 'We've got to make a go
of this.' She paused and then she said, 'Haven't we?'

They didn't look at her.

'Tell you what—'

Clare and Becky raised their heads.

'Shall we go into Ross this afternoon?'

Becky said, 'You said there wasn't any money—'

Nadine smiled.

'I might get some out of the bank. Just a little. We could go to the
cinema maybe. What about that?' She stretched one hand out and
squeezed Rory's nearest one. 'OK?'

He nodded.

'OK, Clare?'

Clare nodded too. Nadine turned full face towards Becky.

'Well, Becky. OK?'

Becky glanced at her. She smiled wanly.

'OK.'

Chapter
EIGHT

THE LETTER HAD COME in the post, along with three bills, some
junk mail and a children's clothes catalogue. Matthew had
handed it to Josie.

'That's his writing, isn't it?'

Josie looked at the letter. It was indeed Tom's writing.

'Yes.'

'You'd better take it then.'

'No,' Josie said. 'I'll leave it. I'll leave it till later, after the interview.'

He leaned over and kissed her, on her mouth. She liked that, the way he always kissed her on the mouth, even the briefest hello and goodbye kisses. It made her feel that he meant them.

'Good luck, sweetheart. Good luck with the interview.'

'I'm nervous. I haven't interviewed for a job since Rufus was two.'

'You'll be great. *I'd* employ you.'

'You're biased—'

'Yes,' he said. 'Hopelessly.'

Josie looked at the letter.

'Tom didn't really want me to work.'

'I want you to. If you want to.'

'I do.'

He glanced at the bills in his hand, almost shamefacedly.

'It'll help—'

'I know.'

'I'm sorry,' Matthew said suddenly. 'I'm sorry so much has to go on—'

'Don't mention her.'

He leaned forward and laid Tom's letter on the kitchen table, weighting it with a nearby jar of peanut butter.

'I'd better go. Good luck.'

'Thanks. I'll ring you.'

The interview had turned out to be very unalarming. The larger of the two primary schools in Sedgebury needed a supply teacher for English and general studies, for two terms while the permanent teacher took maternity leave. It was twins, the head teacher said, so the extended leave was something of a special case. She was a plump woman in a knitted suit whose chief concern, she told Josie, was pastoral care. That was why she had liked Josie's c.v. with its mention of the conference in Cheltenham.

'We can't teach these children anything,' she said, 'until we've taught them a little self-respect.'

Josie nodded. In the school where she had taught in Bath the children, though not inadequately clothed or fed, came from an area of the city where communication appeared almost exclusively to be through acts of casual violence. They had all grown up with it, they were all used to quarrels and frustrations being expressed in yelling and blows, they all accepted physical rage as the common currency. Sedgebury would be no different.

Escorting her out of the school's main door, the head teacher said, 'Of course, your stepdaughter was here. Clare Mitchell.'

Josie was startled.

'Yes—'

'And her older sister was here earlier. The boy was at Wickham, as far as I remember. How are they doing?'

Josie found herself colouring.

'I'm afraid we don't know each other very well yet. I think—they've all settled, in their new schools.'

'Nice children,' the head teacher said. 'Clever.' She looked at Josie slightly sideways. 'You'll find a lot of people knew the Mitchell family, in Sedgebury.'

Josie looked straight ahead.

'I'm becoming aware of that.'

'It's good that you'll be working.' The head teacher put her hands into the pockets of her knitted jacket. 'It will mean you won't have to apologise too much, that you'll have your own status.'

'Apologise?'

'People don't like change.'

'You mean apologise for being Matthew's second wife?'

'It's more being a stepmother, Mrs Mitchell.'

Josie spun round.

She said sharply, 'I didn't have any *choice* in taking them on. It was him I chose!'

The head teacher took one hand out of her pocket and laid it briefly on Josie's arm. 'I know. I'll report to my governors, Mrs Mitchell, and we'll let you know as soon as possible.'

Josie looked at her.

'I really want the job.'

Later, cycling home—Matthew had the car—she knew she shouldn't have made herself appear vulnerable, needy, just as she shouldn't have reacted in any way to the suggestion, however kindly meant, that she was on some kind of local trial as Matthew's new wife.

Sedgebury was proving not only an unremarkable town, but also a rather sullen one; Rufus missed his father plainly and perpetually, and seemed bewildered into passivity at any suggestion that he should make friends with either Matthew or Matthew's children; Matthew's children declined to give an inch in her direction and Matthew seemed helpless in the face of their obduracy; and there was Nadine. Josie gripped the handlebars of her bicycle and took a sharp, self-controlling breath. What had ever, ever possessed her into thinking that Nadine could be kept out of her life, their lives, in fact *any* life? Because of her, Matthew's sister Karen was apprehensive about seeing Josie and Matthew's mother simply refused to. Because of her, Matthew's children were, for the moment, hardly coming to Sedgebury at all, and Matthew minded about this a good deal and was unable to talk about it to Josie. Because of her, a large proportion of the bills that came to the house seemed to require Matthew's embarrassed and furtive attention, and it had occurred to Josie more than once that when—if—she got a job, she would be paying for their lives so that Matthew could pay for Nadine's.

She turned her bicycle up the right-hand concrete strip of the drive of 17 Barratt Road and rode it into the garage. She would not think about Nadine. It was becoming a refrain, like the line of a song stuck in her head, 'Don't think about Nadine.' She got off her bicycle and padlocked it to Matthew's workbench.

Josie put her key in the back door and turned it. The kitchen was quiet and empty, just as she had left it, with breakfast cleared away and the table bare except for a jug of forced early daffodils Matthew had bought her from the market, and the letter under the peanut-butter jar.

She took her coat off, and her gloves and scarf, and put them down in a heap on the kitchen chair. Then she ran water into the kettle and plugged it in. The letter was watching her. Even with her back to it, she knew it was. She put her hand on the lid of the kettle. When it boiled, and she had made herself some coffee, she would open it.

Outside Rufus's school—Wickham Junior—several other mothers waited. Josie knew quite a lot of them by sight now. 'Hi,' they said to each other. 'Bitter cold, isn't it?' Their children came roaring out across the playground at three fifteen. Rufus was almost always nearly last.

'Good day?' Josie said. She stooped and kissed him. He nodded. He nodded most days, having discovered that it averted questions.

'Good,' Josie said. 'I'm so pleased. I went for an interview. It was a nice school, so was the head teacher. I feel quite hopeful.'

Rufus remembered Josie's working days in Bath.

'Will you use the same bag?'

'I should think so. It hasn't fallen to bits yet. Are you hungry?'

'Yes.'

'Would you like it,' Josie said, 'if we went and had a burger?'

He looked up. He was beaming.

'Yes.'

In the burger bar he chose a cheeseburger with chips and a banana milk shake. Josie had a cup of coffee. She watched him carefully extracting the lettuce and tomato from his bun. It was amazing to her that someone who, from babyhood, had had to be bribed and cajoled into eating anything acceptably healthy could possess such luminous skin, clear eyes and shining hair.

'Rufus—'

He looked at her over his bun, his mouth full.

'I've got something to tell you. Maybe—maybe it's easier to tell you here than at home.'

He stopped chewing.

'I had a letter from Daddy this morning—'

He was watching her, waiting, only his eyes and nose visible above the burger bun.

'Darling, I think Daddy is going to get married again.'

It was her turn to wait. He regarded her for a moment and then seemed to abruptly relax. He took another bite.

'I know,' he said, through his mouthful.

'*Do* you?'

He nodded. He swallowed and reached for his milk shake.

'Did he tell you?'

'No,' Rufus said, sucking through his milk-shake straw. 'But she was in the house.'

'After Christmas?'

'Yes.'

'And you—sort of guessed?'

Rufus took another long suck.

'They were laughing.'

Josie looked down into her coffee. A pang she could give no name to clutched her briefly, and let go.

'Did—did you like her?'

Rufus nodded.

'She didn't make a fuss.'

'What do you mean? Of you? Of Daddy?'

Rufus picked up a chip in his fingers.

'She was just there. She's called Elizabeth.'

Elizabeth, Josie thought to herself. Elizabeth Carver.

'What did she look like?'

Rufus considered. He ate another chip. Elizabeth wasn't pretty, but she was OK as well. Sort of peaceful. A bit like Granny.

'A bit like Granny,' he said.

'*Granny!*'

'Not so old,' Rufus said, 'but kind of not showing off.'

Josie looked at him carefully. He looked calm, as if this new development in his life was actually rather welcome.

'Don't you mind if Daddy marries someone else?'

'I wouldn't like him to marry anyone really fat,' Rufus said, licking melted cheese off his forefinger.

'But you don't mind Elizabeth—'

'No,' Rufus said. He picked up his bun again. 'I showed her my bedroom.'

'Oh—'

'Daddy's going to put a desk in there, with a proper lamp.'

Josie picked up her coffee and took a long swallow.

'They want to get married quite soon. They want you to go.'

Rufus nodded.

'I'll write back then, shall I, and say you'd—like to?'

'Yes,' Rufus said. He took another enormous bite of his burger and said through it, 'Elizabeth can ice-skate. She said she'd teach me.'

You can't mind,' Matthew said.

'What can't I mind?'

'Tom getting married again.'

Josie was stacking plates in the sink.

'It's not his getting married. It's this Elizabeth woman—I'll have to share Rufus.'

'Only occasionally.'

'He's been mine and only mine all his life.'

Matthew pushed his coffee mug away from him.

'You don't know that Elizabeth wants to change that.'

'She said she'd teach him to skate—'

'That could just be manners,' Matthew said. 'He's a nice little boy and she's in love with his father.'

'Yes,' Josie said. It was unsettling to think of another woman being in love with Tom. She might not want Tom herself, but the thought of Tom and his house being taken over by someone else was not conducive to a quiet mind.

'It's better for everyone,' Matthew said. He stood up, rattling the change in his pockets. 'Rufus doesn't have to worry about Tom being lonely and you don't have to feel guilty about leaving him.' He came round the table and kissed her. 'It's *good* news.'

She looked up at him.

'It's—just that mother love is such a killer.'

'Father love isn't a picnic, either.'

'Sorry—'

'At least Rufus lives with you.'

'Matt, I'm sorry, I shouldn't have said it—'

'Just think,' Matthew said. He put the back of his hand briefly against her cheek. 'Sometimes, just think before you speak.'

She nodded. She wanted to say to him that, however bad things were for him, being without his children, he didn't labour all the time under everyone else's impossible expectations of him. If he got things right, everyone applauded; if he failed, they shrugged and said, 'Oh well, poor bugger, at least he tried.' Whereas for her, for women . . .

'I've got to go and do some work,' Matthew said gently. 'Just an hour or so. We've got one of those government assessment inspections coming up—'

'I know.'

He kissed her again.

'Thanks for supper.'

He went out of the kitchen, collecting the canvas briefcase in which he kept his papers, and up the stairs to the first floor. With the use of a hooked pole, he pulled down the extending ladder that gave access to the roof space. Up there, Matthew had made himself a study. It was small, and inevitably makeshift, but it was the only space and the only privacy that 17 Barratt Road afforded for his box files and folders. Josie had wanted to adorn it for him, soften it with paint and fabric, but he had declined. It was a working space, a thinking space, and its lack of domestic comfort and natural light gave it a seclusion he valued. It was also becoming the place where he could think freely about his children.

It was no good attempting to delude himself: Josie couldn't see anything likable, let alone lovable, in any of them. To be sure they had given her a relentlessly hard time ever since she had come into their father's life, but Matthew doubted that Josie, even though she paid lip service to the idea, really had any notion at all of the degree of loyalty that Nadine demanded of them. Christmas had been appalling, he knew that. His children's behaviour towards Josie had been equally appalling. And he had been so torn between the two that he had ended up passive, helpless and despising himself for his own weakness.

'Stand up to her!' Josie had cried, on Christmas night. 'Why don't you stand up to her!'

'Because,' he'd said, not looking at her, 'she'd only take it out on the children. Whatever I do, I have to think of whether it'll make it worse for the children.'

He sat down at his desk now and switched on both lamps. The plywood walls he had put up served as pinboards, too, and in front of him was a patchwork of photographs of his children, taken at all ages, in the bath, on bicycles, by the sea, in the garden, asleep, in fancy dress, in solemn school groups. He put his elbows on his desk and propped his chin in his hands. In the midst of the pictures was one he liked particularly of Rory, in pyjamas and a cowboy hat, holding a kitten. Rory must have been about six. His expression was stern, full of protective responsibility. Nadine had rung Matthew several times recently—and always at school—to say that Rory was playing truant. The local farmer had found him in his yard a couple of times, and his school had noticed that, while he was there for morning and afternoon registration, he was often absent for subsequent lessons. She had been loud with reasons for Rory's behaviour but had refused to allow Matthew to do anything.

'Then why ring?'

'Because you're his father.'

'When you'll let me be.'

He had to put the telephone down after that, hurriedly, fearful that the school secretary would hear Nadine's abuse through the thin wall which divided her office from his own. Rory was preoccupying, of course he was, but at the moment Nadine was refusing to let him, or his sisters, come to Sedgebury. They were all at last settling as a new little family and she didn't want them disturbed by contact with a stepmother they detested. Matthew's solicitor had said he must be patient.

'Give it a month or two. If you haven't seen the kids by Easter, then we'll start some action.'

Matthew closed his eyes. Was he, he wondered, romanticising his own children because he missed them? Did he excuse them all the glowering and sulking he knew they possessed in full measure, because their absence was a permanent pain?

'Matt?'

He turned. Josie's head and shoulders were through the opening in the landing ceiling.

'Hey, I didn't hear you—'

'I took my shoes off. Are you OK?'

'So-so.'

'I shouldn't have said that about mother love. I shouldn't have implied—'

'It's all right.'

'I was thinking—'

'What?'

'If they won't come here, do you want to go and see them—at her place?'

He smiled at her.

'I don't think so. The lion's den—'

'Or somewhere neutral. I mean, I don't have to come.'

'You wouldn't want to—'

'I'd like to want to,' Josie said. 'But it's difficult to want to when you're so plainly not wanted in return.'

'I know.'

'Matt—'

'Yes?'

'It's hard, isn't it?'

'Yes. But not impossible.'

'What happens,' Josie said, 'when it does get impossible?'

'I don't know,' he said. He leaned out of his chair and touched her nearest hand, holding on to the wooden frame of the opening. 'We'll have to wait and see.'

Chapter
NINE

'I'LL SELL IT,' Elizabeth said. She stood with her arm through Tom's, looking up at the house she had bought only months before.

'You could keep it and do it up and sell it at a profit.'

'I'm not interested any more,' Elizabeth said. 'I'm grateful to it, but it's not going to be my life now.'

He pressed her arm against him.

'Good.'

'I asked my father if he would like it and he said he had vertigo just thinking about it.'

'What did he say,' Tom said, 'about you marrying me?'

'I think he thinks you're a safe bet.'

'In what sense?'

'Past the male menopause and old enough to know your own mind.'

'I know *that* all right.'

Elizabeth looked back at the house. 'I suppose Dale wouldn't like it?'

'Dale—'

Dale had been very effusive to Elizabeth. They had met several times, always in Tom's company, and Dale had fussed around Elizabeth with cups of tea and extra cushions and conversation. She told Elizabeth how much she loved her family home.

'I've known it all my life, you see. I never really went away, except to school. I hated school. Did you? And I hate this flat I'm in now. It's so impersonal.'

'Why do you mention Dale?' Tom said now.

'Because she said she hated her flat. And she doesn't like Bristol—this is home. So maybe—'

'I don't think so.'

'Too big?'

'Too close,' Tom said.

'To us?'

'Yes.'

'Come *on*,' Elizabeth said. 'We're all grown-up and Dale has her own life, and in any case she's shown no resentment towards me at all.'

Tom smiled. He turned Elizabeth and began to walk her slowly back down the hill.

'Too close for me, then.'

'But you love her.'

'Dearly.'

'What then?'

'She has an overwhelming quality, as you will discover. She can't help needing to know, needing to be involved—'

'Well, she's just been jilted.'

'No doubt,' Tom said, 'for that very reason.'

'I think I'll ask her anyway.'

'Don't.'

Elizabeth stopped walking.

'What are you really trying to say to me?'

He paused, and then he said, 'That I want to be married to you without a permanent extra around.' He put his arm round her. 'Dearest, I'm thinking of you.'

'Are you?'

'I remember Josie saying once—or screaming, to be truthful—that no woman in her right mind ever *wanted* to be a stepmother. I don't expect you want to be one, either.'

'I don't mind—'

'Because you don't yet know. But I know, because I've seen it. We must start as we mean to go on, which is without Dale fifteen minutes' walk away. Rufus is different. He's a child, not a complicated adult. Lucas, being a man, is a bit of both, but he is also independent.'

'My father said—' She stopped.

'What?'

'That there ought to be training courses for stepmothers. Motherhood comes after nine months' preparation with a package of helpful emotions, but stepmotherhood is more like an unexploded bomb in the briefcase of the man you marry.'

'How,' Tom said, 'would he know so much about it?'

Elizabeth pulled up her coat collar.

'He's been reading fairy stories, on my behalf. He says they've made him think.'

Tom was laughing.

'He's wonderful—'

'I know.'

Tom tightened the arm he had round her.

'But *are* you worried about being a stepmother?'

She looked at him. His face was very close.

'Not in the least. We're hardly in Snow White country, are we?'

He kissed her.

'Do you know why I love you?'

'No, of course not.'

'Well, for about a hundred reasons, but the hundred and first is because you are so *sane*.'

Later that day he said, apologetically, that he had a client to see.

'I'll only be a couple of hours. But they're weekenders, so site visits with them are difficult.'

'Of course.'

'Why don't you,' he said, 'have a good look at the house?'

'Heavens—'

'Well, you should. It's going to be your house, after all.'

She pulled a face. 'You've had so many wives in here already—'

'Time to change it round then,' he said. He was smiling at her. 'Time to change it for you and me.'

'Oh,' she said, startled and pleased. 'Oh—'

He kissed her.

'Think about it. Walk round the house, and think about what you'd like to change. Anything you want.'

When he had gone, she sat where she was for a while, at the kitchen table, nursing the last half of a mug of tea. A sweet contentment lapped round her, filling the room. It was hard to believe the last few months, hard to credit that the purchase of a house she didn't really want had drawn Tom Carver into her life. With Tom's appearance a whole new extraordinary world was wheeling slowly into view, revealing itself as not just alluring, but as something she had, at some level, been longing for, for years.

Sitting here in Tom's kitchen—soon to be her kitchen—Elizabeth could acknowledge to herself at last, and with almost confessional relief, that it wasn't just wanting Tom that had overtaken her so powerfully. There was something else, another wanting, the desire for the peculiar domestic power of the married female: the presiding, the organising, the knowledge that one's own decision-making lay at the heart of things. Elizabeth looked round the kitchen, her eye lighting upon this and that, a copper colander, a bottle of olive oil, a jug of wooden spoons, and thought, with a sudden glow of happiness, I'd like an open fire in here.

She got up, poured away the last inch of now cold tea, and put her mug in the dishwasher. Then she opened the kitchen door and went out into the narrow hall, elegantly floored in black and white. From it, the staircase rose to the first floor, where the drawing room was, looking into the street, and behind it, the bedroom where Tom had taken her, just after Christmas for the first time, and then many times since. On a half-landing there was a bathroom for that bedroom, projecting out from the back of the house above the ground-floor utility room, and then the stairs climbed on up to what Tom referred to as the children's rooms—Rufus's room, Dale's room, the room that had been Lucas's.

Elizabeth began to climb the stairs. It was Josie, Tom said, who had painted the walls yellow, a Chinese yellow, a much bolder colour than Elizabeth would naturally have chosen, but she rather liked it. She put a hand out and patted the nearest space of wall.

'You can stay.'

The drawing room was rather different. Pauline had liked it, Tom said, had used it, had chosen the elaborate feminine curtains and the fragile furniture. Josie had disliked it, had almost never entered it and had made the far end of the kitchen into an alternative sitting room instead. There seemed to be no sign of Josie in the room but, instead, a feeling that she had never come in willingly to confront all those photographs of Pauline, on her own, with Tom, with her children, staring down from a portrait over the fireplace in a seventies gypsy dress with her hair in a fringe. Good-looking, Elizabeth thought, gazing up at her, good-looking as Dale was, with the same kind of finish and polish, the same physical assurance. Maybe I can't move the portrait, but perhaps just one or two of the photographs could go, and the curtains, and the frilly cushions? Maybe it would be tactfully possible to suggest to Tom that the room was a bit of a shrine, a little fossilised? She glanced down at the nearest photograph of Pauline. Stealthily, she put out a hand and turned it until it was facing the wall behind it. Then she let out a little involuntary breath of relief.

Tom's bedroom she could bypass. It was comfortable and undistinguished. In his year alone, Tom had allowed a comfortable masculine encroachment of his own possessions to spread across the room, clothes and shoes and compact discs and books. On the chest of drawers stood photographs of his children—there were three of Rufus—and behind them, half obliterated by a postcard reproduction of a Raphael Madonna propped against it, one of Pauline. There were none of Josie.

Elizabeth had only been on the top floor once, at Rufus's invitation, to see his bedroom. He had been very proud of it. He had shown her the aeroplane mobile he had made himself, a model destroyer he had decided not to start until his ninth birthday, the cupboard where he kept his collections, shells and pictures of watches cut out of magazines. Nothing, Elizabeth vowed, would be changed here, nothing would happen that wasn't instigated by Rufus, in case whatever frail sense of continuity that still remained was inadvertently damaged further.

Lucas had not occupied his room for six or seven years. He had moved out when he went to university, only using it as a parking space for the detritus of his life—cushions, music equipment, ski boots, lamps, a tennis racket, posters in cardboard tubes—between academic terms and the long wandering foreign trips he took each summer. With his first job had come his first flat and he had removed some of his possessions. The room felt unused and there was a patch of damp above the window which looked down into the charming little courtyard garden below. But it was a pleasant room, a benevolent room. It was a room that might, in time, become—a nursery.

Elizabeth went out onto the landing. A faint sound from below caught her ear. She leaned over the banister rail and peered down.

'Tom?'

Silence. A motorbike in the street outside was kicked into angry life and the windows, as they always did in response to sudden and uncouth sound, shuddered elegantly. Elizabeth moved across the landing and turned the handle of Dale's closed door. It was locked.

'Nonsense,' Elizabeth said aloud.

She turned the handle again, and shook it. She turned it the other way. It was locked, most decidedly. Elizabeth looked at it. The smooth white paint stared back at Elizabeth as if defying her to guess what was beyond it. She crouched and put her eye to the keyhole. It was quite black, as if taped up from inside. Nothing could be more plain than that Dale regarded this room as her territory, as the place she had always had, as hers, all her life, and the place she intended to keep as hers, whatever.

Elizabeth stood up. Tom had told her about Dale, about the effect of her mother's death on a personality already volatile and needy, about the scene in the shadowy bedroom with Dale hysterical on the bed and Lucas, white-faced with fear and grief, looking on in stunned silence. Elizabeth had felt sorry for Dale, sorry for Tom, sorry for Lucas, all of them plunged into an abyss by the abrupt removal of the linchpin of their family life. She had listened with respectful sympathy. Her own life had never had any such drama in it. She had never felt, as she was now beginning to feel, entering the world of Tom's past and Tom's present, much rawness of emotion. She looked at Dale's locked door and felt, for the first time, a tiny twinge of apprehension that some things—emotional things—might not be capable of being dealt with just by calm and reasonableness.

She turned away from the landing and began to go slowly down the stairs. I must, Elizabeth thought, be myself. I must be allowed to be Tom's wife in my own way, to live in this house as my house. She paused outside the drawing room. I must make that room mine, not Pauline's. Even if one remembers the dead, and with love, one shouldn't live with them as if, somehow, they weren't really dead at all.

She straightened her shoulders. She would go down to the kitchen and start making plans for her fireplace, and she would also go down into the garden and poke about among the unswept leaves from the previous autumn, to see what was lurking there and beginning to stir to life. She descended the last flight of stairs to the hall and went into the kitchen. Dale, in a navy-blue blazer and sharply pressed jeans, was standing by the table, reading Tom's post.

'Dale!'

Dale looked up, smiling. She didn't put the letter in her hand down. She looked absolutely at ease.

'Hi!'

'How did you get in? I didn't hear the bell.'

'Key, of course,' Dale said. She dipped a hand in her blazer pocket and produced a couple of keys on a red ribbon. 'My keys.'

Elizabeth swallowed.

'Do—I mean, do you often do that?'

Dale was still smiling, still holding a letter of Tom's.

'What?'

'Let yourself in—'

Dale said, laughing, 'When I need to. This is my home.'
Elizabeth went over to the kettle, so that her back was towards Dale.
'Would you like some tea?'
'There isn't any. I've looked.'
Elizabeth said quietly, 'I bought some Lapsang this morning.'
Dale looked surprised.
'Where is it?'
'Here.'
'Oh, but tea doesn't live there. It lives in that cupboard, by the coffee.'
'That seems a long way from the kettle—'
'It's always lived there,' Dale said. She put the letter down and replaced the keys in her pocket. 'I see Dad's got across the planning boys again.'

Elizabeth opened her mouth to say, '*Should* you be reading your father's correspondence?' and closed it again. She ran water into the kettle.

'Is Dad out?'
'A site meeting—'
'Damn. My car's playing up.'
'Do you want him to have a look at it?'
'No,' Dale said, grinning. 'I want him to pay for it.'
'But—' Elizabeth said, and stopped. She plugged the kettle in and picked up the packet of tea.

'He started when I was a student and he's just sort of gone on. Look, I'll make tea. You sit down.'
'I'm fine—'
'You shouldn't be doing the work,' Dale said. She came past Elizabeth, opened the cupboard, took out a teapot Elizabeth had never seen before, and went back, past Elizabeth again, taking the tea packet out of her hand. 'Were you looking at the house?'
'Yes—'
'The drawing room's lovely, isn't it? It was the only room Mummy had really finished when she died. The portrait was painted by a friend of hers who was just getting famous, a Royal Academician and all that.'

Elizabeth went over to the window seat, and nudged Basil to make room for her.

'Did you have a good week?'
Dale sighed. She began to bang mugs and cupboard doors about and to clatter noisily in the fridge, looking for milk.
'So-so. I was just a bit tense about the car, all those miles.'
Elizabeth began to stroke Basil's warm, plushy side.

'Surely your company will mend your car for you?'

Dale pulled a face.

'I've exceeded my repair allowance already and I've used it a bit more privately than I'm supposed to. I don't think it's serious but there's something knocking and you can get a bit wound up about that sort of thing on motorways. Dad gave me a carphone, thank goodness, only last week, and that's made a huge difference.' She spooned tea into the teapot. 'Do you know how long Dad will be?'

'About another hour, I should think.'

'The thing is,' Dale said in a confidential tone, 'I rather want to ask him about something other than the car. I want to move. I want another flat.' She poured boiling water into the teapot, and then pulled a chair away from the table so that she was close to Elizabeth. 'In fact, I've already seen one.'

Elizabeth glanced at her.

'Have you?'

'Yes. It needs everything doing to it. I mean *everything*.'

'But your father's an architect—'

'So handy, isn't it? But it's money again, really.'

Elizabeth thought of her house, which she felt an absurd responsibility for because of what it had brought her. She steeled herself.

'There's my house—'

Dale smiled. She leaned over and patted Elizabeth's arm, then she got up to pour the tea.

'Thank you. That's really sweet of you. In fact, I'll confess I went and had a bit of a snoop. But it's a bit *permanent* for me, a house. A bit committed. Do you know what I mean?'

'Don't you want to feel permanent?'

'Not till I've got somebody to be permanent with me. I thought, you see—'

'I know. I'm so sorry.'

Dale carried the two mugs over to the window seat and held one out to Elizabeth.

'Dad's been so supportive. And Lucas. Have you met Lucas?'

'Not yet. We are having lunch with him and Amy tomorrow.'

Dale's face changed.

'Oh. Are you? I didn't know—'

Elizabeth took a sip of tea. Without looking up she said, 'Why don't you come?'

'Why didn't Dad say?'

'I don't know.'

'I spoke to him yesterday. Why didn't he say?'

Elizabeth looked up at her. The smiling composure was gone.

'My dear, I don't know. But come along, come along and join us.'

Dale stared at her tea, her face dark, then she retrieved a smile.

'Yes. Yes, of course I will. And now, if you'll excuse me, I'll just go and fossick about upstairs for some things I need.'

'Of course.'

Dale moved over to the door. By it she paused, looking back over her shoulder. Her voice was very kind.

'Make yourself comfortable,' she said.

Upstairs, it didn't look to her as if anything had changed. Tom and Elizabeth were presumably sleeping together—that was something, Dale decided, simply to avert one's mind from—but Elizabeth appeared to have left not so much as a toothbrush. When Josie arrived and started sleeping with Tom, Dale remembered, she'd arrived wholesale as it were; her clothes in his cupboard, her pots and bottles in his bathroom.

But Elizabeth was different. Climbing the stairs to the top floor and taking her keys out of her pocket, Dale told herself firmly that she must make the effort to remember how different Elizabeth was. She had even made herself say so, as proof of her good intentions, to Lucas and Amy.

'I may not want Dad to marry again, ever,' Dale had said. 'But if he's going to, she's OK. She's different.'

'What kind of different?' Amy said. Amy had liked Josie, who had been kind to her and allowed her to practise new make-up techniques on her. Josie had been fun.

'A quiet professional,' Dale said. 'Very decent. And not clinging. She isn't all over Dad all the time.'

Lucas said, teasing, 'There wouldn't be room for two of you.'

Dale ignored him.

'I feel better, now that I've met her. I really do.'

'She sounds pretty boring,' Amy said.

'She is. But that's fine. Fine by me.'

Lucas had looked at her, a long, hard look.

'She'll still be his wife, Dale, and wives come first.'

'Not always. Not necessarily. Only if they insist on it.'

She put the key into the lock on her bedroom door, and turned it. She could never see her bedroom without emotion, never enter it without a rush of remembering enveloping her, all those years of remembering, intense years in which she had battled with so much, with grief, with longing, with the knowledge that she must one day leave home, and the terror of doing it. When she had met Neil, she had packed up half the room in an extraordinary spirit of release, only taking one photograph of her mother and nothing from her teenage years. She had been exhilarated, proud of herself, congratulating herself on taking only things that would contribute to her future, not detain her damagingly in the past. But even then, even when she left to live with Neil, she had taped up the keyhole and locked the door behind her. Dale's bedroom was full of Pauline.

She went over to her dressing table, her teenage dressing table flounced, at her thirteen-year-old request, in pink and white, and laid the key on the glass-covered top. She looked round her. Composedly, from many angles, her mother looked back at her. Elizabeth Brown was nice, Dale was certain of that; she was nice and decent and a bit boring, but for all that she was marrying Dale's father and, in consequence, Dale's bedroom would have to stay locked. Not just for present privacy, but to safeguard the past. Dale's past: Dale's childhood.

Chapter TEN

'BUT THIS IS THE THIRD TIME,' Clare's form teacher said. 'The third time this week you've said you couldn't do your homework.'

'I can't,' Clare said. She was wearing the approximation of school uniform that most of the kids wore, and the hem of her skirt had come down at one side.

'Is there somewhere at home you can do your homework?' the teacher said.

Clare thought of the kitchen.

'There's a table.'

'Is it quiet?'

It was quiet, Clare reflected, if her mother was upstairs in her studio making clay coil pots which were her new passion. There was clay everywhere. The bottom of the bath was gritty with it.

'Yes.'

'Then really you have no excuse. Your brother and sister have homework, don't they?'

'Yes.'

'Where do they do theirs?'

Clare considered. Becky spent angry half-hours on the floor of their bedroom with music on so loudly it made Nadine scream, and emerged announcing the shitty stuff was done. Rory never seemed to do any homework at all. He took his school bag into his burrow, but Clare didn't think he even opened it. Something in Clare didn't mind school. It was nice belonging, it was nice going somewhere every day that stayed the same, that treated you the same as everyone else. It wasn't rebelliousness that prevented Clare from doing her homework, but hopelessness. Every night, she got her books out and put them in the space she'd cleared in the remains of the last meal, and sat down in front of them. She sat and stared and could do nothing. She couldn't look at words, she couldn't pick up a pencil.

'Clare,' the teacher said. 'You *must do* your homework. Do you understand? You must do it, not because I say so, but so I can see if you understand what you've been taught in class.'

Clare nodded. She felt, in the face of such a reasonable explanation, that she must be truthful in reply.

'But I can't.'

'Do you mean you don't understand it?'

'No,' Clare said. 'But when I get home I can't do anything.'

The teacher regarded her. She looked tired, but then so many of the kids looked tired with unsupervised television sets in their bedrooms and parents too weary for repetitive discipline.

'Is your mother at home when you get home?'

Clare nodded.

'Maybe I should talk to her—'

'No,' Clare said.

'Why not?'

Clare said, quoting Nadine, 'We've got to make a go of it.'

'Because,' the teacher said delicately, 'you're on your own?'

Clare nodded again. Her eyes were filling. She hadn't seen Matthew for six weeks and three days and there'd been a battle that morning when Nadine had wanted to wash the Disneyland track suit and had snatched it from her. Clare had retrieved it from the pile of dirty laundry and hidden it inside Rory's duvet cover. There'd be trouble when Nadine arrived to collect her and confronted her about it.

'Can you have one more try tonight?' the teacher said.

Clare sighed. It wouldn't be any good. She said miserably, 'I just can't think.'

'I see,' the teacher said. She stood up. 'Are you sure I can't talk to your mother?'

'Yes.'

'Well, then I'd better talk to someone else.'

Clare looked up at her, with a gleam of hope.

'My dad?' she said.

In the sitting room of the cottage, Becky sprawled on the sofa. It was broken-springed, and she had padded the places where there were no springs at all with a cushion and an old blanket. The television was on some kids' programme, but Becky could hardly see it because of the snowstorm effect on the screen as the reception was so bad. She didn't care. She just wanted the company of having the television on, the illusion of having people around.

It was cold in the sitting room. The fire wouldn't burn properly. She had rolled herself in the duvet off her bed, but even all wadded up like that she felt cold inside, like you do when you're scared about something. She moved slightly, so that the cigarette packet in her jacket pocket wasn't pressing uncomfortably into her breast, and thought of what else was in that pocket. A white tablet, wrapped in foil, with a bird stamped on one side and a smiley face on the other. A boy at school had given it to her. He'd said he could get a fiver for it but he'd give it to her if she'd go out clubbing with him at the weekend. He was a big, heavy-looking boy from the year above Becky and most of the time that he was talking to her he was looking at her breasts.

Becky wasn't sure why she had accepted the foil packet. It was flattering, in a way, to be asked out, to be offered, as a bribe for going out, membership of a particular group. The boy had a reputation, of course, a name for wanting to go all the way, for refusing to wear a condom, but that made him dangerous, which in turn made him desirable. If she went out with him at the weekend, she couldn't pretend she didn't know what she was in for and, in any case, part of her wanted to be in for it very much, wanted to feel high and wild and sexy. And free. But there was another part. It was a part which had only grown up in her recently. Burdens had arrived, whether she wanted them or not, with her parents' divorce, and the most complicated of those burdens was Nadine. Nadine was a mother, a mother three times over, but she wasn't what you thought of when you said the word 'mother' to yourself. She was more, Becky was coming to realise, like someone who needed a mother herself. Becky could see—she thought the others could see, too, by the way they were behaving—that things were slipping out of control. It wasn't just the household things, it was more a feeling that Nadine didn't know where she was going or what the next days or weeks were for. If Becky went clubbing with Stu Bailey on Saturday night and took her Ecstasy tablet and ended up having sex for the first time, she might feel she was at last flying free, but she'd still have to come home and find Nadine. It might be worth anything Nadine could say or do to get right out of their tangle of troubles for a single night and blow her mind. But then, on the other hand, it might not. You couldn't separate things, Becky was unhappily coming to realise; you couldn't do a thing and then not expect the consequences to come trolling back some time later.

She sat up and took her cigarettes out of her pocket and lit up. Then she took out the Ecstasy tablet and unwrapped it. It looked as innocent as glucose. She sniffed it and then, with a small leap of excitement, licked it. It tasted of nothing. It smelt of nothing. It lay on her palm smiling up at her. It would cost her, it occurred to her, five pounds—her last five pounds to own it, and, at the same time, to be free of Stu Bailey. If she wanted to be free, that is.

She folded the foil back carefully round the tablet and put it in her pocket. Her cigarette tasted sour and tired. She chucked it into the sulking fire. Suppose Nadine found out? Suppose Stu Bailey really hurt her? Suppose . . . Becky flung herself back down on the sofa and pulled the duvet over her head.

That's the fifth time,' Tim Huntley said. He stood, legs astride, hands on hips, in Nadine's kitchen, looking down at her. She was sitting at the table. Beyond her, with a rip in his black school blazer, stood Rory, leaning against the refrigerator and fiddling with the magnets on the door.

'I'm sorry,' Nadine said. Her voice was low.

'A farm isn't a play place,' Tim said. He looked from Nadine to Rory. 'A farm's lethal. It's not just the machines, it's the poisons. You might do yourself harm and you might cause harm too. I've got enough weed-killer there to finish off half of Hereford. And a gun. You're lucky I didn't turn the gun on you.'

Rory bent low over the refrigerator door.

'Sorry—'.

'I should think so. Why weren't you at school, anyway?' He looked at Nadine. 'Why wasn't he at school?'

She was trembling slightly.

'I thought he was.'

'I don't like it,' Rory said and then, muttering, 'It's boring.'

Tim moved forward and leaned on the table.

'That's no excuse. It's the law you have to go to school and it's the law you have to stay there.'

Rory hesitated. Then, with a sweep of his hand, he detached all the magnets from the door and sent them scattering across the floor.

'I can't stay there,' he said. 'I can't stay here, I can't—'

His voice shook a little.

'You got homework?' Tim asked.

Rory nodded.

'Why don't you go and do it, then? While I have a word with your mum?'

Rory kicked the refrigerator.

'I'm hungry—'

'I expect you know where the bread bin is.'

Nadine stood up. 'I'll get it—'

Tim watched her. He noticed, as she sliced the bread and spread it clumsily with peanut butter, that her hands were shaking. Rory didn't offer to help her. Tim opened his mouth to tell him to get off his idle backside, and closed it again. He'd shouted at Rory enough for one day, hauling him out physically from the shed where the tractors lived and ripping his blazer in the process.

'There,' Nadine said. She gave Rory the sandwiches on a plate and then leaned forward and kissed him. 'Don't worry.'

He didn't look at her. He took the plate and went out of the room, letting the door bang behind him. They heard him cross the tiles of the hall and then begin to climb the stairs, his tread slow and unsteady.

'I expect he'll eat it in bed,' Nadine said.

'In bed—'

'He's made himself a sort of bedroom under the eaves.' She looked at Tim. 'Coffee?'

'Please,' he said. He pulled out a chair from the table and sat down on it, resting his forearms on the table top. He looked at Nadine. 'We've been discussing you, Mum and me.'

'Oh.'

'You're not coping, are you?'

Nadine filled the kettle, plugged it in and put two mugs, very precisely, beside each other, on the counter top.

'If it's any business of yours.'

'We're neighbours,' Tim said. 'This is the country, not some bloody town where you can drop dead and nobody'd notice.'

Nadine said nothing. She spooned coffee into the two mugs and screwed the lid back on the jar, very carefully.

'You know what's going on, don't you?' Tim said.

Nadine put her hand on the kettle handle. She bowed her head.

'It's not just the boy pitching off half the time,' Tim said. 'Is it? It's the girls, too. The little 'un looks half starved and the big one's playing around with one of the Bailey boys.'

'Who,' Nadine said tightly, 'are the Baileys?'

Tim grunted.

'You wouldn't want to know. They're a load of trouble. Four boys as bad as their dad. You don't want your girl mixed up with the Baileys.'

The kettle blew a noisy stream of steam into the air and switched itself off. Nadine, holding her wrist with the other hand to steady it, poured water into both mugs.

'Milk?'

'Please.'

'Sugar?'

'Two,' Tim Huntley said. 'Cheers.' He watched her set a mug down in front of him. Then she sat down herself, opposite.

'I take Becky to school every day and I collect her every day and I know where she is, all the time.'

Tim eyed her.

'You don't know what she's doing at school. And you can't keep her shut in for ever.' He thought, briefly, of Becky's overdeveloped, un-girlish figure. 'She'll break loose soon. One trip to Hereford or Gloucester and you'll have lost her.'

Nadine bent her head over her coffee.

'Go away!'

Tim Huntley leaned forward.

'Don't shout because I'm not going. I haven't come to interfere, I've come to help you before your kids really lose it.'

Nadine lifted both hands and put them in front of her face.

'We're getting there, we are—'

'No, lady,' Tim said. 'You aren't. And if I find your boy in my yard again, without my permission, I'm calling the rozzers.'

Nadine took her hands away and stared at him, aghast.

'You wouldn't!'

'I would. For his sake, for yours,' Tim said. 'You look to me like you've had a bit of a breakdown. You should live with other people. Maybe that commune place over towards Hay.' He looked at the clay around Nadine's fingernails. 'Art and stuff. Gardening.'

Nadine closed her eyes. She said, in the most decided voice she had yet used in this conversation, 'I love my children.'

Tim hesitated a moment and then he said, 'There's something else.'
'What?'
'Their dad's a head teacher, isn't he? The lad said—'
'Deputy,' Nadine said with contempt.
'Maybe,' Tim said, cradling his coffee mug. 'Maybe you should let their dad take his turn for a while?'

Matthew sat by the telephone in the sitting room. He sat very quietly, as if his quietness might suggest to Josie, next door in the kitchen, that he was still speaking. He needed her to think that because he needed time to think, himself.

It had been Nadine on the telephone. She seldom rang him at home and Josie had answered the call.

'Hello,' she said, and then her expression blanked. Matthew took a breath.

'I'll get him,' Josie said. She held the receiver out to him. 'For you.'

He took it. Josie was looking at him, as if she wanted something badly and he was supposed to guess what it was. Slowly, he turned his back, putting the receiver to his ear.

'Hello.'

Josie rushed past him into the kitchen and slammed the door, shudderingly. Nadine was crying and crying the other end of the telephone and through the crying she was trying to accuse him of all the things she had always accused him of.

'There's no point to this,' Matthew said, disgusted.

'There is! There is!'

'Then tell me,' he said. 'Cut the abuse and *tell* me.'

He heard her blowing her nose violently.

'They're in bed,' she said. 'They can't hear me.'

Matthew waited. She blew her nose again. Then she said, 'They're coming to you.'

'What?'

'They're in trouble,' Nadine said. Her voice was now a fierce, hoarse whisper. 'They're playing truant and getting into bad company. That's what's happened because you—'

'Shut up,' Matthew said. He was gripping the receiver.

'You made the problem,' Nadine said. 'You got them into this. Now you get them out.'

Matthew took a deep breath.

'You want the children to come here—?'

'I don't *want* it!'

'OK, OK, the children are to come here. Permanently? School and everything?'

Nadine said faintly, 'Yes.'

'Have you asked them?'

Nadine said, spitting the words out separately, 'There isn't any point.'

'Because you don't intend them to have any choice?'

She shouted, 'Because there isn't one! If you don't help, if they go on like this, if something happens, then we'll *neither* of us have them!'

'What?'

'There's someone watching me,' Nadine said unsteadily, 'someone who—' She stopped.

'Might report you?' Matthew said.

Nadine said nothing. He could hear her ragged breathing. Something close to pity stirred in him and then stilled.

'I see,' he said. He glanced towards the closed kitchen door. His heart was rising in him with a sudden, luminous happiness. He said, trying to keep his voice empty of all emotion, 'Do you want to discuss arrangements now?'

'No.'

'Tomorrow? I'll call you from school—'

'OK,' she said. She was beginning to cry again.

He opened his mouth to say, 'Give them my love,' and closed it again, in case his rejoicing betrayed itself. Instead he said, 'Till tomorrow then. Bye,' and put the phone down.

Then he sat there. He sat beside the quiet telephone, with his eyes closed and said thank you, fervently, to somebody. His children back, his children home again, his children where he could encourage them, protect them, supervise them, see them as he hadn't seen them for almost eighteen months in the precious, trivial course of ordinary daily dull family life. He felt almost dizzy, almost tearful. He said their names to himself. He visualised them.

'Thank you,' he said silently. 'Thank you, thank you.'

He opened his eyes. Across the room, the kitchen door stood firmly shut. Behind it, he could hear Josie clattering things in the kitchen and the sound of the classical-music radio station she played all day. He stood up. The first radiance of relief and happiness was dimming slightly. It was no good expecting Josie to greet the news of his children's coming to live with them with anything other than alarm. She might be horrified. She might be angry. She might, even, refuse. Matthew went across the sitting room and opened the kitchen door.

'Hi.'

Josie was washing the saucepans left over from cooking their supper. She didn't turn round.

She said, 'Why does she have to be so bloody dramatic?'

'She is dramatic,' Matthew said. 'And she was in a state tonight. Some kind of crisis. I don't know exactly what because if I ask I get another earful about how it's always my fault—' He came further into the room and stood behind Josie.

'So what's new?'

'Josie,' Matthew said.

She turned round, her hands dripping with suds. She looked at him. His eyes were alight. A small, cold dread settled heavily in the pit of her stomach.

'Does she want you to go there?'

'No . . . Honey, she can't cope. She's sending them here.'

'Here?' Josie said. 'To live?'

'Yes.' He leaned forward and kissed her unresponsive neck. 'Yes, to live here, go to school here. With us. Is that OK?'

She closed her eyes and then said, in a hard, bright voice that neither of them recognised as hers, 'Of course.'

Chapter ELEVEN

RUFUS LAY IN BED and looked at the curtains he had chosen when he was four. They had flowers on them. Blue flowers on a pale yellow background. Now they really embarrassed him. He looked at his desk. It was new. It was sitting there waiting for him when he got to Bath, and it had two drawers and an angled lamp on a hinge, like the ones Tom had in his office. Elizabeth had given him a box of coloured pencils, a huge box with seventy-two pencils in it, all their colours shading gently from one to another like a rainbow. They were artist's pencils, Elizabeth said, and when she was about Rufus's age she had had a box exactly like that.

He sat up in bed. It was very, very nice to be in that bed, in that room, to be alone and quiet. Dale was next door, having suddenly decided to stay the night, but the walls of this house were thicker than the walls of what Rufus thought of as Matthew's house, so it was like being alone.

When he got out of bed and pulled the curtains, he would see the view he knew he'd see, the back of the house opposite across two gardens with a tree between that grew pale green bracts in summer and then dropped them all over the place like tiny primitive aeroplanes.

He got out of bed and padded over to the window, yanking the curtains as far sideways as they would go to squash the flowers up. The tree looked bare still, but a bit fuzzy, because of the new buds on its branches, some of which had minute little leaves beginning to come out of them. Down in the garden below, Rufus could see Basil, sitting by the stone girl with the dove on her hand, washing one paw very slowly and carefully, over and over again.

Rufus went into the bathroom beside Dale's bedroom and had a pee. Then he went downstairs, jumping the last three steps of each flight. His father's bedroom door was open, but the bed wasn't made and there was the sound of an electric razor whining away behind the bathroom door. Rufus sauntered on down to the kitchen.

'Hello,' Elizabeth said. She was already dressed and was laying bowls and plates round the table. 'Sleep well?'

He nodded.

'Are you pleased with your new desk?'

He nodded again. 'Brilliant.'

She was opening cupboards. She said, with her back to him, 'Do you like eggs?'

'Yes,' he said.

'How do you like them?'

He thought a moment.

'Cooked—'

'Yes,' she said. She was laughing. 'But scrambled, fried—?'

He hitched himself onto a chair.

'Scrambled,' he said.

'Won't you be cold, just in your pyjamas?'

He shook his head. He looked at the cereal packets. They were all the muesli stuff Tom ate, nothing decent.

'I don't like muesli either,' Elizabeth said, watching his expression. 'It gets stuck in my teeth.'

Rufus thought of the row of cereal packets at Sedgebury, six or seven of them, all different, all bought by Josie in an attempt to buy something Matthew's children would eat. They did eat them, too, but not at meals. They wouldn't come to meals, but there were cereal bowls all over the house and dropped bits on the stairs and floors.

Elizabeth said now, 'What sort of cereal do you like?'

Rufus jerked his chair closer to the table.

'I like the sugary ones but I'm not supposed to have them.'

'Well, we won't buy any of those then,' Elizabeth said.

Rufus eyed her. She gave him a quick smile and said, 'No cheating on your mother.'

He thought a moment. He said, 'I could tell her about the curtains—'

'What curtains?'

'In my room. They've got flowers on. I hate them.'

'That's different,' Elizabeth said. 'Your room here is yours, for you to choose.'

His face lit up.

'Is it?'

'Of course. I'm not going to break any of your mother's rules about you, but I'm sure you can have new curtains. What would you like?'

'Black, probably.'

'*Black*—'

'Or green. A nice green. Not that sad kind of green.'

Elizabeth broke eggs into a pan.

'I wondered,' Elizabeth said, stirring the pan, 'if you'd like to come out with me this morning.'

Rufus hesitated.

'To see my father. My father lives in Bath. I always go and see him at weekends. I suppose he will be your stepgrandfather.'

Rufus hadn't got a grandfather, of any kind. He only had Granny. Some people he knew had grandfathers who had fought in the war, real soldiers who'd fought the Germans and the Japanese.

'Was he in the war?' Rufus said.

Elizabeth lifted the pan off the cooker.

'He was a prisoner in Italy, for a lot of the war. He was wounded so he couldn't run away and then he was captured. Would you like your eggs on some toast or by themselves?'

Rufus looked at her. It occurred to him unexpectedly that he felt safe, there in the kitchen, with Elizabeth holding the egg pan and talking about her father being a prisoner in a very ordinary voice. Rufus smiled, very quickly, and curled his bare toes round the stretcher of the chair he was sitting on.

'Toast, please,' he said.

Duncan went slowly out of the kitchen and into his sitting room. On the low table, among the piles of books and papers, lay two cans of Coca-Cola and a packet of crisps, purchased at Elizabeth's suggestion,

also his boyhood stamp album and a small microscope he had bought
on impulse, in a junk shop, in case it should appeal to this child
Elizabeth was taking on, because of marrying Tom Carver.

He crossed over to the window and looked down into the street. He
was surprised at how much he did this now, stand at the window and
watch the small comings and goings, the old lady in the top flat opposite who spent all winter in an overcoat and a headscarf, even indoors;
the Chinese family who ran a laundry two streets away and worked all
hours, all week. He glanced down the length of the street now, his eye
caught by some movement. Elizabeth was coming along it, holding the
carrier bag she always brought, full of things she thought he should be
eating, rather than the things he chose to eat. Beside her walked a boy in
jeans and a duffle coat with a neat thick head of reddish-brown hair. He
was walking quite close to Elizabeth, but not touching her, and he was
talking animatedly and Elizabeth was listening. He thought of everything that he had read just recently, of all those fairy stories of stepmoth-
erly malevolence and cruelty, of the betrayal of childish trust, of the
relentless perversion of all accepted notions of maternity. The stories
had shocked him deeply, with their remorseless insistence on the
inevitable wickedness of any woman when faced with the care of children not her own, with their powerful suggestion of a second wife's
witchlike sexual dominance over her husband, a dominance that drove
all thoughts of fatherhood from a man's helpless heart. Duncan looked
down the street. Rufus gave a little skip and glanced up at Elizabeth.
They seemed, Duncan thought, with a small rush of emotion, perfectly
normal together, perfectly comfortable, as far removed from the black
world of spells and curses as they could possibly be. Duncan leaned forward and banged on the window glass, to attract their attention.

'She's nice,' Lucas said.

He was sitting, with Dale, in a wine bar. There were several plates of
tapas on the table between them and Dale had a large glass of red wine.
Lucas had ordered mineral water.

'I know.'

Lucas gave her a long look. She had been very in charge when they all
had lunch together in that restaurant, very much Tom's daughter playing the hostess. Amy hadn't liked it. Lucas had noticed that Amy, who
used to endure things she didn't like mutely, was now beginning to
articulate her objections. She'd said, on the way home from that lunch,
that anybody'd think Dale was Tom's wife, the way she was going on.

'Dad doesn't take any notice,' Lucas said.

'Well, he doesn't protest, if that's what you mean. He just lets it happen. It's what men always do when they don't know what to do—they just roll over and play dead.'

Playing dead or not, Lucas had thought his father looked really happy. He'd looked at Elizabeth a lot, with a kind of profound contentment. It had unsettled Lucas a bit. Not, he realised, because he minded his father's happiness, but because it wasn't what he felt when he looked at Amy. Well, not any more. He used to look at her and feel amazed at having her, but she'd changed from those early days when she'd been such fun, so mischievous.

'Lucas,' Dale said. She had rolled up a piece of mountain ham into a light sausage and was holding it in her fingers. 'Suppose she has a baby?'

Lucas shut his eyes. 'Why do you build bridges you may never have to cross in order to terrify yourself into theoretically crossing them?'

Dale took a bite of ham. 'She's thirty-eight.'

'So?'

'People have babies for ever now. And she's never been married so she may want the works, baby and all. Mayn't she?'

Lucas picked up a stuffed olive and removed its little plug of pimento with the prong of a fork.

'Does it matter?'

'Yes,' Dale said. She put the ham down, wiped her fingers and picked up her wineglass. 'We've been through all that, we've seen it all with Josie and Rufus, we've seen what's really ours being shared out beyond us, with them—'

'Are you talking about money?'

Dale took a sip of wine.

'A bit.'

Lucas ate the olive. He said, 'She isn't a gold-digger.'

'No,' Dale said.

'You don't sound very certain—'

'I am, of that. I really believe she isn't after anything of his. That isn't what scares me.'

'What then?'

Dale took another mouthful of ham.

'It's Dad.'

'What d'you mean?'

'It's that Dad might want to give her things, share things, even if she doesn't ask for them. Things that are really ours.'

Lucas waited. He had told himself, for years, that he didn't want to be given anything by Tom, that he wanted to make his own way as Tom

252

had done, but, as time went on and he saw how hard he was finding it, he had begun to feel that he wouldn't mind some help. He picked up another olive.

'You know,' Dale said. 'You saw how he is with her. You don't have to know him half as well as we do to see how he feels. Especially now that Rufus likes her and she likes Rufus. That's what scares me.'

Lucas raised his head and looked directly at her.

'That he loves her?'

Dale nodded. When she next spoke, her voice was thickened by sudden tears.

'Oh, Lucas, he does. This time, he really, really does.'

'Don't cry—'

'I can't help it,' Dale said. She put her glass down and then put both hands over her face. Under the table, Lucas stretched his feet out and trapped hers between them.

'I'm still here, cupcake—'

She nodded violently, behind her hands. He watched her. In some ways, she drove him mad, and in others aroused his pity as no one else in his life had ever done, pity at the terror of loss which had stalked her since childhood and probably always would, causing her to wreck, inadvertently, the very relationships she most needed. Poor Dale, Lucas thought, poor, driven Dale. He reached out across the table and took her wrists.

'Drink your wine, babe,' he said.

Elizabeth's London flat, she decided, was too big. If she was going, as she now planned, to travel up from Bath on Monday mornings and then return each weekend, she only needed half the space, a quarter, merely a bedroom and a bathroom and a kettle. It should have a porter and a laundry service and a cupboard to hold those sober working suits in which Tom had never seen her, which represented that part of her life which had once seemed almost the whole, but which had now receded.

In all her delight and gratitude at her changed status, Elizabeth couldn't help noticing the relief she felt at the realisation that, as far as her London life was concerned, nobody else need be consulted. Nobody would say to her, as Tom had said to her at the weekend, very nicely, but very decidedly, 'I'm sorry, dearest, but no.'

Probably, she shouldn't have asked him. Or, if she was going to ask him, not so soon, and certainly not hot on the heels of that dreadful lunch with Lucas and Amy and Dale, when Dale had dominated the proceedings and treated Elizabeth as if she were some dear old fondly tolerated relation with senile dementia. Elizabeth had meant to say nothing. She had almost succeeded. She had been able to speak to Tom with real warmth about Lucas, and had then, startling herself, found herself asking if they could move house.

He had stared at her.

'What?'

She was standing in the hall of Tom's house, with her coat on, and her suitcase at her feet, because he was about to take her to catch the Sunday-night train back to London.

'You asked if I wanted any changes. You said we could make changes for your and my life together. Well, I've thought about it and I want a change of house.'

He said in a controlled voice, 'I thought you liked this house.'

'I do. I did.'

'I hope,' he said, 'that this changeableness of affection doesn't apply to people.'

She felt a little surge of temper.

'What a ridiculous and unkind thing to say.'

'Perhaps I feel that the suggestion to leave this house is also ridiculous and unkind. Why do you want to, all of a sudden?'

She took a breath.

'Memories of Pauline, Dale's locked room—'

He looked at her.

'Those have always been here. We'll overcome those. You'll see.' He came closer. 'I'm sorry I spoke to you as I did.'

'That's all right—'

'Dale was silly today. Very silly. But she likes you. She never liked Josie. She'll calm down, stop performing. You'll see. And there's Rufus.'

Elizabeth put her hands in her coat pockets.

'What about Rufus?'

'This is home to him,' Tom said. 'This house is probably the best stability he has just now, the biggest anchor. I couldn't—' He stopped. Then he looked at her. 'Could I?'

Slowly, she shook her head.

'You saw how relaxed he was here,' Tom said. 'How he was with you.'

Elizabeth let out a long sigh. At one point during Rufus's last visit, Tom had found her teaching Rufus the rudiments of chess, and she had felt herself almost drowning in a sudden wash of approval, warm and thick and loving. She glanced at Tom. He was smiling. He leaned forward and put his arm round her, pulling her towards him, both of them bulky in their coats.

'I do see,' he said. 'I do understand how it must sometimes feel to you. But equally, for the moment, for Rufus, it has to be no. I'm sorry, dearest, but no.'

She had been quite angry on the train after that, angry and ashamed because Tom's point about Rufus was not only valid, but one for which she should have felt the utmost sympathy. The trouble was that she couldn't help feeling that Tom was hiding behind Rufus, that Tom, for all his real love for her, for all his commitment to their future, was held down still by the gossamer threads of the past, like a giant in a fairy tale, disabled by magic.

Chapter
TWELVE

WHEN JOSIE HEARD she had got her job, it was better than she had expected. The teacher on maternity leave whom she had applied to replace had decided to stay at home with her twins, and her post had been offered to Josie. In celebration, Josie bought a bottle of Australian chardonnay and put it on the supper table.

'What's that for?' Rufus said.

'To celebrate my job. I've got a job.'

Matthew smiled round the table.

'It's good, isn't it? First try, too. You're a clever girl.'

Becky stood up. She gave her plate a nudge.

'I don't want this.'

Josie said levelly, 'It's chicken casserole. You like chicken casserole.'

'I do not.'

Clare put her fork down. She said in a whisper, 'Nor me.'

She looked at Matthew.

'Sit down,' Matthew said to Becky.

'You can't make me.'

'I wouldn't try,' Matthew said, 'but I would offer you a glass of wine, to toast Josie with.'

Becky said scornfully, 'Alcohol's a drug.'

Matthew looked at Rory.

'Would you like some?'

Rory shook his head.

'Rufus?'

Rufus went pink. He shot Matthew a glance and shook his head, too.

'All the more for you and me, then,' Matthew said to Josie. He took the corkscrew from her and stood up, to take the cork out of the bottle.

'I'm not eating,' Becky said. 'And I'm not staying.'

'Please stay,' Josie said. There was no appeal in her voice.

'Why?'

'So that we can have supper together.'

'I don't want supper,' Becky said. 'And I don't want to be together.'

'Then get out,' Josie said.

Matthew stopped pulling the cork.

'Josie—'

'Get out,' Josie said to Becky again. 'Just go.'

Becky kicked her chair backwards, hard, so that it screeched across the floor and crashed into the nearest set of cupboards. Then she hurtled through the door to the hall and fled upstairs. Behind her she heard her father say angrily, 'What in hell's name did you say that for?' and then someone banged the door shut, and she could only hear babble and confusion.

She opened her and Clare's bedroom door and fell across Clare's bed, which was nearest. She put her face into the duvet and bit a mouthful of fabric, so hard she could almost feel her teeth meet. Then she pummelled Clare's pillow and kicked clumsily against the nearest wall with her booted feet. Bloody cow, she said to herself, bloody cow with her fucking job. How dare she? How dare she wave her bloody job at us like she wanted us to pat her on the back for it?

Why should I care about her and all her bloody cooking and cleaning and poncing about being Mrs Fucking Perfect? Becky picked Clare's pillow up and flung it at the wall opposite where it caught the edge of a picture and sent it spinning off its hook and crashing to the floor.

Becky sat up. She hadn't turned the light on when she came in, but by the remains of daylight left she could see the shards and slices of glass from the picture lying winking on the carpet. It was a picture she had always wanted, a reproduction of a painting by Klimt of an exotic, dangerous, snakelike woman, but Josie had hung it there for her and, in so doing, had at a stroke deprived it of all its allure.

Becky put her heel on the nearest piece of broken glass, and crushed it. Then she pulled her knees up and put her face down on them, and encircled them with her arms.

'I'm fine,' Nadine said, every day, whether Becky asked her or not.

Her voice was often bright and theatrical. 'Really I am. Fine.'

'What about you?' she'd say. 'That's what I really want to know. What about you? Are you getting enough to eat? Is school OK? Tell me what you're doing. Tell me everything.' Some days she rang twice, just as everyone was assembling frenziedly for school in the morning, or ten minutes after Josie had assembled them for supper.

Slowly, Becky raised her head. From downstairs, she could hear the sound of the television. Perhaps Rory had turned it on. Then the phone began to ring. At the sound, Becky felt her stomach tighten and then be filled, slowly and steadily, with renewed anger, an anger so strong she could feel it creeping up her throat, choking her. She stood up, unsteadily. The glass lay at her feet, gleaming and evil. She lifted her feet in turn, clumsily, and began to stamp on the broken pieces. Someone had to pay for this, someone had to suffer for all this unfairness, this pressure, this tension, this agonising disappointment and hurt. Someone, Becky thought, has to be *punished*.

Matthew allowed Clare to do her homework in his attic study. She stayed up there for hours. Sometimes, when he came back from his school—always much later than anyone else—she had been up there since she got home. She came straight in from school, walked past Josie, usually without saying anything, and went directly up to the attic, where she sat in Matthew's chair and sometimes put on one of his jumpers. When Matthew came home, she would come down and run to him and try to get on his knee. If Josie said anything, Clare would say, 'You're not my real mother,' and put her arms round Matthew.

Becky had told her to say it.

'She's not your real mother. She can't make you do anything. Tell her so.'

If they were alone together, just Clare and Josie, Clare didn't have the courage to say it, but from Matthew's knee she could say anything.

'She knows she's not,' Matthew would say, trying to make light of it. 'Poor Josie, having a baggage like you. What a horrible thought.'

'I don't want to be,' Josie said. 'I'm not trying to be.'

'She does mother things, though,' Clare said. 'Doesn't she?'

'Who else do you suggest does them?'

'Our real mother,' Clare said. She held Matthew hard. If she held him hard enough, she didn't have to think of Nadine and the cottage and the lavatory in the shed. If she thought of them, she felt desperate and the easiest place not to think about them, except on Matthew's knee, was in Matthew's attic which held so many things from Clare's childhood that she could sometimes pretend up there that nothing had changed, nothing had broken. She counted the photographs. There were exactly the same number of all three of them, of her and Rory and Becky. But there weren't any of Nadine.

'I wish she wouldn't cling,' Clare heard Josie say. 'I wish you wouldn't let her.'

'She's only ten—'

'It isn't age, Matthew. It's attitude.'

Clare didn't know what attitude meant, but it plainly wasn't a compliment. She was obviously doing something that Josie didn't want her to do, something to do with her father. She didn't sit on Matthew's knee to defy Josie, she did it because she wanted to, she needed to. She didn't refuse to eat Josie's suppers to get at Josie; she refused because those meals made her feel acutely guilty about Nadine, even disloyal. If Josie couldn't see that, Clare couldn't do anything about it, just as she couldn't do anything about her greedy relief when Matthew came home.

Josie lay on her and Matthew's bed. She was fully dressed. She lay quite still, her hands folded across her stomach, and stared out of the window where the fading light and the raw orange glow from the street lamps were producing an effect that was neither lovely nor natural. It was quiet in the bedroom, quiet enough to hear the sounds from downstairs, the murmur of the television, the noises from the kitchen where Matthew was, without much real trouble apparently, making the children wash up. Except Becky. Becky was in her bedroom with the door shut. She had been there since six o'clock, after her mother rang.

Nadine had rung, this time, about money. She had spoken first to Becky, and had then insisted on speaking to Matthew. Josie, grating cheese in the kitchen, had heard him say, 'But *I'm* paying for the children now, you *must* have enough, you *must*.' When Matthew had put the telephone down at last, Josie heard Becky say, with a mixture of fear and rage, 'You can't let her starve!'

'She's not starving,' Matthew said. 'She's just spent everything she had this month and wants more.'

'Then you should give it to her.'

'I give her all I can,' Matthew said. Josie could picture how tired he was looking, from his voice. 'She's only got herself to look after now.'

'Exactly!' Becky shouted. 'Exactly! And whose fault's that?'

Josie heard Matthew's footsteps coming towards the kitchen door. She bent over the grater.

'I'm not talking to you about it,' Matthew said. He opened the kitchen door. 'It's none of your business.'

Becky shoved past him. She stood in the kitchen, glaring at Josie. Josie's hand slipped on the grater and a bead of blood swelled out of her forefinger. She put it in her mouth.

'We're not exactly short round here,' Becky said, still glaring, her voice heavy with sarcasm. 'Are we?'

'Be quiet,' Matthew said. He looked at Josie. 'Are you all right?'

She nodded, her finger still in her mouth. Becky snorted and marched towards the door.

'I don't want any supper.'

'Fine,' Matthew said.

The door banged shut behind Becky. Matthew went across to Josie and put his arm round her.

'Sorry.'

She turned her face into his neck.

'It's OK.'

'Josie, I'm going to have to put her money back up again. I know I shouldn't, I know we've got the children here—'

'What?' Josie said, stiffening.

'I've just said. I'll have to put Nadine's money up again. I gave her less, because the kids were here, but I'll have to increase it again.'

'Because your daughter tells you to?'

Matthew sighed. 'Partly, I suppose. If I'm honest. And with you working—'

Josie shrank away from his embrace. She gripped the edge of the sink and stared down at the blood seeping out of her finger.

'You are telling me that *my* money will help pay for *your* children so that *you* can give more to your ex-wife, who refuses to work?'

'I'd pay for Rufus,' Matthew said. 'If it was necessary.'

Josie turned the cold tap on and held her finger in the stream. She was trembling.

'I don't ask you for a *penny* for Rufus.'

'I know.' He put his arms round her, from behind. She pressed herself against the sink.

'Please don't touch me.'

He took his arms away.

'I've got to behave decently,' Matthew said. 'I've got to juggle all these demands and do the best I can.'

'Except for me,' Josie said. She turned the tap off and wrapped her finger in a piece of absorbent kitchen paper. 'I don't make any demands. So I don't get anything. I do everything for everyone and nobody ever thinks that I have needs, I have hurts.'

'I do.'

'Well, you don't do anything about them. You just expect me to imagine what it's like for you while never even trying for one second to imagine what it's like for me.'

The kitchen door opened. Rufus stood there, holding his maths book. He looked at them.

'Oh,' he said.

Josie said, 'Come in, darling.'

'It's my maths,' Rufus said. 'I can't do—' He stopped.

Matthew moved away from Josie.

'Shall I help you?'

Rufus looked at him doubtfully. Matthew sat down at the table.

'Bring it here.'

Slowly, Rufus approached. He put the book down in front of Matthew and stepped back.

'I won't bite you,' Matthew said. 'I'm useful for maths. If for nothing else.'

Rufus moved a little closer. Josie watched them.

'Show me.'

'There,' Rufus said. He leaned forward, pointing, his shoulder almost touching Matthew's. It was a scene she had longed for, a scene which represented, perhaps, the first quiet, unremarkable step on the road to some kind of relationship between the two people who mattered most in the world to her—and it left her cold. She watched them, and felt nothing. There was no possibility of loving feelings in the face of the rage and despair that filled her now with such intensity.

'I've got a headache,' Josie said.

Neither Rufus nor Matthew reacted. Their heads were close.

'I think you've got these in the wrong order,' Matthew said. 'That's what's stumped you.'

'I'm going up to bed,' Josie said. 'If you put the grated cheese on top of what's in that dish and grill it, that's supper.'

Rufus looked up briefly, his face abstracted.

'Right,' he said.

'See you later,' Josie said. She went out of the kitchen and up the stairs and past Becky's closed door, to her bedroom. Then she lay down, still with her shoes on, and let herself cry.

That must be almost two hours ago. She must have gone to sleep, because she was stiff and her mouth tasted sour, and the tears had dried on the sides of her face. Tears of self-pity, perhaps, tears of anger and impotence certainly. She licked her undamaged forefinger and rubbed away the tear traces. Then she turned her head. She reached out for a tissue from the box on her side of the bed and blew her nose hard. Then she sat up. She swung her feet to the floor and kicked off her shoes. She would go into the bathroom before the children came upstairs, and shower and wash her hair and go downstairs in her dressing gown and make tea and try to be pleasant, ordinary. She stood up and went out onto the landing. The bathroom door was firmly shut and the sound of music coming from behind it was intermingled with the sound of running water. Becky was in the shower.

Under the bedclothes, Rory pressed a lit torch into the palm of his hand, into his bunched fingers. His flesh glowed weirdly, red and fiery. He took the torch away from his hand and shone it out from under the duvet onto a patch of wall.

'Rufe?' he said.

There was silence, He swung the torchbeam until it came to rest on Rufus's bed. Rufus was lying, as he always did, with his back to Rory; the torchlight caught his neck and the collar of his pyjamas.

'You asleep?'

Silence. Rory didn't know why, but he quite wanted Rufus to be awake. He'd always thought of Rufus as a little wet kid, but tonight, in the kitchen, eating supper with just him and Dad and Clare, he'd been OK, he'd been normal. They all had. They'd all just eaten the stuff Josie had left and joshed about a bit and Matthew, despite looking tired, hadn't watched anybody, hadn't ticked anyone off. It had felt different, this evening, without Becky and Josie; it felt as if you could just say things, as if whether you ate or you didn't eat wasn't a big deal. So they all ate everything Josie had left. Then they'd had a water fight, washing up. Matthew had made them mop the floor and Rory hadn't minded. He couldn't believe it, but he hadn't minded; he'd tried to get Rufus's feet wet, and Rufus had yelled and jumped about and you could see he didn't mind either, that he was liking it. It only stopped when Josie came down in her dressing gown. She'd put the kettle on and stood, with her hand on the handle, with her back to them, waiting for it to boil. The kitchen had gone quiet and awkward.

Rory ran the torchbeam all down Rufus's length, and back again. He looked relaxed, as if he really was asleep, not just faking. His wet shoes were jammed behind the radiator, and next to them was Rory's Newcastle United sweatshirt. Rory switched the torch off. It had been odd, this evening, because it had been, well, normal. He rolled over and punched his pillow. It had been fun.

Chapter
THIRTEEN

THERE WAS A PARKING SPACE right outside Tom's house, and it was, in addition, a big enough space for Elizabeth—who was not an experienced driver and had never needed to be a car owner—to manoeuvre into without difficulty. Tom had bought her this car, just like that, easily, amazing her.

'You'll need it.'

'But I've never—'

'You do now. Anyway, I want you to have a car. I want you to have the freedom.'

'I can't believe it.'

He had kissed her.

'You're joining another world. Families have cars.'

Already, Elizabeth liked it. She liked the unexpected status she felt it gave her, the independence, the choice. Even now, lifting the back to heave out the bulging supermarket bags, she felt a small pride she couldn't help relishing. She carried the bags up the steps to the front door in pairs and then locked the car. Then she climbed the steps again and put her key in the front door. It wasn't locked. She turned the handle and pushed the door open.

'Tom?'

'Me,' Dale called from the kitchen.

Elizabeth took a breath.

'Oh—'

Dale came to the kitchen doorway. She wore a scarlet apron tied over a black T-shirt and jeans.

'Been shopping?'

'Yes.'

Dale moved forward.

'I'll help you carry.'

'Dale,' Elizabeth said. 'Why didn't you ring to say you were coming?'

Dale stooped to pick up the nearest bags.

'Please leave those,' Elizabeth said. 'Please leave those and answer my question.'

Dale straightened slowly.

'I don't have to ring.'

'You do now,' Elizabeth said.

'This is my home—'

'Mine too, now. You are welcome at any time, *any* time for any reason, but not unannounced. I need to know.'

Dale stared at her.

'Why?'

'Privacy,' Elizabeth said. 'Not secrecy, but privacy.'

Dale said fiercely, 'This was my home for twenty-five years before my father even met you!'

She turned her back to Elizabeth and marched into the kitchen. Elizabeth lifted the shopping bags from the front doorstep into the hall and then shut the door. She followed Dale into the kitchen. Half the cupboard doors were open and the table was piled with packets and jars.

'What are you doing?'

'What does it look like?' Dale said rudely. She had pulled on a pair of yellow rubber gauntlets. 'Spring-cleaning. I always do it for Dad.'

Elizabeth took her jacket off and hung it over the nearest chair.

'It's my job now, Dale. If it's anyone's. And these are my cupboards and my kitchen. I am, in an old-fashioned expression, to be mistress of this house.'

Dale banged a yellow rubber fist down on the table. She said furiously, 'Oh, that's obvious, you've made that perfectly plain.'

'What do you mean?'

Dale shouted, 'My mother's photographs! My mother's pictures! What have you done with all the pictures?'

Elizabeth said steadily, 'You've been in the drawing room—'

'Yes!'

'And where else have you been? In our bedroom?'

Dale glared.

'Only quickly—'

'Only quickly! Not too quickly, I imagine, to notice that the photograph of your mother is where it's always been?'

Dale was breathing fast. She tore the rubber gauntlets off and slapped them down on the nearest counter.

'The drawing room was her room!'

'The pictures are perfectly safe. They are wrapped up and packed in a wine carton for you and Lucas. The portrait of your mother is still in the drawing room and it will stay there.'

Dale said vehemently, 'It was her room, she made it, she chose every-thing, she was Dad's wife, she was Dad's first choice and our mother—'

'I know all that. I know.'

Dale slumped into the nearest chair and put her face in her hands. Elizabeth went round the table and stood next to her. She looked down at the gleaming dark hair so smoothly tied back.

'Dale,' Elizabeth said, trying to speak gently. 'You're a grown woman, you must use your imagination and maturity a little. I can't negotiate with a ghost like this. I can't compete with something idealised and you shouldn't demand that I do, either. Anyway, aren't you maybe too old to go on believing your mother was a saint?'

Dale stared ahead of her.

'You never knew her. You don't know what you're talking about.'

'You didn't know her very well either,' Elizabeth said. 'You were only a child.'

Dale sprang up and shouted, 'There were hundreds of people at her funeral! Hundreds and hundreds!'

Elizabeth closed her eyes for a moment.

'I don't doubt that your mother was a wonderful person and much loved. That's not the point. The point is that she, tragically, is dead, and therefore, however fondly remembered, cannot influence how we, who are still living, choose to live our lives. When she lived here, this house was hers and she arranged it as she wished to. Now, it's going to be mine and your father's, and we will want to live in it differently.'

Dale bent her head and put the back of one hand against her eyes. She was crying.

'Oh Dale,' Elizabeth said in some despair. 'Oh Dale dear, do try to grow up a little.'

Dale whirled round and snatched several sheets of kitchen paper off a roll on a nearby worktop. She blew her nose fiercely.

'You want to turn us out!'

'I don't,' Elizabeth said. 'All I want is for you to respect my privacy and independence as I respect yours.'

Dale blew again.

'You don't respect my past!'

'I do,' Elizabeth said. She gripped a chairback and leaned on it. 'All I have difficulty with is when you try to insist that the past has more importance than the present or the future.'

'You'll learn,' Dale said bitterly. She untied the strings of the scarlet apron, ducked her head out of the neckband and threw the apron on the table among the boxes and bottles.

'What is that supposed to mean?'

Dale was pulling on a jacket.

'What we had, we'll always have and you can't touch it. You'll never understand us because you can't feel what we've felt, you can't know what we know, you'll never belong. You can try changing Dad outwardly, nobody can stop you doing that, but you'll never change him inwardly because you don't have it in you.'

Elizabeth took her hands off the chairback and put them over her ears.

'Stop it—'

'I'm going,' Dale said. She sounded out of breath. She was rummaging in her bag for her car keys. 'I'm going, and I'll be back. I'll be back whenever I want to because this is my home, this is where I belong.'

Elizabeth said nothing. She slid her hands round her head from covering her ears to covering her eyes. She heard Dale's bag zip closed.

Dale went out of the kitchen and the front doors, slamming both behind her.

What's all this?' Tom said.

He stood in the doorway of his bedroom and peered into the half-dark. Elizabeth lay on the bed, as she had lain for several hours, with the curtains drawn. 'Are you ill?'

'No.'

He moved closer.

'What is it, sweetheart?'

Elizabeth said, without moving, 'You saw.'

'I saw a fair old muddle in the kitchen, certainly. And shopping all over the hall floor. I thought perhaps you weren't feeling too good—'

'I'm not.'

Tom lowered himself onto the side of the bed and put his hand on her forehead.

'Headache?'

'No.'

'What?'

Elizabeth was lying on her side, still dressed, under a blanket. She said, looking straight ahead, and not at Tom, 'Dale came.'

'Did she?'

'She was here when I got back from shopping. She was in the process of turning out the kitchen cupboards.'

Tom took his hand away from Elizabeth's face.

'Oh dear.'

'We had a row,' Elizabeth said. She rolled over onto her back and looked at Tom. 'I told her she mustn't just let herself into the house whenever she pleased any more, and the row began.'

Tom wasn't quite meeting Elizabeth's eyes.

'And how did it end?'

'With Dale saying she would go on letting herself in whenever she wanted to because this was her home.'

Tom got slowly off the bed and walked towards the window, pushing the curtains back to reveal quiet cloudy afternoon light.

'Did Pauline come into it?'

'Oh yes,' Elizabeth said. 'She always does.'

'What did you say?'

'About Pauline? That I couldn't negotiate with a ghost. That Dale was too old to go on believing her mother was a saint.'

'She wasn't,' Tom said.

'I'm relieved to hear you say it—'

'She was very like Dale, in some ways, but with better self-control.' He turned towards Elizabeth. 'Sweetheart. I'm so sorry. Have you been up here ever since she left?'

'Yes.'

'Poor love. Poor Elizabeth.'

Elizabeth struggled up into a half-sitting position, propping her shoulders against the bed's padded headboard.

'Tom, what are you going to do?'

He came back to the bed and sat down beside Elizabeth.

'What do you want me to do?'

She closed her eyes.

'It isn't,' Elizabeth said, 'a question of what I want you to do, it's a question of what you want to do yourself, not just for my sake, but even more for our future sakes, jointly, for the sake of this marriage we're embarking on.'

'You don't sound very enthusiastic about it—'

'It's not lack of enthusiasm I feel,' Elizabeth said. 'It's fear.'

'Fear of what?' Tom said.

'Dale.'

Tom leaned forward and put his head in his hands.

'Oh my God.'

'Can't you imagine?' Elizabeth said, fighting with sudden tears. 'Can't you imagine trying to be married here with both of us straining to catch the sound of her key in the lock?'

'It wouldn't be like that—'

'It might!' Elizabeth cried, sitting up. 'If she got in a state about something, or jealous, or lonely, she might come in all the time, any time, demanding your attention, insisting on her right to come home, informing me, as she did today, that I'll never belong here however hard I try, however much I love you, because I haven't got what you've all got, what you've had. I just haven't got what it takes to make you happy!'

Tom took his hands away from his face and put his arms round Elizabeth. He said, in a fierce whisper against her hair, 'I'm so sorry, so sorry—'

Elizabeth said nothing. She turned her face so that their cheeks were touching, and then, after a few moments, she gently but firmly disengaged herself.

'Help me,' Tom said. 'Help me to decide what to do.'

Elizabeth began to inch across the bed away from him. She reached the far side and stood up.

'I'm afraid,' she said politely, 'that it isn't my decision.'

'Elizabeth, I can't change the locks of this house against my own daughter! Dale was almost born in this house—'

'I know. That's one of the reasons why I wanted to sell it and move to another house, with no associations.'

Tom stood up too. He said, 'You want me to tell Dale—'

'No!' Elizabeth shouted. She raised her fists and beat herself lightly on the sides of her head. 'No! Not what I want! What *you* want for *us*, for you and me, because you can see what will happen if things go on like this!'

'But they won't. These are teething troubles, the shock of the new. We have so much going for us, so much. We love each other, Rufus loves you, Lucas will love you, too, any minute. We mustn't get things out of proportion. Dale's just in a state while she gets used to the idea of you. I'm so sorry she's upset you—'

'Shut up,' Elizabeth said.

'What?'

'Stop talking. Stop mouthing all this stuff at me.'

Tom said angrily, 'I'm trying to explain—'

'No, you're not, you're trying to talk yourself out of having to face what's really the matter.'

'Which is?'

Elizabeth took a breath. 'That Dale is neurotically insecure and possessive, and that if you don't do something about it now you'll have her for life.'

Tom said sharply, 'You have your children for life, anyway.'

Elizabeth looked at him. Against the light, it was difficult to see his expression, but his stance looked determined, even defiant, as if he were challenging her to know better than he did about an area of life she had never experienced, and he had. She walked, with as much dignity as she could muster, into the bathroom, closing the door behind her.

Chapter FOURTEEN

KAREN, MATTHEW'S SISTER, waited at the gates of the school where, Sedgebury's grapevine told her, Josie was now teaching. The same grapevine had informed her that Matthew's children were also now back in Sedgebury, living with Matthew and Josie, and the stories of how they got there ranged from Nadine's being hospitalised after trying to kill herself, to Matthew abducting them from their schools, using his authority as a deputy head teacher to do so. Karen wondered what she was going to say. She'd recognise Josie all right—you couldn't mistake that hair—but she'd only exchanged about ten words with her at the wedding. She didn't have anything much personally against Josie, whatever she'd felt about Nadine. The grapevine that had brought news of Josie's job and the return of Matthew's children also reported a marked improvement in domestic regularity.

Josie came out of the school almost last. She was wheeling a bicycle. Karen moved forward until she was in the centre of the gateway.

'I don't expect you remember me.'

Josie stopped walking.

'I'm Karen,' Karen said. 'Matthew's sister.'

Josie looked at her. She wore black trousers and a jeans jacket. At the wedding, she'd been in green.

'Of course,' Josie said.

'I didn't mean to jump on you—'

'You didn't. It's just that I wasn't expecting—'

'No, I know,' Karen said. 'Sorry.'

'Look,' Josie said, 'I'm afraid I can't stop. I have to meet Rufus outside his school in ten minutes.'

'Can I walk with you?'

'I might have to bike, if the time gets short—'

'Of course. Can we start together, anyway?'

Josie turned her bicycle and began to walk rapidly along the pavement outside the school.

'I thought you were all ostracising me.'

'We are. Or, at least, Mum is. I was just waiting, really. And then—well, we heard rumours.'

'What about?'

'That the kids are back.'

Josie paused on a kerb edge and punched the pedestrian button on a traffic light.

She said shortly, 'They are.'

'For good?'

Josie didn't look at her.

'It seems so. Until—'

'Nadine changes her mind again?'

Josie gave Karen a small, fleeting smile.

'You've got it.'

The lights changed and Josie pushed the bicycle across the road.

Karen said, hurrying beside her, 'How are they?'

'I don't know,' Josie said. 'I feed them and wash their clothes, but they don't really talk to me. Certainly not about how they're feeling.'

Karen put a hand on the nearest handlebar to slow Josie down.

'Are they difficult?'

'In a word,' Josie said, 'yes. They are. I'm not trying to play happy families but they seem to insist that I am. They are actually—'

She paused.

'What?'

'Quite cruel.'

'Cruel!' Karen cried.

'Oh yes,' Josie said. 'Kids can be cruel. One of society's many myths is that stepmothers are cruel, but has it ever struck you that stepchildren can be quite as cruel as stepmothers are supposed to be?'

Karen said uncertainly, 'What about Matt, what does Matt do?'

'He's waiting for us to get to like each other.'

'Is he standing up for you?'

Josie bit her lip. Karen glanced quickly at her. She might be walking like the wind, but it was will-power, not the energy of well-being, that was driving her. She looked tired to death. It suddenly struck Karen that if Josie was in a way rejecting Matthew's children in response to their rejection of her, she might also be haunted by fear that, in time, if things didn't improve, Matthew might reject her, out of ultimate solidarity with his children. She moved her hand, for a second only, from the handlebar to Josie's nearest arm.

'I'm sorry. I didn't mean to pry—'

'You aren't. You didn't. I'm really pleased to see you but I don't know what to tell you except the facts. I'm sorry, but I'll have to bike now.'

Karen said, 'Can I come round?'

'Of course. We'd like it. I'd—I'd like it—'

She pushed the bicycle past Karen and into the road. Then she turned, one foot on the pedal.

'I'll ring you,' Karen said. 'I'll come round.'

'Thanks.'

Karen watched Josie ride away, bent over the handlebars as if to help the bicycle gather speed. There was something about the look of that bent back that made Karen suddenly feel sorry for her, really sorry, as she'd felt about her nice little kid at the wedding. You could see she was fighting, really fighting to keep going, to make things work, but no one was truly on her side. Karen sighed. She hitched her bag higher on her shoulder. There were times, Karen reflected, when it didn't just seem blessed to be single, but also the only way to stay sane.

Josie sat on a low wall outside Rufus's school and leaned against the wire mesh of the playground fence behind it. Rufus's head teacher had asked her to wait inside, but she'd said no, she'd wait in the open air.

'It's serious,' the head teacher said. 'Or, at least, I want it to be very serious for Rufus. It's the first time he has ever been rude to a teacher and I want him to realise, by doing this little task for her after school, that his behaviour is in no way acceptable.'

Rufus, Josie had discovered, had called his form teacher a stupid cow. It had happened after he had been reprimanded three times in class for not paying attention and for distracting the attention of everyone else at his table in a science lesson. He had taken no notice of the reprimands, and had then, when informed he would have to stay in after school as a punishment, shouted, 'You can't make me, you stupid cow!' He was being detained for thirty minutes doing something, the head teacher explained, repetitive, menial but constructive for the teacher to whom he had been rude.

Josie put her head back, against the wire fence, and closed her eyes. She felt so sad for Rufus that it would have been a relief to cry, but she couldn't seem to, as if the sadness went too deep and was too dark and heavy to be assuaged so easily. Poor little Rufus, living in a household where rows, or simmering about-to-be rows, were now almost a daily occurrence, where everybody seemed to be in the exhausted, angry habit of calling each other names, where every detail of daily life, every attempt to live as some kind of unit, had to be fought over. That Rufus should explode today didn't really surprise Josie. She would, she knew, have to explain to these kindly women who taught him what the atmosphere was like at Barratt Road just now and why it should affect Rufus— being used to the relatively calm and civilised world of the only child—so badly. But she couldn't say it now, not today. How could she be surprised at anything having, herself, only the night before, hit Becky?

She hadn't meant to. She hadn't even, until the split second she did it, been aware she was going to. She didn't think she had ever, in her adult life, hit anyone before, but there had been a moment, a ghastly, out-of-control, incandescently enraged moment in Becky's bedroom when she had known that she was literally beside herself, that she was going to do something violent. And she had. She had stepped forward into the chaos and racket of Becky's bedroom and hit her, hard, on the side of her head.

The evening had, on reflection, never boded well. Matthew, perceiving tensions mounting, had announced that he was taking Josie down to the pub on Sedgebury's unremarkable little canal, for an hour at least, away from the house, 'from you lot'. There'd been a chorus of objection then and a flat refusal from Becky to stay with the younger children. Matthew had argued, Becky had shouted, and Matthew, to Josie's intense disapproval, had agreed to pay her. They had then bickered about this all the way to the pub and found, when they got there, that the good weather had brought out hordes of people, spilling out from the pub onto the towpath.

'I don't want a drink, Matthew. I don't want to stay here, I want to go home.'

At home, despite the warmth of the evening, the curtains of the sitting room were drawn and Rory, Clare and Rufus were watching a programme about genital plastic surgery in Hollywood. Becky was in her room, with deafening music on. She had not, as she had been asked, put supper in the oven or laid the table.

'I'll go,' Matthew said wearily. 'I'll go and find her.'

'No,' Josie said. She felt suddenly, dangerously energetic. 'No, I will.'

'Please—'

'It's no good your going,' Josie said. 'Is it? It's no good because you're so *passive*.'

He had shrugged and turned away from her, opening the drawer in which the knives and forks were kept. Josie raced up the stairs.

'Becky!'

She banged on Becky's bedroom door.

'Shove off!' Becky shouted.

Josie opened the door. The room was strewn with clothes and shoes and bags. It was also shuddering with noise.

'Turn that off!'

Becky, who was standing in the middle of the room with a forbidden cigarette in her hand, merely stared. Josie pushed past her and seized her tape player, fumbling for the volume control.

'That's mine!'

'I'm not harming it, I merely want to be able to hear myself speak—'

Becky reached over and turned a knob. The volume of music declined a little, but not entirely. Then she took the tape player out of Josie's hand.

'Thank you,' Josie said. She was trembling slightly. 'Becky—'

'What?'

'You didn't put supper in the oven. You didn't lay the table.'

'Dad never said.'

'No. But I did. I asked you to.'

Becky climbed onto Clare's bed, still in her boots, and leaned against the wall. She blew out a nonchalant stream of smoke.

'You don't count.'

'I live in this house. I run it. I'm married to your father—'

Becky gave a snort of contempt. She trampled down the length of Clare's bed, got off the end heavily and stubbed her cigarette out on a plate on the floor.

'That doesn't give you any rights,' Becky said. 'That doesn't mean anything.' She shot Josie a glance. 'It won't even last.'

'What won't?'

'This stuff with my father.'

'Becky.'

Becky grunted.

Josie found that her fists had clenched. She unrolled them and held them flat against her skirt, against the sides of her thighs.

'Becky, may I tell you something? May I tell you something very important and also very true? If you were to succeed, Becky, if you were to succeed in breaking up my marriage to your father, you wouldn't rejoice. You'd be terrified. Because it wouldn't be a victory, it'd just be a loss, another loss on top of everything you've lost already.'

Becky looked at her. She looked at her for a long, hard time, as if she was really trying to see something, as if she was really trying to understand. Then she flung her head back and began to laugh, great derisive cackles of laughter. For a moment Josie had watched her, had looked at her tossed-back head and her big open mouth and her wild bush of hair, and then, without saying anything because she knew her hands would say it all, she stepped forward and slapped Becky, hard, on the right-hand side of her face and head. Becky had whipped upright, her eyes ablaze.

'You—you *hit* me!'

'Yes!' Josie had yelled, not caring who heard her. 'Yes, I did!'

'Sometimes,' Matthew said tiredly some three hours later, 'I feel I haven't got four children and a wife in this house, but five children. And you're the youngest.'

Josie, staring into the half-darkness of their street-lit bedroom, said nothing. Every instinct clamoured to scream at him that she often *felt* like an abandoned child herself and couldn't he see it, and make allowances for it, but, even as nerve-weary as she was, she could sense that this was no moment to say such things.

Instead she said, in a voice tight with self-control, 'Is Becky back?'

'No,' Matthew said. 'But she will be. She'll go round to a friend's, to give me a fright, but she'll be back.'

'And the others?'

'In bed.'

Josie felt, rather than saw, him stand up.

'Where are you going?'

'To do some work.'

'Now?'

'Just an hour. I may—I may be in for promotion. The head's moving on.'

'Oh,' Josie said faintly. 'Good.' She tried to say something more, something congratulatory and pleased, but, from the place of shame and helplessness where she seemed to have got herself, she found she couldn't. Instead she said shakily, 'Rufus—'

'He's asleep. Rory watched him.'

'Watched him?'

'Rory told him he'd stay awake until Rufus was asleep.'

Josie tried not to hear the edge of pride in Matthew's voice.

'And—and Clare?'

'In bed. Listening to *The Sound of Music*.'

'I see,' Josie said. She turned over carefully, so that her back was towards Matthew's shadowy shape across the room. She whispered, 'I see. Everybody's good, but me. Everybody's behaving well—except Becky who is of course now a victim—but me.'

'What did you say?'

'Nothing,' Josie said.

'I'll be in the attic.'

'All right.'

'Try and sleep,' Matthew said. His voice was kind, but the wrong kind of kind, too impersonal.

She said nothing. She bunched up the guilty hand that had slapped Becky and put it under her pillow. Then she heard the door open and close quietly again, behind Matthew.

'I'm here,' Rufus said now.

Josie opened her eyes. Rufus was standing two feet away, pale and subdued, his uniform very symmetrically in place as if someone had arranged him before he emerged from the school building. Josie held out her arms to him.

'Oh, darling—'

He came into them and stood against her, not fighting her off, but not yielding either.

'Don't worry about it, Rufus, I'll explain to them—'

'No.'

'Darling, they must know it wasn't your fault, they must understand what—'

'No,' Rufus said.

She held him harder. She wanted to tell him that she felt to blame, she felt responsible, that it was her inability to cope with the household in Barratt Road that was causing him to behave in a way that he'd never behaved in before, that wasn't in his nature.

'Look,' Josie said. She let Rufus go a little, so that she could look into his face. 'I know that you don't want to talk about it, but I don't want you to think it's your fault, either. Do you know what I mean?'

He looked at her. His gaze was veiled, almost opaque.

'Do you want,' Josie said, as gently as she could, 'to go and live in Bath again? With Daddy and Elizabeth?'

Rufus sighed. He took a step backwards.

'No,' he said. 'But I like going there. I like—' He stopped.

'You don't have to say any more. Are you hungry?'

'I don't know—'

'Shall we see? Shall we go and look at a pizza, or a burger, and see how you feel?'

'I'm too tired,' Rufus said.

Josie got off the wall.

'Then we'll go home—'

'Yes.'

'Put your bag in my bike basket.'

'I'll wheel it,' Rufus said. He put his hands on the handlebars of Josie's bike and his foot on the nearest pedal and began to scoot away from her.

She said, running after him, 'Matthew said Rory stayed awake for you last night.'

Rufus scooted more slowly.

'Yes. He did.'

It had been weird, really, but kind of, well, nice, too. Rory had said, 'I'll stay awake till you're asleep,' and when Rufus had stared at him, he'd added, 'If you like,' and Rufus had felt embarrassed and pleased and hadn't known what to say, so he'd dived into bed quickly and lain, as he always did, with his back to Rory so that he wouldn't see this disconcerting, well-intentioned watching actually going on.

'That was kind, wasn't it?'

'Yup,' Rufus said, and then he said, 'I'm not allowed to play football for a week,' and scooted away from Josie at speed.

When they reached Barratt Road, he slowed down and walked beside her. He had a little more colour in his face than he'd had when he'd come out of school, and his uniform, on account of his exertion on the bicycle, had a more naturally rumpled look. There would be half an hour, Josie thought, before Rory and Clare returned, and in that half-hour she could indulge, and perhaps assuage, the intensity of her maternal anxiety by spoiling Rufus with hot buttered toast and dry-roasted peanuts.

They had hardly turned up the drive before the kitchen door opened and Matthew emerged, running.

'Matt—'

'Thank God you're back. Where've you been?'

Josie didn't glance at Rufus.

'We got held up a bit. I saw your sister, I saw Karen—'

'Becky isn't back,' Matthew said.

'Not—'

'No. No one's seen her. She didn't go where I thought she'd gone, she didn't go to school—'

'Oh God,' Josie said.

'Come in,' Matthew said. 'Come in, will you?' He took the bicycle from Rufus. 'The police are here. They've been waiting to talk to you.'

Chapter
FIFTEEN

SINCE THE CHILDREN HAD GONE, Nadine had discovered, to her surprise and even disappointment, that the cottage didn't feel so threateningly insecure, just a damp, isolated, inconvenient place to live, and nothing more.

In the first week after their departure, she had been frantic. She had cried and cried, wandering from room to room and making a chart on one of the kitchen walls, to enable her to cross off each day that intervened before she would be able to have them back, for some, at least, of the school holidays. She paced round the telephone, willing them to call her, which they seldom did—prevented from doing so, no doubt—and in a fit of zeal turned out their bedrooms and took all the duvets and sleeping-bags and blankets to the dry-cleaner's, a great fusty multi-coloured mound in the back of the car, giving herself an extraordinary brief sense of happiness and achievement in the process. Then the tears and the energy were followed by gloom, days when she sat at her kitchen table staring out at the moist, milky Herefordshire light, making cups of coffee she didn't drink, and waiting, like a princess in a tower, for Tim Huntley to come down, as he often did, with a covered dish of something his mother had made, and tell her she'd got to eat it.

Tim Huntley had been a lifeline. He was, as a person, almost everything Nadine found incomprehensible—politically traditional, socially conventional, ill-read, obstinate and practical. His manner to her was not dissimilar to his manner to his cows, as if she, Nadine, was a living thing that had to be kept going with regular doses of the right diet and enough simple, foolproof instructions to keep her from swerving off the rails again, getting herself into a situation she couldn't manage. He found her a secondhand kiln, would only take twenty pounds for it, and showed her the way to the commune, where thirty or so people, mostly women and children, lived in organic harmony in a roughly converted barn, growing their own vegetables and weaving blankets of Welsh wool. They looked kindly at Nadine's pots and told her they would be happy to see her any time, whenever she wanted, and that she must bring her children, too, when she had them with her.

Gradually, the gloom lifted. She could even begin to notice the spring coming, leaves unfurling, a clump of small, intensely frilly wild daffodils in the unkempt garden behind the cottage. She even walked up to the Huntleys' farm, to find Mrs Huntley in her kitchen, dosing two lambs with something in a couple of baby's bottles, and thank her for all those covered dishes.

'It's nothing to me,' Mrs Huntley said. 'As long as you eat them.'

'I do—'

'How's that boy doing then?'

Nadine looked at the lambs. They were packed in a cardboard box together, sucking on the bottle with a fervour close to ecstasy.

'He's going to school, I think—'

'That's something.'

'But they don't sound very good on the telephone, they don't like it there, they don't like their stepmother.'

Mrs Huntley pulled the emptied bottle away from one lamb with a rubbery explosion.

'Who did? Whoever liked their stepmother?'

'This one—'

'Now, now,' Mrs Huntley said. 'No tales.' She took the bottle away from the second lamb. 'Would you like to give these two their second halves?'

Nadine found she liked it. The lambs were so comical and endearing in their single-minded obsession with food. Two days later, Tim brought a third lamb to the cottage, and dumped it in a box on her kitchen floor.

'What's that?'

'Something for you to look after. She needs a week of hand-feeding.'

'What if something happens?'

'Then you ring me.'

Nadine sat on the kitchen floor and looked at the lamb.

'She lost her mum,' Tim said. 'You be good to her.'

When he had gone, Nadine mixed the formula he had left and fed the lamb. For the first bottle, she fed her in the box as she had done up at the farm, but with the second one, she scooped the lamb up onto her lap and held her there, feeling her hard little hoofs against her thighs and every muscle solid with concentration. Then she put her back in the box. The lamb wriggled and bleated.

'No more,' Nadine said. 'Not now, later.'

The telephone began to ring. Nadine got up from crouching over the lamb and went to answer it.

'Nadine?' Matthew said.

She turned, holding the receiver under her chin so that she could see the lamb, peering at her over the edge of the box.

'I've got a lamb here—'

'What?'

'I've got a lamb,' Nadine said. Her voice was proud. 'Here in the kitchen. I'm looking after it.'

'Oh—'

'The children would love it. It's only about the size of—'

'Nadine,' Matthew said. 'I rang to tell you something.'

'What?'

'Well, it's OK now, we've found her, but Becky went missing—'

'What!' Nadine shrieked, spinning round to face the wall, gripping the telephone.

'She—well—she ran off. She ran away—'

'Why? What happened, what happened to her?'

'It doesn't matter what happened—'

'What do you mean, it doesn't matter? Of course it matters! It may not matter to you, but it matters to me, what causes my daughter to run away! What did you do to her?' Nadine screamed.

'If you won't let me talk and tell you what happened I'm putting the phone down.'

'No!' Nadine cried. 'No!'

'Then shut up and listen.'

Nadine closed her eyes. She wound her fingers into the telephone cord and pulled it tightly until the flesh went white.

'There was a row,' Matthew said, 'a family row in which Becky participated—'

'I don't believe you!'

'In which Becky participated as much as anyone and which resulted in her leaving the house to go round, I thought, to see a friend, but it transpired that she didn't do that, she didn't go anywhere near anyone she knew—'

'Oh my God,' Nadine said. She disentangled her fingers and shook them to get the circulation going again. 'Oh my God, how could you, how could you?'

'She went clubbing,' Matthew said. 'There's a new club in Sedgebury and she went there. I didn't even know it existed, or I'd have gone to look. I thought she was staying away just to scare me.'

'I bet you slept like a top,' Nadine said bitterly.

'I didn't sleep at all,' Matthew said. 'I haven't slept for nights, not even after we found her. Or, at least, the police did.'

'The police!'

'She hitched a lift. I think maybe she was aiming to get to Herefordshire, but she was found outside Stafford, in a lorry drivers' café. They brought her back last night. She's OK.'

'Where is she now?'

'In bed.'

'Get her! Get her for me! I've got to speak to her!'

'She's sedated. She was fine but very tired, so the doctor's given her something—'

'I must *talk* to her!' Nadine shouted.

'You can't, just now. She's to sleep until she wakes.'

'I demand it! I'm her mother!'

'She'll ring you the moment she wakes up—'

'I'm coming. I'm getting in the car and I'm coming.'

'No, you're not.'

'You can't stop me, I have every right, especially in the face of your neglect, your carelessness, your obsession with your new life which means you can't even—'

Matthew put the phone down.

'Bastard!' Nadine yelled into the receiver. Then she slammed it back onto the cradle. From its box, the lamb began to bleat.

'Shut up!' Nadine said. She was beginning to shake. She put out one unsteady hand and picked up the telephone receiver again, and then, with the other hand and with difficulty, dialled Tim's number.

'Come quickly—'

'What's up?'

'Come and take this lamb. I can't cope, I can't manage—'

'Stay there,' Tim Huntley said.

Nadine nodded. She let the receiver slip from her grasp, and then she slid down the kitchen cupboards she had been leaning against until she was sitting on the floor.

'Becky, oh Becky, poor Becky, poor—'

She gathered her knees up in her arms and put her head down on them and began to shake and whisper to herself.

'I'm so sorry,' Josie said.

She sat on the edge of Becky's bed, towards its foot, as if to sit any further towards the head implied an intimacy she felt she had no right to. Becky lay quite straight, in exactly the position in which she had woken, after sleeping for nineteen hours, with her head turned away from Josie and her gaze fixed on the wall.

'I really am. Whatever either of us said, I should never, ever have hit you and I regret it so much. I am truly sorry.'

Becky didn't move. She lay as if she were wholly unaware of Josie, as if Josie simply didn't exist for her, as if she had never spoken. Josie looked at her face—very pale—and at the dark tangle of hair on the pillow, and then, diffidently, at the long line of Becky's body under the duvet. The police had said Becky had had a bit of a scuffle some time in the two days and three nights of her absence, probably with one of the truck drivers who had given her a lift, but that it hadn't been serious. Becky hadn't been harmed. The doctor who sedated her said that she was a little bruised across the chest, but otherwise all right.

'Are you hungry?' Josie said. 'Would you like something to eat?'

Becky gave the smallest shake of her head. She wasn't hungry or thirsty, she wasn't, at the moment, conscious of any of the usual appetites but only of a curious, weightless, detached calm.

'Becky,' Josie said, 'will you speak to me? Will you at least accept that I am really sorry for what I did?'

Becky neither moved nor uttered. Slowly, Josie got off the bed and stood up. She had told the police that she had struck Becky and they had reacted as if smacks to the head followed by a child search were hardly out of the ordinary to them.

'It happens,' the sergeant had said. 'First sign of an adult stepping out of line, and the kids do a bunk.'

He hadn't looked at Josie while he said it, but at Matthew, and Josie had felt obscurely reprimanded, the one who couldn't cope, couldn't keep a hold on her temper. When the police rang, almost thirty-six agonising hours later, and she answered the telephone, they asked to speak to Matthew.

'Mr Mitchell, please,' they said, 'the young lady's father.'

'But have you—'

'Matthew Mitchell, please. Becky Mitchell's father.'

Matthew had wept when he heard Becky was safe. So did Josie, and Clare. Rufus and Rory sprawled on the stairs and kicked the banisters. Matthew had taken Clare on his knee and then Rory had climbed over Rufus to come and stand by his father and sister and Matthew had put an arm out and pulled him in.

I'm in disgrace, Josie thought.

She went into the kitchen and cried into the sink, holding on to the stainless-steel rim and letting her tears splash down in big drops. Rufus came into the kitchen and leaned on the cupboards beside her.

'You didn't do it on purpose,' he said.

'I did at the last minute. At the last minute, it was definitely on purpose—'

'You can't help the last minute,' he said. 'No one can.'

Josie shot him a grateful glance.

'Thank you.'

'It's true,' he said.

It was a woman police officer who had escorted Becky into the house, and then a woman doctor had come from the Sedgebury practice Josie wasn't yet very familiar with. Matthew and Rory had moved the mattress of Clare's bed to the space on the floor between the beds in the boys' room, and Becky had showered, in silence, and had then taken her prescribed sleeping pills and closed her own bedroom door behind her. Before they went to bed, Josie found Matthew sitting on the base of Clare's bed and gazing at Becky intently, while she slept. There had seemed to be nothing to say to him, just as there seemed, now, nothing to say to Becky.

'Come down, when you want to,' Josie said. 'Or stay there. It doesn't matter. You do what you want to.'

She looked round the room. Becky's boots lay on the floor, beside Clare's teddy bear.

'Sorry,' Josie said again.

'Hello,' Matthew said.

Becky turned her head very slowly on the pillow.

'Hi.'

He came to stand beside the bed, looking down at her. All that sleep and almost nothing to eat had given her a luminous look, almost one of fragility. Beside the bed was a tray bearing an untouched bowl of soup and an uneaten sandwich.

'Josie brought you lunch, I see.'

'I didn't want it.'

He sat on the edge of the bed.

'You aren't ill, Becky.'

She said nothing.

'We can't go on looking after you as if you were ill, if you aren't. Especially if you won't eat food Josie takes the trouble to prepare for you.'

Becky sighed.

'Josie's taking time off work,' Matthew said. 'To be with you. I can't, but she has managed it.'

'I didn't ask her,' Becky said. 'She doesn't have to.'

'She feels she does.'

'That's her problem.'

'No. It's her sense of responsibility. She offered to do it, to help me, for my peace of mind, as well as for you.'

Becky gave the food on the tray a brief, contemptuous glance.

'I'm not eating it.'

'Then I'll tell her to stop bringing it up.'

'Suit yourself,' Becky said.

Matthew put his elbows on his knees and leaned on them.

'I've got something to say to you.'

Becky waited. She yawned. She scooped her hair up into a thick bunch at the back of her head and let it fall again.

'I love Josie,' Matthew said.

Becky froze.

'I want you to be very certain of that. I love her. I want you to be very certain of something else, too. I love you. You are my daughter and I love you.'

Becky made a face.

'But?' she enquired sweetly.

'Not quite but.'

'What then?'

'You seem to think,' Matthew said, turning to look at her, 'that I have to choose between you and her. But I don't. I want you to be as certain of that as you are certain that I love you. I don't have to choose. I can have both relationships. You and her.'

She stared at him.

'You can't,' she said rudely.

'I can,' he said. He stood up. He seemed enormously tall, standing there so close to her bed. 'It's you that can't.' There was a beat. Becky couldn't look at him. Matthew moved away from her bed towards the door.

'If that's what you decide,' he said.

The house was very quiet. Becky sat on the edge of her bed. She was dressed, and felt rather fidgety, but, at the same time, directionless. She was also hungry. Despite Matthew's instructions, Josie had offered her a sandwich at lunchtime, standing at the bottom of the stairs and calling up, and Becky'd shouted above the music she'd started playing again that she wasn't hungry, that she didn't want anything. The thought of a sandwich made her mouth water. She'd found half a packet of crisps in the boys' bedroom and devoured them.

Downstairs, the telephone began ringing. It rang twice, three times, and then Josie answered it. Becky could hear the sound of her voice, but not what she was saying. After a moment or two, the sitting-room door opened downstairs and Josie called, 'Becky?' Her voice sounded odd.

Becky stood up.

'Yes?'

'Becky. Can you come?'

She went out onto the landing.

'Becky, it's your mother—'

'Yes?'

'She—doesn't sound very well, she sounds a bit fraught—'

Becky clumped down the stairs, pushing past Josie. Nadine always sounded fraught, especially if she had to ring Barratt Road, had to risk speaking to Josie. She picked up the receiver.

'Mum?'

Nadine was crying.

'You've got to come—I'm not allowed to come to you, your father won't let me, and now this has happened—I can't cope, I can't manage, you've got to come, you've got to come quickly—'

'What's happened? Are you OK? Are you hurt?'

'I don't know,' Nadine said, her voice ragged with tears. 'I don't know.'

'Jesus,' Becky said. 'Have you taken any pills or anything?'

'No,' Nadine said. 'No. But I need you. I need you here. I need you to come. I haven't seen you since all that happened. I have to see you, I *have* to.'

'OK,' Becky said. Her voice, she noticed, was shaky, as if she was shivering. 'OK.'

'Quickly,' Nadine said. '*Quickly.*'

'Yes.'

Becky heard the telephone go down. She stood for a moment, looking at the receiver in her hand, and then she put it down, too, and walked slowly into the kitchen. Josie was sitting at the table. She looked up as Becky came in, and said in a neutral voice, 'All right?'

Becky hesitated. She put her hand up to her mouth and began to chew at a cuticle.

'Not really,' she said.

Josie said, less neutrally, 'What's the matter?'

'She was crying,' Becky said. 'She sounded awful. She kept asking me to go—'

'To her? To Herefordshire?'

'She said she needed me. She said something had happened.'

Josie stood up.

'Is she ill?'

Becky looked at her.

'I don't know, she just sounded desperate. I—I've got to go, I've got to—'

'How will you get there?'

'I don't know. Train maybe, then a taxi—'

'I could take you,' Josie said. 'I've got the car today. It's outside. I could drive you to your mother's. Just let me leave a note for the others and ring Matthew—'

'No,' Becky said.

'No?'

'Don't tell Dad,' Becky said. 'Please. Just do it. Don't tell Dad.'

'Won't he think,' Josie said, looking at Becky, 'that it's the second irresponsible thing I've done as far as you're concerned, in a week?'

Becky knew her face and voice were full of pleading. She couldn't seem to help it.

'I'll tell him—'

'What will you tell him?'

'That you did it—' She stopped, gulped and then said, 'To help me.'

'You have to eat something.'

'No—'

'Becky,' Josie said, 'take three things out of the fridge, to eat on the journey, while I turn the car round. And leave a note for your father.'

'What'll I say?'

Josie went quickly past her and lifted the car keys from their hook by the outside door.

'I don't know,' she said. 'That's up to you.'

Chapter
SIXTEEN

RUFUS SAT AT THE DESK in his bedroom and contemplated his new curtains. They were green and cream, checked, quite a big check, with a dark green line running parallel to the edge. The line was made of something called braid. Rufus had chosen it when he went to choose the green and cream checks. He felt, surveying his first excursion into interior decor, very satisfied and rather as if he would like to go a bit further now and have a new duvet cover, since the arrival of the curtains had made the Batman print on his bed look babyish. Also a rug. Perhaps a red rug. He would ask Elizabeth. It was she, after all, who had taken him to the curtain place and just let him decide. She'd opened little fat books of pieces of material and said, 'What about that?' and, 'That sort of green?' and, 'I think you said no patterns, only lines, didn't you?' and left him to it.

'Rufus,' Dale said.

He glanced towards his bedroom door. Dale was leaning against the frame. She had shiny black boots on. Rufus looked at them.

'Hello.'

'Very smart curtains,' Dale said.

'I chose them.'

'Excellent choice. Nice desk, too.'

Rufus took his gaze away from Dale's feet and transferred it to his desk top. He kicked at the stretcher bar under his chair. He was never quite sure what he felt about Dale. He knew she was his half-sister, but she didn't feel like someone who belonged to him. In fact, he'd always liked the house better when Dale wasn't in it.

Dale moved from the doorway and went to the window.

'You've got such a nice view.'

Rufus said nothing. He picked up a retractable pen from his desk and began to click the point in and out, in and out.

'It's much nicer than my view,' Dale said. 'I don't know why I didn't choose this room.' She turned round from the window. 'I may be coming back here to live for a bit.'

Rufus stopped clicking.

'Why?'

'I've sold my flat,' Dale said. 'And I haven't bought another one yet. So I think I'll come home for a while and live up here. I could make Lucas's old room into a sitting room, couldn't I?'

'It's full of mess,' Rufus said.

'I could clear that. Perhaps we could put some in here, in boxes, because you aren't here very often, are you?'

Rufus jabbed the pen into the palm of his hand.

'I am.'

'What, once a month?'

'I don't want mess in here.'

'It would be very tidy, all in boxes—'

'No!'

'OK,' Dale said. 'It was just a suggestion.'

Rufus slid out of his desk chair. He wanted to say that he didn't want Dale there at all, he didn't want Dale up on his floor with him, where it was private, he didn't want her living there beside his room when he wasn't there himself, because he was in Matthew's house. But somehow he couldn't.

'I'm going downstairs,' he said.

In the kitchen, Elizabeth was reading the newspaper. She had it spread flat on the table and she had her glasses on and a mug of tea beside the newspaper. She didn't look up when he came in, but she said, 'There's a story here about albino frogs in the West Country. They aren't green, they're orange and pink and white. I shouldn't like that at all.'

Rufus hitched himself onto a chair opposite her.

'Sometimes there's toads in the garden here.'

'Are there?'

'I took a baby one to school once, in some wet stuff.' He began to fiddle with the edge of Elizabeth's newspaper, scuffling the pages about. She didn't tell him to stop. Instead she watched him for a bit and then said, 'Is Dale upstairs?'

He nodded. Elizabeth sighed. She took her glasses off.

He said, 'Where's Daddy?'

'In the office.'

'Dale said she was going to live in her room again.'

Elizabeth looked down at the paper.

'I know.'

'She wants to put some of the junk out of Lucas's room in my room.'

'She can't do that,' Elizabeth said.

'Does Daddy know?'

'Yes.'

'Is he cross?'

'No,' Elizabeth said. She looked at him. 'Don't worry. Nobody's putting anything in your room that you don't want there.'

Rufus wondered whether to say it wasn't just junk he didn't want, he didn't want Dale up there either. He glanced at Elizabeth. She was still looking at him, very seriously, as if to reassure him that nobody was going to say, 'Oh, Rufus is only eight and he's hardly ever here and he won't mind anyway,' and get away with it.

'Shall we go out?' Elizabeth said.

'Out?'

'Yes. We could go and look at something or go for a walk.'

'Could we buy a rug?'

'A rug?'

'For my room. A red one.'

'I don't see why not.' Elizabeth stood up. 'Would you like to go and tell Daddy that we're going out then?'

Rufus hesitated.

'Aren't you going to?'

'No,' Elizabeth said. 'I'm not.'

Rufus slid off his chair.

'Will we be hours?'

'We might be. We might decide to have lunch somewhere.'

'What about Daddy's lunch?'

Elizabeth picked up her handbag and opened it, to put her glasses away.

'Dale can do that.'

Rufus moved to the kitchen doorway and then stopped.

'Is Daddy cross?' he said again.

Elizabeth took a lipstick out of her handbag.

'No,' she said. 'It isn't Daddy that's cross. I'm afraid it's me that is.'

Duncan Brown made himself some soup in a mug. It really was most ingenious, the way a small foil envelope of fawn-coloured powder, faintly speckled, became, with the addition of boiling water, a mug of mushroom soup, complete with little dark chunks of actual mushroom. He stirred it thoughtfully. His late wife, Elizabeth's mother, had always, meticulously, made mushroom soup in a saucepan, starting with mushrooms and flour and butter and going on with stock and milk.

'Am I like my mother?' Elizabeth had said to him today.

'Only to look at, really. Why do you ask?'

'I don't seem to remember her as very maternal—'

'She wasn't.'

'And I want a baby so much!' Elizabeth had cried suddenly, and then burst into tears.

On the way home from work one evening, she had called in at a set of consulting rooms off Harley Street, where she had previously been to visit a gynaecologist who was married to a colleague of hers. Elizabeth had been examined, and had had a blood test taken and, that evening, had been told that not only was everything normal and healthy, but also she was still ovulating.

'Of course,' the gynaecologist had said, 'your chances of conceiving would be even better if you had chosen a strapping boy of twenty-two. But we don't choose these things, do we? They choose us. Good luck, anyway.'

Duncan carried his soup mug and a half-eaten packet of water biscuits into his sitting room. He made his way to his particular chair and sat down in it, holding his soup mug carefully level and putting the biscuit packet down on a nearby pile of books. It was on the small, broken-springed sofa opposite that Elizabeth had been sitting when she had said—quite violently for her—that she wanted a baby so badly.

'Why shouldn't you have one?' Duncan said gently.

Elizabeth blew her nose fiercely. 'Tom doesn't want one. He's had three. He says he's too old. He doesn't seem to see that I badly want one and that I, miraculously, don't seem to be too old at all to stand quite a good chance of having one.'

Duncan got up and poured two generous quantities of sherry into a couple of rose-pink Moroccan tea glasses. He held one out to Elizabeth.

'It's like talking to someone who can't hear me,' Elizabeth said. 'First Dale, and now this. No, he says, smiling and kind and immovable. We don't need a baby, we have each other, we have our work, we have Rufus whom we both adore—true—and we don't need a baby.' She took a gulp of sherry and then said, more wildly, 'But *I* do! I want home and hearth and a *baby!*'

Duncan turned the tea glass round in his fingers.

'Do you imagine the present difficulties with Dale—'

'Oh, don't *talk* about them,' Elizabeth said, blowing her nose again. 'You can't conceive of how demanding she is and how passive he seems to be in response! And I have to be so restrained and tactful, and never expose my true feelings while Dale believes she has every right to impose her own needs and desires all over everyone else, and insist upon our sympathy about *everything*, because once upon a time she lost a mother whom I am beginning to detest with an intensity that amazes me.'

'Goodness,' Duncan said.

Elizabeth took another gulp of sherry.

'It's such a relief to *say* it.'

'And the brother?'

'I rang him,' Elizabeth said. 'I probably shouldn't have, but I was at the end of my tether and I had this mad idea of asking him to stand up for me in this business of Dale moving back in. But when it came to it, I couldn't ask him, I couldn't say. He—'

'What?'

'He implied I'd got to sort it out for myself, and of course he's right.'

'Can you disentangle all this if Tom can't help you?' Duncan said.

Elizabeth sighed. She reached out and placed the tea glass on the dictionary that Duncan used for newspaper crosswords.

'I love him,' Elizabeth said. 'I see how hard it is for him, I see how torn he is, I see how he is burdened with this sense of responsibility he's had ever since Pauline died. I just wonder—if he can see how hard it is for me, too.'

'I expect he can,' Duncan said. 'And he doesn't know what to do.' He watched her. The glow he'd noticed at Christmas, gilding her like a nimbus, had dimmed a little.

'Elizabeth,' he said finally.

'Yes?'

'You're in a corner, aren't you, up a cul-de-sac?'

'Yes.'

'My dear. What are you going to do?'

She lifted the tea glass and drained all the sherry out of it in two swallows.

'I'm going to ask him,' she said. 'Ask him to stand up for me.'

Chapter
SEVENTEEN

THE HUNTLEYS' FARMHOUSE rose redly out of the red Herefordshire earth as if it had, over the centuries, just slowly emerged from it. It was built on a slope, with carelessly arranged barns here and there beside it, and a stream between it and the lane over which Tim had laid a crude bridge made of old railway sleepers. As Becky crossed the bridge, two sheepdogs tethered with long, clattering lengths of chain just inside the entrance to the nearest barn raced forward, barking and leaping. They couldn't reach her by yards, but all the same, Becky kept to the far side of the bridge and made at speed for the gate into the little farm garden.

The door to the house opened before she reached it. Mrs Huntley, whom she had never met, stood in the doorway and regarded her without smiling.

'We wondered when you'd be coming.'

Becky swallowed.

'I've been looking after Mum.'

Mrs Huntley surveyed her. She looked at her unbrushed hair and her jeans jacket and her long, grubby skirt and her unpolished boots. 'You'd better come in.'

Becky followed her. The kitchen was low and small and shabby and clean. On a plastic-covered table by the window were several egg boxes holding weirdly sprouting seed potatoes, and, to one side of them, sat Tim Huntley, in his stockinged feet, eating something from a steaming plate. He gave Becky the merest glance and indicated the chair opposite him.

'Sit down.'

Becky sat. She folded her chipped nails out of sight and put her fists in her lap. Mrs Huntley poured a cup of tea from a pot on the range and put it on the table within Becky's reach. Becky didn't drink tea.

'Thanks,' she said.

'Well,' Tim said. 'What have you got to tell us?'

Becky looked at her tea. She said, 'I—I don't know what happened.'

Mrs Huntley said, 'What did your mother say?'

Becky hesitated. Nadine had been wildly upset, she said, at hearing of Becky's running away and then outraged at Matthew's refusal to let her come . . .

'He didn't,' Becky said wearily.

'He did, he did, he forbade me!'

. . . and then Tim had brought her a lamb and she thought she could cope and then she heard about Becky and panicked and rang Tim and he came and she was hysterical and then he slapped her and lugged her upstairs to bed and then . . .

'What?' Becky said. 'Did he try anything?'

'I don't know,' Nadine said. 'I can't remember, I just know he scared me—he was rough. I didn't know what was going to happen.'

Becky looked away now from both Tim and Mrs Huntley's gaze.

'She—she's not very clear.'

Tim snorted.

'We don't want any nonsense,' Mrs Huntley said. 'We don't mind looking after her, but we don't want any trouble.'

'I came,' Becky said, loudly before her courage went, 'to thank you for getting the doctor.'

Tim shrugged.

'She was hysterical.'

Becky said nothing.

He put a mouthful in, chewed a while and then said, 'She was on the floor when I got there and when I tried to get her up she went for me. So

I slapped her. Slapped her to shut her up.' He took a swallow of tea. 'Then I took her upstairs. She was screaming all the way.' He gave Becky a level look. 'I put her on the bed. Then I went down and rang the doctor.'

Becky looked at her cup of tea. It was thick, milky brown.

She said, 'She's better now.'

'Glad to hear it.'

Mrs Huntley said, 'Did she ring you?'

'Yes—'

'Who brought you? We saw a car, a red car—'

Becky hesitated.

'My—stepmother.'

'That was good of her,' Mrs Huntley said.

Becky nodded. It had been good of her. It had also been deeply disconcerting when they got there and Josie had offered to come into the cottage with her.

'No,' she'd said. 'No, it's OK.'

Josie had looked up at her, out of the car window.

'I'll wait here.'

Becky had nodded. She'd put her hand on the gate, and for a moment had felt she could go no further. She stood there, head bent, looking at her hand on the gate and fighting the urge to turn round and say to Josie, 'Come with me, please come.' She'd won. It had taken her some time, but she'd won. She'd gone up the path to the cottage's back door and in through the kitchen and up the stairs, step after step, to find Nadine lying in bed with her eyes closed. It was only then that she'd screamed, it was only then that she'd allowed herself to admit that she'd found what she dreaded to find: Nadine dead in bed because Becky hadn't got to her quickly enough, because Becky was living somewhere else instead of here in the cottage.

After that, it was awful. Nadine opened her eyes and said something but Becky couldn't stop screaming and her screaming brought Josie running in from the car and, at the sight of Josie, Nadine just went ballistic and there was a horrible brawling scuffle that made Becky so sickened, so ashamed that she'd gone from screaming to utter silence in a second. Josie had managed, at last, to free herself, and Becky had followed her, despite Nadine's demands and pleadings to her not to. They'd stood, shaking, by the car.

'You'd better come back with me,' Josie said.

Becky shook her head. 'I can't.'

'Look,' Josie said. She was leaning against the car, as if she couldn't quite stand up without its help. 'I know any remark I make will sound to you like a criticism of your mother, but will you be safe?'

'Oh yes,' Becky said. She turned her face away. 'She's—she's never done anything like that before.'

'I can't leave you here like this, alone with her. I must get a doctor or something.'

'OK,' Becky said. Her shoulders slumped a little.

'It's Saturday tomorrow. Maybe Matthew could come—' She stopped.

'I'll ring,' Becky said. 'I'll ring and tell you.'

She'd stood in the road, watching Josie drive away slowly. When she was out of sight, Becky turned and went back into the cottage. Nadine was standing by the kitchen table, her hands folded in front of her.

She said, very clearly, as if she'd been planning it, 'I'm very sorry.'

Becky said nothing. She went past Nadine to the sink and leaned over it to open the window.

'About everything,' Nadine said.

Becky breathed in the air coming in from outside.

'There's a doctor coming.'

'I don't need one,' Nadine said. 'I've seen the doctor. Tim got her for me. I've got antidepressants and some sleeping pills. I'd taken some of them before you came.'

'Typical—'

'What is?'

Becky turned round. 'To ring me and then take sleeping pills which are meant for the night anyway.'

Nadine stared at her.

'I said I was sorry. I am. Very sorry.'

'I don't care,' Becky said.

She moved over to the refrigerator and opened the door. Inside were a few things in brown paper bags, a cracked egg on a saucer and a carton of long-life apple juice.

'What are you going to do?' Nadine said.

Becky slammed the refrigerator door shut again.

'I haven't decided.'

'Will you stay?' Nadine said. Her voice had an edge of real anxiety. 'Will you stay and keep me company?'

Becky glanced at her. She touched the breast pocket of her denim jacket and let her hand linger there for a moment. On the journey, Josie had stopped for petrol, and when she got back into the car, after paying, she'd handed Becky a packet of Marlboro Lights. She hadn't said anything. Nor had Becky.

'I'm going out,' Becky said.

'Where?'

'I don't know. A walk maybe.'

'Will you be long?'

'No,' Becky said.

'I need to talk to you,' Nadine said. 'We need to talk all this through.'

'Sorry,' Becky said. She went across the kitchen to the door to the outside. 'I'll stay till you're better. I said I would. But I didn't say I'd talk.'

'You've been here a week,' Mrs Huntley said now.

'I know.'

'What about your schooling?'

'It was the end of term today. Anyway, I'd been off school—'

Tim Huntley dropped a wedge of bread onto his cleared plate and began to push it round with the fork.

'What about your dad lending a hand with all this?'

'He can't.'

'Why not?'

Becky looked straight at him.

'She wouldn't let him.'

He put the wedge of bread in his mouth.

'So it's down to you?'

Becky shrugged. She stood up, holding the edge of the table. 'I'd better be getting back.'

Tim Huntley stood, too.

'Give us a call. Any time.'

'Thanks,' Becky said.

She went out of the farmhouse, while they watched her, and then, at a safe distance, past the barking dogs and over the sleeper bridge to the road. The stream was full and the hawthorn hedge was frosted with bright green leaves, each one neatly cut out, as if with embroidery scissors. Becky took her cigarettes out of her pocket and put one in her mouth. It was the last but one in the pack that Josie had given her a week ago. She paused to light up and then walked on, blowing blue smoke into the clear air.

Nadine was sitting on the grass in the garden, under an apple tree. She had her glasses on, and, in her lap, a pile of 'Teach Yourself Greek' books she'd found in the local junk shop. She looked up as Becky came in through the gate.

'How was that?'

'OK,' Becky said.

'Are you going to tell me about it?'

'There's nothing to tell,' Becky said. She leaned against the apple tree. 'Tim was eating and they asked how you were.'

Nadine took her glasses off.

'I'm fine.'

'For now,' Becky said. She put her hand on her jacket pocket. One left. Save it for later. She slid down the tree and sat with her back against it, holding her knees.

'No, I really will be fine now. Summer's coming—'

'You shouldn't live alone,' Becky said.

'What?'

'You heard me. You shouldn't live alone. You can't cope.'

Nadine turned on her a gaze full of distress.

'Oh, Becky—'

'You can't,' Becky said. She looked up at the sky, through the apple tree's branches. 'And—' She stopped.

'And what?' Nadine said, her voice sharp with apprehension.

'And,' Becky said, her gaze still on the sky, 'I can't live with you any more. Not permanently. I can't cope with you either.'

'I haven't got it,' Matthew said.

Josie turned. He leaned in the kitchen doorway, still in his jacket and tie from work, but the tie was crooked and loosened. He came into the room, pulled a chair out from the table and sat down. Josie pushed another chair next to him and slipped into it. She took his nearest hand.

'Oh, Matt.'

'They said that, although I had all the required experience and qualifications, they felt that because of my family circumstances this wasn't a good moment in my life for me to take on extra responsibility. They said that kind of thing several times over in various ways until I felt so dysfunctional by implication I could hardly sit up. The injustice of it—'

'I know.'

'I don't mean the injustice of not giving me the job, I mean the other injustice, the weaselly insinuation that my family circumstances are too much for me now when they used to be far, *far* worse.'

Josie lifted the hand she held and put it against her face.

He leaned forward and kissed her.

'We needed this promotion,' he said. 'We needed something positive to happen, something to show us we'd turned a corner.' Gently he took his hand out of hers. 'Where are the children?'

'Out,' Josie said. 'Clare and Rory are next door and Becky's gone to see a friend.'

'Is—is it any better since Becky came back?'

'It's quieter,' Josie said.

'Only that?'

She looked down at her hands. Something had arisen in her mind during that drive back from Herefordshire, something which she was not yet ready to tell Matthew about. Something had changed, something in her perception of Matthew's children had altered, and while she considered it, and what to do about it, she wanted to keep it private. She'd thought, often and often, of Becky's face as she got out of the car, outside Nadine's cottage, of Becky's figure dwindling in the driving mirror as she drove away after that hideous scene. She had not expected Nadine to be so violent. Nor had she expected her to be beautiful. Nor—and this was the most astonishing nor of all—had she expected there to be a real, a palpable reluctance between herself and Becky to part. A glimmer of hope had flickered, faint but unquestionably there.

'Josie?' Matthew said,

She looked up at him.

'I'm really sorry,' she said.

'I know. So am I.' He stood up. 'I just feel—'

'Please,' Josie said, interrupting. 'Please don't say any more. Please don't. This is a disappointment, but it's not something worse than that, it's not as bad as things have been.'

He gave her a small smile.

'Maybe.'

He went out of the room. She heard his tread going up the stairs and into their bedroom and then the sound of a drawer being opened while he looked for a sweater to wear instead of his jacket. Then she could hear the clatter of the extending ladder being pulled down, to give him access to the attic.

She looked down at the kitchen table. There was a postcard from Rufus to Rory showing a picture of the Roman baths in Bath. He'd got rollerblades, he said, and it was raining a lot. His handwriting was small and cramped. Love from Rufus, he'd written at the bottom. Rufus had rollerblades. Perhaps the nice Elizabeth had bought them for him.

The door opened. Becky, holding a small carrier bag from a music shop, came in. Josie looked up.

'Hello.'

Becky nodded.

'I saw Dad come back.'

'He's upstairs,' Josie said.

'I'll go up—'

'Becky,' Josie said. 'Becky, would you do something for me first?'
Becky eyed her.
'What?'
'Would you get the others from next door?'
'Why?'
'I've got a reason,' Josie said. 'I wouldn't ask you to do it if I hadn't.'

Becky hovered uncertainly for a moment, and then she went out of the kitchen and Josie could hear her boots clumping down the drive.

Shortly, the outer door opened again, with a bang.

'Thank you for coming back.'

They all three looked at her.

'It's two things, really,' Josie said. She moved the chair which Matthew usually occupied, at the head of the table, and sat down in it. 'Do you want to sit down, too?'

Becky closed the door and leaned against it, her hands behind her back. Rory stayed where he was, squatting over his laces. Clare came forward and sat at the table.

'I don't know if this is the right moment to say what I'm going to say,' Josie said. 'But it seems quite a good moment. I'm afraid your father hasn't got his promotion.'

They stared at her.

'I don't need to tell you how he feels,' Josie said. 'And what you say to him and what he says to you about it is your affair. But it's given me a chance to say some things I maybe couldn't say if nothing had happened.'

Rory got up very slowly and slid into a chair beside Clare.

'The thing is,' Josie said, and stopped. She pushed her hair behind her ears and said abruptly, 'We don't have to be a disaster. Really we don't. Maybe we've got a sort of chance now. Maybe we could start, well, mending things after all that breaking. If—if we stopped being afraid of being a stepfamily, that is.' She folded her right hand over her wedding ring. 'I know I'm not your mother. I never will be. You've got a mother. But I could be your friend, I could be your supporter, your sponsor. Couldn't I?' She took her hands off the table and put them in her lap. 'I really just want to say that we may be a different kind of family, but we don't have to be worse. Do we?'

Becky came away from the door. She moved only a few steps, until she was standing behind Clare.

She said, blurting the words out, 'What about Mum?'

Josie took a breath.

'She'll have to find a way. Like we all have to.'

She stood up slowly. They didn't watch her.

'You ought to go and see Matthew,' Josie said. 'He's the one in need right now.'

'OK,' Rory said. 'OK, OK.'

He sprang up and darted past her and wrenched open the door to the hall. Clare followed him and their feet stampeded up the stairs. Becky watched them. She stayed where she was. Then she said, gesturing awkwardly towards the kettle, 'Would you like a coffee?'

Chapter EIGHTEEN

DALE'S POSSESSIONS almost filled the landing on the top floor. They were very orderly, labelled boxes and bags and plastic carriers, stacked tidily against the walls. Rufus's bedroom door was open, and inside, on the floor, lay Dale's television and video recorder and a small mountain of the items out of Lucas's room. Lucas's room had been cleared in order to make way for the sofa from Dale's flat and a low table and lamps and a stack of posters in rimless frames. Dale's own bedroom door was closed and locked.

It had all happened in five days. Elizabeth had gone back to London on Sunday evening. She had spoken to Tom several times throughout the working week. He had said nothing about Dale, nothing about Dale's possessions. Elizabeth hadn't been surprised. One of the agreements they had reached at the end of a distressing conversation about Dale was that Tom would indeed do something about her, but must be left to do that thing, whatever it was, in privacy.

On Friday night, Elizabeth had returned to Bath. Tom, as usual, came to greet her at the station. He looked tired. His manner was guarded. He said, trying to make light of it, 'I'm afraid I'm not doing very well. But at least it's only temporary.'

'What d'you mean?'

'You'll see,' he said.

She went straight upstairs when they reached the house. She knew what she'd find when she reached the top and, sure enough, she found it, except that its orderliness was more assertive than she had bargained for. She stood and looked, with both rage and despair, at the blatant, unmistakable evidence of Dale's relentless purpose.

She glanced at Rufus's room. Lucas's skis and poles and his tennis racket were piled on the bed and Rufus's new red rug was almost obscured under a haphazard clutter of splitting bags and broken boxes. The order that prevailed among Dale's own possessions was plainly not a courtesy extended to anyone else's. Elizabeth ran into Rufus's room and somehow manhandled the television and video recorder out into the small remaining space left on the landing. Then she began to seize the bags and boxes randomly, almost running in her breathless hurry to get them out of Rufus's room and dump them, anywhere, anyhow, among the symmetrical piles on the landing. She started to throw things, hurling them out of the door and letting them clatter and slither where they fell, pictures and books, plastic sacks of clothes and bedding, a shoebox of old cassette tapes. Then she grabbed the skis and the tennis racket in a great unwieldy armful and, staggering out of the room with them, flung them, banging and thumping, down the stairs.

'What in hell's name is going on?' Tom said.

He stood at the foot of the topmost flight of stairs and looked upwards. Elizabeth chucked the final cushion.

'What do you bloody *think*?'

Tom stepped over a tennis racket and moved a ski from where it lay, jammed crosswise across the staircase.

'Dale isn't living here,' he said. 'Please don't be so melodramatic. She isn't living here. She's living with a friend. She's got nowhere to put anything until she finds a flat, so I said—'

'Oh!' Elizabeth cried in exasperation. 'Oh, don't *tell* me what you said! I can imagine exactly what you said! You said all the reasonable, placatory, surrendering things you have so disastrously said to Dale for twenty years. What d'you mean, she isn't living here?'

'She isn't.'

Elizabeth gestured wildly towards Lucas's bedroom door. 'Then why make a sitting room of this? Why do expressly what Rufus didn't want, the minute his back is turned? Why keep *her* door locked? Why be so utterly, bloody provocative if she doesn't actually intend to move back in here and watch you and me like a hawk?'

'Elizabeth,' Tom said. He closed his eyes briefly, as if summoning the patience to deal with the kind of unreasonableness that no civilised man should ever be required to deal with. 'Elizabeth. Will you please stop screaming and simply *listen*? I have spoken to Dale, as you requested—'

'As we agreed!'

'As you requested, and she asked if she might just store things here for a few weeks until she finds a flat. She is living with a friend called Ruth, with two young children, in Bristol. She has looked at three flats this week and is viewing two more tomorrow. The invasion of Rufus's room is only temporary, and it will be restored before he next needs it.'

'You are a fool, Tom Carver, if you believe any of that. And you're not only a fool, but you're weak.' Her voice rose. 'Dale can do what she bloody well likes with you because you are completely, pathetically *weak!*'

He looked up at her. His expression was neither friendly nor unfriendly but empty, as if he didn't recognise her, as if her insults meant nothing to him because they were, in fact, perfect strangers to one another. Then he turned and went, with great dignity, downstairs. Elizabeth watched him go and when he was out of sight round the curves of the staircase, she stepped over the trailing leads of the television and the scattered contents of various bags and boxes, crossed to Rufus's bed and lay down on it, face down on the Batman duvet cover he so strenuously wished to exchange for something more sophisticated, and held on to it, for dear life.

'I'm sorry,' Tom said.

He had laid two places, opposite one another, at the kitchen table, and lit candles. There was an opened wine bottle, too, and a warm buttery smell. He took Elizabeth in his arms.

'I really am sorry.'

She laid her face against his shoulder, against the dark blue wool of his jersey. She waited for herself to say 'Me, too'. It didn't happen.

'It was unforgivable of me,' Tom said. 'Especially on a Friday night with you tired and me cross with myself.'

Elizabeth sighed.

'How did it happen?'

'When I was out,' Tom said. 'On Wednesday. I was out, meeting a new client who wants to make a house out of an eighteenth-century chapel, and came back to find a note. Then she came the next day and sorted things out a bit, and told me about Ruth.'

Elizabeth extricated herself from Tom's embrace. She said tiredly, 'I don't believe in Ruth.'

'She exists.'

'Oh,' Elizabeth said, 'I believe *that.*'

'Sit down,' Tom said.

He pulled out a chair on the side of the table where Elizabeth usually sat, and pressed her gently down into it.

'I bought skate. Skate wings. I knew you liked them.'

'I do.'

Tom put a bowl of salad on the table and a yellow pottery dish of new potatoes. The potatoes were freckled with parsley. Elizabeth looked at them. She wondered, with a kind of detachment, if it was normal to remember to garnish potatoes with parsley or if, and particularly this evening, it had a significance, a subtle message from the parsley chopper to the parsley consumer about the extra trouble taken and all that that implied, about love being expressed in practical details because it was sometimes so impossible to express it more straightforwardly.

He put a plate in front of her. The skate lay on it, darkly glistening, beside a wedge of lemon.

'Thank you,' Elizabeth said. 'It looks lovely.'

He sat down opposite her.

'You look so tired.'

She picked up her knife and fork.

'That's crying.'

He said, with warmth, 'You're wonderful about Rufus.'

'Tom,' she said, cutting carefully into her fish, 'let's not talk about him. Let's not talk about children, any children.'

He smiled.

'Of course,' he said. He picked up the wine bottle and reached through the candles to fill her glass. 'This chapel I saw is fascinating. It's rather classical in design, pedimented and so forth. A lovely building, full of light, all grey and white panelling. Badly decayed, of course.'

Elizabeth took two potatoes out of the yellow dish.

'Can I see it?'

'Of course. I'd love to show it to you. It's listed, so we have to make practical rooms out of the vestry and back quarters and leave the chapel itself as a living space.'

Elizabeth looked up suddenly.

'What was that?'

'What?'

'Something,' Elizabeth said. 'The front door—'

Tom got half up. There were quick footsteps in the hall and then the kitchen door opened.

'Hi!' Dale said.

She was smiling. She carried her handbag and keys in one hand and a bunch of stargazer lilies in the other. She swirled round the table and pushed the flowers at Elizabeth.

'For you.'

Elizabeth took a breath.

'Oh—'

Tom was standing straight now.

'Darling—'

'Hi, Daddy,' Dale said. She spun back round the table and kissed him.

'You didn't say you were coming—'

'I didn't know,' Dale said. She winked at Elizabeth. 'I didn't know until I got back and found that Ruth's hot date from last night was still there, wearing nothing but a bath towel. Ruth didn't exactly say push off but she hardly needed to. Hey, don't stop eating your supper.' She bent briefly towards Elizabeth's plate and sniffed extravagantly. 'Smells *wonderful*. What is it?'

'Skate,' Elizabeth said.

'Dale,' Tom said. 'We are having supper together, Elizabeth and I—'

Dale bent forward again and lifted the lilies from Elizabeth's lap.

'I'll put those in water for you.'

Elizabeth closed her eyes.

Dale ran water noisily into the sink 'I'm not going to interrupt you,' she said. 'Honestly, I had some soup, I'm fine, and I've got so much to do upstairs you wouldn't believe.'

'Tonight?' Tom said. 'Now?'

She turned from the sink, the lilies dripping in her hands, her hair and teeth and eyes shining

'Honestly,' she said again. '*Honestly*, Daddy. Have you even *seen* it up there? I promise you it's going to take me a couple of hours just to make enough space to *sleep*.'

Dale was singing. Elizabeth could hear her clearly from the kitchen two floors below. She had a good voice, light but true and sweet. She was singing along to a CD of the score of *Evita,* and the sound came spiralling down the house, rippling through open doors, flowing everywhere. As a sound it was quite different, the complete opposite, in fact, of the sound that Dale had made the night before when she discovered the havoc that Elizabeth had wreaked on the top floor. That had been terrible; screams and howls of rage and outrage, thundering feet down the stairs, cascades of furious tears. Elizabeth had sat in her place at the table, and declined, mutely and stubbornly, to have anything to do with what was going on. It was Tom who had attempted to soothe Dale, Tom who had gone back upstairs with her to help her sort out the muddle. Elizabeth wondered if Tom could hear the singing now in the basement. He had been down there since four or five that morning, when he had given up all attempts at trying to sleep and had slid out of bed, trying not to wake Elizabeth who was awake already and pretending not to be in order not to have to say anything.

She had taken coffee down to him about eight. He had been sitting, wrapped in a bathrobe, in front of his drawing board, looking at drawings of the chapel. He took the coffee and put his other arm round her, still looking at the drawings.

He took a swallow of coffee.

'I'm afraid of what you're thinking,' he said.

She moved herself gently out of his embrace.

'I'm afraid, too.'

'Shall we—shall we go and look at this, this morning?'

'Yes,' Elizabeth said.

He took her hand for a second.

'Good.'

Half an hour later, he had come into the kitchen to leave his empty mug on his way upstairs to shave and dress. Elizabeth was sitting at the table, already dressed, reading an arts supplement from the previous weekend's newspaper. Tom bent, as he passed her, and kissed her hair.

She said, 'Breakfast?'

'No thanks. I've got about another half-hour to do downstairs before we go. Can you wait?'

'Yes.'

'You don't mind waiting?'

'No,' Elizabeth said.

She had tidied up the kitchen and fed Basil one of his tiny gourmet tins. He had eaten it seemingly in a single swallow and had then heaved himself onto a kitchen chair so that he could gaze pointedly at the milk jug and the butter dish. It was then that the singing began. Elizabeth was just stooping to tell Basil, in a voice of profound indulgence, that he was the greediest person she had ever met, when the first wave of sound came rolling lightly down the stairwell. She straightened.

'It's Dale—'

Basil seemed entirely indifferent. He leaned his chins on the table edge and purred sonorously at the butter.

'She's singing,' Elizabeth said out loud in amazement. 'She's woken up and found herself to be exactly where she intended to be and she's singing. In triumph.'

Basil put a huge paw on the table, next to his face. Elizabeth knelt beside him. She put her forehead against his furry reverberating side.

'I can't bear it. I can't.' She closed her eyes.

'Dearest,' Tom said from the doorway.

She looked up.

'Are you ready?' Tom said. 'Shall we go now?'

The chapel stood in a side street in the north of the city, balanced precariously on a hill, between a short row of shops and a terrace of neglected houses, mostly divided into flats. In front of it, separated from the street by iron railings and a locked iron gate, was a rectangle of unkempt grass.

The chapel had handsome double doors under a nobly pedimented porch. Tom put a key into the lock and turned it.

'There.'

Elizabeth peered in. There were windows down both sides, a second tier of them running above a graceful gallery. The nave space was empty, except for debris and a little huddle of pitch-pine pews below a magnificent panelled pulpit.

Elizabeth walked forward, her feet grinding on the dust and fallen plaster.

'It's lovely.'

'I thought you'd think that.'

She leaned on the back of one of the pitch-pine pews.

'Do you feel excited, every time you get a new commission, every time you look at something like this, that you can rescue?'

He walked past her and gave the panelling of the pulpit a professional pat or two.

'Not as much as I did.'

Elizabeth slid her hands back and forth along the pew back. It was slippery with varnish, ugly in so elegant a place.

'Tom.'

He didn't turn from the pulpit.

'Yes?'

'I can't marry you.'

He leaned forward and put his forehead against the pulpit, one hand still resting against the panelling.

'You know why,' Elizabeth said.

There was a long, complicated silence and then Tom said, indistinctly, 'I warned you about Dale.'

Elizabeth brought her hands together on the pew back and stared down at them for a moment. Then she looked up at Tom.

'Yes,' she said. 'You did. You told me not to offer my house to her. You warned me that she might try to overwhelm me, to overwhelm us.

But—' She paused and then said, very softly, 'You never warned me that you'd do nothing to stop her.'

Very slowly, Tom took his head and his hand away from the pulpit and turned round to face her.

'I love you,' he said.

She nodded.

'I didn't know,' Tom said, 'I never dared to hope that I could love anyone as much again. But I have. I do. I love you, I think, more than I've ever loved any woman.'

Elizabeth said sadly, 'I believe you—'

'What about Rufus?'

Elizabeth shut her eyes.

'Don't—'

'You'll break his heart—'

'And mine.'

'How *can* you?' Tom shouted suddenly. 'How *can* you let this—this single aspect get to you so?'

'It isn't a single aspect,' Elizabeth said steadily. 'It's a fundamental. It colours everything and you know it. I think I understand something of your position, but I also think nobody can change things but you.'

His face was eager.

'I *will* change things!'

'How?'

'We'll move, we'll do what you wanted, another house, another city, a baby even. We'll start again, we'll put distance, physical distance, between ourselves and the past—'

Elizabeth shook her head. She said unsteadily, 'It doesn't work like that.'

'What do you mean?'

'You can't—shed the past just by moving. It comes with you. You only deal with things if you face them, challenge them.'

'Then I will!' Tom cried. He put his arms out to her. 'I will!'

'Tom,' Elizabeth said.

'What?'

'There's another thing.'

He dropped his arms.

'Yes?'

She came round the pew she had been leaning on until she was only a foot from him. He didn't try to touch her. Then she put out both hands and held his face and leaned forward and kissed him on the mouth.

'It's too late,' she said.

Chapter
NINETEEN

'JUST TALK TO ME,' Elizabeth said.

She was lying on the broken-springed sofa with her eyes closed. Duncan got up to move the curtain a little, in order to shade her face from the afternoon sun.

'What about?'

'Anything,' Elizabeth said. 'I just need to hear you, saying things.'

Duncan looked down at her.

'I don't think you slept much last night. I'm afraid that bed is hardly comfortable.'

'It doesn't matter. At the moment I couldn't sleep on twenty goose-feather mattresses.' She opened her eyes. 'Oh Dad, what did I do wrong?'

He took her hand and wedged himself onto the edge of the sofa beside her.

'You didn't do anything *wrong*. You may have done things out of innocence or lack of experience, but not things you should blame yourself for.'

Elizabeth looked out of the large-paned window at the high bright early-summer sky.

'I certainly didn't know about Dale.'

'No.'

'He's afraid of her,' Elizabeth said. 'Can you imagine that? He's her father and he's afraid of her. Or, at least, he's afraid of what will happen if he stands up to her. He thinks that if he confronts her with her own destructiveness he will destroy her. So, he's trapped. Whichever,' Elizabeth said with a flash of bitterness, 'she's won.'

Very gently, Duncan unfolded Elizabeth's hand from his own and gave it back to her.

'Do you know, I don't think it's just Dale. Or just Dale's temperament. I don't think that's the sole reason.'

'Oh?'

He sighed. 'I think it's maybe the myth of the stepmother, too. Unseen forces, driving her, affecting you, affecting Tom, everyone.'

Elizabeth turned on her side, putting her hand under her cheek.

'Tell me.'

'There must be something behind the wicked-stepmother story,' Duncan said. 'There must be some basic fear or need that makes the portrayal of stepmothers down the ages so universally unkind. I suppose there are the obvious factors that make whole swathes of society unwilling even to countenance them, because of the connotations of failure associated with divorce, because, maybe, second wives are seen as second best and somehow also a challenge to the myth of the happy family. But I think there's still something deeper.

'It's as if,' Duncan said, turning to look directly at her. 'It's as if stepmothers have come to represent all the things we fear, most terribly, about motherhood going wrong. We need mothers so badly, so deeply, that the idea of an unnatural mother is, literally, monstrous. So we make the stepmother the target for all these fears—she can carry the can for bad motherhood. You see, if you regard your stepmother as wicked, then you need never feel guilty or angry about your real mother, whom you so desperately need to see as good.'

Elizabeth drew a long breath.

'Yes.'

'And we exaggerate the wickedness of the stepmother to justify, in some human, distorted way, our being so unfair.'

Elizabeth sat up, putting her arms round her bent knees and leaning her shoulder against Duncan's.

'I find all that very convincing.'

'Do you?'

'Yes,' Elizabeth said. 'Except that I can think of an exception.'

'Can you?'

'Rufus,' Elizabeth said.

'Oh, my dear—'

She put her face down into the circle of her arms, and said in a whisper, 'I still have to tell Rufus.'

The pub was full. Tom saw Lucas almost immediately, taller than most people and with a preoccupied air, standing by the bar.

'Gin and tonic?' he said to Tom, almost without turning.

'A double,' Tom said.

Lucas glanced at him.

'Two double g and t's,' he said loudly to the barman.

'I thought you drank vodka—'

'Like you,' Lucas said, 'I'll drink anything just now. In any quantity.'

'It's kind of you,' Tom said, 'to sympathise so—'

Lucas glanced at him again.

'I'm afraid it isn't all sympathy.'

The barman handed up two glasses of gin and two tonic-water bottles, held by their necks.

'I'll take them somewhere,' Tom said, 'while you collect your change.'

He took the glasses and bottles from the barman and, holding them above his head, threaded his way towards a bench at the back of the pub.

'Why couldn't we meet at home?' Lucas said, joining him and stuffing his change haphazardly into his jeans pocket.

Tom handed him a glass and a tonic-water bottle.

'You know why.'

'Isn't she out at work?'

'She's taken this week off.'

'Oh,' Lucas said. He poured the whole of the tonic into his glass and put the bottle under the bench. 'Staking her claim.' He took a swallow of his drink. 'It just means I'll have to tell her separately.'

'Tell her what?'

'Amy's left me,' Lucas said.

Tom stared at him.

'Real soap-opera stuff. The ring and a Dear John waiting on the table.'

Tom put his drink down on the floor by his feet. He leaned forward and put his arms round Lucas.

'Oh, dear boy, dear Lucas, poor fellow—'

Lucas let his head lie briefly against his father's.

'It was a shock—I don't mean I don't feel it, I feel awful, I feel utterly bloody, but I can't pretend I didn't see it coming.' He pulled himself gently out of Tom's embrace. He said, 'I wasn't putting her first. Or second, really, if I'm honest.'

'I'm so sorry, so *sorry*—'

'Yes,' Lucas said. 'Thanks.' He gave Tom a quick, sidelong glance. 'Same boat, then.'

An expression of pain crossed Tom's face. He bent to retrieve his drink.

'Maybe.' He paused, and then he said, 'Did Amy blame Dale?'

'She blamed my attitude to Dale.'

Tom leaned forward. He said earnestly, 'But is it Dale? Is it just Dale?'

Lucas took another mouthful of his drink.

'I suppose,' he said slowly, 'that it is. I've come to see that I don't think I'll ever find love here; I can't somehow, around Dale. That's why I'm going to Canada.'

Tom's glass suddenly shook in his hand.

'Canada!'

'Yes,' Lucas said. He looked down. 'Sorry.'

'Why Canada?'

'The new company that's bought the radio station owns stations in Canada. They said would I go because they couldn't keep me on in England and I said no, at first, and now I'm going to say yes.'

'Where?'

'Edmonton,' Lucas said.

Tom put his free hand across his eyes.

'Sorry,' Lucas said again.

'No, no—'

'It was Amy going that finally did it. And, well, thinking that we were all going backwards somehow, back to somewhere we should have moved on from.'

Tom took his hand away and gave himself a little shake. He said, a little unsteadily, 'Good for you.'

'Thanks.'

'I mean it. I just wish—' He stopped.

'You can't, Dad,' Lucas said. 'There's Rufus.'

'I know, I didn't mean it, really.' Tom looked at Lucas. 'Where has Amy gone?'

'To Manchester. She has some idea of a new life there.'

'She might be right.'

'I think,' Lucas said sadly, 'she was right about a lot of things.'

Tom dropped his eyes to his drink.

'And Elizabeth,' he said quietly.

'What is she going to do?'

'Go back to London. Buy a house instead of a flat. Get promoted to the very top of the civil service.'

'Has she moved out?'

Tom gave a small smile.

'There was almost nothing to move. You never met anyone less imposing of themselves on anyone else. She left her car parked outside, tank full of petrol, keys on the hook where she'd always hung them. I find I'm desperately hunting for traces of her. Anything.'

'Don't, Dad.'

Tom gave himself another little shake.

'Will you see her again?'

Tom lifted his glass and drained it.

'Yes,' he said. He put his glass under the bench and stood up. 'She's coming down next week, to see Rufus. She wants to tell Rufus herself.'

Dale had made osso bucco. She was chopping garlic and parsley and lemon rind with a long-bladed knife as she had seen television chefs do. The smell was wonderful. She hoped, when Tom came back from this mysterious drink with Lucas, he would say how wonderful the smell was, and not, as he had done the last few days, appear not to notice the effort she was making, the way she was trying to show him that she knew he was in pain, and was sorry. She heard his key in the lock, and began to chop faster.

The kitchen door opened.

'Hi!' she said, not looking up.

Tom came slowly over to the table and dropped his keys on it with a clatter.

'How's Lucas?'

'You might as well hear it from me. Amy's left him,' Tom said.

Dale paused in her chopping for a second.

She said quietly, 'You mean she's walked out?'

'Yes.'

'Maybe,' Dale said, 'maybe in the long run, it was the right thing to do?'

Tom pulled a chair out from under the table and sat down heavily.

'Put that knife down.'

'What?'

'You heard me.'

Carefully, Dale laid the knife beside her green-speckled mound on the chopping board. She looked at Tom. After a moment he raised his head and looked back at her with an expression she did not recognise.

'Satisfied?' Tom said.

She was truly startled.

'Sorry?'

'I said are you satisfied?' Tom said.

'What d'you mean?'

He leaned forward.

He said, in a voice so raised it was almost a shout, 'You've seen off Elizabeth, you've seen off Amy. Are you satisfied now?'

She gasped.

'It wasn't me!'

'Wasn't it? Wasn't it? Making it perfectly plain to a nice girl and a wonderful woman that your brother and father would never belong to anyone else but you?'

Dale was horrified. She leaned on her hands over the chopping board, breathing hard.

'I didn't, I never—'

'The keys?' Tom demanded. 'The invasion of this house? Your bloody possessions staking your claim louder than words could ever do? Making Elizabeth feel always and ever the outsider, the intruder, and Amy too?'

'Don't,' Dale whispered.

Tom rose to his feet, leaning on his side of the table, his face towards her.

'You're not a child,' Tom said, 'though God knows your behaviour would disgrace most children. You're a grown woman. You're a grown bloody woman who won't accept the loss of childhood, the need to make your own home, your own life—'

'Please,' Dale said. 'Please.'

Tears were beginning to slide down her face and drip onto the chopping board.

'And because you won't accept those things, you want to make Lucas and me live out the past with you, over and over, never mind at what cost to us, never mind the suffering, never mind losing probably the best person—do you hear me, the *best* person—I have ever known, never mind, never mind, as long as you, Dale, have what you think you want.'

Dale began to sink down behind the kitchen table, crumpling softly onto the floor, her arms held up around her head.

'Please, Daddy, don't, don't. I didn't mean to hurt, I didn't—'

'But you did hurt!' Tom shouted. 'You caused terrible, deliberate destruction. *Look* at what you did!'

Dale unwound her arms and leaned against a table leg.

'I wasn't doing it to hurt someone else. I did it because I couldn't help it, because I couldn't breathe otherwise.' She heard Tom sigh. She said in a steadier voice, 'You don't know what it's like, what it's always been like. I've fought and fought, I've tried not to be—' She stopped, and then she said, 'Sorry.'

There was a silence. She glanced sideways under the table and saw her father's legs, planted slightly apart, cut off across the thigh by the table top.

'Daddy?'

'Yes,' Tom said. His voice was tired.

'I'm sorry. I'm really sorry.'

Tom sighed again, a huge gusty sigh, and his legs moved out of her sight, across the kitchen towards the window.

'Oh Dale—'

Slowly, she got to her knees and held the edge of the table, pulling herself up, peering over. His back was towards her, his hands in his pockets.

'Daddy?'

'Yes?'

She held the table edge hard and whispered fiercely across it.

'Don't leave me.'

Rufus sat up in bed. He had been surprised, but not very, not to find Elizabeth in the house when he arrived. Tom explained that she sometimes had to work late and thus had to get a later train, on Fridays. What had surprised him, and not very pleasantly, was to find Dale in the kitchen, where he had expected to find Elizabeth, in a dress he disapproved of, with almost no skirt at all, frying sausages. She said the sausages were for him. She said this in a very bright, excited voice, as if he ought to feel pleased and grateful, and then she kissed him and left the smell of her scent on him which he could still smell now, even though he'd scrubbed at the place with a nailbrush. After he'd eaten the sausages—which were not the kind he liked, being full of herbs and stuff—Tom offered to play chess with him, which was very peculiar. They'd played chess for a bit, but it hadn't felt right, and then Dale had come prancing back in in even more scent and announced in a meaningful voice that she was going out now until much, *much* later.

It was better when she had gone. Tom poured a glass of wine and gave Rufus a sip and Basil managed to lumber onto the chessboard and knocked all the pieces over. Rufus kept yawning. He didn't seem able to stop. Tom had asked, after a while, if he'd rather wait for Elizabeth in bed, and, although as a general principle he liked to hold out against bed as long as possible, he'd nodded and gone upstairs and washed. Then he'd climbed into bed and wondered, with a dismalness that dismayed him, why his new curtains and his red rug and his desk didn't seem to fill him with any satisfaction at all.

It seemed ages until Elizabeth came. He heard the front door open and close, and then murmuring voices. He imagined Tom taking Elizabeth's luggage from her, and perhaps her jacket, and offering her a glass of wine. They'd probably go into the kitchen and talk for a bit, while Tom got started on their supper, and then Elizabeth's feet would come running up the stairs, and she'd sit on his bed and he might be able to hint, at last, at some of the things that troubled him, about finding Dale there, about the feeling in the house, the oddness in his father. He picked up a Goosebumps book that he'd left lying on his duvet earlier. Tom didn't like him reading Goosebumps, he'd said they didn't stretch his mind enough, but sometimes, Rufus thought, his mind didn't in the least want to be stretched.

'Hello,' Elizabeth said.

She was standing in his open bedroom door, wearing a navy-blue suit.

'I didn't hear you,' Rufus said.

'Perhaps these are quiet shoes—'

He looked at them. They were so dull, they certainly ought to have been quiet. Elizabeth came over and sat on the edge of his bed. She didn't kiss him, they never did kiss, although Rufus thought sometimes that they might, one day.

'I'm sorry I'm so late. How are you?' Elizabeth said.

Rufus thought. Usually he said, 'Fine,' to ward off any more questions, but tonight he felt that questions might almost be welcome. He jerked his head towards the wall behind him.

'Dale's living here.'

'I know.'

He sighed.

'Does she have to be my sister?'

'I'm afraid so. She's Daddy's daughter, just as you are his son.'

'But it feels funny—'

'I know,' Elizabeth said again.

Rufus began to riffle through the pages of his Goosebumps book. 'Will it be long?'

'Dale being there? I think it might be. I don't think she likes living alone.'

'And I,' said Rufus with some energy, 'don't like living with *her*.' He glanced at Elizabeth. Her face was very still, as if she was thinking more than she was saying. 'What are you going to have for supper?'

'I don't know—'

'Isn't Daddy cooking it?'

'No,' Elizabeth said. 'He offered, but I'm going round to Duncan's.'

'Why?'

'Because—because I'm not staying here.'

Rufus stopped riffling.

'Why?'

Elizabeth put her hands together in her lap and Rufus noticed that she was clenching them so hard that the skin on her knuckles was greenish white, as if the bones underneath were going to push through the surface.

'Rufus—'

He waited. He stared at Batman's face, spread across his knees.

'Rufus, I don't want to say this to you, I don't want to hurt you and I don't want to hurt myself or Daddy or anybody, but I'm afraid I can't marry Daddy after all.'

Rufus swallowed. He remembered, briefly, the registry office last year and the registrar with gold earrings and the picture of the Queen.

'Oh,' he said.

'I would like to explain everything to you,' Elizabeth said. 'I'd like you to know all the reasons, but for one thing it wouldn't be fair, and for another, I expect you can guess most of them.'

Rufus nodded.

He said kindly, 'It doesn't matter.'

'Doesn't—'

'There's people at school whose parents aren't married. It doesn't matter.'

Elizabeth gave a small convulsion. For a second, Rufus wondered if she might be going to cry, but she found a tissue in her pocket and blew her nose instead.

'I'm so sorry—'

He waited.

'I'm so sorry,' she said, and her voice was unsteady. 'I'm so sorry, Rufus, but I'm not going to live here any more. I'm going away. I'm not marrying Daddy and I have to go away.'

He stared at her.

He heard himself say loudly, 'You can't.'

'Can't—'

'You can't go away,' Rufus said. 'You can't. I *know* you.'

She blew her nose again.

'Yes. And I know you.'

'Where are you going?' Rufus demanded. His throat felt tight and swollen and his eyes were smarting.

'Oh, just London,' she said. Her hands were shaking. 'I expect I'll buy a house with a garden and then my father can come and stay with me at weekends.'

'Can I come?'

Tears were now running down Elizabeth's face.

'I don't think so—'

'Why not?'

'Because it wouldn't be fair—to Daddy, to you even—'

'It would!' Rufus shouted.

'No,' Elizabeth said. She was scrabbling about in her pockets for more tissues. 'No, it wouldn't. It might make you think things were going to happen, when they weren't. It's awful now, I know it is, but at least you *know*, and it's better to know.'

'It isn't,' he said stubbornly. He put his fists into his eyes, like little kids did. 'It isn't!'

He felt her get off the bed.

'Go away!' he shouted, his fists in his eyes. 'Go away!'

He waited to hear her say, 'All right then,' or, 'Goodbye, Rufus,' but she didn't. She didn't say anything. One moment she was there by his bed and the next she had gone and he could hear her quiet shoes going quickly down the stairs and, only a few seconds later, the front door slamming, like it did when Dale went out.

Slowly and stiffly, Rufus took his fists away from his eyes and eased himself down in bed, onto his side, staring at the wall. He felt cold, even though it was summer, and rigid, as if he couldn't bend any more. The wall was cream-coloured, as it had been for ages, for ever, and on it Rufus could still faintly discern where he had scribbled on it, in black wax crayon, and Josie had scrubbed at the scribble. The thought of Josie made the tears that had been bunching in his throat start to leak out, dripping across his nose and cheeks and into his pillow, and with them came a longing, a fierce, unbidden longing, to be back in his bedroom with Rory, in Matthew's house.

Josie came all the way down to Bath, to collect Rufus. She'd offered to when she heard about Elizabeth's leaving.

'I'll come,' she'd said. 'It's no bother.'

Tom had let her. He'd been grateful. She'd arrived with her stepson, an unfinished-looking boy of perhaps thirteen whom Rufus had been suddenly very boisterous in front of, as if he were extravagantly pleased to see him, and couldn't say so. They'd gone up to Rufus's room together, Rory holding Basil.

'He's great,' Rory said to Josie. 'Isn't he? Why can't we have a cat?'

'I expect we can—'

'When we get back,' Rory said. 'Can't we? A kitten?'

'Two kittens,' Rufus said.

'Go away,' Josie said, shaking her head, but she was laughing.

Tom made her coffee. She was very nice to him, sympathetic, but her sympathy had a quality of detachment to it.

'I'm sorry it's happened,' she said. 'I'm sorry for Rufus.'

Tom flinched slightly. He couldn't say how awful it had been, couldn't admit to Josie how Rufus had longed for her arrival, his bag packed for twenty-four hours previously. She was pleasant, but a little guarded, and only at the end, when she was getting into the car and the boys and Rufus's possessions were already packed inside, did she say, as if in fellow feeling, 'Don't be deluded. Nothing's as easy as it looks.'

He went back into the kitchen after the car had driven off and looked at their coffee mugs, and the empty Coca-Cola cans the boys had left. Rufus had said goodbye hurriedly—lovingly but hurriedly, as if the moment needed to be dispensed with as quickly as possible.

Tom sat down at the table. Dale had put a jug of cornflowers in the middle of it, cornflowers and some yellow daisy things with shiny petals. Perhaps she would, unthreatened, calm down again, calm down to a point where she might again venture on a love affair and this time, oh so devoutly to be wished, with someone who could handle her, could skilfully convert her fierce retrospective needs into, at last, an appetite for the future.

'Until then,' Tom had said to Elizabeth, 'I'm responsible. I have to be.'

She'd said nothing. She'd given him one of her quick glances, but she hadn't uttered. She had, she made it plain, no more sympathy left for his abiding sense of guilt about Dale.

He stood up, sighing, and walked slowly down the room. The door to the garden was open and on the top step of the iron staircase was a terracotta pot, planted with trailing pelargoniums by Elizabeth, pink and white. Tom looked past them, and down into the garden.

Dale was down there. She was crouched against the statue of the stone girl with the dove on her hand, crouched down, with her arms round her knees. She was waiting, just as Pauline used to wait, for him to come and find her.

Chapter
TWENTY

KAREN WALKED SLOWLY up Barratt Road. It was hot, for one thing, and for another, she had offered to collect some dry-cleaning for Josie, and although it wasn't heavy, it was uncooperative to carry, slithering through her arms in its plastic bags, or sticking to her skin in unpleasant, sweaty little patches. She'd told Josie quite a lot recently, about her and Matthew's mother, as well as about her job and the love-hate relationship she had with it, and about Rob, the Australian dentist, newly arrived in Sedgebury, who was displaying the kind of interest in her nobody had shown for ages. She found that Josie was very easy to talk to.

She'd cut her hair off, too. Karen had been amazed. One day there'd been that heavy coppery mane that seemed almost to be Josie's trademark, and the next day it was gone. Two weeks later, Becky had done the same thing. If Karen had been amazed about Josie's hair, she was absolutely astounded at Becky's.

'Is that a compliment, or what?' she said to Josie.

'I don't know. I'm trying not to work that kind of thing out because I always get the answers wrong. But she looks good, doesn't she?'

'Yes,' Karen said. She was gazing out of the kitchen window at the lawn, where Becky was playing with the new kittens. 'Yes,' she said.

They were doing all right, Karen thought, especially if you compared it with only three months previously. The house, which was too small for all of them anyway, looked thoroughly lived in, sometimes over-lived in, but the children's friends came round now and rode skateboards up and down the sloping drive or kicked footballs against the garage wall or lay in the girls' bedroom, with the curtains closed, and music on. Matthew had sunk an empty food can in the back garden, and was teaching the boys how to putt with golf clubs his father had given them. Karen was observing her father with some amusement. When she had started going round to Barratt Road, he'd always cross-examine her when he next saw her.

'How did you find them, then?'

'Who?'

'Matthew and Co. The kids. You know.'

Karen would pretend to be looking for something in her bag.

'Fine.'

'Working hard, are they? Going to school? Not playing truant?'

'Dad,' Karen would say, 'look. If you want to see how they are, you go and see for yourself.'

And, in the end, he had. First, he'd sent the golf clubs round and then, after he heard that Nadine had bought herself a large, second-hand mobile home, and parked it at some commune near the cottage, and was helping to grow vegetables for the people there, he somehow seemed to feel that he was no longer shackled by the conventions of first loyalties. He had gone round to Barratt Road saying he'd be ten minutes, and he'd been over an hour. He'd given the boys a golf lesson, he said, and Josie had made him a cup of tea. When Karen's mother had begun on him for going round at all, he'd said, 'Not going is your loss, Peg, and no one else's,' and walked out of the room.

Now, Karen thought, you'd think he'd never had a qualm. He mended things for Josie that Matthew didn't have time to mend, promised Becky a hundred pounds for Christmas if she stopped smoking, and told the boys he'd make them members of Sedgebury Football Club's junior league next season. He began to tell Karen things, as if he knew more about them than she did, about Matthew having met the newly appointed headmaster and finding him sympathetic, about Rufus's father planning to take him to Legoland, in Denmark, later in the school holidays because there were complications at home, about Becky saying she would spend a week at the commune with her mother, but refused to promise more until she'd seen what it was like.

'Nadine still rings,' Derek said. 'She rings all the time.'

'From a caravan?'

'She's got a mobile. She rings from her mobile.'

And, Karen thought, no doubt she always would. Josie said she never mentioned Nadine to the children unless they spoke of her first, but she couldn't help noticing that, when she telephoned now, there was often a palpable reluctance to go and speak to her.

Karen shifted the dry-cleaning bags, peeling them off one bare arm and transferring them to the other. She sometimes wondered what part Matthew had played in all this, how much he had stuck up for Josie, or his children, how hard it might be to relinquish entirely the old habit of acquiescence to Nadine to buy even a few moments of peace. Josie didn't talk to Karen about that. She was very open about most things, about herself, about Rufus, about Matthew's children, about her first marriage, about the complex remorse she had that she'd done nothing to help the woman who'd almost become Rufus's stepmother . . .

'But what could you have done?'

'Nothing, probably. But I would like her to have known that it wasn't her fault, and that Rufus really—loved her.'

. . . But she never spoke of her relationship with Matthew. Karen could understand that. She could see, very clearly, that, if you were going to build any kind of relationship in a small house largely lacking in a general *esprit de corps*, you had to give it such privacy as you could, for any hope of success. Watching them, Karen thought, they weren't doing badly. They were facing in the same direction, certainly, and she felt they would get there in the end because they wanted to, they intended to.

And these thoughts, which preoccupied Karen sometimes with interest, if not with any particular urgency, were beginning to encompass another one, one that Karen, less than a year ago, thought she might never have. Sometimes, when she went to Barratt Road, she found she had an idea. It came to her, walking into the house on an ordinary day, as she was about to do on this ordinary day, and finding the kitchen in chaos, laundry on the line, the television yattering to nobody and Josie in the midst of it all, that she looked less foreign than she used to, more familiar, less superimposed on someone else's background. She was beginning, Karen thought, to look almost as if she belonged there, as if she had the beginnings of a sense of belonging herself. And it occurred to Karen, watching her, that, in time, even the children would come to feel she belonged there, too. For the last time, Karen shifted the dry-cleaning bags from one arm to the other, and turned up the drive on which an upturned skateboard lay like a beetle on its back. She glanced up at the house. Almost all the windows were open. One day, she told herself, one day.

JOANNA TROLLOPE

It was her interest in the part played by the wicked stepmother in fairy tales that prompted Joanna Trollope to write her latest novel, together with the astonishing discovery that, by the year 2010, there will be more step-families in Britain than the traditional kind.

Having decided on the novel's subject, Joanna Trollope then embarked on her usual practice of talking to people about it. 'For no novel I have ever researched before did people talk so openly and feelingly as they did for *Other People's Children*,' she recalls. 'The stuff poured out of them: the pain, the difficulties, the bewildering unalterable fact that children continue to love the most impossible parents.'

Apart from all the emotional turmoil, lack of privacy emerged as a major issue. 'I think privacy is one of the things that's hardest to achieve in family life—particularly in a rather artificially slammed together family,' she says. 'The courtesies have to be observed. One woman said to me, "I had to go and buy a dressing gown—I realised I couldn't walk around the house wearing nothing but a bath towel."'

What emerged as a result of all Joanna Trollope's conversations 'were several curious facts and an amazing amount of common feeling. Boys, it turns out, make easier stepchildren than girls. Men see their role as keeping the peace and making money; women see their role as being expected to do the near-impossible: to mother and yet not to mother the new, frequently hostile children in their care.'

Joanna Trollope says that when she actually sat down to write *Other People's Children*, it almost wrote itself. 'I devised, as I always do, a cast list and places for them to live and work and play in. Then—again, as I always do—I plotted the first half-dozen chapters and the end, to ensure that I would know where I was going, although I am never entirely sure how I will get there. And as I wrote, a love affair began to develop, a love affair I hadn't planned but which bore out the essence of so much of what I had learned through all those weeks and months of research. It is the love affair between the little boy of eight and the woman who he believes will be his stepmother.'

Joanna Trollope firmly agrees with one of the major conclusions in *Other People's Children*. 'Stepfamilies can be a big success, for the simple reason that those in them have to work at the relationship.'

319

ANITA BURGH
ON CALL

Following the tragic death of her husband, Chrissy Galloway decides to return to the nursing profession, and to take up a job at St Edith's Hospital in her home town. St Edith's is under threat of closure and Chrissy finds herself drawn into the fight to save it. But this desperate struggle is soon dwarfed by affairs of the heart and a personal drama that threatens her reputation—and even her life.

PROLOGUE

FOR ONE HUNDRED AND TWENTY years St Edith's Hospital had stood on the top of South Hill, as if standing sentinel over Fellcar, a small town in the north of England.

Erected at a time when no building was regarded with civic pride unless suitably crenellated and turreted, St Edith's was a fitting testament to the stonemason's art, even if its maintenance was proving expensive. The Italianate windows, their surrounds decorated with a latticework of stone, let in too much heat in summer and cold in winter for the comfort of those inside. The people viewed the building with various emotions, dependent on what had happened to them, or those close to them, within its granite walls.

To some it was a source of hope and happiness; to others a place of despair, to be feared. For a lucky few it was merely handy for checking the time as they glanced up at the large clock tower, which was known as Old Tom's, but few knew why. For everyone the idea of Fellcar without St Edith's was difficult to envisage.

The closure of St Edith's was a rumour that had circulated at regular intervals since the end of the Second World War. Until now Fellcar had been a marginal parliamentary seat, and no government had been prepared to take on the townsfolk who, at each hint of such action, became mightily vocal in their disapproval. Fellcar was marginal no longer, and St Edith's was yet again under threat.

CHAPTER ONE

IT ALWAYS RAINED on Thursdays or, at least, on the important Thursdays in Chrissy Galloway's life. She'd been born, 'with far to go', in a dramatic June storm. When she'd left home for good, on a Thursday, she'd been soaked to the skin. It was also unfortunate to have chosen that day of the week for her wedding, when dress and photographs were ruined by a torrential downpour. There was little she could do about the day of her husband's funeral, but inevitably the gloom of the day was accentuated by drizzle. And now she peered out of the window at Fellcar station, through the driving rain, and remembered that it was *that* day.

The line shuffled forward as a cab pulled into the station yard, its wheels spraying great arcs on the passengers who had rushed out too eagerly for it. Chrissy pushed her holdall along the floor with her foot.

What, she wondered, had changed here in the sixteen years she'd been away? It wasn't that she expected things to be as they had once been. They couldn't be. Her leaving and then marrying had altered not only her life but her parents' too. They had set up new routines and taken on new interests, of which she was not a part. Then, three years ago, her father had died, at a time when she was looking closely at how she felt about many things in her life. She'd wanted to ask his advice—but she'd left it too late.

Another taxi pulled in. The queue moved.

How many of her schoolfriends were still here? Only a few, no doubt: they had whiled away many hours planning how to escape from boring Fellcar. Chrissy had eagerly left for London and her teaching hospital, discarding the past without a regret. Now, however, after so many upheavals in her life, she needed its familiarity.

At her interview at the hospital last month she'd felt a stranger in her home town. She'd only herself to blame: she'd not returned often enough. The problem was that she and her mother had never got along. Iris had fussed over her and nagged her as a child and as a married woman. No doubt she'd meant well, but the constant interference had driven Chrissy away. At the funeral of Chrissy's husband, Ewan, Iris had been hysterical—far more so than at her own husband's burial—and

Chrissy had known then that she could not see too much of her until she had recovered a measure of equilibrium in her own life.

Lynn was the only friend she could be certain still lived here. They exchanged Christmas cards. Although she was looking forward to seeing her again, she was also nervous in case they didn't get on any more. If she thought about it, what did they have in common? Lynn had married Terry Petch, a builder, and Lynn had sent a photo of them standing in front of the bungalow he'd built with its net curtains, flowering cherry and silly name. Chrissy, meanwhile, lived in affluent muddle in a Cornish village, in a house so pretty it appeared on postcards. Lynn had two children and Chrissy had failed miserably on that score. And Lynn was happily married and Chrissy was widowed. Still, they had nursing in common.

Finally Chrissy was at the head of the queue. Clutching her bag she dashed through the rain and into the next taxi. She was looking forward to the drive ahead and seeing the town again, the mix of building styles that had evolved over the centuries.

Down by the harbour they drove past the sixteenth-century fishermen's cottages, now gentrified beyond recognition. The fine Regency Assembly Room loomed ahead; beyond were solid Victorian villas, converted into offices now, and the Grand Hotel. High on North Hill were the expensive middle-class houses, one of which was her mother's. In just over three hundred years the fishing village of Fellcar had grown and it was now a town of some fifty thousand people.

'You look deep in thought, miss.'

Chrissy looked up to see the taxi-driver, reflected in the mirror, watching her.

'I was remembering the amusement arcades down on the front and they've all gone.'

'Ages ago, miss. We don't get many trippers, these days.'

The driver stopped chatting as he negotiated the busy roundabout at the base of South Hill, and they began to climb up the steep incline on which stood St Edith's.

'Daft place to put a hospital, I always say. If you're ill, by the time you've climbed the hill, you'll be dead. Cost-effective, I suppose.' He laughed, pleased with his remark, which sounded too practised.

Chrissy looked out of the window as they passed the hospital where she was to start work in a week's time.

'You're from round here, then?'

'Yes.'

'You married?'

She had to smile. Another thing she had forgotten was the curiosity of the natives.

'No.' Since Ewan's death, she had learned not to say she was widowed: it led either to an embarrassed silence or to an outpouring of sympathy, which she found difficult to deal with.

'Got a job?' They were motoring across the moor now, which crept to the cliff edge in this part.

'I start work at St Edith's in a week's time,' she said carefully. She knew that if she said she was a nurse then not only would she be told the driver's ailments but those of his wife and children.

'What, as a secretary?'

'Bigton is next left along that lane. The last house.' She had neatly sidestepped his question.

'Bet it gets a bit blowy up here.'

Chrissy felt a surge of excitement as the taxi bumped along the unmade road on the top of the cliff, through the hamlet of Bigton Wyke, which everyone knew as Bigton only. The cab swung onto the small driveway, past the lopsided, five-bar gate to End Cottage.

Chrissy climbed out of the taxi and stood looking at the building. Her house, her very own! She felt a surge of peace and contentment, emotions she had not experienced for too long.

The corridor stretched ahead, and from the tall windows shining cubes of light illuminated the well-worn floor. Kim Henderson, bringing up the rear of the group walking along it, wondered how many square metres of space such long, wide corridors wasted. A tidy sum, he reckoned, enough for an extra ward or department, no doubt. He looked up at the false ceiling, put in to save on heating, and the administrator in him approved such measures, the admirer of Victorian architecture mourned such necessities.

He smiled at a young nurse who had stepped aside to let them pass, and looked over his shoulder, admiring her retreating figure. He cannoned into his boss, Craig Nutting, who, with the others, had stopped in front of the large front door of St Edith's.

'Watch where you're going, matey. Ignore the crumpet!' Craig said good-naturedly.

'Sorry.' Kim felt himself begin to blush. He grinned apologetically at the only woman in the group, but Glynis Tillman, the hospital's clinical services manager, indicated by the set of her lips, the arching of her brow, her disapproval of anyone leering at *her* nurses.

'Thanks for your time, Glynis.' Craig's hand was reluctantly shaken.

'My pleasure, *Mr Nutting*.' She emphasised his surname.

Kim looked away, embarrassed for his boss being put down, but when he glanced back Craig seemed not to have noticed. One by one the others took their leave of her.

'Thank you, Miss Tillman.' It was Kim's turn. He'd known her for years but he'd never lost the feeling of awe he had for this woman.

'Give my regards to your aunt when you see her.' She smiled at him.

'Today—we're having lunch together.' Kim followed the other men outside.

'Phew! What a tyrant! Is she normally like that?' asked the oldest.

'Afraid so, Minister. The trouble with Glynis Tillman is that she thinks she owns this hospital. I've always thought what she needs is a bit of how's-your-father, know what I mean?' Craig Nutting, the Thorpedale and Fellcar NHS Trust's chief executive, smirked.

The other two men laughed, but Kim became interested in the shine on his shoes. He liked Craig, but there were times when he thought him a total prat. In his early forties and still ambitious, he had lank, russet-coloured hair, and the pale skin of one not used to daylight.

'So, Minister, what do you think?' Craig was saying. Joke over and back to business.

The round, pasty face of Jake Shortley, the Junior Minister for Health, crumpled with concern. He rocked on his heels in the way of one making portentous decisions; at least, that was what he hoped the others would think. 'I'd like the figures. Let's say on my desk before Christmas?'

'And when do you think we can expect a decision?' Mark Fisher, the local Member of Parliament, asked. He had a worried expression and was sweating slightly.

'Now, now, Mark,' said the Junior Minister, 'you know as well as I do these matters take time.' Kim, noting the Minister's smile, realised he could afford to bestow such a smile for Fisher was regarded as a back bencher of no note, idle and unlikely to make waves whatever the Minister decided to do about this hospital. 'Is that clock right?' the Minister asked, looking up at the tall bell tower. 'What a monstrosity!'

'Don't let the electorate of Fellcar hear you say that—you'll halve my majority!' Mark Fisher protested. 'That tower was raised by public sub-scription in memory of a certain Alderman Thomas Yates, a gentleman of propriety, long forgotten by all but his descendants. It's known as Old Tom's, even if few know why.'

Kim looked uncomfortable and wished he didn't. He tried to smile, but it didn't quite work.

'Hell, I'm sorry. You're a Yates, aren't you, Kim?' Mark Fisher put his hand on Kim's sleeve.

'No, I'm no relation. My aunt was related through marriage, that's all. I don't mind what you say.' But he did mind. He'd always been proud of his tenuous link with the old buffer.

'I'd no idea you were so well connected, Kim,' said Craig.

'Well, gentlemen, I must be off.' The Minister swung round towards his car.

'A pleasure meeting you again, Mr—' He shook Craig's hand. 'And, of course, you as well, Mr—' With a faint nod he acknowledged Kim.

'Safe journey, Minister.' Craig waved as the Minister was driven away. 'Slimy, inadequate creep!' he said to the departing car.

'I thought you liked him,' Kim said, puzzled.

'Me? You have to be joking. What I could tell you about that useless little turd would make your flesh creep. You'll learn, Kim.' Craig put his arm about him in a comradely way.

'Nobody likes the toad. Twists himself into all manner of contortions rather than commit himself. Word has it he's got a bit of skirt in these parts. Not that his wife or the tabloids have twigged yet.' Now that the Minister had gone, Mark Fisher appeared to be bursting with confidence.

'But you'll be setting that little matter straight at some time, Mark?'

'Depends, Craig. We've things to discuss—alone.' Mark looked at Kim.

'I've got a lunch appointment.' Kim felt suddenly in the way.

'Your dad's one of the local GPs, Dr Henderson, isn't he, Kim? I know him, nice bloke,' Mark said, as if to make amends, as they walked towards the car park. 'So, what did you think of the old battle-axe?'

'Miss Tillman? Bit on the rigid side, isn't she? But you've got to admire her, haven't you? I mean, she really loves St Edith's.' He wasn't sure why, but Kim felt it was better if he didn't let on that he knew Glynis.

'That's something you'll learn. She's a pain in the arse.'

'Still, you can understand her attitude. At her age it wouldn't be easy to find another job like the one she has here. And I agree with her, I don't see the point of closing this hospital. It works, it's needed.' Kim was far from happy at all the talk of St Edith's being closed. It had always been there, throughout his life, a comforting presence.

'It's inefficient,' Mark offered.

'Then make it efficient,' Kim said, a shade too diffidently for his comment to have substance. He was nervous since he was new to this job and already did not like what he was discovering. 'If we closed St Edith's could Thorpedale absorb all the intake?'

'No problem. Need a bit of shaking down, but not impossible.'

'And what would happen to this building?'

'You do go on, Kim. I told you, the other day. Apartments. Nice little earner for the Trust,' Craig said, as he unlocked his car.

'Still, it would be a shame, wouldn't it? A fine old place like this, which has served the community all these years . . .'

'Don't get sentimental on me, Kim. We've got to be practical. Cuts have got to be made, waiting lists have got to be shortened and that's an end to it,' Craig said.

Twenty-two was no age to kill oneself. But, given the way that Buck Marston was weaving his way across the forecourt of the Fox and Fiddle, that seemed to be his intention. '*Happy Birthday to me!*' he was singing as he searched for his keys.

'Buck! You're too tanked up to drive,' Wayne Freeman shouted.

'Mind your own sodding business,' Buck yelled back.

'We ought to stop him, Jason.' Wayne turned to his brother.

'He'll be all right. He's driven pissed enough times. Why, that car probably knows its own way home!' But Wayne, less drunk than the other two, did not look too sure. 'Come on. It's nothing to do with us.'

'You're right, it's down to Buck, isn't it?'

Andrew Basset was in a hurry to get home. He was feeling pleased with himself: it had proved a shrewd move changing jobs—his commission would be double here, enough to consider taking out a mortgage. He'd collect details of the house on the estate that Rachel had set her heart on. If he got a move on perhaps they could be in for Christmas! He laughed with excitement at the idea.

He wouldn't have chosen Fellcar himself, too quiet by far. But, with the baby on the way, Rachel wanted to be closer to her mum.

He pressed the eject button as the cassette came to a halt. Fumbling, he dropped it on the floor. He glanced down just for a second to locate it, his car wavering over the white line as he did so. The man in the car behind hit his horn in warning.

Andrew looked up just in time to see Buck's banger sweeping round the bend towards him, too fast and too far over on his side.

The combined force of the two cars crashing together made a hideous noise, as metal tore at metal, shards were separated and flew through the air with the force of bullets.

The Accident and Emergency Department of St Edith's, known to the town simply as Casualty, was quiet. In her office Sister Betty Greaves was taking this lull in the population's mania for damaging itself to have a cup of tea and to catch up on her paperwork. The amount of information the managers required grew constantly. Betty could see that some statistics were relevant. However, other information demanded, she felt, was pointless: how many left-handed patients and how many six-footers were treated, were some she remembered.

'Yes, Margaret, what is it?' she said, to a young student nurse who had knocked nervously on her door. Although she was irritated at being interrupted she spoke kindly.

Nurse Margaret Harper was a Project 2000 nurse, and this was her first week in the department. This system of training, brought in in 1990, with the intention that all nurses would be trained under it by the year 2000, was more academically weighted than Betty's own training had been. These students spent longer hours in the classroom than at the hands-on learning on the wards Betty had enjoyed. Many staff rejected the new regime, and the unfortunate students, with ill-concealed irritation. Betty was aware of how frightened most of the nurses were when beginning a placement on A and E. They could never be sure from one minute to the next what they might see, what they might be asked to do, and if they would know how to do it.

'Sorry, Sister, but there's a young woman in cubicle two. She's got severe abdominal pain. Staff isn't back from lunch and the patient says it's getting worse.' Nurse Harper's eyes looked alarmed.

'Has the duty houseman seen her?'

'No, he popped off for a coffee—it was quiet, you see. She's not pregnant, though. I tested her urine,' Margaret said proudly.

'That's very good, Nurse.' Betty smiled as she bleeped the doctor.

The doctor back, with Margaret Harper dispatched to help, Betty returned to her reports. It was ten minutes before there was a further interruption. Freddie Favour, their consultant in A and E, barged in.

'I've got another one for your statistics.' Freddie was waving a letter. 'That young woman in cubicle two—peptic ulcer or I'm a Dutchman.'

'Which GP referred her? No, let me guess—Dr Giles Middleton.'

'The same. Up to his old tricks. So pop it on your list, Betty dear. I'm off to pen a note to him, while I'm still steamed up about it.'

If this hospital or this department closed it would be the Dr Middletons of this world who would have helped it on its way, Betty thought. Everyone knew that GPs sometimes referred patients to A and E not only to jump a waiting list but also as a way of getting a patient admitted if a ward was full and so closed to routine admission. They knew that she and her staff would move heaven and earth to get a sick patient a bed. But doctors like Giles Middleton were thinking not of the well-being of their patients but, rather, of their pockets. If GPs from a fund-holding practice referred a patient to a specialist, the practice paid for the consultation and treatment. However, if they referred patients as an emergency, and if the hospital doctors decided to admit, the hospital paid. It was becoming harder for the hospital to keep to its budget. This year already they were heading towards serious overspend. The Dr Middletons were helping to distort the figures: St Edith's, always at risk from closure, appeared to be out of favour with too few referrals.

At the first ring of the telephone she picked it up. 'A and E. Sister Greaves here . . . ETA? . . . Fine.' She replaced the receiver, alerted the resuscitation team and the consultant, and walked out into the main area of the department. 'Margaret, is Staff back yet? Right. There's been a serious RTA. Two victims, both will need the Resus room.' And she bustled out with a terrified Nurse Harper, who had never seen an accident, in her wake.

The doors to the outside hissed open at their approach just as the ambulances ground to a halt and the patients were unloaded. Betty quickly assessed both men, looking for the least hurt to give to Margaret to accompany to the resuscitation room. It was not an ideal situation since the young woman lacked experience, but as yet there was no sign of the teams who were on their way. There was no one else to call upon: she was lacking two members of staff. Since both patients were unconscious and had the same ashen colour, there was nothing to choose between them. 'You take that one, Margaret,' she ordered. A white-faced Margaret Harper trotted alongside the trolley accompanied by the ambulance man.

Forewarned of the severity of the men's injuries, the department was buzzing. The consultant and his housemen were joined by the registrar, the resuscitation team, and on their way were the 'head' men—the neurosurgeons—with the 'bone' men—the orthopaedics team—in hot pursuit, with anaesthetists and X-ray personnel bringing up the rear.

It was controlled pandemonium in the starkly lit resuscitation room. Buck and Andrew were rapidly attached to equipment supplying vital oxygen and fluids, while other machines clicked, whirred and flickered the progress of their vital signs. Orders were barked as the group moved in an urgent and familiar routine.

'There's not a hope in hell here.' Freddie Favour stood up from leaning over one of the young men. 'Try to get hold of the relatives before it's too late for him to be a transplant donor.' And he turned his attentions to the other.

'Margaret, go through his clothes, find out his identity and bring it to me. Then clean him up,' Betty ordered.

But Margaret Harper stood by the trolley, her face white, tears streaming down her cheeks. 'But he's so young . . . I never saw anything like this . . .' she wailed.

Betty nodded to a staff nurse, Dawn Allyson, as she entered the room, and told her to take over. 'It's all right, Margaret. Come with me. It's hard the first time. It doesn't get better but you just get more used to it. Come and sit down,' she said softly, remembering her own reaction all those years ago when she had been just as scared and just as sickened.

Glynis Tillman, in overall charge of St Edith's, an elegant woman, immaculate, her posture rigidly perfect, had been at her desk since seven thirty that morning. She was smartly dressed in a navy suit with a crisp high-collared blouse, which looked rather like the old uniform of a senior sister which, in truth, she would have much preferred to be wearing. This alteration in dress for senior staff was just one of the many changes she had seen in her profession, few of which met with her approval.

She was studying the surgical-bed allocations and matching them against the proposed operations listed by the various surgeons to be done next week. She was not aware that she frowned as she worked; the lines caused were the only ones on her fine-boned, pale-complexioned face. It was a difficult task, but it should have been simple: a surgeon had a fair idea of his patient's progress and when he or she was likely to be discharged, so knew when he could admit a new one to take their place. But chance invariably interfered with neat order. An unexpected deterioration of the recovering patient; a patient catching a cold and having his operation cancelled; the acute illness of someone who didn't even know they were poorly in the first place—any of these occurrences and the whole system was in danger of collapsing.

In the past, the beds were kept empty, always ready for emergencies. Now all were booked to achieve the highest occupancy rate possible. The problem was that when an emergency cropped up and a bed was required, a patient booked in had to be cancelled. It was not a pleasant duty to tell patients that their admission was cancelled and that another date would be allocated. If a spate of A and E admissions happened, as had taken place this weekend, then the juggling began.

Glynis attacked her chart with a rubber. Fortunately, with Russell Newson, the orthopaedic surgeon, going away for a week, she should be able to resolve the influx with no cancellations.

ON CALL

Standing on the terrace overlooking the steep garden, Kim Henderson watched his aunt climb the steps. 'Want a hand?' he shouted down.

'I'm not on a Zimmer frame yet!' Harriet Yates, known as Floss, though no one could remember why, called in reply. 'Bloody cheek,' she said, as she reached the terrace.

'You'd have moaned if I hadn't offered.'

'Indubitably.' Floss grinned. 'What's the point of getting on if you can't be a cantankerous old cow when you want? Kiss?' He had to bend to kiss her cheek. 'You're early.' They were entering the large house.

'Meeting ended sooner than we expected. Rumour has it that the Minister who came has a bit of skirt on the other side of Thorpedale. He was certainly in a hurry to get going.' He helped his aunt out of her coat. 'This is wet.'

'Sling it over the radiator. Nap and Jo, did you miss me?' she called with delight, as two elderly and overweight bulldogs shambled towards her. 'If there's one thing both Napoleon and Josephine loathe it's the rain—it *disgusts* them. Now, large gins are in order, don't you think?' Floss led the way into her drawing room.

'Small. There's a meeting at St Edith's this afternoon.'

He stood in front of the window in Floss's drawing room in the large, rambling mansion on the top of North Hill, as she busied herself with the drinks. Kim's monthly lunch with his aunt was something to look forward to. He enjoyed her company and he knew that she adored him as substitute for a child of her own—even if she loved her dogs more. Floss was unconventional; it never failed to amaze him that his conventional, rather prissy mother and Floss were sisters.

He took his drink from her. He sipped it gingerly for even Floss's small gins could still be lethal.

'Have you seen my prune-faced sister? She doesn't like you coming here, you know.'

'I didn't know you'd seen her. She didn't say.'

'Oh, I haven't—never do if I can help it. A friend told me Fiona had been carping on.'

'How's the hip replacement?' he asked, to change the subject. He hadn't much time for his mother either, but he always felt uncomfortable if Floss sounded off about her.

'Look.' She swung her leg high. 'Brilliant, isn't it? Russell Newson should be sanctified.'

'He's a good surgeon. We're lucky to have him. I've heard his wife would prefer they moved to London.'

'He'd never go. He likes it here—he told me so. In any case, all those waiting lists you read about at other hospitals would upset him, he's so conscientious.'

'Thorpedale and Fellcar have horrendous waiting lists. It's staff shortages mainly. I mean—'

'I didn't have to wait. I was in hospital within two weeks. All this waiting-list stuff's an exaggeration.'

'We're working on the lists, but I put in a word for you and so did Dad.'

'You what? You arranged for me to jump the queue?'

'Something like that,' Kim said, with pride.

'You interfering creeps! You had no right to do that.'

'I thought you'd be pleased.'

'Pleased! I'm incandescent with rage. You know I'm a Friend of St Edith's. You've compromised me, made it look as if it's an advantage if you're a Friend. I don't know if I'll ever forgive you.' She turned away with an angry gesture.

'Aunt Floss, I wouldn't do anything to upset you, you know that.' Kim was horrified. 'You're right, I should have consulted you, but when I saw you in such pain I had to do something, don't you see?'

Floss shrugged her shoulders. 'Oh, well, it's done now. I'll forgive you, but next time something goes wrong don't interfere. Ever!' She wagged a finger at him and smiled, her anger quickly over.

'I promise. Honest.' He held up his hands defensively and grinned.

'Then we shall eat. Come.'

In the dining room the table had been beautifully set for two by Floss's cook-cum-housekeeper. Smoked salmon and vegetable terrine was finished and replaced with roast pheasant.

'Scrummy. Beats hospital food.' Kim tucked in enthusiastically.

'How's the job?'

'Not what I thought it was going to be. I suppose I had an idea I'd be helping people. All we seem to do is make everything more difficult. All the medical staff think of is the patients. Then we come along with our "unit controls" and "rate of throughput", and it's their patients we're talking about. I thought we'd work together, but instead it seems to be "them" and "us" and outright sniping and warfare. It's getting me down.'

'Oh, sweetie, I *am* sorry. Then you must change it. Make waves. I would. If you see something you don't like, then speak up.'

'You would. I'm different. I mean—' He stopped.

'What? What is it? Tell me.'

'I think they're planning to sell off St Edith's.'

'Oh, don't worry, that rumour comes each year like the swallows.'

'But it's worse than that. They want to privatise the hospital.'

'Who? Who's planning this? The government?'

'Individuals. My boss for one.'

'Report him.'

'I can't do that!' Kim looked appalled at the idea. 'He has lots of faults but he's fair to work with. And I can't snitch!'

'Only he wants to ruin a perfectly good hospital. I shan't let this happen!' Floss banged the table.

Kim concentrated on the palm of his hand.

'Who else, Kim?' Floss asked softly.

'My father's partner, so I'm forced to presume Dad too,' he said finally.

'Cooee! Anyone home?'

'Gran! I wasn't expecting you. How lovely,' Chrissy, waiting for the removal van to arrive, exclaimed. Her grandmother, a basket hooked over her arm, bustled into the kitchen. 'Oh, this is nice, I like oak. When's the furniture coming?'

'The removal men are due any time.'

Her grandmother was unpacking the cleaning materials in the basket.

'Do I see coffee in there?' Chrissy asked.

'It's only instant. Don't let your mother know you've had some.' Daphne Galloway snorted derisively, as she spooned coffee granules into two brightly coloured mugs. 'It's all my Frank's fault, I'm afraid. He could be an insufferable and snobby little creep.'

'That's your son you're talking about,' Chrissy said reprovingly.

'I'm not saying anything I didn't say to him when he was alive. He must have driven your mother mad with his pernickety ways. It's no wonder she's enjoying the liberation.'

'Is she? Liberation from Dad?'

'Don't listen to me. I'm just rambling. It's my senility,' Daphne said, with the confidence of one who had nothing of the sort. She began to laugh, but she started to cough.

'Are you all right, Gran? You're not still smoking?'

'No. I gave it up,' she managed to say finally. 'It's just a bit of cold left over. Can't seem to shake it off.'

They sat on the window seat, their coffee mugs in their hands, and both looked out of the window at the rain and mist outside.

'There really is a wonderful view out there if only we could see it.'

'You don't have to justify your purchase to me, dear. Mind you, I bet it'll be parky up here in winter.'

They sat together in companionable silence. Outside the wind had strengthened and the sea mist had increased in billowing swirls. There was a pervasive dampness in the air, and Chrissy hoped it wasn't often like this, or she might end up regretting buying this house.

'Why have you come back, Chrissy?' Daphne asked.

'I don't really know. Just a vague feeling that this was where I wanted to be. After all, "East, west, home's best." Isn't that what they say?' She trotted out the glib words in a light tone, not wanting to explain anything, not even to this woman she loved.

'Do you want to talk about it? About Ewan?'

'No, Gran. If you don't mind.' Chrissy pointedly looked out of the window at the mist, rather than at the other woman, to avoid seeing the sadness in her eyes.

'Where's Mum?' she asked, when the moment had safely passed.

'She's gone to get some champagne and Harpic. I'm sure the house won't be up to your mother's high standards. What's that?' The elderly woman looked up sharply at the sound of a large vehicle inching down the narrow lane.

'The removal men are here,' Chrissy said.

Two hours later, the last of Chrissy's possessions had been unloaded just as Iris drove her Volvo estate through the gates.

'Chrissy!' Iris kissed the air beside her daughter's cheeks. 'Finished unloading already?'

'There wasn't much, I've sold a lot of stuff. I like your hair.'

Iris patted her newly cut and highlighted hair and laughed skittishly. 'Poky little place you've bought. Personally I think you're mad.'

'Excuse me, Miss Galloway.' The foreman of the removal men approached Chrissy, a form in his hands for her to sign. Chrissy accepted the men's good-luck wishes and dug in her pocket for the tip.

In the kitchen, her grandmother was unpacking and washing china, and her mother had begun to make sandwiches.

'Why did that man call you Galloway? Your name's Watson.' Iris waved a cucumber at her accusingly.

'Not any more.'

'Well, what a thing to do!'

'Iris, leave her alone. What she calls herself is up to her, not you,' Daphne intervened. 'You took your time.' She changed the subject abruptly.

'I had to go out to Sainsbury's.' Iris sounded defensive. She turned back to Chrissy. 'When your father died, I didn't change back to my maiden name.'

'Right, I'll start on the packing cases in the sitting room.' Chrissy stood up, not wanting to get into an argument.

In the next room she knelt on the floor and began to unpack the first of the cardboard cartons. First out was a china cat, won for her by her father at a fair when she was eight. Its body was encrusted with a scattering of brightly coloured flowers. 'Are you sure that's what you want?' her father had asked at her choice of prize.

Had he been as difficult as her gran had said? How could the perfect father she'd known be anything but a perfect husband too? She placed the cat on the coffee table.

From the box she took an intricately engraved silver bowl. It was the first present Ewan had given her. She'd been overwhelmed by his generosity. She'd been so happy, so proud of this new, unbelievably handsome, talented boyfriend. She sighed as she placed the pretty bowl beside the gaudy cat. Two such different objects from the two most important men in her life. Her conservative, careful bank-manager father could never have been expected to understand the free-spirited, dangerous man in his daughter's life—he'd never stopped worrying over her well-being. If only he'd known, if only she'd talked to him.

'You need the light on.' Iris flicked the switch and everything in the room looked even sadder.

'My possessions look as if they've come from a car-boot sale.'

'They'll be fine in a few days when they've settled. Tea's ready, or, rather, the champagne is. Pity that ghastly cat didn't get broken.'

'I love that cat.'

'A taste bypass.'

Chrissy laughed as she followed her neat-figured, cashmere-dressed mother back into the kitchen.

Cucumber sandwiches, a cake-stand crammed with cakes, china plates and crystal flutes awaited her. 'How sweet of you, Mum.'

'Oh, it's nothing.' But her mother looked pleased at the praise. 'Gracious, I nearly forgot. The hospital phoned this morning. They said you were to phone back.'

Chrissy covered the surge of irritation she felt at her mother's vagueness as she went to the phone.

'Was it important?' Iris asked innocently, when she returned.

'You could say it was. There was a hospital management meeting they wanted me to attend this afternoon.'

'I'm *so* sorry.'

'Never mind. I'm to see the clinical services manager tomorrow instead,' she said.

'What a mouthful,' her grandmother said. 'I remember when Gladys Simpson was matron of St Edith's. Everyone was terrified witless of her—but, by God, that hospital was run like clockwork. And she cared. Patients felt they were important.'

'Instead of just "throughput".'

'That isn't what we're called these days?' Daphne looked horrified.

'I don't know why you've come back to such a tinpot operation. That hospital just lurches from one crisis to another,' Iris said.

'Mum, we've been over this. I'm more than happy with this job—after all, it's what I've done all those courses in oncology for.'

'What's that when it's at home?'

'Cancer, Gran. They've a staffing crisis and have asked me to do some nights to help out for a couple of weeks.'

'Won't you find nights tiring?'

'It will only be for a couple of weeks. The builders are behind with the new Oncology Ward. Once that's done I'll only do nights in rotation. Anyway, won't this cottage be super when I've finished with it?' Chrissy steered the small talk.

'I'll never understand why you bought it. It's small and dark and stuck out here.' Iris looked about her disparagingly.

'I like it. What would you have preferred? That I lived with you?' Chrissy said, preparing herself for the inevitable argument.

'No,' Iris said hurriedly. 'That wouldn't have worked.'

'Exactly,' said Chrissy, but, illogically, she felt hurt. Iris had certainly changed since Frank Galloway's death.

Although the meeting had not yet started, the atmosphere was already hot and heavy in what had once been the hospital governors' board-room. Now it was where the senior doctors, nurses and managers of the Thorpedale and Fellcar NHS Trust met—too often, in the opinion of the majority present.

This meeting at St Edith's had been called unexpectedly by Craig Nutting. No one had been too concerned initially. Until they read the agenda. Tucked away among the items for discussion was one that had jumped out: Managing Disinvestment, grey-suit talk for *cuts*. The heads of departments were talking among themselves. Some were quietly resigned, others were noisily adamant that their departments would be making no further cuts.

'Anyone know where Matthew Kersey is?' Craig Nutting asked irritably, looking up from the stack of papers in front of him. His expression was resigned when no one answered since the medical staff and the managers did not get on. 'It might be an idea to start this meeting an hour earlier, then we might all get here on time,' he said acidly.

The door opened and Russell Newson, the consultant orthopaedic surgeon, mouthed his apologies. 'Thanks so much for coming, Russell. So kind of you.' Russell took his seat, ignoring the sarcasm. Kim Henderson, sitting at Craig's right hand, moved in his seat, from embarrassment at the animosity that was obviously mounting.

'Right. No point in waiting. The minutes, Tiffany.'

As Craig's secretary droned out the minutes of the previous meeting, Glynis Tillman studied the others present. The medical staff sat at one side of the table, the administrators at the other, as if they were two teams, which in truth they were. And that, of course, was no way to run a hospital, as she knew well.

Her sharp eyes noticed that Russell Newson's eyes were closed. Glynis was worried about him. They were all overworked, but Glynis saw more than tiredness in Russell. Recently he had become withdrawn and, she did not think it was her imagination, sad.

Late as always, the joy of Glynis's own life, Matthew Kersey, general surgeon, entered the room. The quieter he tried to be the noisier he was, she noted with indulgent amusement.

'S-o-r-r-y,' he mouthed to all, tiptoeing across the carpet and barging into a side table, which rocked alarmingly, causing the Victorian inkwell, fortunately empty, to crash to the floor. There were muffled laughs and Craig rolled his eyes heavenwards with frustration.

'My apologies, ladies and gentlemen.' Matthew bowed as if he was an ex-student of the Royal Academy of Dramatic Art rather than of University College Hospital, London.

Glynis smiled, aware that in anyone else she would have found such clumsiness intolerable. Fortunately, the only spare seat was beside her.

'Miss Tillman,' he acknowledged her formally.

'Mr Kersey,' she replied, laughing inside at their subterfuge. It never failed to amaze her how they had got away so long with their relationship undetected.

The meeting settled again and it was Craig's turn to drone on. Only the faces in the large oil paintings of former hospital governors appeared to be taking any interest. However, once he got on to cuts and acquisitions the change in the meeting would be electric.

'By the way,' Craig said now. 'Next month I've arranged for the time-and-motion bods to have a dekko at A and E.'

'No!' Freddie Favour, the A and E consultant, was on his feet.

'Got a problem with that, Freddie?'

'You know damn well I have. Why, when things are hard, is it always A and E that faces closure?'

'Did I say that, Freddie?'

'No, you didn't, but we're not stupid.'

'If there *are* to be cuts—I did only say *if*—then I admit A and E is, in my opinion, the logical one to go for. We have an ageing community here, we have other priorities to think about.'

'I can see where you're leading, Craig. The old can't be patched up, is that what you're saying? Do they take up too much bed space, not fast enough "throughput" for you?' Freddie was barely controlling himself.

'If you're thinking along such lines then presumably the Orthopaedics Department will be the next at risk. Take away the car-crash and sports injuries, and the majority of our patients are elderly,' Russell said.

'There's only so much money in the kitty, Russell, me old mate. Decisions have to be made.'

'I didn't come into this profession to treat patients on financial rather than clinical grounds,' Russell said, to a murmur of approval.

'I'll tell you how money can be made,' Freddie said.

'I'm all ears, Freddie.' Craig smiled.

'A and E is being abused by certain fund-holding GPs in this area. They're referring patients to us as casualties to save on their own funds. Talk to them.' He burrowed in his briefcase and produced a folder. 'Study that. Those are our admission figures for the past six months. Look at Dr Middleton's in particular.'

'Not my responsibility, old boy.'

'I'll study them.' Kim put out his hand.

'That wouldn't be proper, Kim. I'll see to it.' Craig grabbed the file. 'Kim's father is the local GP, Dr Henderson. We don't want any conflict of interest, now do we?'

There was a swell of noise as each head of department began to add their needs.

'Look, all of you, keep your hair on! All I'm trying to say is we're running in over budget. Cuts are going to have to be made. Speaking for myself, the logical one is A and E. But,' he held his hand up, warding off the uproar that threatened, 'I'm open to suggestions on any savings. I want you all to look at your budgets, see where savings can be made next year, and if I could have them before Christmas. Ta. As from today no replacements to be taken on for positions vacated.'

A great roar of 'No!' filled the room.

On days like this, Glynis could wish she had chosen a different profession. As demands on the service got greater and were not matched by the necessary funds, the arguments got worse and more frequent. It was appalling that such talented people should have to spend so much of their valuable time trying to balance the books, she thought, as she looked with concern at her colleagues.

Russell Newson worked methodically, packing a large holdall. He looked about the room, checking to see if he'd left anything out. He felt exhausted. If only he could ignore the administrative side of his work and be free to concentrate on surgery alone. Still, that was the luxury he'd be enjoying in this coming week.

'Have you ever thought that I don't want you to go?' His wife Sabine, prettily blonde, pouting and dainty, appeared in the doorway. Russell looked at her and responded with a derisive snort. 'You don't believe me, do you?' A tear emerged from one blue eye and rolled down her cheek, followed by another. 'Why don't you answer me? Russell, please!' Russell, unmoved, watched her. 'Please, speak to me!'

'There doesn't seem any point any longer. And do me a favour, turn off the waterworks.' Russell began to ball a stack of socks into pairs.

'You don't care what I think, do you?' She sobbed dramatically.

'Not particularly. And don't forget, Sabine, I know that you can cry at will. You've tried that trick one time too many.'

'I hate you!'

'Then you won't mind my going. I'm doing you a favour.'

'I only hate you when you're like this. When you won't listen to me.' She grabbed the bag from the bed and tipped the contents onto the floor. 'Don't go!'

Russell wrestled the bag back from her. He began to repack as if nothing had happened.

'What do I have to do to make you notice me?' Sabine's voice was becoming shrill.

He turned and faced her. 'Sabine, you don't want *my* attention. I *have* to go. I promised. I can't let them down.'

'What about *me*?' The tears began again just as the telephone rang.

Russell answered it.

'Mr Newson,' Milton Curtis, his senior houseman, said, 'it's Mrs Norman. She's complaining of pain.'

'Milton, what were your instructions?'

'To refer everything that worried me to Phil. But I just thought . . . I mean Mrs Norman never complains. Since you were the surgeon—'

'Phil is competent to deal with any complications. Now, if you'll excuse me, I've a plane to catch.' Russell replaced the receiver. He was upset. These endless scenes with Sabine were wearing him down.

'I'll give you a call,' he said finally.

'Why, thank you,' Sabine said sarcastically, no sign of a tear now.

'God, he's a cold sod, I never know what's the best thing to do,' Milton said. 'If I didn't tell him I'd be in the wrong, but when I do . . .'

'At least you've covered your back,' Lance Travers, the Orthopaedic Department's new junior houseman, said from the desk where he was finishing making up the patients' notes for the day.

The door swung open and Russell Newson entered the office. He nodded at his housemen, who hurriedly jumped to their feet.

'Mrs Norman's notes, please.'

Once the notes had been found, he wheeled smartly out of the office and into the corridor that bisected the ward.

All was dark in Mrs Norman's ward, apart from the blue light that glowed over her bed—always an indication that procedures would be necessary through the night.

'Good evening, Mrs Norman. I'm told you're feeling a little poorly?' Russell smiled down at the elderly woman.

'I don't want to make a fuss, Mr Newson.'

'You're not, but even if you wanted to, why shouldn't you?' Russell sat on the side of the bed. 'Now, this pain. Is it a dull ache or a nasty sharp one?' He took her hand in his and gently, kindly, urged out of the worried woman her symptoms.

Minutes later, in the office, he said, 'She's all right. I've written her up for an increased dose of morphine later if she persists in complaining. I don't think she will. I think she's frightened. Keep an eye on her temperature. Half-hourly obs to be on the safe side. I'll see you in a week.'

As the aeroplane flew over the Alps towards Bosnia, Russell looked out of the window at the mountains below. The moon was shining on the snow and the peaks looked close enough to touch. Momentarily he longed to be able to step out of the plane, lie down and let the snow enfold him.

'You all right, Russell? You look a bit doomy.'

He looked up to see Georgie Wallace, a theatre nurse, smiling at him, proffering a whisky. 'Purely medicinal, of course.'

He grinned as he took the plastic cup from her. She sat down beside him, settling herself as if for a chat.

'You're turning into a mother hen, Georgie.'

'It's just . . . Russell, you've changed, you know, in the past year. You can tell me what's bothering you, I'd never breathe a word.'

'Georgie, if there was anything bothering me you'd be the one person I'd turn to for a dollop of counselling. There's nothing. Just the same boring old me.' He forced himself to smile at her.

'I'm not fooled, you know. Still, have it your own way.'

'You're looking a bit peaky yourself.'

'I'm pregnant. A laugh, isn't it—at my age?'

'You're not *that* old, for heaven's sake. Is this good news or bad?'

'Mixed. I never expected to be, not at forty. And until I found I was I didn't even know I wanted to be. But, well, I've come round to the idea. The sad bit is, this'll probably be my last trip. I've enjoyed them. It's been real medicine—patching up innocent people, real victims. Instead of people who, a lot of the time, have brought misfortune on themselves, drinking, eating, smoking too much.'

'Falling off skis. Smashing up cars. But it's not for us to judge, is it?'

'I never did before. But after coming to Bosnia everything changed. I began to despise a lot of my patients.'

'Deary me. Sounds as if it's time you got out,' he said teasingly.

'Georgie, anything left in that bottle?' Ship, the anaesthetist, called from in front.

'A bit.' She stood. Russell watched her move along the gangway. What a comfort it would be to unburden himself to someone like Georgie. But it wasn't his way.

Iris Galloway lay in Bob's arms and felt content. She touched his face gently, as if making sure he was there. As he kissed the tips of her fingers she sighed.

'That was a big sigh. Any problems? You can tell me, you know.'

Iris looked at him. 'I can't believe you're real.'

He sat up. 'So, what's the problem? Worried about what your daughter will say?'

'No,' she lied. 'It's none of Chrissy's business. Shall I make a cup of tea?'

'Do you know what made me fall in love with you, Iris? You're the only woman I've ever met who understood the need for a cuppa after a good fuck.'

'Oh, Bobby. You're so bad!' She slid from the bed and slipped on her dressing gown. 'And how about a bacon sarnie?'

'At this rate I'll have to propose!'

In the kitchen, the cherry tree outside the window clicked against the panes as it was lashed by the storm. She was still smiling as she busied herself with kettle and frying pan. She smiled a lot these days. And all thanks to Bob.

When she thought of her husband now, it was with a dreadful anger. Why, for all those years, had their lovemaking been a quick, groping coupling once a week on a Saturday? What would have happened if she hadn't met Bob, and the wonderful uninhibited world he'd given her? He only had to look at her and she felt her nerve ends start tingling. And when he used language never allowed in this house before, she felt a wave of sexual excitement that was almost unbearable.

She'd hoped to say something to Chrissy about him today—a hint, perhaps—but how could she say, 'Chrissy, I've met this man, he's giving me the most wonderful love, real sex for the first time in my life, and by the way he's fifteen years younger,' with Frank's mother sitting there? She sighed loudly as she placed the bacon on some bread. Chrissy would see it as a betrayal of her sainted father, she was sure.

Iris pushed open the bedroom door. Bob was pretending to be asleep, sprawled naked on Frank's side of the bed. She liked that bit best of all. It was as if she was cocking a snook at Frank beyond the grave.

Daphne could not settle. She'd taken paracetamol, but her head throbbed and sleep would not come. One moment she was hot, the next shivering with cold. She put the electric fire on, closed the window against the storm and climbed wearily back into bed.

She knew she should have seen the doctor. She knew why she hadn't. She was afraid to be ill. She couldn't bear the thought of being dependent on anyone. 'Not yet, dear God, not yet,' she said aloud. She sighed deeply and winced from the pain of it. She couldn't fight, not any more.

St Edith's, standing exposed on the top of South Hill, was being buffeted with ferocity. As the storm intensified the rain lashed at the old granite, beat against the tall windows.

On Ward 2, the elderly fretted and moaned. Gwen Fortune, having a nightmare, woke screaming into another.

'There, there, love. It's only a nasty old storm,' the student nurse crooned as Gwen screamed on.

'Can't you shut that stupid old cow up, Chelsea?'

'She's frightened, Jazz.'

'I'll give her something to be frightened about.' And the staff nurse lashed out and slapped Gwen hard.

'Jazz, you shouldn't have done that!' Chelsea Mottram's own hand shot to her mouth with shock.

'Well, I did! And it worked, didn't it? Any complaints?'

Gwen slumped back on her pillows, and cowered with a new fear. She began to cry silently, tears rolling down her wrinkled cheeks.

CHAPTER TWO

IN THE MORNING, following the storm, the sun was shining and everything looked fresh.

Chrissy inspected her face in the bathroom mirror. Since she had turned thirty, she checked for any wrinkles that might have sneaked up on her in the night. She was not neurotic about being thirty-four—she looked younger, anyway—and she was not dreading being forty. And yet, each morning, the search was made.

She crossed the tiny landing and entered her bedroom. It was this room that had sealed her decision to buy the cottage. Its sloping ceiling matched the walls, which were covered in a paper patterned with blue, white and yellow daisy-like flowers, and the curtains matched.

Chrissy sat on the floor and propped a mirror against the wall. She rubbed in her moisturising cream and applied a light foundation. A touch of beige eye shadow, a flick of black mascara, and her dark brown eyes shone. She outlined her full lips with pencil and filled in with bright lipstick. Lastly, she coiled her long, straight, dark brown hair into a neat, heavy bun.

What to wear? She wanted to look smart without overdoing it. She finally chose a mid-calf brown tweed skirt, which she topped with a black polo-neck sweater and a short brown velvet jacket. She pulled on black leather boots, looked at herself in her mirror and decided she would do.

A quick coffee and an apple were her breakfast as she waited for a taxi. She leafed through the local paper and saw a car that might suit her at Potter's Garage. She would go there after her meeting.

Glynis Tillman smiled. 'Cancellation, Saturday possible,' said the message, signed 'A. B. Hausmann', Matthew Kersey's pseudonym.

For sixteen years their secret had held. Yet the odd snatched evening, the rare weekends—if they were added together this romance had been going probably for only a year in hours spent together. It was sad that this was how it was. These days she found herself often thinking of her retirement, and the loneliness she expected it would bring.

Not this weekend, though. Incredibly he would be free for her birthday on Saturday. She'd long ago resigned herself to not seeing him then—that was a family day. Lord, how much she had accepted. She clutched the message to her, her excitement no different from a teenager's, even though she was forty-six this week.

'Come.' She looked up, flustered, as if whoever was at the door would be able to read her thoughts.

'The new F-grade sister has arrived,' Sister Shelagh Morris, her deputy, said.

Glynis crossed to the door to the outer office.

'Miss Galloway?' she called.

Chrissy jumped to her feet and in her confusion dropped her handbag. Confronted with this smart, somewhat imperious woman, she was glad she'd thought out carefully what to wear.

Glynis held the door wide open and Chrissy stepped into the room.

'Would you care to sit?' Glynis indicated one of the chairs. 'I'm sorry I wasn't here in August to interview you personally.'

'They told me you were on holiday,' Chrissy said.

'Yes. Well . . .' Glynis hid the annoyance, which still rankled, that such an important appointment had been decided in her absence—the deft hand of Craig Nutting at play. 'Unfortunately the Oncology Ward's delayed—builders, you understand.'

'Yes, Sister Morris telephoned and warned me.'

'We've the added problem that one of our junior sisters has had to leave abruptly and a senior sister is having to take early retirement.'

'Yes, she told me that too. I don't mind being a float pro tem.'

'You seem to know everything, Miss Galloway.' Glynis gave a glacial smile.

'Only what she told me. I hope you had a nice holiday,' Chrissy added lightly, to try to dispel the chill atmosphere that was building.

'It was most cooperative of you to agree to help out.'

'My pleasure.' If Chrissy had known how unfriendly the woman was she wondered if she would have been so keen to help.

'I'm worried that you will find yourself with patients whose conditions you may be unfamiliar with. It's the main problem with nursing staff specialising.'

'Don't worry, I'll muddle through,' Chrissy said encouragingly.

'That is what I fear, Sister.' The voice was deep-frozen with disapproval. 'Could you outline your career to me thus far?'

'Well,' Chrissy began, 'I worked for two years as a staff nurse at my teaching hospital, University College, Male Surgical and Oncology. I left to do my midwifery at Addenbrooke's in Cambridge.'

'Why not at UCH? An excellent maternity hospital.' It was at this point that Chrissy registered the clinical services manager was wearing the familiar silver and blue brooch of her own hospital. Chrissy relaxed.

'Well . . . I met a fella.' A frown flashed across the other woman's face and all thoughts of swapping anecdotes about their old hospital faded. 'After my midwifery I applied for a post on the Oncology Unit and made that my specialist subject. Then I married and my husband did not want me to work.'

'You're a widow?'

'Yes, my husband died two years ago. Then I thought I'd like to get back into the profession. I did the Back to Nursing course. I chose an oncology ward to do my placement on. I was fortunate to get a permanent F-grade post at my local hospital. I saw your advertisement. I wanted to get away—so, hey presto, here I am.'

'You are fully recovered from your husband's death? I ask because nothing must come between you and your work. Nothing must interfere with your care of your patients.'

'I'm fine.' Chrissy looked down at her hands. She allowed herself a small smile, since she knew that staff shortages were becoming a nightmare and, with her experience, she'd been an ideal candidate. She said nothing, though. Let this woman play her power games, if that's what she wanted.

'I should explain that I belong to the old school, Miss Galloway. I will not have anything worn other than the designated uniform. I expect total dedication. Whereas some of my senior staff are happy for staff junior to them to use their Christian names, I am not one of them.'

'But of course, Miss Tillman.' This woman must be one of those who was having trouble moving with the times. Chrissy was certain the sister had taken an instant dislike to her.

'Is there anything further you wish to discuss?'

'I've been thinking I would like to start a support group for my breast-cancer patients. As I'm sure you're aware, research is beginning to show that those who have this help live longer.'

'Funding would be difficult,' said Glynis, mindful of Craig Nutting's warnings. But, seeing Chrissy's disappointment, she added hurriedly, 'I think it sounds a splendid idea.' Chrissy wondered if she had actually said something that had met with Miss Tillman's approval.

'I wouldn't mind running it in my own time.'

'Then you have my permission. Would you like me to take you on a tour of the hospital?' Glynis was already standing. She smiled at last. Chrissy got to her feet.

With Kerry in bed and her teenage daughter, Katya, out with friends, Mo Fordham was enjoying a bath before Robbie returned from the pub and took her out for a meal to celebrate her thirty-fifth birthday. How the hell she'd got to that age was a mystery to her. One day she was twenty, newly wed, life stretching before her, and wham! here she was, the big four-oh just round the corner. Whoever had written 'they lived happily ever after' should have been shot. Did anyone ever achieve such a stage? She doubted it. She and Robbie hadn't. You had to have time to be happy, time to sit back and realise you were, and time was a commodity they had always been short of. Mo, with the house, the children, her teaching job, had had little time left for fun.

They were drifting apart, she knew it. Sex was a rarity. What made that worse was that she didn't mind its infrequency. Robbie had always worked long hours, but now in the free time he had he was often out. In the past when he'd invited her to go with him to the pub or the club she'd always said she hadn't the time. Now he never bothered to ask. And now, she knew, often he wasn't at either. 'He's got a bird!' she said out loud. There. She'd allowed herself to say the unthinkable. She'd sensed it for a couple of months now.

Come on, it's your birthday. Stop this! Think about it tomorrow.

She washed her arms and her neck. She began to soap her left breast, her hand flat and moving in a rhythmic circular motion. Suddenly, she froze, sitting completely still, not even breathing. She took a deep breath and gingerly touched herself again. Waves of fear started accumulating in the top of her head and then trickled down her body. She got out of the bath. In front of the mirror she tried again, hoping that by standing upright the lump she had felt would disappear. It didn't. She sat on the lid of the lavatory seat and began to shake.

Glynis poured herself a whisky and added water. She selected Mahler's Third and put it on the CD player with the volume low. In the kitchen she checked that the chicken with tarragon was not drying out. She looked at her watch. He wasn't late yet, not by his standards.

On her return to the sitting room, she took out a folder from her briefcase. She began checking the rows of figures in front of her. Ever since the management meeting she had been working on this, trying to make savings for the next financial year.

While being the first to agree that economies should be made wherever possible and that waste must always be guarded against, she felt now that every decision was money-led. The needs of the patients were becoming lost, almost unimportant, against Mammon. She had always been determined that in her hospital it would be the clinicians who made the medical decisions and not the 'suits' with their clipboards and calculators. It was a stand that was becoming harder to maintain.

An hour later, her task still not finished but feeling weary, she looked at her watch. He wasn't coming, that was evident. She had been mad to believe he'd make it.

She stood up purposefully. In the small dining room, the table laid with her best silver, she lit the dark green candles.

Her first course was Dublin Bay prawns with an aïoli sauce. She sat at one end of the table and wished she'd removed his setting from the other. She stacked his unused china, silver and glass quickly. In the kitchen, she served herself a portion of the chicken and poured a glass of the Gewürztraminer she had chosen specially.

She had no one to blame but herself. On nights like this she had invariably to remind herself that this was her chosen life and to stop feeling sorry for herself. Sixteen years ago she had been well set on her promising career. She had had several chaste relationships for she had been a beautiful young woman—naturally blonde, with eyes of a remarkable blue, effortlessly slim with cheekbones that were envied. But none of those men had meant more to her than her career. Her work had been everything, until she'd met Matthew. Nearly six years younger than her, he was newly qualified, a junior houseman at the prestigious UCH. She was enjoying promotion to junior theatre sister.

Some people meet and know they have met their destiny. So it was with her. They had negotiated with other staff to arrange an off-duty weekend. In a hotel in the New Forest, to his astonishment, he found she was still a virgin. It was a present she gave him, together with her love, for life. It was to be her last truly happy weekend. On their last night together, he confessed that he was married. He did not love Wendy but had married her because she was pregnant—a mere month before he'd met Glynis.

Glynis's world was shattered at his words. He assured her that, once the baby was born, he'd ask for a divorce and they'd marry as soon as possible. But instinct told her it would not happen. Wendy's baby was stillborn, and Wendy could not be told about Glynis—not until she recovered from her understandable depression.

Wendy never did recover. Her depression lurched on. A year later she was pregnant again—even though he'd said they never slept together. He'd explained that Wendy had got tipsy one night and seduced him. Glynis made herself believe him. This child was born with a defective heart. Again, she agreed, Wendy could not be told.

He took a post as registrar in general surgery at Inverness. Six months later, she followed him. It was as well she had, for she was the nurse in charge when, during a routine gall-bladder operation, he had made a mistake and the patient had died. In the subsequent inquiry she was able to cover up for him. It was not an incident she was proud of—a blot on an otherwise perfect career. But where Matthew was involved—when morality and love clashed—love won.

Wendy tired of the Highlands. Matthew moved to a consultancy at Fellcar. Another discreet six months later Glynis followed. Fortunately Wendy liked Fellcar, so Glynis took promotion until, two years ago, she had been appointed to the post of clinical services manager.

Patrick, the sickly son, grew into a healthy rugby-playing teenager. Glynis had waited patiently until two years ago, when, at her prompting, Matthew finally confessed to Wendy. Wendy ranted, begged and entreated. Matthew told her he was sorry, and drove to Glynis to tell her they were free. The remainder of that night they had spent making love and planning their future together. She had tried to mirror his confidence but had found that doubts were not easily eradicated.

She was right. During the day, the news that Matthew Kersey's wife had been brought into A and E was phoned to her office. Wendy had taken an overdose. She was saved. Then her unmarried sister, Jenna, had moved in with them so that Wendy was never alone. Matthew felt he could not risk leaving her, not yet.

On nights like this Glynis could see clearly the hopelessness of her situation—something she tried to keep buried deep inside her. *Matthew would never leave Wendy.* But Glynis's love for Matthew was genuine. And so she endured. *Endured.* What a harsh word to describe her anguish. And fear loomed; fear of what the future held, how she would survive.

Her meal lay untouched. She felt such a dreadful sadness. Tears, which she never normally allowed herself, tumbled down her cheeks.

Mo Fordham was beginning the preparations for the roast. She hoped the familiar Sunday routine would help stem the fear that swirled around inside her. It didn't.

This fear was not like the normal day-to-day variety that, for a mother, was part and parcel of living. Were the kids safe? Would Katya let her know before she did anything silly with a boy? Often she'd joked that if these disappeared she'd have to find something else to worry about. If only she'd known!

There was no stopping the tears that slid down her cheeks. How would the children manage without her? How could Kerry, eight next birthday, cope if she was not here? And Katya needed her more than ever now. Her legs felt weak and she sat down on the kitchen stool, then, hearing Katya call from the hall, she shook herself, forcing herself to look in control. She quickly began to peel an onion.

'Mum, guess what?' Katya rushed into the room, hair flying. 'Mr Stevens says he's going to start up a club for us.'

'Can I join?' asked Kerry, appearing in the doorway.

'No. It's only for teenagers. Brats aren't allowed.'

'Mum, that's not fair!' Kerry began to wail.

'Stop it! Both of you!' Mo shouted, and the tears began again.

'Mum, what is it? Why are you crying?'

Mo wiped at her eyes. 'I'm not crying, silly. It's the onions.'

'Oh, is that all? Can I join?'

'I expect so. Now, if you're not going to help, clear out.' She shushed her daughters away and began to peel the potatoes. She was lucky with her girls—oh, they argued, but that was understandable. Otherwise they were good and helpful. So whoever—she gulped. She wouldn't even allow such thoughts to enter her head.

'I'm off.' Robbie's head appeared in the doorway.

'When will you be back?'

'Hope you've cheered up by the time I get back.' He ignored her question, he often did these days.

Last night's birthday celebration had been a disaster and it had been her fault. Robbie had tried hard with the evening. They'd gone to the Lotus Blossom—and everyone knew how expensive that restaurant was. And he'd bought her a red rose. There, he'd given her a CD to play on the mini-deck he'd given her before they left home. And then they'd gone to the Indigo to find all their friends gathered there as a surprise.

She wondered if his fling was over and he was making amends. But soon she was wondering if this was being done out of guilt. But such concerns didn't bother her nearly as much as her breast. She had tried to join in the banter and the fun, but she couldn't.

'Anything wrong, Mo?'

'You down in the dumps, Mo?'

As one friend after another questioned her, she forced a smile.

'Feeling my age . . .'

'You look really sad, Mo. Anything I can do to help?' Ashley Straw, Robbie's friend and partner in their central-heating company, leaned over her, looking anxious.

'Honest, Ash, I'm fine.'

She could fool the others, but not Robbie.

'What the fuck's got into you? Aren't you ever happy?' he'd whispered angrily into her ear.

'I'm fine. A bit tired,' she'd said, while longing to have the courage to shout, 'I've got a lump in my breast and I'm frightened I'll die,' but she didn't. 'Sorry,' she said instead.

He'd driven her home in silence and shot off into the night. Mo was still awake when he came home as dawn broke, but she'd pretended she was asleep . . .

Once the potatoes were on she made herself a coffee and sat at the kitchen table. If only her mum was alive or she had a sister to talk to. She had friends, but no one to whom she felt close enough to unburden.

Chrissy had the whole of Sunday planned. As she pottered about she found her concentration wavered and she became aware of a strange feeling of unease that would not go away. It intensified into a certainty that something was wrong.

When she called her grandmother there was no reply. It was worrying: Daphne rarely went out and certainly not on a Sunday. This decided her and she called a taxi.

Two bottles of milk stood ominously on the doorstep of Daphne's house. They had often nagged her about the danger of a key on a piece of string inside the letterbox, but today, as she fished for it, Chrissy was relieved that her grandmother had not listened to them. She pushed the door open and called out. No response.

Chrissy felt sick with apprehension as she ran up the stairs.

'Gran, it's me.'

Daphne was lying on her back, her mouth agape, her face flushed. Gingerly Chrissy touched her hot forehead. Her eyes opened and she looked at Chrissy with an unfocused stare. She coughed and winced with obvious pain.

All the years of training, all Chrissy's knowledge were covered by a great blanket of fear.

'What . . . are you . . . doing here?' Daphne asked, with difficulty.

'It's me,' Chrissy said inanely. 'You should be sitting up.' Sense began to edge back into her mind.

'I'm comfortable . . . as I am, thank you—' But she began to cough and to struggle to sit up herself. Chrissy helped her grandmother upright.

'Here, sip some water . . . Can you lean forward, I'll plump your pillows up . . . There, isn't that better?' The familiar nursing actions began to calm her.

'I'll be all right . . . now . . .' The painful cough intervened.

'Try not to talk, Gran. Try to relax.' Chrissy felt her pulse, noting its speed. 'I'll go and call the doctor.'

'No fuss . . No . . . not on a Sunday . . .' But the effort was too much and Daphne slumped back onto her pillows, exhausted.

'It's his job to come,' Chrissy said briskly. And to prevent further argument she quickly left the room.

In the hall she tapped her foot with impatience, as, having heard her call rerouted, she had to listen to it ring and ring.

'Yes?' a man's voice said abruptly.

'Dr Henderson?'

'Middleton.' The voice offered no further explanation.

'I'm calling on behalf of Mrs Galloway—seven, Princes Row. I think you should call, she's running a temperature, she's—'

'Bring her to the surgery tomorrow,' he said brusquely.

'I'm a nursing sister at St Edith's, Dr Middleton.' She listed all the signs she had observed. 'Mrs Galloway needs to be seen. In my professional opinion, you should be in attendance as soon as possible, *Doctor*.' With that she slammed down the telephone on its cradle.

Ten minutes later Daphne was sitting up, hair brushed, with a clean nightie on. Chrissy had done a quick tidy-up, for the thought of the doctor seeing her room in a mess was bothering the old woman.

'I'm fine. I don't need a doctor. You'd better call and put him off.'

'You do need him and it's too late, he's here,' Chrissy said, as she saw a car pull in to the kerb in the street below.

Dr Middleton was handsome, arrogant, and in his early thirties. His disdainful expression told Chrissy clearly how angry he was with her for having the temerity to tell him his job.

'You were right to call me, I'm sorry,' he said later, in the sitting room, where he was writing out a prescription. He smiled at her now, a mixed smile, half apologetic and half flirty.

'That's all right. It *is* Sunday.'

'I'm amazed I haven't seen you around—someone like you.' The smile this time was smooth and practised.

'Is it lobar pneumonia?' she asked, distancing herself.

'Afraid so.' He finished writing the long prescription.

'Shouldn't she be in hospital?'

'I think she's better off here. You're here.'

'But I do work, Doctor.'

'I find old people recover faster in their own environment,' he said.

'Not clogging up beds and eating into funds, you mean.'

'Look . . . I'm sorry. I don't make the rules.'

She wanted to argue with him and tell him to make a stand, to care, but she knew there was no point. He'd decided. And probably Daphne *would* prefer to be here.

'I'll stay here today and tonight. Then my mother can take over,' she conceded.

'Any problems, let me know. I'll arrange for the community nurse to call.' He was on his feet, all smiles and amiability. She stepped towards the door.

In the narrow hall, he held his hand out to her and held hers a fraction too long. 'Well . . . I hope to see you around.'

'Inevitable,' she replied, looking down at the floor. She opened the front door and stood back to let him pass.

Lynn Petch was late. She looked at her watch as she began the steep drive up North Hill. She had arranged to collect the surgery keys from Dr Henderson and she had less than an hour before Terry would begin to throw a wobbly over his Yorkshire puddings. The man was a saint, she decided, as she manoeuvred her car through the gates of the large, expensive home of the practice's senior partner. She pulled her coat closer to her and waited for her ring on the doorbell to be answered.

Dick Henderson, tanned from many hours on the golf course, came to the door. He unclipped the surgery keys from his key-ring. 'You shouldn't be giving up your Sunday.'

'I'm not doing that, just an hour of it. If I don't get the pharmacy order done now I shall be catching up for the rest of the week.'

'Family well?'

'Great, thanks.' There was nothing Dick Henderson liked more than natter and she had Terry to get home to. 'Thank you, Dr Henderson.'

She drove back down the hill to the surgery and left the car in the street. It took all her courage to enter the empty building. There weren't many drugs stored here that were of any use to addicts, but the addicts did not know that—as she was well aware. Two years had gone by since she'd been attacked here by a crazed drug addict. Still, she straightened her shoulders, no point in dwelling on that. She entered her office and took her drug stores book from her desk. From the doctors' surgeries she took their scheduled-drug books in which they entered which drugs they had used, on whom and when.

In the treatment room she unlocked the drugs cabinet. She quickly counted the ampoules and checked the resuscitation equipment. Then she turned her attention to the nonscheduled drugs. She noted those that needed reordering and returned to her office.

Back at her desk she began to make out the prescription for the pharmacist, ready for one of the doctors to sign. It seemed a lot of temazepam had been used. She should check it out on the computer, but, then, Terry was waiting.

A stealthy noise outside her office made her heart helter-skelter. She held her breath. Quietly she opened the instrument drawer and gingerly removed a scalpel. She blessed her rubber-soled loafers as she tiptoed towards the sound coming from Dr Middleton's room.

The door was open. She sighed audibly at the sight of Giles Middleton hunched over his bag.

'Oh, you gave me a fright!' she said, feeling foolish.

'What the hell!' Giles Middleton swung round to face her. 'Are you spying on me?' he asked angrily.

'Don't be silly. What a thing to say!'

'I'm sorry, Lynn. I don't know why I spoke to you like that. I suppose you gave me a fright too.' He laughed, but it sounded false. 'Just replenishing my bag.'

'I must be going. Terry's cooking the roast.' She returned to her office and locked the door. 'Bye,' she called as she let herself out. That was odd, she thought. Why had he looked so guilty?

Giles Middleton ran up the stairs two at a time.

'I thought you'd gone for ever,' the woman said from the bed.

'Not likely.' Quickly he began to remove his trousers.

'Anything important?'

'No, just a silly old cow with pneumonia. Look what I've got for us, though.' He held up a carton of pills in one hand; in the other he had a bottle of vodka. 'Treats!' He laughed as he jumped onto the bed.

Russell Newson stood outside the bleak, shell-pocked building that passed for a hospital here in Bosnia. It was unseasonably warm, with no smell of winter in the air.

'It's a brilliant day, isn't it?' Georgie said. 'We're going for a walk—join us?' she pointed to the group of volunteers walking towards the gate.

'Sure. A break will do us good. Where are we going?' Russell asked.

'Apparently there's a spectacular waterfall a kilometre that way.' Ship pointed along the steep valley, heavily wooded with pine trees.

'Is it safe? What about the mines?' Georgie enquired.

'If we keep to the paths we're safe—they've been cleared.'

The group set off along a path beside the fast-flowing river. One by one they removed their padded jackets as the heat got to them.

'So, where's this famous waterfall?' Russell pretended to complain.

'Listen,' Ship said. They paused. Ahead was the unmistakable roar of tumbling water. They quickened their pace. Suddenly the trees were bigger, the undergrowth lush. The waterfall cascaded down between the high rocks of the gorge.

'Look at that!' Georgie exclaimed.

That view was the last thing that she saw, as a mine hidden at the side of the path exploded and then another, triggered by the first, then a third. The noise was magnified as it ricocheted from one rock of the gorge to another, while birds, calling hysterically, flapped away from the disaster. In the unnatural stillness that followed, two of the party stood rooted in shock as they saw the carnage in front of them.

CHAPTER THREE

MO FINGERED the numbered disc in her hand nervously as she sat in the doctor's waiting room. She shouldn't have come on a Monday morning, the busiest day of the week. She should have made an appointment, then she could have seen nice Dr Henderson. Instead she was to see young Dr Middleton and how was she to talk to a total stranger about her worries? Mo was working herself into a state, but she could do nothing about it. Her fear had a momentum of its own, pulling her along with it as she held on to its coattails, unable to let go.

The loud click of the number indicator rattled and a buzzer sounded.

As she entered his surgery, Dr Middleton was tapping at his computer. She stood waiting, but when he did not acknowledge her she sat down. Her legs seemed to have lost all strength. He said, 'Good morning.' Mo felt her mouth dry, and nodded in greeting. 'And what seems to be the problem?'

Mo swallowed hard, forcing herself to speak. 'Well . . .' she began, in a whisper. She coughed and tried again. 'I've found a lump in my breast.'

Less than five minutes later she emerged into the reception area, white-faced and looking close to tears.

At that moment a nurse appeared. 'It's Mo Fordham, isn't it? Hello. How are you?' Lynn Petch smiled kindly at her.

'Lynn!' Mo felt relief surge through her. But she wished she didn't sound so kind, she feared it would make her cry.

'Are you all right? Do you want to come into my room for a minute?'

'Please.' Lynn ushered her into her office.

'You sit down there. Now, what's the problem?'

Mo's hand went to her left breast and she cradled it. 'I've got a lump here. It's scared me witless.' She shuddered. 'The doctor said he'd make an appointment but I don't know what for or when. I hope it's soon. I can't wait long in this state.'

'I understand totally. Look, Mo, if I were you I'd make an appointment for a private consultation.'

'We can't afford to go private.'

'Not just the one consultation? It'll save the agony of waiting for a hospital appointment. Dr Stratton in Thorpedale is a sweetie. Shall I get Dr Middleton to make an appointment for you?'

'That would be great. There was so much I wanted to ask, but he didn't give me the time.'

'Then ask me. I might be able to help,' Lynn said.

'I'm not holding you up?'

'I've got all the time in the world for an old schoolfriend,' Lynn lied smoothly.

Sabine Newson let herself into her house. Having dropped her shopping on the floor, the first thing she did was to check the answering machine. A dozen calls were waiting for her.

All the messages were from an RAF hospital in Lincolnshire, giving a number, which she now dialled and waited impatiently to be connected. She'd be late for her hair appointment at this rate.

'Mrs Newson? I'm the sister in charge. I'm sorry, but I'm afraid we have your husband here.'

'But he's in Bosnia.'

'He's been in an accident. A mine. We've done a brain scan and can see no apparent damage. We have to do further tests.'

'Can't he be moved?'

'It would be inadvisable. As it is—well, I'd rather you came.'

'What is it? I insist on knowing.'

'He won't speak to us, Mrs Newson.'

'Won't speak? What do you mean? Is he damaged?'

'No, not physically.'

'You mean mentally? Then he'd be happier here, in his own hospital.'

'But, Mrs Newson, I really can't—'

'I know what my husband would want. I'll leave it to you to arrange.' Sabine replaced the receiver.

'She's a lot better, Mum. We caught the pneumonia early enough. She's nattering like nobody's business today.' Chrissy and Iris were standing in Daphne's hall.

'Is there anything to be done?'

'The nurse has been and gave her a blanket bath. I suggest a little light broth for lunch. The bedpan's in the bathroom.'

'I can't lift her! She should be in hospital.'

'She can get on the bedpan, she just needs a steadying hand.'

'Can't you stay?'

'No, Mum. I'm going to pick up a car I bought on Saturday. I didn't get much sleep last night with Gran. I want to try to rest this afternoon otherwise I'll be worse than useless on my first night. I'll phone later this afternoon. OK?'

'No, it's not OK, but I suppose it'll have to be,' Iris said petulantly. 'We'll have to make some other arrangement if this situation is to continue.'

'I forgot. Did you have a nice weekend?' Best to ignore her mother when she was like this.

'Brilliant.'

'Where were you?'

'At a would-be writers' seminar in Bournemouth.'

'I didn't know you wanted to write.'

'You don't know everything about me.' Iris was giggling at how easy it was to lie as she closed the door on her daughter.

The bright red BMW was handling a treat, Chrissy thought as she drove along the narrow lanes that crisscrossed the top of the cliff. At the junction with the main road into Fellcar she stopped and sat waiting her chance to find a gap in the traffic flashing by.

The road was busy, which was odd for a Monday night in November. Everything shuddered to a halt as she joined the line of traffic held up at the big roundabout on the outskirts of town.

ON CALL

She had left home early, not wanting to be late on her first night of duty. It was as well she had. As she approached St Edith's, glancing at her watch she saw she had only ten minutes left to park.

Not quite late, she rushed into the office to be told where she was to be placed that night. A stony-faced Shelagh Morris was waiting for her.

'How kind of you to come, Sister Galloway,' she said sarcastically.

'I'm so sorry, Sister. The traffic was heavy—I didn't expect that.'

'You should allow enough time for any eventuality.'

'There's a pop concert out at the old holiday camp—that's why.' A staff nurse she had not noticed on the far side of the office spoke up.

'So *that's* what it was.' Chrissy smiled her thanks to the other woman, who was tall, with an enviable figure, short fair hair and an attractive strong face. 'Do I know you from somewhere?'

'I don't think so. It's probably me face—a common old one I've got.' She spoke in an exaggerated West Country accent and grinned good-naturedly. 'Dawn Allyson,' she said, holding out her hand to Chrissy.

'Is there any chance of any work tonight?' Shelagh sighed.

'Yes, of course, sorry.' Chrissy fiddled with the ornate silver buckle on the belt of her navy-blue uniform, a sure sign that she was nervous.

'Dawn, you're on Male Surgical and, Sister Galloway, you take Neurology and you'll need to keep an eye on Orthopaedics—there is no senior nurse on duty. I suggest you both get going.'

'Are you helping out during this staffing crisis, like me?' Chrissy asked, as she and Dawn walked along the long corridor from the office.

'No. I'm a bank nurse.'

The bank nurses were the hospital's pool of staff, trained and auxiliary, set up to save the expense of fees payable to an agency. They could be called on at any time when staffing levels were low.

'I'd hate the lack of security of a nurse bank,' Chrissy shuddered. 'I mean, if you're ill you get no sick pay, isn't that so?'

'That's right. Must be bonkers.' Dawn grinned. 'Truth is, I came up here for an interview—for a job I didn't get—but I liked it and decided to go on the bank in the hope that a position might turn up.'

'I wish you luck.' Chrissy felt uncomfortable, wondering if the post Dawn had failed to secure was her own. 'This looks like Neurology.'

'See you at the lunch break, perhaps?'

Chrissy pushed open the door of the darkened ward and walked quickly towards the office, from which light streamed.

'Anyone know anything about her?' she heard someone ask.

'No, except she's a widow,' an older voice answered.

'Sod! Then she'll be as old as the hills. Just my luck!'

Chrissy paused in the doorway. Two nurses stood at the desk. The colour coding of the belts told her that the older one with the dark red was a senior staff nurse. The nurse with a black-and-white striped belt was a senior nursing auxiliary.

'Not quite that old,' she said, with a smile that broadened as she saw the surprised and embarrassed expressions on their faces. 'I'm sorry I'm a little late, I'm still learning the ropes,' she said to the red-belted nurse, who she knew would be day staff and waiting to give her the report on the patients' condition before handing over the responsibility and the keys.

They sat at the desk and Senior Staff Nurse Jo Baker opened the report book. 'We're waiting for Trish Walters. She's a Project 2000 student,' she explained to Chrissy.

'More trouble than they're worth, that lot! They're scared witless of the patients, hardly dare touch them, as if they'd bite or break,' Auxiliary Nurse Stella Gibson complained.

At this moment they were interrupted as a young woman rushed into the room. Her cap was askew and her apron was wet.

'What happened to you, Trish?' Jo Baker asked.

'It was the bedpan thingummy,' the younger girl answered, looking mortified.

'Can't you even empty a bedpan without flooding the system?' Stella Gibson sneered.

'Then after report I suggest you show her, Nurse Gibson,' Chrissy said sharply, quickly reading the woman's name badge. 'I'm ready, Staff, when you are.' She sat waiting for the handover to begin. She was more relaxed now, as the familiar routine swung into action. A detailed report on each of the patients on this ward—condition, medication, problems to watch for, treatments required and state of mind. After that, Chrissy toured the ward with her night nurses, walking quickly, torches pointing towards the floor, used momentarily to check those asleep, chatting to those awake.

With diseases of the nervous system dividing into medical and surgical conditions, there was a good mix. Half a dozen were post-operative, several were in for observation after accidents. Most serious of all was a young man hideously damaged in a car crash, who had been moved from the Intensive Care Unit because there was nothing more that the unit could do for him.

Chrissy and her nurses approached the side ward where John 'Buck' Marston lay, hooked up to the machines that were all that stood between him and death. An agency nurse had been brought in to work exclusively with him for he needed constant monitoring.

Two relatives sat by Buck's bed: a woman whose worry for her son had made her look elderly before her time; and a younger one, smartly dressed and carefully made-up.

'Mrs Marston?' Chrissy asked. Both women turned to face her.

'Yes?' they said in unison, their faces showing a glimmer of hope that here was someone new, who'd make their darling better.

'I'm Sister Galloway. I shall be on duty tonight. Have you everything you need? Some tea?'

'We're fine, thank you.'

'We think he's looking a bit better, and he just squeezed my hand, I'm sure he did.' Buck's young wife spoke quickly, urgently.

'Really? That's good,' answered Chrissy, knowing it was of no note, that such involuntary movements were common. She felt a heel, half of her knowing she should not give false hope, and the other half unable to stop doing just that.

Once the patients had been seen, Chrissy checked the various rooms that were part of the ward: the sterilising room, the showers, lavatories and the sluice.

Trish Walters and Stella Gibson were in the sluice. Stella, with bad grace, was demonstrating the bedpan-washing machine. 'Hi,' she said, on seeing Chrissy cross the tiled floor to check the fire-escape door.

Chrissy saw Stella's quizzical look. 'I was on a ward once where the fire door was left open. A drunk got in and terrorised the patients,' she explained.

'Nasty.'

'Could have been. But it left me with a bit of a thing about them.'

With the ward settled to her satisfaction, Chrissy took the lift to the next. Orthopaedics was quiet. Chrissy quickly checked the patients. All were sleeping. She made sure that the two young and inexperienced auxiliary nurses felt able to cope. She made a note of the times when drugs were prescribed and when she would be needed here to check them and to supervise their administration. Returning to Neurology, she made herself a cup of coffee and searched for some biscuits.

'Are you having breakfast here?' Dawn Allyson caught up with Chrissy, who was trudging along the central corridor of the hospital with the other bedraggled-looking night nurses. All the smartness of the night before had been erased, as with feet aching and faces grey with fatigue, they trooped along. It was half past eight.

'I might, but I must call my gran's first.' Chrissy had planned to go straight to Daphne's, but she needed to make friends here too. It was important to be one of the team as soon as possible.

On the telephone her mother was short with her, but, reassured that her grandmother was much better, she rejoined Dawn.

'How was your first night?'

'Fine. Nothing untoward. A good beginning.'

'Is that Buck Marston still alive?'

'Yes. Sad, isn't it? At first I didn't realise his wife was pregnant.'

'Silly sod. Did you know that the bloke in the other car died? His wife is preggers too.'

They entered the large canteen, which was busy. The noise of the assembled night nurses chattering was like a starlings' moot. Chrissy selected scrambled eggs, toast and coffee. Dawn had coffee only.

'Dieting?' asked Chrissy.

'No, skint. Once I've paid for my bedsit there's not a lot left over.'

'Are the rents in town that bad?'

'Yes—there's a shortage of accommodation. I'll have to wait for my great-aunt to pop her clogs before I can think of buying.'

Chrissy felt a flush of guilt at how fortunate she was as they took their seats, each placing her bag on the floor beside her. She took a plate and began dividing her eggs onto it.

'You don't have to,' Dawn objected.

'I want to.' As she began to eat, she tried to shut out the voice of guilt inside her head. 'God, I'm tired. I'd forgotten what it was like.'

'You haven't been nursing full-time, then?'

'Yes, I did the Back to Nursing course, but I was working at a much smaller hospital.'

'You mean you got *out* from this hideous profession and you *chose* to return?' Dawn's eyes were wide in mock astonishment.

'My husband died. I had to do something.'

'Sorry,' Dawn said, looking down intently at the eggs. 'Tactless fool!'

'How were you to know?'

'I did know, though—everyone here does. You know these places, hospitals breed gossip like a super-bug. I just forgot.'

'Try and forget again—for me. It's all right, I can talk about him.'

'Was it an illness?'

'No, an accident.' Chrissy chose not to elaborate.

'Can I join you?' A staff nurse carrying a tray of food sat down.

'Sure. Chrissy, this is Jazz Poundman. Care of the Elderly.' Dawn moved her chair to give the newcomer more room.

'She applied for your post, didn't you, Jazz? They fell about laughing.'

'About as much as they did when you applied!' Jazz retorted.

'I'm sorry, both of you,' said Chrissy. So she had been right about Dawn applying for her job—oh, hell.

'Don't be,' said Dawn 'I only applied because I thought it was expected of me. And I didn't think I'd get it.'

'It was too soon for me, too. I just thought I should show willing. Sugar, please.' Jazz proceeded to spoon some into her tea.

'That's it, Dawn. If you applied for the same post, that's when I must have seen you.' Chrissy felt quietly satisfied that that little mystery was solved. 'At the interview.'

'Probably. Sugar's bad for you, Jazz, or has no one told you?' Dawn grabbed at the bowl.

'God, I hate old people,' Jazz said, snatching it back.

'Isn't it difficult for you working with them, then?' Chrissy asked.

'There wasn't anything else.' Then she leaned forward, as if bored with the subject. 'What about Russell Newson, then?'

'What about him?'

'I thought you heard everything, Dawn. He's been blown up by a mine in Bosnia.'

'Never!'

'Ghastly business.' Jazz's face showed her eagerness to be first with the news. 'Two people with him were killed, another lost a leg.'

'Is he seriously hurt?' asked Dawn.

'Not a scratch on him, he was in shock, though. They've done a CAT scan—nothing untoward. He was flown into an RAF hospital. But apparently he's being moved here.'

'Is he the orthopaedics surgeon?' asked Chrissy.

'The very same,' said Dawn. 'He's a cold bastard, but good-looking. Unfortunately for us he's very much married to the divine Sabine. All the men *drool* after her. Doesn't leave much for you and me.' Dawn laughed, and then stopped abruptly as if thinking she'd been tactless.

'I was going to ask you what the talent was like around here,' Chrissy lied smoothly. The last thing she wanted was a man in her life, but she'd warmed to Dawn and didn't want her upset.

'Dire! I'm sorry, I didn't think,' Dawn said. Jazz looked curiously from one to the other.

'No problem. Still, I must be going.' Chrissy stood and picked up her bag.

'She seems nice,' Jazz said, as they watched her leave. 'She's too flaming attractive, of course. There's something odd about her husband's death. A lot of rumour, if you know what I mean.'

'No, I don't know,' Dawn said, in a bristly way.

'Suit yourself.' Jazz shrugged her ample shoulders.

'How would you know anything, anyway? Cornwall's miles away.'

'My aunt lives there, works at Trelisk. Poor Ewan,' Jazz said darkly, and then refused to say another word.

'You took your time getting here!' was Iris's welcome.

'Is that a statement or an accusation?' Chrissy laughed, but stopped as she realised her mother was not amused. 'Gran all right?'

'Of course she's all right. Had a boiled egg and soldiers.'

'What a relief! I'll just pop and see her before I get going.'

Iris grabbed her daughter's arm. 'You're not going anywhere. *I'm* going.'

'But, Mum, I'm whacked. I've got to go home and go to bed. You'll have to stay.'

'I don't *have* to do anything. She's no longer my relation, she's yours. For years I've done my stint, put myself out. No more! Now, if you don't mind . . .' Iris was buttoning her coat.

Chrissy moved quickly and put herself between the door and her mother. 'We've got to sort this. How about I go for, say, four or five hours' sleep and come back to relieve you this afternoon?'

'No.' Iris took a great interest in pulling on her gloves.

'All right, then.' Chrissy was having to make a conscious effort to keep her annoyance under control. 'I'll stay this morning and you come back this afternoon and I'll kip then.'

'Do you not understand? Then I'll have to be straight. I don't want to do this. I don't even like the old bat—I never have.'

At that point the argument was interrupted by a sharp rat-a-tat-tat on the front door. Standing on the step was a community nurse. Iris took the opportunity to sneak past her daughter, saying a cheerful 'Good morning,' to the nurse.

'What about tonight?'

'Sorry. No can do.' And with that Iris climbed into her Volvo.

'Hi! I'm Janis Thompson. Problems?' They shook hands. Janis was smart in her pink and grey uniform.

'It would seem my mother is not available to sleep here tonight and I'm on nights.'

'Couldn't you phone the hospital and take this night off?'

'My second night? That would go down like a lead balloon.'

'Mothers! They can be such a pain. Look, let's sort Mrs Galloway out and then see what we can come up with.'

Chrissy followed Janis up the stairs and realised, with relief, that for the moment someone else was in charge.

'Mrs Galloway. How are you? Had a good night?' Janis spoke with a cheerful briskness.

'I feel an old fraud. I should be up and doing.'

'You're staying put.'

'Not when—' But Janis popped a thermometer in Daphne's mouth, putting a stop to further argument.

Fifteen minutes later Daphne was bathed, her bed changed, her hair done, and she was sitting up and looking much better.

Janis entered the kitchen having made a phone call.

'I'm sorry. There's little the surgery can do to help you. You know, limited funds and all that . . .' She shrugged apologetically. 'Hasn't your grandmother got a friend or a neighbour who'd sleep over?'

'She keeps very much to herself, and the neighbours—well, it isn't like it used to be. I doubt if there's anyone left she really knows.'

'Your gran's so much better, you know. She's probably all right to be left. After all, she's got a phone extension by her bed.'

'I couldn't leave her. I wouldn't be able to concentrate. Is there an agency where I can get someone?'

'There's one in Thorpedale. You might have to pay travel costs too—it could be expensive. Still, you don't need a nurse. A nice kindly body would do.'

Mo, her clothes back on once more, took a seat and waited for the doctor to finish writing his notes.

'As you are aware, Mrs Fordham, you do have a lump in your left breast.' Dr Stratton looked up from his notes. 'I'd feel happier if you had a mammogram and an ultrasound done. I can arrange an appointment for you at the Beacon Hill Clinic.'

'I see. The problem is, Dr Stratton—I mean, isn't the Beacon private? I don't think we could afford that. I did explain.'

'Yes, I realise. But if you could stretch to just this little extra—about eighty pounds—it would set your mind at rest. Even if I make you a priority appointment at the hospital there's sure to be a delay. It's probably nothing, but better to be safe, don't you think?' He smiled kindly at her. Mo did a quick calculation in her head.

'When?' she asked.

'This afternoon,' he replied. 'For the best.'

Mo felt as if the walls were moving, as if her guts had melted.

'So soon?' she said, almost in a whisper. 'I'd better then, hadn't I?' She tried to smile but it was as if her lips were paralysed. Her mind raced: this doctor wouldn't have suggested so quick an appointment unless he was already convinced of the worst. 'Then if you could make an appointment for me? Thanks,' she managed to say, and longed to burst into tears but controlled herself.

'Have you someone to go with you?'

'No. I'm fine. Really.'

'You have told your husband about this worry?' he asked kindly.

'Yes. I have. Of course I have.' Even as the words tumbled out she knew they sounded false.

'He has a right to know, Mrs Fordham. And a worry shared—you know what they say,' Dr Stratton said. Mo knew he hadn't been fooled for one minute.

'What a day!' Lynn Petch collapsed into her chair and held out her hand for the cup of tea Terry was offering her. 'You're a mind-reader.'

'Not enough to know what you want for supper.'

'No problem. I got us a Tandoori chicken on the way home.'

'Brill. So, why was today worse than usual?'

'Well, it's Middleton. I think he's up to no good. For one he's having an affair with a patient. Worse, though, I think he's nicking drugs.'

'Shit! Are you sure?'

'Not yet. It took me time to twig. I noticed there was a lot of temazepam used and yet we'd had a big order in not long ago. At first I thought, winter, need for tranquillisers, depressed patients. Then I remembered that lecture on drug abuse at Thorpedale police station. The inspector told us of a craze for taking temazepam mixed with alcohol. You get a high, but even better you get a second high some time later. So I was checking his files. He finds a chronic patient on supplementary benefit who doesn't have to pay for his drugs and orders in his name then the bastard gets them for free.'

'What are you going to do?'

'I don't know. Speak to Dr Henderson when I find out which patient he's fiddling on.'

'Be careful. Make sure before you crash in with accusations.'

'I will, don't worry. But I have to sort it out. Don't forget, I've got access to the drug cabinets also. Before I know where I am I could be being accused of nicking the stuff.'

Chrissy felt as if her brain had been replaced with cotton wool. She'd hardly slept—not that Daphne had been demanding, it was just that Chrissy couldn't relax. She'd got overtired, she realised.

Chrissy walked to her allotted wards. Neurology and Orthopaedics again. Thank goodness she need not worry about her gran. Liz Boxtree, from the agency, was a kindly, middle-aged woman, working part-time as a care assistant. Chrissy was sure they'd found a treasure.

As she passed one of the side wards a beautiful young woman, Senior Staff Nurse Jo Baker's arm about her, walked into the corridor. Chrissy stood back to let them pass.

'With you in a minute. Sister.' Jo said.

In the office Chrissy glanced at the report book as she waited. She saw that Buck Marston was still hanging on.

'Sorry about that.' Jo said, coming into the room. 'Poor woman's distraught. Now. The report.' She sat down opposite Chrissy, whose staff— Auxiliary Nurse Stella Gibson and Student Nurse Trish Walters—had gathered about her with notebooks in hand.

'Who is she?'

'Our VIP's wife. Her husband's the orthopaedics consultant—Mr Newson.'

'Ah, yes. I heard. The mine blast in Bosnia.'

'They're still running tests galore. The trouble is, he's not speaking. They feel he can but won't.'

Chrissy did not look forward to nursing Mr Newson. If there was one thing that filled a nurse's heart with dread it was having to look after a fellow professional. She settled back to listen to the rest of the report.

When the day staff had gone, Chrissy made her rounds of the patients, Stella and Trish behind her.

At the sight of Russell Newson in the side ward, the greeting she had been about to make froze on her lips. For the colour of his hair, the way it flopped forward, made him look like her dead husband's double.

'Hello, I'm Chrissy Galloway. We haven't met,' she finally managed.

He raised his head to look at her. She saw that he wasn't like Ewan at all: his face was not as handsome but stronger. He had sad, troubled dark brown eyes; Ewan's had been an untroubled blue.

She was not sure why her heart should be racing. But as he looked at her she saw the expression in his eyes change, as if he recognised her, was about to say something. She waited, but he remained silent.

Nights on the wards passed either with a mind-numbing slowness or in a frenzy of activity. Consequently as she, Stella and Trish sat with cups of coffee in the almost silent ward, Chrissy felt uneasy as she waited for the inevitable chaos to begin.

'Quiet, isn't it?' Stella looked up from her knitting.

'The lull can't last.' Chrissy stood up. 'I think I'll just go and check on

Orthopaedics. Then I shall go for lunch.' She left the office.

Chrissy paused outside Mr Newson's door. She would have liked to go in to see if she could get him to talk. There was another reason too: she'd just like to see him again. She shook her head at such ideas and went to check on the agency nurse and her seriously ill patient.

'Everything under control, Jolene?'

'Buck's a bit restless.'

'Any idea why he should be like that? Have they changed his medication?' Buck's bed was brightly lit and looked like a small island in the darkened side room. 'Do you need all these lights? Maybe that's what's disturbing him.'

'Oh, really, Chrissy. How can the lights disturb a vegetable? In the next twenty-four hours he'll be—'

'Jolene, a word please,' Chrissy interrupted. 'In the corridor, now!' She held open the glass-fronted door for the other nurse to pass.

'Nurse Gardner, were you never taught not to speak like that in front of a comatose patient? You know that hearing is the last sense to go. You do not speak of vegetative states, or death, in front of such a patient. I forbid such talk on my ward.'

'I'm an agency nurse—you can't speak to me like this.'

'These patients are my responsibility. I'll speak as I see fit.'

On Orthopaedics, Chrissy found elderly Mrs Norman in the kitchen, making herself hot chocolate.

'My, Mrs Norman, you're doing so well. Can I help you?'

'No, thank you, Sister. I've got to manage when I get home. Isn't it amazing what they can do these days? I'd have been in a wheelchair a few years back. But, thanks to Mr Newson and his hip replacements, there's life in the old girl yet.' She laughed and swung her leg to emphasise the point.

'Now, clever as you are, you can't manage crutches and hot chocolate. Let me help you.' Carrying the cup and saucer, Chrissy walked slowly back to the side ward with Mrs Norman.

'Try to sleep,' Chrissy said, as Mrs Norman settled on the pillows, with a contented sigh.

In the canteen, Chrissy was just about to take a bite when her bleeper buzzed. Here we go, she thought, as she dialled the ward.

'What's happened, Stella?'

'It's Jolene. She's gone. She said you'd no right to speak to her as you did and pissed off. I can't leave Trish alone on the ward and who's to special Buck?'

'I'll be up straight away.'

'What did you say to her?' Stella, watching over Buck, was all agog when she got back to the ward. Trish was standing looking anxious.

'Nothing to warrant this. How irresponsible of her,' Chrissy said. 'Trish, you'd better go for lunch now. Could you get Stella and me some sandwiches? Be quick, we need you. Right, Stella, I'll special Buck. Have you phoned around for a replacement?'

'There isn't one available.'

'Well, let's just pray nothing else turns up. Anything else to report?'

'Mr Newson woke up. Jolene left a bit noisily, if you get my drift.'

'Did he need anything?'

'Peace and quiet, he said.'

'He spoke?' Chrissy said with astonishment.

'So he did! In all the drama I hadn't registered.'

'I'd better check him.' She tiptoed into his room and up to his bed. He was asleep. As she watched him, her hand stretched out as if to stroke his face. She stopped herself just in time. What on earth was getting into her?

Quickly she returned to Buck, and began the endless round of checks on him. Jolene had been right, he was very restless: one of his arms was twitching and at intervals he grimaced. Chrissy had seen this before in patients who, not having moved for weeks, suddenly became active as if agitated, as if they knew that death was near.

Twice Stella appeared needing medication checked for patients who had woken and were complaining.

'This is ridiculous, we need another nurse here. Are you sure there's no one?' Chrissy whispered.

'No one. *They* don't give a stuff.'

'Mrs Tomley will need turning in a few minutes.'

'Trish won't be long. She might be a bit thick but she's willing.'

Stella grinned, aware that she had made a positive statement about a Project 2000 nurse, even if a shade grudgingly.

'There were no sandwiches left. Sorry.' Trish had returned.

'Help Stella with Mrs Tomley then,' Chrissy said.

Buck's blood pressure was fluctuating. Should she call the doctor? She checked the chart again: it had been like this for some time now. Her bleeper vibrated. She picked up the phone by Buck's bed.

'Sister Galloway speaking,' she said quietly into the receiver.

'Sister, can you come quickly? It's Mrs Norman, she's ill.' The nurse on Orthopaedics spoke urgently. 'Like she's having a fit. I don't know what to do!' Chrissy could hear the rising panic in the woman's voice.

'Call the houseman, say I told you to.'

Seconds later her bleeper vibrated again.

'Yes?'

'Lance Travers here. I've just had an hysterical auxiliary nurse on the phone. Something about Mrs Norman—it can't be, she's going home tomorrow. Why can't you check it out?'

'Because I'm tied up here, Doctor. Otherwise I would have.'

'This is too much.'

'Too right it is, Doctor.' But she was talking into a dead phone.

'Stella,' she whispered down the corridor. Stella appeared from the darkened ward. 'We shall have to risk leaving Trish on the ward for a minute, while you watch Buck. There's a panic on Orthopaedics.'

Chrissy ran up the stairs two at a time. Mrs Norman's screened-off bed was ablaze with light. She parted the curtains. She was too late. Mrs Norman was dead.

Once Lance Travers had confirmed the death, Chrissy straightened Mrs Norman's body, closed her eyes and mouth and covered her serene face with a sheet.

'Have you any idea why Mrs Norman died? She seemed to be doing so well,' she asked Lance.

'Must have been an embolism somewhere—you know, a clot waiting to happen. Russell's not going to be too happy about this.'

'I don't think he should be told. We don't want him upset.'

What a night this was proving to be, Chrissy thought, as she raced back to the Neurological Unit. Buck was still twitching.

'He moaned just now,' Stella reported. 'A bit like a whiffly snore.'

Chrissy giggled. 'There's a fine medical description.'

'Sorry, but that's what it sounded like. I think he's coming round. But the doctors said he never would.'

'It's an unwise doctor who says "never". You OK here? I'll just check the others.' Quickly she went round the ward. Trish Walters was managing well. Sometimes, she thought, being short-staffed could turn into a good thing. The nurses simply had to manage and discovered a confidence in their ability they had not realised existed.

The light from the side ward attracted her attention. She saw that Russell Newson was sitting up in bed, reading. She tapped on the door before entering.

'Is there anything I can get you, Mr Newson?'

'Ah, it's you!'

Chrissy stood rooted to the spot. He said it as if he'd been waiting for her, in a way that made her heart race ridiculously.

'Tea or hot chocolate?'

'Why is it that whenever a nurse sees a patient awake they automatically offer tea?'

Chrissy decided she had imagined that moment of intimacy. 'What else is there?'

'Sympathy, perhaps?' He looked up at her with a quizzical expression.

'We dish that out in great dollops too. I'm glad you're talking again. Any reason why you weren't?'

His doctors would still need to know why he'd been silent.

He looked away, and she feared that he was about to lapse into silence again. He sighed. 'Have you ever been tired—Chrissy, isn't it? I don't mean physically but mentally?' He turned to look at her. 'So tired you just wanted to escape from everyone and everything?'

'Yes, I have.' She balanced herself on the side of the bed.

'Why?'

'Oh, something happened and I felt I had no reserves to deal with it.'

'And what did you do?'

'I went to the New Forest for a weekend by myself. It was bliss.'

'Did it help?'

'It did. But it was temporary. I had to go back and found the problems had multiplied. Maybe there's never an escape.'

'Same here. Substitute hospitals for hotels!' He laughed. She liked his laugh. 'I don't know why but I didn't want to talk to anyone. I couldn't make myself do it. But you're right. The problems still exist.'

'It must have been a dreadful experience—I mean the mine.' She spoke diffidently, needing to know professionally what had happened, but remembering that when she'd been traumatised prying was the last thing she'd wanted.

'Chrissy, I suggest you write in your report—because that's what you're snooping for, isn't it?—"The patient admitted he'd been fooling all along and just wanted some peace and quiet." How about that?' He sounded bitter.

She hid her disappointment that he seemed suddenly irritated with her. 'Maybe I will.'

'I'll be off tomorrow. Then you needn't worry about me any more. I want to get back to work—that's the best solution. I feel—'

'Well, well, well, what a pretty sight. Am I interrupting?'

Chrissy swung round to see Sabine leaning against the doorjamb. She jumped from the bed knowing she looked guilty even though there was nothing to be guilty about.

'You're pissed.'

'And I'm pleased to see you too, dear Russell.' Sabine entered the

371

room with a provocative, sexy walk. 'Decided to talk, have we? I didn't think you'd be quiet for much longer.'

'If you'll excuse me,' Chrissy said.

'Yes, go. We don't want you here, do we, Russell?' Sabine giggled.

'God, you can be such a bitch. I don't want *you* here.'

'But I *am* here,' Chrissy heard Sabine say, as she closed the door on them. She felt stupidly put out that his wife had come. What bothered her most of all, though, was the surge of pleasure she'd felt when Russell so obviously hadn't wanted to see his wife.

'No! Not that path . . .' she muttered to herself. Involvement with anyone, let alone a doctor, and a married doctor at that, was the last thing she needed. She settled at the desk and pulled the report book towards her. She was imagining things, she—

'Come quick!'

Chrissy looked up to see Trish standing in the doorway.

'What on earth is it, Trish? Calm down.'

'It's Mrs Tomley. I think she's dead.' And Trish burst into tears.

CHAPTER FOUR

THE EXHAUSTION Chrissy felt came in waves. By the time she had completed the paperwork involved with the patients' deaths, reported to the day staff and been to the main office, she was too late for breakfast. Even if she had finished in time she knew she wouldn't have gone. A death was always the main talking-point in the canteen. Two deaths, both unexpected, both patients under her supervision—no, she could not have dealt with the chatter. As it was, she knew she would go over and over in her mind the care, worrying for fear they had made an error until the results of the post-mortems came through.

'You're up! That's marvellous,' Chrissy said, having found Daphne sitting in her favourite chair in the back room, the television on.

'You look dreadful!'

'Thanks a bunch.' She began to unbutton her coat.

'Stop that. You're going home to get some sleep. I'm fine now.'

'Who said you could get up?' Chrissy asked suspiciously.

'The doctor—he came before morning surgery. It was Dr Henderson, I'm happy to say, not that terrible Dr Middleton. The community nurse helped me dress and get downstairs and Liz is coming to put me to bed tonight. Now, you buzz off before you fall over. Bad night?'

'You could call it that! Heard from Mum?'

'No,' Daphne answered, thin-lipped with disapproval.

'I don't understand her.'

'Don't you? I do. She's never liked me and that's the truth.'

'Oh, Gran, that's not so.' Chrissy was aware that she hadn't quite disguised her lie.

'And she's got a fella.'

'Mum? You're joking!' Chrissy laughed.

'I'm not. She's attractive—why shouldn't she?' The words sounded reasonable, but her expression said otherwise.

'I understand, Dad's been gone a long time now.'

'Oh, it's not that.' The old lady waved her hand dismissively. 'It always amazed me she put up with my son as long as she did. Miserable old sod, he was.'

'Gran,' Chrissy said warningly.

'It's the truth. You can't go through life inflicting your opinions on everyone like he did. He was a little martinet.'

'He was a good dad.'

'And a strict one.'

'Because he cared. I thought Mum loved him,' Chrissy said sadly.

'Maybe she did once but, come the end, I don't think so.'

'I never saw them argue. Never heard him raise his voice.'

'He didn't have to. He got at her with calm reason—dripping away like a Chinese torture. "You're putting on weight." "You're too thin." You name it, he'd have said it. He wanted to undermine her confidence so she stayed because she thought no one else would want her.'

'That's awful!' Chrissy felt her face stiffen. She could have been describing Ewan. If her father had been like that too, even if Chrissy had not been aware of it, had some instinct made her search out someone similar? 'Then why do you disapprove of her having an affair now?'

'I reckon he's married, that's why. I can't get my mind round one woman taking another's husband. Why are you crying?'

'It's odd.' Chrissy wiped a tear from her cheek. 'Listening to you, it's like Dad's died all over again. Why is it people are so often not what they seem?' She knew the tears had come for many reasons, not just this new knowledge of her father.

'I'm sorry, I shouldn't have gone on like that. Not when you're so tired.'

'No, I'm glad you told me. I mean, you end up looking foolish, don't you? Everyone else knowing and not you.' She looked down, not wanting Daphne to see the pain in her eyes.

'You're holding back on me, Chrissy. It never does any good. You can talk to me. It's about Ewan, isn't it?'

'What gave you that idea? No. I was sad about Dad, that's all.'

She stood up, wanting to get out of here quickly. 'Still, if you're sure you're OK, I'd better get going. You're right. I'm so tired.'

'**W**hy wasn't I told?' Russell looked angrily at his houseman.

'It was thought best not to bother you.' Lance played with the end of his stethoscope.

'For heaven's sake, Lance. A patient who shouldn't have died and you call that *bother*?' Russell could feel his anger begin to build. 'Who decided? You?'

'Chrissy Galloway, the new sister. She didn't want you distressed.'

Russell, who'd been sitting on the side of the bed, stood up. 'Get me my clothes. I've got no clothes. I'm discharging myself. I need—'

'What? You're not leaving, Mr Newson?'

'Just do it.'

Lance scuttled out of the room. Russell was furious. How dare that woman make such decisions for him?

Fully dressed now, two at a time he took the stairs to the Orthopaedic Ward. The appearance of Russell sent the staff into a tailspin of anxiety.

'Russell, what the hell—' Sister Tina Newport came forward.

'Mrs Norman's notes, please.' He held out his hand.

'They've already gone to the main office. No doubt there'll be an inquest. I mean—'

'Any ideas why she died, Tina?'

'Who knows? An embolism? You know how it is—'

'Did Milton Curtis see her?'

'Honestly, Russell, I don't know. You know this isn't my ward. I'm doubling on it.'

'This bloody place is falling about our ears. Can you get Curtis here? I'll just check my other patients.'

Normally this was where Russell was happiest. Chatting to patients, reassuring them and planning procedures put everything else out of his mind. Except that today it wasn't working. He couldn't seem to concentrate. He retreated to the office and sat leafing idly through notes he wasn't reading.

'You look done in, Russell. Are you sure you should be doing this?'

'I'm fine, Tina.' She was an old friend of many years, but he hoped she'd go so that he could be alone to think. Instead, she sat opposite him.

'You should be in bed, resting.'

'Don't you start.' He managed a grin. 'Mrs Norman complained of pain before I left for Bosnia. I should have taken more time with her.'

'Then you'd have missed your plane. Come on, Russell. Most patients complain. How were you to know?'

'This small voice inside me tells me I *should* have known.'

'You're not God, Russell.' Tina smiled slyly. 'Ah, Fraser. Hello!'

Russell looked up to see Fraser Ball, the consultant neurologist, in the doorway. 'Tina, you called him, didn't you?'

'I had to, Russell.'

'I'd have preferred you stay a day or two longer,' Fraser Ball said.

'I'd rather go, Fraser. I'll rest better out of here.'

'You're not planning to come back to work?' Fraser looked relieved.

'I'm not stupid, Fraser. I realise I need a few days off.' He hadn't realised anything of the sort until coming here and finding himself so disorientated.

'Well, that's different. Shall I call Sabine to come and collect you?'

'No, don't,' he said sharply. 'I'll get a taxi.'

Russell climbed the staircase that swept in a graceful curve to the upper floor. He'd had doubts about buying this house, preferring the old to the new, but this stairway had clinched it. Sabine had clapped her palms together with excitement in that childlike way he'd found so endearing—once. 'Oh, I shall love sweeping down that!' And, loving her and wanting to indulge her, he'd agreed to buy.

He entered the guest room, which had been his room for over a year now, and found, to his consternation, that he felt exhausted. He sat on the bed. He must counter this. He'd work out an exercise routine to build himself up.

He put his arms behind his head and lay back, looking up at the ceiling. It wasn't just his strength he needed to sort out, there was much else he had to resolve. If last week had taught him anything, it was that he could no longer accept second best. Life was too short.

The door opened and Sabine, exquisite in an Armani suit, stood in the doorway.

'Russell, darling, what are you doing here? No one told me.'

'I told them not to. I didn't want you to collect me like a parcel.'

'Russell, what a silly thing to say—a parcel!' She crossed to the bed.

'You'd have felt more emotion if it had been.' He snorted.

'Russell, don't be grumpy. You're home now. I'll look after you.' She moved until her legs were against the bed, he moved further over to the other side. 'Russell, don't shrink away from me.' She looked downcast.

'Sabine, who do you think you're conning? You don't love me. You like what my money gives you, that's all.'

'Russell, that's not true. I begged you not to go to Bosnia.'

'That was a game, Sabine. Making me think you cared still.'

'You're not well, Russell. Don't upset yourself.' She put out her hand.

'Don't touch me! Don't come near me! You reek of sex!' he hissed.

One more night and then two nights off, Chrissy thought with relief, as she drove up the steep slope of North Hill to her mother's house. The high hedge of beech, which her father had planted years ago, was now fully mature. She loved this house. Built in a cottage style, earlier this century, it had dormer windows, was thatched and had a cosiness about it that belied its size. She supposed at some point her mother would want to sell it. Not only must it be worth a small fortune now, but with five bedrooms and four reception rooms it was far too big for her.

'It's only me!' Chrissy called as she let herself in with the key she still had.

'Oh!' Her mother appeared at the door of the breakfast room, which in turn led into the kitchen. 'You could have knocked.'

'I'm sorry. I didn't think. I mean, I had the key, I just—' Chrissy was taken aback by her brisk tone. 'I thought I'd come and report on Gran.'

'How is the old bag?'

'Much better. Up and about, if a bit wobbly on her pins.'

'It'll take more than pneumonia to bump off that old girl.'

'Mum!'

'I told you how I felt.' Iris blocked the way into the breakfast room.

'I'm still adjusting to it. It came as a shock.'

'Life's full of such little surprises.'

'I know,' Chrissy said. 'Any chance of a coffee?'

'It's not actually—'

'Iris? Where've you buggered off to?' a man's voice called.

'"Convenient"? Is that what you were about to say, Mum?' Chrissy smiled, wanting Iris to know she didn't mind if she'd got a bloke.

'Oh, hello. Sorry. I didn't know you'd got a visitor.' A short, but broad-shouldered, fair-haired man had appeared in the doorway.

'Well, you're here now. Bob, this is my daughter, Chrissy. This is Bob.'

Chrissy knew she looked taken aback; her mother having a boyfriend was one thing—but so much younger! 'Hi!' she said lamely.

'You'd better come through.' Iris led the way. On the kitchen floor, protected with sheets, were the hob covers of the Aga and other bits and pieces from its insides. 'Bob's a plumber. Want a coffee, Bob?'

'No, I was coming to say I'm just off to the builders' merchants. I'll leave you two to have a natter. Bye, love.' He kissed Iris full on the mouth, winked at Chrissy and was gone.

'He seems nice,' Chrissy said. She sat at the pine table.

'Bit young for me. Was that what you were thinking?'

'No,' she lied.

'Good. Then don't. He's here to stay,' Iris said, that brisk tone returning, and busied herself with making coffee.

'I didn't say a word. Good luck to you. I'm really pleased for you, Mum. I think it's lovely.'

'Really?' Iris placed the coffee cups on the table. 'Well, that's a relief. I've been telling myself I didn't give a damn what you thought, but of course I did. Chrissy, I can't tell you how happy he's made me. I feel reborn. I didn't know love—you know—could be so wonderful.' Chrissy squeezed her mother's hand, not sure what to say, never having had this type of conversation with her.

'Gran told me that Dad made you unhappy. Is that true? I need to know, Mum.'

'I wasn't *that* unhappy, I just wasn't happy. And now I realise it was all grim. It's made me angry with him. I feel sort of cheated. You probably don't understand.' She laughed self-consciously.

'I do, actually.' Chrissy paused, but knew she wouldn't explain how. 'Was he controlling?' she asked instead.

'Yes. He needed to control everything, what I wore, how I did my hair, the central-heating temperature.'

'I didn't know. That's what I find difficult to grasp.'

'He got far worse after you left. That's why you were unaware.'

'Maybe all this explains why you've gone off Gran.'

'If I'm honest, I never got on with her, I just pretended for the sake of peace, and then, after Frank died, I pretended out of convention. Then Bob made me look at things differently, and you're back and I don't have to bother.'

'I wish you would bother. I can't sleep for worrying.'

'I've been selfish, haven't I?' Iris replied. 'I'll pop in later and check on her.'

They sat drinking their coffee, chatting amicably. Chrissy found it strange. They had never been friends, never close, and yet in one hour everything seemed to have changed. She liked it, she decided.

So many of the female population of Fellcar wanted to be a 'Friend of St Edith's' that, to give everyone a chance, they were divided into teams who alternated.

Leader of her particular group of a dozen volunteers, from the start Floss Yates had determined to make them the best; certainly on their days the flowers were more artistically arranged and she made sure the library trolley had an interesting selection of books. She personally checked the trolley, laden with sweets and toiletries, which toured the wards, and had glowed with pride when she'd overheard two visitors swear that even the tea tasted better when Floss was in control.

Floss loved this hospital. Her involvement had begun thirty years ago when her child had died less than a day after he was born here. Floss had remembered the kindness and dedication of the staff. When she had learned that the latest hi-tech incubator might have saved her son, she had been galvanised into fund-raising to buy one so that other babies might be saved. She had never wavered in her devotion.

Floss tapped on Glynis Tillman's office door for their weekly chinwag.

'Everything fine?' Glynis asked, as she fussed over the tea.

'Running like clockwork,' Floss replied to her old friend. She'd spent a few sleepless nights. She was still undecided whether to discuss her nephew Kim's worries about the hospital with Glynis.

'Thanks—two sugars,' she said, handing back her cup to Glynis.

'What do you want to talk about, then?'

'First, I think we need to recruit more Friends. We're all middle-class and we all mean well, but I think we need a cross-section and some younger women, too, to help with the children and teenagers. And I've been wondering if we shouldn't start self-help groups within the hospital—women who've had hysterectomies or breast cancer, say, to talk to patients in for treatment. Set their minds at rest. That sort of thing.'

'The new oncology sister suggested the same thing—she's very keen. There are so many possibilities, but funding might be difficult. We're coming in over budget.'

'What's new?' Floss snorted and picked up a biscuit.

'What else did you want to raise?'

'Oh, yes.' Floss sipped her tea. 'I've heard—from a very reliable confidential source—there's a plan afoot to privatise St Edith's.'

Glynis felt the blood drain from her face.

'Privatise St Edith's?' she said.

'A group—I don't know who—will ensure that the hospital is not cost-effective. Its closure will be inevitable. Their plan is that a so-called property firm will buy it. It will remain empty for a time but not long enough for the medical infrastructure to collapse. And then, hey presto, it will be sold to a company—American, no doubt—and will reopen as a private hospital, but one willing to deal with the NHS as well since Thorpedale General couldn't possibly take the overflow.'

'Good Lord.' Glynis slumped back into her chair. 'What do we do?'

'We stop them, of course. We start a "Save Our Hospital" campaign immediately. Nip their little scheme in the bud.'

'But who?'

'We have to find out. We've got to stop their greedy tricks, Glynis.'

Mo, sitting beside the bed, looked about the ward. Every bed was occupied by women with gynaecological problems. It was drab, the radiators chipped, the bed curtains torn. Without realising it, she grimaced.

'Pretty ghastly, isn't it?'

Mo swung round. Behind her stood a tall, blonde-haired staff nurse, a clipboard clutched to her chest.

'A little. Bit depressing, yes,' Mo said.

'Not for much longer. The new Oncology Unit opens next week, hopefully. I'm Lesley Bing. Now, if I could just check you in.'

Patiently Mo, for the umpteenth time it seemed, trotted out her details.

'Why can't the first form I filled in follow me around?'

'You went private, didn't you?'

'Yes, I did,' Mo almost whispered, feeling defensive, sensing she was being criticised. 'I couldn't deal with any waiting, you see.' Lesley did not reply and began to wrap the cuff of the blood-pressure machine round her arm.

'What's oncology mean?' she asked, unable to deal with the silence.

'Let me put this thermometer under your tongue.' That done the nurse began to pump the cuff. 'It comes from the Greek *onkos* meaning swelling or a mass. From that root comes oncology—the study of tumours or, in other words, cancer.' Briskly she packed away the apparatus. She began to take Mo's pulse.

Mo sat rigid. She felt as if the oxygen was draining from the air, making normal breathing difficult.

'Everything's fine. If you could change into your night clothes and pop into bed the doctor will be round to see you.'

'Nurse. I—' Mo stopped at seeing Lesley's distracted look. 'Oh, nothing,' she said; she wasn't even sure what she wanted to say.

'Any questions, don't hesitate.' And Lesley swept away.

'Hi! I'm Yvonne. Want to talk?'

Mo looked up to see a woman in her forties in a purple dressing gown, not the ideal colour for her given her yellowish-grey pallor.

The last thing Mo wanted was to talk, but out of courtesy she smiled. 'I'm Mo,' she said.

'Are you all right?'

'I'm fine. Really—' Mo felt the tears she had been fighting well up. She shook her head. 'I'm not fine at all. I'm so scared.' She fumbled in her locker for the Kleenex she was sure were there.

'Here.' Yvonne handed her the box. 'Don't let her get you down, she does it to everyone.'

'It wasn't her fault. I asked her what oncology meant and she told me.'

'The C word? You hadn't said it to yourself? Got used to all that tumour talk and its-probably-a-cyst-or-benign crap. That it?'

'I hadn't said it out loud. Does that sound silly? It was like if no one said it about me, then it wasn't cancer.'

'I know they keep saying it to you, but it probably *will* be all right. I've seen so many come and go here and for the majority it *is* just a lump. Quite honestly, Mo, it's the not knowing that's the worst. If it is cancer, at least you'll know what you're up against. You haven't talked to anyone, have you? You should. What about your husband?'

'He's the last person I'll tell. He's terrified of hospitals.' She took a deep breath. 'And, in any case, we're going through a dodgy patch. This would probably make him take to the hills.'

'Then you'd be better off without him. Mine did that. Said he was afraid of disfigurement—'

'Have you? I mean—' Mo floundered, unsure what she could say.

'Had cancer? A mastectomy? Yes, I have. And it's not the end of the world, Mo. I like to think there's more to me than a pair of tits.'

'Oh, Yvonne.' Mo was laughing genuinely now.

'You know what you find out in hospital? There's always someone worse off than you . . . That puts everything into perspective sharpish.'

'Will this biopsy hurt?'

'Nah. Bit of an ache, that's all. You'll be out of here tomorrow.'

'They told me, and then a two- or three-week wait for the results. God, that's going to be awful.'

'Keep busy. Go shopping.' She stood up. 'Come along to the day room and meet the others.'

'I hope you didn't mind me inviting myself?' Chrissy asked Lynn.

'It's lovely to see you at last. Terry's really sorry he missed you but he's had to go to a Rotary meeting.' She led Chrissy into the L-shaped sitting room. 'Is a drink out of order if you're going on duty in a couple of hours?'

Chrissy glanced at her watch. 'If you've got any white wine, a glass would be lovely.' She noticed the table in the short bar of the L was set for two. 'Where are your children?'

'They've gone to my mother's. I'm lucky, she looks after them when I'm working. They wanted to sleep over.'

Lynn opened a bottle of wine and poured some into a crystal glass, which she handed to Chrissy. 'I'll have some soda, just to join you.' She poured herself a glass.

'You didn't open the bottle just for me, did you?' Chrissy asked, wondering if Lynn had a drink problem.

'Don't worry. I'm not an alcoholic,' Lynn said. She'd read Chrissy's mind. 'I just can't drink. A glass of wine and it goes straight to my head, so I rarely do. But anyhow, welcome home, Chrissy. I hope you'll be happy here.' Lynn lifted her glass in a toast.

'Thanks. How nice.' Chrissy smiled affectionately at her.

As they ate supper Chrissy caught up on news of their old schoolfriends. Lynn seemed to know where everyone in their class was, what they did, who they'd married and how their children had turned out.

'You're amazing!' Chrissy laughed.

'Not really. I've just stayed put so people contact me.'

'They'd have had a problem finding me, that's for sure. In Cambridge we kept changing flats. Once we got to Cornwall, that's when we settled.'

'I was sorry to hear about your husband. But you must be sick to death of people saying that when they don't know what else to say.'

'Oh, Lynn,' Chrissy sighed. 'You're right—it is difficult.'

'Do you like to talk about him or not?' Lynn asked bluntly.

'Not.'

'Fine. You're taking on the new Oncology Unit, aren't you? You must look out for Mo Fordham—she was Moira Daly, do you remember her?'

'Yes, I do. Masses of dark curls. Went to do teacher-training.'

'That's right. I'm probably being unprofessional, confidentiality and all that, but she's in now having a biopsy—breast.'

'Poor Mo. But she's married?'

Lynn pulled a face. 'Robbie's a right bastard—he's always played around. Good-looking, though. How's your gran? You didn't say.'

'She's much better, thanks.'

'I hear you had a run-in with the loathsome Dr Giles Middleton?'

'Bit conceited, I thought.'

'Conceited! You can say that again. But he's a lousy doctor—poor Mo, he put her through the wringer. And he's having an affair with a patient. Do you know Russell Newson?'

'Yes. I nursed him when he came back from Bosnia.' It was ridiculous, she thought, how at the mention of his name she felt an excited surge. Get your act together, she told herself sternly.

'Have you met his wife Sabine—sweet and adored by all?'

'I've seen her around. She's very beautiful.'

'Well, it's she who Giles is having a ding with.'

'No!'

'Madness, isn't it? You'd think no doctor would ever risk it with so much at stake.'

To her shame Chrissy could not hear enough of this gossip. And later, driving to work, she berated herself for the pleasure she felt that Sabine was not as perfect as she seemed. Poor Russell, how awful for him. But even as she thought this she knew she smiled.

Glynis had been reading, but she was unable to concentrate. Floss Yates's warning about the hospital being privatised kept racing about in her head. Logic told her that such double-dealing was possible, these days: she had weathered too many changes to be surprised by anything at St Edith's. How could Floss know of such matters? This doubt had been something of a comfort, seeming to prove that it was all gossip until she remembered Craig Nutting's new assistant—what was his name? Kim Henderson—and his father was a GP, whose wife was Floss's younger sister! That was where such information was coming from, undoubtedly. And, if so, it had to be taken seriously.

At a ring on the doorbell she looked at her watch. Nine o'clock.

'Matthew!' she said, pleasure etched on her face. 'What a lovely surprise. Come in, do.' She fussed about him, seating him and pouring him a large Scotch. 'You're late. You must be tired.'

'An emergency—perforated gastric ulcer. Nasty.'

'Where was your registrar?'

'Flu. You, my darling, are a sweet mother hen. Come here.'

Autocratic, dignified Glynis did as he bid. She knelt at his feet, looked up at him with eyes that brimmed with adoration. A surge of excitement flashed unbidden through her body as he leaned forward and kissed her on the mouth. A couple of seconds later she sank back on her ankles, struggling to disguise the disappointment that engulfed her, as he returned to his whisky. They so rarely made love these days. He was often so tired, he worked far too hard. But accepting these matters did not stop the longing in her.

'Another drink?'

'Just a small one.' He watched her as she crossed the room to the drinks cabinet. 'Thanks.' He took the refilled glass. 'You look a bit down tonight. Problems?'

That he should have noticed gave her such joy. And what luck that he had come. Matthew knew most things that were going on.

She related Floss Yates's conversation to him. 'Such a worry.'

'Bit far-fetched, don't you think?'

'Her nephew is Craig Nutting's new assistant. She didn't say, but it *has* to be him who told her.'

'What would he know? He's probably only a glorified clerk. No. Don't worry. Closure, yes, that's always a fear, but we'll get round that, don't worry.' He laughed and immediately she felt better.

Then he stood up as if to leave.

'Do you have to go?' she asked, the closest she could get to begging him to stay.

'Sorry, darling. Wendy's on her own.'

She closed the door, and the cottage sank back into its silent loneliness.

It was set to be a troublesome night. In the office Chrissy was being asked to keep an eye on Care of the Elderly.

'Three wards? That's impossible,' she protested.

'It will have to be possible, I'm afraid. Jazz called, she's locked herself into her flat—she'll be late,' the administrative sister said. 'The firemen can't get to her for a couple of hours so she's got to wait.'

'But it's not right.'

'Not a lot is in this profession at the moment.'

Dawn commiserated with Chrissy as they walked to their wards.

'I mean, if something goes wrong who gets the blame?' Chrissy said, worriedly, as she turned into Care of the Elderly.

'See you at first lunch?'

Russell sat in his sitting room, a half-empty bottle of whisky beside him. On his lap were a stack of papers, which he was working through methodically, jotting figures on a pad.

'Do you want supper?' Sabine appeared, dressed in simple, but expensive, as he well knew, white jeans and T-shirt.

'No, thank you.'

'You're sulking, aren't you? Come on, Russell. We can work this out.'

He looked at her, blankly, as if too tired for emotion. 'I'm deciding what is a fair distribution of our assets. I've spoken to the estate agents.

They're coming tomorrow to value this house.'

'We can't sell this. I love it. I won't move out. You can forget it.'

'If you want a large cash settlement from me you'll have to agree.'

'You don't mean to go ahead with this? I've said I'm sorry. I'll never be naughty again. Promise. I want to stay with you.' She stood contrite— the big blue eyes appealing. He wondered why he'd ever found her little-girl-lost act attractive. She thought she could play him along as she'd done so many times before. She could not accept that she'd lost the power to manipulate him.

'Oh, Sabine! Don't you understand? I don't want you back. You want Giles, then have Giles. I'm finished with you.'

'Russell, I love you.' She fumbled in her pocket for a handkerchief.

'You don't love me, I doubt if you ever did.'

'That's not true. I was lonely . . . That's why . . .You *know* that's why. You were always working, I hardly ever saw you.'

'Sabine, you're pathetic. How do you think the bills get paid? The Porsche bought? This house?' He turned back to his pad and pen.

She snatched the pen. 'Stop this! You don't mean it.'

'Oh, yes, I do, Sabine. I've suddenly woken up to what a stupid prat I've been. No more. We'll get divorced. Now. No hanging around. If you don't comply I'll name Giles as co-respondent. You understand?'

'Christ, you're a cold bastard, aren't you?'

'Where you're concerned, yes,' he said simply.

Sabine's car screeched to a standstill outside the block of flats down on the seafront. She got out, went to the door of the block and stabbed agitatedly several times at a bell-push.

'Who the hell's that?' The intercom came tinnily to life.

'Giles, it's me. Let me in. Please!'

The buzzer sounded and she pushed the front door open. She ran up the stairs.

Giles was waiting in his open doorway. 'Where's the fire?'

Sabine did not reply but flung her arms round him and clung to him like a blonde limpet. 'Hold me, my darling.'

'With pleasure,' Giles said into her hair, and hugged her tight. Sabine sobbed uncontrollably as he led her into his apartment and sat her on the sofa. 'Poor darling. What's happened? Tell me. Shush . . .' He comforted her. Slowly the sobbing subsided.

'Oh, Giles, my darling, I'm so afraid . . .'

'Who's frightened you?'

'It's Russell. He's so angry.'

'He hasn't hit you?'

'Oh, Giles . . .'

'The bastard. How could he? A sweet little thing like you. I need a drink.'

As he poured two brandies, Sabine cried quietly.

'It was awful, Giles. I don't know where to start—you do love me, don't you? Tell me you do.'

'I do—' Giles looked at his drink and knelt in front of her.

'No, properly. I need to hear you say it.'

'I love you,' Giles said, as if such words were a foreign language.

'I love you too, Giles. Oh, so very much.' She leaned forward, kissing him long and hard. His hands searched under her T-shirt for her breasts.

'No, darling, I must talk to you. He wants a divorce. He says he is going to name you in his petition unless I comply.'

Giles sat back on his haunches. 'What? How did he find out about us?'

'I told him '

'You did *what*? You stupid cow. Oh, shit!'

'But, Giles—you said. You just said you love me.'

'Because you told me to. Don't you remember we agreed—no strings, just good *fucking fun*! Look, you've got to deny it was me. You've got to say you'd made it up to make him jealous.'

'But why should I? Can't we live together, as I've dreamed?'

'Then you can dream on. If he names me, the next stop will be the GMC—you're a patient! Don't you understand? I could be struck off.'

'But I love you,' she wailed.

'And I don't love you. Now, shut up and let me think!'

Matthew Kersey let himself into his house. He opened the door of the drawing room. 'Hi, my sweet ladies, I'm back.' He crossed the room and kissed his wife, Wendy, on the cheek.

'A drink?' Jenna, his sister-in-law, was quickly on her feet.

'In a moment. I've a call to make. What's for supper?'

'I cooked you boeuf en daube,' Jenna said.

'What a dream your sister is, Wendy. What would we do without her?'

In his study he dialled a number.

'Craig? Matthew here. Problems,' he said. 'You'd better arrange a meeting. That stupid old cow Floss Yates has got wind of our plans.'

'Mrs Galloway. It's Liz Boxtree. I care at night for the older Mrs Galloway. I do hope I'm not disturbing you.'

'Of course you are! It's midnight!' Iris did not hide her irritation.

'I'm sorry, Mrs Galloway. Truly. But my car's broken down. Mrs Galloway's on her own.'

'Didn't you call her?'

'Yes, I've phoned several times through the evening. She says she's all right. But I'm worried. She sounded woozy—she's taken sleeping pills, she told me. She doesn't usually. I wondered if you could go round?'

'OK.'

'You will? Oh, that's taken a weight off my mind. Thanks.'

'What's the problem?' Bob asked, as he slid towards her.

'I've got to go round and check the old girl.' Iris began to get up.

'Not now.' Bob's voice was husky with longing as he searched for her breast through the folds of her negligee. 'Give her a ring,' he whispered.

The phone rang. Lying on the floor of her bedroom, Daphne tried to inch towards the bedside table to pull the telephone down by its flex. But the pain in her leg was too severe. She slumped back on the floor, but had enough wits left to pull at the eiderdown so that it fell across her. But she could not stop the tears.

'Can't you sleep, Mrs Fortune?' Chrissy, who'd been rechecking the patients on Care of the Elderly, stopped at the side of the bed.

'I haven't had my suppository, Sister,' Gwen said, in the tremulous voice of someone who was afraid.

'You haven't?' Chrissy looked at the old lady and saw her move away from her ever so slightly. She sat on the edge of the bed. 'Anything wrong, Mrs Fortune? Something's bothering you. Tell me.' She took hold of Gwen's hand and squeezed it gently. 'Are you afraid of going to sleep?' she asked, since often the old, she knew, were convinced they would never wake up.

'Where's the plump nurse?'

'Nurse Jazz Poundman? She isn't here, Mrs Fortune. I'm in charge.'

Gwen Fortune's body slumped with evident relief. Chrissy frowned. 'Is it Nurse Poundman who bothers you?' The old lady lay silent. 'You can tell me. Come on, what is it?'

Mrs Fortune's lips pursed as if her mouth was preventing her from saying what her mind wanted her to.

'I'll check about your suppository.' Chrissy spoke reassuringly as she moved away from the bed.

'Sister. Thanks for calling me Mrs Fortune. It makes a nice change.'

Chrissy found Chelsea Mottram, the student nurse, loading a trolley with clean linen.

'Chelsea, I've been talking to Mrs Fortune. You don't call her by her Christian name, do you?'

'No, I don't, we were taught not to. But Jazz does.'

Many of the elderly clung to formality, which made them feel more dignified. Some nurses took it upon themselves to use their Christian names thoughtlessly. Chrissy decided to have a word with Jazz. 'By the way, Chelsea, Mrs Fortune says she didn't have her sedative.'

Chelsea paused in loading the trolley. 'She did. I poured her a glass of water and watched her take it.'

Chrissy's hand shot to her mouth. 'Nurse, that particular sedative is given as a suppository, normally inserted at the other end of the body.'

'Oh, no!' Chelsea looked horrified.

'It'll take longer to work, that's all. I'll go and tell her that the doctor decided she shouldn't have it tonight.' Chrissy suppressed a smile.

With no sign of Jazz Poundman, there was no way Chrissy could go to the canteen. She'd grab a coffee and some biscuits in the kitchen on Neurology instead.

Lance Travers had beaten her to the percolator. 'Hi!'

'Aren't you on the wrong ward, Doctor?'

'I'm covering for the neuro houseman. There's an emergency. Looks like a brain haemorrhage. She's just been sent up from A and E and Fraser Ball's on his way.'

As she made her way to the ward Mrs Marston appeared in the side-ward doorway. 'Sister. A minute. Buck's—'

'Mrs Marston, if you could wait a moment I'll be with you as soon as I can. The consultant's due.'

'*You must come.*' Mrs Marston was pulling at her, and Buck's wife was standing in the doorway of the side ward. 'Sister, Buck opened his eyes. He did. Honest. And his eyes followed me across the room. He's coming round, isn't he? Oh, God, I'm so excited!'

Cheryl Marston burst into tears. Chrissy put her arm round her just as the main ward door opened and Fraser Ball strode in.

'Mrs Marston, we have an emergency just in,' said Chrissy.

'I can manage, Sister.' Fraser swept on. Chrissy appreciated his attitude. If Buck *had* woken up he had now returned to his previous state.

'He was awake!' said Cheryl.

'I'm sure he was,' Chrissy said reassuringly.

'Sister,' Fraser Ball called from the door, 'about the new patient.'

'Doctor!' Buck's mother was on her feet in a trice.

'Mrs Marston,' he said, with weary patience. 'Lance, call theatres to prepare as quickly as possible. Yes, Mrs Marston, what can I do for you?' He stepped into the side ward.

'It's Buck, he's coming round.'

Fraser looked questioningly at Chrissy.

'I wasn't here,' she said.

'He's been opening his eyes all the way through. It's not significant. I did explain to you—'

'Cheryl?' A weak voice sounded. All four swung round to face the bed. Buck, his eyes open, smiled vacantly. 'Where the fuck am I?'

Though she was pleased for his family, Chrissy could have wished that Buck had chosen another time for his reawakening. In the small side ward, all was chaos since Buck—silent now for a week—could not, it appeared, stop talking. His wife and mother were beside themselves with excitement.

'We must try to keep him quiet,' Chrissy said anxiously.

'Quiet? What do I want to be quiet for? I've been asleep a week. You sure it was a week, Cheryl? You're not having me on?'

'No, Buck, honest!'

'And you remember nothing?' Fraser asked as he took Buck's pulse.

'Not a bean. I was in the pub. Next thing I'm here. And it's now!'

'I think you should leave, Mrs Marston.' Fraser spoke quickly and kindly to Cheryl. 'He really does need his rest. It's hard, I know. But you do want the best for him, don't you?'

'Put like that, Doc. Oh, I could hug you!'

'Five minutes to say good night, then. Sister, a word.'

Chrissy led the way to the small office. 'I'm to call the police—night or day, they said.'

'Leave it. They can talk to him in the morning. Meanwhile, he should be sedated. I don't like this. Far too sudden. Prep the other patient. I'll go and scrub up.'

'The prescription for Buck, Mr Ball—'

'I'll write it up in the morning.'

'But I can't—'

'Oh, Sister, for Christ's sake, if we don't get that young woman on the table and draining soon it'll be curtains for her. Get Lance to write it.' And Fraser was gone.

'Have you seen Lance Travers?' she asked Staff Nurse Alex Oldham, who had chaperoned the new patient from A and E.

'No, he left just after you.'

Of Lance there was no sign. Nor could she raise him on the telephone.

By now Buck was in a high state of excitement, trying to get out of bed, pulling at the cannula in his arm.

'If you don't calm down, Buck, I shall forbid visitors for a week,' she said, in her sternest voice. 'Now, get back into bed. And I'm sorry, but you two must go—you can see how overexcited he is.'

Allowing them a few more moments alone, Chrissy tried once again to find Lance. She dialled the theatres, only to be told that both doctors were scrubbing up. She could hear Buck laughing and shouting as she explained her problem to the theatre nurse.

'Well, if Fraser said to give the drug, I'd give it. He'll back you up.'

Chrissy held the telephone, looking at it as if to find an answer. 'Alex,' she called out, 'I need to check a drug that Fraser ordered but forgot to write up. It's irregular, but Buck's going to kill himself if he's not sedated.' She unlocked the scheduled drug cabinet and drew up the required dose. She wrote up the dosage, which she and Alex initialled. 'We shouldn't be put in this sort of position. If anything goes wrong it's us who get it in the neck, not the doctors,' Chrissy fretted, aware what she was doing could cost her her job.

On Orthopaedics the patients were all asleep. Wearily, Chrissy returned to check Buck, who was finally sleeping peacefully. The telephone's light flashed. It was the theatres staff phoning to report that the new patient was in Recovery, that everything had gone far better than they had hoped. One of the happier tasks that night was to search out the husband and to let him know his wife had come through the operation and was as well as could be expected.

Almost leisurely after the night's dramas, she made her way back to Care of the Elderly. As she entered the ward her bleeper sounded.

'Oh, Sister—thank heavens! It's Mrs Fortune.' Chelsea grabbed at her hand. 'She's dead!'

Chelsea was right. Mrs Fortune was most decidedly dead.

'What's that draught?' Chrissy asked, as she emerged from the bedside. 'It's coming from the sluice.' Quickly she walked in that direction. The sluice door was wide open to the fire escape.

'Did you open this, Nurse Mottram?'

'No, Sister. It was locked. Don't you remember? You locked it.'

'Busy night?' a voice asked from the shadows, as she and Chelsea walked back to the nurses' station.

'Jazz, is that you? Where the hell have you been?'

'Can't manage without me?' Jazz laughed good-naturedly. 'Sorry I left you in the lurch. But I'm here now.'

'I'm sorry I snapped—it's been a bit fraught here. Mrs Fortune's died.'

'Unexpected! I thought she was doing well. Still, you never know with the elderly, do you? You get on. I'll do what's what here.'

'Thanks. I've called the houseman.' There seemed little point now in discussing the matter of using Christian names when patients didn't like it.

Chrissy redid her make-up to give herself courage. She had resolved that this morning she would brave the canteen. If she hid, every time there was a death on her shift, the staff would have something to gossip about. She must stop being so paranoid. Everyone was so busy talking when she joined the queue at the self-service counter that no one noticed her.

'Do you realise that since she joined she must have doubled the death rate in this hospital?' a nurse in front said.

'*Death Stalks the Wards*. Can't you just see it in the tabloids?' Her companion laughed, but on seeing Chrissy standing with her tray, she blushed and shoved her friend in warning. The silence that followed was oppressive, Chrissy thought, placing coffee and toast on her tray.

'Well, I feel sorry for her,' she heard from one table as she passed by.

'Maybe she was just careless.'

Chrissy settled at an empty table by a window. She wanted to stand and shout out her innocence, to yell at them to give her a chance. Instead she ate quickly and then left the room, aware of the sudden silence as she did so.

Chrissy sat outside Glynis Tillman's office. She felt sick to the pit of her stomach. The only bright spot that morning had been Lance Travers appearing and filling in Buck's prescription chart for Fraser so she hadn't had to confess to the day staff her actions in the night.

'Sister Galloway, come in. You look tired.' Glynis ushered her in. 'You have a problem?'

'Yes.' Chrissy stood stiffly, awkwardly.

'Coffee?'

Chrissy shook her head. 'No, thank you. I need to talk.'

'Well, tell me what's upsetting you.' She spoke kindly.

'I don't know where to begin,' Chrissy said. She was already worried that, rushing here without thinking things through, she might be making matters worse for herself.

'I presume it's about the sudden deaths on your wards. Unfortunate, but you mustn't let it upset you. Deeply distressing, but something we, as professionals, have to learn to deal with.'

'In the canteen this morning . . . they were talking . . . Miss Tillman, they think I killed the patients.'

'Sister! Really! What a thing to say! Don't you think you're overreacting?' Glynis said briskly. Chrissy remained silent. 'You know how gossip spreads in hospitals. The post-mortems will show cause of death and then the spiteful remarks will stop.'

'But why me? Others were on duty those nights.'

'Because you are the newest person here—an unknown quantity. Because you are the senior. Because—' Glynis stopped.

'Because what, Miss Tillman? What were you about to say?'

'Nothing, Sister, I had run out of causes.' Chrissy gave her a bleak look. 'Are you aware, Sister, that there has also been a spate of pilfering of patients' possessions?'

'I've heard, yes. Why? Are they accusing me of that too?'

'Oh, Sister, come, come. I only asked to ensure that you made your patients aware of the problem and told them to lock up valuables.'

'I'm sorry. I'm just on edge.'

'You're nights off now, aren't you?'

'Yes.'

'Well, try to get some rest. You're exhausted and imagining things, I'm sure. It's been decided, in any case, to put you on your new ward next week. It isn't quite finished, but there's plenty to be done.'

Chrissy sat gazing into space. Why the sudden change of plan? Did they think it was safer to put her on that *empty* ward? The panic returned. What did Miss Tillman know? Chrissy wanted to explain everything to this woman. She opened her mouth to do so, but suddenly changed her mind.

'Is there anything else you want to say?'

'No. Why should there be?' She spoke defensively.

'Nothing. I just wondered.' Glynis looked at her as if not convinced. 'I'm always here, Sister, if you need me.'

By now Chrissy was so late her gran would think she wasn't coming. At the sight of a parked ambulance her heart plummeted. 'Oh, no!' she cried. She parked her car and ran up the road, impervious to the slight drizzle which was falling. As she reached the house the ambulance, its light flashing, drove away. A worried-looking Liz Boxtree stood on the pavement.

'Chrissy, thank goodness you're here. I phoned the hospital, they said you were off duty. Mrs Galloway had a fall.'

'How? When?'

'Must have been in the night. Luckily she managed to cover herself with an eiderdown so there's no hypothermia.'

'What are you talking about? What happened?'

'Broken thighbone. Poor lady, how she got through the night—'

'What do you mean? Where were you? How could this happen?' Chrissy felt anger take control of fear.

'Didn't your mother tell you? I phoned last night when I couldn't get here. My car wouldn't start. She promised to go round. First thing this morning I phoned. When your gran didn't answer I borrowed my sister's car and drove straight over and found her.'

'Are you telling me my mother didn't turn up?' Chrissy's face and voice were etched with shocked disbelief.

'I'm afraid so. She did promise me she'd look after her. Honestly.'

'Liz, I believe you.' Chrissy put out a comforting hand. 'Thank you for coming so promptly. I must go with her.'

A and E was not busy, so when Chrissy, followed shortly by Liz, walked through the door, they entered an almost deserted department. Of Daphne Galloway there was no sign. The receptionist told them to take a seat. Liz took Chrissy by the arm and led her to a row of empty chairs.

'I'll get some coffee. Black? White? Sugar?' Liz asked.

God, what a day, Chrissy thought, as she watched Liz doing battle with the coffee machine. She'd kill her mother, the selfish bitch. A broken thigh at Daphne's age was serious. If she was kept immobile too long the pneumonia could easily return. She could die. Chrissy shivered.

'Here you go.' Liz handed her the polystyrene cup of coffee.

At the sight of the A and E sister, Chrissy jumped to her feet.

'My gran—how is she?'

'She's shocked, understandably. She has a compound fracture—we're prepping her for surgery now. You've been on nights, haven't you? Go home and get some sleep. There's nothing you can do, you know.' Betty Greaves spoke kindly, aware of how helpless Chrissy would feel.

'Can I see her before I go?'

'Of course. Come this way.'

Daphne looked so small in the high bed, its cot sides up, her face as pale as the white hospital gown.

'Chrissy, I'm sorry,' she said, in a croaky, parched voice.

'Don't be silly, Gran. You'll soon be racing up the supermarket aisles again in no time.' Chrissy could hear that she sounded half-witted and that Daphne would not be taken in. The situation was serious.

A nurse hovered with a small tray containing a syringe.

'Gran, they want to give you an injection. It'll make you feel woozy and take all the pain away.' She leaned over and kissed her. 'Bye, Gran.'

'She's only just recovering from pneumonia,' she said to the sister, once they were outside the curtained cubicle.

'Don't worry, she told us. She's a feisty old lady, isn't she?'

'The best.' Chrissy turned abruptly away. She wanted to cry.

The conversation in the nurses' home flowed back and forth over various topics, but every so often returned to Chrissy and the deaths.

'What have you got against her, Jazz? You talk as if it's cut-and-dried and she bumped them off in some way.'

'I've got nothing against her,' Jazz said, looking affronted.

'You could have fooled me.' Dawn laughed.

'You must admit, it does look fishy. In any case, I know what I know.'

This had exactly the result Jazz wanted: immediately she was the centre of attention. She smiled enigmatically as they plied her with questions. What did she know?

'You're like ghouls! Oh, all right, then, I'll tell you. Her husband, Ewan—guess what he died of?'

'What?' they roared with impatience.

'Well . . .' Jazz milked the moment. 'Ewan Watson died from an overdose of insulin, that's what!'

CHAPTER FIVE

THE SEA BELOW THEM sparkled; the wind whipped skittishly about the cliff top. The December sunshine was, for most people, uplifting after a damp and drab November, but apparently not, judging by their expression, for the two men who stood on the green.

'Is it necessary to talk out here?' Craig Nutting complained. 'It's parky enough to freeze the old proverbials off a brass monkey.'

'We're meeting the others. They teed off a good half-hour ago. We're to meet them in Yates's copse.' Matthew Kersey heaved his bag of clubs onto his back, scowled at Craig and set off to the next hole. Craig puffed up behind him.

'Whose idea was it—all this cloak-and-dagger malarkey?'

'Mark Fisher's. He says he's got most to lose if it comes out.' Matthew lined up his ball.

'Little shit. MPs think they're so sodding important.'

'He reckons the papers would focus on him. Tory sleaze reawakens—all that tosh. The rest of us would remain fairly anonymous.' Matthew looked up from addressing the ball.

'And jobless!' Craig laughed. 'If jobs were to be lost it wouldn't be his, he'd make sure of that.' Craig sliced his ball, throwing a divot in the air, and watched it fall wide of where he'd aimed.

Two holes later they peeled off the green and disappeared down a slope into Yates's copse, where they found Mark Fisher sitting on a log, smoking nervously, while Giles Middleton leaned somewhat languidly but elegantly against a tree.

'What's the panic?' Giles pushed himself away from the tree and sat on a log.

'Your partner's son, Kim Henderson, is Craig's right-hand man and he's singing like a canary. That's the panic.'

'I don't see how. Kim doesn't know anything.' Craig looked as relaxed with the situation as he felt.

'He must know something, or why would Floss Yates, Kim's aunt, tell Glynis Tillman she'd heard the hospital was to be privatised?' Matthew snapped at him. 'Are you sure Kim hasn't seen a file?'

'There's no file—I'm not a berk. And even if he heard me on the phone to one of you he couldn't have twigged. There's no way—'

'Have you sacked him as I suggested?'

'Oh, really, Matthew! On what grounds? In any case, he's unsackable. He's a civil servant.'

'What do you suggest we do? Forget the whole project? Yes, that's probably the safest.' Mark looked ill with tension.

'Of course we don't give up. We've nothing to hide, we've done nothing—as yet—but sow a few fears and alarms,' Craig said.

'I'll start referring all my patients to the hospital, OK? Forget A and E for a while.'

'No way, Giles. You do that and if we're not careful the bloody hospital will start making a profit and where will that leave us?' Craig thumped Giles matily on the shoulder.

'It's only a matter of time before something's said to me—you do know that, Craig.'

'No, Giles. If we start acting differently it looks suspicious. You tell your patients to toddle along to A and E to circumnavigate the waiting lists. You're a good doctor with only the best interests of your patients at heart,' Craig cajoled him. 'Stop worrying. As for you, Mark, what have you done other than to point out to the Minister that St Edith's is running at a loss and, as its MP, you wouldn't create a stir in the House of Commons if it was shut down, right?'

'Well . . .' Mark placed a cigarette in his mouth and lit it before speaking. 'Well, I might have hinted that if it closed there might be something in it for him.'

'You moron!' Craig spat out at him. 'He's an incorruptible bloody socialist!'

'I didn't tell him the plan,' Mark whined.

'The man's not daft—he'll put two and two together. At the first whiff of something afoot he'll stop you dead in your tracks.'

'Hadn't we better calm down? This'll get us nowhere. Does anybody know anything about the Minister?' Matthew asked.

'What, a spot of blackmail?' Craig perked up at this notion. 'Rumour has it that he's got a bit of skirt the other side of Thorpedale—the husband's a defrocked Tory MP.'

'Brilliant! So why are we worrying?'

'That's down to you, Mark. A little threat if he looks the least bit iffy.'

'And the rest of us?'

'Business as usual, gents. I'm off to New York next week—a few exploratory talks, if you get my drift.'

'What if Floss starts banging her drum?'

'Deny everything, Giles, it's the only way. They'll be too busy gossiping about the alleged hospital murders to worry about this.'

'Hardly murders, Craig,' Matthew objected. 'We're still awaiting the post-mortem results on that. Bet you it's all a storm in a teacup.'

'Who? What, Matthew?' asked Mark.

'Three patients died unexpectedly and the finger of suspicion is pointing at the sister in charge at the time,' Matthew explained. 'Unfortunately for her, her husband died in somewhat similar circumstances. The police hauled her in for questioning.'

'And we're employing her at St Edith's?'

'She wasn't charged, Mark.'

'Makes you think, though, doesn't it?'

'Exactly,' said Craig. 'Where there's smoke . . . It couldn't have happened at a better time for us, gents. A handy smoke screen which I suggest we keep pulled. Maybe a few post-mortem reports should get lost in the deluge of paperwork. Now, if you gents don't mind, I'm calling it a day and wending my way back to the bar. Coming?'

Floss Yates stood in the hallway of the clubhouse and looked out of place. Dressed in black she stood out dramatically from the golfers in their peacock-bright clothes. 'Kim!' she called out, as she swept towards the bar, spotting her nephew and waving excitedly. Holding the hand of a pretty young woman, he made his way towards her and introduced Tiffany Lester, daughter of the resident professional golfer, to his aunt.

'So, you're Tiffany. What a pretty name. And you, my dear, call me Floss. Now, Kim, the drinks, chop-chop.'

Settled at a table by a window, the niceties dispensed with, Floss folded her hands in front of her. 'So. To business. Tell me all.'

'We nearly left. Our boss, Craig Nutting, was on the forecourt. If he'd seen us together—phew!' Aha, thought Floss. So Kim's in love. 'He was here with Giles Middleton.'

'Interesting. But I need to know how you know their plans.'

'Tiffany had better explain.'

'It was by accident, Floss. In our office the computers used to be fixed to act as a telephone and fax machine as well as for e-mail. Anyhow, Craig decided he didn't like it, "not secure enough" I remember him saying. So he ordered me to close it all down, which I did, and we returned to using ordinary telephones and fax machines. I don't know how it happened—Kim and I think a new cleaner must have seen the unused telephone jack points and put them back in the machine. We had a bad storm the other night and the modems might have been activated by that.

'Anyhow, I was working in the outer office and suddenly I heard Craig dialling and I could hear everything he was saying next door as it was issuing out of my computer. He was talking to the local MP about selling the hospital. Then he said he'd fax him and to stand by the machine and to destroy it immediately he'd read it. It came out on my fax modem as well. I didn't like what he was saying—so, here it is.' From her handbag Tiffany took out a print-out of a fax detailing the hospital's budget and handed it to Floss.

Floss saw, under one column headed 'Real', was listed a long row of figures. Under a second, headed 'Massaged', was another.'

'What a clever girl you are, my dear. How smart of Kim to recognise it in you.' Floss smiled warmly at the couple.

'Are you going out?' Mo asked, as she cleared the supper dishes.

'I thought I would.' Robbie looked down at the newspaper he was holding, but not before she registered the shifty expression she'd almost come to expect.

'Only I need to talk to you.' She folded the tablecloth.

'What about?' he asked, with a hint of suspicion.

'Katya, Kerry. Bed,' she ordered. 'I want to talk to your father. In private,' she said, as Katya opened her mouth, about to argue. Reluctantly, they left the room.

Mo turned to find Robbie standing at the kitchen door about to go through it. 'No, Robbie, please. I really do need to talk to you.' She knew that if she didn't tell him now maybe she never would. 'Last week when I told you I'd gone to your sister's—well, I hadn't.'

He moved back into the room at that. 'Really, so where were you?' he asked, a suspicious look on his face.

'In hospital.'

'Hospital? St Edith's? What for?' He sat down.

'I found a lump in my breast. I went in for tests. I'm waiting for the results.' She was amazed how calm she felt, how prepared she was for him to walk out.

'Mo, I'm so sorry.' He was round the table and his arms were about her and he was holding her tight. 'You should have told me. You shouldn't have coped alone. Why didn't you tell me?'

'It's silly, but . . .' Her voice was muffled, held as she still was against his jumper. Gently he pushed her slightly away so that he could hear what she was saying. 'If I told anyone it would make it real.' He let go of her and sat down abruptly.

'Shit!' He put his head in his hands.

'Robbie, I'm sorry.' She stroked back his hair, which had flopped forward. At her touch his body tensed. Why? Was he afraid of her and *it*? Afraid he might catch it? He slumped in the chair. There was a despondency in his attitude that told her that she'd ruined something for him. Had he made plans that this news altered? She knew from his first reaction that he felt genuine sorrow for her, but suspected that a lot of it was for himself now. She sat down too. She would have liked to hold his hand, but stopped herself, feeling that he must have time to come to terms with things. As she watched his shoulders heave, certain he was weeping, she marvelled at how strangely detached she felt. She said nothing, waiting for him to control himself, unable to be sure how many of the tears were for her.

'Useless support system, aren't I?' he said eventually, fumbling in his jeans for a hanky.

'It's the shock. I understand.'

He blew his nose noisily. 'It happened to a mate of mine—his wife got it. You don't expect it to happen to one of your own, do you?'

'No. I've talked to doctors. It's not a death sentence any more—there *are* treatments. It can be beaten, you know. And nine out of ten lumps are nothing ominous—and we don't know for sure that it's malignant. I should have waited for the results before I even mentioned it.'

'You're right. There's no point in getting upset, not until the results are through.' He sat straighter in the chair. 'It's just—I think we need a drink. Rum and Coke?'

'Lovely. Best get a couple down me in case I have to go into hospital. No drink there!' She laughed.

'God, you're brave.'

'No, I'm scared silly. What were you about to say? Just what?'

'Oh, nothing.' He busied himself with the bottles, but not before she saw a look of shame flit across his face.

'What is it, Robbie? We have to be straight with each other—especially over this.' She was aware that her heart was thudding: what if he was about to confess about his bit on the side?

'It was just . . . I thought . . . What if—' And he circled his own chest with his hand as he stood looking sheepish, afraid and, she didn't think it was her imagination, guilty too.

'If I have to have a breast off?' She spoke lightly, almost with relief that it was this and not the other that was bothering him. 'There's no point in even thinking about it until we know what's what, is there?' And she, who normally sipped at her rum and Coke, drank greedily, for once, in need of it, wanting to obliterate this big fear from her mind. The loss of her breast she sometimes thought was an even worse prospect than death.

'If it had to happen—my breast, I mean—I'd still be me, wouldn't I?' she said, looking straight at him. He shifted his gaze. In that second she knew he would not be able to cope with this; that she was on her own; and knew instinctively that she would manage—how, she wasn't sure, but she would.

'If you don't mind, I'd promised I'd pop round to Lynn Petch,' she lied.

'Oh, I see.' He stood up. 'Then you don't mind if I go to the pub?'

'Not at all, Robbie. You must do what you want.'

She watched him leave. She felt sad, but she was not surprised.

Chrissy was working alone in her ward; as yet there were no patients, just empty, unmade beds, nor had she any nursing staff to help her. She looked up from the lists on her desk in her office. The view from this ward was lovely: sea from the windows on one side, and at the far end, where her office and the day room were situated, sea and what was left of St Edith's garden. She hadn't known until she'd come to this ward that the cottage in the grounds below was Glynis Tillman's quarters.

She returned to her lists. There was so much to organise, with her first patients due on Monday. The linen cupboards, kitchen and sluice room were all complete and checked. Chrissy had been overjoyed to find that Floss Yates, whom she had known all her life, was in charge of allocating funds from the Friends of St Edith's coffers. With her help she'd been able to arrange a good library of books and videos, and some prints to hang on the walls.

She would make this ward as pleasant as possible, she had resolved. The very word 'cancer' struck fear into the soul of even the most stalwart. It was her job to alleviate that fear and give the treatments, and thus the patients, the best chance of success. 'Plants', she scribbled on her list and underlined the word with a flourish, as if making the point. She was a great believer in nature helping to soothe.

From her eyrie she could see the car park below. She saw Russell Newson striding towards the hospital. She'd heard he was popping in occasionally to see his patients but doing no surgery yet. She'd seen him once or twice and each time her heart had betrayed her, racing. At night, her thoughts often turned to him. She did not understand why, she hardly knew him. She looked up to check the time. She'd managed two relaxed hours working away contentedly. It couldn't last, of course: staff were joining this weekend, and then what? She sighed with weariness. It was all getting too much for her—again. She was fully aware of the conversations that stopped at her approach; the oblique looks people gave her when they thought she would not notice. Just like it had been in Cornwall, in the village street, the shop. That had been a black time she thought she'd never survive. But she had. She knew she hadn't killed Ewan. That thought had kept her steady. Now again the same nightmare. Yet she'd done no wrong—she must cling to that knowledge and hold her head high. Her shoulders slumped. Easier said than done.

Only last night, when she'd visited her grandmother on her ward, she'd walked straight into a drama.

'That's her! That's the one what killed poor Gwen Fortune,' an old woman in the next bed had screeched loud enough for all to hear. Chrissy had stood rooted to the spot, unable to move, unable to speak.

'That's my granddaughter you're insulting.' Daphne hauled herself up in the bed.

At least this galvanised Chrissy into calming her just as the staff nurse, Jazz, lumbered up and restrained the other patient.

'Don't be silly, Thelma. That's our nice new Sister Galloway you're insulting.' Jazz's voice was bubbling with amusement. 'Now, get back into bed, you stupid old bitch,' she said in a lowered voice, but loud enough for Chrissy and Daphne to hear.

'You're a disgrace, Nurse.' Daphne spoke for Chrissy.

'And what's your problem, Daphne?' Jazz grinned as if being told off was welcome excitement in her dull routine.

'Speaking like that. And I'm Mrs Galloway to you.'

'Jazz, please . . .' Chrissy began.

'What?'

'Oh, nothing,' she said, too tired and demoralised to pursue it.

Back in her office, Chrissy shuddered at the memory—it had all been so unpleasant and worrying—for Daphne, once Jazz had left, slumped back on the pillows, fighting for breath. She was glad she hadn't rowed with Jazz, who, when called for her help, had acted swiftly and calmed her grandmother.

'I thought I'd find you here.'

'Floss, lovely to see you. Come in. Fancy some tea?'

'No tea. I'm the senior Friend on duty and I'm up to here in tea. But I *had* to find you. We must do something *immediately*! I was in the office and outside I heard two bitches gossiping about you. Appalling!'

Floss plonked herself down on the seat beside Chrissy's desk.

'Floss, that's sweet of you. I can't blame them—three deaths in a row like that and after Ewan's death, well, it's human nature, I suppose.'

'Don't be so infuriatingly reasonable. It's criminal of them and it has to stop.'

'What's worrying me is that the results of the post-mortems should be through by now and they're not. The delay points to them being inconclusive and so they must be doing further toxicology tests. That can only mean the patients were murdered.'

'Oh, Chrissy, who'd do a thing like that here, and why?'

'That's what I can't puzzle out. I don't know anyone here, so how can anyone hold a grudge against me?'

'Maybe someone's jealous of you getting this job. Mind you, that would be an extreme reaction—knocking off patients to get at you. Don't worry, they probably all three fell off the twig quite naturally. I'm going to have a word with Glynis and tell her to tell the pathologist to pull his finger out—oh, Lor', that's a rather unfortunate choice of phrase, isn't it? Anyhow, I'll go and find her now.'

'There's no point, Floss. I saw her leave her cottage a good half-hour ago. I can see all manner of comings and goings up here.'

'Seen Matthew Kersey snooping about? Matthew and Glynis go back a long way.'

'You're joking?'

'No. They're very discreet, but a few senior staff know. He's a creep and she's a fool. Speaking of which, seen your mother recently?'

At the mention of Iris, Chrissy looked away. 'We're having a little local tempest, over Gran's accident.' It was a mild way to describe the full-blown row they'd had. She felt she'd never forgive her mother, not this time.

'The trouble is, when a woman of your mother's age discovers sex, good manners go flying out the window.'

'You know? What don't you know, Floss?'

'Nothing of any importance. By the way. Christmas Eve—I'm having a party. "Save St Edith's from Unscrupulous Creeps" the invitations will say. You're invited. Coming?'

'I'd love to,' Chrissy said. A party was the last thing she wanted. All the same, she wondered if Russell would be there.

From her briefcase Glynis took a copy of *Nursing Times* and settled to read it. Once the train was in motion she'd put it away and allow herself to think of the weekend. She could hardly believe her luck. Matthew had called to say he was going to London and would she care to join him?

They were well beyond Fellcar when she lifted her head to find Edna Greenbank, the senior theatre sister, sitting opposite her.

'Going to London?'

'I'm led to believe that is the destination of this train.' She knew she sounded pompous and cool—she intended to.

'Christmas shopping?'

'Yes. I hope to do some present-buying.' But she smiled to herself: she hoped she wouldn't be out of bed long enough to shop!

'I'm glad I've bumped into you in this way, Glynis.'

Well, I'm not, Glynis thought. She looked pointedly out of the window.

'I've a problem that I'd like to discuss with you. It's about Matthew Kersey.'

Glynis knew she reacted too quickly as, abruptly, she turned her head to look at Edna, eyes wide, before she could stop herself. 'What about Matthew?' she said, anxiety in her voice. Was it her imagination, but was a sly smile playing around Edna's mouth?

'I've spoken to him in a roundabout way and he was very annoyed with me. Understandable, I suppose.'

'Edna, my dear, I do wish you'd get on with it.'

'There are two things, actually. He's borrowing theatre equipment to use in his private practice and he's not paying for it.'

'I'll have a word with him.' Oh, Matthew, he could be so silly. He'd done this in the past and she'd had to reprimand him, and he'd laughed and kissed her on the mouth in her office, which was always so deliciously exciting. 'And the other?' she said, feeling almost light-headed at that particular memory.

'I found him with the anaesthetic nurse in the rest room, in a rather compromising situation.'

Glynis said nothing, for she could not. She was aware only of the pounding of her blood through her body.

'I mean, what he gets up to in his private life is none of my business—but in the hospital, on hospital property, then I think it is.'

'Hospital property?' Glynis was aware she whispered the words.

'The bed in the rest room. At it like hammer and tongs.'

Glynis felt the blood drain from her face, a dizziness seeping over her. Suddenly she knew she was going to be sick.

'Glynis, are you all right?' she heard Edna call after her as, buffeted from side to side by the train's motion, she struggled to the lavatory.

Why was it that reality failed so often to live up to one's dreams? Chrissy thought, as she opened the small window of her sitting room. The acrid smoke, the only result from the fire she had lit on the hearth, seemed not to notice this escape route. She pushed her hair back from her face in a gesture of frustration, unaware that in doing so she had smudged her face with soot. She began to cough for the smoke was pungent and thick. She put on her Barbour and green wellies and let herself out of the back door. She stood for a moment, breathing deeply, enjoying the air. The sun was shining, even if it was bitterly cold. She'd take a walk and let the smoke clear, she decided.

Out in the lane she turned towards the cliff path. On walks like this she should have a dog to run and snuffle along beside her. As a child she'd often walked these cliffs with her father and for a short time with their cocker spaniel, Fluff.

She crossed the cliff, stumbling on the tufty grass before reaching a cluster of rocks on the cliff's edge. She sat on a flat stone and shivered— from cold or memories? She gazed down at the sparkling sea far below her and was aware that she wanted to cry. She pulled her Barbour closer. So many problems . . . the worry . . . the sense of isolation. Then the tears came. She let them fall, made no attempt to stop them. Who was there to see? What did it matter?

'Excuse me. It is Chrissy, isn't it?'

Chrissy, recognising the voice, put her hand in her pocket to search for a hanky, not wanting anyone to see her like this.

Russell Newson crouched down. 'Will this help?'

Chrissy was sure she was incapable of speech.

A neatly folded handkerchief was being offered to her. Confusion, embarrassment and excitement were playing tag in her mind. She patted at her eyes and blew into its folds.

'I'm so sorry. I don't know what got into me. I'll wash the hanky.'

'No need. I'll leave you alone if you want. Or you can talk, if you want. Or I'll take you for a drink.'

Even without seeing his face she knew he was laughing at her. She raised her head and risked looking at him. He really laughed this time. 'Did you know your face is covered in what looks like soot?'

'My fire, it was smoking.'

'Ah, that explains everything. Can I help? I'm good with fires.'

There it was again, the amusement, which made her feel a lot better.

'That would be very kind of you,' she said, clambering to her feet.

'I never expected to see that lovely sight here!' Chrissy said, as she entered her sitting room to see a log fire burning and Russell efficiently tidying the hearth. 'I'd virtually given up on it.' She placed steaming bowls on the coffee table. 'Are you sure soup's enough? It's from a tin,' she asked. 'The bread's fresh.'

Russell laughed.

'What's so funny?'

'Your honesty, I suppose. Tinned soup will be lovely.' He lowered himself onto the rug, his long legs stuck out in front of him, and leaned his back against an armchair. She pushed the basket of rolls towards him, then sat on the floor.

'What were you doing on the cliff?'

'Part of my getting-fit regime. I try to walk a couple of miles a day. Today I decided to trek up here. I always envied whoever lived in this cottage.'

'You did?' She sounded surprised. 'My cluttered little cottage? As you can see, I'm a bit of a muddler.'

'Understandable when you have to be so organised in your work.'

'I hadn't thought of that. Thanks. Now I'll know what to say to my mother when she nags. More soup?'

'No. That was lovely.' He shifted so that he could throw another log on the fire. 'Why were you crying, Chrissy?' he asked quietly.

'I wasn't. It was the wind—in my eyes. You know.' She was on her feet, stacking the dishes. She had to get out of the room, she didn't want sympathy. She didn't want him to delve, didn't want him to be kind. She'd begin to cry again, she knew she would.

'Coffee?'

'If it's no trouble.'

He was reading when, composed now, she returned from the kitchen with the coffee.

'You like poetry, I see.' He looked up at her, tapping the slim volume he held in his hand. 'I'm afraid this stuff's a bit over my head.'

'Really?' She wasn't sure how her response sounded. All she knew was that she wanted him to put that particular book aside.

'A real doom merchant this bloke, isn't he? A bit twisted, I'd say. E. M. Watson. I can't say I've ever heard of him.'

'You wouldn't have. It was privately printed. He was my husband.' Her hand shook and she spilt the coffee. 'Oh, look what I've done!' And she was on her feet again, but this time so was Russell.

'Chrissy, I'm so sorry. I'd no idea. I'd never have said—' He stepped towards her. She retreated from him. 'The name, it's not yours—I—'

'How were you to know? Don't be silly,' she replied, more in control now as she ran to the kitchen to fetch a cloth to mop up the coffee.

'You're fully recovered, then?' she asked briskly as she returned, putting on her professional mantle as a defence. 'No trouble sleeping?'

'What's that? Sleep, I mean.' He pulled a face.

'Didn't they give you pills?'

'Hundreds of them. I don't approve of them, though. If I douse the nightmares with chemicals, they'll be lurking there, waiting to pop out at me again. Somehow I've got to face what happened. And beat it.'

'You'll need help. You can talk to me if you want,' she said, her professional hat on.

'And why should I tell you? You won't confide in me.' He smiled so that any hint of criticism was dispelled. He put his head in his hands and sighed. They sat in silence. Then he shook himself slightly, as if reaching a decision. 'It's Georgie who haunts me the most. She was with me in Bosnia. She was a great nurse and a wonderful woman. She'd just found out she was pregnant. She was so happy, and then *boom*.' He slapped one hand into the palm of the other. He looked so sad as he spoke that she leaned forward and took his hand in hers. 'I didn't mean to cause such panic back here. I just didn't want to talk. I think now I was scared I'd lose control if I did.'

He held her hand more firmly. 'If people you respected and liked were lying dead and wounded and you without a scratch, how would you feel?'

'Relieved and, I suppose . . . I'm not sure . . . Guilty?'

'Exactly. Why not me? That's what I have to come to terms with.'

'And are you?'

'Yes, slowly. I know I'll never explain it to myself, never forgive myself. I'm beginning to understand it's something I'll have to learn to live with. Sod of a world, though, isn't it?'

'I think part of becoming mature is accepting just how unfair life is.'

'Have you had to accept? It's your turn now.'

Chrissy withdrew her hand from his.

'I'm not used to confiding. I've always worked out things alone.'

'Maybe you should change tack—try another means.' He spoke gently, coaxing her. She looked at him and suddenly she wanted to tell him, wanted him to understand.

'You heard about the deaths on my roster? Well, I'm being blamed for them. It got to me, that's all.'

'That's ridiculous. You'll be saying next that they think you murdered them. Gave them a deadly overdose.' He laughed at the idea.

'They do.'

His laughter ceased abruptly as if a switch had cut it off. 'Oh, come on, Chrissy. You're not serious?'

'I am,' she said softly.

'But the post-mortems will prove otherwise. Why, look at my Mrs Norman, she had a massive stroke. And—'

'She did? No one told me.' She sounded indignant.

'I'm not surprised you're annoyed. You should have been told.'

She sighed. 'I think they know about my husband. And they're putting two and two together and coming up with five.'

'Why should they be interested in him?'

'Ewan killed himself. He stole insulin from his diabetic mother. He didn't mean to kill himself, I'm certain. He wanted a little coma, that was all. He thought he could dose himself and not damage himself.'

'But why?'

'To punish me. He liked playing games like that.'

'What had you done?'

'Left him. It was the day after he shot a dog.'

'He did what?' Russell exclaimed.

'He killed a dog, God knows. Perhaps because I was feeding it and growing fond of it. It galvanised me. I went to the hotel in the New Forest—remember I told you about it?—to decide what to do. I knew I had to leave him if I was to survive intact. But he wanted me back. Of course, as soon as I heard what had happened, I came running—just as he'd planned. He was dead. I was arrested.'

'Why, for God's sake?'

'He left a note with his mother—I suppose just in case. In it he said if anything happened to him I was to blame.'

'Charming.'

'She called the police and I was carted off for questioning.'

'And you think someone at the hospital knew this and let the cat out of the bag.'

'Exactly. Maybe the nutter who's bumping patients off.'

'Oh, come on. Chrissy, you don't know that.'

'It happens.'

'It does—but so rarely. Think it through. Who do you know at the hospital who's got such a grudge against you they'd set you up?'

'I've racked my brains. I'm not aware that I know anyone there.'

'Look, Chrissy. First thing on Monday, go to the office—demand to know the results. Talk to Glynis. She might seem a cold fish but, in fact, she's very kind and extremely fair, and this isn't a fair situation.'

'No, it isn't, is it?' She smiled at him, relieved that he understood.

Glynis had recovered her composure. She had returned from her rush to the lavatory white-faced, apologising profusely. 'I don't normally have takeaways—last night was an exception. But never again!' She'd taken her seat, hoping she'd managed the incident well enough.

'I thought it was something I'd said that had upset you.' Edna leaned forward with a serious expression.

'I'd rather not speak to Matthew. I find these matters so distasteful. Let's leave it to Fraser Ball. He's the senior physician, after all. You've spoken to the young nurse?'

'Well, no. Like you—it's rather indelicate . . .'

'Let's leave it to Fraser.'

'As you think best, Glynis.' Edna looked puzzled at the other woman's apparent and uncharacteristic delegation of responsibility.

Once Glynis was safely in her hotel room, she stood motionless for a second. Then her legs gave way and she fell to the floor, weeping.

She had no idea how long her emotions gushed from her in a torrent, but she rode the storm, feeling emptiness engulf her, until eventually the crying stopped. She sat up, exhausted and in despair, and contemplated the wreckage of her hopes and longings. All her past, her sacrifices, for what? And how often, when friends had been suffering, had she trotted out the cliché that nothing was ever a waste? All experience was valuable. Now she shivered. Time, life, love, devotion—what had they given her? Nothing!

She was as she was because of him. Contained, distant, so that no one would know. And why? To protect Matthew. And what had it done to her? Isolated her, given her a life of snatched hours of happiness that punctuated the loneliness. Why had she bothered? He hadn't. She shuddered.

Five hours on, Matthew Kersey arrived at reception. 'My name is Tillman. I've a room booked. Has my wife arrived?'

'Mrs Tillman has checked out, sir. Early this afternoon.'

'Are you sure?'

'Yes, sir.'

'Where did she go?'

'I wouldn't know, sir.'

Matthew swung round towards the bar and ordered a large gin and tonic. What could have happened? He didn't like this at all—he needed to talk to her, to try to counteract the gossip of Floss Yates. What had he done recently that might annoy? Of course, there had been the incident of the nurse in theatres when Edna Greenbank had barged in. But he'd sorted that, even if it had cost him an expensive suite in a country-house hotel. He thought he'd banged some loyalty into Edna!

Glynis sat at the dining room of a hotel north of Fellcar. She'd chosen this hotel since it held no memories of Matthew, as so many other places did. She had booked in for several days. She needed time to reappraise how she felt and how she was to deal with *her* future.

Mo looked round the empty ward. She was the only patient to have been admitted so far. The staff nurse had explained that the other patients would be coming up from the Gynaecology Ward, where they'd been housed before this special unit had opened. Mo had wandered round the ward on the top floor of the hospital. The views were sensational, one side looking out at the sea and the other looking down on the town. It was light and airy, and the sludgy green paint that dominated most of the hospital had been replaced by cream and pale yellow. The bed curtains were primrose and white check and nice paintings hung on the walls. She had been able to choose her bed and had opted for one that overlooked the sea. She sat on the chair by the window, opened her magazine—and read nothing.

Everything was moving too fast. It was as if she wasn't to be given time to adjust to one lot of bad news before she was hurtled into the next bleak scenario.

She had attended the clinic last week. The young doctor was pleasant enough, she couldn't complain. While he was speaking to her, his manner was odd, detached. He didn't seem to grasp how shocking his words were to her, how devastated he was making her feel. And as he spoke she sensed that she was no longer in control of her own future—that from now on things would be decided for her. He'd told her she was to come into hospital for her lump to be investigated further. This lump was to be removed and tested to see if it was malignant or not and her lymphatic system was to be checked too, and if that was involved, she would need a course of chemotherapy as well as radiotherapy. However, he'd ploughed on, she was most fortunate: normally she'd have had to wait for a bed, but since the new Oncology Unit was open she could go in on Monday.

It wasn't until afterwards that she had realised she hadn't asked him anything. What did the chemotherapy involve? Where were her lymph glands? Why was it that the minute she entered a doctor's surgery she became an empty-headed idiot?

'Hi! Hit the jackpot, have you?'

Mo looked up to see Yvonne Clarke in a wheelchair. Her colour was even worse, Mo saw.

'Sorry? I don't understand?'

'Further tests? Aren't you the lucky one!' Yvonne laughed.

'Oh, yes, my lump's coming out.'

'Did you tell your old man?'

'I did. It wasn't easy. He was very sweet but frightened.'

'So, he didn't do a runner?'

'No. But I have this sneaky idea he wished he could.'

'And the kids?'

'At my sister-in-law's. She's being a brick. She's bought me all these books on alternative healing.'

'Burn the lot!' Yvonne said, with a dismissive wave.

'Oh, I couldn't do that. There might be something in one of them—you never know. At least I'd feel I was doing something for myself.'

'There's no harm in the diets. It's all the positive-thinking crap that gets on my left *and* right—if I had them, that is!' Yvonne laughed.

'But all the research shows that people with a positive attitude to life have less chance of getting cancer.'

'*Less chance of getting* is the operative phrase. What if you've *got it*? What gets at me is giving people false hope. So you meditate and you visualise your malignant cells until you're crackling with positive thoughts. And still it spreads. So did you fail? Is it your fault you're bloody well dying?' And to Mo's horror Yvonne burst into tears.

'Oh, Yvonne. What is it?' And Mo was on her feet and putting her arm round the sobbing woman's shoulders just as Chrissy appeared.

'Oh dear. Yvonne, are you in pain? Can I help?' Chrissy looked questioningly at Mo.

'We were talking about positive attitudes to cancer and she suddenly burst into tears.'

'I think you'd better come with me, Yvonne. Let's find that bed you chose. Maybe a little rest. It's been a busy day.'

'Why do nurses have to be so patronising? I'm not a child. I'm a fully grown woman. So treat me with some respect, OK?'

'I'm sorry, Yvonne. I didn't mean to sound like that. Come on, let's get you back to bed.'

Mo watched as Chrissy pushed the wheelchair out of the ward. Sadly she realised that Chrissy hadn't even recognised her. Had she changed so much?

It was rapidly turning into one of *those* days, Chrissy thought, as she pushed Yvonne back to her bed.

'I went OTT just then, didn't I?'

'Understandably,' Chrissy answered. 'You're tired.'

'Too right I'm tired,' Yvonne said as, with difficulty, she hoisted herself out of the chair. 'I don't want any more treatment. I'm sick of feeling grim. I'm going home.'

'But, Yvonne—'

'No buts, Chrissy. What's the point? The doctor this morning was straight with me. I'm off. Even in this sodding contraption.' She pointed at the wheelchair. Chrissy smiled at the woman whose courage had moved everyone who'd dealt with her over the years.

'One thing, Chrissy. I shouldn't have carried on like that in front of the new patient. Don't tell her, will you? Mo might be one of the lucky ones, after all.'

'Not Mo Fordham? What must she be thinking of me?'

Half a dozen phone calls dealt with. An influx of patients sent up from Gynaecology and settled in their beds. Three new patients were welcomed and admitted. Only then was she free to get back to Mo.

'Mo. I'm sorry. It's the ward's first day up and running and I want everything to be perfect. And then I behave in this fine way—not welcoming an old friend who's a new patient.' She sat on the bed and took a photograph from Mo's locker. 'Are these your girls? They're so pretty.' And for a while they talked just like the old schoolfriends they were, not like patient and nurse, thought Mo.

'Now, did Nurse Bing explain things to you satisfactorily?'

'No, she didn't,' Mo said baldly. 'She was busy,' she added.

'I'd better explain it for you then. Everything is done under a general anaesthetic so you'll feel nothing. As you know, the lump will come out. Lumpectomy—a grand name, isn't it? And the surgeon will also remove tissue in the immediate area as a precaution. If, and I only say if, it's malignant then your lymph glands, here,' she indicated on her body, 'will be checked to make sure nothing has spread. If it's just the lump involved then you'll have six weeks of radiotherapy. You come into Outpatients for that. However, if the lymph glands are affected you will need chemotherapy as well as the radiotherapy. A simple lumpectomy and you'll be out before you know it. With the lymph system involved you'll be in longer.'

'If I need chemotherapy where do I go?'

'You'll come here to this ward . . .' And Chrissy explained the courses the doctors might take, although she knew that Mo was absorbing only a fraction of what she was telling her.

'Just now, Yvonne said trying other things was a waste of time.'

'You mean alternative therapies? Some patients are helped enormously, others aren't. But please let us know what you intend to do and never stop your medication for an alternative. If you feel something is doing you good, then it's certain it is.' Chrissy heard herself trotting out the careful line.

'So why was Yvonne so angry?'

'Yvonne was fed up. We all get fed up, don't we?'

'You talking about me? I heard!'

Chrissy and Mo turned to see Yvonne walking towards them. She leaned against the bed. 'I've come to say goodbye and good luck.'

'Are you off? But I thought—'

'Nah. Just seen the doc. He was surprised I was so much better—said he didn't want me cluttering up a bed.'

'And the wheelchair?'

'Taken away. He told me I was being a lazy cow. Now, Mo, my love, don't let these buggers get you down.' She bent down and kissed Mo on the cheek. 'Right. I'm off before they change their minds.'

'I'll see you off.' Chrissy walked beside Yvonne. As soon as she passed out of sight her legs buckled. Chrissy caught her and supported her, calling out to a passing nurse to fetch a wheelchair.

'That was very brave of you, Yvonne.'

'Nah. Nothing to it. I had to make amends, didn't I?' Even as she began to smile, it failed and converted into a grimace.

Dawn appeared in the kitchen doorway, a glass of wine in her hand.

'Would you like me to lay the table?'

'Bless you. Here.' Chrissy handed her cutlery and glasses. All that was needed was to wash the salad.

'It's kind of you to invite me,' Dawn said, as she returned.

'My pleasure. It can't be much fun in a bedsit.'

'You can say that again! This is a lovely cottage. Mind if I snoop?'

'Be my guest.'

'None of your husband's paintings are on display.'

'Well, no. I—' Chrissy paused. 'How did you know Ewan was an artist?' she said instead.

'Everyone at the hospital knows. Jazz Poundman's the oracle where you and your husband are concerned. Her aunt's a nurse in Cornwall.'

In the kitchen Chrissy clattered about as if the noise of crockery and oven doors slamming could obliterate talk of Ewan and Jazz. Already she was regretting that she had felt sorry for Dawn and invited her to supper. If she was going to go on about those two all evening she'd live to regret it. *Stop it,* Chrissy's inner voice said sharply. She leaned against the sink and forced herself to calm down. She must stop getting in a state like this when Ewan was mentioned.

'Here we go. Sainsbury's finest.' She held the pie in front of her, all smiles as she returned to the room. They settled to their meal.

'Shall I do the honours?' Dawn replenished their glasses.

It was an age since Chrissy had spent time alone with a woman friend, and she found she was enjoying the light-hearted gossip, the talk of clothes and men. As Chrissy got another bottle from the fridge she discovered she'd already had too much to drink and was weaving slightly. She went back to the sitting room where they were now ensconced in armchairs either side of the inglenook.

'I love a fire like this.'

'Russell Newson fixed it for me—or rather, showed me how to light it without dying of smoke inhalation!'

'I didn't know you knew him—socially, that is.'

'Oh, I don't. He was on the cliff, out for a walk. Then he rescued me from the smoke. He's rather dishy, isn't he?'

'He's married. Married men mean only one thing—disaster.'

'Can't I look?'

'You can look but don't touch!' They shrieked with laughter.

'It must be awful losing the love of your life as you did. Just awful.' Dawn shook her head in sympathy at the thought.

'Well . . . I hated my husband,' Chrissy said suddenly.

'Chrissy, I'm so sorry. I didn't mean—'

'No, I've never really told anyone except the police—not everything.'

'Why did you marry him, if you don't mind my asking?' Dawn said.

'I loved him in the beginning—he was so alive, so good-looking, so attentive. He gave me the confidence I was lacking. But then . . .' She stopped and sat gazing into the fire. Quietly Dawn rose, and sat on the rug at her feet. She took Chrissy's hand.

'Talk, Chrissy, love. It'll help you. You can trust me.'

Chrissy's shoulders slumped. 'Trust? What an innocent little word. I *trusted* him with my life and love, and he shattered it all. He'd given me all that love and tenderness just to take it away again. He became jealous, possessive. I couldn't go to the shops, take a phone call without a grilling afterwards that could go on for hours. He opened my mail. Then he began following me. I thought I was going mad. Then one day I knew I had to get out or one day he'd kill me. So I ran away—to be on my own to think.' She sighed deeply.

'And that was when he killed himself?'

'Yes.'

'It must have made the guilt intolerable.'

'Unbelievable—but I think I'm getting out of it now. I'm sure he didn't mean to die.'

'Why do you say that?' Dawn was still holding her hand.

'Because we had a fishmonger who always called on Tuesdays. If I wasn't there he made himself a cup of coffee. I think Ewan planned for Ted to find him and rush him to hospital. I'd be contacted and rush back to him full of contrition. Only he chose the day Ted's van broke down and he was too late for Ewan, who was dead when Ted got there.'

'How dreadful for you.'

'I couldn't grieve. I just felt relief. I didn't have to be frightened any more. I realised I'd wanted him dead without knowing it—that's where the guilt lies. Look, I shouldn't be loading all this on you.'

'Why not? I'd like to think I was your friend.'

'Bless you, Dawn. Oh, really, this is silly. Let's round the evening off with a brandy. Just talking I feel better already.' Chrissy was on her feet and finding the bottle. She felt exhausted now and longed for bed and sleep, but she also felt strangely light, as if the talking had removed something—bitterness or guilt, she hoped.

CHAPTER SIX

LYNN COULD NOT FAIL to notice the frigid atmosphere in the surgery as she went about her work. For nearly a week now she'd been left out of conversations and people left the staff room when she walked in.

'I felt I had to say something,' Lynn said to Ella Thompson, the other practice nurse, when she found her in the kitchen one day. 'This thing is just dragging on.'

'I think accusations with no proof are snide.'

'The pharmaceutical orders show there's something amiss,' Lynn said defensively.

'That could be a clerical error,' Ella said, looking uncomfortable.

'Come off it, Ella. You know that's not so.'

'It could be anyone, not necessarily Giles. Why pick on him?' Ella looked indignant now. Lynn was aware she had a soft spot for Giles. 'You've no proof. You said that at the meeting. You should have checked it out more thoroughly, Lynn, on the computer.'

'I did. It wasn't down to any of the likely patients.'

'There you are, then.'

'No. Computer files can be altered.'

'Then the date, when it had last been altered, would show.'

'None of the dates is different from the consultations.'

'There you are, then,' Ella repeated, insufferably smug now.

'It could mean that the date on the document was changed too, to match the automatic dating on the machine.'

'Then you'll have to check with the appointments book.'

'That'll take for ever.' Lynn looked aghast.

'Then you shouldn't have started all this, should you? Not if you weren't willing to see it through.'

'It's not that. It's time. I really thought you'd understand, Ella.'

'I hate to see a good, dedicated doctor accused like that. You're lucky he isn't suing you for defamation of character. I still can't believe it. You, of all people. You were always so professional. Now, if you'll excuse me, I've got a diabetics clinic to run.'

Lynn was hurt. She and Ella had always respected each other. Now here they were sniping. Maybe she had been a fool.

'Sod that!' she said to the empty kitchen. She'd stay after work. Ella was right. She'd have to check the appointments against the computer.

It was quiet in the surgery, except for the rustling of paper as Lynn leafed through the appointments book, checking each patient's notes on the computer to match their attendance. She'd been at work on this task for nearly two hours and had only just got started on the Gs.

'Lynn?'

Her head jerked up, she clutched at her chest. 'Giles! You gave me such a start.' She felt embarrassed at being caught out.

'It's late for you still to be here. What are you doing?'

'It's your day off.'

'I needed a book. You still checking me out?' He grinned.

'Not necessarily, but there has to be a discrepancy somewhere. I've got to find it, Giles.'

'I understand that. After all, because the pharmacy list is your responsibility you're under a cloud, aren't you?'

'Giles, I'm so pleased you understand that. No one else seems to.'

'I don't want us falling out, do you? The atmosphere here this past week has been pretty grim, hasn't it?'

'I'd agree with that.' Lynn looked sad.

'Honestly, Lynn, it's not down to me. I don't know what's gone on but I promise you I've done nothing wrong.'

'Then there's all the more reason for me to check these records out.'

Giles looked thoughtful. 'Fancy a drink?'

'I don't drink.'

'What, never? Come on, just this once. Show we're friends again.'

'Just a little one, then.' Lynn didn't want a drink, but if Giles was willing to make the peace it would be churlish of her to refuse.

Giles reappeared with two glasses of whisky. They clinked glasses. 'Here's to a speedy resolution,' he said, smiling smoothly.

Half an hour later Lynn was driving home and going over the problem in her mind. The trouble with Giles was that, in his presence, everything he said seemed right. It was when she was away from him that the doubts crept in. She peered through the windscreen. The lights at the side of the dark road seemed to be moving. The trouble with Giles— She shook her head. She'd just thought that, hadn't she? She felt hot and wound down her window. The car veered across the road. Lynn slammed on the brakes just as a car with a flashing blue light screeched to a halt beside her.

ON CALL

'How are you, Gran?'

'I'm fine.'

'You don't look it.'

'No need to be personal.' Daphne laughed, but her laughter disintegrated into coughing. Chrissy picked up her emtpy water jug.

'I'll pop along to the kitchen and fill this up.'

'Bless you. I've been dying for a drink.'

Jazz and an assistant nurse were in the kitchen.

'Come to see Daphne?' Jazz asked.

'Mrs Galloway? Yes.' Chrissy ran the tap. 'Some old ladies like to be addressed formally, I'd have thought you'd know that, Jazz.' She spoke calmly as she rinsed out the jug.

'And most prefer we use Christian names,' Jazz defended herself.

'But not my grandmother. Why didn't you ask her?'

'I wasn't aware you'd been posted to this ward, Chrissy.'

'Don't like the criticism, Jazz? Well, I'm sorry, but while my grandmother's a patient here, I'll be taking an interest. And while I'm about it, don't you think the water jugs should be checked?' She turned back from the sink just in time to see Jazz poking her tongue out at her. 'Oh, Jazz, really. Why don't you grow up?'

'I should watch it, if I were you, Chrissy. Your track record hasn't been *that* impressive so far, has it?' Jazz smiled sweetly.

Chrissy could feel anger growing, but forced herself to control it and did not answer back. Nurses like Jazz made her mad, she thought, as she returned to Daphne's bed. There were always one or two like her and it was a mystery why they had become nurses in the first place.

'There you go.' Back at Daphne's bed she poured a glass of water.

Daphne gulped thirstily at the water. 'Oh, that's bliss. Better than a gin and tonic any day.'

'Gran, are you often without water?'

'Too often. They're idle cows. And that Jazz is a bully. You have to pee to order too. You can't get a bedpan when you need one. Call themselves nurses—they're a disgrace to your profession.' Daphne was plucking at the top sheet of her bed with agitation.

'I had a word with Jazz about the water.'

'Oh, Chrissy, you never did!' Her fingers clutched at the linen. 'Now she'll have it in for me, you can bet on that.'

'I'm sorry. I don't want to cause you any trouble.' With a shock, she understood that her grandmother was scared. 'Gran, are you frightened about something or someone?'

'Me? Frightened?' Daphne looked away, biting her bottom lip.

415

'If you are you must tell me, so I can help,' Chrissy coaxed her.

Daphne sat silent. Chrissy thought she was not going to speak but eventually she took a deep breath. 'Only of that bitch Jazz—she gives me the willies!' And Daphne shuddered.

'Gran, I'm going to have to do something about this.'

'Are you sure you have to? Who will you speak to? Sister? That won't do you any good. She's so sweet she wouldn't believe you.'

'Then I'll talk to Glynis Tillman. She'll sort it out.' She glanced at her watch. 'Heavens, look at the time. I'm setting up a self-help group this evening.'

'I hope they're paying you overtime.'

'No, I volunteered. There are not enough funds in the coffers.' She stood up and moved the chair she'd been using back against the wall.

It was cold and raining when Chrissy left the hospital and made for her car. She was feeling pleased: the first meeting of her group had gone well. Her main worry had been that too few would turn up. In fact, there had been twelve. She was only sorry that Mo had been too groggy from her anaesthetic to attend.

Chrissy swung out of the car park. Along Hursty Avenue, the road ahead was blocked by a badly parked car and a police car, its lights flashing. In the headlights, she saw a wet and wan-looking Lynn Petch. She was out of her car in a trice.

'Lynn, are you all right? Have you had an accident?'

'Who's that? Who are you?'

'Officer, what's happened?'

'Are you a friend of this young woman?'

'I am. Is she hurt?'

'No, but she's coming to the station. She won't give us her address.'

'I would—I can't remember it, honest.' Lynn was slurring her words. She was obviously drunk. Chrissy felt she could not leave her friend in this state.

'She lives in Timber Lane, Officer. Number forty-two. I'll come to the station with you, if you want, Lynn?'

'Please.'

Chrissy decided to telephone for Terry.

'Lynn? Drunk? I don't believe it,' he said, his voice a mixture of disbelief and indignation. 'Lynn rarely drinks—a glass of wine, maybe, but that's all and that's usually when she's safe at home.'

'Yes, Terry. I understand.' Maybe Lynn was a secret drinker despite her protestations that she didn't touch the stuff.

ON CALL

Sabine stood in the heavy rain in the middle of the driveway.

'I know you're in there, you bastard!' she yelled as she hurled a handful of gravel at the window of the second-floor flat. Most of it missed and rattled the panes of the flat below.

The window was flung open. 'What the bloody hell do you think you're doing?' An irate man's head appeared.

'It's all right, Trev. I'll deal with this.' The front door had opened and Giles stood there. 'Sabine, don't you ever do that to me again,' he said, ominously quiet. 'I told you on the phone I couldn't see you. Don't you understand?'

'Why couldn't you see me? I know it's your day off.'

'I had other things to do. Now, please will you leave? I've had a difficult day.'

'Don't make me, Giles. Please let me stay with you. I can't deal with the atmosphere at home. I want to move in with you.'

'Sabine, be a good girl. Just go home. I'll give you a bell.'

'But you won't. You're tired of me, aren't you?' She pouted, as her lovely eyes filled with tears.

'I think we should see less of each other—just for the time being. I don't want any fuss—or trouble.'

Sabine stamped her foot as Giles went inside and closed the door.

Terry held the steering wheel so tightly that his knuckles showed white. His mouth was set in a thin line. Easy-going, tolerant Terry was angry. Lynn, beside him, was crying quietly.

'Oh, for goodness' sake, shut up sniffling.'

'I can't stop.'

'Of course you can. Just pull yourself together. If there's one thing I loathe and despise it's drunk drivers.'

'I'm not drunk! How many times do I have to say it?' Lynn slumped back. It was difficult to talk: the words emerged slurred and the effort required seemed to have exhausted her.

'Can't you hear yourself? You're pissed as a rat.' Terry drove onto the hard standing outside their house. He turned to her. 'You, of all people. I never expected to see you in this state.' And, switching off the engine, he climbed out of the car, slammed the door and marched into the house, slamming the front door with equal ferocity.

Lynn sat in the car, shocked. She knew she was not drunk, but if she wasn't what had happened to her? It was all too difficult to work out, especially with her mind in such a muddle—and suddenly all she wanted to do was sleep. So she did.

As she waited for the doorbell to ring Glynis was quite calm. She felt rested after her few days away and, after the storm of emotion, she felt almost detached, as if this drama was happening to someone else.

It amused her when at the first trill of the bell she checked her watch and saw that he was punctual—the first time in their relationship.

'Good evening, Matthew.' She held open the door for him.

'Darling—where were you? I waited and waited. Were you taken ill?'

'No, I wasn't ill. If anything I would say I'd begun to recover. A drink?'

'A large Scotch, please.'

'Is that wise when you're operating tomorrow?'

'You've never queried my drinking before.' He sounded offended.

'As I've not queried many things. But as you wish.' She poured a generous measure of Highland Park whisky, but nothing for herself.

'You're acting a bit strange, Glyn, my love.'

'Am I your love, Matthew? Truly?'

'Of course you are. What a thing to say after all these years!'

'Yes, it has been a long time. Maybe too long. Is that why you were discovered in a compromising position with a young nurse last week?'

'My darling, what *are* you going on about? Me? With whom, what, when?' He laughed confidently, as if at a good joke.

'Edna Greenbank confided in me the circumstances she'd found you in—"going at it hammer and tongs" was the way she described your actions.' Glynis thought how smoothly she had trotted out the words that had led to the breaking of her heart.

'Oh, really! Edna, of all people. Is that all? Darling, I've never told you this before because I didn't want to upset you, but Edna has had a *crush* on me ever since she joined the hospital staff. I'm forever fending her off. It's all in her imagination, nothing more.'

'If, as you say, she has a crush on you then why would she tell me?'

'God knows. To make you jealous, perhaps. To get you to kick me out of your life. I don't know.' He shrugged easily, as if the whole incident was of no importance.

'But, if that were the case,' she turned to face him, 'that would mean she knew about us.' She frowned deeply.

'Dear Glynis, if truth be told, I reckon half the hospital knows.'

'Surely not? Oh, how dreadful,' Glynis said, with genuine distress.

'Why? I'd like the whole world to know about us and our love for each other. It saddens me that we have to live as we do.' He leaned forward and took her hand in his. 'I'm proud of your love for me.'

At his words the calmness and control deserted Glynis and to his horror, as well as her own, she began to cry. It was not a noisy crying, but a silent weeping that shook Glynis to the core and was all the more heart-rending for its silence.

It was late when Russell drove back from the country club where he had been for a swim. He was pleased with his progress, each day managing to swim and walk further without the fatigue of last week returning. And now that he had made resolutions about his life and marriage, he felt a new burst of mental energy too.

He thought of Chrissy. It was strange the effect she had on him. He hardly knew her and yet knew that when he did get to know her he would like what he would find. But Sabine and the mess that was their marriage had to be sorted out first—Chrissy had to know that he wasn't playing adulterer's games.

Nothing was as straightforward as he had anticipated, though. He'd had no way of knowing how disturbing it would be to have to continue to share his home with Sabine. He'd presumed that this affair of hers with Giles meant that she'd wanted the end of their marriage as much as he did. Instead, he was learning that Sabine, faced with the end of their marriage, was clinging on to it, almost with desperation. Her mood-swings and emotional outbursts were exhausting. She could be contrite one moment, yet hurling a glass at him two minutes later. He'd reached the conclusion that things with her lover were not running smoothly.

On the last stretch of his journey up North Hill, he wondered what his next move should be. As he pulled into his drive he saw with irritation that every light in the house was burning—one of those petty things Sabine did these days just to annoy him.

Inside, he stood in the sitting-room doorway and looked about him with disbelief. The room was a shambles and his first reaction was that they had been burgled. But when he entered Sabine's room and saw it was neat and immaculate, while his was devastated, he knew that no criminal had been involved—just his wife.

His clothes were ripped, his books torn, paintings were defaced, his LPs were scratched, his CDs dented, his aftershave and toiletries spilt everywhere. Little of what he owned remained intact.

He turned on his heel, ran down the stairs and hurtled out into the night, into his car, and drove like a demon to get away from the hatred and the loathing. The furies of outrage raced in him. God, how he longed for peace and quiet.

He drove through the pouring rain. He'd planned an aimless drive, just something to do to tire himself out. The road he was on petered out.

He stopped and looked about him. He'd had no intention of coming here and no recall of how he'd got here.

He ran through the rain and knocked on the door.

'Hi!' He tried to smile but he was too tense to manage it. 'I hope you meant it—that I could call again?'

'Of course I did. Come in.' Chrissy held the door open.

'Is it too late?'

'Yes it is.' She laughed. 'But come in all the same.'

'I hope you don't mind. I decided to go for a drive and my car just seemed to head this way. I saw your light on—'

'I was late back,' she answered. 'Are you all right, Russell? You look very pale.'

'Me? Yes, fine.'

He did not look it, she thought. 'Well, I was just getting a bite to eat. Do you want some? It's only an omelette and salad.' She led the way into the kitchen.

Russell began to say no when he suddenly realised he was hungry. 'Heavens! I haven't eaten all day. An omelette sounds great.'

'You're hardly going to recover your strength if you don't eat.'

'Yes, Nurse,' he said obediently, as he followed. He sat at the small pine table and watched her as she added extra eggs to the bowl and beat them into the mixture.

'I wish you wouldn't look at me like that, you make me nervous,' she said, half laughing with embarrassment.

'I didn't know I was.'

'Would you care for a drink? There's a bottle of wine or some beer in the fridge.'

'Wine sounds great.' He was glad to have something to do. While Chrissy cooked he poured the wine. Sitting in the warm, his glass in his hand, he felt the tension begin to peel from him. By the time she placed their supper on the table he felt relaxed, the storm of anger spent.

'Why did you forget to eat?'

'I don't know. Preoccupied, I suppose,' he answered. He had no intention of burdening her with his problems. And, in a way, he felt ashamed of what had happened. Something had pushed Sabine to the edge. He hoped it had been Giles and not something he had said or done—he had no room for any more guilt. He had failed her, hadn't given her the happiness she yearned for. But it didn't look as though she had found it with Giles either. He sighed mightily.

'Gracious, you sound as if all the world's problems are on your shoulders. What a sigh.'

'Did I? Not for much longer.' That was the way he must go—stop the guilt, the who did what to whom. Get out, he told himself. Suddenly he smiled. 'It might have been once, but no more.'

Chrissy wondered what had happened to make him look so sad and she wished she could lean over and hug him. She longed to know why and what, and if she could help in some way. She suggested they move into the sitting room, where she served coffee and he settled by her fire once again. They sat back on the comfortable chairs and soon they were away, chattering about music and books they liked. But then a silence fell and again she couldn't think of a thing to say.

'I like talking to you. I find it easy,' he said out of the blue.

'You could have fooled me for the last ten minutes.' She laughed, and immediately wished she hadn't, for his face became expressionless as if he were retreating. 'Only joking!' she lied, hurriedly.

'Were you? I thought—oh, it doesn't matter.'

'What did you think, Russell? Please tell me. I didn't mean to offend you.'

'No, I'm sorry. I'm being oversensitive. It was just—the other night I felt we were comfortable together. And I thought tonight would be easy too. And I hoped . . . But really—' He stood up. 'It's not important.'

Chrissy wanted to put out her hand and stop him leaving. She wanted to explain, to get close to him—only she was afraid to.

'Your coat,' she said, to cover her confusion.

'Thanks.' He put it on quickly and stepped out into the hall.

'Russell.'

'Yes?' He turned to face her.

'Please come again.' She knew she blushed.

'Is that what you want?'

'I do . . . It's difficult to explain, but when you've been trampled on it takes time to get up again,' she said, and hoped he understood.

'I'll see you, then,' he replied, and she presumed he hadn't.

The light from her hallway cut a bright swath across the garden but was not strong enough to reach the cliff top beyond so neither of them saw the figure crouching behind a gorse bush.

Lynn Petch was having difficulty in making out who was speaking on the telephone to her, so muffled was the voice.

'I'm sorry, I can barely hear you.' There was a noisy harrumphing along the line. 'Oh, it's *you*, Dr Henderson. You sounded as if you were down a mine-shaft.' She laughed, but as she listened the laugh was not repeated. She sat down with a bump on the chair beside the telephone table. 'No, I don't understand,' she said. 'You can't do this—' But she spoke to herself, cut off. She'd been sacked. She exhaled slowly.

'Who was that?' Terry looked up from his bowl of Weetabix.

'Dr Henderson. My P45's in the post.'

'You what? He can't do that.'

'He can. Apparently he can terminate my contract for unprofessional conduct. Getting breathalysed is sufficient.' Lynn sat at the table, picked up the teapot and poured herself a cup.

'You seem quite calm about it.'

'I'm stunned. I'm still taking it in.'

'Well, I see their point.' Terry pushed his cereal bowl aside.

'Thank you so much for your support,' she said bitterly. 'I won't go on about it, Terry. I understand how you feel. But I promise you I wasn't drunk. I'd had less than half a whisky. I think it was spiked. And I really would appreciate you believing me.'

'I wish I could, Lynn. But I just keep thinking you could be dead— and in my book that shows how little you must think of us. Now, if you'll excuse me.' Terry was on his feet, his chair pushed back, and he left the room. She heard the front door close. In thirteen years of marriage that was the first time he had left without kissing her goodbye.

Lynn could have slumped there at the table, bewailing her fate and the unfairness of it all. Instead, she stood up, collected the blood sample the police had given her, and picked up her car keys.

Her first stop was in Thorpedale where she delivered the vial to an independent laboratory to be analysed. Then she drove back to Fellcar. She swept through the practice door into her own office, where she saw Giles Middleton bent over the drawers of her desk.

'Lynn!' he said. 'Hi.'

She was glad to see that at least he looked embarrassed. 'Giles.' She nodded slightly. 'Are you looking for something? Can I help you?' she said, with heavy irony.

'I've always liked your desk. I was just checking to see if it was empty yet.' He stood up straight and leaned against it.

'My, my, you're behaving like a rapacious relative when the corpse is still warm.' She began to take off her coat. 'As far as I can recall your desk is identical to mine. Not much point in swapping, is there? Come on, Giles, you were snooping, weren't you? Frightened I'd solved how you fiddled the drugs ordering?'

'Watch it, Lynn.' He wagged a finger at her, which annoyed her.

'No, Giles. It's you who is going to have to watch it.'

The door opened and Dick Henderson bustled in.

'Lynn, there was no need for you to come here. We could have parcelled up your possessions.'

'I needed to come, Dick. I have property here I don't want others to see.'

'Anything pertaining to the patients like computer print-outs is practice property. Nothing can be removed.' Giles stepped forward.

'Why would I be interested in patients' files if I'm not going to be working here any more?' Her voice was raised.

'Now, come on, Lynn, there's no need to be like this. It might help if you could tell us what you want from your desk,' Dick Henderson said, with the expression of one who loathed scenes.

Lynn crossed the room and opened a lower drawer. 'Cuff links for Terry's birthday.' She waved the box at them, then opened another drawer and fished out a folder. 'My bank statements, so Terry wouldn't see them and spoil the surprise. Satisfied?'

'There. You see, Giles? Nothing wrong there.' Henderson smiled.

'Dick, you've sacked the wrong person and I shall prove it.'

'If you do, then of course I shall apologise and you'll be welcome back here.' He smiled indulgently at her.

'I wouldn't come back here, not if you doubled my salary. I've given you years of loyal hard work and you don't even have the decency to come and see me and hear my side of the story. I'm glad to be out of here.' She stumbled through the door and rushed to the main entrance. She didn't want them to see she was crying, to know how hurt she was.

Safe in her car she had to sit for a second, controlling her emotions until she was safe to drive.

She decided to do a shop at the local Tesco. She trundled the trolley up and down the aisles, hurling food into it.

'Lynn, hello!'

Hell, she thought, put her head down and pushed the trolley swiftly away from the voice.

'Lynn? What's the matter? It's me.'

'Oh, Chrissy, I'm sorry. I thought you were a patient. Rather, an ex-patient.' And her eyes filled with tears.

'Lynn, love. What's the problem? Do you fancy some lunch?'

'That would be nice. Yes, that's just what I need.'

'Right. See you in the Fox and Fiddle in twenty minutes.'

'An old friend who's in a bit of a state is joining us, if you don't mind,' Chrissy said to Floss Yates, as the pub landlord led them to their table.

'Why should I? I like talking to you young people. And I adore solving others' problems,' replied Floss.

'Lynn!' Chrissy waved at her friend, who was standing looking uncertain in the doorway. She moved across the crowded room towards them. 'Do you know Mrs Yates, Lynn?'

'Not really, though I've seen you around. I thought—' She turned to Chrissy, about to explain that she'd assumed they'd be alone.

'Lynn, please join us, you look done in.'

'You sit by me, my dear.' And Floss manoeuvred her bulk along the seat to make room for Lynn. 'Before we sort out what's ailing you, let's order. The pie and a burgundy, or would you rather have claret?'

Floss insisted on doing the ordering, even though Lynn protested she couldn't eat a thing and didn't drink. Floss was a bit like a tank when she'd decided something.

'Now, my dear Lynn, what's the problem? Tell Floss.' She smiled at Lynn, took her slim hand in her podgy one and squeezed it. Lynn felt a blanket of kindness enfold her.

'Well, you see . . .' Lynn relayed her sorry tale. 'And I'd bet everything was down to Giles spiking my whisky,' she finished.

'Lynn, I'm so sorry. How awful for you.'

'You believe me?' Lynn sounded surprised.

'Of course.'

'I'm so happy someone does.' Lynn picked up her bag from the floor. 'At least I've got these.' She pulled out the folder she'd taken from her desk. 'Copies of the computer pharmaceutical files on the last few patients of Giles's that I didn't have time to check.'

'Clever girl.' Floss beamed approval.

'Has it crossed your mind, Lynn,' said Chrissy, 'that that road you were on is residential? How often do you see police cars there? I was just wondering if they'd been tipped off—by Giles presumably.'

'Then we must find out,' said Floss.

'But how?' Lynn looked pleased and doubtful at the same time.

'Leave that to me, my dear. I've excellent contacts in the local constabulary. Ah—the pies. Now, tuck into that.'

Lynn suddenly found she was ravenous.

'There's something else. I overheard Dr Henderson and Giles Middleton having a row one night when I was working late. I heard Dr Henderson shout, "You do that, I'll report you to the GMC." When Giles yelled back, "You wouldn't dare. If you do I'll kill you," the old man said, "I'm warning you, Giles. You go ahead with this hospital plan, I'll bury you."'

There was a clatter of a knife and fork as Floss, of all people, suddenly lost interest in her food.

ON CALL

As the doctor, Sol Brown, spoke to her, his voice seemed to be coming from a long way away. Mo could hear him, but she felt oddly detached, almost as if he was talking about someone else. Her hand was being squeezed in a gesture of comfort by Chrissy, who was sitting beside her.

'Do you understand, Mrs Fordham?' Sol looked across at Chrissy, his expression one of concern.

'Mo, Dr Brown needs to know if you've taken in everything he's said.'

'Oh, yes, sorry. I feel a bit strange. No, I understand I'm to have radiotherapy for six weeks and, because my lymph glands were involved, chemotherapy too. How long will I have to stay here?'

'You can go in a few days once your wound has drained, and then your treatment can be conducted as an outpatient.'

'But I'll be here with you on this ward, Chrissy?'

'Of course. You're not feeling too bad?'

'No. My arm's sore, otherwise I'm in top form!' She laughed but the other two frowned, afraid she was tipping into hysterics.

'Mo, it's best to talk freely about all this. Try not to bottle things up,' the doctor advised.

'I shall become the local breast-cancer bore, don't worry.' She knew that if she didn't laugh she risked bursting into tears.

'Is there anything else you need to have explained, Mo?'

'Just—' These words would be difficult to form. Even as she thought what to say she felt as if her stomach had turned to liquid. 'I was wondering—if—well—perhaps—how long—' Somehow she forced the words out.

'I always tell patients that prognosis depends on what sort of patient the disease has.' He smiled kindly at her. She smiled back, if puzzled by what he meant.

'Thank you, Doctor,' she said. 'You've been very kind.'

Chrissy and Mo watched him leave the ward.

'Are you all right? Anything I can get you?' Chrissy asked.

'Nothing.' Mo swung her legs to the side of the bed. 'It's really odd, but in fact I'm fine. I was a bit wimpy just now but, Chrissy, do you know? It's almost a relief to know. Now I'm aware what I'm up against, what's to be done. I've got a focus, something to fight.'

'That's the spirit. See what the doctor meant? Your illness chose a fighter. Fancy a cuppa?'

In the ward kitchen Chrissy put the kettle on.

'Hi, Chrissy.'

She turned to see Dawn Allyson standing in the doorway. 'Hello.'

'Reporting for duty, Sister.' Dawn grinned. 'I'm your new staff.'

'Dawn, that's wonderful! I called the office earlier today and they said I had to wait for a replacement.'

'I was summoned by La Tillman. She said that as I was the only bank staff nurse available she was sending me to you. Then I asked if they were advertising this as a permanent post—if so I fancied applying. She went all po-faced—she's in a right old crabby mood today.'

'There's to be no recruitment until further notice, that's why.'

'That would explain it. Though she needn't have been quite so sniffy with me. "Nurse Allyson, when that time comes we shall be looking for someone with extra training in oncology." '

'Have you done oncology as a speciality?'

'Well, I started, but something got in the way, you know how it is,' Dawn said. 'Yes, a fella!' She grinned.

'Where were you?'

'Plymouth.'

'Well, we need you and how. Lesley Bing is going on maternity leave next week. That's why I wanted someone now so she can settle you in before she leaves.'

Chrissy poured boiling water into the teapot. 'I do hope they won't move you again. Tell you what, when Glynis *can* recruit again, apply for the post. I'll be involved with the selection, after all.'

'Would you do that? You're a brick.'

'Depends on your nursing.'

'Of course. But that doesn't worry me, I'm one of the best.'

'Can you hold the fort here? I've got an appointment with Glynis in five minutes.'

'Good luck.'

Chrissy picked up the tea tray. 'I'll just give this to the patient.'

'Do you always make the tea, Sister?' Dawn quipped. 'You'll be swabbing the floors next.'

'We're so short-staffed that on this ward everyone mucks in,' Chrissy replied. 'When I get back from Glynis I'll show you around.'

When she reached Mo, a short, stocky, blond-haired man was sitting on her bed and holding her hand, a look of utter bleakness on his face. She placed the tray on the bedside table.

'Your tea, Mo. Would you like a cup, Mr Fordham?'

'No thanks,' the man replied.

'I'll leave you two, then.' She turned and walked away.

'Oh, Ash! She thought you were Robbie.'

'Wish I was,' Ash said seriously.

'Dear Ash. Best not to think it.' Mo squeezed his hand comfortingly.

'Yes, Sister Galloway, what can I do for you?' Glynis ushered Chrissy into her office and indicated the seat she should take. Once again Chrissy felt like a schoolgirl in the headmistress's study—convinced she'd done something wrong when she knew she hadn't.

'I'm afraid I've come to complain about Staff Nurse Poundman.'

'Oh, really?' One slender eyebrow was raised questioningly.

'You realise I'm not happy doing this?'

'If you're not happy with it, then why do it?' Glynis asked sharply.

Chrissy felt as if she had been slapped. She hadn't expected quite such a bald reaction. 'Because I feel I owe it to the patients.'

'So?' Glynis looked irritated.

'If you're going to be this dismissive there doesn't seem any point in my continuing.' Chrissy half rose.

'I apologise,' Glynis said easily. 'Please continue.'

Chrissy sat down again. 'My grandmother is on Nurse Poundman's ward. She is afraid of her and she says other patients are too. She calls the patients by their Christian names, which a lot of the elderly do not like. And standards are sloppy.'

'For example?'

'Empty water jugs. Bedpans reluctantly given.'

'We have never had any complaints about the care of the elderly before. Jazz Poundman has been a hard-working, dedicated nurse. Did you speak to the sister in charge?'

'No. My grandmother says she wouldn't believe me.' Chrissy shifted uncomfortably in the armchair. 'Don't you want to know when things aren't right?'

'Of course,' Glynis said coldly. 'Anything untoward in my hospital is of concern to me. But there are procedures. You should have complained to the sister in charge and then, if matters weren't rectified, to me.'

'I'm sorry. I thought this was the best way. I'll be sure to observe the correct procedure in future. So am I to go back and report to the sister?'

'No, it's too late now. I shall investigate personally. I shall let you know my findings.' Glynis stood, a sign of dismissal. 'You should be warned, Sister, that your actions are quite likely to lead to bad feelings. And since you're—' She turned away.

'What were you going to say? That I was already unpopular enough, what with all the gossip about me?'

'I never listen to gossip, Sister. I'm interested only in facts,' she said, turning back.

Chrissy stood and faced Glynis, puzzled. She'd thought her a fair woman, if a rigid one, but today she appeared to be vindictive. She squared her shoulders. 'Are the post-mortem reports on my patients in?' she asked.

'I've seen nothing. They must still be with the pathologist.'

'Aren't they taking a long time over them?'

'Are you complaining about that too?' Glynis responded.

'Thanks for nothing!' Chrissy said, and slammed the door after her.

Glynis slumped at her desk and sighed. She'd handled that so badly. She didn't know what was happening to her—but then she did. She despised herself for her behaviour last night with Matthew.

When working at the hospital in Cornwall, Chrissy had thought herself rushed off her feet. She could laugh at that notion now. Life had been one long holiday compared with her workload here, she thought, as she prepared to drive up North Hill to her mother's house.

'I thought you'd fallen off the edge of the world,' Iris said sharply in greeting.

'I'm sorry. I've been so rushed recently I haven't even finished unpacking,' Chrissy replied. She could have pointed out that her mother could just as well have contacted her, but she didn't. The last thing she wanted was a further falling-out with her mother.

'Any news on those odd deaths you were fretting about?'

'Nothing,' said Chrissy, feeling her face tighten.

'Maybe someone did bump them off. Wasn't you by any chance?' Iris chortled, but Chrissy did not join in.

'Mum, it's hardly a joking matter, is it? The gossip in the hospital is like a plague. It's getting me down.'

'Well, you must expect that after Ewan. Suspicion'll never leave you,' Iris said bluntly, as she sat down opposite Chrissy, who was huddled in what had once been her father's wing chair. Then she changed the subject. 'Do you want that chair?'

'This one?' Chrissy fingered the dark blue velvet. 'I don't know where I'd put it.'

'Then I'll sell it. I'm getting shot of everything—furniture, house, the lot.'

'You can't do that! Not this house. Oh, Mum.' Chrissy was appalled. 'Where will you go? Something smaller?'

'No, I'm buying a boat and sailing the world. It's what I've always wanted to do.'

'I'd no idea you liked sailing or that you'd ever done any. Still, if it's what you want,' Chrissy said unconvincingly. 'But how will you manage? I mean, what do you know about sailing?'

'Bob's coming with me. Sailing's his hobby. Didn't I say?' she added, with wide-eyed innocence.

'No, you didn't.' Chrissy was upset, and doubly so when she realised that she was far more perturbed at the thought of her family home being sold than of her mother leaving.

'So why are you here? You so rarely come to see me.'

'Gran.' There seemed no point in prevaricating. 'She hates the hospital. I want to get her into a nursing home. She'd be happier.'

'So, do it, if that's what she wants.'

'Yes, but they cost an arm and a leg and her pension won't cover it. I can help a bit, but I'm pretty stretched. I was wondering—'

'No, is the answer. I can't afford it. I shall need every penny I can raise. Boats—good ones—don't come cheap and I'll have to invest to give me an income.'

'Gran needs our help now. She's old and infirm.'

'Probably does, but why should I do anything?'

'For the very good reason that she's Dad's mother, and Dad got where he did because of the sacrifices she made when he was a boy. You wouldn't even be going round the world if it weren't for Gran. Dad would never have left you everything if he thought you wouldn't look after her.'

'You do things in life you want to, not because you're expected to.'

'That's not right, Mum. I can't believe I'm hearing this.'

'I'm grabbing at happiness before it's too late. I've paid my dues a thousand times over. Now I'm reaping my reward. And don't even think of lecturing me. My mind's made up.'

Chrissy stood up. 'No. I won't waste my breath.'

The changes in her mother had taken place too swiftly for Chrissy to accept easily. How could she be so blatantly egocentric?

'Drat!' she said outside, at dropping her keys. She bent to search for them in the road as a passing car approached and picked out her bending form in its headlights.

'Chrissy, hello!' she heard Russell call as he slammed his car door shut and walked speedily up the hill towards her. 'What are you doing here?'

'This is my mother's house.'

'I didn't know that. I live down the hill. I've just been to your place.'

'I haven't been home yet.'

'Fancy dinner?'

'Oh, I don't know. I'm tired and—'

'Please, Chrissy. I want to apologise about the other night. I was stupid.'

She grinned at him. 'Yes, you were rather.'

'I was tired. It had been an awful day. Can we try again?'

'OK. But I've got nothing in the house.'

'No, I meant may I take you out? Have you eaten at Chez Sylvie?'

'I'll have to go and shower and change.'

'What if I come and pick you up in an hour?'

'Lovely,' she said. To her surprise he bent forward and kissed her cheek. 'Actually, it'll be better if I meet you at the restaurant.' And then, knowing she had sounded a little tense, she added lamely, 'I'll be less flustered.' They were standing under a street-lamp and clearly visible to Iris, who was watching from an upstairs window, and to Sabine who was watching from two doors further down.

A serious staffing crisis was looming, there was no doubt of that, Glynis thought, as she worked on her ward allocation charts. Christmas was fast approaching, and nurses with young families would not be prepared to work over the holiday. A and E was most vulnerable, and they would have to pray that no major incidents would stretch the department to its limits.

There were times when Glynis could quite happily have throttled the Craig Nuttings of this world. If he hadn't banned recruitment last month she would still have a problem, but not as acute as this was becoming.

'Come,' she said, to a rap at her door. 'Problems?' she asked at the sight of an anxious-faced Edna Greenbank.

'You could say that. Remember the nurse I told you about—the one I found bonking with Matthew Kersey?'

'Of course.' Glynis winced inwardly at Edna's choice of words.

'Well, how can I run a theatre when one of my nurses keeps having to throw up? She's pregnant. By *him*.'

Glynis paused, almost imperceptibly, as she assimilated this news. 'How would you know that for sure? It could easily be someone else.'

'No, I believe her. She also tells me you haven't had a word with her. Does that mean you haven't had a go at Matthew either?'

'I did speak to Matthew. He denies the incident.'

'You're having me on!'

'No. That is what he told me. I have no reason to disbelieve him.'

'Glynis, when will you wake up? The man is a serial adulterer. He's making you the laughing stock of the whole hospital.'

'How could that be? Don't be so silly.' Glynis stood up. 'Edna, I know that you are infatuated with Matthew and that obsessive jealousy has motivated these accusations.'

To her consternation Edna laughed. 'And what cock-and-bull story has he been telling you? Look, Glynis, I'm not jealous. I'm sorry for you. You obviously love Matthew and he doesn't deserve you. Stop wasting your life on a creep like him.'

'Edna, I don't know what you mean.' Glynis clung to the clichéd words as if they were a life raft. 'Now, if you wouldn't mind, I've work to do. I'll see what I can do about a replacement bank nurse for you.'

Edna stood. 'Suit yourself,' she said.

When the door had closed Glynis sat still, gazing into space. And then she began to take stock.

In a strange way, what Edna had told her had come as no surprise. She found she was even sorry for the young pregnant nurse, and wondered what she would have done if she'd ever found herself in the same position.

The most surprising discovery of all was that she was calm. She wasn't, for the moment, hurt. Instead, she found that she was disappointed in Matthew. *Disappointed*. What a lame word for the ending of such a passionate affair. For it was the end, she knew. There was no going back.

Chez Sylvie was a French restaurant caught in a time warp of thirty years ago. It was warm and welcoming on such a bitterly cold night. Red-and-white checked tablecloths matched the frilled curtains at the windows. On each table stood a wine bottle heavily encrusted with years of dripped candlewax. Strings of obviously artificial garlic and onions hung from the ceiling. No nouvelle cuisine was served here: instead there were generous portions of food of the French countryside—thick, nourishing soups, hearty casseroles and stews. Accordion music issued from an eight-track stereo system.

The restaurant had always been popular but just recently, with the swing back in fashion, it looked chic again.

'Can you imagine? One has to book a table. Sylvie's doing so well.' Floss flicked her napkin onto her lap and eagerly picked up the menu.

'She deserves it. The food is so consistently good.' Glynis poured herself a glass of water from a carafe.

'You look a bit peaky, Glynis, are you all right?'

'I'm fine.'

'You'll say that on your deathbed, no doubt. What's up?'

'Staffing levels are bad. I think we're approaching crisis level.'

'You should be used to that particular worry, my dear. So what is it?'

Glynis, who would never normally have confided in anyone, looked at Floss, her kind face, her warm brown eyes, and suddenly felt a need

431

to unburden herself. As her sad story unfolded, she found it rather comforting to share it.

'Well, at least it makes it easier for me to talk to you about a rather distressing matter. I've found out more about the proposed hospital closure and it's certain that Matthew is one of the conspirators.'

'Floss, nothing surprises me any more,' Glynis said, with a sad, weary smile . . . and Floss leaned over and quietly told Glynis of her plans.

'Do you see who's sitting over there?' Russell leaned towards Chrissy. 'Our beloved clinical services manager with Floss Yates.'

'I hope they don't see us. I don't think Glynis approves of me.' She played with her napkin. 'I'm being silly. Let's change the subject. Tell me, how are you feeling? You look so much better, less strained and tired.' She smiled tenderly at him.

'I'd forgotten what it's like to be smiled at like that. As if you care.'

'Of course I care—what an odd thing to say.'

'You wouldn't think that if you were me.'

'Gracious, I can almost hear the violins!' She laughed lightly. 'What's got into you? You're handsome, successful, your patients adore you. Half the nurses drool over you.'

'I wasn't talking about them. I was meaning someone special.' He put his hand across the table and covered hers. Quickly she removed it. 'Why is it that whenever I get close to you you react as if I'm Jack the Ripper? It's confusing.'

'I'm sorry, I don't mean to. It's . . .' She shook her head almost defiantly. 'No. That's not true. The truth is that I'm scared to let us go any further.'

'Scared? Of me? What have I done?'

'Nothing.' She looked miserably at her plate. She longed to tell him that she ached to be held by him, kissed, loved—but she knew that her brain would not permit her body to do what she wanted. Too much pain, too much humiliation, too much mental abuse stood in her way. 'I don't think it's right to be involved with a married man. I shouldn't really be here now.' She knew she sounded prim and precious, but didn't know how else to explain herself: how she feared she'd be hurt and disillusioned.

'I'm getting divorced,' he said abruptly.

'But you still live in the same house as Sabine.'

'If that's what's bothering you then I'll move out tomorrow. Will you accept me then?' he asked eagerly. Chrissy looked frightened, her large brown eyes startled. 'It isn't just that, is it? You need to talk, my darling.

Who better than me? I promised myself I'd be patient and not rush you, but I've got to say it—I'm falling in love with you, I'd never hurt you. All I want is to care for you.'

'*Bonsoir*, Russell. 'Ow lovely to see you.' Sylvie's heavily accented English interrupted him. 'Ze special tonight . . .' And she listed the dishes of the day. Chrissy relaxed, as if some danger had passed. Russell sighed, aware that a moment had slipped away.

Certainly that evening it did not return. They ate their meal with enjoyment, drank their wine with pleasure.. They talked of many things, Russell having made a conscious decision that he must not move too fast with Chrissy or he would lose her.

'And you say Glynis has heard nothing about the post-mortem reports? This is ridiculous. If you want, I'll sort it out. The pathologist is a mate of mine.'

'Would you? If you could find out something for me it would be such a weight off my mind.'

After coffee and petits fours, Chrissy began to feel for her handbag on the floor. 'I think I should be going.'

'Already?' He sounded disappointed.

'I'm on early shift.'

Russell paid the bill and they walked to where their cars were parked.

'That was a lovely meal, Russell. Thank you,' she said, as she stood by her car.

'I'm glad you enjoyed it. We must do it again.'

'I'd love to.' She opened the car door. She wanted to invite him back for a nightcap, but after she'd rejected him how could she? Not that she'd wanted to put him off. It seemed she could not stop herself doing it. She climbed in and put the key in the ignition. He closed the door behind her and bent down as the window slid down.

'I was wondering—' He stopped.

'Yes?' she asked, expectantly.

'Oh, nothing,' he replied. 'See you.' He'd been about to ask if he could follow her car home and congratulated himself on the self-control he'd exerted. He walked across to his own car.

All the way home Chrissy berated herself for her stupidity. She had to erase Ewan's damage from her mind. Logic told her that she wasn't fat; the mirror told her she wasn't ugly; her birth certificate showed she was still young; she ran a demanding ward so she was not stupid; Russell enjoyed her company so she could not be boring. Oh, yes, she could think it through logically. Then why was she afraid to let Russell near her—to touch her skin, to see her naked? She knew the answer only too well; given an endless diet of criticism the most confident woman would end up as she had.

She turned into her gateway and got out of the car. She paused a second, enjoying the smell of the wind, then she unlocked the back door, entered her kitchen and stood stock-still. The room was exactly as she had left it. Nothing was out of place. And yet Chrissy was certain— someone had been here while she was out.

CHAPTER SEVEN

'SORRY, RUSSELL, I can't help you. My reports have gone to Thorpedale.'

'Thorpedale? Why not here?' Russell asked into the telephone.

'It's normal for a copy of any post-mortem we perform to be sent to them, but I'll tell you, Russell, I was surprised when they requested that *all* copies be sent and none to go to Fellcar.'

'Any idea why that should be?'

'Well . . .' There was silence. 'I'd rather not say.'

'So you did find something untoward. Which patient?'

'Look, Russell, don't push me, please. Ask Craig Nutting what's up. He's the one sitting on them.'

'But, Jim, it's me—we go back a long way.'

'Not far enough, Russell,' he said, and hung up.

Russell sat at his desk, picking at the edge of the blotter. Jim was edgy and hiding something, he was sure.

He swivelled the black leather chair, picked up the telephone and punched in the numbers for Fellcar Hospital. He asked to speak to Fraser Ball, the consultant neurologist.

'Fraser, it's Russell. Your Mrs Tomley, the sudden death, have you heard the post-mortem result?'

'Now you mention it, I haven't. I must chase it up.'

'Was it totally unexpected?'

'In neurology we're always prepared for the unexpected.' Fraser laughed. 'But I was surprised. I thought she'd made a good recovery.'

The Care of the Elderly consultant could shed no light either. 'Old people, Russell, you can never tell. But thank you for reminding me.'

Lynn slapped the letter from the laboratory down on the table in front of Terry.

'Now what have you got to say?' she asked, hands on hips, her stance aggressive, but the effect spoilt by the wide grin on her face.

Terry read the single sheet. 'This report says you were well below the limit.' He looked up at her. 'I'm sorry.'

'I think this proves my point. You know me, I've never been able to take alcohol—one gin and I'm anybody's! But it takes a whole drink to do that. Yet a couple of sips of whisky and I'm falling down drunk? There had to be something else in that whisky.'

'But if there *was* something else, wouldn't they have picked it up in the blood test?'

'Not if they weren't looking for it.'

'Bloody mystery to me. What are you going to do now?'

'I've two options. I've spoken to Glynis about joining their nursing bank. And I've got an interview today at the Mimosa Nursing Home.'

'Why not try to get your old job back?'

'I wouldn't work there if they paid me double. But I'll get an apology from Dick Henderson before I'm finished.'

'What do you think's got into him?'

'He's tired and I don't think he cares any more. I think he loads too much of the work on Giles and so he's stuck. He can't control him any more and Giles can do whatever he wants.'

'But apart from the drugs what's so sinister?'

'Giles is permanently on the fiddle. I couldn't prove it, but I bet he takes bribes from the pharmaceutical companies. Certainly the reps spend longer with him than they do with Dick.'

'But that business about sending patients to the Accident Department to jump the queue—that's a good thing, isn't it? And he's saving the practice money.'

'I agree, but I doubt if the hospital sees it that way. But any savings made at the practice should be ploughed back into it. I'm certain they aren't. Henderson has to know about them—he's the senior partner—so what's the game? I reckon they share the money and put it in their pockets. Maybe that's another reason why Henderson lets Giles get away with murder—he knows Giles could blackmail him with what he knows.'

'Have you proof of this?'

'No. I've worked it out.' She tapped her skull.

'Then keep mum or you could land up in trouble. Promise?'

'I promise,' she said, but under the table she crossed her fingers. She'd already told Floss Yates her theories.

'Russell, well, this is an honour. Come in and take a pew.' Craig indicated a deep leather chair opposite his desk. 'What can I do for you?'

'I'm told you have the post-mortem reports here on two former patients at St Edith's, Mrs Tomley and Mrs Fortune.'

'Were they late patients of yours?' Craig asked, cockily.

'No, but—'

'Well, then, I can't tell you anything, can I? You wouldn't want me to divulge confidential information, would you?'

'Good God, man. I'm a consultant there. Once the results are sent over I shall know all about it, whether they're my patients or not.' He knew that he was pulling rank in an unpleasant manner. There was something about this weaselly man that made him act like this.

'Of course you'll know. But now? Sorry, no can do.' Craig was enjoying this. What had started as a delaying tactic had all the makings of bad publicity for the hospital. It couldn't be better.

'But why the delay?'

'Wheels within wheels, Russell old boy, you know how it is. They must have been important patients. Everyone wants to know about them—even good old Glynis.'

'Of course she does. This delay isn't fair on the staff.'

Craig's eyes lit up with immediate interest. 'Got an interest in the staff? One member in particular? Is it that pretty little new sister I've heard about? The one whose husband died in rather odd circumstances? Are you sure you're safe there, Russell?'

Russell longed to hit him, to wipe off that supercilious grin. He stood up. He had to get out of this room before he lost his self-control.

'Going?' Craig looked artificially surprised.

'There seems little point in continuing this conversation.' He turned and walked to the door.

'One little snippet, Russell. Tell that sister she'd better start looking for a lawyer . . .'

As he shut the door, his face rigid to disguise his shock, Russell heard Craig laugh as if he'd just cracked the best joke ever.

As Chrissy came out of the front door of the Mimosa Nursing Home, Lynn was approaching.

'We do keep meeting in odd places!' Lynn began to laugh, then stopped. 'Love, what is it? You look so tired.'

Chrissy shrugged. 'Have you got all day?'

'Long enough. I'm early for an interview.'

'Oh, I don't know. I'm worried about so many things. One, I could deal with, but they've all piled onto each other. I'm so afraid I'll start making stupid mistakes because of everything else.'

'And what's everything else?' Lynn coaxed once they were settled in the front of her car.

'There's my grandmother . . .' And she related her worry about Daphne being afraid in the ward and that there was no way she could afford nursing-home fees.

'Then there's my mother . . .' And without mentioning Bob she told Lynn how Iris had changed, so much so that she barely knew her any longer. 'On top of that there's been a spate of sudden deaths at the hospital and I know the finger of suspicion is pointing at me . . .' And she had of necessity to explain about Ewan and his death. She would like to have discussed Russell and her mixed emotions—wanting and yet fearing involvement and, the biggest stumbling block of all, Sabine. But she didn't, she couldn't go that far. She sighed deeply.

'What else is there? That sigh says it all.'

'It's probably my imagination, but—oh, hell, I feel stupid just saying it. I think someone has been snooping about in my cottage.'

'Good heavens! Have you been to the police?'

'And say what? That I've got this *feeling*? They'd laugh.'

'With your responsibilities you need to have some help through all this, or something will give. Why not talk to Floss about it? She knows everyone.'

'I might do that.'

'I would. And get yourself a fella—that's what you need. Someone to snuggle up to and confide in.'

'You reckon?' Chrissy laughed for the first time. She looked at her watch. 'Oh, my God, Lynn, your interview—you're hopelessly late.'

'Oh, forget it.' Lynn waved her hand. 'You've made my mind up for me. I'll take the bank job on Care of the Elderly at St Edith's. I'll keep an eye open for your gran, so that's one less worry for you.'

'That's wonderful news! But I thought they weren't taking on any more staff for the time being?'

'I reckon Glynis decided it didn't cover bank nurses.'

'Bless her. And you, Lynn, really are an angel!'

Mo was up and about on the ward, pushing the trolley to which her intravenous infusion was strapped in front of her.

'I hear you're feeling less sore,' Chrissy said to her.

'Much better, thanks. I looked out for you this morning.'

'We work a shift system. I'm on now until ten. Was it anything in particular?' she asked. Mo nodded bleakly. 'Come into my office and we'll talk it through.'

'A friend came to visit me last night. I told her about me having chemotherapy and she said I was mad to agree to it, that her mother had had it and it made her feel worse and it didn't work—and she died anyway.' Mo looked doleful and close to tears. 'She said when they give you chemo it's the last resort.'

'Well, that's a load of rubbish to start with. Times have moved on. We get amazing results these days. And, in any case, this course of drugs is preventive. No one can be a hundred per cent sure that your operation removed all the cancer cells. These drugs are to be given to you to mop up anything that's left which, in any case, might not be there. You see?'

Mo relaxed visibly. 'But . . .' And she stiffened again. 'She said I'd feel so sick I'd want to die.'

'Some people feel nausea, others don't. Some get indigestion, others don't. And if you do feel sick, we have drugs that can help you. Let's sort that out *if* it occurs.'

'OK.' Mo still sounded doubtful.

'Mo, do you remember when you were pregnant all you heard were horror stories? You'd have thought that no one had ever had a normal birth. Well, having cancer is a bit like that—everyone has a gory tale to tell. Try to ignore them and talk to us who know.'

'I'm so glad it was you on this ward.'

'So am I! Still, you're lucky, you've got a supportive husband—that helps immeasurably.'

'Me? He hasn't even been to visit me. He's too scared of hospitals.'

'But the other night—'

'That was a friend, Ash. He's my husband's partner.'

'Oh, I'm sorry. Only, the way he was looking at you—I thought . . .'

Mo blushed. 'I think he's got a soft spot for me. Still, I'm keeping you from your work.' Mo changed the subject to cover her embarrassment. She stood up to leave. 'You've helped a lot. Thanks.'

Dawn appeared in the doorway as Mo left. 'We've got a bit of a problem, Chrissy. Pharmacy say they haven't had the ward order, it's due today. And Mr Hobbs says he told you he was a diabetic but he didn't get a special diet meal.'

Chrissy's shoulders slumped. Dawn approached her and put her arm round her. 'You've got too much on your plate at the moment, Chrissy. Why don't you go home early? I can cover for you.'

'Would you? I could do with an early night. You're a treasure.'

'No problem. You can do the same for me one day.'

ON CALL

Chrissy had been a nurse long enough to know that it was wisest always to cover one's back. Something she hadn't done that night when she had given Buck Marston a drug that the doctor had only verbally ordered. Now she was on her way to the office to report that she was leaving early.

'Sister Galloway! Cooee! Sister!' a voice called.

Chrissy stopped at the next flight of steps down. 'Mrs Marston. How is your son doing?'

Mrs Marston puffed up to the landing. 'He's a blooming walking miracle, Sister. He's zapping about like a racing driver. Can't wait to get out of here.'

'And his head?'

'Well, there never was much in there to start with, but he's had no more fits. Mr Ball's very pleased with him.'

'And your daughter-in-law?'

'A boy, two nights ago. I'm like a Yo-yo visiting her then Buck.'

'Do give her my congratulations, won't you?'

'I will. We're hoping that they'll both be home for Christmas.'

'Let's hope it will be a happy Christmas for you.' She paused, remembering the other family that, because of Buck, would not be having a jolly time. 'And the police?'

'Ah, well, as I said to Buck, he should never have been drinking, so he must take the consequences. We hope, because of his injuries, they'll be lenient. You know—that he's suffered enough.'

'I see.' Chrissy edged towards the stairs. Once she had started Mrs Marston was difficult to stop. 'If you'll excuse me . . .' She ran down towards Miss Tillman's office to explain why she was leaving her shift three hours early.

'You're not going down with anything?' Glynis asked kindly, in contrast to her tone at their last interview.

'No, I don't think so. I'm very tired. I haven't been sleeping well.'

'Because of the post-mortem reports? I've chased them up. We shall receive them tomorrow.'

'Thank goodness.'

'Chrissy, I think I should tell you. The police are bringing them. Sit down. You look very pale.'

Chrissy exhaled. 'I didn't want to hear anything like that,' she said, as she groped for a chair.

'I'm sure we'll find a plausible explanation and that they're only involved in a routine capacity.'

'I hope you're right,' Chrissy said, though she doubted it.

439

'Chrissy, there's something else I wanted to talk to you about. It's none of my business, but . . . well, I saw you with Russell Newson the other night at Chez Sylvie.'

Chrissy stiffened. 'So?' she said, trying to sound defiant and failing.

'Mr Newson is a married man.'

Chrissy got to her feet. 'You're right, it's none of your business.'

'Please, Chrissy. I'm concerned for you. Please sit down.' Reluctantly Chrissy did. 'I don't want to see you hurt by a married man.'

'He's just a friend.'

'Then I hope he stays one.'

'I'm sorry, Miss Tillman, but I really—'

It was Glynis's turn to breathe deeply, hardly believing what she was about to do. 'I speak from experience, Chrissy. I became involved with a married consultant. For sixteen years I believed he would leave his wife for me. I've been a fool and I've been duped.'

'It's costing you dear to talk to me like this, isn't it?'

'It's not in my nature to discuss my affairs.'

'I appreciate your concern, I really do. But please don't worry. I've no intention of getting involved with Russell. I've too much else to worry me, I can assure you.'

After her session with Glynis, Chrissy popped in to say good night to her grandmother and to tell her that Lynn Petch was joining the staff and would keep an eye on her. Despite leaving her shift early, once she had driven home, it was almost the time she would normally have got back. So much for an early night, she thought, as she walked to her back door.

'Mrs Galloway, might I have a word?'

'Heavens!' Chrissy stopped dead in her tracks, her heart pumping with fear. 'Gracious, you made me jump!'

'I'm sorry, but I need to talk to you.'

Chrissy sighed as she put the key into the lock. The last thing she needed was a confrontation with Russell's wife. 'You'd better come in. You'll catch your death of cold in this wind. Have you been waiting long?' she wittered, and realised she was nervous. Why? What had she done wrong? Not much. A couple of evenings, one dinner out—hardly adultery. 'Do you want a coffee?'

'No. I wish you'd just sit down and listen to what I have to say.'

'Right. I'm sorry.' Chrissy, flustered, removed her coat and sat down obediently, not registering how rude Sabine had sounded, thinking only of how beautiful she was and how elegant.

'I love my husband.' Sabine stood on the hearth-rug and leaned forward defiantly. She swayed slightly and Chrissy wondered if she was drunk. 'So? You hear?'

'That's very nice for you,' said Chrissy.

'Then leave him alone. He's mine. You're ruining everything.'

'Look, I think you're under some misapprehension here.'

'You've been seen with him.'

'Yes. He took me out to dinner the other night.'

'There you are, then!' Sabine tossed her head triumphantly.

'I was told you were separated. In which case—'

'That's a bloody lie. Did Russell tell you that? The bastard. I want you out of my husband's life. You understand?'

'I'm hardly in it. He's a friend, that's all.' This was so silly, thought Chrissy, and, in a distorted way, it was even funny.

'They all say that. You know about all his other bits on the side?'

'No, I don't.' Chrissy was not finding this so amusing now.

'Oh, you poor dear. Didn't know he's St Edith's own Casanova.' Sabine sat down. 'I'm so sorry. If only I could have got to you earlier and warned you.' Her eyes filled with tears. 'I can't tell you the times he's pulled this little trick—that I don't understand him, that he's lonely.'

'If he does this, then why do you stay with him?' Chrissy sat rigid, disappointment, betrayal, anger playing tag in her mind.

'Because I love him . . . What can I do? It's the tender trap, isn't it?' she said. Tears were rolling down her cheeks. Chrissy fetched the Kleenex box and handed it to her, and stood beside the chair while Sabine sobbed, feeling ineffectual, not knowing what to do or say.

'He's destroying me and he'll destroy you too, if you let him.'

'Look. I'm sorry about this, but you seem to have got the wrong end of the stick. I'm not having an affair with your husband. I've problems of my own to sort out—I don't have room for a man.'

'It's like an illness with him,' Sabine sobbed. 'It's difficult for him to resist. You know—an important consultant, a busy hospital full of frustrated nurses.'

'Oh really?' In Chrissy's experience nurses had a marked degree of cynicism where doctors were concerned and, in any case, the man Sabine talked about didn't sound like the Russell she knew. Was she such a hopeless judge of character? She smiled to herself. Why did she need to ask herself that after making such a huge mistake over Ewan?

'Will you promise to drop my husband and give my marriage a chance?'

'Look, Sabine. I'm sorry you're unhappy, I really am. But nothing has happened between Russell and myself. If you won't believe me . . .' She shrugged her shoulders.

'Oh, I do. If that's what you say.' Sabine was on her feet again, no longer tearful. 'I'm sorry to have bothered you,' she said, with dignity, and allowed Chrissy to show her to the door.

After she'd gone, and Chrissy had locked the house, she made herself a cup of hot chocolate. As she sat at the pine table, mulling over the scene, she jumped at a noise from outside. Tentatively she pulled back the curtain and peered out at the darkness. She was edgy. The feeling that someone had been here snooping wouldn't go away. Maybe it had been Sabine trying to find out more about her, her sadness for her marriage making her act crazily. 'Oh hell!' she said aloud. She couldn't deal with these dramas.

When Chrissy awoke a slight breeze lifted the curtains. She heard the soft murmur of a calm sea after last night's high winds. She stretched contentedly. And then a bleakness descended as she remembered.

It was far from being a good day. The police were coming, which could only mean the post-mortem findings were suspicious. No doubt the gossip would move up a gear, and the whispering would intensify. At Fellcar she had hoped for a new start. Now she had this new nightmare to contend with alone.

If only she could see Russell, she thought. He would calm her in his logical way. She knew she yearned for him—there was no point in denying it . . . but she knew she was wasting her time dreaming of him. He was married, he'd lied about his marriage, Sabine had said. Like so many men, he was not to be trusted. And yet . . . Chrissy believed in him, sensed he had told her the truth. It was difficult to switch that off and make herself distrust him. She buried her face in the pillows.

'Fancy a coffee, Chrissy?' Dawn called to her in the car park, as Chrissy parked and Dawn locked her bicycle.

'I don't think so. Better get straight up to the ward.' Chrissy looked about her, searching shiftily for people who were talking about her.

'Chrissy, you've got to face them sooner or later.'

'Hell, am I that obvious? But, Dawn, it's so hard. I can't.'

'Yes, you can. I'll be with you. If I hear one whisper against you I'll belt them.'

'You are kind.' Arm in arm they walked into the hospital and down the stairs that linked it with the canteen.

There was a perceptible drop in the noise level in the room as they entered the canteen. 'Morning all,' Dawn said loudly and led the way to the servery.

Once they had their trays they looked about them for a space.

'Over there.' Dawn pointed to a table where Jazz Poundman was holding court.

'I'd rather not,' said Chrissy, but Dawn was already forging ahead towards the table.

'Don't often see you in here, Chrissy,' Jazz said, moving her chair with a scraping noise to make room for the two newcomers.

'You know how it is. I'm always in a rush, Jazz.'

'Have you seen the fuzz? One of them's to die for. The sergeant—wow!' Jazz fanned herself with a napkin. 'Been in with Tillman for an hour now. Exciting, isn't it?' she boomed.

'An excitement I could do without,' Chrissy said quietly.

'I expect so, Chrissy dear. But, then, you've got more to worry about than the rest of us, haven't you?'

'What are you implying, Jazz? Out with it.' Dawn faced her.

'Moi? Nothing, Dawn. What makes you think that?' Jazz batted her eyelashes in a parody of wide-eyed innocence.

'Come on, Dawn, let's go.' Chrissy put her hand on Dawn's arm.

'No, Chrissy, I want to know what she's getting at.'

'I'm not saying anything that other people aren't saying. Mrs Fortune died in iffy circumstances. Similar to someone's husband, that's all.'

Chrissy pushed her chair back and grabbed her bag. She made quickly for the door.

Dawn caught up with her on the way to the hospital building. 'You shouldn't have left like that.'

'Why not? I didn't want to hear any more snide remarks.' They entered the building.

'It's as if you had something to hide, that's all.' They began to climb the stairs. 'It would have been better if you'd faced them out.'

'That's a matter of opinion. But thanks for your help. I appreciate it,' she said, as they pushed open the swing doors of the ward. Halfway down the corridor she saw Russell.

'Sister, might I have a word?' he asked formally.

'I've yet to hear the night staff's report.'

'Just a minute. In private.' He looked hard at Dawn.

Her office would be full of staff, the kitchen busy.

'The linen cupboard will be quiet.' Chrissy led the way and held the door open for Russell.

'God, this takes me back to my youth—trysts in the cupboard!' He grinned at her, but when she did not respond he became serious. 'What is it, Chrissy?' he asked, concerned.

'I've only a minute. What did you want?' she said coldly, when what she wanted was to fling herself into his arms.

'I thought I should see you as quickly as possibly. I called several times last night, but your phone was constantly engaged.'

'I was tired. I took it off the hook.'

'Oh, I see. Only I went to see Craig Nutting yesterday. There is a problem with—'

'I know. Mrs Fortune. Or that's the buzz in the canteen.'

'How do they find these things out? Craig said something odd. He suggested you get a good lawyer.'

Chrissy felt as if the floor would give way under her.

'I took the liberty of phoning a friend of mine, Henry Yates. He's a good lawyer. I just thought, since you were new to the area, that you wouldn't know who to turn to.'

'His father was our family solicitor.'

'Of course. I'd forgotten you were born here. I'd have come round, only I didn't want to appear to be pushing myself on you.' He looked all ways but at her.

'Just as well. I was asleep,' she lied.

'Chrissy—I—' He put out his hand, as if longing to touch her.

'I've work to do, Russell. If you'll—'

'Chrissy, you're backing off again. Why? What's happened?'

'Nothing.' And she turned away.

'Tea or coffee, Inspector Webster?' Glynis asked of the grey-haired man who sat opposite her. The hair, she decided, made him look older than he was. The lack of lines on his face, his clear brown eyes, put him a good ten years younger than it implied. 'Coffee or tea?' she repeated, flustered at her unexpected interest in him.

'Either. In this job you take whatever's on offer.' He laughed.

'Well, I usually have coffee at this time.' She picked up the phone and ordered it. 'I just can't believe the culprit could be a member of staff. There's no doubt?'

'The poor woman had well in excess of two hundred units of insulin in her blood. That's a massive overdose, isn't it? And I'm afraid it's not unknown for a serial killer to be in a hospital.'

'But St Edith's?' Glynis frowned and George Webster longed to tell her not to worry, but didn't like to.

'I'll need everyone's personnel notes. We'll be as quick as we can.

Sergeant Townley, who is working with me, will set up an office here at the hospital, if we may?'

'The boardroom would probably be best.'

'There are two things I'd like to discuss in confidence, Miss Tillman. You have a Sister Galloway working here?'

'Yes. And I feel I must say that there was gossip about the poor woman right from the start. Her husband killed himself using insulin. But she was investigated by the police and found innocent. Once the gossip started I checked for myself. It's most unfortunate..'

'How do you regard her?'

'She's a highly competent sister, conscientious and hard-working. I do not believe that she could have been involved in Mrs Fortune's death. Why did you mention her first?'

'We've been doing a bit of homework,' he said, not mentioning the anonymous phone call they'd received accusing Chrissy of murder. 'I'd like to start with interviewing the staff on that ward.'

'You said there were a couple of things you wanted clarified?'

'Yes. Do you know why the notes were sent from the pathologist to Thorpedale—to the desk of Mr Craig Nutting?'

'I've no idea. We had to chase them up ourselves. Maybe because of the circumstances . . . But, then, you should have been notified.'

'Mr Nutting apologised, said that it had been a mistake and that the papers got stacked, unnoticed, with a pile of others. But who chased them?'

'I did, and the consultants—Mr Ball, Mr Green and Mr Newson.'

'Why did Mr Newson find it necessary to chase them up? I gather he was informed last week that there was nothing suspicious in the death of his patient, Mrs Norman.'

Another frown flickered across Glynis's face. 'I've no idea,' she said firmly. But George Webster had seen the frown and made a mental note that the beautiful, calm-looking Glynis Tillman was probably lying.

There were five outpatients in for chemotherapy. Chrissy spent the morning settling them and explaining to Dawn the various doses of the forceful drugs. Once the drugs had been administered, the patients needed constant monitoring, and their spirits needed checking too.

Today half of her could concentrate on the patients but the rest of her was in tumult, worrying about herself. The phone call she dreaded finally came. She left Dawn in charge of the ward.

'Take a seat, Sister Galloway. Do you fancy a cup of coffee?'

'No thanks,' she said. Her hand wasn't steady enough to lift a cup.

She wished she had said yes, since the inspector looked disappointed. Maybe he was hoping to take a break. 'I've just had a cup, thanks,' she added, knowing she was trying to ingratiate herself with him.

'Right. I think the best thing is if you tell us about the night Mrs Fortune died and what, if anything, you noticed.'

'Well, that night—' She had to stop and cough, since her voice sounded husky, as if she had a cold. 'I had three wards to supervise.'

'Three?' He looked at her in disbelief. 'How can you look after three wards? Were they on different floors?'

'You learn to walk fast,' she said, with a tentative smile, and was rewarded with one in return, which helped her feel a little bit better.

'Is this normal?'

'No, but the staffing levels are low here. Everyone has to do more.'

'So what happened that night?'

She told him that Mrs Fortune had been agitated, but said she did not know why, that the elderly often were.

'Had she any complaints?'

'She didn't like her Christian name being used.'

'You weren't on the ward when she died?'

'No. Neurology had a problem with one patient and an emergency admission. Once they were settled I returned to Care of the Elderly. Nurse Mottram met me and told me that Mrs Fortune had died.'

'Who was on the ward apart from her?'

'A couple of auxiliaries. Staff Nurse Poundman was late on duty. She arrived just moments after me.'

'She was locked in her flat, I hear?'

'Yes. She'd had to wait for the firemen.'

'You're sure she was locked in? It's common to be locked out, but *in*?'

'That's what I was told.' She was puzzled. 'I suppose . . .' Her voice trailed off.

'What do you suppose, Sister Galloway?'

'Well . . . I don't want to get anyone into trouble . . . I suppose she could have been skiving and made up the story about the fire brigade— but that's only my idea.' She looked uncomfortable.

He sat back, his face mirroring his disappointment. He made notes and added an asterisk to check with the Fellcar fire brigade.

'And nothing else was untoward?' He looked up from his pad.

'Yes. I felt a draught. The fire-escape door was open, and I knew I'd locked it. I always check—it's a phobia with me. Years ago, at another hospital, an intruder had got in that way. That was all.'

'Was this before or after Nurse Poundman arrived?'

Chrissy thought. 'I'm sorry, I can't remember.' Which was true. She couldn't remember the sequence of events that night in such detail.

'You've no suspicions as to how this tragedy happened?'

'None,' she replied. It was not fair to mention the complaints about Jazz.

There was silence as Inspector Webster wrote some more. Strange, he thought, as he made his notes, that she hadn't mentioned Mrs Fortune was afraid of Jasmine Poundman—everyone else had.

'Would you say Nurse Poundman was a good nurse?'

'I don't know her work well enough. She can be a little brusque with the patients,' was the only criticism Chrissy allowed herself.

Inspector Webster scribbled some more, deciding this woman was fair, unlike some of her colleagues, in haste to accuse her. She might be the culprit, but he'd bet a year's pay that she wasn't.

'Thanks for your help, Sister.' He smiled up at her.

'Is that all?' She looked astonished.

'For the moment.' He began to pack up. 'Time for lunch.'

Chrissy made her way back to the ward deep in thought. Did the shortness of her interview mean she was off the hook? Or did 'for the moment' mean she was she going to be hauled back?

She heard someone running up behind her.

'Chrissy, how did it go?' Russell had caught up with her. She stopped dead, her face rigid from self-control.

'Fine, thanks.' She did not look at him and began to walk again.

'Chrissy, what is it?'

'Nothing.'

'When a woman says that, a man is a fool to believe it!'

Chrissy stopped and turned to face him. 'Your wife came to see me, Russell. She told me she loved you and wanted her marriage to work. I think it's best if we don't see each other.'

'But it's all lies, Chrissy! Please.'

'Look, Russell, the state of your marriage has nothing to do with me. Let's make sure we don't do something we'd regret.'

'I don't believe this! That woman is evil. She—'

'Russell, I don't want to be involved with a married man. OK? Now, if you'll excuse me, I've a ward to run.'

His lunch with Floss had been very productive, thought George Webster as he got into his car. Things were obviously awry at St Edith's—not only the possible murder of Mrs Fortune, but the plans to close it. He'd have to make a point of seeing this Craig Nutting. He'd hardly got a foot in the door before Floss was telling him not to listen to the gossip surrounding Chrissy Galloway—it was all lies.

He was more than interested in the news he'd gleaned from Floss that Glynis was single. His wife had died ten years ago and it had been a long time since he'd been so attracted to a woman. He wondered if it was conceit on his part that he'd sensed a spark of interest in her too.

Then there was the interesting matter of Dr Middleton, Matthew Kersey, Craig Nutting and their nefarious schemes. It was looking certain that this investigation had been deliberately delayed by Nutting. And Giles Middleton had a lot to answer for about a certain Lynn Petch and a spiked drink.

It always intrigued him how often one investigation led him into various other dubious actions. Circles within circles, he thought as he parked his car outside the hospital.

As he crossed the car park he saw Glynis Tillman. 'Ah! the very person.'

'Your investigation is advancing, Inspector?'

'Slowly. I wanted to talk to you, Miss Tillman.'

'Please, my name is Glynis,' she said, and felt ridiculously skittish.

'George,' he replied. 'Might we have dinner together tonight?'

'Why, George, how kind. I should love to.' She smiled.

'I don't know Fellcar. Do you have any suggestions?'

'Chez Sylvie is excellent—and not too expensive.'

'Right, Chez Sylvie it is,' he said, deciding, with such consideration for his pocket, he liked her even more.

As she dressed to go out Glynis felt elated—and foolish. 'I've only just met the man,' she said to her image in her mirror, but she could not control the mischievous smile. Why was she so confident that this evening was to be one of significance? Stupid, when she thought how she had been fooled by Matthew. Acknowledging her past weakness did nothing to quell this feeling. She double-checked that she had her bleeper with her—she was the manager on call tonight. Chez Sylvie was close enough to the hospital for her to get there within minutes in the unlikely event of disaster striking. Shame she wouldn't be able to enjoy any wine.

'Without doubt that's one of the nicest meals I've had in a long time,' said George, as he helped Glynis on with her coat.

'Sorry?' she said, for the bistro was crowded now with an influx of late diners and she could barely hear him.

'I'll tell you outside,' he yelled.

Sylvie escorted them to the door. They thanked her for the meal.

'Tell me, Sylvie, there's the most lovely smell in your restaurant tonight. What is it?' Glynis asked.

'Ees zee jasmine, zee joss sticks for zee garz—'

Before she had finished there was a mighty roar, accompanied by a blinding flash of light, as an explosion ripped through the restaurant.

The explosion ricocheted against the opposite houses, shattering glass in its rush to be free. There was a momentary silence and then the screaming and shouting began.

Glynis sat up, puzzled. She felt shaky, but otherwise unhurt. She got to her feet. 'George!' she called out. 'George!' With increasing panic.

'Glynis, over here.' Despite the pandemonium he'd heard her and she him. She was by his side in a millisecond.

'George, are you hurt?'

'I think—my—leg—' he said, with difficulty and in obvious pain.

She knelt down and gingerly felt both his legs. A warm patch on the right one and the awkward angle of his trousers gave a warning. 'Don't move, George.' She stood upright, took off her coat and rolled it like a bolster and wedged it against his leg. From her handbag she took some nail scissors and quickly ripped open his trousers.

'Those are new.'

'Then you'll have to buy newer,' she said promptly. 'Ah. That's a relief. No arterial blood. Stay as you are. I'll see if I can help. The ambulances must be on their way.'

'You'll catch cold.'

'I'll be too busy to be cold,' she said briskly, looking about her at people lying on the ground. 'Don't move,' she ordered.

'I wouldn't dare.' He grinned at her through the pain.

'Oh, really!' She laughed before assessing the first of the wounded.

Chrissy was just about to turn into her lane when she heard on the radio about an explosion in town. She reversed and sped off in the direction of St Edith's. When she arrived it was to find organised chaos in the A and E Department as a fleet of ambulances disgorged the wounded.

'How many injured?' she asked the first nurse she saw.

'I'm not sure, but they've put in motion the Major Incident Plan. There's been a bomb at Chez Sylvie. Everyone on call has been pulled in.'

The waiting area was heaving. Nurse Margaret Harper was having little success in trying to persuade patients who were already in attendance before this influx to leave if their problems were not acute. Already patients' relatives, alerted to the accident by the newsflash, were beginning to pour in. This added to the overcrowding so that the ambulance crews were having difficulty in getting their trolleys through the milling, noisy throng.

'Everybody. Listen. Per-l-e-a-s-e!' Freddie Favour, the A and E consultant, had jumped onto the receptionists' counter and was clapping his hands for silence. He achieved a modicum. 'Look, everyone, we need order to treat the patients. All relatives to follow this nurse.' He pointed to the staff nurse. 'You'll be asked to wait in a room where the police will take your details. You will be informed of developments there. Those patients with non-urgent conditions, please go. If you're worried, contact your GP. We have to treat the badly injured first. Thank you.' He jumped down. 'Where the hell's the manager on call? There's no organisation, no central office set-up. What in God's name is going on?'

'The manager on call is Miss Tillman. She's not answering her bleeper,' Sister Betty Greaves explained. 'But we've contacted the next in line and I've had the switchboard alert all staff on standby.'

'Glynis? Not responding? It's not like her.' Freddie bent down over a patient.

'Sister, I'm sorry, I was delayed.'

'Glynis, are you all right? You're covered in dust.' Betty turned to see a dishevelled Glynis.

'I'm sorry. I was there, you see. Right. Have all senior staff been notified? Social workers? The Friends? The chaplain?'

'Being done, Glynis love. Don't you think you should sit down and take it easy, you've had a shock.'

'I'm right as rain. I'd better set up a press information desk.'

'Freddie, will you persuade this woman to sit down?' Betty said.

'What, stop Miss Tillman in her tracks? I'm not man enough for that.'

'Mr Favour, you are a tease!' To everyone's astonishment, Glynis almost giggled.

Triage nurses assessed patients the minute they were wheeled in. The more seriously wounded were weeded out for the doctors' immediate attention in the resuscitation rooms; others were wheeled into cubicles.

In cubicle three, Chrissy found a young girl lying patiently. She checked the notes at the bottom of the trolley. All it contained was her name and age, eighteen. No checks had been done on her.

'Hello, Amber. How are you feeling?' she asked, while noting the girl's extreme pallor, the thin film of sweat on her face.

'I'm fine. There's others . . .' She closed her eyes and shuddered.

'They're being looked after. Now, does it hurt anywhere?'

'Nowhere. I said, I'm fine. I shouldn't be taking up this space. It's my birthday. Dad took me out. Mum wouldn't come—they'd had a row.' She bit her lip.

'I'm sorry. But happy birthday anyway. Now, you just lie back. I'll take your blood pressure.' Chrissy did not like the girl's colour. She wound the cuff round Amber's arm: her blood pressure was alarmingly low. Her pulse was racing wildly. Chrissy feared she might be bleeding internally. She hit the emergency buzzer.

'She's gone into shock,' she said to the houseman who appeared.

With Chrissy he began to push the trolley towards the resuscitation room. A nurse took Chrissy's place and she returned to the cubicles she'd been allocated.

'Nurse!' A woman grabbed Chrissy's arm as she passed. 'My daughter! Have you seen my daughter?'

'Your daughter's name?'

'Amber Nicholls. It was her birthday. Her dad and I had had a row.' At this point the woman burst into tears. 'I can't find my husband,' she said, in a gruff voice through her sobs. Chrissy looked wildly about her. This woman needed help.

'Floss!' she called with relief at the sight of her and several of her kindly Friends of St Edith's. 'Could you?'

'Certainly. Now, you come with me, my dear. I'll see what I can do for you.' And taking the woman's hand Floss led her away.

In cubicle four Chrissy stood transfixed. On the trolley was the inspector. She clutched her throat. Why should she feel guilty at seeing him? Pull yourself together, she told herself.

'Hello, Inspector. What's the problem?'

'Broken my leg—compound fracture, no arterial involvement.'

'My, you sound as if you know what you're talking about.'

'My friend Glynis told me. If you've got patients worse off—'

'A compound fracture is nasty enough, Inspector,' she said gently, as she collected together equipment to clean his wound. 'Do you know what it was? I heard a bomb.'

'Gas explosion, I reckon. Sylvie said something about a smell before the whole kybosh went up.'

'Now, I'll try not to hurt you.'

'What have we here? My name's Newson, orthopaedic surgeon. Sister.' He nodded formally.

'Mr Newson,' she said politely.

Together as a team, they set to work on the inspector's leg.

It was three in the morning. The staff room was crowded as the exhausted doctors and nurses had a quick cup of coffee before dispersing and leaving the regular staff to cope.

'Thanks, everyone who came in—we'd never have managed without you.' Freddie Favour lifted his coffee mug in salute to them.

'At least we showed that our Major Incident Plan works,' Betty Greaves said, satisfied.

'Bit of a kerfuffle at the start, Betty. I think when the next major incident happens the first thing we do is have someone on the door controlling where people should go,' Matthew Kersey pointed out. 'I had to fight my way in.'

'The problem there, Matthew, was that the manager on call was delayed,' Betty explained.

'Well, he or she damn well shouldn't be delayed. What sort of excuse did they have?' Matthew said irascibly.

'It was Glynis. She was at the restaurant.'

'She should have been here, not living it up at Chez Sylvie.'

'Oh, come on, Matthew. Glynis could hardly have known she was about to get involved in an incident of this magnitude. That hiccup apart, I think we can congratulate ourselves that we handled the emergency brilliantly.'

'And they threaten us with closing this department? It doesn't make sense,' said Russell. 'It would have been a lot worse if they'd had to be transported to Thorpedale.'

'Too right,' several agreed.

'Anyone seen Glynis?'

'She went up to the Orthopaedic Ward with the police inspector.'

Betty was rewarded by a *wow* from the group. 'Holding his hand!' The next *wow* was deafening. Slyly she glanced across to see that Matthew looked very put out.

Chrissy walked across the car park with Betty and Dawn.

'Well, thanks for your help. Hope we didn't mess up any plans.'

'No, I was only going home to a hot bath and bed, which is what I'm going to do now.' Chrissy reached the car.

Over Dawn's shoulder Chrissy saw Russell approaching. She willed the women to move on, but they lingered.

'Good night, ladies,' Russell called over. She would like to have thought he looked straight at her, but she knew he didn't.

They'd worked well together, smoothly, professionally, she thought on the way home. But that was all. She'd be lying to herself if she thought there had been a look, a touch, a message from him. But what right had she to expect any interest from him now? It was she who'd told him she didn't want to be involved. She banged the steering wheel. Only it wasn't so! She wanted him, she wanted to be with him, she was falling, had fallen, in love. Now it was too late. She'd thrown it all away. Oh, if only Sabine would leave, run away, disappear . . .

'So, you're off?' Chrissy asked Mo.

'Until the next time. The doctor says I can wait to start my treatment until after Christmas. I'm determined we'll have a good one this year.'

'You've earned it. Do you need transport?'

'No thanks. My husband's coming to collect me.'

'Gracious. He's taking the risk of entering a dreaded hospital? I'll see you before you go.'

Chrissy returned to her duties, even though she felt as if she was in a heavy diving suit of fatigue. She must watch herself today and double-check everything. It was hardly surprising she felt like this—she'd enough on her plate to last most people a lifetime. One thing she knew: she had to keep busy. She pulled a large plastic apron over her uniform and went to find some nursing to do.

'Mrs Fordham's ready to leave, Sister.' An auxiliary popped her head round the door of the side ward where Chrissy was.

'I'll be right along. Ask if she can hang on a minute.'

Her task completed, she went to say goodbye to Mo.

'We'll miss you, Mo,' she said cheerfully. 'Hello, Bob. What a surprise to see you here.' She smiled at her mother's lover.

'I didn't know you knew my husband. This is Robbie,' said Mo.

Chrissy looked up sharply. 'Your husband?' Bob looked trapped.

'How do you know Robbie?' Mo asked brightly.

Chrissy's mind raced. Bob looked everywhere but at her.

'I met him at my mother's . . . He's been doing some work for her.' From the corner of her eye she saw Bob, or Robbie, relax.

'An Aga, wasn't it, Bob? My mother's going round the world in a boat, Mo.' She was aware she sounded false, but normal speech had deserted her.

'Lucky her. I wish I could do that, don't you, Robbie?' Robbie didn't answer. 'Oh, Chrissy, I must go. Look at the poor man, he looks green. He's so terrified of hospitals.' She walked round the bed and kissed Chrissy goodbye. 'Try and pop in for a drink over Christmas.'

'Yes . . . Yes, I'll do that,' said Chrissy, motionless with shock.

Mo didn't expect to feel so exhausted. As Robbie helped her from the car she had to hang on to the car door for support.

'You all right, love?' Robbie hurried round to her side.

'Just a bit dizzy. It's the excitement of coming home. Where are Katya and Kerry? I'd hoped they'd be here.'

'They're still at my sister's. I thought it was best.'

'I'm not going to be an invalid, Robbie. I'm going to start as I mean to go on. This business is not about to beat Mo Fordham.'

'Jeez, you're something else,' he said, as he took her arm.

'No, not really. I'm just having to come to terms with this—thing.' Out of deference to him, she refrained from saying 'cancer'. She must be patient with him. She wasn't the only one with adjustments to make.

'Tea?' he asked, as he settled her in a chair. She smiled up at him, unused to him fussing over her. It looked as if some things were changing here. She looked about the sitting room as he disappeared into the kitchen; it was tidy and he'd made an effort. She made herself more comfortable in the chair. Her shoulder was still sore, but she'd have her tea first, then do some exercises.

She closed her eyes for a moment. Maybe, she thought, what had seemed to be such a catastrophe might turn out to be a blessing in disguise; might bring them all back together again as a family should be.

A sound made her open her eyes. Robbie was standing in front of her, staring at her. It made her feel uncomfortable.

'Can't find the tea bags?' She smiled up at him.

'There's no easy way—'

'Yes, there is—just make sure you boil the water.'

'I'm leaving.'

Mo stared back, a smile in place. He looked like a little boy standing there, head bowed, guilt written all over his face.

'I'm sorry,' he added. 'I wish it could be different.'

'When?' she asked, after a pause.

'I moved my stuff out last week.'

'You'll be staying in Fellcar?'

'No, Portsmouth.'

'Alone?'

'No.'

'I see.'

Mo wasn't surprised, but was she hurt? She wasn't sure.

'Are you all right?' She noted he asked quite anxiously.

'I'm absorbing the news.'

'You seem to be calm about it,' he said suspiciously.

'We haven't been getting on, I was aware of that . . . it's just . . . well, I can't exactly congratulate you on your timing.'

'I know everyone will think me a shit, but would you want me to stay with you out of pity?'

She flinched at the word. 'No. So, how am I to manage?'

'You said you didn't want pity.'

'I did—but a bit of loyalty might have helped.'

'This isn't easy for me, Mo. I feel a bastard. I really do.'

'And the kids?'

A frown came over his face. 'I've told them. They cried.'

'You told *them* before *me*? How dare you? I suppose your sister knows too!' she shouted, angry now in a way she hadn't been initially. His not answering confirmed her suspicions. 'Thanks, Robbie, oh, thanks a bunch.'

'I'm sorry.'

'You keep saying that. If you really were you wouldn't be doing this, would you? When I'm in the hospital who'll '

'Look after the kids?' he interrupted. 'My sister says she will. She'll move in.' He looked pleased, as if he expected her to congratulate him on his forethought.

'And money?'

'Ash has bought me out. You can have all of that. And you'll have the house and your job.'

'And what if my treatment doesn't work and I can't teach?'

'I'm sure it will. You'll be all right, Mo. You know you will.'

'I know one thing. It would almost be worth dying just to cock up your plans.' She laughed. 'And I know something else.' She stood up and faced him. 'You're a creep, a waste of space. I shall be glad to see the back of you.' She turned away.

'I'd hoped we could be friends.'

'Friends? You and me? Hell will freeze over.'

'I'm sorry—' He turned.

'Who is she?' she asked, as he got to the door.

'Iris Galloway. Your ward sister's mum.'

At that the room rocked for Mo.

'Did Chrissy know?' That would be one betrayal too many.

'No,' he said. 'She thought I was just the plumber.'

Mo heard the front door slam, the car drive away. She waited for the grief, for fear, for tears. Nothing came. She knew instinctively that whatever she decided now would affect the rest of her life.

'I don't need him,' she said aloud. She had two things to survive now:

her illness and his abandonment. She looked in the mirror over the fire-place and saw the determined set of her chin. 'I'll surprise everyone! I'll do it alone!' she said, in a voice tinged with triumph.

'He's married, Mum.' Chrissy stood in the centre of the kitchen, her expression serious with concern for her mother.

'Oh, don't be silly, I knew that!' Iris retorted.

'You knew? Do you also know he's got young children?' She sounded shocked.

'So?'

'His wife's got cancer. She's a patient of mine.'

'So Bob said.'

Chrissy sat down. 'Mum, I don't believe this. What's got into you?'

'Nothing. It's not my fault she's got cancer.' Iris lifted her chin in a defiant gesture. 'She didn't have it when we started this relationship. It's too late. What's happened has happened.'

'Mum, please listen to me. Mo is a sweet woman, brave, devoted to her children, ill. This just isn't fair.'

'Life has a habit of not being fair.'

'But don't you see the sort of bastard this shows Bob is? To even con-template leaving her at a time like this?'

'He's not a bastard and don't you dare say he is.' Iris's face was distorted with anger. 'It's not his fault all this has happened. We fell in love . . . His marriage was over, finished.'

'I wonder if he thought to tell his wife that?'

Iris poured herself a drink. 'I've got a buyer for the house,' she said calmly, turning to face her daughter. 'We're leaving. Going down to Hampshire to look for our boat.'

'So you're still off?' Chrissy looked away. 'But it's Christmas! God, Mum, you're so selfish. Don't you see?'

'I'm fed up with being bloody unselfish.' Iris's voice exploded with anger. 'Now it's *my* time—at long last. I spent my youth living with your boring father, bringing you up, knowing you loved him more than me—don't bother to deny it, I always knew.' As she listed her grievances her voice became shriller.

'Don't talk such rot,' Chrissy yelled back, her own voice staccato with her mixed emotions.

'It's the truth. At least I'm not a hypocrite like you.'

'I beg your pardon?'

'How you have the nerve to talk to me like this. Your lover's married.'

'I haven't got a lover!'

'No? What about Russell? His wife's heart is broken—by you.'

'How do you know all this?'

'Poor Sabine came to see me. Begged me to ask you to leave her husband alone. But I'm different from you, I'm loyal and I don't stand in judgment on others. I told her it was none of my business, as Bob and I aren't yours.'

Chrissy stood up. 'I've told Russell I'm not seeing him any more, that I don't think it's right.'

'Oh, aren't we the pious one?' Iris smirked.

'I've never slept with him.'

'Well, you make a habit of that, don't you?' Iris got to her feet.

'What does that mean?'

'You know.'

'I *don't*. Tell me. I insist.' The two women glowered at each other.

'Ewan.'

'What the hell has Ewan got to do with all this?' Chrissy said.

'You made his life hell with separate rooms, didn't you? No wonder—'

'No wonder what?' She stepped towards her mother, anger plain in her face. 'What is it you long to say, Mother?' She could feel a mounting hysteria that matched her voice.

'Very well then, since you insist. That he turned to others for comfort, of course,' Iris shouted.

'Oh, yes? Since you claim to know so much about my marriage, who in particular? You've got quite a choice.'

'Me for a start.' Complete silence attended this remark until it was broken by Iris. 'I thought that might wipe the smile off your face.'

A flash of memory of Iris's extreme grief at Ewan's funeral seared Chrissy's mind. Surely not. No. Not this—this was too much.

'And when did this happen?' Chrissy said coldly. 'We hardly ever saw you.'

'On a rare visit to Cornwall. You liked your long walks with your father so we took the opportunity!'

'How very strange when Ewan didn't even like you.'

'What a spiteful bitch you are, Chrissy.' Iris slapped her hard across her face.

Chrissy did not flinch. 'What I find odder is that he didn't tell me—he always did, you know. He wouldn't have missed the joy of telling me he was having it away with my own mother!'

Iris hit her again, harder. 'Sorry, Mum, I don't believe you.' Chrissy fled from the room, from her childhood home and, she was sure, from her mother's life.

'Chrissy, what is it? Why are you crying?' Daphne, sitting in a chair beside her bed, squeezed Chrissy's hand.

Chrissy looked down at her smooth hand held by her grandmother's lined and gnarled one. The contrast upset her even more. Her gran had always been there for her. What would she do without her? Who would she turn to?

'There was a girl last night, she said she was fine, but an artery ruptured and she died—I felt so helpless I—'

'Listen, Chrissy. You're doing what you told me that as a professional nurse you could never allow—you've let her death get to you. Why? Are you sure you're not grieving for this girl because of something else? Has something else happened? You can tell me.'

She looked across at the old woman, blinking through her tears.

'It's a long story.'

'I've got the time. Where else is there for me to go?' Daphne asked.

'He's called Russell. He's married.'

'Ah, well, I'm all ears.'

She started diffidently, knowing how intransigent her grandmother was about adulterers. But, as she talked, her confidence grew and finally she declared that she thought she was in love. 'No, that's wrong. I *am* in love,' she stated, more than said.

'Do you think he's an honest man?'

'Yes.'

'Then if he says his marriage is over, why don't you believe him?'

'His wife came to see me and begged me to get out of his life.'

'Wives tend to do that. I should have it out with him. If a marriage is over there's no patching up will put it back together again.'

'But Mum said—' And then she told her grandmother the last of what was bothering her. 'Finding out things like this shakes the foundations of my life. How can I ever believe anything or anyone ever again? I've had to adjust to Dad not being what I thought he was. Now this, my own mother.'

'Phew, her and Ewan? In her dreams! You're too naive, Chrissy. Just because you're truthful, it doesn't mean everyone else is. She's lying to you to annoy you.'

'But why?'

'God knows with Iris. Maybe she's jealous—you're young and she's middle-aged.'

'But she's got Bob.'

'How long for? When she gets a bit longer in the tooth he'll be off.'

'Oh, Gran, I'm so confused.'

'My advice is simple. Talk to Russell, but keep a little bit of cynicism in store, just in case.'

Chrissy laughed, her tears forgotten now. 'What would I do without you, Gran?'

As soon as she got home, Chrissy checked Russell's number in the telephone directory. She sat for some time studying the phone before she picked it up then replaced it. Several times she went through this ritual. But finally she dialled, praying that Sabine would not answer. 'It's me,' she said when she heard his voice. 'I need to talk.'

She waited for him to arrive. At the ring of her doorbell, she ran downstairs with a pounding heart.

'Thanks for coming,' she said, holding the front door open for him.

'It sounded important. What's up?'

She stood in the middle of her sitting room, certain he could hear the banging of her heart, knowing that this was a moment that held her whole future. She turned and faced him. He looked so tense, a worried frown on his face.

'The other night at the restaurant—you said—only I wasn't sure if you meant it—and then . . . None of this is sounding as I planned it to be.' He waited patiently. 'I think I've fallen in love with you,' she blurted out. She smiled nervously as still he stood watching her. 'Sorry,' she said.

His laugh was a short burst of relief. 'I thought you'd got me here to say you never wanted to see me again. Why do you say sorry when you're making me so happy?' He stepped towards her, but she took one step back.

'I thought you must be fed up with me. One minute I'm obviously longing for you and the next pushing you away.'

'It's been a tad confusing—but the circumstances have hardly been ideal.'

'I think we should talk about that, if you don't mind,' Chrissy said. He took her hand in his, and gently kissed it. 'That's why I asked you here. I've got to know where I stand. I didn't mean to tell you I love you. It just sort of came out.'

He still held her hand. 'I'm glad you did,' he said softly.

'It's so silly. We've only known each other a few weeks.' She pulled away her hand.

'A few days, a few weeks. What's the difference? I knew in the first *minutes* of meeting you that you were something different.'

'But your marriage? I mean, I'm not prying, I need to know.'

'You've every right to know.' He sat down on one side of the inglenook. She sat opposite him. 'I've been so miserable. I couldn't get you out of my mind. And when you said Sabine had been to see you. Lying to you!' He shuddered. 'My darling, my marriage has been truly over for more than a year. We've had separate rooms all that time. I know that's what married men say—it's quite a cliché, isn't it? In my case it's true. But you've only my word for it.'

'So, whose fault was it?' she asked. She knew it was a sneaky question, that marriages fell apart for a thousand reasons, but his answer would tell her so much.

'You can't apportion blame. It was my fault as much as Sabine's. If I had been the husband she wanted and needed, she wouldn't have strayed.' Chrissy relaxed against the cushions in her chair at the apparent honesty of his answer.

'We should never have married in the first place. I suppose you could say I fell in love with her wonderful legs. But there was so little we had in common. I bored her, I was soon aware of that. She liked dances and discos. I preferred home and a good book. I pretended, even to my friends, that all was well with us. And Sabine is a great actress so everyone thought we were perfect for each other.'

'So why did Sabine choose you?'

'She's had a hard life. Her father deserted them, mother liked to drink and there was little money. She wanted all the nice things. I was rich, I was security for her.'

'How sad.'

'It is. I felt guilty, I suppose, that I wasn't what she had dreamt of.'

'When did she start playing about?'

'Three months after we were married. I found a letter from a lover. I suppose I just wasn't good enough in bed for her.'

She loved him for that admission and what it must have cost him to make it.

'So, why does she want to hang on now?'

'She's afraid of losing everything I can give her. She's in love with my wallet, not me.' He laughed a short, bitter little laugh.

'But you wouldn't leave her short?'

'Oh, no. I've given her the house. I was packing to move out when you called—against my solicitor's advice. But I thought, it's best to get on now as quickly as possible. I can buy another, smaller house.'

Or move in with me, she thought, but sense told her not to say it yet. But, oh, she hugged the thought to her.

'Thank you for telling me, Russell.'

'Been my pleasure.' He laughed ironically. 'Now, I need to know about

Ewan and what happened to make you so afraid of love.'

Chrissy looked into the fire, wondering how to explain the inexplicable. 'Ewan liked playing cruel games with me. He was possessively jealous and set out to demoralise me so that I'd think no one else would ever want me.'

'He didn't succeed.' He grinned, leaned forward and stroked her cheek.

'Looks like it.' She chuckled. 'He was handsome, a brilliant artist, charming. Everyone thought how lucky I was. Looking back, I don't understand why I put up with it. He loved to tell me about other women and what they'd do in bed, unlike me! He said I was a failure there. The possessiveness became intolerable. Then he shot the dog and I ran and the rest you know.'

He stood up and pulled her to her feet. 'So we're both lousy in bed?'

'It sounds like it,' and she laughed, but not for long for his mouth was on hers, his arms about her and he kissed her full and hard in just the way she'd imagined in her dreams.

Somehow, she could not remember when or how, they climbed the stairs. In bed beside her he lifted himself on one elbow and looked down at her with such gentleness and love in his face that she almost cried out with joy.

'Chrissy, I'll never hurt you—never,' he said.

'I know, my darling. I know.' And she put her arms up to him.

Her fear of not pleasing him lasted only seconds before her body seemed to melt into his as he caressed, kissed and loved every part of her. Nerves that had been dormant so long were thrillingly activated. And when, finally, he entered her, her body rose in rhythm with his as they rocked and thrust, and together climbed the levels of pleasure to climax, and then again and again.

Satiated, twined in each other's arms, they fell asleep.

Once in the night Chrissy woke with a start and sat bolt upright, suddenly afraid. Then she heard his gentle breathing, laughed at herself, snuggled back into his arms and was quickly and contentedly asleep.

The sun woke her—they had overslept. She lay, watching his face, for several minutes. She felt so happy, so complete, so relaxed.

Gently, so as not to wake him, she slipped from the bed. In the kitchen, she filled the kettle and spooned the coffee into the cafetière . . . Her heart lurched. On the worktop stood a teapot. Gingerly she put out her hand and touched it. It was warm.

Her screams woke him and he thundered down the stairs wrapped in a sheet. He found her wide-eyed with terror pointing at the teapot.

'Oh, Russell. Who is it? I never drink tea!'

CHAPTER EIGHT

THEY SAT IN RUSSELL'S MERCEDES outside the police station.

'They didn't believe me. You do realise that?' Chrissy turned and faced him.

'They were useless. They thought it a joke.' He started the car, then swung it into the road.

'Where are we going?'

'Henry Yates—my lawyer.'

'Oh, Russell! It'll look as if I'm guilty. I've done nothing. Why should I need a lawyer?'

'A precaution, that's all. You needn't worry about cost, I'll see to that.'

'You damn well won't.' She was so annoyed she sat up rigidly in the seat. 'I pay my own way.'

'OK, OK.' He took his hand off the wheel and mockingly fended her off. 'I was only trying to help.'

'Well, thanks, but no thanks.' Everything was ruined, she thought miserably. Last night she'd been so happy and content with him. But then, upon finding the teapot, all that had collapsed like a flimsy house of cards. And all the old anxieties had rushed back led by distrust. What if he was playing games with her? What if he'd got up in the night and made the tea—just to scare her? She looked at him from the corner of her eye. A smile played round his mouth and made her stuff one hand to her own mouth to stop her from crying out. Ewan had smiled like that when he'd had a private joke; Ewan would have thought it highly amusing to frighten her witless.

'What's funny?' she asked, and hoped her voice did not sound as squeaky to him as it did to her.

He glanced across at her. 'Funny? Nothing.' He looked back to the road. 'I'm happy, that's all. Well, actually, that's everything. I can't believe you wanted me.' He placed his hand on her thigh. 'You've made me the happiest man in the world—I know that sounds like a cliché but the words haven't evolved to say what I mean, what you've become to me in such a short space of time.'

'Russell, if only—' He sounded sincere, but then—

'It's a bad time for you, Chrissy. But don't worry, it'll get sorted. And then we'll have the rest of our lives together.'

She wanted to believe him, needed to love him, to have someone to rely on, to care for.

Mo woke and lay in the bed, their bed. This was the beginning, the challenge, she thought. She'd expected not to sleep but she had and felt refreshed by it. She wondered where he was.

She sat up. There was nothing to be gained by lying here. She had things to do and, given her new circumstances, she had to find ways round doing them. She was going to have to learn to pace herself, conserving her energy. She must list the priorities. The first adjustment she would have to make would be with her home. She'd always been so houseproud; now she was going to have to learn to let things slide. She'd always been so particular about the food she'd put into her family: no convenience food for them. But now her days of standing in the kitchen for hours at a time were over too. She'd have to take short cuts.

Downstairs, over a cup of tea, Mo made a list of people she needed to talk to. She'd phone the bank and ask the manager if he could call round—she'd be in funds and needing advice. She added Ash's name: she had to know what the true state of the business was. Maybe she'd like to reinvest in it—maybe she could do the paperwork.

Mo pulled the phone towards her and dialled her sister-in-law's number. She could hear the embarrassment in Sue's voice.

'If you could bring the girls back, Sue. I'm a bit sore to drive.'

'Do you think that's a good idea? I'm happy to have them.'

'I need them here.'

'Yes, of course. But how will you manage?'

'We'll manage fine.' And, as she said it, she knew she would.

Sabine was not having a good morning. Russell had not come home last night and, checking his room, she saw he'd begun to pack his belongings. So he'd meant it. She was scared—of a future alone, of having to manage her own affairs, of not having a man to rely on. She crossed the hall to answer the ring on the doorbell. 'Giles!' she exclaimed with relief. 'Come in.'

'You evil bitch!' he shouted, waving a piece of paper at her.

'Giles! Whatever do you mean?' She stepped back in hurt surprise.

'The GMC—you reported me, unprofessional conduct with a patient! That's what you've done.'

'Giles, I never did. You must believe me. I wouldn't hurt you, you know that.' She would like to have added that she loved him, but sensed that it was not what he wanted to hear.

'If it wasn't you, then who was it? Russell?'

'I doubt it. He wouldn't do anything mean like that.'

'Well, if it's not one of you, who was it?'

'Someone at the surgery—another woman, perhaps?'

Giles looked thoughtful. 'One of the nurses might have. She'd have cause.'

'Then shout at *her*.' She looked close to tears which, for once in her life, were genuine.

'I'm sorry. I panicked when I picked up the letter. I saw my whole career in ruins. I apologise.' Giles looked contrite, she noted, so she let him take her hand.

'That would be awful! Is there anything I can do to make it easier for you?'

'Get divorced in double-quick time and marry me—they might see things differently then.'

'My darling, of course I will,' she said, in an unseemly rush. 'I'd be so happy to be your wife.'

Giles looked somewhat taken aback at the speed of her reply. She moved quickly to his side. 'I'll make you the happiest doctor in the world.'

'I couldn't give you a home like this—ever.' She did not like the doubt in his voice.

'But, my darling, with you I wouldn't need any of this,' Sabine said breathlessly, and for the time being she meant what she said.

Fiona Henderson replaced the telephone receiver on its cradle with a thoughtful look.

'Who was that?' Dick Henderson asked, as he ambled into the hall looking for his medical bag.

'That was my sister, inviting us to her Christmas party.'

'Floss? Good heavens! We've not been asked for years—ever since she accused you of exerting undue influence on your mother and her will!'

'Why must you repeat that slander?' she snapped.

'Because it's true,' he muttered. He was rather fond of Floss and regretted not seeing much of her. Long ago he had concluded he'd pursued the wrong sister.

'She wants something,' Fiona said. 'She was particularly insistent that you were there. What have you been up to?' she asked, in an accusing tone, honed by years of despising her husband.

'Not a thing.' He held up his hand as if swearing an oath. 'Honest.'

'You're late.' Fiona handed him his bag. 'What are you waiting for?'

'Oh, I don't know. I don't want to go to work, I suppose. This Lynn Petch business has upset me. I wish she'd never left.'

'Left? She was sacked by you, or don't you remember?' she said tartly. 'Get her back. Offer her her old job.'

'I tried. She won't come back. She's got a new job at the hospital.'

'I can't say I blame her—leaping to wrong conclusions, it's so typical of you, Dick. It's that Giles Middleton you should have got rid of. I never trusted that young man. Now he's sniffing about that poor Sabine Newson. I do hope you won't have to get involved in this GMC hearing.'

'Oh, I'm sure I will.'

'What happened about the missing drugs? Did you solve it?'

'I fear Lynn might have been right and that Giles has been nicking them. I suppose I'm going to have to have a word with him.' He sighed.

'Report him to the GMC.'

'What? A fellow doctor? I couldn't do that—he's a colleague.'

'Don't talk such prattish rubbish, Dick. You'd be advised to. Cover your back or he'll take you down with him,' she said ominously.

In his car he relaxed and grinned broadly. He had no intention of telling a living soul that it was he who'd tipped off the GMC about Giles and his goings-on. That way, he'd not have to sack him and put up with all the legal complications that might bring. And he'd come through still regarded as good old Dick! 'Serve the bugger right,' he said to himself as he bowled down the hill.

Daphne Galloway sat in the chair beside her bed, conscientiously doing the exercises the physiotherapist had taught her.

'My, you're working hard.'

'I want to get out of here, Lynn. Nothing personal, though!'

'Don't push yourself too hard, will you?' Lynn smiled fondly at the old lady. 'Do you know where you're going after here?'

Daphne's whole body slumped dejectedly. 'No. I wanted to go somewhere like the Mimosa but . . .' She rubbed thumb and first finger together.

'Have you heard of the Escalls Trust? You could will them your house, then they'll look after you but you stay in your own home.'

'But I wanted to leave it to Chrissy—I've little else to leave her.'

'If it's a choice between inheriting a house or your well-being I know which Chrissy would go for. Talk to her about it.'

'Nurse Petch, are we going to be gossiping all day?' Jazz Poundman appeared suddenly. 'There's work to do or haven't you noticed?'

'Just coming, Staff,' Lynn called. 'Now, Mrs Galloway, you stop worrying. Everything will work out.' She straightened the counterpane on Daphne's bed and checked her water jug before she left the side ward.

'Well, thanks for ambling along,' Jazz said unpleasantly. 'When I say jump, you jump, Petch, understood?'

'No, Poundman, I jump for no one. I was reassuring a patient.'

'What? Telling the old girl that her precious granddaughter isn't about to be arrested? Was that kind?' Jazz smirked.

'I think, Jazz Poundman, you should watch your mouth. You could get into serious trouble saying things like that.'

'Me? That's a laugh. I'll tell you this just once, Petch. Watch it! You're new here and it won't do you any favours to be sucking up to Chrissy. You'll end up getting tarred by the same brush. Meanwhile, Mrs Bantam needs her pre-med. If you don't mind?'

Lynn decided not to pursue this tit-for-tat.

Lynn was with Mrs Bantam until her general anaesthetic had been administered. As she left the main theatres she looked at her watch. It was time for her lunch break, but she'd go back to the ward and make up a post-operative bed for the patient first.

On her crepe-soled shoes, she made barely any noise as she turned into Mrs Bantam's ward, where she was the only patient. Jazz Poundman's large bottom was in the air as she rooted in Mrs Bantam's locker.

'What are you doing?' Lynn asked.

'Do you have to creep up on people like that? You nearly gave me a heart attack!' Jazz laughed, and she stuffed a hand under her apron, but not fast enough. Lynn had seen the roll of notes in her hand.

'What's that?'

'What's what?'

'You know. That money. Whose is it?'

'Oh, this money?' Jazz said, with innocent surprise. 'Really, Lynn, you should have checked. The old get confused and there must be a good hundred quid here that the old bat had stowed away in her locker. Someone could have stolen that. Now, if you don't mind, I've work to do.'

'Stay there,' Lynn ordered as, taking up the bell pull, she tugged it. 'Get Sister,' she ordered the nurse who appeared. 'Tell her I've found Nurse Poundman stealing from a patient's locker.'

Floss was in her element when organising her annual parties. The electricians were wiring the huge pine tree in the garden with the fairy lights that were always a feature. Glasses and cutlery were inspected for shine.

The flower arrangements were admired. Each gaudily wrapped present was checked for the correct name tag. The champagne had to be sampled as, of course, did the food, which had been delivered by the caterers. Floss never left anything to chance, nor did she rely on others to check things for her. Her parties were famous for their high standards.

Only when all this checking was done did Floss, much to the relief of her staff, disappear into her library to make telephone calls.

'But I said I'd be there, Floss.'

'Yes, Jake, but I'm just reassuring myself. I'd be so devastated if you didn't appear.' The Minister of Health's name was ticked with a flourish and another number dialled.

'But I said I'd be there, Floss.'

'Yes, Angus, but I'm reassuring myself.' She repeated the previous dialogue before ticking the name of the chairman of the Fellcar NHS Trust.

Then she checked that her favourite police inspector and newspaper editor were still coming. And finally that Craig Nutting, Matthew Kersey, Giles Middleton and Mark Fisher, the local MP, had not made other arrangements, which might have spoilt everything.

'Now!' she said aloud, clapping her hands with happy anticipation. She would decide which dress she would wear.

'Buck, don't go out. Stay with us,' Cheryl Marston begged.

'I told Wayne I'd meet up with him.'

'But you're not totally recovered. You know what Mr Ball said—to be quiet, no rushing around.'

'I don't have to listen to a deadhead like him.'

'I wish you hadn't discharged yourself.'

'Another day in that place and I'd be in the loony bin.'

'You promise you won't drink anything?'

'Nah. Don't worry.'

'You know what Mr Ball said about drinking when you're on pills.'

'Oh, for Christ's sake, Cheryl. I'm meeting Wayne for a coffee. We're not even going to the sodding pub.'

'All right—keep your hair on. It's just that I love you.'

'Do you feel happier now you've got a lawyer?' Russell asked Chrissy, as they stood on the steps of Henry Yates's office.

'He's very pleasant. And he certainly made me feel more confident.'

'Don't find him too pleasant, will you?' Russell put his arm possessively round her shoulder. 'I wouldn't like that.'

'Don't crowd me, Russell, please.' She shuddered.

'What the hell?' He dropped his arm.

'I'm sorry,' she said, confused.

Russell took her gently by the shoulders and sat her down on the steps. 'Now, listen to me,' he said sternly. 'Ewan is gone. I'm here. I'm not Ewan. I'm in love with you and I'll want to kill any other man who touches you. It's called jealousy. Where you have love you have the other. Understand?' She nodded sheepishly. 'Because I'm jealous does not mean I'm going to turn into a monster, twisted and cruel. Got it?' She nodded again. 'I shall not open your mail, listen to your phone calls, snoop in your life. I will trust you with this love, with my soul.'

She smiled up at him. 'I'm becoming neurotic, aren't I? I do love you. I don't want the past to hurt us.'

'It won't, if you'll let go of it.'

'I don't hold on to it—or him.'

'Don't you?' He bent down, crouching in front of her. 'When we made love you were tense. You were expecting me to hurt you. The bastard was in our bed. Now, Chrissy, I understand why but it's time to stop being afraid, to allow yourself to be loved and to live—with me, preferably.' He grinned.

'God, I'm so lucky to have found you.'

'Then loosen the guilt. That's what's anchoring Ewan in your life. It was not your fault he died. Get that straight and we can move on.'

'I'll try. I will. I need you.'

'And I need you.' He pulled her to her feet and hugged her hard. They started walking down the street.

'The solicitor wasn't happy with you moving out of your house.'

'He didn't have to live with Sabine.'

'Where will you stay?' she asked, wishing she had the confidence to invite him to move in with her.

'I was rather hoping with you.'

'I didn't like to ask you.'

'Why?'

'In case you said no.'

'And pigs might fly! In any case, I don't think you should be on your own—not with all that's going on and your poltergeist!'

Chrissy, who'd been smiling, stopped. She'd been truly happy, for a moment. But reality had rushed back in with her fears in hot pursuit.

Glynis was supervising George Webster's discharge from the ward.

'What do you think of my plaster?'

'It's fine, but you're having a wheelchair.'

'I've got crutches.'

'Wheelchair,' Glynis said firmly, and George grinned broadly, knowing that the owner of such a voice was used to being obeyed.

'This is kind of you, Glynis. I could easily go back to the hotel.'

'Nonsense. I wouldn't hear of it.' She began to push the wheelchair towards the lift.

'Hang on.' He put up his hand. 'Why are you aiming for the front door? My temporary office is thataway.' He pointed in the direction of the boardroom.

'I thought you should rest today.'

'I've an investigation to conduct. Push me there or I'll get out and hobble.'

'You are a most intransigent man.'

'Since you are the female version, my dear Glynis, you can easily recognise it in me. Good morning, Sergeant,' he said, as she wheeled him through the large mahogany double doors.

'Boss! I'd expected you to be laid up for days.' The sergeant stood, flustered, looking anxiously at the table, which he'd covered with papers.

'Having a sort-out, I see. Anything of interest?'

'Quite a development, sir. A staff nurse on Care of the Elderly was seen behaving oddly with a roll of fivers from a patient's locker.'

'No! When will they learn not to keep their valuables with them? The nurse's name, Sergeant?' Glynis asked.

'A Jasmine Poundman.'

'Oh, no!'

'You know something about this nurse, Glynis?'

'I had a complaint about her from Sister Galloway. I spoke to Jazz but fairly ineffectively—we were short-staffed and I couldn't risk her storming out.'

'What was the complaint about?'

'Bullying. It's rare, but it does happen. But stealing!'

'We don't know that yet. Of course, Miss Poundman denies everything and says she was collecting the money to put in the safe.'

'Which she could have been, of course.' Glynis sat down.

'Hang on. Wasn't Poundman the nurse who was locked in her flat the night of the murder? Was that checked with the fire brigade?'

The sergeant began to shuffle papers.

'You didn't do it, did you?' George asked, resignedly. 'Then I suggest you do it now, immediately.' The officer dived for the telephone as if his life depended upon it.

Something kept Glynis rooted to the spot. George was furiously making notes. Glynis watched him and realised how much she wanted to look after him. But she reined in such ideas. Hadn't she been fooled enough for one life?

'The fire brigade have no record of helping a Miss Poundman that night, sir.'

'Right,' said George. 'She might have a reasonable explanation for the money, but she'll have one hell of a job explaining away the Fellcar fire brigade. Looks like we've got her.' George rubbed his hands in glee.

Each day Mo felt better. The scar had healed well. She was able to plan her Christmas which, she was determined, was going to be a day to remember for Kerry and Katya. She was making her shopping list when she was interrupted by the doorbell ringing.

'Ash! What a lovely surprise. I've telephoned you a couple of times but you're always out.' She held open the door for him.

'Sorry, but I've been so busy, what with—' He stopped as they entered the kitchen.

'With Robbie having done a runner.' She put the kettle on. 'It's all right, Ash. I can talk about him. I won't collapse in hysterics.'

'Mo, you're something else. I'd like to strangle the bastard. I don't understand how he could leave you now, what with . . .'

'The cancer? Really, Ash, you're going to have to learn to finish your sentences,' she teased, but then she became serious. 'Look, Ash, we'd been heading towards a breakup for years. I don't know why it wasn't working, but it wasn't. It takes two to make a marriage and two to break it. Had he stayed with me out of pity that would have been humiliating. I can make it, and that's a promise.' She stood up to attend to the coffee.

Ash sat with the expression of a man who did not know what to say. He coughed awkwardly. 'About the business.'

'Yes?' She placed the coffee cups on the table.

'When Robbie put the proposition to me, I said yes.' Ash looked shifty.

'Perhaps it would have been better if you'd talked to me,' she chided gently. 'I might have wanted to be in partnership with you. It's what I wanted to talk to you about. I could do the accounts and type estimates.'

'Mo, that would be marvellous.' Ash was grinning from ear to ear. 'It won't be too much for you?'

'There'll be days when I'm on my chemotherapy when it probably will, but I reckon that having a goal, having a share in a business, might help to keep my mind occupied.'

'Mo, I've a confession to make. I don't know how to tell you . . .'

Mo tensed, afraid of what he was about to say.

'It was me who suggested buying Robbie out. I thought if he's going to go he will, and if I arranged the loot for him he'd go further. I've been in love with you for years, Mo. And I want to be there for you and care for you and the girls.'

Mo exhaled. 'Ash, you're the sweetest man in the world. But please don't rush me. Not now. It's not the time,' she said quietly.

'Does that mean you're not interested in me?'

'No, Ash. I like you more than I can say, but with everything so uncertain—give me time, Ash.'

Despite everything, Chrissy felt vital and alive. Last night had been endless making love and exploring their feelings for each other. She wanted to be home with him, not here. As she went about her duties she kept glancing at her watch, the hands of which did not appear to move.

She checked her dress for Floss Yates's party which was hanging behind the door in the linen cupboard. The plan was to shower and change here so that there'd be no need to go home. She wasn't getting off duty until ten, so Russell would go ahead of her.

'Dawn, you go off. I can manage here,' she said to her staff nurse. 'You must have Christmas shopping to do. If you're quick, you'll catch the shops.'

'You sure? Well, I have got one or two things to do.'

'Shoo . . . before I change my mind.'

Five minutes later Dawn popped back.

'Guess what? They've arrested Jazz Poundman.'

'Jazz? What for?'

'Murder! Isn't it exciting?'

Chrissy sat down with a sigh. 'Thank God for that,' she said.

Chrissy slipped on her stiletto heels and put on the stiff black taffeta dress she'd bought specially for the occasion. The zip jammed.

Twenty minutes later, despite the night staff's efforts to mend the zip, Chrissy was back in her uniform, driving hell-for-leather to her cottage.

She ran up the path, fumbled her key into the lock, hurtled up the stairs and flung open the door of her wardrobe, riffling through her clothes.

As she grabbed a long-skirted black suit her hand froze. She held her breath and listened. Suddenly she gasped. She could hear someone breathing—on the stairs!

If noise was any indication then this party of Floss's was an enormous success. The decibel level was deafening.

Floss, resplendent in a scarlet-sequinned trouser-suit, which did nothing for her figure but much to raise the festive spirit, wafted about introducing here, interrupting there, joking and teasing, laughing uproariously.

Tonight she'd taken particular joy in insisting that her stuck-up sister meet, and be pleasant to, sweet Tiffany. She enjoyed dropping the hint that it would please her if Kim and Tiffany were to marry and produce another generation of heirs for her fortune.

'Russell. You came. What have you done with Sabine?'

'She's with her lover. Giles Middleton.'

'You are joking, Russell? So the rumours were true?'

Floss was slightly put out when Sabine arrived with Giles. She was a stickler about social niceties. So she proceeded to ignore the woman, as if she wasn't there. This was a new experience for Sabine and put her in a sulk. 'Don't forget, library at eleven, Giles,' Floss ordered.

Floss had always liked George and was pleased to see Glynis arrive with him. Now, that's the sort she should have been involved with all these years—strong, dependable, with a sense of humour and wid-owed—highly suitable. Floss took an inordinate pleasure in introducing him to Matthew Kersey, who blustered his annoyance away. Floss was quite cool when she greeted Wendy's sister, Jenna, a supercilious woman she'd never taken to and who—she'd always kept this to her-self—for at least two years now had been having an affair with Matthew. What a two-timing creep he was, she thought angrily.

Craig Nutting strode around with obviously satisfied pleasure. He thought he'd cracked it, had finally been accepted by nobs like Floss. We'll see, Floss thought, as she waylaid Mark Fisher, and reminded him she'd like a 'little talk' in the library.

The party motored on, creating its own momentum.

'Floss, might I phone Chrissy? She should be here by now.'

'Be my guest, Russell.'

The night staff told him that Chrissy had left half an hour ago, and Floss's was ten minutes from the hospital. He dialled her cottage.

Chrissy wanted to answer the phone on her bedside table, but was too scared to move. If she did, whoever was on the stairs would know for sure that she was there . . . and yet she could ask whoever was calling to get the police.

In one swift dive she crossed the room, ready to pick it up.

'I don't think so.' A hand pressed the cradle rest disconnecting the call.

Chrissy swung round. Then she laughed with relief. 'Dawn! What are you doing here? You almost gave me a heart attack.' The laughter died as Dawn lifted her hand, which held a hypodermic syringe.

'But, Chrissy, that was the idea!' Dawn laughed, but there was no mirth in it. 'First I'd like to explain a few things to you. Let's go downstairs, shall we? Open a bottle, perhaps? You first.' And, with deceptive gentleness, she pushed Chrissy towards the staircase.

Floss waited in the library, standing by the log fire.

One by one they entered, and each in turn was invited to help themselves to a drink.

'Right. Is everyone settled?' Floss beamed round the group. 'I've a few words I want to say to you. Glynis, are you comfortable there?'

'I'm fine, Floss, really,' said Glynis. She was worried, concerned that Floss's plan might misfire, but Floss was grinning as if she was enjoying the prospect of the game ahead.

'Right. Dick, Craig, Giles, Matthew and Mark—the game's up. You've been found out!'

'What the hell are you going on about?' Dick, Floss's brother-in-law, looked annoyed.

'What game?' asked Craig, smiling contentedly.

'Sorry?' Giles looked uncomfortable.

'Is this a form of charades?' Matthew sounded puzzled and Mark Fisher said nothing, but looked nervous.

'As you know, I'm a Friend of St Edith's and I see it as my duty to stop your little plan to privatise the hospital. You will—forthwith.'

A swell of male voices objected in unison. Floss called for silence. 'Your plan to run down the hospital services, sell the building, buy it back as a private hospital and take a lot of money off the NHS. That little plan.' She smiled sweetly at them. 'I want an undertaking from you all tonight to stop what you're doing or I go to the relevant authorities— who, I should point out, are all here tonight as my guests, if you haven't already noticed.'

'Look, Floss, have you gone barmy? There is no scheme that I know of. Now, can I get back to the party?'

'No, Dick. You may not.'

'He's not in on anything.'

'How interesting, Mark. Then if he's not in on anything there's something to be in on, is there?'

'You bloody fool, Mark,' Giles snarled.

'I didn't mean that,' Mark blustered. 'I meant he's not one of our group.'

'I'm glad, but if he's not directly involved he's guilty of not being suffi-ciently concerned about his fund-holding practice to stop certain dis-crepancies—of pocketing, instead of ploughing back, any savings made.' Floss, making a stab in the dark, was gratified from his expression to know her assumption was right. 'I suggest you retire, Dick. You're too tired and lazy to have the responsibilities that go with your job.'

'Floss! You go too far.'

'My dear Dick, I haven't even started. Now, Mark, I think I should point out to you that Jake Shortley, the Junior Minister for Health, is in the drawing room. Would you like me to call him? You could have a little chat.'

'No, no, that won't be necessary,' Mark said.

'Oh, yes? You reckon old Jake will go along with you? What about when his leader finds out about his bit of skirt? Craig, if you'd checked your facts, you would have found out that the woman Jake visits on a regular basis is his sister, who suffers from MS. But then there's you, Craig.'

'You've got nothing on me.'

'Haven't I? Glynis, the faxes, please.' She slapped them down in front of him. 'Pretty incriminating, don't you think? And then, of course, we've the tapes, of your phone calls. I especially liked "Burn the papers" . . . So dramatic, just like a spy film!'

'Wouldn't stand up in court.'

'It won't have to, my dear, now will it? You will tender your resigna-tion. You can do it tonight if you wish. The chairman of our NHS Trust is out there. Now, Giles.' She turned to face him.

'I don't even work at the hospital. You've got nothing on me.'

'Haven't I? It might not be illegal to abuse the referral system of patients to the hospital. But stealing drugs and spiking Nurse Petch's drink. I'm sure the chief constable and that nice Inspector Webster will be . . .'

'Outside having a drink, we get the picture. But you can't prove it.'

'Oh, no? Glynis, the computer print-out of the medical records of poor Mr Spike, aged ninety-four—if he were still alive, that is. And'—she held up her hand to prevent him speaking—'I know from my own researches that it was you who reported poor Nurse Petch drunk. The analyst's report showed traces of temazepam. My, Giles, you do have a thing about that particular drug, don't you? Of course, the GMC will lap up all this info. And we'll have to tell them about the bribes you've taken from the pharmaceutical reps. Not very attractive, Giles,' Floss said darkly. 'You've been very quiet, Matthew. Cat got your tongue?' She turned to face him.

'This is very entertaining, Floss. What am I supposed to have done?'

'You were part of the plot.'

'Prove it.'

'I can, if I want.' Floss crossed her fingers behind her back. She had no proof, but she was determined to get him for the way he'd treated Glynis who, she saw, had suddenly stood up.

'Of course, Matthew, I'm sure the authorities would be most interested in that little mishap of yours on a patient in Inverness.' Glynis smiled nervously. 'You do remember, when you accidentally cut into an artery?'

'You blow the gaff on that then your career would be ruined too.'

'Yes. I was wrong. It would be just punishment.'

'We wouldn't even need that information, Glynis,' Floss interrupted. 'I can, with your permission, Glynis, tell poor duped Wendy about you. How about that?'

'Ha! She's known all these years. I told her I had to keep in with Glynis or she might blow the whistle on my mishap in Inverness. Why should I bother with the old bag for any other reason?'

Floss saw Glynis wince at his words, then bravely lift her chin. Nothing more could hurt her, she thought.

'But Wendy knows nothing about your affair with her sister, Jenna, does she? Glynis, come.' She held out her hand to her friend. 'We shall leave you gentlemen to your deliberations. I want an undertaking, in writing, by midnight or we will have another little powwow in here with the relevant chiefs.' And she swept from the room with Glynis in pursuit.

Dawn sat opposite Chrissy, the syringe at her fingertips, a glass of champagne in her hand.

'Sorry I can't toast you a long life,' she said. 'This is good. Vintage. You can easily tell the difference, can't you? Ewan always said that.'

'I was right. I *had* seen you before, in Cornwall. Fleetingly. He pointed you out to me.'

'Yes. I was brunette then. That's why you weren't sure if we'd met. And, as I said, I've a common face.'

'You haven't. You're very attractive.'

'Don't waste what's left of your breath trying to get round me.'

'Russell will be here any minute.'

'No, he won't. I heard you arranging to meet him at Floss Yates's. There's no hurry—enjoy your champagne.'

Chrissy lifted her glass to her lips, but only sipped from it. Her pulse was racing and she was sweating as terror seeped through her.

'I bet you thought it was Jazz who bumped off old Fortune?'

'But you were on duty that night.'

'Easy-peasy. I slipped into your ward when no one was looking and opened the fire escape. Then I ran down from my ward to your ward.'

What was so chilling, Chrissy thought, was how normal Dawn sounded, not mad at all. Yet she had to be mad, didn't she?

'But why? Why kill that poor old lady? Do you like killing?'

'No, not particularly. You don't understand. I wanted to get to you. If they hadn't arrested Jazz, we wouldn't be here now. I wanted you to rot in prison, really.'

'But why? What have I ever done to you? Because I got the oncology job and you didn't?'

'Good God, haven't you twigged yet? Ewan, of course. He was my lover. We had a wonderful relationship—deep, spiritual. I understood him, you never did.'

'But, Dawn, I didn't kill him. I promise you that was all a dreadful mistake. He didn't mean to kill himself.'

'Oh, I know that. You see, I did.'

'I'm sorry?' Chrissy tensed in the chair, gripping the arms.

'I killed him.'

The walls of the room moved as if they were made of elastic. Chrissy felt hot then cold. The carpet became a blur.

'That shook you up, didn't it?'

'But the note?' Her voice sounded weak in her ears. She was afraid she would faint and then what? As if she was reading Chrissy's mind Dawn picked up the syringe and played with it. Suddenly she lunged across the space between them. Chrissy pressed herself back in the chair away from the needle, a drip of fluid at its tip, which she watched as it wavered an inch from her face. Dawn laughed and then sat down again.

'Oh, Ewan wrote the note. At his mother's. I was there—I took the insulin from her bathroom cabinet. He was devastated when you bolted. He thought you'd gone for good. He wanted you back. He wanted you rather than me.' Dawn jerked her head as if such words were difficult to say. 'I wanted all the things you had—the house, the lovely furniture, the money. We had money once, you see, until my father lost it all. Lloyd's, you know,' she explained in that normal voice. 'And Ewan. If he didn't want me he certainly wasn't going to have you. I persuaded him that if he did what I said, he'd get you back. I told him that I would inject him with just a little insulin, enough to make it look like a suicide attempt—only I gave the bastard the lot.' She laughed at that, her eyes glinting with excitement.

Chrissy looked at Dawn with horror. She felt so desperately afraid. And then came the memory of Ewan, the pain he'd caused her alive, the guilt when dead. She remembered the whispering looks, the innuendoes. The adrenaline of terror forged with the adrenaline of rage.

'You evil, mad bitch!' she screamed. She dived for the syringe but Dawn had grabbed it and was waving it, making Chrissy weave away from its lethal contents as, both standing, they danced a deadly dance.

With one leap Chrissy crossed the rug, got hold of a hank of Dawn's hair and tugged, and Dawn's laugh became a yelp of pain, which turned into a scream of agony as Chrissy's teeth sank into her arm and the syringe dropped to the floor. Chrissy's swept it up and held it out in front of her.

'Now, how's it feel?' Without taking her eyes from Dawn she backed towards the phone. Before she reached it the door burst open.

'Chrissy, are you here? What are you doing? Floss said—'

'Russell,' she called out, relief bubbling in her voice. For a second she glanced away. Dawn raced past her, past a startled Russell in the doorway, out of the cottage and down the path. 'Catch her! She wanted to kill me!' Chrissy yelled, as she set off in hot pursuit.

Russell overtook her as they pounded across the turf of the cliff.

'Dawn!' she screamed, but the wind tossed the name away.

Dawn turned once on the edge of the cliff, silhouetted in the moonlight. She seemed to wave before she leapt into oblivion.

The night was long. Of Dawn's body there was no sign and the search for her had been cancelled until the morning. At the police station they had encountered a tearful and unusually subdued Jazz, being released from custody. Then they had to make their statements. Finally they were alone.

'Oh, Russell, will Christmas ever be joyful again?'

'I'll make sure it is—for you.' And he kissed her passionately, desperately, determined to kiss the pain and fear away.

St Edith's stood sentinel above the town. The patients stirred restlessly in their beds in their drug-induced sleep. The nursing staff scuttled about, finishing the preparations for Christmas tomorrow.

A and E was busy: a car crash, a drunken fight, a couple of domestic eruptions. Freddie Favour, who only hours before had played Father Christmas at Floss Yates's party, frowned over the figure on the treatment table. Nothing could stem the blood pouring from the young man's chest cavity where the steering wheel had ripped into him. The smell of alcohol was all pervasive.

'No seat belt, I suppose. Silly fool.'

The nurse at the patient's head finished cleaning the blood away. 'I know him,' said Freddie. 'How do I know him?'

'It's Buck—Buck Marston. He was in last month in a coma.'

'Why did we bother?' said Freddie. 'There'll be no coma this time.'

In maternity, Rose Noelle Basset pushed her way into life and cried lustily. Her mother Rachel's euphoria was marred by sadness that her husband, Andrew, was not here to greet his daughter. And she cursed Buck Marston and wished him dead for taking Andrew from them.

The lights were fewer now as sleep and order settled back. There was a solidity about St Edith's in the bright Christmas moonlight, as if the building knew it was safe—for the time being.

ANITA BURGH

Anita Burgh has lived such a varied and colourful life that she is never short of a good background for her novels. She experienced an extraordinary childhood. Born into very modest circumstances in Gillingham, Kent, she was evacuated at the age of two to Lanhydrock, in Cornwall, where she spent five years as an honorary member of Viscount Clifden's family. 'This was an idyllic time and my first taste of the high life. It was not until I returned to our terraced house with no bathroom and the first doodlebug raid took place, that I fully appreciated the reality of war.'

At eighteen she became a student nurse at University College Hospital, London, an experience she was able to use in *On Call*. During her nursing training, she met the Honourable Peter Leith. She says she had no idea at first that he was an aristocrat but simply fell madly in love. 'When you marry, whoever you marry, he's your prince isn't he?' she says. They had three children, but Anita Burgh found the class prejudice in England more and more of a strain. 'It was the women who were the most difficult,' she recalls. 'They never stopped reminding me I was an outsider.' Now, however, she can exact her revenge by putting them in her novels whenever she is in need of a villain. The marriage to Peter, now Lord Burgh, ended amicably and they were divorced in the early 1980s. 'We just drifted apart,' says the author.

None of the old acquaintances from her married days features in

On Call, but the author herself is very much present. 'I'm always in my books usually a bossy person! But it is only after I've written them that I recognise myself. In *On Call*, I'm Floss Yates, the woman with the two bulldogs, Napoleon and Josephine, the lady who thwarts the privatisation of St Edith's.'

On Call was just started when someone she knew was diagnosed with breast cancer. 'I decided to combine my nursing knowledge with the feelings and emotions of my friend. I found it a difficult book to write, particularly the breast cancer scenes, as I didn't want to cause any unnecessary concerns to anyone suffering from the condition. I wanted to be positive.'

Unfortunately, Anita Burgh is no stranger to hospitals as a patient. She suffers from arthritis in her right elbow. Until a few months ago she had written all her novels in longhand, but when this became too painful she faced a major crisis. 'How could I stop writing? If I stopped, my head would explode from the characters and plots inside it!' Necessity led her to discover the perfect solution: a voice-activated computer program called Dragon. Happily, this has enabled her to write more than she ever did before.

Today, Anita Burgh has a flat in Cambridge and a wonderful old farmhouse in Auvergne, France, which she shares with her partner and business manager, Bill Jackson, her dogs, a daughter and granddaughter. For a few months each year, her ex-husband and best friend joins them.